©2003 David King

Original Artwork and Cover Design
Back Cover Art 'Over the top, 1st July 1916'
By Rob Macauley
©2003 King Lion Publishing
103 Adelaide Street
Blackpool
FY1 4LU

FA Memorial Plaque courtesy of the National Football Museum
Photograph by Mick Arther
©2003 King Lion Publishing

Published by King Lion Publishing 1st edition 2003

Printed Concept and Design Solutions

ISBN 0-9545215-2-8

ABIDE WITH ME.

Book One:

My Country's Service

IN REMEMBRANCE
OF
THOSE WHO TOOK PART
IN THE NATIONAL GAME OF
ASSOCIATION FOOTBALL,
AND GAVE THEIR LIVES
IN THE CAUSE OF RIGHT
AND JUSTICE
· IN THE GREAT WAR ·
1914-1918.

"GIVE ME LEAVE TO LIVE AND DIE
IN THIS OPINION, THAT HE IS NOT
WORTHY TO LIVE AT ALL·WHO
FOR FEAR OF DANGER OF DEATH,
SHUNNETH HIS COUNTRYS SERVICE
AND HIS OWN HONOUR."

FOR FRANCES

'What though the radiance
Which was once so bright
Be now forever taken from my sight,
Though nothing can bring back the hour
Of splendour in the grass,
Of glory in the flower,
We will grieve not, rather find
Strength in what remains behind;
In the primal sympathy
Which having been must ever be;
In the soothing thoughts that spring
Out of human suffering;
In the faith that looks through death,
In years that bring the philosophic mind.'

IN MEMORIAM.

Greater love hath no man than he
that lays down his life for his friend.

The gospel of St. John. Ch.15v 13.

In our times, as the new century begins to find its way, to establish its separate identity from the last, seeking new goals, new steps towards a more civilised state, it is an opportune time to pause, to reflect upon how we have travelled thus far, to whom we owe a debt, to acknowledge such, to reaffirm our gratitude.

If the word 'football' is mentioned in conversation, it provides for a whole range of comment, from 'great' to 'boring', from 'oh no not football again' to 'weren't United fantastic last night'. Football brings forth images of rampaging hooligans, of scandalous incidents scattered over the years. Alternatively it conjures memories of great disaster, Munich, Ibrox, Valley Parade, Hillsborough.

Yet it is our national game, played and watched by millions, men and women alike. Britain has had its success, now we no longer speak merely of '1066' and all that but of '1966' and all that, also. One reminds us of our frailty, the other of an invasion by a score of other Nations who, one by one, retreated from our shores defeated by their superior host.

We also recall the deeds of Celtic, Manchester United, Nottingham Forest, Liverpool, Arsenal, Chelsea, Leeds and Spurs, all triumphant in Europe, bringing glory to themselves and their Country.

Then occur the victories of the small teams, the demolition of the greats by minnows. Almost every year it happens, at virtually every level. An obscure never heard of team beating one from the Conference, even perhaps, from the Football League. In turn, the accomplishment of a Conference side, or third level team sweeping aside a club from the Premiership.

Occasionally such a victory brings one of these small fry to fame by reaching the semi-final of the FA Cup. Yes it still happens and for a while it is the topic of conversation in pubs, clubs and homes throughout the land.

Football at one time or other touches us all. At times it can entirely consume a town or city, or a village. During the nineties Wycombe Wanderers, having a gate of not much more than four thousand, found the entire local population supported them really. Over thirty five thousand of its citizens descended upon Wembley to watch in disbelief and delight as their local hero the talented Dave Carroll coached by the ever-effervescent Martin O'Neil demolished a bemused Preston defence. Thus they were left

8

to languish in the basement of the Football League whilst Wycombe progressed 'ever onwards and upwards'.

Today, Preston, in their turn, have leap-frogged over Wycombe and are pressing for their rightful return to the premier flight. Such is football, up and down but hardly ever stagnant.

Consider though another time, when this great game and those who played in it were asked to set aside their pleasure, their ambitions, their search for fame and achievement to come to the Nation's aid, to defend her shores against a belligerent, pitiless foe having millions of highly trained soldiers at its command, and possessing the most terrible of weapons.

They were asked and they came. They stepped forward in their hundreds of thousands, fit, fleet of foot, agile, strong, full of courage. They rallied to their Country's cause, voluntarily, brimming with hope and possessing the resolution not to return until all was safe once more, where, in freedom and peace, they could again kick a ball goalwards whilst the roar of the crowd edged them on.

Thus it was. In 1914 there were over three-quarters of a million men registered with the FA. They were overwhelmingly amateur. These men formed the spine of Kitchener's 'New Army'. Over twenty thousand football clubs immediately ceased playing while their men prepared to go into barracks, then overseas.

Three battalions, composed entirely of registered footballers were formed, comprised of over three thousand men. In addition the Association raised thousands of pounds towards the provision of its serving members and to aid their families. They served their Nation, these footballers, and they died too. In their hundreds of thousands they died, mostly in the ghastliest manner. They died or were maimed both in mind and body.

These brave young men bade their families, and all they loved, farewell, then left their familiar shore, most never to return. Today they sleep in a foreign field, making richer the earth wherein they rest, known or unknown.

This is their story. Not, of course, the story of them all. It is a tale of one small team from a quiet Derbyshire town laid out at the foot of the Pennines. Just the tale of a few but in the telling it is the tale of them all. Contemplate, in the reading; bring back the memory of those young warriors. "Lest we forget."

Lest we forget indeed, for it is not only within the individual that the memory dims. When the FA came to move from their premises in Lancaster Gate they dismantled their memorial to the fallen footballing heroes of The Great War. I asked many times over if anyone knew of its whereabouts without success.

It was only when I was engaged in discussions relating to the launch of this book, with Hugh Hornby of the National Football Museum in Preston, that I was informed that it had become part of their archives. I was shown a small dusty room and, sure enough, there it was, covered up in a corner. It was as if I had found the Holy Grail. Now, God willing, it will once again take up a place commanding recognition and respect. You, who pass it by, as you visit this magnificently constructed venue that celebrates our footballing past, pause and add your respects to those who recovered it and gave back, to the fallen, their memorial.

Further, as you play the game, or watch from the stands, or in the comfort of your home, safe, secure, free, for just a moment, even if for only a fleeting second, remember them. Then, once a year when you watch the FA cup final, be sober of mind when the Hymn is sung, for although its origins lie deep in the past, it was first sung in tribute to those who did not return from war, or, without a limb, could no longer play. As the words flow, hope as so many of those young men wished, that should you ever face such peril, he, in his mercy, will abide with you.

"Where is death 's sting? Where, grave your victory?
I triumph still if thou abide with me "

FOREWORD

Behold, a pale horse
And he that sat upon him,
His name was Death
And Hell followed with him.

Book of Revelation: ch6 v.8

Madness engulfed the world. Events escalated out of control, powered by their own dynamics. Politicians had gambled, and lost, having no control over the dice. Generals, clothed in their finest and their own self importance, wielding their batons, struck their puppet Kings, Emperors, and civil Ministers, dumb. Engineers trundled out their latest, finest, machines of death and handed them over to the grateful Generals. Men, simple men, for the most part, thrilled by patriotism, the quest for fame, glory, honour, swept to the flag and were swept away.

It was insanity, a madness, eventually stilled only through sheer exhaustion, even then but partially and temporary. It devastated and eclipsed an entire generation. It was the manifestation of Revelation, the Apocalypse; the four horsemen let loose, War, Pestilence, Famine and Death.

It was a time of legend, of deathly blunders, offset by deeds of unbelievable courage, love and sacrifice. Now the years have travelled on, the memory dims. The mist descends, confusing myth with fact. The dead sleep covered by the mud of Flanders, the Somme, Verdun, Paschendale, Gallipoli. Forsaken millions lie in graves, unknown, unrecovered, having no consecrated resting-place. They are known only to God. The bureaucratic mists envelop to disguise the truth, concealing the evidence. All begins to fade, people cease to care, to respect their memory. Two short minutes once a year. Too much to ask.

Their time has passed, these countless dead, yet but for them what would we be. Of whom and to what would our souls, our beings, be slaves, be commanded by, be given to.

Still though, there are stories to tell, to grasp the imagination. Stories which demand to be told. From out of the confusion that was those times, laboriously unravelled, comes this tale, a solitary tale, but in its telling it becomes the story of them all. As they live again through these pages, pause and reflect. Be grateful that you did not live through such a time. Pray that such a day will never come again.

This was the age of the great crime, plotted by a few dark men. Through the death of one of their own they provided the excuse to begin the terror. To the world the Austrian autocracy was grief stricken for their

12

Franz and Sophie. Yet, in truth, these two unwitting murdered souls were the price the Emperor paid to give him the legitimacy that allowed Austria-Hungary to sweep up ambitious Serbia hence gaining unhindered access to the Adriatic. Poor unsuspecting Franz and Sophie being driven to their assassination, bringing with their doom, the death sentence for millions.

At last the veil is drawn away and we see what little puppets those leaders were, gazing at train time tables, scrambling to be the next to sign up for mobilisation, to issue ultimations, while in Vienna a guilty few were hiding the greatest secret of the century.

Sherlock Holmes observes that when everything else has been examined and eliminated, then what is left must be the truth. Young Princip, a Bosnian, not a Serb, infiltrates the Black Hand, un-be-known to them the instrument of Austria-Hungary, He fires two shots. Two shots, two deaths, preordaining those countless others.

Just how far did the conspiracy spread out its tentacles? Berlin? probably, for the Kaisers' men were straining at the leash, they had been for years. In 1914 Europe was a heaving arsenal. Dreadnoughts waiting to set sail. Krupps and Skoda impatiently waiting to compose their 'constant anger'. Scores needed to be settled, ambitions to be fulfilled, fulfilled by the efforts, sacrifices, and the executions of ordinary men and women, they too unknowing victims of this heinous plot.

Yet, paradoxically, from this great evil sprung some of the greatest examples of human courage, of selflessness, that history records. As with troy, another war begun of treachery, there emerged the Hectors, the Achilles, the Ajax. Many times over they stepped forth upon the stage of war, bearing their testament to courage, to valour. Victims they were, but likewise victors, stepping out into no-man's-land, with authority, leadership, example and apparent fearlessness.

Such a man was Billy Thomas. A man of conscience, of morality, knowledge and skill. He was a man who loved and was loved, who found his resting-place amongst Kings and Poets. Thus he represented his generation, surrounded by grieving, loving, respectful mourners, few of whom knew him, but all believing that they did so.

Billy was a family man the beloved of his wife Sally, her parents also. His mother worshipped him, had sacrificed everything for his well being. Numerous friends, such as young Jimmy Jones took example from him. In his short life he had become an icon, a role model. The kindness of Lucille Bertois, the advice given to him by Robert Blatchford, The work given freely by Colin Russell, each in turn give witness to human generosity and kindness. Each plays their part.

My Great Grandfather Gideon Livingstone, he is also to be mentioned, for he in many ways is the pivot for the drama. He unravels much of the secrecy, he keeps many of the characters together, ensuring that essential letters and documents would one day come back into the public domain, to be selected, collated, and brought together exposing the essential facts.

This too is also the story of the football team that died. The team whose poise, skill and gentlemanly conduct graced the emergent Football League for a few short seasons then vanished into obscurity, its players having, in the main, answered the call. Like that other team from that city just a short train journey away, over forty years later, they were a bright beacon, the flower of their generation, giving all they had to their chosen sport. Now they gave all they possessed to their Country, to the coming conflict. The war accepted their offered gift. Today most of them lie in Flanders Field, or Picardy, deep beneath the blooms of poppies, red crimsoned poppies, whose seed was germinated by the agitation of the very guns that claimed the lives of so many of them, that immortal, 'band of brothers'

Now all that remains to speak of their deeds on the football field are the bland impersonal records, and, hidden away in obscure library archives, contemporary reports from local reporters of their day. Thus the student of those records, examining the history of Glossop North End, notes a familiar pattern. The remorseless swing of the pendulum. The team rises to excel, achieves its high point then falls into obscurity, typical of a team from a small town. What the studious young person will not know is the story behind the facts. For those you have to look elsewhere.

Glossop entered the football league in 1898, when two new teams were added to the second division. Immediately, guided by their inspired captain Herbert Rothwel, they caused an upset by instantly gaining promotion to the top flight, together with Manchester City. It was a moment of footballing history, for it was the first time that promotion had been gained through nothing other than the team's efforts during the season.

The feat was also unique in another aspect, never before, or since, has a team from so small a town climbed to so high an elevation. The town that gave the team its name boasted a population of merely twenty five thousand. The distinction is Glossop's; it will probably never be surpassed.

In its day the feat was viewed with such high pride that the town issued a commemorative medallion, which portrayed a lion and crown together with the club motto "Virtas, Veritas, Libertas". It sold in hundreds. This was decreed, to be the Club's high point of success. It was relegated after just one season. From that time to the outbreak of the First World War, Glossop meandered in the second division.

In 1914 the call went out. Almost to a man the members of the team rallied to the flag. By the end of that season not one of the original members of the team that started the season remained playing. They were all in France or training in barracks. The team eked out the season with elderly veterans and boys to young to volunteer. They were outplayed on almost every occasion, finishing the season at the foot of the table.

The war claimed most of this brave little team. Come its end, they had either returned home carrying injuries that prohibited them from ever playing again, or resting by the banks of the Somme, and other battlefields, they had become but memories, their names graven on memorials. Thus the team disappeared from the annals, just a footnote in football's history. It was as if the town, in her grief, did not possess the heart to resurrect a new team. Just a footnote, without reason, 'Virtas, Veritas, Libertas.

The role played by literature scatters these pages. Milton and Lyte, the poet and the hymnist. Their words bringing together comfort and spirituality, a sure and certain knowledge, that however comes the end, there is everlasting peace, eternal life. They, with their words deep in Gospel, assure us that nothing overcomes faith, nor hope, nor love, especially love. Nothing, not even parting or death.

This story begins in France, where much of it is later played out. Not the damp, dismal, Northern France of Picardy and the poppied fields of Flanders, but the warm, safe tranquillity of Southern France, the town of Nice. Here by the graveside of an English cleric, whose final work threads its solace through these pages, as it has done so elsewhere, for so many years, the story begins. Francis Lyte, composes his final words which, like the deeds of Billy Thomas and his gallant comrades, are immortal.

> *"In life, in death oh Lord,*
> *Abide with me,"*

CHAPTER 1

Liftest me up from the gates of death,
That I may shew forth all thy praise.'

Psalm 9.v.13-14.

The life of Henry Francis Lyte was ebbing away; coming to its close, there was no pain, no loss of mind or acute sickness. It was a general lethargy, weariness, signalling a gentle but certain close to his mortal existence. God was truly beckoning. Soon that stairway to heaven would open to him lined by Angels. Strong, immovable, irresistible, his faith dwelt within him, sure and certain of his resurrection, his predestined appointment to reside with his maker.

Henry's life had been one dedicated to his maker, to his faith; a life of service to God, spreading the good news, evangelising the eternal truth of salvation "For God so loved the World, He gave his only begotten son that whosoever believed in him would not perish but gain eternal life," Lyte's strength came from within, his steadfast belief in the one true faith, in which God is with you, fortifying you, bringing strength, comfort and inward peace.

Now, as his last hours approached, he meditated. God had blessed his life here on Earth. In his last years he had been provided with a sanctuary in this inspiring corner of the Earth. Here he had comfort, warmth and bounty. Indeed this was an inspirational place of abode where the Mediterranean Sea gently kissed beaches of pure white sand that stretched far away into the distant horizon. He concluded that Nice was an imitation of Eden, a taste of Heaven on Earth. It was as if Paradise had been regained in a likeness to the days before Adam sinned.

The sea had never been far away during Henry's life. His youth had been spent on the Hampshire coast, his father being a captain in the Royal Navy. Above the fireplace in their small cottage by the shore there hung a large print displaying the Battle of Trafalgar. The memory of this great battle scene, which so endured, was not of the mighty Victory, her guns ablaze, closing in upon its helpless French foe, but of two unfortunate souls clinging to a fragile scrap of flotsam. They were inches from death, their strength draining. Yet, while they clung to the wreckage they had hope of this life. In his boyhood Francis had often wondered, 'did they pray and if so to whom and for what? Did they ask for divine intervention to save them from a watery grave, or perhaps they pleaded for their redemption in the next world, with a word to God to protect the ones they were leaving behind.'

The painting and the dilemma facing that wretched stranded pair of unfortunates had often been the subject of discussion between him and his mother. Yes his dear mother, through which he became familiar with 'the book of Common Prayer', and Hymns Ancient and Modern, During long winter months, when only the two of them were sat by the fireside, he would read to her from the Psalms, Pilgrims Progress, or Milton. He owed a lot to his mother. God's first gift to him, after life had been breathed into his frame.

Later, when he reached his twenties, such memories drew him towards a life in the Church, of service to God. Now, here upon the edge of death, his past dedication, coupled with his faith, was to sustain him. He was reaching out towards the bridge that separates this World from the next. For one last time in his life he became inspired to take up his pen, to see where inspiration would lead him. He comprehended how the act of dying and peace came together with faith and hope, side by side. God would reside with him all through this coming final journey leading him to his eternal rest, where, reaching out, he would touch the very face of the Creator.

His Bible, life's constant companion, as ever, lay close by. Taking the book in his hands, Henry sought out the Gospels. He came upon St. Luke. There was something about the poetic flow styled by the physician, which found empathy with the cleric. Delving more deeply, he turned the pages towards the last chapter inscribed by this, his most favoured Apostle. He read Luke's description of the resurrection of his Saviour, the empty tomb, the Angels in the garden appearing to the two Marys and Joanna.

Now his eyes arrived at his most favoured scripture. The story of the journey to Emmaus, where two despairing Disciples, walking from Jerusalem, encounter the risen Lord. Unaware of whom it is who walks amongst them they invite Him to partake of their evening meal. Henry's eyes came to a halt, they closed on his most loved verse. He read aloud.

And they constrained him saying,
Abide with us,
For it is towards evening, and the day is far spent.
And he went in to abide with them.

He stared at the verse, then; at long last, it came to him why he had always found so much inspiration in this particular passage. It was, he concluded, because his entire life's journey, his mortal aspiration, was to attempt, throughout his life, the merit of salvation, which was, for him, the earned right to abide with his Lord. Now, near to death, he knew, he was certain, that the fulfilment of the wonderful scriptural promise was, for him, about to gain totality, his inheritance, to rest for all time with God, to abide with Him. Over and over, in front of his eyes, the exaltation came, bringing with it immortal assurance.

Words and phrases passed by, drifting in front of Lyte's eyes, finding form. His final hymn now found conception, from birth, through life, to the day of death. For the next hour or so he gazed out from his study window towards the passive azure sea. Periodically his eyes would drift towards the blank leaves of paper; he would then survey the room mentally sketching lines and form. Now, at last, came the time to draw together his inspirations. Turning once more to his desk, he trimmed a nib, placed it in the sooty ink and began to stroke the paper.

'Abide with me, fast falls the eventide'

The sun was now setting over the western sky, fast; as if warning him how quickly time was ebbing away. Streaks of red, amber and gold shot out across the water, mingling with aquamarine and blue. Light, whispery feathered clouds fled towards the horizon. No breeze was perceptible. A pair of Harriers swept passed, with apparent effortless ease, ever upwards, driven by an invisible thermal, their meek mating mewing hardly perceptible to his ear.

Suddenly, as is the case on such days, the sun dipped its last rays below the distant sea. The heavens lit in all the glory that man's perception could comprehend, contrasting with the grey that now skated away across the land. That familiar ominous, sombre, grey, the colour summoning, encouraging the presence of death, which each day the Earth experiences this drawing of a veil about her. Daily, countless eyes cast skywards towards the diminishing light of the heavens before they become the realms of stars. Now came the darkness, consuming the landscape, yet, spite of dread, all was tranquil, calm.

'The darkness deepens, lord with me abide'

There were times during Henry's lifetime when he had been badly let down by others. He had planned, then organised, when, at a crucial point, when others were needed to fulfil a previously promised obligation; they were not forthcoming in their duty. It seemed that at times like these, such misfortune was the inevitable lot of a cleric. Now he made comparison with these unfortunate experiences and contrasted them with the surety of his trust in God. Earthly matters consisted mainly of futile struggle, tempered by passing, fleeting, success, soon to fade and dim. Yet within Lyte was an inner strength, surging out from his physical frailty, and that power, prayer, brought upon him God's ever-loving presence.

' When other helpers fail, and comforts flee,

Help of the helpless, oh abide with me.'

Five ageless verses were composed that day, before his quill came to rest. Later, that very night, came to him the reward of Heavens Mansions. Angels were gathering to guide his soul to the presence of his Maker, therein to abide, leaving his freshly drawn lines to adorn the paper, lines that were destined to bring aid and comfort to countless others for generations to come. Thus he passed from this world, 'with calm of mind, all passion spent.

CHAPTER 2

'Guide me oh thou great Jehovah,
Pilgrim through this barren land.'

J.Hughes 1870-1932

'No man is an island,' so observes the poet. Then came the machines, and few places existed in isolation. Appearances could be deceptive. A town sheltered on all sides by steep barren moorland, largely self sustaining, its works engines powered by the swiftly flowing river's current, can appear to exist, to thrive, in splendid isolation

Life's progress, in industrial terms, in social terms also, still had the capacity to march forward apparently unhindered by the lack of contact with the outside world. True, technology had brought the railway, canals, roads too, and with these modern methods of conveyance came raw materials from all over the country, the world even. Wool, cotton, dyes, to feed the ever-insatiable mills, timber and explosives for the quarries, which, in turn, were manufactured into finished goods, which returned to that outside world few of its inhabitants seldom saw.

Then would come the time that the world at large no longer required the results of the town's labour and the machines would grind to a halt bringing idleness and poverty in its wake. At such a time, the emergent town comes to realise that it is no longer isolated, it has become part of the new industrial age where geography no longer protects it from the outside. The world is suddenly a much smaller place.

The town now comes to compete with its neighbours. The mill owners begin to build splendid mansions for themselves, with their ever-increasing wealth. Houses are built of a far less grand nature for their thousands of workers. Civic pride is established through its infrastructure, churches, libraries, schools, technical colleges, courts and police stations, sustaining order and education which all have their place in providing and shaping the other essential element that such a community requires, a skilled, sober, obedient disciplined workforce.

The Romans controlled their populace through paganism, loyalty to the Gods, the Emperor, supplying sufficient bread and creating an illusion of contentment through the circus. Mankind learns from the past, so it is believed. Maculey's 'Lays of Ancient Rome', Gibbons, should have taught him that even at an empire's height unforeseen powers can bring the greatest edifice crashing down in ruins.

It is often when Mankind reaches a pinnacle, his influence reaching out in all directions, his technology and inventiveness bringing him apparent superiority, that he becomes vulnerable. His navy, his army, may have conquered all before him, but often it is then that defeat overcomes him. His pride, his sense of splendid isolation and superiority infuse the circumstances, the accidents, and the blunders, which conspire towards his downfall.

Life's qualities can appear to be grand, progress uninterrupted, wealth and power multiplying year after year. Then destruction descends upon the land without warning and Rachael weeps for her children, without comfort, for they are no more. Structures come crashing down; the established order is questioned. Rulers struggle to save what they can, sometimes retrieving sufficient assets to continue but, inevitably, historians can look back observing the time, even the day, when the disintegration began.

Such a day of destiny came for many of the empires and dynasties of Europe on that fatal day June 28th 1914. The Kings, Emperors, the political leaders had reached a pinnacle of world-wide power and influence. They commanded with a great air of self-assurance, a belief that with their new machinery, new technology, they possessed control over the very elements. That day in the summer of 1914 changed everything.

Glossop in the spring of that year appeared to both flourish and thrive. Generally it was a place of contentment providing facilities for most of its population's needs. The town itself housed about 25,000 souls mainly workers in the weaving mills, the dye works, the quarries and the mines. It boasted but one main street running from east to west, the primary route by means of the snake pass, twisting and turning over the Pennines, from Manchester to Sheffield.

The railway had come of course. Irish navigators had built the great tunnel at Hadfield sixty years before. In evidence over fifty of them lay in their graves within the grounds of the small Chapel built where they encamped, whilst the wondrous engineering feat was in course of being constructed. The line could have continued straight through to Manchester but Glossop was deemed to be important enough to be provided with its own spur over the viaduct at Dinting, from where it reached into the heart of town.

The Dukes of Norfolk, the Howard's, were the great local landowners. Gradually, as the town expanded, the municipality, and the new breed of industrialists, vastly increasing the urban area, acquired land from them. Consequently many of the streets were named after this ancient family of aristocrats. The centre of town became Norfolk Square, which was dominated by the railway station, The George Hotel and The Norfolk Arms.

The Parliamentary Constituency had been entitled, somewhat imaginatively, 'High Peaks'. Tory influences still reigned supreme, even in the face of the Liberal ascendancy, but the Partington dynasty was beginning to encroach upon its majority. Political loyalties tended to split down religious lines with the Partingtons, their industrial friends and the mill workers being Nonconformists and Liberal, whilst adherents to the established Church, usually gave their allegiance to the Tories. The present Member of Parliament was Captain Hill-Woods, a man who studied his power base, the threats to it and acted out any course designed to protect it.

Most of the shops were sited in High Street East. Here you could purchase almost anything providing, of course, you had the money. However, work was plentiful at the moment, the mills were still expanding and for those who were fit and in good health, life was bearable.

The mill owners, had become aware that a captivated workforce, living in factory housing, tended to be more loyal, so surrounding the factories they constructed strong adequate stone dwellings having basic but planned sanitation. For as long as a worker was loyal and diligent he had a house for himself and his family and, in addition, wages to spend.

Temperance was a well-preached sentiment echoed from the pulpits of the many Chapels that had been built, usually with donations provided by the industrialists. Their names, or their wives names, were inscribed on the foundation stones by the entrances, reminding the congregation to whom they were indebted.

The Independent Chapel in Fazackerly Street was one such establishment. Pastor Gideon Livingstone had been its resident preacher since its consecration in 1895. Although at Chapel meetings at the Manse he was persistently reminded of the Chapel's reliance for funds from its major benefactors, he was truly an Independent. His forefathers had been preachers for centuries, stepping out of the Presbytery of Scotland, inheritors of the free worshipping Bunyanites.

To him a man's life was a variable of Christian's in his progress to the Celestial City. A man might work hard, an essential ethic, he would marry, have a family, undertake his duty, then have to confront all the temptations, iniquities, false friends and dangers that allied and combined together to destroy his immortal soul. A Christian combated this array of serpents with prayer, by reading and understanding the Bible, attending services, and keeping both sober and honest.

Still, the God of the Christians was a benevolent, charitable, loving, God. He did not expect a man to live honestly, if his toil could not feed and clothe himself and his family. A man could not obtain a sound grasp of scripture without a good education, a high level of literacy. Women could not retain that high standard of morals expected of them, unless they, in turn, were respected and given rights of free speech, decision making and representation.

22

Gideon would not have described himself as a Christian Socialist, but he came close to being just that. He knew all his flock intimately. Their homes, he visited regularly. He shared their joys and sorrows, triumphs and disasters, their failures and successes. His flock had become his extended family; he loved every one of them.

It was his lasting goal to have a school built next to the Chapel so that the children of his congregation could all be guaranteed high levels of literacy, numericy and Biblical morality. The Library was situated opposite the Chapel. It was well stocked and provided excellent facilities. If its services could be enhanced by organised schooling based around his Chapel, all the children of the congregation could have an excellent start to life, having possibilities of accomplishment.

Nathaniel Hawkins, together with his wife Elizabeth and daughter Sally were regular attendees to the services of Pastor Livingstone. The family owned and ran a large hardware and haberdashery store in High Street East. Both husband and wife worked on the premises and recently their eighteen-year-old daughter had begun working with them, serving, stocktaking, and making up accounts.

Nathaniel's father had been a peddler, supplying the needs of itinerants or people coming to market, he would travel to Sheffield buying quantities of cutlery made from the new Britannia Metal. His caravan was full of the necessities of life pots, pans, utensils, and fabrics. Mary, his wife, would make and mend garments, while his stone wheel, that he took everywhere with him, would sharpen all kinds of implements. Nathaniel could remember, as a young child, turning the handle that powered the wheel whilst queues of people waited in turn for their requirements. Eventually Nathaniel would have inherited his father's business, or branched out on his own, but when he was eighteen fortune, in the guise of Elizabeth Watts, came his way.

Elizabeth was the daughter of a local mill manager. She had been provided with a good education, in female terms. She assisted her mother who was a renowned seamstress. In turn Elizabeth inherited her mother's skills and her workmanship was in great demand. It was a pair of tragedies that brought Nathaniel and Elizabeth together. Firstly, his father's horse died. The constant strain of climbing the snake pass, fully laden, became too much for the poor beast. He passed away one day in a meadow above Glossop while his owners were attending the summer fair.

Samuel, Nathaniel's father, had been a frugal man. Unlike so many itinerant salesmen he was both temperate and a Chapelgoer. When in Glossop, he attended Pastor Livingstone's Independent Chapel, which was now newly consecrated.

On the steps of the Chapel the following Sunday he informed Gideon of his problem. The Pastor sympathised, but, as was his way, he also put his mind towards resolving the situation. Within an hour he came down to the centre of town where the family sat around an iron pot, upon which, a good savoury beef stew was boiling away.

"Samuel, a word if you will".

The Pastor's request led to the two men walking out of earshot for a short while. When they returned Nathaniel's father was all smiles. He shook hands with his Pastor, friend and mentor, then came back to the caravan.

What happened next was to change Nathaniel's life forever.

"Travelling days are over missus."

Samuel announced this groundbreaking news to his startled wife, as if he were simply passing the time of day.

"We're going to put down roots, have a house, mebbee even a shop. Pastor Livingstone has it all planned out. I catches the train to Sheffield, brings back me goods, sells 'em here in the town. Woman we're going to put down us roots".

Mary, Nathaniel's mother, was surprised, yet she was overjoyed.

"I'm sorry we lost the poor horse me dear, very sorry, but it was the will of the good Lord."

She put her arm around her good husband in reassurance.

"We shall prosper here me dear, I knows' we will. Glossop be a goodly place with plenty of opportunities for the likes of us."

So it came to pass, 1895 became the year that Nathaniel began a settled life. He also married, beginning a relationship that established a successful business and produced a daughter, Sally.

Elizabeth Watts was also affected by death that year. Her father died. Gideon presided over the funeral and on the following Sunday announced the passing of this well-known member of the congregation. As fate would have it Nathaniel was sitting next to Elizabeth when the obituary was proclaimed. Elizabeth began to weep and Nathaniel passed his handkerchief to her, which she accepted.

After the service she sought him out, handed back the fragment of linen and thanked him. Nathaniel's mother was within earshot. She came over, offering her condolences to the bereaved girl and her mother. She then invited the two women to share in their Sunday lunch, which was accepted, albeit reluctantly.

During the meal both mothers realised that they shared mutual skills, which led to Mary suggesting to her husband that the widow, should come and work for them in their new establishment. Within the year Elizabeth and Nathaniel were married and expecting a child. Thus Sally was born in 1896 into a successful family, possessing a thriving and expanding business.

By 1910 Nathaniel controlled the enterprise, in partnership with Elizabeth, his parents having both passed on. Elizabeth's mother was to die in 1912, from which time she began to expand, quite dramatically, the fabric facet of the business. Sally introduced herself to this aspect of work and soon it became apparent that she had inherited artistry from her mother and both her Grandmothers. She developed into a talented seamstress, an asset to the shop.

A son had been born to Sally's parents in 1910 but he had died of influenza when only two years old. Sally, therefore, was the sole inheritor of the family's growing wealth. By 1914, 'Hawkins Ironmongery and Haberdashery' was the emporium to visit for most of the townsfolk of Glossop when wanting such supplies.

Two years prior to the demise of the poor horse, which so paradoxically had brought settlement to Nathaniel's parents, Joshua Thomas, a young man of barely twenty seven years, sat spellbound as Pastor Gideon Livingstone, produced an inspirational address at an open air evangelical revival meeting. The Pastor had been called to Glossop by his denomination's circuit in Manchester.

Here he felt God's calling. Having established with a number of local illuminaries, who felt the need for an Independent Congregation in the town, he had already been granted land near to the library for a Chapel and was now fighting to raise the money to build his visioned dream, a permanent place of worship. Meanwhile, he reasoned, if there was not, as yet, an establishment for the people to come and hear the word, then he would take the word to them.

This particular Sunday God had been very good indeed. The crowd had gathered under a cloudless sky. It was late spring, people were standing, some even sitting, in a meadow emblazoned with the colours of wild flowers, edging their faces skywards through the cropped, luxurious, dark emerald, grass. It was a huge congregation, several hundred souls, each eager to hear his words of wisdom and consolation. Gideon felt full of the Lord. He had his platform, his Hymnals, his bellows blown organ powered by two enthusiastic young boys and his bible. God had, in his mercy, given Gideon the tools, now he had to justify his vocation.

This day he performed splendidly. He gave a sermon on 'The Parable of the Sower' and related it to the building of his vision. He explained that money alone does not build a Church, "people build Churches.' His appeal was to the benevolence to those surrounding him. Between them they possessed the skills to raise a house of God, who among them would help him in this great task of the Lord?

His words were splendid; they struck a chord with his flock. People of many crafts came forward to offer their time and talents. This young preacher had brought them the message of salvation, they, in turn, could offer no less than their sweat to assist in the building of his house of God.

One such was Joshua Thomas. He had been completely enthralled by the words and the challenge of this man of God. He explained to Gideon that he was a skilled mason who had helped to construct many of the grand municipal edifices of Manchester. He had come to Glossop to play his part in the erection of the new Victoria Hall, which was being built to commemorate the diamond jubilee of Her Majesty.

After Pastor Livingstone had given the crowd the Lord's blessing, the crowd began to disperse. Now the young mason approached the preacher to offer his services. Gideon felt overjoyed. He contentedly considered that if this young man was serious with his offer, most of the needs of the project were in place. He had the site, planning permission, architectural drawings, some money, and even the promise of raw materials. Offers had flooded in from labourers, decorators, weavers, carpenters, builders, all in one day, more by far than was needed. It had been like the parable of the loaves and fishes; he was humbled at what God had performed through him.

Now the Lord was providing him with a volunteer master mason. Even the Pharoes were not so provided. Their craftsmen were slaves. True, these charitable workers were also free of cost, but they came of their own free will. God had indeed been very good today.

The new recruit explained, "Of course Pastor, I shall only be available on holidays and Sundays and perhaps some evenings when it is light"

Gideon was shocked. "Surely you do not propose to work on the Sabbath", he exclaimed.

This outburst did not seem to act as a deterrent, for the reply came, "but Pastor you work on the Lord's day."

"Yes I do", came the reply, "but I am doing the Lord's work."

"And I", the young man countered, "when I am carving stone for a new assembly of God, of my own volition, free of any pay, whose work am I undertaking?"

Gideon was speechless, a rare occurrence. With all his training, all his knowledge of scripture, such a proposition had never occurred to him. Yet this young man was correct. Manual work, brutal work, if entered freely into for God, could be every bit as pure and holy as the words he uttered every Sunday with his entire intellectual strength and purpose. Of course this young man was right. The sounds of hammers, shovels and stone chisels could be heard on a Sunday, if they were taking part in erecting a new house of God. The sound was no different than a Hymn or a Prayer; it praised God just as wonderfully. The scent of sweat, drifting towards Heaven, Would be as incense to his sacrifice. Yes, it would be so. His Chapel would be built on Sundays, especially on Sundays, just as on any other day. Praise the lord!

"son", replied Gideon, "you are of course correct. You will be praising God with your hands and tools, as if they were closed in prayerful supplication. It shall be enacted so. Work will be carried out for Him on Sundays. Yes it shall, especially on the Sabbath."

He felt a sense of humility; it was as if the Almighty was reminding him that in doing his work, Gideon should know, there is always an answer to any obstacle presenting itself. The young man before him, had taught him, shown him, how biblical bureaucracy would not impede God's work. It was as if Christ was standing before him saying, "I am about my father's business."

"And where can I contact you?" Gideon asked.

"Number 4 Talbot Street", came the reply.

"And what is your name?"

"Why its Josh, Joshua Thomas, Pastor. I always wondered why it was that my good parents named me so, after all it was Joshua who destroyed Jericho, brought down its walls. I build, I carve straight and true, strong and permanent, ironic is it not?"

"Not at all", contradicted Gideon with a smile. "In destroying Jericho, Joshua built a Nation, a Nation of the Lord."

"Well Pastor, I never thought of that, a Nation of the Lord eh?"

"The very same Joshua, a Nation of the Lord."

They shook hands; a handshake that put the seal, on so much that was to pass. The Chapel was built. Scores of the emergent congregation toiled on the structure, making it blessed, consecrating it with their sweat, sweat freely given for God. Joshua Thomas, true to his word, toiled endlessly. His was the keystone that held together the entrance arch. He carved the foundation stones that identified the luminaries whose contribution had been financial. His was the final elaborate coping stone set solidly atop the little spire pointing towards the heavens, in company with several smaller finials splendidly erected atop each gable. These represented the last structures of human creation between the congregation and their God. It was here that Joshua scribed his name, out of view from the people below, yet the first evidence of human dedication observed from the heavens.

The Chapel was dedicated, the congregation installed, but Gideon did not forget the open-air meetings. As the years marched on, he still held them in the summer. They reminded him of the generosity of his God and how he would never cease to find new facets within his faith.

Joshua Thomas became a regular attendee at services, always on his own, immaculately dressed. He was ever there to aid the less fortunate of the congregation. If a widow's roof leaked or a chimney needed repair, one word from Gideon and he was there coming to the rescue. He practised his Christianity. His faith, hope and charity gave example to others, especially his charity.

There was however one aspect of his life that bemused Gideon. He was always alone. No family, no close friends. It was true that Joshua was never without people coming up to him, greeting him, thanking him, but he never seemed to have anyone close. Gideon would hear of his exploits of kindness from others, for Joshua would never speak of them himself. He was alone at home, a bachelor, seemingly without any family or relations. He was never without work; toil seemed to be his life. Yet, Gideon mused, had not God said of Adam, 'it is not good that Man should live alone.' Gideon pondered much on this dilemma; eventually he decided to attempt a match.

On discovering that Joshua had now reached his twenty ninth year he put his mind to the problem as a matter of urgency. His thoughts centred upon Gladys Potter. She was twenty-five years of age and had spent all her adult life looking after her frail widowed mother. This vocation had overridden all others, meaning that all young men who had ever approached her with enticements, and there were several, had all been sent packing.

Now, recently, her mother had passed on, leaving her alone. Gideon spoke to his wife Ruth, whom, he felt would have a better insight into his plans. One evening he confessed to all his machinations.

"Well Ruth, what do you think?"

Silence reigned for a while, then his wife spoke, "Gideon, it's a marvellous idea. You will have to be very clever though, Gladys is a shy young thing."

Then she entered into the conspiracy. In a voice scarcely above a whisper she made her proposition. "Let us see what a woman's perspective can achieve. Leave the problem with me for a day or two."

Duly, Ruth made a visit upon Gladys at her home. The place was spotless, if somewhat sparse. Ruth was attempting to discover if any repair jobs were in need of remedy and eventually she discovered one. When Gladys took the large iron kettle from off the range she placed it upon a stone platform at its side. It was loose, making the kettle unstable.

"You will have to get that seen to Gladys", she remarked in a matter of fact tone, "I know, I shall ask Joshua Thomas if he would be so kind."

"Oh I don't know", Gladys stammered, "Mister Thomas is always so busy helping everywhere and he works so many hours, I couldn't ask him."

"But you are not going to", concluded Ruth. "I am, or perhaps the Pastor will."

Gladys continued to protest but gradually Ruth warmed her to the idea,

"Perhaps", she added, "in return, you could help Mr. Thomas, after all he is a bachelor who, I am sure, would appreciate the assistance of a woman from time to time. After all, now that your mother has, sadly, passed away you must have a lot of time to yourself"

Gladys thought for a moment, then replied with confidence, "You are right Mrs. Livingstone. If Mr. Thomas would be kind enough to help me with a few things that have needed attention for quite some while, I would be able, if he wished, to return his kindness by aiding him in some tasks. Sort of mutual assistance."

"Quite right," agreed Ruth, "Quite right."

As her husband had spoken upon, many years before in that initial open air meeting, when he had first met Joshua, the Gospels speak of a Sower who went forth to spread his seed. So it was that Joshua and Gladys came together. The seed scattered by Gideon and Ruth fell on good ground and, in its growing, brought forth abundance.

Just a few weeks later Joshua came knocking on the door of the Manse to speak with his Pastor. Gideon led him into the study where the nervous, unsure, stuttering member of his flock blurted out his feelings and wishes.

"Pastor, I need to speak upon a delicate matter. You may know that I may have been doing some work for Gladys Potter."

Here he blushed as if he was admitting to a grievous sin. He continued self-consciously.

"Pastor, nothing is amiss, I have not taken any advantages of her I assure you, but I have come to the conclusion that she would make a wonderful wife. How do I tell her that Joshua is willing, after all she may refuse me and I don't think that I could take a refusal easily."

Gideon smiled, he was highly amused.

"I do not think that will be the case at all Joshua. Let us just say that I firmly believe your suite will be greeted in a positive manner."

Here Gideon omitted to reveal to Joshua that a similar conversation had taken place between Ruth and Gladys just the day previously.

Good marriages are made in heaven, or so it is said. Thus it could be observed upon regarding the union of Joshua and Gladys. Plotted by the leaders of their Chapel, their communion became loyal and loving, enduring till death and after. They were married in August and their son Billy was born in June the following year, 1896. It was a complicated birth and no other children followed but the pair were inseparable and so proud of their son. Gideon and his accomplice Ruth, isolated in their knowledge of their conspiracy, were very pleased with their deed, becoming ever more so as the years went by.

Joshua proved a model father and husband, diligently overseeing the needs of his family. The house in Talbot Road was well furnished and provisioned even if the plumbing and the water closet never quite reached the standards that he sought. He used to confide to Gladys that one day every home would possess an inside bathroom, with all the rooms heated to the temperature that its occupants desired. Gladys used to smile at what she considered to be "fanciful notions", but she enjoyed her new life, her family and her husband.

She thought him so handsome and, blushing to herself, so desirable. He presented himself so well, both at home and to the outside world, and had, of late, taken to displaying a resplendent moustache, of which, he was so very proud. In their intimate moments he inquired of her, "did it suit him?"

"Of course", she would reply, "You are the most handsome man in Glossop, the best husband a woman could wish for."

Joshua's skills were in great demand. The work he had undertaken at the Chapel had come from within his very soul. He had excelled himself. The result was so fine that others who wanted classic stonework undertaken would seek out his services. Late Victorian society witnessed an explosion in Gothic and Classic styled building. Municipalities and factory owners vied with their competitors to build ever more grandiose edifices. It was an age of engineering accomplishment, combined with ever increasing wealth for the capitalist investors and those Boroughs wishing to make their mark.

Towns would explore areas well outside their jurisdiction to build reservoirs and pumping stations, designed to provide clean and plentiful water supplies for their citizens. Places like Liverpool and Warrington explored Wales, flooding Her valleys, to bring a sustained flow for their populace. Architects were commissioned to design these grand ventures, which in their grandeur would create an immortal monument to their vision.

Such was a particular scheme conceived by the city fathers of Stoke on Trent. Their population had expanded greater than most and water had become scarce. Peter Billington, an eminent engineer and architect was commissioned to solve the problem. He found the answer with the discovery of huge underground recourses in the Woore valley. It required a massive pumping station, a complex that would speed millions of gallons to Stoke each day, to be stored and distributed in strategic towers, which then supplied every house and factory in the region. The City fathers approved the plan but they wanted the facility to command a special awe. To this end they insisted upon a massive entry portal being constructed, immortalising their patrimony, elegantly carved by one of the Country's great stonemasons

Billington took up the challenge. He had his budget to keep within, so he had to obtain a mason who was both highly skilled and came reasonably priced. That was when Joshua Thomas came to his attention. Philip Partington was expanding his weaving manufactory and had asked Billington to provide both designs and costing. They were meeting in the Liberal Club to discuss progress when the architect revealed his dilemma over the Stoke project. Partington told his guest of the craftsmanship of Joshua and it was not long before Glossop's famous stonemason was being propositioned.

"Build this and you will be immortalised", stated the architect somewhat in his typical grandiose manner. It will mean at least two years creative endeavour. You will also have two other masons at your disposal to carve the mundane stonework leaving you to sculpt the flourishes."

"You make it sound as if we shall be constructing the Pyramids", mocked the young mason.

"We shall be my young friend but our work will be of far greater use than the originals."

Joshua constructed his portal; it stands to this day. Taking the road from Woore, passing the Dorothy Clive Gardens towards Stoke, the pumping station dominates the valley. It cleaves the woodland and the surrounding hills. The tourist stops to admire it, not knowing that it took the life of its creator.

For over two years the train sped Joshua from Glossop to Stoke every two weeks. He would work for eleven days, then come home for three. He shared the food and living quarters of the labourers, supervising the carving of the stone whilst sculpting intricate details himself. Blocks would be cut, matched and faced before being placed into their designated position and secured, in much the same way as they had been for centuries.

The accident came when the construction was almost complete. The scaffolding was in course of being dismantled. The engines were undergoing their inaugural trials. All was on target for the commissioning to commence in five days time. Suddenly, without warning, the main boiler, providing the steam for the engines, exploded. A pressure valve, which had stuck, went unnoticed, revolving the dial into the red. The subsequent blast was catastrophic. The entire engine shed was demolished. Joshua was one of three men who were killed. He just happened to be passing when the blast occurred. A brick hit him full in the chest killing him instantly. When Billington was informed of the accident he was most put out. It would take several weeks to replace the boiler, additionally, he would have to inform the relatives of the dead and, either organise their funerals, or the transportation of the bodies back to their hometown.

Subsequently, it was arranged that the train should transport Joshua's body back to Glossop. Gideon Livingstone had been instrumental in taking responsibility for many of the arrangements, relating the news to Gladys and, with his wife, devoting much time to her comfort. Gladys was inconsolable, devastated unable to comprehend what was happening.

Duly, it was the Pastor who met the coffin at the station, walking in front of it all the way to the Chapel, where it was to lie for two days until the internment. People were lining the streets all through the solemn journey, displaying the respected esteem that he was held in by the community. The cortege stopped outside Joshua's home in Talbot Road where Gladys, composed, displaying great dignity, joined the procession. Supported by Ruth she walked the rest of the way to the Chapel. Young

Billy now approaching six years of age, stayed close to his mother, holding her hand. As they turned into Fazackerly Street, Nathaniel, his wife and young Sally stood silent and still displaying their respects, Sally saw the pathetic, confused little urchin, he, in turn, noticed her. She smiled softly at him, full of empathy; he smiled back then turned his gaze again to stare stoically forward towards the Chapel. It was the first time that their eyes had met and, in their meeting, something stirred that was to endure.

Tears flowed down Sally's cheeks that day, tears for a crumpled little boy grief stricken over the loss of his father. Many more of her tears would flow for him over the years, but there would be smiles also, smiles and joy, profound joy. For Billy memories of that torrid journey would remain with him for the rest of his life.

The funeral was a memorable affair. The Chapel overflowed with mourners. Dignitaries from Stoke and Glossop attended. Gideon excelled himself with his oration. It was a sincere eulogy coming from a man who considered himself privileged to have been a friend of the master stonemason. No other person had known Joshua Thomas so well or knew of his countless kindnesses better than he, other than, of course, Gladys. Now, as he spoke he was certain their dear departed friend enjoyed a crown of glory, in the presence of his maker, provisioned of eternal peace, in heaven.

Today, Joshua lies at peace, in sight of his Chapel's spire, together with Gladys, his devoted wife who for the rest of her mortal life, never let a day go by without thought of him. She found reflected in their son, so much of her beloved husband, now upon him was showered all the loving devotion she possessed.

Joshua had saved well, and had a sustaining life insurance policy. The City of Stoke also granted her a widow's gratuity. Together with work that Gladys found with Partington's mill, the mother and son fared reasonably well. Gladys kept up her regular attendance at Chapel, mirroring her Billy's diligence. Consequently the young boy became well versed in the Bible and his faith, firstly in Sunday school, where occasionally he would smile sheepishly at little Sally Hawkins, then as a member of the senior congregation.

Both mother and son would visit Joshua's grave every week, where Gladys would converse with him, upon her love for him and the progress of his boy. Now a headstone stood over him, crafted by two of his fellow masons. It gave his name, his years; together with the names of those he had left behind. A space had been left for Gladys, together with the inscription 'A craftsman of great imagination'. For the master stonemason, who had capped so many spires came the hymnal plea inscribed along the base of the memorial.

'Shine through the gloom,
And point me to the skies.'

CHAPTER 3

'The child is father of the man.'
William Wordsworth. 1807.

Frank Potter tutored at the technical college, a large neo classical building which had been constructed in commemoration of the Diamond Jubilee of Queen Victoria. By the time of the death of that great monarch it had become the establishment that all boys aspiring to serve a worthwhile apprenticeship, or skilled trade, aimed to qualify for. Students would take a selection examination at the age of twelve or, alternatively, attend one day a week whilst working.

Frank had once worked at Partingtons Mill, but after an accident he had lost the necessary agility to continue. Therefore, when an opportunity became available, he had applied for the position of mechanical engineering master. His technical knowledge and practical experience had got him the vacancy.

With his wife and two daughters, he resided in North Road, which being the last northerly exit from the town, to the moorland above, it overlooked the daily bustle below and extended a view to the far hills opposite, where they dropped away towards Hadfield. Frank had lived in this house as a boy and would often fondly remember watching, with his mother, from the top of the garden as the steam train wound its way across Dinting Viaduct towards the station. Memories of his youth, his house were precious to him, remembrances of himself and his sister blackberrying or merely idling the summer days away in the meadows above; two of them brother and sister, glorious days.

Gladys Thomas and her son Billy were now his only other blood relatives, outside his immediate family. Since her sudden bereavement a year ago he had taken it upon himself to keep an eye on them both.

Young Billy was almost eight years old and growing into a strong healthy lad. He was proving to be a great source of strength and help to his mother. Gladys had obtained regular 'outwork' from Partingtons. It did not pay very well, in fact it was a pittance, but it supplemented the savings that her husband had left, together with a small pension, so they lived relatively well.

They carded hooks and eyes. Gladys would sew the eyes onto the cards and Billy would pass on the hooks. There were four dozen of each to a card and their front room would be full of gross upon gross. They worked together every weekday evening, with Gladys continuing their toil whilst Billy was attending the National School. All this labour would earn them the grand sum of nineteen shillings a week. Very little, but it provided Billy with good clothes and a decent diet.

Sunday had become a family ritual since Joshua had passed on. Frank and his family attended the Anglican Church in Fauvel Street. His wife had always been a member of the Anglican Communion so Frank had come over to the Parish Church when they were married. Both the Anglican and the Independent Chapel services ended at similar times so Frank and Gladys would meet at the top of Talbot Street and return to his home for Sunday lunch. It provided a most welcome break for Gladys who often felt lonely and depressed during the week, especially when Billy was out of the house. She was good friends with Helen, Frank's wife, and they would often sit together for two or three hours after lunch, whilst Frank would take the children walking, discussing their hopes and fears.

Frank's house had a long steep garden which, at the top, linked to that of his neighbours. There they had taken down the hedges and the three men used the land for a jointly owned pig. Every year a newly acquired piglet was obtained, fed on scraps and swill gathered by the three families and fattened up. Come Easter the pig would be 'put to sleep' as Frank would describe the undertaking to his daughters. For a long time thereafter, all three families would eat 'like Kings' for weeks. The pig was 'manna' from the Lord, nothing was ever wasted.

For this coming Easter weekend, Saturday had been designated, 'Pig day'. For the past year Billy had been helping to feed the ever-growing animal by collecting potato peelings and other vegetable scraps from houses all along Talbot Street. The little lad had a small wheelbarrow with which he would call to collect the scraps and empty the bins. By the time he got to his Uncle's, the barrow would be full to overflowing.

Billy would carefully empty the swill into a large copper receptacle that had once been used for washing, ensuring that the mess came to the boil for at least an hour. Thus he fed the boiler with sticks, stirred the ever increasingly unpalatable mixture until it was ready. Then the grateful pig partook of the feast. Billy had come to provide so much swill that Frank and his neighbours had considered extending the sty and having two pigs next year. It was also agreed that Gladys should be given a good leg joint, some bacon and a sausage of black pudding. Next year, if Billy kept supplies coming in they would be more generous.

This coming week Billy was to be initiated into the annual ceremony, which accompanied the dispatch of the poor animal. When the boy arrived the following Saturday morning, his barrow brimming with 'mysteries', he saw that the boiler was already lit and the water simmering. He took away the wooden lid and began to shovel in his collected goodies. It was then that Jimmy Jones, the son of one of Uncle Frank's neighbours, came running up.

"Come quickly Billy, we've got two new piglets, they are running around, squeaking and everything."

34

The boys ran to the top of the garden where sure enough three men and two other boys were looking over the pigpen admiring the new additions.

The'be both Gloucester Oldspots, the'be", observed one of the men.

"Particularly good for loin bacon", informed Uncle Frank. "They develop large broad backs."

Billy watched the two small piglets running around like mad things. He was fascinated "Reckons I shall have to bring even more swill in future, Uncle Frank."

"Reckons you will Billy, reckons you will."

The old pig was quietly grunting away in the far corner of a neighbour's garden. He had a strong rope around his neck, which was staked to the ground. Having served out his tenancy, he was now ready for his last excursion.

"Well," reflected Mister Jones, "happen its time we were off."

Michael Jones, Jimmy's father, saw the raising of the pig as a co-operative venture. He was a professed Christian Socialist, a member of the Independent Labour Party.

"Keir Hardie, would approve of this", he informed Frank. "It's a workers co-operative we are, that's a fact. brother citizens showing their solidarity with each other, sharing the fruits of our labour, without exploitation."

"Except for the pig of course", chipped in Mister Fennyworth, the other neighbour and partner in the venture of raising the pig.

"Happens you be right there John", Michael agreed.

All was now ready. A procession left Lord Street, proceeding off towards the moors. Three men followed by four boys and a pig. John Fennyworth carried a lump hammer, the instrument of death, delivering the fatal blow. Two of the boys pulled a hand cart containing a pair of large zinc plated bins and an enamel bowl, together with a saw, a long butcher's knife and a quantity of grease-proof paper, all the required, essential materials. The poor pig, the sacrificial lamb, the scapegoat, waddled overweight, seemingly little aware of his impending fate. Occasionally he would try and stop to root out some delicacy from the roadside but Jimmy, who held the rope, just pulled and the unfortunate animal would fall back into line just quietly complaining to himself.

It was then that Jimmy let out a plea in exclamation, "I bags the bladder", he declared, most determinedly.

"The bladder?" enquired Billy, "and what would you want that for?"

"Well the bladder is taken out carefully so as it's not damaged or punctured. Then it's tubed by the valve and me Mum makes up a ball from some of the skin. Then she puts the bladder inside, laces it up, then pumps it up. Makes a proper football it will. Wait and see, a proper black and white spotted football." Jimmy felt so triumphant. He had bagged the bladder.

The procession progressed to the designated place where a low wall met an adjacent trench. The ditch was used by the man responsible for catching the blood in the enamel bowl. The pig would be stood above the trench whilst Mister Fennyworth hit the unfortunate creature over the head. Death, hopefully, would come instantaneously, but the heart would continue to beat for a few minutes.

The throat would then be slit and the pumping of the heart would drain the body of its blood. Once it had stopped dripping the carcass would be slit from the neck to the rear, exposing the entrails, which would be fastidiously extracted. Two stakes would then be stretched out across the beast like a cross to display the organs, which were then cut away kidneys, heart, liver and lights.

The ceremony was enacted faultlessly. The four boys stood on the wall to observe the ritual. Billy was amazed; the pig went without a struggle, without a sound. Then all was cut up, the only waste being the entrails, which spilt into the trench to be left for the crows. It was so efficient. When the bladder was dislodged it was given to Jimmy, still bloody and warm. He was the richest boy in the Kingdom, holding up his trophy with pride.

"Well boys, you be initiated into the mysteries of the pig."

Mister Fennyworth took the undertaking very seriously, as if they had become members of a secret society. It was the first of a number of such occasions for Billy and his friends. The killing of a pig, by a trench, cut apart, his entrails and organs exposed, prefiguring what they would experience when they became men living in trenches across the sea.

For now, both for Billy and Jimmy, their only concern was in the making of the football. Mrs. Jones worked on the sacred object for a week. She carefully cured the bladder making sure it retained its elasticity. She then selected the finest part of the skin, the back, soaked it in brine, cut it into hexagons and stretched it on a frame to dry. It was then stitched into shape encompassing the bladder. Finally Michael pumped it up and tied the laces. It was a perfect football.

Jimmy was overjoyed. "Thank you pig", he whispered to himself, "thank you God for the pig."

The ball lasted for years; finally it found its destiny, like that of its grateful recipients, on a field far away, inspiring others onto their final goal. From time to time it found itself in need of repair, but it served its purpose many times over. Billy and Jimmy learned many of their early skills using the ball donated, so generously, by the pig. It was seemingly always with them, the black and white patches serving to remind them from whence it came.

As the years went by the dubbing utilised to waterproof the skin and keep it supple, led to the colouring becoming a uniformly dark Brown. The ball proved the unifying element, from around which began a lifelong friendship. Its source was often spoken of when they were elsewhere, stood in other trenches, deep in mud, being confronted by other similar yet even more tragic sights, as the slaughter of the pig, the destruction of men, mass destruction of men.

Frank would go down to the football ground on summer evenings with the two boys, while they practised their skills. Sometimes Jimmy's father would join them and they would make up two teams. It could become very competitive. On rainy days the ball could become very heavy if the water breached the dubbing that was used to protect it from becoming sodden.

Walking down to the ground one evening in 1906, Michael spoke to Frank of the coming General Election. "Who are you going to support Frank?" enquired his neighbour.

"Well I have listened to you over the past years Michael, shared many a pig. Reckon I shall support the Socialist candidate. He won't win, not this time, but he deserves my support."

"What's a General Election?" Jimmy whispered to his friend.

"It's when people gets to vote for that Hill-Woods, to be our MP", replied his friend.

"Oh" and Jimmy continued to dribble the ball along the road.

Billy held back, listening to the two men.

"The Clarion van is coming to Glossop this Saturday", Informed Michael, "You coming down Frank?"

"Certainly will", came the reply, "Should be interesting."

"Can I come too? I want to see that Clarion Van as well." Billy was forever eager to gain new experiences, this sounded interesting to Uncle Frank, and it should be for him.

"Why yes, of course you can." affirmed his Uncle.

The Clarion Van was a beautifully crafted affair. Like many of its sister vans, it had been entirely constructed by volunteer labour. It was drawn by the most magnificent, strong, handsome, Shire Horse, brown and white, immaculately groomed and owning a grand flourishing tail. Inside, the van was fitted with an iron stove whose chimney projected from out of the roof. The entire interior was decorated in panels of green, red, blue and yellow, composed of delicate, elegant, scrollwork. The front of the van was equipped with detachable doors and a platform allowed anyone addressing the crowd to project four feet above their audience.

Billy arrived with Uncle Frank, finding himself propelled along by the eager crowd of men and women curious of the 'goings on'. The caravan had been parked at the top left-hand side of Norfolk Square. It was adorned with banners proclaiming 'Socialism Now!' and 'National Union of Women Workers.'

So many people were gathered that it was impossible to get within thirty yards of the van. Billy skirted the crowd, he wanted to inspect the horse, which had been tethered close by 'The Moon And Sixpence.' He was amazed at the size of the beast it towered above him. It was magnificent, having such a shiny well-groomed coat.

"Want to stroke him?" enquired a man standing by, "He is very mild mannered, won't kick or bite. Just touch him gently and speak softly to him."

Billy tentatively began to stroke and sure enough it never moved.

"His name is Hercules because he is so strong."

"Who was Hercules?" asked Billy, totally fascinated with the gentle giant.

"He was the strongest of all the Greek heroes", explained the stranger.

Billy was becoming absorbed with this man and his horse "Who were the Greek heroes?"

Now a question came from the man. "Do you not have a library here in Glossop?"

"Of course. I have never been in there but I know it is full of books and things."

"Don't you read at all?" came the next question.

"Yes I do. I have read Treasure Island, Kidnapped, and Christmas Carol. I've read Treasure Island three times."

"That's good", the man replied. "Tell me, what is your name?"

"Why, it's Billy Thomas and I am eleven years old"

"Well Billy, take my advice, go and join your library, look at all the books, find what interests you and read. You will be forever glad you did so. Now I have a book right here with me, which I want to give you. It is a present to you. It might not suit your taste right now, but it could interest you in the years to come."

With that he handed over the book. Billy looked at the cover, 'Merrie England'

"Thank you very much sir. I promise that I shall read it, thank you."

"You are very welcome Billy. Tell you what, would you like to look after the horse? I have to make a speech."

"Yes", agreed Billy, "I will stay here until you come back."

Just at that moment a man approached, "Mister Blatchford, we are ready for you now."

"Coming right away", replied Robert Blatchford and away he went to the van.

Billy stayed by the horse for nearly an hour, together with the rest of the crowd, he remained hushed, as promised, a studious guardian of his charge whilst his new found friend spoke. There were times when the crowd erupted spontaneously into applause and Billy automatically clapped with them. The eleven year old boy understood little of what was spoken upon, but retained elements of what he heard, which came back to him in later years. This charismatic man, he would always remember with gratitude, for a day spent with a wonderful animal, but mostly he would be grateful to Robert Blatchford for introducing him into the world of books.

He would also remember how the crowd displayed its appreciation. when Robert Blatchford's oration came to an end, with the summation.

"In this world there is plenty for all by far, no need of starvation, no need of poor housing. We need a Government possessed of the will to sweep away the slums, it could be achieved in a few short years. This task would help in solving another blemish of society, that of unemployment."

"The factory owners, the mine owners, the railway owners, they are also part of the problem. Sweep them all away! You sweat for so little; they idle for so much. These are their values, representing their society. Well, I implore you, sweep it all away, knock it all down, rebuild it nearer to our hearts desire. Bring into being the new Socialist order. From each according to his ability, to each according to his need. Where is the fault in that? I exalt you, where is the fault in that?"

The crowd was enthused, it surged forward each member of the mass wishing to grasp the hand of this Socialist Messiah. Robert Blatchford shook hands with so many that day, increasing adherents to the Socialist cause.

He had also stirred the emotions and aspirations of an eleven-year-old boy, transforming his life. Two key things would happen, firstly Billy would come to read all manner of books and secondly, subconsciously, in his mind, would be stored the essential elements of Robert Blatchford's speech. 'From each according to his ability, to each according to his need.'

The people had begun to disperse. Hercules stirred as if he was impatient to be re-hitched to the van and be on his way. Billy began to stroke the horse once more speaking softly to him as Mister Blatchford had instructed.

"Well Billy, you've done a grand job there, a real grand job. Not everyone of your age would have stood his duty like that. What say you Belle?"

This enquiry was addressed to a tall substantial woman standing by his side.

"Well, I think this young man will make a fine comrade one day," and she put her arm over one of Billy's shoulders.

Billy could discern the aroma of delicate scent coming from the ample white blouse of the grand lady. "I heard you speaking before Mister Blatchford" he remarked, "tell me what is the Suffrage and why haven't women got it?"

The lady smiled upon him.

"Robert, what have you found here? Not only a grand young comrade to guard Hercules but one who grasped the essence of what was preached."

She turned to Billy, bending down until their eyes met on a level. "My name is Belle Maloney. I spend my life travelling the country attempting to reason with people over rights for women, meaning, the right to vote, equal wages for equal pay, equal rights in education, working conditions that will allow both men and women to be together deciding affairs of state. I do not only campaign for the Suffrage, but for real equal rights between the sexes, then and only then we, both men and women will obtain true freedom and justice."

Much of this, of course went over poor Billy's head, Belle did tend to preach somewhat, sometimes forgetting to whom she was speaking. That is not to say that every word sounded out without a message striking home.

"Do you know?" he informed the lady rhetorically, "I live with my mother, the two of us on our own. My Dad, he died a few years ago and my Mum she works so hard. She is always so tired, yet she tells me she would vote and things, if she could. That's the truth too, I know she would. I always get told by her that living will get better for me and her if I learn all I can, putting what I learn to good use. "

Coming from the mouth of a babe he sounded profound, "Billy you are wise before your years," concluded Mister Blatchford. "You do as I advised and get down to that library, read good books, lots of good books."

Robert Blatchford shook Billy's hand. Belle gave him a hug. He stayed watching as they hitched Hercules to the van, then waved frantically as they left. He waited till all disappeared from sight going in the direction of Manchester, accompanied by a group of Clarion cyclists.

Billy felt sad at their leaving. It had been an exciting day, out of the ordinary. He had fallen in love with Hercules, hoping, one day to meet with him again. He concluded that the advice he had received was sound, he would indeed join the library. Now, however, it was time to run up to the football field and see if he could find Jimmy. Giving his leave of Uncle Frank, who was participating in illuminated discussion with a group of men, he turned to run towards the railway station.

Gladys sat attentively that evening listening to her son, telling of his days adventures whilst they carded the hooks and eyes. His chattering was unceasing. By the time they had been working for two hours, she felt that she had been there in the square herself, so graphic and detailed had he reported matters to her. The caring of the horse, the speeches, Mister Blatchford, Miss Maloney, she felt that she knew them intimately and had listened to their speeches personally.

Before he went to bed that night Gladys promised Billy that, come Monday, immediately after school, she would take him to the library and sign up his membership. In truth, she was very pleased with her son. He seemed genuinely enthused towards his book reading project, as he had christened it. Again she was minded of Joshua, beloved Joshua, a well-read man himself.

Over the years, Billy was to witness a number of Clarion rallies, either at election times, or when strikes broke out. There were other times also; on hot summer afternoons when meetings were organised to recruit new members and to re-commit existing ones. Billy came to realise exactly how firmly the Clarionettes were dedicated to their socialist cause.

Billy did join 'The Men's League For Women's Suffrage', but, in truth, by then Football and work consumed his life and his membership was merely a token. The real accomplishment of that first Clarion meeting was how it resulted in introducing to him the great wealth of knowledge, wisdom and entertainment that the library gave him. He became obsessed, spending hours leafing through the reference section and diligently reading the two books each week that he was allowed to take home.

At first it was fiction that attracted him. He read the remaining works of Robert Louis Stevenson that he had yet to encounter, followed by, R. M. Ballantine. Mark Twain, moving up to Thomas Hardy, the Brontes, Dickens, where 'Great Expectations' enthralled him. Characters from other of the master's books brought forth differing emotions. Uriah Heap, he hated, how could a person say one thing and, dishonestly act so differently? Little Nell, life could be so cruel to the weak, the kind, the innocent.

In three years Billy had taken out, and read over two hundred books. The librarians had come to respect him. He always brought back his volumes on time and in good order, often remarking on their contents. They would recommend books to him.

"Billy, there is a great new book in this week, 'The Iron Pirate.' Billy would thank them, later informing his providers how engrossed he had been reading of the rogue Dreadnought. He encountered Jules Verne, Alexander Dumas, H. G. Wells, Elizabeth Gaskell, George Elliot, whose 'Silas Marner', gave him an insight into principle, honesty, and what was for him, at this time, love. Then, one day it happened, he found poetry.

It all began with Lewis Carroll, 'The Walrus And The Carpenter', the dreaded 'Jabberwocky.' Looking along the shelves he found Lord Byron, 'Beppo', 'Don Juan', and long to remain in his memory, 'Childe Harold's Pilgrimage.' Then came the most reprehensible of creatures, 'The Jackdaw of Rheims.' This he found in 'The Insgoldsby Legends', from which he learned from heart 'Bloody Jack Of Shrewsbury.'

Now all you young Ladies beware,
All you young Ladies beware,
And don 't you go down no glen
With harum, scarum young men,

41

For you really can 't trust one in ten.

He thought upon that for a long time, what on earth could young men be not trusted upon when girls were concerned, some more years would pass before he gained an inkling. Next came the works of Oscar Wilde. On this occasion the librarian was unsure whether it would make suitable reading for one so young, 'considering what the author was caught doing with that young Lord what's his name'. Eventually, after leafing through the pages the lady relented somewhat reluctantly and Billy sped away with the volume wondering just what they were afraid he would read.

He merely found beautiful words, wonderful short stories and a rather silly play about an absent minded young man called Earnest. Then he read the 'Selfish Giant', and was filled with sadness, yet learnt word for word. The following Christmas he related it to the gathered school, parents and governors. His performance was faultless, Gladys felt so proud sitting in the audience alongside Gideon Livingstone and his wife. The Hawkins family also, all three of them, were deeply impressed.

Now his poetic exploration became more sophisticated. Tennyson, The Light Brigade swept across the page, galloping into glory whilst being thundered at and volleyed upon. Yet the same author brought him, the tragic infatuated lover of Sir Lancelot, his 'Lady of Shallot'. Through this he came upon the Arthurian legends, The Green Knight, Sir Galahad, the brotherhood of The Round Table, their deeds of chivalry, the quest for the holy grail, their destiny with death. Finally, Wordsworth's 'Imitations of Immortality' found a lasting place in his memory.

'Splendour in the grass,
Glory in the flower'

From myth and legend came the history of the British, and those Races that had influenced its destiny. Greeks, Romans, Saxons and the dreaded Vikings, Dickens, with his 'Child's History Of England', gave him the basic facts surrounding his heritage. Yet not all her leaders were heroes. He was, for instance, informed of that fat, fornicator of a Monarch, 'who was a blot of blood and gore upon the English throne'.

History was full of kings, soldiers, sailors, and adventurers. Harold less an eye, Henry the Fifth, with his Welsh archers, Elizabeth, Drake, Raleigh, the Armada, Clive Of India, Napoleon and Wellington, Balaclava, South Africa, Doctor Livingstone, whom, he wondered, just might be related to his Pastor. England, he discovered, was the centre of the World. The atlas proved it to be so. All those pink areas covering the globe, controlled by her Navy, her great battleships.

Industry and invention, all the Nations of the World stood in the shadow of Britannia. Cotton, steel, steam, the railways, tunnels bridges.

James Watt, Thomas Telford, Isambard Kingdom Brunel, Stephenson, with his Rocket, Arkwright with his Mule, Billy met all of them, learned of their skill, their achievements, courage and their sacrifice.

Yes, he was part of the greatest Nation on the face of the Earth, possessing the greatest Empire ever carved out upon the Planet. Statesmen, writers, generals, admirals, the greatest were all of Britain's soil. Billy was so proud to be a part of it all, ascending above the ordinary mortals who inhabited other parts of the Globe.

Then came the day. It was in his fifteenth year. Upon clearing up his bedroom he re-encountered 'Merrie England.' He turned the pages to read that all was not projected as stated in the history books. There was another side. This was a world of heartless employers, poverty, sickness, unemployment, exploitation, and injustice, enacted upon those who did not own any of the 'means of production'. This book challenged the way things were. 'Merrie England', with all its wealth and power did not offer happiness, for nothing was shared. Just a few had almost everything; the rest had to struggle for a pittance.

Long hard hours worked in pits, factories and quarries, yet still people were unable to feed themselves and their families. 'Merrie England', brought Billy back to reality. He now wished that he had read it earlier, for here he discovered the paradox. Reading had given him all that knowledge, literature, history, geography, the Arts, but the books in the library were chosen with the purpose of providing selective knowledge. There was another side to the England that all those books had failed to explain to him. Yet the exposition had been here at home, in his bedroom, all the while, 'Merrie England.'

Sitting here, the book on his lap, he recalled that day four years previously when he had encountered The Clarion Van, Hercules, Belle Maloney and Robert Blatchford. He clasped the book tightly and in a soft voice, just for his own hearing he whispered, "thank you Mister Blatchford, thank you very much."

Thus, two events had brought great influence to bear upon his life. The killing of the pig, which had provided the football and, his meeting with Robert Blatchford opening up to him a world of purposeful literature. There was now to occur a third event, which happened due to the inclemency of the English climate, on a cold, very wet Saturday morning in the library. It was the first time he ever spoke to Sally Hawkins with any purpose.

It was June in the year 1910, one of those summer days when the sun remains obscured from sight and the rain sheets sideways down from the Pennines drenching and chilling anyone who is brave enough to venture out. The cold seems to penetrate the very bones, not because the temperature has slipped below freezing but due to its unexpected, unseasonable nature. An English summer's day all to often defrauds its recipients with an inhospitable discomfiture, that extends shivers deep into the frame of its uncomfortable victims.

Not even Billy would practice football on such a day so off he ran to the library, borrowing his mother's old battered umbrella. He had left Gladys at the house preparing some more hooks and eyes for carding promising her that he would work all that coming evening until all his share of the work was completed. Now, armed with a slab of bread and jam, he made his way to the palace of books, eager to explore new discoveries.

He had yet to realise how high a level of education he had attained, although, his Uncle Frank had begun to consider his potential. Some Sunday afternoons the two of them would converse, with Frank listening to his young Nephew. Often they would discuss the latest book that Billy had read. The latest combination of 'Merrie England', Walt Whitman and a history of the American civil war had brought about a discussion on democracy and poverty.

Billy's skills in argument were in their formative mode, idealistic and simple. It is the way of the young who observe tradition, bureaucracy and prejudice as the sole barriers to change and improvement, which once swept away, inevitably lead to the solutions their idealism demands.

What impressed Frank was his Nephew's ability to quote from sources and to make a judgement. For example, the differences within the society of the emerging United States and the community that he lived in. How his conclusions had been formulated, Frank could only guess at.

Billy was talking, making sweeping statements.

"We have a society of servants and masters. America is a land of equals. Not all might be equal in ability or possessions, in fact they most certainly are not, Uncle Frank, but they do not have barriers of social stigma, laid down like we have. We sing:

'The rich man in his castle,
The poor man at his gate.
He made them high and lowly
And ordered their estate.'

President Lincoln contradicts this. In his Gettysburg address he states:

'We hold these truths to be self evident,
that all men are created equal.
That Government of the people,
for the people, by the people,
shall not perish from this land.'

Billy continued in his explanation. Lincoln's Republic had just defeated the Confederacy in the bloodiest battle of the civil war; a war designed to set free the slaves. His belief was that everyone had rights of representation that governments should work on behalf of every single member of its citizens, equally.

Frank did not want to destroy what he saw as a young boy's illusions brought about through over simplistic analysis, yet he did want to inform his Nephew how impressed he was at him being able to take two statements of contrasting sentiment and of diverse sources, to use them in creating an argument.

"Well Billy", he said , in an encouraging and positive manner. "You have certainly read well and, what is more important, remembered what you have read. What you accomplished then was a very clever form of argument. However, not all in life is so black and white, people, society does not undergo change, merely through the expression of noble sentiments.

The reply, which followed, brought a lasting impression to Frank Potter.

"I know Uncle Frank, Mark Twain taught me that when I read The Adventures of Huckleberry Finn."

Quite so", replied his Uncle, "Quite so Billy."

Frank now realised that Billy could produce logical, mature assessments, even if they contradicted his own point of view. Billy was now fifteen years of age and this next year would be crucial for his development. What to do with such a boy?

Circumstances thus far, had allowed Billy a full education, both technical and literary. Although he helped his mother to earn extra income through their home working and he assisted several local farmers at harvest time, now was the time to think upon his future career. Frank decided that this coming week he would have a considered discussion with his sister on the matter.

The young boy, who now ran up the imposing entrance to the library, was indeed the object of much thought in the mind of his Uncle Frank. He was now about to enter the contemplation of another who fate was about to thrust in his path.

Such was his enthusiasm that he was quite unaware of the slightly built young girl waiting to be attended to when he handed in his returns upon the reception desk. Placing two volumes in front of the startled librarian, a volume of Lear's nonsense poems, and Conan Doyle's, early adventures of Sherlock Holmes.

"Do you have anymore Sherlock Holmes please?" he enquired.

"Wait just a minute Billy", pleaded the voice behind the counter. "Just let me finish seeing to this young lady first."

"Oh I am so sorry", said the admonished lad and, turning to the girl being served he added, "Sorry miss, I didn't see you there."

As he was speaking he realised who the girl was; it was Miss Hawkins, Sally, from the Chapel.

The librarian, Mrs. Lloyd, did not realise that they knew each other. She introduced them. Billy, this is Miss Sally Hawkins, like you she reads a lot, but, fortunately, she is more steady than you are."

"Well I am very sorry for butting in Miss Hawkins."

Here Billy turned towards the girl as he spoke and something inside him stirred. He had never noticed girls before except as dull uninteresting creatures having nothing in common with boys. However this young lady now produced within him a feeling of sheepishness, mixed with another sensation which seemed to make his heart beat faster. He knew his face had gone very red, leaving him, for the moment, lost for words.

Sally Hawkins possessed endless strands of long, glorious, fair hair, together with large deep blue eyes. She was slim and well developed for her fourteen years. It was she who, in a very grown up manner, formally stretched out her hand.

"Well, Billy, I am very pleased to meet you."

She spoke, in an apparently mocking manner, formal, keeping her hand extended towards him.

"Likewise, I'm sure Miss Hawkins", he stammered, then, without realising why, he added, "and what do you like to read?"

There was no chance for Sally to reply, for Mrs. Lloyd interjected, "Billy I have kept back the best of all the Sherlock Holmes novels for you, 'The Hound of the Baskervilles'."

"Oh I have read that", announced Sally, triumphantly. "It is a very good book, full of mystery and has an unexpected ending. It takes place on Dartmoor with mists, bogs and mountains always in the background."

"That is very well described Sally", remarked Mrs. Lloyd, then added, "Billy, you will enjoy it very much."

"Well thank you Mrs. Lloyd." Billy was taken aback that Sally had read something that he had not. "What are you reading at the moment Miss Hawkins?" Billy was hoping that it would be something that he had read so that he could counter the literary advantage that the girl had gained over him.

"I am going through the novels of Sir Walter Scott at the moment." came the reply.

This was a further drawback for Billy; Scott was an author he had not read. "What book in particular?" he asked pretentiously, appearing to know of the novelist.

"The Fair Maid of Perth."

"Oh that, it sounds like the kind of book that only a girl would read." He was becoming very defensive now.

"Not at all", interjected Mrs. Lloyd. "The book is set in Medieval Scotland. It is all about treachery and intrigue finishing with the most ghastly fight between thirty people of two different Clans, fighting to the death, a fight where almost all are slaughtered."

Here Billy felt he was on stronger ground. "It has similarities with Macbeth then. Seemingly whenever the ancient Scots met each other, they plotted, and killed one another."

"Quite so, agreed Mrs. Lloyd. Then an idea came to her, "Sally, why don't you show Billy where the Waverley novels are?"

"I would love to", answered the girl in a pleasant and agreeable manner. "Come on Billy."

Billy followed her like an obedient puppy, brought down to earth by this slightly built girl almost a year younger than himself. Now however, together with his newly found modesty. came a sense of excitement, he would like to spend some time with Sally, perusing new books.

That morning the two of them spent over three hours together each discovering new aspects of literature and reading. Mrs. Lloyd observed them from the distance of her counter, very pleased with herself for bringing two young people of like minds, and interests together.

Within a year, Billy and Sally had read much of what the other had found rewarding. They conversed for hours in the library on what they had just read. Mrs. Lloyd would watch them and listen, noting how, in their mutual shyness, their conversations remained formal and discursive, seldom straying from the realms of material that the library offered.

It was to be the poet Milton who awakened an unspoken, little understood tension between them, a phenomenon that would not find resolution until years in the future. Pastor Livingstone had been speaking upon original sin and the inevitable, subsequent, imperfections that it had created in Man's character. He had quoted from 'Paradise Lost'. The following Saturday, Sally discovered the relevant volume. Sitting next to each other the pair read with growing interest and curiosity.

The blind composer of the rhymless, epic, heroic, English verse, found two new adherents in Billy Thomas and Sally Hawkins. For the next three weeks they read and explored their reading, a process that gave birth to an awakening, a deciphering of the secrets between male and female that usually comes from gradual practical experimentation. The story unravelled, as the great poem progressed it became as thrilling and tense as any novel they had previously read.

Satan gathers together a monstrous horde, a vast army of devilry. Legion, upon legion rise up to challenge the might of Heaven. They are miserably defeated, scattered to hell, there to await the next opportunity to strike at he who did first create them. They arise a second time for Satan has heard that a paradise has been created, within which God has placed his greatest creation, Man. Satan is determined that this new wonder shall join in the fall from grace to which he and his host have been condemned. Man's downfall will mirror his own. Meanwhile, in Eden, God creates, for Adam, a partner, Eve. She is beautiful and perfect in Adams eyes.

As Sally and Billy read each in turn one to the other, they both became expectant of an oncoming revelation. Sally, had now come to look at her Saturdays in the library as the highlight of her week. In many ways the books, the library possessed had become peripheral, it was Billy who was the centre of her reason for coming.

In Billy's heart also, something was stirring. He was mostly unsure of what it was, but he knew that Sally's company was becoming a very important part of his life. Little they knew, merely two weeks were left to them of this idyll among this oasis of books. Sally was reading. God had formed Eve from Adam's rib.

Before me, Woman is her name,
Extracted; for this cause he shall forego
father and mother, and to his wife adhere;
And they shall be one heart, one flesh, one soul.

Here Sally paused; there was a meeting of eyes, blue and brown, boy and girl, innocent, yet somehow knowing a force was binding them together. Sally closed the book.

"Time for me to go now Billy, See you next week."
It was a statement, not a question; it brought a nonchalant, passive reply.
"Yes, of course."

They left together, parting at the foot of the steps, each the owner of new thoughts, new feelings, each in wonderment of the day and what had been revealed to them. The following week came Sally's announcement; a declaration, which brought such devastation to the wretched boy.

"This is going to be my last visit to the library for a considerable time. My parents are going to send me to a boarding school to finish my education. I am going to St. Elphins, in Darley Dale, which is simply miles away. So today, I have to hand in my books and leave without a single volume."

Billy was devastated, seeking to understand the implications of what his friend had said. He found it impossible. Sitting down, staring at a blank wall he uttered not a word.

Sally came over to him and put her arm on his shoulder. It proved a soothing remedy. Reaching out, he took her hand, looked into her eyes to discover that Sally was as upset as he was. Putting her hand to his lips he gently kissed it, then embarrassment took over and the hand dropped away having been released.

That morning the pair talked, and talked, never attempting to seek out a book. They spoke of the times they had spent together in the library, of the past books they had introduced to each other. So intense was their conversation that they were completely unaware how quickly the time had flown. Suddenly Sally discovered it was the hour for her to go. Their eyes both glistened, she shook his hand, kissed his startled cheek, and turned to go. Hesitatingly, the distraught girl turned back hugged the bemused boy, then turning for the last time, went over to Mrs. Lloyd, thanked her and left. As she went out of the door, the librarian noticed Sally taking out a small white handkerchief to pad her eyes.

Mrs. Lloyd turned back to observe Billy sitting gazing out towards the door which had stubbornly, unusually, remained ajar. In later years, remembering that door, she saw its status as symbolic, displaying that only a chapter had ended, not the entire story.

For now Billy appeared so bereft, so alone. She knew that boys like Billy who were academic, always having an open book before them, tended to be solitary in nature, sensitive. Sally had become his fellow traveller, exploring life together through the world of books. Now she saw him entering a period of great loneliness, drifting as if a sailboat, without a compass, through the doldrums.

Mrs. Lloyd approached him speaking kindly in a softly spoken voice. "Well I do not suppose young Sally will be away for ever and, when she comes back home, I would think that one of the first things she will do will be to visit here. Billy uttered not a word. He just nodded in assent and went back to his book. He had found a volume of Tennyson, reading the Knight's oath.

To love one woman only
And to cleave to her, and worship her
With years of noble deeds
Until he won her.

Now he determined upon a task. Swearing solely within the earshot of God he pledged to win Sally Hawkins, if necessarily through years of noble deeds. Yes, he would cleave to her. He sought out the word in the dictionary, 'cleave to, in union with.' With noble deeds he would one day win Sally Hawkins and be in union with her. There was little insight of any physical connotation composing his oath, among Billy's thoughts that day, but he was aware that it meant the two of them would, one day, be inseparably linked. For now, that comforting vision was enough for him.

It was to prove to be almost four long years before Billy was to have another deep conversation with Sally. They would meet occasionally on the Chapel steps but time and parents would prohibit more than a perfunctory and nominal greeting.

His reading of books never slackened though, indeed in many ways it increased. Within two years, he had read all of Scott's works. He reasoned, correctly, that one day he could, perhaps impress, young Miss Sally Hawkins, with a profound knowledge of the author. The other aspect of his academic nature began to develop, taking a distinctly technical turn, especially in the field of engineering and physics. He was accepted as an apprentice at Partington's, swiftly gaining a reputation for being skilled in the ministering of maintenance and fault finding of complex machinery.

Complex skills on the football field were also being mastered. Together with Jimmy Jones and the inevitable football, he was starting to become noticed. The 1912-1913, season saw him gaining a regular first team place playing for Hadfield. Jimmy whom, if the truth were known, had practised much longer and harder than his friend, had been signed as an apprentice with Glossop North End. It was cleaning out the changing rooms and the players boots in the early days, but gradually the Manager Jack Lloyd, husband of the sympathetic librarian, together with some of the senior players, began to realise Jimmy's dedication and talent. It would not be long before Jimmy was playing regularly for the first team.

It was a blustery day in March 1913, that Billy walking casually past the ground spotted Jimmy having a practice session, with one of the stars of Glossop's team. It was none other than Tommy Fitchie. Billy knew this because he had recently been given a cigarette card displaying Fitchie's photograph, together with his details. He was an avid collector of football cards and pestered anyone he knew who smoked that brand which portrayed the steadfast sailor and the Dreadnought, or the cheaper Woodbines.

Jimmy spied Billy and called him over. He introduced his disbelieving friend to the famous man. "This is my friend Billy, Mister Fitchie, he is excellent at football."

Tommy Fitchie went through the motions of grasping the young lad's hand. "Hello Billy, and you, like my young friend here can play brilliantly, yes?"

Tommy was incessantly being informed of promising players', but although he had often been shown footballers who were good amateurs, never had he discovered high-class talent from out of the blue. Today was to prove differently.

The reply, when it came was full of confidence. "Well I have played with Jimmy for years. Now I play for Hadfield's first team."

"Hadfield eh?" came the reply. "Best we see what you can do then. What position do you play in?"

"Centre forward."

Centre forward, ninety five per cent of young boys were centre forwards. This did not bode well. "Let us see then. Take a penalty shot against me Billy, do your best."

"If it is all right with you Mister Fitchie, I shoot better from further back."

'Cheeky little beggar', thought the Scottish international. "Right then wherever you want to take it."

Billy stepped back almost to the eighteen-yard line and over to the right. He placed the ball walked back about eight paces and ran. The ball was struck firmly but not accurately. It was going wide of the mark and high to the left. Fitchie stood still, making the same mistake that others had made before and would do so again. The ball dipped, curved and entered the goal inches inside the top corner. The Scotsman was flabbergasted, bemused even. A fluke?, well he would see.

"Try that again Billy."

"Yes sir", came the reply. "From the right side this time, if that is all right?"

"No problem."

Well it was a problem. Fitchie was ready this time but even so the ball defeated him again. He noticed that on this occasion, Billy struck the ball with his left foot. The ball appeared to be coming straight towards him but then it curled upwards and outwards tantalisingly escaping his outstretched fingertips and entering the goal.

'This boy has something', he thought, 'best see what else he can do.'

Fitchie was coming towards the end of his playing career, one which stretched back over twenty five years. He had witnessed the birth of the professional game and seen the game grow in popularity and sophistication. Now, having survived a couple of cartilage injuries he was preparing for his retirement, hopefully to take up coaching or even management.

As the next hour progressed the young man began to impress him more and more. At the end with the two lads having run rings round him, he had decided to inform one of the team's scouts.

"Let us see how this lad performs in a team environment", he said to himself. He remembered his early days playing in the streets of Glasgow, running back to his home in the Gorbals, his knees grazed, clothes caked with mud, his poor mother pleading with him to try and keep his clothes from damage and muck, his drunken father clipping his ear for no apparent reason.

Football had allowed Tommy to rise above the hapless throng that wearied and drank their lives away aimlessly leaning on street corners waiting for the bars to open or for the chance of a few days work.

He had been spotted by a scout working for Queen's Park soon becoming a permanent fixture on matchdays, commanding the field at Hamden Park. The highlight of his career came when he played for his country against the immortal enemy, England. His talent was self-evident and soon he was playing in the colours of Woolwich Arsenal, followed by the famous colours of the emerging Tottenham. Now, in his twilight playing days, he was lending his talents to this little town south of Manchester, struggling in the Second Division.

If he put a Scout Billy's way and gave him a chance, his experience in football would have come full circle. He would speak to Nathaniel Hawkins as soon as possible. Hawkins was a good scout, able to discern the exceptional from the merely talented.

Fitchie bade the boys good day, wishing Billy all the best for the future. He felt he had achieved something worthwhile, hoping that the lad would play well in front of Hawkins. Perhaps he would see the lad again, soon, playing in the colours of his present team.

Poor Tommy Fitchie, he was not aware at the moment in time, but his next match was to prove his last. A bad tackle would lead to a re-occurrence of his ligament injury and he would never fully recover from it. He would, however, become a gifted coach assisting his national side during one of its few periods of pre-eminence over its ancient foe to the south.

In contrast, Billy's future was to take a brief, yet glorious turn. Soon crowds would be clamouring to see the town's newest and brightest star. The young man who could curve the ball both left and right, up and away. Billy's time was coming.

CHAPTER 4

Sport that wrinkled Care derides,
And Laughter holding both his sides.
Come, and trip it as you go
On the light fantastic toe.

John Milton 'L' Allegro'

Nathaniel passed through the entrance of the High Peaks Conservative Club, an imposing building of mock Victorian Gothic style that succeeded in its purpose of dwarfing and intimidating those of the uninitiated who entered its hallway. The shopkeeper who extended his talents and time into scouting out for new players for his town's football team was seeking out Mr Hill-Woods, the local MP and benefactor of Glossop North End.

They had arranged this meeting to discuss the young player that Nathaniel had been monitoring, young Billy Thomas, whom he was ready to enthuse upon having been so impressed by the exhibitions of skill, dexterity and agility that the player undoubtedly had at his command.

In the past, Nathaniel's ability to spot new local talent had provided the club with a number of players who eventually succeeded in gaining a place in the first team. One had even been recently purchased by one of the big clubs adding much needed revenue to the accounts.

Hill-Woods sponsored the team, not so much because it was a real interest of his, but it had become a means whereby vital votes came his way aiding him to keep ahead of the Liberal dynasty which was the Partingtons. The franchise was extending all the while. Soon, he believed, heaven forbid, it might even extend to women. He had covered for this eventuality utilising his wife, together with her wide ranging web of charity work, the churches and her women's groups.

The football team had cost him considerable sums of money over the years but it was well supported, playing far above the level expected from a small town of less than twenty-five thousand souls. He respected the ability of Nathaniel Hawkins to seek out new talent and for free at that. Subsequently, when the man displayed so much excitement over a potential new player in a manner far more enthusiastically than he had ever before witnessed, it gained his immediate attention.

"Well Nathaniel", the MP, began, "Who have we found this time?"

A waiter brought drinks to the table, Scotch for the Anglican MP, fruit juice for the temperant, non-conformist Nathaniel.

"Young Billy Thomas," came the reply. "A member of our congregation, father killed in an accident whilst in charge of constructing stonemasonry at a water pumping facility near to Stoke on Trent. He is a promising engineer by all accounts, can strip down and re-assemble a Hattersley in less than a day I believe."

"And football?", enquired the MP

"It's astonishing." replied Nathaniel, "Truly astonishing. He has both pace and complex ball skills, but most of all he can kick a ball that is able to swerve in a curved line. He plays with both feet so the opposition has no idea which way it is going to travel. Beats the keeper every time. The young man trains hard, so his fitness is superb. I tell you Mr. Hill-Woods, unless we sign him, forthwith one of the big clubs will discover his existence and we shall lose out."

Nathaniel had successfully touched the three major nerve ends that electrified and drove the MP, the scent for a good commercial proposition, becoming associated with bringing a new talent to the team and, finally, being involved with intrigue. The young man's future and development never entered into his mind. Billy Thomas was merely an instrument in the cause of his advancement.

He decided. "Better get Jack Lloyd to have a look at him, then, if he is suitably impressed, get him signed on professional forms. Minimum wage mind."

"I shall see Jack first thing tomorrow Mr Hill-Woods," Nathaniel assured him. "Young Billy Thomas will be on the books before the end of the week."

Nathaniel left the Club, having succeeded in his aim. "I should be feeling very pleased with myself." he thought. That being so, he considered, then why did he have such a bad taste in his mouth?

He deduced that it was due merely to being in the very company of Hill-Woods. 'Not a very nice man at all', he concluded. His insight had seen through the MP, a man entirely centred on his own ambitions. Nathaniel was not to know such at this very moment but it was to be exactly these kind of urges, multiplied and magnified nationally and internationally that would all to soon culminate in the deaths of millions of young men on land, the sea and in the air.

Men of power, driven in likewise manner to Hill-Woods, would soon light a fuse, whose subsequent explosions would erupt year upon year bleeding the Nations of Europe white, whilst the politicians, the generals and the Kings postured and paraded, extolling ever greater sacrifices.

Few envisioned the coming storm, a maelstrom that would descend upon sleepy little towns and villages, much like Glossop, bringing with it pitiless destruction, death and famine. A wind was advancing, complete of black menacing clouds, dragging the youth of a generation away to pointless sacrifice. The catalyst was being compounded, giving birth to the unstoppable juggernaught of Mars. Soon it would be setting out upon its journey towards the annihilation of an age.

Yet, for now, in England and Glossop, spring, then summer was advancing glorious and bountiful, providing long days of balmy sunshine and warmth. It was as if a merciful God knowing what catastrophe the foolishness of Man was to bring down upon himself, was allowing a short respite, a time of luxuriance before the apocalypse came, full of fury, its energy composed of a single aim, the destruction of a generation.

True to his word, Nathaniel met with Jack Lloyd. Jack was approaching his forty fifth year, yet he was still fit and lean. Football was and had ever been his life. Since his late teens he had either played the game or had been a manager. He was born in Sheffield. One of his earliest memories was of his father playing in a match at Bramall Lane under electric lights. Jack was eight at the time sitting cross legged virtually on the pitch surrounded by thousands of other spectators watching a novel game played under four giant illuminated lamps, one in each corner whilst away from the ground all was pitch black.

The year was 1878 and the game had progressed. Now professionalism was ascendant. The days of the famous amateur sides, The Wanderers, The Royal Engineers and Oxford University were past. It was true that sides like Corinthians could still spring a surprise, but, in general, it was the teams composed of full time professionals that took the honours. Now a good player could command £125 a year and a team would pay a signing on fee of as much as £4,000. for a new star performer. Football was becoming big business.

Jack himself had experienced a great career, winning an 'FA Cup' medal with Sheffield Wednesday in 1907. He then moved to Manchester United and repeated the performance two years later. In between times he had assisted the fast emerging premier team to a league championship win, carving up opposing defences alongside the immortal legends Billy Meredith and George Wall, two of the greatest wingers of their age. In his final playing season, United won the league once again when Jack was partnered by the man he regarded as the finest forward ever to grace the game, Enoch West.

That was in 1911. It was during the following closed season that Jack sustained a leg injury, ending his professional playing career. Positive as ever, he decided to enter management. It was at this time that Hill-Woods heard of the availability of the accomplished player and asked him to come and oversee his struggling team. Jack jumped at the opportunity and since then had kept Glossop functioning in the Second Division on a very tight budget.

It was generally acknowledged that the team was performing well above the assets it possessed in an increasingly demanding world. Jack stored great pride in this achievement. The man who had won two FA Cup medals and two league championships could still derive great pleasure in observing his protégés succeeding on the field of play. Whilst he was in charge of team affairs, he was convinced that Glossop would stay on the footballing map.

Jack, like Hill-Woods, respected Nathaniel's assessment of new talent so once he had heard him describe the abilities of young Thomas his interest was fully gained. He went to observe two matches and saw for himself just how the player confused and bemused opposing sides. His conclusion agreed with that of Nathaniel. Billy Thomas was a gifted, indeed magical performer who, with guidance, disciplined training, and the opportunity to play alongside other quality footballers, could reach the very top of the profession. He agreed to accompany Nathaniel to Billy's home with a proposition, one hundred and twenty five pounds a year for an indefinite contract.

Gladys was a little unsure of the proposal that her son should leave off his apprenticeship to enter the uncertain future of football but she respected Nathaniel, being an Elder of the Chapel. He had, in the past; given her advice, and it had always turned out to be sound. With his mother in agreement, it took little to persuade Billy that signing the contract was a good move, particularly as he was assured that Mr Partington would be spoken to, leaving the certainty that he could return to his old profession if matters did not turn out well. Mr Hawkins further professed that Billy would progress beyond Glossop, that soon other, more famous, clubs would seek him.

Billy went to the ground the very next day, signed the contract, and was introduced to the team. Immediately he was kitted out to begin a training session. Except for Jimmy Jones he had not met any of the other players in the team. Jimmy was now in his second season with the club and had established a regular place in the first team at right half.

Training consisted of the usual mixture of physical exercises and the practice of ball skills. Before the hour was out Billy had undergone press-ups, running several circuits of the field, passing formations, dribbling by corner posts, shooting and heading practice. Billy became absorbed in every aspect of the regime quietly without undue demonstration, thoroughly enjoying himself. Eventually Jack Lloyd broke up the collective and organised his players into specialist groups, to practice skills pertinent to their particular field placing.

It was now he introduced Billy to Terry Causer, the first team goalkeeper.

"Take some shots from about twenty five yards with your special kick Billy, let us see what you can do."

"Yes coach", came the reply, and Billy ran to the side of the penalty area while the keeper prepared himself.

The ball was stationary, five yards outside of the area, as the new recruit ran up to it. He struck it with his right foot and it sped away passing the top left corner of the goal when it began to swerve fooling the unfortunate Causer and ended inside the netting. Thus Glossop's keeper became the first professional keeper to be fooled by this new phenomenon in footballing skill. He would not be the last. The demonstration was to be repeated several times that morning with both the left and right feet, high and low shots, swerving accordingly. Eventually Causer could judge the balls deviation by watching the foot as it was struck managing to save half of the attempts upon his domain.

Jack Lloyd had been observing this torment of his prime keeper and now decided to bring a new dimension to the contest. He asked one of his wingers, Mickey Stapeley to centre some crosses onto Billy's feet. This was a speciality of Stapeley and he was soon winging accurate crosses onto the feet of the new Glossopian who repeated on the run what he had performed when the ball was stationary. The ball beat Causer almost every time. Billy's accuracy, coupled with his deceptiveness, was just far too good for the experienced sentinel of the net. Soon other members of the team joined in to service Billy with crosses, lobs and half volleys watching them leave the boot of their new shooting wizard.

Not one of them had quite seen such a display before. Soon they all began to analyse how Billy achieved this curving spectacle with the ball. They nodded approval with every succeeding example, anticipating exactly how his skill would affect the team's performance in its coming matches.

Eventually Jack called for a break.

"All right", he cried out. "Get cleaned up and meet in the club house in half an hour for tactics."

He was pleased with the morning's work, extremely pleased.

As the week progressed it became evident, to Jack Lloyd, that Billy was impressing his fellow team mates to the extent that when he decided to place him in the line-up, the boy would fit in well. He trained hard with a dedicated attitude towards instruction and advice. There was no evidence of Billy considering himself as a prima donna. His shooting skills continued to impress his colleagues.

Causer was eventually heard to admit. "Billy I am so glad that you are going to be playing with us. I only have to face you in practice, not in matches. I, for one cannot wait to be alongside you in a competitive match, perhaps even against Barnsley on Saturday."

Astutely, Hill-Woods gave out a press release for the Thursday edition of the Chronicle that a new player of exceeding talent from the locality had been signed, would be playing this coming week, who would amaze all those lucky enough to be present to witness the event. This annoyed Jack Lloyd intensely, though he realised the sound financial premise upon which it was made.

Hill-Woods was to be proved correct in his assessment of the promise of new excitement that his press statement would create. The local footballing fraternity was in ferment. Saturday the 21st of March 1914 was to see a far larger crowd than usual, complete of anticipation, enthusiasm and overflowing with patriotic fanaticism. The highly charged mass streamed towards the north of town, confident that they were about to be a part of a memorable spectacle. It was as though Billy was a famous gladiator about to enter the arena. They would salute him or dismiss him according to the level of pleasure his efforts and talent gave them. Such is the fickleness of the football supporter.

There was also the political background, against which the match was being played. The pronouncements of the ever-increasing warmongers were beginning to enter into the psyche of the populace. The sense of forthcoming tragedy subconsciously possessed their minds. Football provided a welcome distraction from this dismal outlook and provided a diversion of achievement by association from what was for many of them, a depressing monotonous life.

The National Press had published just a few days ago a speech by Lloyd George describing the new European arms race as 'organised insanity.' Calls were being made in Parliament for compulsory military service. The Russian Government had announced the doubling of its standing army. Speakers from the emerging Labour Party were calling Winston Churchill's baiting of Germany, through his proposals to increase the strength of the Royal Navy, 'a danger for the security of the Country and for world peace.'

All these factors, combined with troubles at home, Ireland, the Miner's strike, the ever present Suffragettes now destroying paintings in national galleries and bombing Yarmouth Pier encouraged many to retreat inwardly into a life where entertainment, alcohol and frippery dominated their desires. For a large section of the town's working population that meant football, a need to be associated with success by reflecting in the victories of their local heroes.

Kick off was at two o'clock and an hour earlier witnessed Nathaniel Hawkins passing through the doors of his emporium, accompanied by his daughter, leaving it in the capable hands of his wife. He to was on his way to the match. Sally had been eager to accompany him ever since Billy's name had been published announcing his debut for the team. She had now completed her schooling at Saint Elphin's, and was keen to observe just how the young man, who as a boy had shared so many hours with her, deeply engrossed in reading volume upon volume in the library, had matured to become a potentially famous footballer.

They had seen little of each other since her return, a few glances across the aisles in Chapel, some formal words on the weathered steps after the service. Once, last summer, they had sat down together during the annual summer picnic that the Chapel had organised. Billy, very bravely she thought, had brushed an extremely large orange and black furry bumblebee from her shawl. Whether it was because of shyness or something else, she knew not, but Billy had uttered scarcely a word. Somehow a distance, a formality, had grown between them. It hurt her in an unexplainable way. She hoped that soon they could meet and talk together in the unreserved manner they eventually achieved, those years ago. If he played well today it would give her the perfect excuse to go over to him tomorrow and congratulate him.

Nathaniel's thoughts were of vastly differing sentiments. News of the latest Glossop signing had reached the ears of an old friend of his, a certain Arthur Parker. They had known one another for more than thirty years, playing matches together in their youth, before Arthur went on to develop a successful professional career with Manchester United. They now employed him as a full time scout. It was his policy to keep his eyes and ears open all the time where football was concerned. Thus he was coming today to view for himself the new talent that the jungle telegraph was gossiping over. If the young man turned out to be as skilled and talented as rumours were led to believe then, after watching him over a number of games, he would encourage his employers to purchase him as quickly and cheaply as possible. Teams, the likes of United, were now attempting to obtain dominance of the game through their purse. Men of the calibre of Arthur Parker undertook the window shopping, before their bosses moved in clasping a chequebook.

The two men met at the station, just a few hundred yards from the ground. They greeted each other and coyly began to fence.

"Well Nathaniel, who have you discovered now?"

"Just a local lad", came the reply.

"More than that, I hear", retorted Arthur. It was his job to gain intelligence of the quality of new blood entering the smaller teams that scattered Manchester. He held contacts; it never took very long for him to receive reports from training sessions if a player of promise was emerging.

"Well", mused Nathaniel, conjecturing that a gifted player of Billy's quality would shine whether he burnished him or not, "You will be in a position to judge for yourself shortly won't you?" He gave Arthur a sly enigmatic grin.

"Just so, Nathaniel. Just so."

The crowd became ever more dense as they approached the ground surging in its impatience to enter, each member keen to claim a good place to watch events unimpeded. A considerable number of supporters from the opposing team had made the short trip over the Pennines their blue and white colours much in evidence as they made their way singing out praises to their heroes.

It was indeed going to be a large crowd, exceeding the six thousand that Hill-woods was hoping for. The Barnsley supporters were full of confidence. Their team was performing well this season having good prospects for promotion, a skilful squad with a reputation for dogged defence and swiftly breaking attacks.

It was but two seasons ago since they gained the FA Cup for the first time, the most gruelling campaign on record. Their victory came after four replays, three of which went to extra time. Barnsley eventually won by a single goal over the unfortunate West Bromwich Albion.

Several stars of that winning team would be appearing today. Dicky Downs, the legendary full back, feeding the wing halves, Utley and Glendinning, who if strategy went according to plan, would cross the ball for Harry Tufnell, the division's leading scorer, to execute his magic. Everything was truly set up for a most intriguing encounter. Nathaniel, for one, was experiencing more excitement prior to a game than he had felt in many a year.

The game started scrappily with the ball often going out of play forbidding any momentum to build up. At last, after fifteen minutes, Barnsley gained a corner, which almost resulted in a goal. The game was picking up. The pace began to increase, chances being offered and declined at both ends. At last, on the half-hour, Glossop's central defender, Walter Stapeley set paceman Jimmy Knight speeding down the left wing. He crossed; the ball fell at the feet of the man so many had come to watch, Billy Thomas. He took the ball, magically dribbled round two defenders, with a dexterity and deception, which brought spontaneous applause from all over the ground. He guided the ball into the penalty area only to be promptly brought down from behind, dispossessed and left flat on the ground.

Nathaniel felt disgruntled but he knew that his new protégé would have other chances today. He did not have long to wait. Barnsley conceded a corner; the ball was floated over the heads of attackers and defenders alike. It came down on the far side, finding Billy's right foot, which drove the ball back towards the goal as if propelled by a flash of lightning. It appeared to be going wide. Now a curious manifestation occurred, the ball climbed and curved. Instead of going out of play it sneaked into the top left-hand side of the goal.

The Barnsley defence stared in disbelief, their keepers mouth agape. They were all absolutely certain that the ball was going wide, so how did it end up in the back of the net? Glossop's new forward had scored a fluke, through a freak gust of wind or some similar manifestation. Either way, it mattered not; the referee was pointing to the centre spot, Glossop one, Barnsley nil.

Arthur Parker turned towards Nathaniel. "How did he achieve that?"

Nathaniel merely shrugged his shoulders. "You have seen very little yet Arthur "Wait till the second half."

Young Sally was squeezing her father's hand. "Has Billy scored?" She was full of delight anticipating Nathaniel's reply.

"Indeed he has", beamed the team scout, justification filling his mind, he was beginning to feel that God was going to be very good this day.

Football is rumoured to be a funny game; those who inhabit Olympus use it to amuse themselves, by thwarting the expectations of those humans who make the game their life. Within five minutes of the restart a glaring error from Causer gave Barnsley the easiest of equalisers, silencing the North End supporters.

However, the Glossopian 'Peakites' were not to be downhearted for long. This day was destined to witness deeds, which were to enter into local folklore, often to be recalled by those privileged to be part of the event. Many a pint was to be gained through the retelling of the spectacle in pubs and clubs for years to come. The day when Barnsley came to town, retreating back over the Pennines in a state of shock having been given a salutary lesson in how the game should be played.

Glossop's forwards began to pepper the Barnsley keeper with shots as if he were a clay pigeon. To his credit he withstood the barrage, defying his tormentors time upon time. In truth matters could have been resolved so differently. Barnsley were consistently breaking away and it was only through a supreme effort from right back Montgomery that stopped a further goal being added to the Barnsley total.

Now began the period when the match changed its character and entered into legend. It started with Stapeley. He trapped the ball near the halfway line, drawing the Barnsley defenders towards him. Now he passed the ball square to Jimmy Jones who sent it through to Tommy Toward who, in turn, centred with pin-point accuracy onto Billy's left boot, which instantly fired it passed the despairing keeper and into the net.

Glossop two, Barnsley one.

Parker was becoming very interested in the phenomenon that was Glossop's new striker. "He shoots with his left foot as well as his right", he observed.

Nathaniel, his pride growing by the minute, merely replied. "Yes he does Arthur, yes he does."

The game was now going to pass to a level that would take it to the realms of mythology in future years. Within five minutes of the restart Stapeley once again captured the ball. This time he floated it over in a smooth lazy lob that found Billy's chest. Taking out all the momentum of the ball Billy allowed it to drop onto his right boot, flicking it over to his left providing the necessary bounce. From at least thirty yards he let loose a powering driving shot which was ever leaving the hapless keeper to become embedded in the bottom right hand corner of the net.

The crowd erupted. This young man playing in his first team debut, in front of his own crowd, had scored a hat trick.

'What a trio of goals', considered Nathaniel. 'This is going to give Arthur considerable scope for thought.'

Arthur, indelibly impressed, but never speechless, exclaimed. "That shot veered to the left whilst dipping. It was as if it contained bottom spin like you can get with a tennis ball in fives. How is that possible?"

Nathaniel simply mused to himself. Now he knew for the first time in his life the meaning of the expression, 'the cat that's got the cream', for now, in the first time for an age, Glossop were in complete command of a game and it was his lad who was turning out to be the star performer. Billy was inspiring the entire team to raise its game. Glossop were in full flight as if each member of the team were dancing with the ball. Now Stapeley once again dispossessed the Barnsley centre, passed to Toward who, in turn, magnificently dropped the ball onto Billy's head. Propelling himself forward, stretching out his neck, Billy guided and drifted the ball over the hands of Cooper the Barnsley keeper and saw it droop down below the crossbar.

'The Chronicle' was to report the following week that 'the crowd went wild with delight, reflecting the riotous manner of their team on the pitch.'

Barnsley were now completely dispirited. Just before full time Glossop's Dave Barnett scored a fifth.

Nathaniel summarised the feelings of all the Glossop supporters who now gave vent to an exhibition of unsuppressed euphoria. "What a day, what a great day. Well Arthur, I told you that coming here would be well worth your while. What a day, what a performance. Let us go to the pavilion. I will introduce you to our chairman, patron and MP, Hill-woods. Let me give you some advice, however do not appear to be too interested in Billy just yet. The man strikes a hard bargain, a very hard bargain."

Hill-Woods had also, of course, been watching his new signing. The effect of Billy Thomas and his performance on the crowd had not gone unnoticed. He decided that he must quickly find the Chronicles' sports correspondent, acquainting him with the major role that he had played in obtaining the services of their new sensation. The MP realised that such an outstanding player would be soon spotted by one of the major teams. Offers would come pouring in to acquire his services.

Whatever happened, he would like to see the player making the team sheet for the rest of the season, while his scouts were seeking out other talent. He could then dispense with the services of Thomas after a few games of the next season, bringing a huge profit to his enterprise without creating too large a gap in the squad.

Meanwhile he would bait his hooks and leave a few fish dangling at the end of his line. A Dutch Auction was always the best method of gaining a maximum price. For now Hill-Woods would enjoy the after match euphoria, glowing in the glory of his part played, a role that he was enhancing by the minute.

When Hill-Woods espied Arthur Parker, the chief scout of Manchester United, entering the pavilion accompanied by Nathaniel Hawkins, his cup overflowed. He was aware of the past association of these two aficionados, and, observing the illuminated conversation between them, concluded it would be an opportune moment to join them. What a time to appear patriotic to the club. If he could manipulate the local reporter to overhear the subsequent conversation, so much the better. The fact that once other scouts had been made aware of the extra ordinary talent Glossop now possessed, leading to an inflation of the player's value: the fact that the pressure would build until even he could no longer withstand it, would in no way detract from the gratitude felt towards him by his football loving would be electors.

The subsequent farce was enacted precisely in the manner Hill-Wood foresaw. The two men approached him, a reporter following in their wake. Hill-Woods made a great play of voicing that is only concern was for the young player and the Club. He explained how young Billy now needed personal development whilst Glossop enjoyed further displays of his excellence in numerous games to come.

The MP succeeded in every aspect of his elaborate plot. Next week's paper would paint their MP as a sporting savour, a local patriot, a generous benevolent provider, the man to support once again when the next general election was called. Thus Billy Thomas became a pawn in a game destined to end in a manner not one of the participants could wish or foresee.

Eventually the actors of the scene headed home. Hill-Woods full of himself, convinced of his ability to manipulate people and events in whatever direction he wished. A certain local sports journalist wound his way knowing his script would create the best story scribed for the paper in years. Nathaniel Hawkins paced along Norfolk Square escorting Sally who was incessant in her constant excited witterings upon her re-established hero. Billy too came home to his beloved mother, glowing in the praise so heaped upon him.

The train sped Arthur Parker home to Manchester. Here he would spread the news of the day's events and the central part played by the undoubtedly skilful, but unassuming man whose magic with a ball put four goals past the best defence in the second division.

Meanwhile, on the other side of the continent, a disparate group of young revolutionaries were gathering in what they supposed was the height of secrecy. They were no less illuminated and excited than their English counterparts. It had just been announced that the heir to the throne of Austria-Hungary would be visiting their city in three months time. After much agitated discussion it was agreed that an attempt should be made to assassinate him. Three of their group volunteered the task. One of these, a sickly consumptive youth who had been planted within their midst, by the Austrian's themselves, would bear more influence upon the life of Billy Thomas than any of those that had marvelled at his performance that day, pondering over his future. He was Gavrilo Princip. The city was Sarajevo.

CHAPTER 5

'Give me leave to live and die in this opinion,
That he is not worthy to live at all
Who for fear of danger and death
Shunneth his Country's service and his own honour.

Inscribed upon the base of the FA. War Memorial.

August the fourth dawned clear, bright and golden. The harvest that enriched the fields surrounding the town bore overburdened stems, carrying burgeoning swollen ripened ears of grain, complete of the bounty gained from years of agricultural practice that, although it required enduring toil, gave a rich reward.

It was a Tuesday, traditionally a day when Jack Lloyd gave his players a rest from his diligent pre-season training schedule. Billy had consequently agreed to spend the day helping to layer some hedgerows with Jimmy. They were to meet by the library and walk up through the old town, then up into the narrow winding lanes leading to the hills above. It was here that Jimmy had been provided with some work to perform. With luck when they reported to the ground this coming evening, Jack would allow them as much as a further weeks rest, leaving them the opportunity to work in the fields above town until the following Monday.

Billy had just enjoyed the most exhilarating long weekend. On Saturday he had assisted his mother in re-decorating the parlour. His wages, though not extravagant, were now considerably higher than those of a mill hand, allowing him to contribute funds towards both his keep and in improving the home. On Sunday the Chapel service was a curious mixture of the sombre and elation. Young men and girls were buzzing like bees on the Chapel steps attempting to assess the situation. The Royal Navy had been mobilised, leading to screaming headlines being displayed from the newspaper hoarding.

Word got round that Germany had declared war upon France in addition to its previous pronouncement on Russia. This had led the British Government to warn the Kaiser not to violate Belgian neutrality or encroach its ships towards the Channel.

Thus, the significance of this Tuesday morning was not lost on the two friends as, leisurely, they ambled towards their place of work. They both felt that before this day's end grave new developments would ensue, bringing with them heroic, historic conclusions. Now walking alongside the perfumed summer hedgerows, tune-filled with winging fledglings, garlanded by pink wild roses overlaid alongside ripening blackberries, the threats from overseas seemed to belong to another world. The placid pastoral Derbyshire country lanes provisioned so great a contrast to the ravaging mechanised turmoil that was unravelling overseas.

Yesterday had been August bank holiday. As usual Glossop hosted its traditional outdoor fair in Norfolk Square. Rows of colourful stalls of all description were scattered along the cobbles from the station to the Moon and Sixpence. A Merrie-go-round acted as the central attraction, together with a set of swing-boats and a steam organ. Providing rides for over excited children was a traction engine towing a trailer, many of its occupants experiencing a mechanically powered ride for the first time. Laughter filled sticky faced urchins, full of the halfpenny candyfloss, or the toffee-apples that were being peddled along with the treacle toffee and cream fudge, shone out behind the barrier of the trailer as it ambled along both East and West High Streets.

Billy, of course, was dressed in his Sunday best, an immaculate new suit of dark blue pinstripe. He sported a colourful yellow Paisley cravat, spats and perfectly polished black shoes. Indeed he represented a perfect example of handsome English youth that all young ladies of his age were subconsciously desirous to have escort them on their arm. He came strolling into town with his mother whose primary function this day was to assist in the running of the Chapel stall.

Most of the Churches and religious organisations together with the town's charities used the August fair to sell produce and crafts donated by their members and rotas were organised allowing each stall to be managed throughout the day.

Being a bank holiday, the main shops were all closed leaving Elizabeth Hawkins and her daughter to share in the manning of the Chapel's outlet. Trade was brisk, a marvellous sale of cakes, confections, jams, pickles, apples and pears all produced or donated by the congregation, concocted in their kitchens, or harvested from their gardens. Fortune was to decree that Billy's mother was to relieve the pair allowing him to meet with the girl who so occupied his thoughts.

Mrs Hawkins and Gladys exchanged pleasantries while Billy took the opportunity to greet Sally.

"Good morning Miss Hawkins", he said sheepishly, not being brave enough to use her Christian name in her mother's presence.

"And good morning to you Mr Thomas", replied Sally highly amused by his discomfort. It reminded her of the little boy who found communication so difficult that first day in the library.

"And good morning it is." The boy spluttered out, his predicament becoming more graphic by the second.

Sally smiled at him, attempting to ease his evident embarrassment, hoping she could persuade him towards conversation.

"It certainly is", the girl confirmed. "Shall you be enjoying the fair this afternoon Mr Thomas?"

"Certainly", confirmed Billy. He was gaining slightly in confidence now, yet he knew that one slight sign of disapproval would put him right back into his shell like a terrified tortoise. He offered further information to the delicate girl that had stolen his heart without any knowledge of her so doing.

"I like the August fair, you never know what you might find."

"That is true", Sally agreed, recalling the stories that her father told her of the years when he and his parents had travelled to such events all over the north of England, never missing the annual August celebrations of Glossop.

"People come here for the fair from all over England", she added.

Elizabeth had completed her conversation with Gladys. They had exchanged all the current gossip and information at their respective disposal. Now Sally's mother wished to make a tour of the fair. However she made an observation that caused her to pause. Over the past weeks it had come to her notice that her daughter became extremely animated whenever mention of Glossop's new star player came into conversation. She had also noticed Sally staring at him during services at Chapel. From what she knew, Billy Thomas was a pleasant young man who possessed a bright future. She also knew that he commanded the respect of her husband.

It was now that a mischievous, romantic scheme entered her head, bringing a warm inner glow to her almost as if she were a young girl herself. She would give Sally the opportunity to spend a little time with this man whom, she was sure, her sole offspring was taken with in no uncertain manner.

"Why don't you two go off and explore the fair together? she invited. "I want to buy a few things and see one or two people. Perhaps we could meet back here in a couple of hours?"

Billy and Sally gazed at each other, not knowing what to say. Eventually it was the young man who broke the silence.

"Why I would love to escort your daughter Mrs Hawkins. It would be a great pleasure."

"And you Sally?" enquired the Machiavellian.

"Yes mother." The coy reply came from a blushing, totally self conscious girl who had been handed all she had yearned for since the day she left St. Elphin's, though she would never have been brazen enough to admit so, even to herself. To be in the company of dear Billy, her Billy as she so often thought of him in her private thoughts, brought a sensation of deep emotion from within her. Her gratitude for her mother was only surpassed by her joyful anticipation of Billy's undiluted company. "Off you go then, you two." Her mother's command needed no further urging. Elizabeth gave Gladys a sly knowing look as the pair vanished into the crowd.

67

For a while the two departed offspring wandered through the fair aimlessly in profound silence. Their was a tension between them created by the years of separation, in which both of them formed fanciful notions of the other's feelings towards them. Now that they were alone together, even if that solitude was in a vast crowd, what if their aspirations were not mutual?

Billy, for one, was grateful for the distraction that the numerous side-shows afforded. He tried his hand with the dartboard, without success. Sally gave effort to throwing a hoop over a square block having a grotesque Staffordshire figurine perched upon it, also without reward. They wandered on, almost without noticing they were now clasping hands.

Then it came into sight: the stall that Sally just knew Billy would undoubtedly overcome. It consisted of an old bicycle tyre suspended from a rope. Potential contestants were challenged to shoot a football through it from twenty yards without touching the sides and causing the obstacle to move. One successful attempt and a small inconsequential prize was on offer. Two victorious efforts brought a small figurine. Three triumphs however and a magnificent pair of figures mounted on horseback beckoned.

Billy checked the ball. It was old, a little soft but he thought the challenge reasonable. Handing over a threepenny piece, which was the fee demanded, he took up his position. The first shot flew straight and true, through the centre of the tyre, not even threatening the edges. Billy was pleased, at least now Sally would have a small memento of their excursion. With a certain confidence he placed the ball for a second time, having been handed it back by a somewhat disgruntled attendant. Smoothly, with little apparent effort, the result of the first shot was repeated. The feelings of the owner of the attraction were now rapidly elevated from the merely disconcerted to the deeply troubled. Not one single person, in ten years of his guardianship of the tyre and the ball, had ever been successful three times out of three. The Staffordshire figures were worth over three pounds, more than a days taking, alarm bells now began to ring in his head.

"Here you are son." Billy was handed back the ball once again. "Make sure it's placed behind the line now."

Tension mounted inside Billy's breast. Sally also felt her pulse beat faster. She saw Billy as an ancient chivalrous champion taking up her cause which now pivoted on a single exploit.

Quite a crowd was gathered round. Many of them recognised their new local footballing hero; they expected great things. Billy felt that he was being given the responsibility of taking a crucial penalty in a game it was essential to win. Truthfully, it was infinitely more important that he repeat his past two efforts, than any achievement on a football pitch. This was for Sally; his entire frame now possessed an urgency that could only be assuaged by presenting his lovely companion with the pair of figures. This poor imitation of a ball would fly directly into the target, please God, please, please, God.

Taking his time, he stepped back and shot. As if directed by Cupid himself the ball sped straight as one of his mythical arrows passing through the target precisely as its sender intended. The tyre remained absolutely static. Instantly the audience erupted in spontaneous applause recognising the complete accomplishment of Billy's endeavour.

The stallholder knew he was beaten. Deciding to make the best of the outcome, he took down the figures that had been his companions for an age and the covetousness of countless other competitors who had eyed them with hopeful ownership and, with full ceremony presented them to the latter-day Olympian. Never was a fairground prize more eagerly accepted. To the great pleasure of those who were witnesses to the epic event, Billy in turn handed his trophy over to the young girl by his side. Sally protested time and again at being offered the wonderful prize but her champion would not be dissuaded. She accepted, providing Billy with a kiss on the cheek in return, his happiness was complete.

Jack Lloyd had been in the crowd watching the spectacle. Coming up to his new star pupil, he congratulated him.

"Well done Billy, I see you have been keeping up with your practice."

Billy acknowledged his kind words with a faint embarrassed smile. He was feeling proud, full of contentment, yet, in Sally's scented company he contained far less confidence than when amidst the presence of a whole team of his fellows, and to those who knew him well, it showed.

Mrs Lloyd smiled inwardly, young Billy may have reached manhood but he was still a small boy in the presence of Sally Hawkins. Some things would never change. Jack merely observed matters through manly eyes. He was full of satisfaction and pride, understanding how his interest in Billy Thomas was becoming personal, his very own protégé, almost the son he never had. He also recognised the look that the daughter of Nathaniel Hawkins wore when gazing at her companion whilst he presented her with his skilfully gained token of affection. It was recognised for what it was, admiration. Conjecturing, he concluded, 'this could lead to other things.' Doffing his cap without a further word, he escorted his good lady into the crowd.

The two hours granted to the couple soon passed. In no time at all they were back in the company of their parents. Not that their time had been wasted. After his success with the football, Billy had taken Sally, who had provided ever more delightful company, on a swing-boat ride. Additionally, she was now laden with two coconuts as well as the figures so skilfully won.

"Why Sally, what have you got there? enquired a genuinely curious Gladys.

The two mothers were standing side by side, in truth they had gossiped happily for most of the time that their children had been away together, reliving anecdotally, scenes from their respective offspring's childhood. Many a confidence had been exchanged to the later embarrassment of the pair.

As a result of the question an animated babble ensued, revealing all the details of the afternoons adventures. Sally was illuminated, her mother never quite seeing her in such a state of emotional turmoil like this before. Elizabeth sensed that this would not be the last time that the pair would so enjoy each other's companionship.

Nathaniel arrived and the whole saga was repeated for his benefit. He was both impressed by Billy's achievements and pleased that his daughter had enjoyed herself with such an accomplished escort. His joy for his daughter was only spoilt by the contrasting gravity of the news that he brought with him.

"I am afraid that the news is grave", he began, feeling the stigma of being the bearer of bad tidings at a time when those around him were displaying such happiness. "Our Government has informed Germany, that Great Britain is prepared to abide by its undertaking signed in the treaty of 1839 regarding Belgium. If the Germans do not respect the integrity of Belgian soil, then we shall go to war in defence of the little country. Our Navy is at this very moment steaming towards the Channel to defend the shipping lanes.

His news silenced all those within hearing distance. It was apparent that all the warnings of the past few months were coming to pass. Britannia would soon be at war against a terrible foe. Nathaniel could only remark. "No good will come of this, no good at all." Lord Grey, the Foreign Secretary had issued a statement, which had come over the wire as Nathaniel was leaving the newspaper office, it reflected his thoughts precisely. "The lamps are going out all over Europe, we shall not see them lit again in our lifetime."

It was subsequently a sombre parting between the two families that evening, bringing heavy hearts to the young couple who had so enjoyed themselves. When Billy awoke on that last day of peace destined to be granted to England for over four years, his satisfaction with yesterday's events in Glossop was complete. He had shown off, he knew, but not too obviously. Dear Sally appeared so happy as she left him, posturing her emblems of his triumphant campaign. That morning, as he climbed the hills above the town, his only thoughts were of when he would next set eyes upon this lovely girl whose fellowship he now so treasured.

They at last arrived at the pre-ordained spot only to discover three men already laying the hedges. One of them, whom Billy recognised as a devoted supporter of the football club, came over to the pair offering his hand.

"Howbe Billy, Jimmy. Coming to partake of some proper work eh?"

The rhetoric was not composed of any malice but came attendant with a warming smile. He was acting as messenger for the absent landowner, feeling very important addressing two men who he alternatively cajoled or encouraged every week from the terraces as the mood or the game took him.

"Boss says he would be most obliged if you both could take up scythes to reap the two small fields over the way. Says you done it affore."

"Yes, of course, a pleasure", stated Jimmy. "Have you got stones, string and a knife?"

"Reckons all you need is on the cart." The labourer pointed to a handcart nearby and turning started back to continue his own duties.

"Reckons we'll see you come break, we been left cider by boss."

"Give us a shout then when it's time", pleaded Jimmy, following Billy towards the cart.

They collected their tools and began the harvest of the nearest field. Most harvesting by 1914 had become mechanised. Yet the machinery was cumbersome meaning that in inaccessible places or where the fields were small the corn was still cut by hand. The scythe, perfectly honed and balanced effortlessly, cut a swathe through the stalks with a crackle and a swish. In the hands of an expert the harvest would lie in pristine rows ready to be gathered and bound. Later these two friends would observe German machine gunners reap a human harvest in much the same way. Happily dark sights as these were still some time off. Today it was golden rows of corn that absorbed their attention.

The practice was for the two men to cut a double swathe across the field then, using the string, bind the harvest into bundles placing four upright together at opposite points of the compass which encouraged air to circulate, and the grain to dry. Finally the stacks would be collected on huge high sided trailers and taken away for threshing, which isolated the grains, and eventually milled into flour

Nature's providence had so overflowed this summer that almost every stalk remained upright creating easy access to the scythe. The pair progressed swiftly, with the sun beating upon their exposed backs whilst the endless swish of their implements brought down the ears of grain to the ground. Excepting for the monotonous sound of stems yielding to the scythe, of a slight breeze disturbing the leaves upon two oaks that reigned upon the near southerly horizon, or the family of spiralling buzzards high above them no sound was heard. The men worked away in silence. Only the sounds of autumnal fecundity lazily disturbed the day. Today each man was engrossed in his own thoughts and in his work. It was only when work ceased at the appointed time, for food, drink and rest that any conversation took place.

By this time Billy and Jimmy had sliced and stacked over half the first field's crop. Upon hearing the welcome shout they needed no further encouragement, they immediately made way to the cart. Five wooden mugs were placed on a large flat slab of granite, filled to the brim with cider. Each man unwrapped a linen bundle exposing his lunch, wedges of bread, cold mutton and cheese, nothing fancy but sustaining and satisfying.

The man who had spoken earlier was older than the rest, balding, grey, in his fifties. Agricultural contracting had been his life or, if work was short on the land, he sought work in one of the local quarries. He was generally a sober man, a good timekeeper, hard working and reliable, rarely knowing unemployment. His name was Albert Griffiths. The younger pair were his sons, Peter and Paul. All three were Anglicans and Tories.

With the ground being both warm and dry the five men sat down in a circle to eat. Conversation soon turned to the latest news.

"Well sons, seems you may be called up and off to camp." Albert was very proud of his sons. At home they kept fit exercising, often going to camp to train, or footslogging on the parade ground adjoining the Drill Hall. Paul was a particularly cracking shot; able to send off fifteen rounds a minute using his immaculately oiled Lee Enfield. His RSM said he made his rifle sound like a machine gun. Peter was not far behind his brother in expertise having had a year less training.

It was Paul who replied. "Well we were told by the drill sergeant last Thursday that if hostilities do break out we would be called directly to barracks in Chester. He said that all England needed was her Territorials being added to the Regulars and together with Frenchie we would have they Huns beat real proper affore Christmas. Come home all heroes we will Pa', real heroes."

Peter, never slow in entering conversation, provided confirmation to his brother's assertion. "That's right Pa', the visiting Captain explained that them Germans is having to fight on two fronts. The Ruskies have over two million men, two million! They be all marching towards Fritzie. He reckons we'll all meet up by the shores of the Baltic in a couple of months. The Hun's bitten off more than he can chew this time."

All the time, while his brother was enunciating this detailed assessment of how the war would be all over by Christmas, Paul was nodding in enthused agreement. He added. "Also, our Navy is going to tie up the Germans at the entrance to the North Sea. It will sink any warship or merchantman daring to come out. Within weeks they will be starving and our Captain told us that this great General bloke Napoleon said that armies march on their stomachs. No, the Hun's had it, can't fight if you's hungry."

This all sounded very plausible to Billy. "So as far as your officers are concerned, the Germans are going to lose very quickly if we join in the fight."

"Well it's a certainty I reckon", affirmed Paul. "We goes over, fires a few shots, takes our big guns and they will start a running."

None of the five men were to know until later that evening, but just as Paul was issuing forth, German troops were racing through Luxembourg towards Bastogne. From the east, by rail, a huge siege gun, greater than any possessed by the British or French had been brought up to the Belgian frontier merely twenty miles from Liege. Before they were to return to work that afternoon, the first shell weighing over a ton, had been fired towards that hapless city. Germany, ignoring Britain's warning, had unleashed its Valkuries from out of the monstrous mouth of a beast named after the wife of its creator. Big Bertha had announced the arrival of modern warfare, a conflict between men and machines, a contest of flesh against mechanised metal from which there could be only one outcome.

Five men, isolated from momentous events, toiled under the August sun, working till eight O'clock. At the end of their day's labour, they gathered together and taking turns with the cart, descended to the town.

One large cool shandy, before going home, was the order of the day for Billy and his friend. They waived goodbye to their fellow workers and walked towards the Moon and Sixpence. Sitting inside, cooling down, they discussed the lunchtime conversation.

"Do you really believe a war with Germany could be that easy?" Jimmy was full of foreboding. It was just a few weeks previously that he was watching the Kaiser opening the great Keel Canal from the bridge of a mighty battleship. Germany, to him, was a modern country armed to the teeth.

"Well his argument sounded plausible."

"So perhaps there will be no need for us to volunteer."

"Perhaps", Billy responded thoughtfully. "Perhaps not."

They drank the welcoming shandy, sensing the dawn of great events with no little trepidation, then parted, each going home to his family, homes which were familiar, comfortable, occupied by loved ones, welcoming. It was a blessing, that they possessed no conception of just how soon it would be when they would bid farewell to their surroundings to embrace a harsh unnatural world, in a land seemingly far away of which they knew little. It was three hours later when Prime Minister Asquith announced that Britain was at war with Germany.

The next day the two friends met Albert nearby to his home to assist in hauling the cart back to their place of work. It was here that they both heard, for the first time, of the state of war that their Country had entered into. Paul came rushing up from the vendor who sold papers by the station, shouting excitedly and waving his copy of the Mirror. His father grabbed it from him impatiently. Two seconds later he proclaimed what they all guessed.

"That's, that that then, we be at war me boys. "What's to do now then?"

Paul declared. "We shall report to the drill hall tonight Pa'. Get us our instructions."

To this Peter added. "No doubt we shall be full-time soldiers before much longer."

During the lunch break, Billy read the paper from beginning to end. Despite the re-assurances of Peter and Paul, Billy felt a deep unease, coupled with a sense of guilt. As matters were, two of them here were going off to defend their country while He and Jimmy would stay at home to enjoy playing football and carrying on with their lives as normal, whilst others would be risking their lives on the battlefield.

Over the next two weeks, this sense of being inactive, whilst others were facing danger, grew. News of early German successes intensified the guilt. This was but a fraction alleviated when the team got together for pre-season practice. Initially, the army issued posters requiring only a small number of volunteers. By the second week of war matters had changed dramatically. The Chronicle was now carrying an urgent appeal to swell the ranks.

YOUR KING AND COUNTRY
NEED YOU
A CALL TO ARMS
An additional 100,000 men
To His Majesty's Regular Army
is immediately necessary
in the present grave emergency
JOIN UP NOW

Jack Lloyd got his team together for a talk. The country needed patriots, he told them, patriots at the front and patriots at home. Men were needed to fight; they were also required at home. It was impossible for an army to fight without equipment, ammunition, clothing, food and something to fight for. He explained that the mill worker, the collier, the farmer, all were as important to the war effort as the fighting man was. Footballers could play their part as well. When soldiers got news of home they would find assurance in normalcy, in the knowledge their loved ones were flourishing, That meant their football teams as well Manchester United, Aston Villa, The Arsenal and, yes, Glossop.

"Think of the war effort as a team affair", he invited. "When I compose a team, it has to be balanced, goalkeeper, full backs, half backs and forwards. The soldiers at the front have to score against the enemy, to shoot straight, to knock him out. Now, unless he is served with the ball or, in his case, guns, bullets and food, he cannot keep going."

Jack did not know if he was making any sense to them, but at least he had their attention.

"So lads, the better the workers at home work, in providing the necessities for the front, the quicker the war ends. Workers need rest; they also require entertainment, to keep pride in their hometown. That is where you come in. Show the people at home and the soldiers abroad, that all is well here in Glossop, that life continues."

For a while there was silence, each man unwilling to be the first to respond. Then William Causer, who was the longest serving member of the team, stood up.

"Mr Lloyd, what you say makes sense. I say, let's continue as a team for now, train hard, do our very best, make the town proud of us. All of us know someone who has gone off to fight, Let us play for them. If things get worse then we can look at matters again. For now, I say, we get behind Jack and show people what we can do."

His words gained general approval, becoming a consensus as others added their opinions. Jack, with satisfaction, concluded the meeting.

"Lads, that is settled then, now let's get out there and prepare for the season. I will monitor events, if the need arises we shall meet again for further discussion. Also, anyone who wants a private word they can see me at any time in full confidence. Now, let us get on with training."

The team filed out, their doubts, for the time being, dissolved. A determination now came upon them, a resolve to strive to greater purpose, to shine in the new order that was wartime England.

In unison with the rest of his re-invigorated team-mates, Billy had been assured by Jack's words. He would continue with his career for now and prepare for the first game of the new season due on the fifth of September. Anything could happen, he reasoned. Perhaps the Germans might think again, now that they faced three great powers determined to thwart their every aggression. At this moment, even little Belgium was giving Germany a bloody nose.

In the first few weeks of the war the newspapers printed scant reports of Allied casualties whilst exaggerating German setbacks and fatalities. It seemed to the uninformed observer that matters were progressing well. All that was needed was one great Allied victory and the Germans would be sent packing back across the Rhine, pleading for peace. Even at this late hour the general population was living in total ignorance of the slaughter to come.

The reality of the developing situation at the front, in contrast to the expectation built up by the media, could not have been more stark. Within two weeks of the new season, Billy's life, along with so many others, would be transformed; innocence and illusion would be swept away by the evidence of his own eyes and ears.

The first match of the season found Glossop at home against Derby, the match viewed by many as the local 'grudge match.' On this occasion, everyone was gossiping in illuminated fashion, no matter where they came from, needing to find out how others elsewhere in the country were reacting against the now increasingly alarming news coming out of Belgium and France. The match was almost of secondary importance in spite of the large Derby contingent pouring out of the railway station onto the cobbled square.

For a while it was business as usual, the Countymen marched towards the ground singing the praises of their team and forecasting the immediate and profound demise of Glossop in the face of such wonderful players possessing the most marvellous skills. Over six thousand watched the match that day, a bad tempered game only assuaged, for the Glossopians, by the single goal of the match which was scored by their side, through a free kick from Tommy Toward. As was usual, both teams were rusty at the beginning of a new campaign, with new players fitting into place alongside unfamiliar team members. A poor game, but two points for the home side, Jack Lloyd was most pleased.

Nathaniel Hawkins, together with Sally, attended the match. To him it appeared that Billy's mind was elsewhere, his performance was undoubtedly muted. However, he reasoned, the young player could not be expected to provide a star exhibition every week, his play would get better, he was sure.

Since that lovely day at the fair, Sally spoke to Billy every Sunday on the steps of the Chapel. Their conversation became the highlight of the week. She discovered that the young boy she had left so traumatically, virtually sobbing, in the library had now grown into a sophisticated, polite, highly intelligent young man. He displayed great charm and appeared most attentive. She saw him as extremely good-looking in an innocent way, her inner feelings becoming invaded with sensations that came from an attachment that was far above mere friendship. Sally now knew she was in love, deeply, shyly, confusedly, but certainly in love. Recollections came flooding back of those past times in the library on Saturday mornings. The truth dawned upon her, she had been in love with Billy Thomas for years.

For the moment Sally enjoyed but five minutes each week in his company, this required rectification, her problem was how. Not one of their encounters would pass without Billy making enquiry of the figurines. Sally would confirm they took pride of place upon the piano in the parlour, which seemed to please Billy bringing a smile, displaying no little element of pride to his handsome face. The girl earnestly wished to invite Billy to tea that he may see his trophy for himself, yet somehow could never muster the courage to ask, by the time she felt so armed to do so, he was gone escorting his ever present mother. If she did but know, the young man longed for her to provide some insight of her feelings but each week passed with continued disappointment.

Elizabeth, never lacking in her observation, noticed the couple's shy extended reticence, and determined upon speaking to Nathaniel on the subject. The opportunity came one evening when Sally went out to a newly formed ladies sewing evening where comforts were produced then sent off to their adopted regiment, The Cheshires.

Evenings were becoming cooler, so Elizabeth lit a homely fire. She prepared tea with tea-loaf, laced generously with butter, Nathaniel's favourite snack; a treat prepared for him over countless evenings of married life. Nathaniel turned up the gas lamp and began to read. The house contained a wide selection of books, mostly volumes from the classics or poetic works. Tonight Nathaniel was idly leafing through an anthology of English verse.

"What are you reading dear?"

Elizabeth often brought out her sewing on evenings like this while he read verses to her. Firelight and romantic poetry recited by her beloved Nathaniel, it was on nights as these, Elizabeth realised how much she was still in love, was loved.

"Thomas Grey, his 'Elegy in a Churchyard.'"

"Would you read me a verse please Nathaniel?"

He read:

The boast of heraldry, the pomp of power
And all that beauty all that wealth ere gave,
Awaits alike the inevitable hour,
The paths of glory lead but to the grave.

"Very true Nathaniel, very true, apt."

"Yes it is", Nathaniel agreed. He was feeling morbidly reflective of late, recollecting how the events of the year slowly, but seemingly inevitably, had taken control out of the hands of moderation and common-sense, remorsefully fuelling the engines of war, projecting national hysteria to so great a level of hatred, all reason vanished. Now the young men were going, or would soon do so, jubilant, fearless, full of hope. He knew not how it would all end.

Elizabeth passed him his teacup together with a generous helping of his favourite delicacy. Sitting down she took advantage of her husband's silence.

"Can I speak a little of Sally?" she enquired

"Of course, Elizabeth." Nathaniel put down the book, took up his cup and, facing his wife, and became the height of an attentive listener.

"Sally is taken with young Billy Thomas. I am sure of it. Do you have any thoughts upon the matter Nathaniel?"

Her husband considered for a while before making his reply.

"Well Billy is a good enough lad, with prospects too. He is dedicated to the pursuit of excellence. Jack Lloyd speaks very highly of him. Billy is modest; he goes to Chapel each week out of conviction, not from habit of

77

that I am sure. In addition, he is good to his mother. I would certainly trust him with Sally's emotions and her reputation. But."

"But what?" The demand came from Elizabeth in a short terse question warning her husband to proceed with due care.

"Well"

"Well what?" Elizabeth's voice was displaying anxiety mingled with not a little rising frustration. 'She has an undoubted agenda', considered her besieged spouse. 'How to make reply?'

"The truth is, it's this war. People's lives are going to change. Many lives are going to end much before their time; war does this, especially the kind of conflict I believe we are going to face.

"Very true, Nathaniel my love, but should such a prospect become an obstacle for two young people attempting happiness? I do not think so. This war could come to dominate every aspect of life if we allow it so."

"You are right of course", Nathaniel concluded, knowing that the solution to the dilemma confronting him was to seek dear Elizabeth's opinion.

"What do you consider we should do my love?"

"That is simple, invite him to lunch one Sunday, and see where it leads."

The response was so immediate that Nathaniel just knew that his astute partner had decided upon this now announced course of action long before this day. His only option was surrender, to give up any illusion that this was a discussion. In the face of so determined a woman it would be foolishness indeed to contemplate even the slightest hint of objection. He would allow his wife her head, let her intuition guide them.

"Whatever you say my dear. I leave the matter entirely in your hands. Whatever your plans, I am sure they will meet with success."

"Why Nathaniel, thank you. I will keep you informed of any developments, I assure you."

"Thank you Elizabeth." The reply was emitted from a man experiencing great relief. He now picked up his volume signifying that the audience was concluded.

Elizabeth settled back down to her sewing. She was fully content, now Sally could be spoken to and plans put into operation. In contrast Nathaniel was troubled. Ever since Billy had played his first home game for Glossop, Nathaniel was aware that this talented player had become a pawn in the affairs of Hill-Woods. Now, in addition, the young man could find himself powerless in the larger world, a world which soon, he was certain, would demand more and more youths to feed the furnace of conflict.

He recalled how, just a few days after Billy's debut, his 'tour de force', news came of the potential for war that was contained within the Balkans. It was on the fourth of April that Albania called up its reservists, threatening Greece with invasion. Next Russia announced a further increase in its war budget of five per cent, following Serbian atrocities being reported being enacted upon her Albanian Moslem minority. By the beginning of June a full civil conflict had erupted in Albania, with the city of Durazzo coming under siege.

The final match of the season witnessed Billy putting two more goals past a visiting defence. This time the hapless team was Nottingham Forest who lost three goals to one. A crowd of more than eight thousand, almost a third of Glossop's population, attended the game, enthused by the team's resurgence largely emanating from the boot of their latest signing. It was here that Nathaniel came to realise the true potential of his discovery. What he did not know, or could, was how short lived it would all be.

The very evening following that memorable last game of the 1913-1914, season, a secret meeting of the Serbian Black Hand movement was in session in Sarajevo. Its leader Slobodan Karavich had chosen three of his most fanatical followers to make separate attempts on the life of Franz Ferdinand, heir to the throne of Austria-Hungary. Supporters in the Bosnian hierarchy had supplied the group with details of the streets and times that the motorcade would pass. Both countries wanted greater freedom and the potential for expansion, and though little love was felt between them, on the principle of 'my enemy's enemy is my friend', co-operation was forged, making them allies of convenience. Plans were sealed that evening which finalised the fate of millions, together with that of most of the crowned heads of Europe.

Within hours the inner cabinet of Austria-Hungary would know the outcome of the conspiratorial group. Their agent provocateur, Gavrilo Princip reported to his controller, who sent coded dispatches to Vienna. Princip was not happy; he was but the third choice for making the attempt. Surely one of the others would succeed before he could fulfil his opportunity. Come June the twenty eighth, Franz Ferdinand would be dead. Gavrilo still hoped it would be his gun that placed him in the pages of history. Full of hope, he went back to his apartment to strip and clean his weapon. He knew not that his masters, needing to arrest and execute some scapegoats to cover up their part in the murder, would ensure that his role would be simplified, whilst that of the other would-be assassins, was to be made impossible.

The world carried on with its affairs completely innocent of the chain of events unravelling at the behest of fanatics and tyrants. Saturday the twenty eighth came with a deceptively glorious sunrise all over Europe. In England trains were full of people setting off for the coast, making up walking parties, trekking the fells, having picnics or merely enjoying their gardens. 1914 was fast becoming the best summer for decades all over the continent.

The motorcade was drawn up on the out skirts of the city. It had been a long journey from Budapest, over three hundred kilometres taking six hours. Franz Ferdinand, not unusually, was in a bad temper. He had not wanted to make this journey anyway, but his advisors were overpowering in their persuasive insistence, informing him it was a great wish of the Emperor. Franz had never been on good terms with his despotic uncle, a self-indulgent capricious man, who manoeuvred formal precedence, thus forbidding his children ever to inherit the throne. He knew he was a stopgap unwanted convenience needed to continue the Habsburg Dynasty, an errand boy. This was one such errand a flag-waving trip to a Moslem infested outpost of the Empire, literally God forsaken.

Here they were approached by the Sarajevo chief of police together with an overbearing ingratiating escort of local dignitaries. The pompous black uniformed man walked up to the car where the Heir Apparent sat; saluting he laboriously welcomed His Imperial Excellency to the humble city. Next he organised the procession. These provincial heathens completely disgusted Franz Ferdinand but, for now, his distaste was disguised. The open car in which Franz and his beloved Sophie were to be revealed to the populace was to travel third in the extended procession, he was informed that huge crowds were waiting to greet them, persuading him to suffer the ceremony and patiently acknowledge the peasantry who so longed for a glimpse of their Sovereign.

The procession progressed so slowly. People were lining the streets in increasing numbers as they advanced. They were certainly enthusiastic, the cheers becoming louder with each street they passed; perhaps the day would not be so intolerable after all. Now, however, events were to take a dramatic turn. Suddenly a man, successfully avoiding the guards, sprang out from the crowd, pointed a gun at Franz and pressed the trigger. Having, unknown to the assailant been previously tampered with, it jammed, not more than two yards from the eminent visitor's head. The increasingly frenzied, now doomed man pressed the trigger four more times before being overpowered yet no report came from his weapon, no bullet left the barrel. The Empress elect screamed; the Heir Apparent felt nauseous, a warm moist sensation spread from his loins, and trickled down his leg.

Uniformed officers instantly smothered him, surrounding the car creating a protective screen. Others were forcing the would be assassin to the ground and wilfully dragging him face down across the cobbled street. All was embarrassment in the aftermath, the supposed protectors offering the most profuse of apologies, lining each side of the vehicle, watching and waiting, ensuring no second attempt could be made.

At least five minutes elapsed before the chief of police announced that all was clear, everything under control and proclaiming the procession should continue with all expedition to the City Hall. These were fine sentiments, yet impossible to initiate for a new problem faced the convoy. The crowd, now swollen from curiosity, massed in such numbers that they advanced at a crawl.

Sophie turned to her husband, imploring him. "Franz, do something, if another assassin is lurking, we shall be defenceless."

The Archduke attempted consolation. "Don't worry my dear, it will take more than a Slav peasant to kill the likes of us, inheritors to the throne imperial."

Sophie was re-assured. She both loved and trusted her husband, a mutual emotion. The couple had married without the approval of the Dynasty, which deemed her far beneath the status required to be the spouse of the inheritor of the imperial throne. The rancour from the state was so intense towards their union that it was decreed their offspring to be illegitimate in regards to attaining the highest Habsburg title thus forbidding any son of Franz from gaining any status he so enjoyed.

Seeing his wife smile at his words, Franz squeezed her arm gently. "There, there my dear, we will soon be at the City Hall, all is safe."

Unfortunately, what had started out to be a bad day was about to get worse. No sooner than the words were uttered than a large black oval object landed in the car at their feet. Instantly, Franz recognised it to be a bomb. For a second time that day fate intervened. An observant guard, not a member of the conspiracy, reacted with lightning speed, grabbed the device and threw it with all force in the direction of the river. Unfortunately, it did not reach the water, exploding on the bank, seriously injuring a number of bystanders.

Fury welled up within the Archduke. "Imbeciles."

He was shouting uncontrollably, his eyes virtually dislocated from his head, his face purple, brimming with rage. "Get us out of here before we are all killed."

Instantly the car accelerated irrespective of any in its path, many of whom received injuries as a result. The driver sped them towards their destination, where a host of illuminaries awaited them, gathered on the steps.

Franz Ferdinand was in no mood for ceremony. On being greeted by the Mayor, he exclaimed in somewhat less than diplomatic terms the incidents, as he perceived them. "Two Slav pigs have tried to kill me. I was forced to eject a bomb from the car myself or my wife and I would now be dead."

This lie was to persist for years, assisting in the elevation of this bad tempered, inadequate man, to that of an innocent martyred heroic sovereign whose sole concern was the protection of his beloved wife, so gaining, posthumously, a reputation for quick thinking and selfless bravery.

In reality, the Archduke and Sophie were intensely relieved to be inside the building in relative safety. Here he could also relate his tale of trial which became ever more intense with repetition, exaggerating on each occasion his personal role in events. He dominated the luncheon of dignitaries, accepting the accolades heaped upon him, illuminating his brave conduct of the morning.

The function was completed, the toasts and speeches performed, the hands all shaken. Now it was time to leave, trepidation once again began to rise within his Excellency. He had changed his hose and underclothing. It would do no good to repeat his past bodily function in the face of another exposition of personal danger.

On the steps all the couple's hosts bid them 'bon voyage.' It alleviated their concern somewhat when the Chief of Police informed them that their route was now greatly altered, thus foiling any further attempts on their lives. Now placated, becoming calm, the Archdukes dignity returned. He duly thanked the officer who so diligently, with much foresight, and short notice, had re-arranged affairs to further ensure his safety and, together with his wife, re-mounted the car.

The convoy moved off, again with the royal car in third position. Soon they arrived at the place where they were to divert from the original route. According to plan the first two vehicles changed course. Not so the car containing Franz and Sophie they continued along the originally designated path, now without the protection of the leading vehicles. Franz Ferdinand was alarmed, shouting at the driver to change direction. No response came; the vehicle sped on ignoring the pleas of the pair in the back. They were now both doomed. As the car reached the next corner, it slowed down almost to a stop.

Immediately, a young thinly built black bearded man ran up to the car pointing a pistol. At point blank range a volley signalling an emanating bullet was released. The projectile struck the Archduke full in the chest. Instantly, instinctively Sophie spread herself over her husband to protect him. A second shot entered her back, rupturing the heart, instantly killing her. The nearest guards rushed towards the pair gently pulling Sophie's dead frame away from the beloved man she had fruitlessly tried to save, her lifelessness all too apparent. Her husband was alive but fading fast.

He managed to speak some words, his last." They have solved the problem of me; I trouble them no more. Now they have their excuse." Here his eyes glazed over and he met his God.

Words from a man having the knowledge that life for him was to continue elsewhere, the sentiments were never to reach the public domain. Total secrecy was demanded from Vienna. Her foreign minister, Von Bertold, personally taking charge of the crisis which he knew would develop, for he would initiate it, according to an agreed plan involving others in the Government, the royal household, and chief of the armed forces, General Franz Conrad Von Herzenborg, who became responsible for ensuring that their conspiracy remained out of the public domain.

The driver of the royal car was immediately taken from the scene. He was pleased with his days' work having complied exactly with his master's instructions providing them with the exact planned outcome. On the pretence of being rewarded and the need for him to lie low for a short while, he was brought back to a secure house deep in rural Austria to be feted for his work. Like so many others over the next weeks, he was lied to and eventually betrayed. On the day war was declared between Germany and Great Britain his body was found drowned in a small lake outside Spittal. The incident never even made the local press such was the gravity of news elsewhere.

As for Gavrilo Princip, he was immediately arrested, photographed with those who had apprehended him, the scene being telegraphed across the world. By Sunday his staring fanatical face would gaze out from newspapers all over the globe, contrasting dramatically with the postured reverence of the murdered pair. Condemnation was universal. In Britain 'The Times', exclaimed, somewhat sanctimoniously, 'It shakes the conscience of the world.' The Daily Chronicle was to conclude, more accurately, 'It has resounded a clap of thunder over Europe.'

The principle contributor to the crime in the uninformed eyes of the world was provided with a strange existence for the rest of his life, dying of natural causes in 1918, unique among the other hapless, publicly acknowledged, conspirators who were dispatched with all haste. Gavrilo Princip was kept alive because his manipulators felt his testimony might be needed if events, in a complex situation took a direction that, for the moment, could not be foreseen. By the time he breathed his last, millions lay dead on the battlefield, or maimed for life as a direct result of the two shots fired from his gun.

From the moment of the assassination the guilty politicians began to contrive events. By the thirtieth of June the Black Hand society had been exposed, pointing the guilt for the outrage directly at Serbia, providing Austria with all the excuse it needed to deal with its small, yet capricious and turbulent neighbour. Clearing her proposed action with her powerful ally Germany, Austria sent a harsh ultimation to hapless, though proud, Serbia with the full knowledge that it would not be accepted. Von Bertold well knew his demands would be ignored which, in consequence, would provide the justification for invasion, occupation and retribution.

Back home in England, Nathaniel, along with the rest of humanity, was never to gain knowledge of the true nature of the plot. Intrigue, and speculation surrounded the assassination but never got close to the truth, which was so dastardly in its connivance, that years later with all the evidence that time provides, none have ever completely unravelled it. What Nathaniel could follow was the manner in which a transparent line of tragedy followed in progression, allowing the settling of scores and realising long held ambitions.

Nor were matters unfolding merely from the camp of the central powers. On July the fifteenth a French delegation met with their Russian friends in St Petersburg to re-affirm the long held alliance. Despotic autocrats and professed egalitarian republicans clung to each other desperately hoping that their evident joint strength would be sufficient to deter any aggressor.

Meanwhile the situation in the Balkans rapidly deteriorated. Austria broke off all diplomatic ties with Serbia on the twenty-fifth, quoting her perception of an unsatisfactory reply to the ultimation. In response Serbia mobilised her forces, signalling reluctance to acquiescence. The tinder box was open, the flint in hand, now all that was needed was the first spark to strike, destined not to be long in coming.

By the time Nathaniel was meeting up with Billy and Sally at the August bank holiday fair, Austria had invaded Serbia, Russia was proceeding to her borders with over a million men and Germany poised to invade France through Belgium and Luxembourg. Inevitably, as so many enlightened prophets had forecast, war was about to explode all over Europe.

Against the background of these historic manifestations Nathaniel allowed Elizabeth her head regarding the encouragement in the development of an understanding between his daughter and Billy Thomas. In truth he was pleased, even when considering international affairs and the logical consequences of war, how it is prone to make widows, now he awaited personal family developments as impatiently as he sought news from the world stage.

Two young people gradually finding confidence to discover the emotions and hopes of the other were now as driftwood on the sea of events. 1914 possessed a dynamic all its own, dictating the destiny of the couple. In France, by the banks of a river called the Marne a tragedy was being played out that spread its tentacles far afield eventually to reach little Glossop, curled up beneath the Pennines.

By the middle of August, six whole divisions of the British Expeditionary Force had arrived in France, near to the Belgian border. The gallant soldiers of that small country, outgunned, outmanned, obsolete in the terms of modern warfare, withstood the invader inflicting large casualties, costing him time, equipment and manpower. The Prussian response was to smash everything before him utilising overwhelming force combined with brutality. By these means was Brussels occupied and pivoting here the Germans swung into France sweeping towards Paris. In front of them the British were in full retreat heading back towards the sea.

Now an incredible reversal of fortune occurred, later referred to as the miracle of the Marne. The Germans became overstretched, leaving them woefully understrength to fully carry out their original plan. The grubbing they had received from the Belgians, the forces they were persuaded to release for the Russian front in the face of a more resourceful eastern enemy than anticipated, coupled with the French threat to Alcace-

Lorraine, meant that they could never brush the Channel with their sleeve as Schlieffen had directed. Their forces turned before Paris, pushing west to link up with their southern pincer, thus exposing an extended flank. The British, who by now had gained reinforcements from a number of territorial battalions turned to face the weakened enemy, by the banks of the Marne. Soon the Germans would be in full flight pursued relentlessly by a bulldog gnashing at their heels.

Peter and Paul Griffiths arrived just in time to take part in the battle. The battalion was placed on the right flank of the British forces; therefore they found themselves next to the French, a motley citizen force that had streamed out of Paris utilising hundreds of taxis. They were amateurs but also patriots angry at the German desecration of their beloved France. They were the Valois, they were dangerous.

On the morning of the ninth of September the Cheshires were ordered to advance, not to stop until the enemy had been driven across the Marne. This plan unlike so many that were to follow was a complete success. The British swept the Germans over the river then beat the Germans in a chase to the Belgian city of Ypres, meeting up with the French and Belgians who secured the line to the coast. The 'Miracle of the Marne' was a great victory for the Allies yet, it was to cost the lives of both Peter and Paul, the first of the sons of Glossop claimed by the war.

The dawn of battle brought a mist, which lowered visibility to less than one hundred yards. On the given signal from their Lieutenant, the brothers advanced alongside their comrades with bayonets fixed to the famous Lee Enfields. They had advanced about five hundred yards and were approaching a small copse. Here the officer ordered the charge and they were racing towards the woods. The Germans spotted them at last. Fire from a pair of Spandau machine guns halved their force in less than thirty seconds.

The Lieutenant lost his nerve decided that the woods could not be taken and ordered a retreat back into the friendly mist, which beckoned safety. As the Platoon turned Paul was hit and fell. Peter was running, eyes to the fore so he did not realise immediately that his brother was no longer with them. The troop came to a stop when the officer deemed it safe enough to regroup. Now Peter looked around for his brother, immediately he became aware that Paul had not made it back.

Shouting Paul's name he ran back into the mist. Within a few yards he virtually fell over his brother's lifeless form. Instinctively he knelt down to take hold of him. Now in a semi-trance he held no perception whether his brother was alive or not, As gently as possible he placed Paul over his shoulder and began to carry him towards the security of the British lines. The German machine gun opened up once more. Two bullets struck Peter full in the back, one destroying his left kidney. Miraculously he kept going, staggering back to where his comrades were. He arrived collapsing under the weight of his dead brother's body. The wounds were mortal; he died in a field hospital two days later.

Conditions were not as confused here on the banks of the Marne, as they were to be during later battles of this war. Casualties did not reach horrendous proportions of Ypres or the Somme allowing for all the recovered casualties to have a civilised burial, identified with named crosses and a Christian blessing. The two brothers were interred next to each other. Today they lie, still together, side by side, names among masses of other names, their headstones displaying their regimental arms and identifying the Military Medal that was Peter's award for his deed in gathering up his brother in the face of unremitting enemy fire.

It was over a week later that Billy was passing Norfolk Square and spotted Albert Griffiths sitting on a bench, gazing at a newspaper trancelike, tears falling on the page, his hands clenched in fists as if he was about to tear the sheets to shreds. He walked up to the distraught man with no inkling of what was to transpire.

"How are you today Mr Griffiths, have you heard from your sons?"

Albert made no reply; he simply passed the paper to Billy. There, graphically portrayed on the front page, were photographs of Peter and Paul in uniform.

"I was told of Paul's death four days ago. The next day news came to me of Peter. They died together, Peter having gone back to rescue his brother who had been shot. He was killed trying to rescue him. Buried together they be, gone, they be gone, my two boys, they ain't a coming home. Here you read it Billy, I don't want it."

With a gesture, half of anger, half of grief, he thrust the paper on the bench, placed his hands in his pockets and walked off, inconsolable. Billy looked after him, tempted to follow to offer condolence. Wiser council came to him; he thought it better to leave the bereft father with his grief. Taking up the paper, he sat upon the bench and began to read.

It was, he remembered, not much more than a month since he was harvesting with these two men. So self-assured they were, convinced they were going off to beat the Hun, and be back home as soon as you knew it, covered in medals and glory. Now all that covered them was the soil of a French field. Despairingly he turned the pages seeking other news. The appeal glared out at him, a petition that was to change his life.

CHAPTER 6

Farewell happy fields,
Where joy for ever dwells;
Hail horrors, hail.

Paradise lost Bk: 1.

Upon reaching home, unutterably distressed by his conversation with Joseph and the news of the death of Peter and Paul, Billy made a quick excuse to his mother and rushed upstairs to his room. Again he opened the Chronicle, to see the two young men gazing out from the page. They were so dignified, so strong and determined staring sternly forward, upright as if nothing could pass or overcome them.

Billy considered: 'It is the like of these two brothers who are fighting this war, not only for King, and Country, but for me and, yes, Sally also.' He felt wretched, was it indeed true that others were protecting him, fighting his battles and those of whom he loved, whilst he was here, safe in Glossop, playing football? Leafing through the pages the appeal glared out at him. The call, designed by the editor in collaboration with Hill-Woods and constructed in the largest type at his disposal, drew him as a moth to the flame.

Young Men
Between the ages of 19 and 35
YOUR COUNTRY NEEDS YOU
Time is precious and the need is great.
In this terrible time every man who is
capable should rally to the flag
Glossop has sent but 500 sons
It is not enough.

This imposing proclamation, followed by an editorial seemed composed of language appearing directly aimed at Billy.

'Young unmarried men, will you share in the fight and in the glory?' It is a fight for liberty, honour and freedom. Now is not time for games and amusements. Your Country calls you in her direst hour.'

Billy stopped reading for a moment to consider, he was feeling increasing discomfort almost cowardly. He continued along the column. By the time he had concluded the inducement was filling him with shame that he had not enlisted but, instead, had continued in his preparations for the new season.

'Do not wait, or hesitate, delay could be fatal. Join the army at once until the war is over. Employers, help your men to enlist. mothers, send your sons. The stronger the army the sooner the victory.'

'Join the army at once.' The words taunted Billy, challenging him, shaming him. That night he slept, his dreams filled with morbid spectres. The mud encrusted skeletal remains of Peter and Paul arose from their pitiful graves to question him. Why were they in death when he roamed the hills of home? How could he profess to love Sally when he was not prepared to defend her but leave matters to the likes of them, now dead and in their graves. All night they, and their fellow regiment of the lost, visited him. When he awoke, with dawn well broken, he recalled his entire nightmare, and recoiled.

He got up as tired as he had retired. It was the morning of Friday, September the fifteenth, a day that was to prove to be one of profound destiny, both for him and scores of other young men of the town. With all haste he washed, shaved and gulped some milky oats. He then grabbed his coat, shouted goodbye to his mother and headed for Norfolk Square. Something told him a crowd would be gathered there, and so it transpired. Coming past the station he saw that hundreds of excitable people were milling around.

Billy's old foreman from Partington's came over to him. "Just like the end of the Boer War. Joining up Billy? Going to the 'Call of arms rally' tonight?"

"Of course", came the reply, then he hurried off to see who else was around the square.

During that morning Billy met with many of his friends and old workmates. They all declared they were going to the rally. He discovered that the main speaker was to be none other than Hill-Woods himself, there would be singing, bands, 'everything'.

Billy stayed in the square for over an hour, shaking hands, being clasped by unknown middle aged ladies extolling him to enlist. Without exception, he assured them he would do so that very evening at the rally. Tiredness, a feeling of an oppressive atmosphere, encouraged him to graduate towards the edge of the massed throng. He drifted away, finding himself walking along High Street East. For the moment an overwhelming urgency invaded him, he needed solitude, or, the least to be away from the bustle of the madding crowd. Soon his steps would take him to Cliffe Road where he could hike up to High Field, spending the rest of the morning in reflection and enjoying the fragrance and serenity of an autumn meadow, bereft of any other human presence.

His route took him by 'Hawkin's Stores'. Here fate decreed that Sally would be coming out of its doors at the precise moment he was passing. Billy practically fell over her.

"I am so sorry Miss Hawkins." He was spluttering, both embarrassed and pleased simultaneously. Having discomforted her, Billy was compounding the felony by becoming incoherent. He needed to reverse matters without delay.

"I was in my own world, pondering upon the coming recruitment rally at the Town Hall tonight. When the moment comes I shall go forward to volunteer my services to the army."

Sally replied with a gasp, not one word escaped from her lips. She just looked at him, filled with empathy for his well being. The longer she stood there the more her feelings transcended from the sympathetic towards an inwardly incomprehensible intuition of foreboding, from the subconscious to the all too apparently aware. There, upon the pavement, Sally came to the realisation that unconditionally, her life, her love, her happiness, could never be separated from the man standing before her. She was overwhelmed with an insufferably intense yearning, welling from deep inside her. Now, right here and now, she had to plead with him to reflect upon his avowed intent, to prevent this lovely man from placing himself in harm's way. She would use his newly created key position in football to dissuade him, diverting his attention away from her real motives.

"But Billy", she implored. "The team needs you. You are their best player by far. What would they do without you?"

In response, Billy reiterated the sentiments of the newspaper's appeal.

"It is not now the time for amusements and games. My country needs me."

"And so does Glossop." Sally was now possessed of heightened panic. By the second it was growing inside her invading every part of her being.

"At least Billy, take time to consider. Father tells me that this war could last a long time, years even. It could cost a great many lives."

"But I must, and shall do my duty."

"And your duty may be at home. You are your mother's only child, and she widowed with no husband to console her. Think of her Billy, think of her." In truth Sally wished to add, "and think of me", but her nerves disallowed that sentiment.

During this frank exchange of views, Nathaniel was observing them from inside the shop. He could see how distressed his daughter was becoming and decided to join the pair outside.

Opening the door he greeted the young man whom he knew to be the unwitting source of his daughter's distress.

"Good morning Billy, what excites you so today?"

"I am going to enlist Mr Hawkins, at the great rally tonight."

Nathaniel had already been informed of the meeting, of its purpose. As a member of the Glossop Chamber of Commerce he had been requested to attend. His presence would add to the support to the call to arms.

"Very good Billy, very good for you. Sally, myself and her mother shall all be there, unless, of course, Sally stays here gossiping instead of undertaking her errands."

Billy blushed: "Sorry Mr Hawkins, I did not mean to detain her."

"That's all right Billy, not your fault I am sure. This daughter of mine just cannot resist a good gossip. Just like her mother she is, could chat away all day. Sally, say goodbye to Billy."

"Goodbye Billy." The instructed reply came sadly, sheepishly, unwillingly. Full of a great sadness, of apprehension she did not want to go and leave this man who had so weaned her heart from her, captivated it and now held it in his protection. For now, faced with her father, mockingly authoritative, she needed to retreat.

She did with a final enquiry, More of a spoken hope than a question. "Perhaps I shall see you tonight Billy?"

"Hopefully you shall Miss Hawkins, Hopefully you shall."

With that final remark, Billy touched this forelock in respect to both father and daughter and turning, went on his way.

"Off you go then." Nathaniel could see how hurt Sally felt, he wanted her on her way. Duty to her tasks would alleviate any thoughts filling her head surrounding Billy Thomas. His hope was a forlorn one. Not a minute of that day would pass when Billy Thomas would cease to invade the thoughts of his daughter. Conversely, what he could not know was that it was mutual. Billy, wove round most of that day dazed by the vision of Sally which so graphically implanted its impression before him.

Sally crossed over the road, upon her errands, without further word. Billy looking over his shoulder watched her moving away. She walked, the gentle breeze causing her skirt to flutter, pressing her blouse pronouncing her chest, mirroring his palpitating heartbeat. As she moved Sally swayed as a meadow in May, pretty, enticing, her darling buds, full of intrigue, suggesting reward to the brave. He shook his head, what must he be thinking of!

Yet, as he looked back, Sally's head also turned. From a distance their gaze met. She smiled, somehow he knew it to be special, special to him. The girl raised her hand in a wave, she smiled again, one of the few times in their future togetherness that the gesture would be accompanied by that expression. He smiled back and even though the distance was now considerable, he knew, she knew, their worlds, their lives, laughter, joy and tears, were forever linked.

The rally was a grand affair, all political parties were represented, Labour, Liberal and Conservative. The President of the Glossop Liberal Party Mr Henry Partington chaired the meeting. There were two main speakers Mr Hill-Woods, M. P. for High Peaks, who would make the final call to arms, and a visiting Socialist, Mr Victor Grayson, one time rogue MP for Colne Valley and a Clarionette. He had been recruited because of his standing amongst those from whom most was expected.

The Town Hall was full, many having to stand in the aisles, the entrance or even on the pavement outside. Mr Partington stood. Instantly the audience became silent, expectant. He made a proclamation. "I call upon our very own Mr Tom Shepley to open proceedings with Jerusalem."

William Blake's famous anthem, sung in a fine Tenor voice, both haunting and evocative, was heard in intense silence, moving all who heard the words. To some it proved beyond all doubt that God was an Englishman, to others it was a plea, a vision for a better world. The second chorus reached its conclusion, sentiments of a long dead English poet married to the music many considered to be her greatest composer.

Henry Partington considered that just the right atmosphere had been struck for the introduction of his first guest. Victor Grayson was a renowned Socialist, if such a description was not an oxymoron. Indeed every political ideal Grayson stood for, Partington considered an anathema, why even many of his own Labour colleagues had disassociated themselves from him due to his long held extreme views, together with stories of more than one dalliance with a female admirer. That aside the man was universally acknowledged as a hypnotic speaker, capable of holding a crowd in the palm of his hand. Grayson's charisma had already brought thousands to the colours, if he could be as persuasive this night all well and good, if his politics got out of hand he could curtail him from the chair.

Partington rose, scarcely had he begun to introduce the elegant relaxed supremely confident man on his left than a mass of cheering broke out at the rear of the hall, Grayson obviously possessed more than a few supporters impatient to hear their man. They held little respect for the one introducing him, and were stating their sentiments. After a few cursory sentences, Partington gave way, handing the auditorium over to the peacock philanderer.

Taking out his pocket-handkerchief, in a gesture half-mocking towards the speaker who had so generously introduced him, Grayson, smiling to his audience took centre stage. Recollecting some of the words of Blake, he began.

"I could use that great anthem as a polemic, making a purely class conscious point. That will lie for another day, for this day we are here as Englishmen and women first and last. Class, the politics of party have their place but it is not here. England, the whole of the lands comprising these British shores, ladies and gentlemen, comrades, is in dire danger from a foe more wicked, more determined and far more dangerous than many comprehend. Germany is an evil state, led by a blood-covered despot who will not cease in his labour of conquest and destruction until all good, capable Englishmen and women are under his heel. I appeal to you, rally in resistance to the tyrant to give him a sound thrashing, sending him back across the Rhine attendant of shame and defeat."

Grayson had an alternative agenda to those others on the platform, who represented all that was politically despicable to him. He was determined to be an oasis within this desert of capitalists that encompassed him. True, his exhortation would achieve the same result as that of Hill-Woods and his ilk. The difference was that he would send men off to fight knowing the real reason why they should do so.

This war was developing into much more than merely military conflict. It was a force for change, possessing a dynamic, which, at its conclusion, would leave the world much, altered. The applause now died down, he continued.

"A few short weeks ago, the Germans were storming through Belgium and France. It appeared no force could withstand them. They considered themselves to be the mightiest army ever assembled upon the face of the world. Then they confronted the British! This small regular army, comprised of men from the tenements and hovels of town and country, these few, these happy few, turned to face the juggernaught. Their allies, the exhausted French and Belgians, were reeling before the foe, yet this small band of brothers turned like lions at bay. They selflessly attacked the remorseless grey wave, first halting it, then chased it as it fled. For an immortal hour they, alone, prosecuted the war. I tell you!, our Army, our Navy, are the best in the world"

This last sentiment brought forth rapturous prolonged applause. It was sometime before he could continue. When he did so it was to send home a most telling point. He spoke softly.

"Yes the best in the world. Not because Britain commands the most mighty of ships, as she surely does, or supreme weapons for the field of battle, of this there is no doubt, for they are built from the blood and sweat of the most skilled workforce ever assembled. The ultimate reason, ladies and gentlemen, is because these forces have been drawn from the classes that are most impoverished, cast from out of the foundry of endless toil."

Unease was beginning to well inside Henry Partington. No argument, this renegade Socialist was enthusing his audience, but what he was preaching was verging on revolutionary agitation. If he was unhappy with Grayson's sentiments so far, his unease was about to grow. The oratorical pugilist continued.

"I exclaim to you, exhault you, remember their example, their sacrifice, their determination, their struggle which leads us towards victory, for it will succeed in a far greater aim. When these champions come home, together with all the rest who volunteer to be part of their great company, class shall be no more. There shall be only grades determined by ability.

Neither shall there be greed, nor poverty. Society shall be governed by this premise; from each according to his ability, to each according to his need."

Here his supporters, Frank Potter among them, shouted their affirmation. Billy Thomas felt the stirrings within his memory of a speech made long ago by the man who allowed him to guard Hercules the Clarion horse. Little he knew, how the speaker before him now and Robert Blatchford were comrades of long standing. Victor Grayson's final words would echo in Billy's ears upon another time, at a place not far from this hall. They would be spoken by Billy himself, having come home for a short time from that cauldron here so graphically described.

Victor Grayson, full of the knowledge that his message had not fallen on stony ground, concluded.

"Therefore, rally all you young men of England, stiffen the sinews, summon up the blood: from this place, at this hour join the fight for it is a great crusade. Then, when your duty is fulfilled, the enemy lies at your feet, come home and build that long yearned for Jerusalem!"

Rapturous acclamation erupted from every corner of the hall, Victor Grayson, son of Socialism, had urged these Miners, Quarrymen, Weavers, all those who toiled so philanthropically for their masters welfare, to come to the colours. They would undertake his plea, not so much for Monarch or Realm, but for the secret scripture of the poor, the promise that, at war's end the old would pass away to be replaced by a new Heaven, a new Earth.

'Enough of this egalitarian claptrap', decided Partington. He recognised that Grayson had crossed a divide forbidden to both him and Hill-Woods, reaching deep into the hearts and minds of the unwashed. Enough of that. now leave it to the established leaders of the land to conduct the rest of the undertaking. He would now pave the way for another political foe one, he knew, he would eventually defeat. Grayson's words would soon be forgotten, in the tumult to come.

"Ladies and gentlemen, may I now introduce to you that great patriot of long standing, Captain Hill-Woods. First I give you our own Mr. Tom Shepley once again with his singing of Rule Britannia."

The much-acclaimed local Tenor was once again greeted with furious applause. He filled the hall with the familiar stirring words, the audience joining in the chorus with frenzy and gusto. Time after time the lines were repeated with growing enthusiasm, coupled by cries of 'hurrah' and 'encore' when any lull threatened to end the performance. Finally, from sheer exhaustion, Tom Shepley sat down, to lasting cheers and applause.

Without further introduction, Hill-Woods stood, before the hypnotised audience, he wanted no pause between his appeal and the ending of Shepley's performance, nothing would allow for any dilution of sentiment.

"No, I say no!, never shall Briton's be slaves."

The crowd, already full of adrenaline from the words of Victor Grayson, Jerusalem and Rule Britannia were ready to be transformed into a baying mob. Hill-Woods now merely spoke words to assist the process.

"If there is one type of slavery worse than another, it is the type suffered in Germany today. The German people suffer an iron yoke of militarism that would never be tolerated by us freemen living in England. Yet it is the most earnest desire of the German Kaiser, together with his high command to, by force of arms, inflict their values upon the whole of Europe, including Britain. People of Glossop, never doubt, if Germany were to win this war, you would all be enslaved by a foreign power, his foreign laws and his foreign values. We would all become slaves to his capricious will."

Hill-Woods took a sip of water, allowing himself to drown in the nectar of applause that greeted him. He was warming to his theme, now to develop it.

"Shall we sit idly by, allowing ourselves, our loved ones, to become slaves?"

The reply came back to him. From all parts of the hall frenetic repeated cries resounded, shaking the very foundations. "No! no,! no! never! never! never!"

He extolled them further. "Shall our young men stand idly by?"

"No! no! no!"

The sound now reached the platform of cries coming from outside the hall drawn out of the throats of the masses who had not gained entry.

"Will all you young men answer the call to the colours?"

"Yes! yes! Yes!"

The crowd were playing into his hands, taking upon a spontaneous, chain reaction of self inducing hypnosis, becoming almost crazed with enthusiasm. Hill-Woods was very pleased with himself. Never had he been so successful in manipulating an audience before, impatiently he wanted to see where his final plea would lead.

"So young men of England, her dearest and her best, will you join up in service of your Country today, here and now? Men of Glossop, I implore you, do your duty. Mother's of Glossop, wives of the men of Glossop, sweethearts, sisters, urge your men to do their duty."

He paused, looked about him, the air was thick with tension, caused by his entreatments. Summoning up all his resources he made a direct plea to the women present.

"Who here will urge their men to do their duty?"

In response, every female voice hearing him screamed: "We, will, we will!"

His cup overflowed, Hill-Woods was convinced that now he would complete his task The night was going to end most successfully. He brought his voice down to just above a whisper, becoming serious of tone, uttering each word slowly.

"Well, men of Glossop, your women have spoken, do not I pray you let them down. Let it not be said of Glossop that the women were willing but their menfolk shirked. Sign up to the colours tonight, now, this very moment. All is prepared for you to do so. Ladies and Gentlemen may I introduce you to Sergeant Flannagan, he and his team have all that is necessary upon their persons to enrol you, and God speed all who volunteer."

Not one person remained seated as a well moustachioed man, full of military posture, sporting Khaki, emblazoned with three stripes on his upper arm, stepped onto the stage. Adulation reigned, also envy from those young men who saw what effect his bearing had upon girls, for whom, so many of them hid secret desires.

Partington judged that now was the correct time to bring proceedings to a close. Catching the eye of Hill-Woods, who nodded in knowing assent, he stood for the last time.

"We shall now close with the National Anthem. Mr Shelby; if you please."

"God save the King." The words rang through the hall and out onto the streets, echoing throughout the town while hundreds of delirious young men prepared to sign an agreement designed to consign all to many of them to oblivion.

Billy joined the queue, the jingoism having completely consumed him, sidled by Jimmy, equally under the thrall of the words and music.

"It's great Billy, great. We are all going to be heroes in uniform, all the girls will be after us, all keen to be seen on our arms."

Billy reflected, he only wanted one girl to notice him, to wish to be seen walking out on his arm. All through the meeting he had sought her out, without success, neither Sally nor her father could be seen. Now his time came in the queue. Stepping forward, he made the oath, signed the proffered slip of paper and then conducted to adjacent room for his medical.

A cursory examination followed, lasting all of two minutes, followed by questions on eyesight, hearing and general health, culminating in a request to touch his toes which, forthwith, he proceeded to successfully accomplish. Rising up he was ordered to straighten his back whereby he was informed that he was now duly accepted as a recruit and ordered to report to the Drill Hall at 9.00am sharp on Monday morning. Departure for training camp would probably take place within the week.

It was now that the suddenness of it all dawned upon Billy. Within a week he could be far away from Glossop, there was so much to do. He needed to find Sally, tell her all, of his feelings, his leaving. Jack Lloyd, he too needed to be informed, oh, and his mother, how to tell her that her son was now a private in the Chester Regiment and off to undertake his duty?

Jimmy came running over to him. "Looks like tomorrow will be our last game for a while, at least for Glossop."

"Looks like it." Billy began to fill with some regret. His fans, his friends, his football, Sally, it could be an age before his eyes set upon her once more.

Others began to mill around. Someone suggested a street party, a mobile one being transported from Pub to Pub.

Young Bill Carney commented. "It will be one to remember."

Billy merely nodded, shook hands with his soon to be army comrades and left for home. As he was passing the Station he noticed the first speaker who had so roused the crowd that night. He was coming from the George and crossing the square, presumably to catch a late train.

"Good evening Mr Grayson."

"Good evening to you comrade."

Billy had not been so addressed in that way since Belle Malony had called him such all those years ago when he was guarding Hercules.

"It was a good meeting Mr Grayson, you were extremely inspiring, I enlisted you know."

Victor Grayson came towards him, Billy thought he staggered, as if he were a little drunk.

"I hope that was not on my account comrade. My conscience would not allow me be the instrument of such a decision."

"Not at all, my decision had already been made."

Billy could now smell the whisky on Victor Grayson's breath, he was somewhat the worse for wear. Grayson indicated to a railway bench and both men sat down.

"I meant it you know. This war could be the catalyst for the transformation we Socialists have been advocating all these years. It could bring down Kings, Empires, the very capitalist system itself you know."

"I agree."

"You agree?"

"I agree."

"Well, well: then all is not lost. If some of you are going off believing that, then, just perhaps, my recruiting work is not being wasted."

"Certainly." Billy was finding suitable words difficult to come by.

"What's your name comrade?"

"Billy Thomas."

"Well comrade Billy Thomas, I am most pleased to meet you."

A hand was offered to Billy. He grasped it, shook it gladly. As he did so he heard the whistle of the coming train as it went over Dinting viaduct. It would arrive within five minutes.

"No one has addressed me as comrade since the day I met Robert Blatchford near this very spot over eight years ago, at least none as enthusiastically as you Mr Grayson."

"You have met comrade Blatchford?"

"Certainly." Here Billy quickly related the story of Hercules, Of Belle Malony, of the Clarionettes.

"Comrade, Robert Blatchford and I have been fellow travellers more years than I care to remember I sit here in esteemed company.

The train now drew in, gave a huge release of steam and came to a halt. Victor Grayson got to his feet with a little difficulty.

"I shall walk with you to the train Mr Grayson."

"Thank you, most obliged, call me Victor."

"Let's go Victor, it only stops for a couple of minutes."

The two men walked towards the single carriage that the engine pulled this time of an evening Billy opened the door, allowing Victor Grayson to enter with ease. As the door closed the new occupant let down the window.

"Billy, never let the exploiters grind you down. They will use every opportunity to do so, take my word."

Pressure came once again to the pistons, the wheels raced round seeking traction with the rails, slowly the carriage pulled away.

"Never Victor, never, they will not get me."

Victor Grayson shut the window and sat down. He was alone in the carriage. Once again, he knew, he had drunk too much, but he had disguised it well. 'Best of luck Comrade Thomas, best of luck.' He drifted off to sleep, it had been a long day.

Billy got home before the train crossed over Dinting, not knowing the circumstances where upon he would once again meet Victor Grayson two years hence under a moonlit sky, damp and cold in a trench in France by a river called the Somme.

Next day he awoke at eight, dressed, breakfasted and without telling his poor mother any of the previous evening's events, left the house to report for pre-match training. Whilst changing, the entire conversation was of the great rally. Billy soon discovered that about half the team, together with most of the reserves, had enlisted. They all agreed to meet that evening for a celebration such as Glossop had never before witnessed. However, firstly, they would go onto the field of play, beating today's opposition, before going off to France to thrash the Hun.

Their opponents were Birmingham, a team that usually drew a large crowd. Not today, although the weather was perfect for both playing and watching the game, the crowd was poor. So many of the usually loyal citizens of Glossop were, no doubt, nursing sore heads or were preparing for their imminent departure.

Nathaniel was in the crowd, accompanied by Sally. She already knew Billy had enlisted and was keen to see him play in what could be his last game with Glossop for quite a while. Poor Sally, she was not aware but today would see the very last match ever played for Glossop by Billy, together with most of his team-mates. This phenomenon also extended to Birmingham. It was ironic that this very day the national press were insisting such meetings as this should be suspended for the duration of the conflict. Practising the game of football should be replaced by practice with the bayonet.

Paradoxically, today's match turned out to be a great game, one long held in the memory by those privileged to witness it. An age was passing, a time when the game was worthier than the result, sportsmanship greater than success, the whole greater than the individual. This day, these young gladiators of the ball, challenging, tackling, dribbling, deftly deceiving, out-manoeuvring their bemused opponents, playing strategic, thoughtful, Corinthian football, displayed on the field those attributes that soon other challengers in other places would come to both fear and respect.

For the moment, before this sparse crowd of fortunate onlookers the two teams, evenly matched, strove for initial advantage. The men from the Midlands were fast, surging forward time after time, testing keeper Causer to his utmost limits, shot upon shot.

As is so often the case, in a game where fortune reigns, undeservedly, it was Glossop who went into the lead by purchase of a fine goal from Bill Carney which sailed fast and high into the net. His senses heightened, Billy began to conjure hope that this day would witness a fine victory. Birmingham had a history of being a bogy team in their confrontations with Glossop. In all the years of their meeting, he could not remember Glossop once being victorious, perhaps today would provide a watershed.

Disappointment however was not long in coming. Before halftime the scores were level, the Birmingham forward, Tinkler, successfully slipping round the stranded Glossop keeper to simply tap the ball into the home net. Thus it remained until ten minutes of the second half was underway. Years later the next goal would be discussed in public houses and clubs whenever Glossop and football was recollected in conversation.

This goal was to restore Glossop's lead, it was also the last that Billy would ever score for his home team. It found its creation with a fine piece of pick-pocketing by Tommy Toward who whipped the ball away from a Birmingham forward, leaving him comically stranded to the great delight of the home spectators. Dribbling the ball from out of his own goalmouth, passing two other Birmingham players, Tommy ran the entire length of the left wing. without slowing down he crossed the ball into the centre of the opposition's penalty area. It found Billy's feet and, seemingly by magic, was juggled from left to right as a confidence trickster would display his talent with three cups to a confounded speculative audience with much the same outcome. The defence lost sight of the ball as it left Billy's feet heading, inevitably, goalwards in its legendary swerving flight, searing passed the fingertips of the keeper.

With its telling, over the years, the goal that restored Glossop's lead would grow wondrously. A tale spoken by old men long after the coming conflict had been resolved and the shadow of the swastika was foretelling the advent of the next part of the great tragedy that was Europe during the first half of the twentieth century.

Glossop, a goal to the good, but fortune was to explore another aspect of her temperament. Two quick goals for Birmingham and they now possessed the advantage It appeared that the visitors would now take all the honours. Fate, it is said, is a fickle mistress, she also responds to the emotions of men, their need for recollection that is not all gloom. This day she gave all those present a gift, a game for the memory, of even honour.

Glossop bore down upon the Birmingham goal threatening its security on countless occasion, to no avail. Eventually Carney and Knight linked up with complimentary passing moves which split the opposing defence asunder and allowing Knight to whip the ball behind the isolated Keeper for young Carney to simply nod in. Three goals each, at that it was to remain. Saturday the 16th of September, 1914, honours even between two teams that had pushed themselves and each other to the highest limits. Fate also made a further decree that day, deeming history would never allow them to meet again in the competitive arena.

The whistle blew, an age passed. Players, officials, fans, they all congratulated each other. More, they looked to their fellows, who delighted in this beautiful expression of human endeavour, for mutual support in the coming time of trial. Competitive they had surely been, hard, professional, certainly, giving of all their skill and energy. Soon, they knew, many of them would meet on another field. Together, they would be seeking out a mutual enemy who did not play by any rules recognised by civilised society. A game, not with a ball, but utilising bombs, bullets, and shells under the tutelage of no referee in a game of life and death which would not cease with the blowing of a whistle.

Tradition demanded that, after a match, the whole team would plunge together into a large communal bath then go to the pavilion together for hot drinks and refreshments. Here they would reflect upon the character of the match, its salient points and lessons to be learned, with Jack Lloyd and the management. After the analysis they would then be given their instructions for the coming weeks training schedule.

Today, although they felt it had been a good game in which their performance was high, the mood was sombre. All present knew that it would be a long time before many of them would meet together, here in Glossop, playing football. Conversation was, understandably, muted. Jack was making the rounds, giving encouragement to those who had volunteered, shaking hands; feeling as if he was saying goodbye to his very own sons.

Mr Hill-Woods, now using his honoury title of Captain, was also congratulating those who had enlisted as a result of his call to the colours. Nathaniel Hawkins and his daughter were together adding to the farewells. It was inevitable that Billy and Sally would come face to face.

"Congratulations on such a good game Billy."

"Why thank you Sally." Billy felt an urgent need to sit her down and talk. "Can I get you a cup of tea?"

"Thank you Billy, thank you very much, just what I need."

Billy went away, soon coming back with the tea, together with some biscuits. They were about to sit down when Hill-Woods and Sally's father came over. Nathaniel was looking embarrassed, very uncomfortable.

Hill-Woods pronounced. "Let us all sit down here, I have something to say to this young man."

Billy had never been in close conversation with Hill-Woods before. His family, being non-conformists and either Liberals or Socialists, the exact opposite of the Conservative Anglican would, ordinarily, never come into contact with his like. None-the-less he did as he was bidden and awaited the pronouncements of the team's Chairman.

"Billy, Nathaniel and I have been thinking. You are your mother's only son. You have become a famous citizen, a key member of the team. Now, there are many exceptions being given to local men who are their family's only bread-winner. We could arrange a Magistrate's order rescinding your assignment to the colours. Billy, you could stay at home, with all honour, continuing with your career."

The address was somewhat removed from the truth, a not unusual facet of statements made by the MP In reality, Nathaniel had voiced what he thought to be the unethical nature of the proposition now confronting Billy. Hundreds had volunteered the previous evening. It just so happened that Billy was of more use to Hill-Woods at home than at the front. He need not have worried, Billy Thomas was made of sterner stuff than his tempter imagined.

Billy stood up, tall, erect, facing the Captain. It was true that he had pondered his situation, he was yet to inform his mother, when he did so she would overwhelm him with tears, not a scene to look forward to, ensuring the good woman, that all would be well. It would be harder for him to face Gladys Thomas, than a whole regiment of Captain Hill-Woods.

"I thank you sir. I thank you for considering my situation, but I cannot accept your proposition. You see Captain, I would not play well thinking of all the others doing their duty, being covered in glory, helping to defeat the enemy while I stayed at home playing football. No I reckon we all go over, win the war, and when the job is done, only when it is done, do we come home. Then together with creating a better world for all to live in, we create a new team which will embark on wondrous things, perhaps even win the division, get promotion and this time stay there. Sir, I say these things with all due respect to you but no power or persuasion will divert me from this path"

Hill-Woods was speechless. He was aware of many wives and mothers who had attempted to dissuade their menfolk, how a few had already made applications to renege upon their signatures. He automatically thought that a young lad like Billy with such good prospects before him, would jump at the prospect, especially coming from a high illuminary as he. The MP was about to counter Billy's reposte when the young upstart interrupted.

"Sir, my mind is made up. I shall go off to camp next week, train to the best of my ability and do my duty. Would you have me do otherwise sir? I implore you, give me leave to live or die in my Country's service."

Hill-Woods knew he was beaten. Standing up, he faced Billy and reluctantly shook his hand, then, silently, he went off to talk elsewhere, his scheme to keep control over this particular investment was in ruins, added to which, he had been publicly humiliated, or so it seemed.

When the Captain was finally out of ear-shot, Nathaniel stood up. He also shook Billy's hand.

"You are a brave man Billy Thomas. It is easy for a man to sign up in the frenzy of a patriotic gathering, another matter altogether when he re-iterates his intention in the face of an alternative enticement. God keep you Billy. I hope all goes well with you. See you and your good mother at Chapel tomorrow."

Nathaniel now turned to his daughter, a devious plan forming in his mind.

"Sally I have to speak to the others who are leaving us. Perhaps Billy, you would be kind enough to escort my daughter home for me?"

There were times, considered Nathaniel, when he excelled himself, acting with the highest of intuition and insight, the kind Elizabeth so often displayed. This, he felt, was such a time, his wife would be so pleased with him. Billy responded immediately.

"Sir, I shall be most honoured to escort Sally home, she will be very safe with me."

Here he found the courage to muster a further proposition.

"May I ask Sally if she would care to walk home through old Glossop, unless, of course, you need her home quickly?"

"No Billy, I have no objections at all."

Then he enquired of his daughter rhetorically. "Sally?"

"Yes father, I would love to."

She turned and smiled at the young man who had so bravely faced both the stern temptations of the MP and her father in one afternoon.

"Let us go Billy, before you become embroiled in another confrontation."

Billy now felt as if he were king for a day. Nathaniel Hawkins had been so supportive of him over the last six months, taking him from an obscure life as an engineer in a cotton mill and a part time footballer, to a full time professional who had famous clubs seeking his services. Now, additionally, he had been entrusted with the companionship of his only daughter, the very girl that had composed his most intimate thoughts for what seemed an age.

Old Glossop was the site of the original medieval village. For hundreds of years it had been the first place of refuge and welcome to travellers or pilgrims, even armies coming over the Pennines from the east coast. It was the gateway to Lancashire, Cheshire, The Midlands and Wales. Below, the main town of Glossop had grown around the rapidly flowing brook, streaming out of the hills onto Dinting where it linked up with other rivulets coming down through Hadfield and Hollingworth.

This fine old settlement, displayed its history, traditions and myths which mingled with the Autumnal essences of ancient trees, complete of gold speckled leaves, now one by one losing contact with their host. Resplendent berried hedgerows mingled with the warmth of a cloudless Indian Summer's afternoon, intensified the trembling of fingers, which had permitted the slightest of brushing touches to produce burning sensations, which heightened expectancy to make more eager the awaited, stealthy, apparently accidental strokes stoking latent emotions and passion.

Now an awakening physical, yet mutually understood urgency was becoming instilled within their breasts. Innocence was facing fecundity, two star-crossed souls initiated the ageless transformation from childlike delight to impassioned love. They wandered idyllically in each other's presence, yet they were self-conscious that a new most profound link was being formed. Their souls were becoming mated long before their bodies would be so joined.

Billy found the need to express himself, yet, as with his body, his mind was trembling, he was even stuttering in his thoughts. He needed to find a point for conversation that appeared not to be too crass. Sally's beautiful pink hat, which crowned her delicate head, so appealed to him. As they began to walk along Fauvel Road towards the crossroads he complimented her. He also, without any verbal suggestion proffered his arm, which was accepted. His reward was the linking of Sally's hand onto his wrist. In this manner, they progressed towards the old Church and the ancient monument that proudly stood before its entrance. It was mounted atop a raised plinth, an obelisk summitted by a cross, prefiguring so many more that soon would be erected in towns, villages and cities throughout the land.

"Wonderful isn't it? They say it is Saxon, it has stood on this spot for over a thousand years, unbowed by any threat. That it stands to this day is evidence to the character of our Nation and its People."

Sally gazed at her young companion. She saw him echoing past deeds of courage and daring. Her lovely man, at the foot of this cross of ages, she was in awe.

"Why Billy, that is so romantic, so heroic." She squeezed his arm with both hands.

They stood silently before the cross, close together, physically side by side, their hearts beating in unison, each with the other, welded ever towards a single destiny. For an hour they strolled round the old town, then, by unspoken agreement, now hand in hand, they walked over the meadows alongside Hurst Brook. They were completely alone, the small stream on one side the meadow on the other. Billy held Sally's hand firmly, they gazed at each other as they ambled along the path. Thus they continued as the afternoon drew to a close, looking only at each other, their smiles charged with inward speculation.

A country style indicated the end of the path. Billy climbed over first, then grasping Sally's waist he lifted her clear of the obstruction. Once she was again safely upon firm ground, Sally did not back away but stayed in anticipation, still being held by Billy. She extended her neck towards him and kissed his cheek. A surge of delight rose within Billy. Instinctively he placed his hand upon her chin and gently kissed her lips. Sally responded, what Billy had intended to be merely a short, touching wistful brush evolved into a complete passioned expression giving the two young lovers their first physical token of belonging.

As their lips separated all Billy could utter was her name over and over. "Sally, Sally, Sally."

The girl made not a sound Silently gazing at the young man full of awe and wonder, not merely of him but of the entire experience. The kiss filled Sally with an intensity both divine and exquisite, yet noble, without any sense of sinning. Her response had been willing, full, leaving nothing back. It amazed her, this place would forever be special, holy even, this scene, the young man with his strong arms, his gentle provocative touch, all was very special indeed. Sally now knew, with all certainty that she was embarking upon an unknown adventure full of intrigue, exploration and delight.

Suddenly, coming out of his sublimnity, Billy realised that they were no longer alone which brought his natural instinct for duty to the fore. The couple had emerged onto High Street West with all its bustled throng typical of a late Saturday afternoon, here the couple once more walked with her hand on his arm, formal and respectable, typical of the pose adopted by a newly courting couple. Billy was aware of some embarrassment, Sally also, but the rapture they were experiencing far excelled any self-consciousness they possessed. They were now fully engrossed with each other, empowered with longing, embraced by love.

Approaching Norfolk Square, they were spotted by a number of Billy's team-mates who were making a rapid exit from the George. Their demonstration of jollity and the level of their out of tune attempts of singing, quickly led the pair to realise that copious amounts of alcohol had been going down the throats of all present. Billy just knew that both of them were in for some suggestive barracking, his estimation was correct.

"Why Billy, you lucky sly beast, we wondered where you had gotten."

Billy's face flamed: "Only out for a stroll, just taking Miss Hawkins home."

Young Bill Carney, noticed a red smear on Billy's left cheek. Taking full opportunity of being one of the boys, he pointed towards the offending mark.

"Better not let Miss Hawkins' mother catch you with her daughter's lipstick on your cheek then."

Here he scuttled behind Jimmy Jones, just in case he was to become the centre of wrath from the enraged object of his torments. Billy decided, to the great relief of his companion, that the best way of treating such taunts was to ignore them. The couple passed by the revellers, climbing the rise towards Charles Street.

The group called out once more, this time in a serious vein.

"Coming down to the Square tonight?"

"Wouldn't miss it for the world. see you at seven"

So untangled from their inquisitors, they managed their escape. Sally stopped, pulled out a small linen handkerchief, moistened it with her tongue, and wiped away the evidence of their embrace.

"There, all gone, and no one any the wiser."

She was to keep that scrap of stained cloth for the rest of her life, just as it was.

Far too soon, they were at the front gate of Sally's house, still holding hands, not wanting to part or let go of each other. The house was surrounded by green railings, the abode of a successful family. Billy saw it as forbidding, the object that was now to separate them. People were passing by on both sides. Turning to face his beloved girl, the young man felt that he should merely shake her hand, perhaps touch her cheeks briefly with his lips. That was exactly what happened.

"See you in Chapel tomorrow?"

"Of course Billy, I simply will not be able to wait."

Re-assured, Billy placed his lips on those delightful cheeks for one last time. Sally reciprocated.

"Goodnight my love, till tomorrow, Parting brings forth such sweet sorrow."

They were back in the days of the library, as if nothing had ever separated them.

"Shakespeare?"

"Romeo and Juliet."

"Two houses, each alike in dignity."

"Quite."

With that one last kiss was planted upon the cheeks of his goddess and Billy, with more reluctance than he could bear, turned down Charles Street towards his home. Neither he nor Sally observed that the net curtains of the front living room fell back as Elizabeth Hawkins reclined once more into the chair she had vacated just a few minutes before. Her enigmatic smile was still being worn when Sally entered the room.

That evening, an elated Billy Thomas did the rounds with his friends, The George, The Norfolk Arms, The Moon and Sixpence. Later these would be the places he could remember, other similar establishments were simply a blur. He would not be able to remember his staggered walk home, or the sight of his astounded, speechless, angry mother waiting by the door. The stairs must have been climbed, for he awoke later in his bed, but it was beyond his recollection. Events were erased not solely by the alcohol but by an inexplicable mixture of celebration cocktailed with an underlying trepidation of the future. These Spartans feverishly revelled in the anticipation of being in uniform, tempered by the awareness of an unsure outcome when, at last, they would have to face the foe.

This throng of doomed youth, gathered that night in the Square, singing out its anthem. Being both congratulated and feared for, they passed away the evening united in abandoned gaiety. Within six short years, three hundred and seventy seven of them would have their names inscribed upon a monument in this very place. Here, yearly, the people of the little town would gather, together with their bereaved families and friends, to remember them, as they were this night, youthful, fresh, talented, full of hope, marching off to meet the enemy and finding their end 'in a small corner of a foreign field.'

CHAPTER 7

Such night as this I have never passed;
Heaven awakes with all her desires
Whom to behold but thee.

Paradise lost Bk. V.

A young man's constitution, even an inexperienced one like that of
Billy Thomas, is capable of consuming an astounding amount of alcohol,
particularly if he is drinking with a pack of his peers, where each one is out
to prove that they possess an adult frame. They had all drunk 'as men', and
who could contradict them, offering, as they undoubtedly were their lives,
on behalf of Britannia, placing themselves in harm's way, defying the guns
of an enemy state. A heady mixture providing ideal receptacles for
countless pints of the strongest beer.

It was Billy's virginal night of experiencing alcohol taking over
his bodily stability and his verbal outpourings, and the same could be said
of most of his revelrous co-felons. As the night bore on they became ever
more boisterous and outlandish, sometimes becoming less than respectful
to passers by, particularly female ones who were often invited to supplant a
kiss upon one reprobate or another. Yet, for this night, the town was theirs.
The local constabulary, realising this was a one-night affair, showed
constraint, often in the face of the most blatant provocation. The Chief
Constable, a father of two strapping lads himself, reasoned that if a young
man was about to go voluntarily to serve his country, then he could be
allowed this short time of merriment.

Those under his command, therefore acted with considerable
restraint and tact, attempting to ensure they reached their homes safely
without becoming the victim of pickpockets and the like, those scavengers
of the night who contain no principles upon selecting their next victim,
other than he be as drunk and incapable as makes for an easy prey. Thus the
main responsibility of uniformed officers that night was to escort as many
brave warriors home to their waiting worried parents. Such an escort, it was
later to transpire, led Billy Thomas safely home. He would never remember
the solemn instruction.

"Goodnight lad, mind out for your mother now, she will clip your
ear as soon as look at you."

Yes he had drunk copiously, totally out of character. In later years,
upon coming home from the front to fulfil his dream, he would recall this
night, such as he could, and find no explanation, or excuse, for his conduct.
The drink had undoubtedly been consumed, what he was to discover during
the next few hours was the all too apparent truth that neither the stomach,
nor the head can cope with such misuse forever. As the night progressed his

body began to reject the fermenting toxins, to fail in combating the attendant dehydration. Eventually, the inevitable results of abuse began to come to the fore, vastly outweighing any enjoyment or release that his unrestrained over indulgence had provided.

His turn came, it was time for repentance, time to pay for his night of uninhibited imbibing of that substance which he had been warned upon so many times to avoid, and which, truthfully, he had never seriously experienced before.

He awoke in the early hours, dazedly extracting from out of a fitful range of dreams, full of melancholy, dismal disposition and doubt. Bile flavoured his mouth and the room gently tossed in a whirling jig. Nature was calling, uncomfortably pressing his bladder. Somehow, he knew, he had to find the strength and stability to stagger down the stairs and outside to the little house.

Twilight was encroaching, slowly gaining momentum over the retreating darkness. The clock struck seven, or was it six? He made his way out into the garden; the brightest of the stars still shone through leading his befuddled brain to contemplate whether they appeared the same in France. The door to the privy greeted him and he swept through, falling to his knees.

Being both relieved and sick, with the sour odour of vomit about him, shivering in the frosted air, the reprobate regained his bed slamming onto the mattress. Now, full of remorse, he promised himself, his God and anyone else who might remotely help him in his direst hour that never, ever, ever, would he behave in such a way again. Never, never, honestly would he consume the devils nectar in as like manner, seriously, honestly, truthfully, God, mother anyone, but please good Lord the host of Heaven have mercy on him now.

Slowly, blessedly, consciousness left him relieving the unbearable symptoms that distressed him so. Physical release however was immediately replaced with rambling nightmarish images, which flooded his brain. He was in a foreign land, engulfed with mud crushed by noise. Everything hurt, terribly, insufferably. He was screaming without giving utterance, surrounded by corpses he knew were his friends. Peter and Paul rose up to greet him. They were pleased to see him, hoping that soon he would be keeping them company in their dread abode. Now they were dragging him to his doom, he cried out for help but no sound escaped from his lips.

Suddenly, an angel came to fill his dream with light, sweeping away the clinging, oozing, mud that constantly beckoned and threatened him. The light became brighter, a clear white radiance, defying the grotesque images of the dead who could only exist in the darkness. The Angel turned, she had Sally's face and smiling she led him away from this land of the damned. He gained clean verdant pasture, free of the vale of

107

death. Here Sally let go his hand, smiled once more and vanished. He awoke and lo' it was a dream.

He now felt much better physically than had been the case a few hours previously, and with the improvement in his wellbeing his rationality returned. The clearer his mind became the more he was filled with doubt and uncertainty. Fear, in opposition with hope, two fellow travellers competing for his attention. Both had been his companions throughout the night alternatively providing torment then aspiration, they were with him still, only now he was awake.

Had he really signed up to go to France, throwing his cap in the air along with so many others? Had he truly drunk all that ale, bought for him by so many people? Had Sally really let him hold her and kiss her, taken his hand and coupled her fingers with his in that exquisite manner, smiling all through that blessed walk with eyes only for him? Of course, he concluded, it had all happened, just as he was remembering so. He was successfully separating dream from reality, and now the truth dawned.

Sitting up in bed, he was starkly aware of how much he had undertaken. Plans must be made, so little time was left to him before he, inevitably, would be swept away from Glossop, leaving England, coming to a foreign shore to fight on behalf of God, King and Country. He would be fighting for Sally also, Sally, ever for Sally.

The idea came to him slowly, yet firmly formed. Today was Sunday; he would present himself for Chapel as never before. Billy was always particular about his appearance on Sundays, but today, despite still hosting the presence of after effects from the previous night, he would attend Chapel before his God and his fellow congregation as never before. Sally would be so proud of him, with Sally's parents too suitably impressed. He would delight in the beloved girl spearing him with pleasured glances all through the service.

His mother was moving around downstairs, startling him into action. She heard him move.

"Tea Billy?" It was a question that came together with no little tone of disapproval. He knew that sooner rather than later he would have to face his mother's wrath. He must compose himself.

"Five minutes mother."

Shamefacedly, he came down into the kitchen. He timidly offered his morning greeting and decided the best course was to shave immediately, his mother would never interrupt whilst he was using the razor once the daily implement of his father. He remembered how 'Dad' would meticulously strap the blade against the leather thong hanging by the sink. Now he was, in his turn, repeating the routine whilst mother brought him the kettle of boiling water from the range.

Gladys watched him as he stood in his vest, lathering his face with the brush and soapstick which seemed to last forever. Her anger was rapidly subsiding, so full of love was she for the young man, here looking identical to her beloved Joshua, mimicking the daily function that had engrossed her all through their happy years together.

Nonchalantly, the boy enquired. "Do you think I should grow a moustache?"

"I think it would suit you Billy. It was the first thing I noticed about your father, his was a real monument, glossy, bushy, manly. Joshua used to love me trimming it for him whilst I cut his hair. Every first Monday in the month I would attend to it, right here in this kitchen. Oh that I could trim it now. Billy you are my present from him, the blessing he left for me. Joshua would be so proud of you, the man you have become, your talent with a football. I can see him now, he would be reading of your exploits every week in the Chronicle, extracting the reports and pasting them up in a book for posterity. Billy, your mother is twice blessed, my son a star, my husband a shining light in the heavens. A life's gift, the two best men in the world."

Billy turned round to see that his mother was gently weeping, looking into the flame within the grate. He knew that he could not tell her about yesterday, his volunteering, not at this moment, here on his own, perhaps Sally would come with him when he told her. The bringer of such bad news could not also be the provider of the comfort that his mother was surely going to need.

A determined course of action now came to him. Mother was going to his father's grave before coming to Chapel. They would always go together once a week, but sometimes Gladys felt the need to visit her Joshua on her own where she could speak to him of matters concerning her. Today was one such time; mother and son would meet in Chapel, once she had shed her troubles upon her husband's grave. Billy glanced at the clock, 9.35, Sally would be leaving her house in ten minutes, it was important to appear to be approaching the corner just as she and her parents were closing their gate.

"Are you going to Uncle Frank's as usual."

"Yes Billy"

"Well mother I shall not be coming today. Jimmy and I are probably meeting at the Club with some of the other lads."

Gladys was surprised but not unduly concerned. Of late Billy had begun to alter their time-honoured arrangement of walking together to Frank's house for Sunday lunch.

"What about your dinner?"

"I will be alright mother, don't worry I'll not starve."

Before his mother could protest further, he had grabbed his jacket and was heading for the door.

"Got to dash."

No sooner had he left than he realised an emerging problem. Someone could mention to his mother the events of yesterday. His mind flew to a possible scenario, "Your Billy, you must be very proud."

Considering he should tell her, he paused, thinking to return. The dilemma hit him, tell his mother and miss Sally. It was to be the first occasion that someone else preceded Gladys in his priority, he turned again towards his rendezvous full of anticipation and expectancy.

Fortune was with Billy this Sunday morning. He did not have to check his paces or retrace his steps. Exactly as he turned the corner of Charles Street and Fazackerley the three objects of his proposed collision were at their gate. Luck, or fate, either, he was indebted to both, Sally was standing there beside him, arms linked to her mother with her father alongside. Sally whispered to her mother and dropped behind to meet with the fortunate youth.

Tipping his hat, Nathaniel Hawkins acknowledged Billy

"I hear that you young men had quite a street party last night. If you all make the same impression in France, the Germans are not going to last long."

Elizabeth added.

"Your mother must be very proud of you Billy."

To this last remark the guilt ridden juvenile could find no response. He hesitated, able solely, to utter mumbled formalities.

"Thank you sir, good morning to you Mrs. Hawkins."

"And good morning to you Billy."

The latter greeting was issued, with an encrypted, tone together with an enigmatic smile; the same manifested expressions, which confronted her daughter the previous evening.

Sally took Billy's arm in the now familiar manner whilst covertly providing it with a fondly administered squeeze.

"Oh Billy, Billy."

The girl's expression of delight in being with him on her perambulation to Chapel increased his sense of the victorious outcome of his plot. The morning was going exactly according to plan. The joyous pair walked side by side, silent but full of gestures, smiling contentment. They reached the Chapel steps, still enraptured in each other's presence. Traditionally Billy would stand at the back of the Chapel, together with the other young male reprobates, whilst the family Hawkins would sit in their favoured pew, four rows from the front, on the left.

"Why not sit with us today, Billy."

The invitation from Elizabeth came as a complete surprise to the charmed lad whose Sunday morning was developing into his best ever. Now a further invitation from Sally's mother was about to place the cream upon his cake.

"Would you like to come back with us for Sunday lunch Billy. Sally can prepare some extra vegetables and there is enough beef for an army."

Sally's sense of joy was complete; Nathaniel was surprised, but pleased that, at last, a resolution could be made regarding his daughter's undoubted feelings for Glossop's finest footballer. Billy was virtually speechless. He could merely mutter his grateful acceptance in a muffled voice.

"Thank you Mrs. Hawkins, thank you very much, you are most kind."

Sally squeezed His arm once again. This time it was a sign of her excitement. As they entered the Chapel, she let go of him, not uttering a word, her flashing azure eyes, however, expressed the alpine height of her delight. Seeing Sally so illuminated, so full of exquisite anticipation, in turn, drove Billy to an altitude of pleasure that had never entertained him before.

The mood of the couple was in stark contrast to the sombre resilience, mingled with adventurous trepidation, portrayed on the faces and in the subdued voices of the young men gathered in the rear. It appeared that like him, they had volunteered, almost to a man. Billy shook hands with most of them, as he went past the gathered throng, most of whom echoed sentiments from Friday's meeting. The recruitment Sergeant had reaped a very fruitful harvest indeed, his uniform and the young ladies response to it being most effective. Were some of them, Billy conjectured, like him, now experiencing more rational considered emotions, which they were keeping quietly within themselves?

He dwelt but a fleeting moment on these thoughts, for his mind returned to Sally, the prospects of a delicious lunch, perhaps to be followed by a magical afternoon. As he took his place with the Hawkins family he was greeted more enthusiastically than usual. Today a changed congregation possessed a unity, a more open expression of friendship than traditionally, far more reflective, supportive.

Pastor Gideon Livingstone climbed the steps of his imposing pulpit an edifice of dark sturdy English Oak that, somehow, reflected the Nation's present expression of strength, resilience and stature made manifest in these challenging times. The congregation became deathly silent, the atmosphere pregnant with an incomprehensible tension.

Gideon had passed most of the night deep in contemplation, wondering how to conduct this morning's service. He too was in attendance at the rally on Friday night, coming back to the Manse steeped in mixed emotions. Considering himself to be a patriot, he was full of pride in the outpouring of duty displayed by those young men all around him who were unconditionally putting their lives in danger for God, King and Country. Yet this was tempered by a fear that the coming days would see the conflagration, with all it's assembled, increasingly massive armies, grow into an apocalypse never before witnessed in the history of mankind.

Surely, he concluded, the time was now come, when, together, as the Bible solemnly warned, War, Death, Pestilence and Famine were to be let loose from Hell, to descend upon the World, adding to the woes brought by the armies of men. Of one thing he was sure, before this fury was dissipated, the World would become changed forever. Kingdoms, Republics and Empires would give birth to endless rows of graves, attended by countless grieving mothers, fathers, sisters, and wives. Nations would fall, as Lord Grey observed, the lights would go out, possibly for a generation. Against this his faith sustained him, lights may go out but not The Light of the World. Christ would not desert Mankind even if Mankind deserted Christ.

These grave times gave a preacher of the word his greatest challenge. To bring comfort and spiritual sustenance upon the flock of Christ was the primary aim, followed by the instillation of concepts of forgiveness towards enemies. He had to mellow mindless chauvinism and to fortify souls. During the early hours of that Sunday, at much the same time as Billy was expelling the toxins within his digestive system, Pastor Livingstone knelt by his bedside whilst his wife remained fast asleep, blissfully unaware of his prayers for guidance. Softly, his voice not more than a whisper, he prayed as he had heard his father do so on an occasion when he was about to preach against the imprisonment of a number of collectivists. The year must have been about 1875, for Gideon could not have been more than ten years old, but it had left a lasting impression. Ascending the pulpit, on the morrow morn, in muffled tones barely perceptible to his congregation, he made a plea to his God.

"Lord, Thou knowest what I must do this day. If I should forget Thee, I pray, do not forget me."

Through his late father, the plea of Oliver Cromwell had brought him the essence of his coming address. Saint Paul was going to provide him with his text. Gideon had always admired Paul. Now here reading through his letter to Timothy he found what he required. Gideon explained to those sitting below the context of his reading.

"Paul finds himself imprisoned, his life is soon to end. He is betrayed, given false assurances, yet, in this, his darkest hour, his faith sees him through. He contemplates, a profound paradox whilst incarcerated in his small, dark, cold, damp cell."

'My release is imminent, my reward is due.
I have fought the good fight, I have run the race,
I have finished the course, I have kept the faith.
There is now reserved for me a crown of righteousness.'

Gideon was now full of inspiration. Taking his text and the context in which it was written he transported the message to the background of present events.

"Politicians overseas have failed their people. They are, for the most part, evil ambitious men. Our Country is surrounded on all sides, betrayed by the cynical smile of one who though related to our Monarch has not one ounce of his worthiness. Now the need arises for the strong to defend the weak. Think of little Belgium, she represents the wounded man set upon by brigands and discovered by the Good Samaritan. Britain must now become the Good Samaritan of Europe. Yet, by so being we are sending our young men into the fiery furnace. We must pray that God will protect them as he did Daniel."

Here he paused; once again his voice was lowered, almost to a whisper.

"We must also pray for those who are left behind, those who through their love and devotion, shall sustain the brave at the front. Never shall we cease in our prayers during the dark days, which surely lie ahead of us. With God's good grace, he shall protect them in the darkness and bring them safe home, stronger than ever before, their faith enhanced they shall be nearer to Him."

For the first time ever, Billy was truly enraptured by a sermon. Looking around the congregation he could see it was spellbound, Sally's heart was pumping uncontrollably she was so uplifted by the enscriptured words. Pastor Livingstone was showing her what she must do. Whatever Billy needed to sustain him, anything at all, she would give. He would not be allowed to leave Glossop, to step into the hell of battle without the knowledge, given in the most profound way, that he was loved by Sally Hawkins, would forever be loved by her.

The sermon came to its end, the Pastor was drained, a great calm had descended upon his flock, attuned to his oratory, It had given them assurance, hope and unity. Gideon gave the Blessing and announced the final hymn.

We shall sing the great song of comfort given to us from the pen of Henry Francis Lyte. 'Abide With Me.'

Familiar to all, the soothing words of comfort filled the Chapel. As the verses progressed Billy was uplifted, absorbed. Here were sentiments that he knew would help to sustain him in the days ahead, times full of trial and trepidation, danger as his constant companion. More, he would be living day after day without Sally. Enemies would be all around him. sorrow too, sown from loneliness, yet here an assurance, a solace came to him, through the inspired words of the hymn.

'I fear no foe, with thee at hand to bless,
Ills have no weight, and tears no bitterness.

113

He was enriched, consoled, reassured, and ready to go from this place of worship and undertake his duty. Together Billy and Sally strolled out of the Chapel. As they walked down the steps both were coming to the realisation that their togetherness, their years old acquaintance, was transcending far beyond friendship towards an exclusivity that, one day, not too far hence, would find a new level of intimacy.

In front of them Mr and Mrs Hawkins, together with Billy's mother, thanked Pastor Livingstone, exchanged pleasantries, and continued towards the street. Now their offspring shook his hand, self-consciously, displaying to the whole congregation that they regarded themselves as a couple.

Gideon could see, as so many of his flock had also observed, how a special aura now surrounded the pair, portraying a special unity of heart and mind. For the moment, he was sure, it was pure. He felt it would remain so until other decisions were made between them, bringing God's recognition and approval to their coupling. For the moment he was aware that the boy needed God's special blessing as did so many others of the congregation this day.

"Wherever you go Billy, whatever confronts you, the good Lord will go with you. He will bring his countenance upon you, protect you and keep you to Him. Just be sure that your faith walks with you. Remember your prayers and you will be sustained. Sally, it is for you to be a companion of Hope. Hope will never leave you whilst your trust is with our God. Remember this and all will be well. Billy, come and see me before you leave, and bring this young lady with you. God bless you both.

Pastor Livingstone was to repeat similar sentiments to other young couples, husbands and sons that warm Sunday morning. As he did so a terrible foreboding came upon him. Somehow he was being forewarned that he would not see many of these young men again.

At the base of the steps the two families met. Billy explained to his mother that he had been given an invitation to lunch with Sally's parents. Immediately Elizabeth extended the welcome to Gladys, who graciously declined on the grounds that her brother Frank and his wife were expecting her. She embraced both Billy and Sally, displaying her knowledge of their new closeness and shook Elizabeth's hand in a gesture of friendship and left, walking towards the Library junction. She was heavy of heart. Of course Gladys now knew that her son was to leave her, she needed some consolation, some sympathy, Frank would help.

Lunch was a sumptuous affair. Billy consumed everything he was offered, ensuring to make compliments and express gratitude whenever appropriate. When the meal had ended, the very last possible mouthful of apple pie consumed, he was ordered to go and sit down in the front room with Nathaniel while Sally and her mother cleared away. Here he gained the opportunity to pose a request.

"Mr. Hawkins, would you mind if I walked Sally out this afternoon.?"

The reply, when it came, brought Billy surprise, contentment and a sense of being chastened all at the same time. After a long pause Nathaniel spoke with wistfulness and in considered manner.

"Yes Billy you may, but first I need to say something. You see, Sally is our only child. We lost one other, he was stillborn you see, a boy child you know. His loss makes Sally so special to us, precious, unique. Be very careful with her, look after her, take no advantages and be home for tea, say five thirty. Be kind to her Billy, she is very taken with you, I can tell."

Here Nathaniel offered his daughter's first and as fate decreed, only suitor, his hand. Billy clasped it and, looking directly into Nathaniel's eyes, he promised the concerned father that Sally would not come to any harm in his company. this appeared to assuage Nathaniel's concerns.

"I am sure of that Billy, very sure."

As if on cue, Sally and her mother came into the room and Nathaniel informed his daughter of Billy's request, and that he had provided limited permission. Elizabeth was gleeful, not awaiting a reply from Sally she made an assumptive enquiry.

"Where will you go?"

"Wherever walking takes us. We shall see you at five thirty. Come on Billy, no time to waste, let us be on our way."

Elizabeth thought in an almost audible mode, 'you little madam.' Together with her contemplations came an attendant inner smile.

Within ten minutes they were climbing above the town, leading on towards the Sett Valley and leaving the urban sprawl behind. Autumn was in full splendour, rich of colour, the leaves knowing they would soon have to lie upon the ground, yet persistent in their obstinacy, refusing to leave their host, giving mother Earth a prism of her countenance. The corn, long since ripened, had all but been harvested leaving stubble not entirely bereft of grain. A flock of Lapwings, beaks facing windward, mixed with poaching pigeons, were gleaning what grain they could muster. Oblivious to any other purpose in life they were determined to accrue as much sustenance as was possible before the coming days of bleakness, or the plough, which would bury this treasure forever.

Warm and glorious, benevolent, calm, this Indian summer's afternoon blessed Billy and Sally with a glow, mirrored by their own. Hand in hand, silent, they gazed over the hedgerows watching the busy birds in their frantic gathering. Alongside the verge, the wild grass had brought forth long dry feathery splays of perfect bloom. Sally began to pluck a number, lazily stroking her cheek with the sensual fronds. They shimmered silver and gold, flecking in the sunlight. The young man noticed how the plumes rustled as they fed along her face, how the heads of ungathered grass waved in the breeze in tune with Sally's hair.

The world was a perfect place, here, among his Derbyshire hills with Sally Hawkins, the girl he had loved all these years. How much he did love her, more than life, more than any ambition. Yes even more than football, Billy Thomas loved Sally Hawkins. Without her as his life's companion he would shrivel like withered wormwood, drooping despondently in a wintry marshland. Without Sally Hawkins he would come to exist in a slough of despond, a burden of loneliness upon his back, dragging him down to the depths of despair.

Today however, in this warm, almost sultry afternoon, amidst a grand display by countless fleeting Swallows gathering in preparation for their long journey south, escaping the long cold dark days of winter, Billy harboured total contentment. Beside him, her hand in his, was Sally, his Sally, smiling, happy, laughter filling her eyes. This was their time, yes their time, time for him to gather his thoughts, his courage, it was the moment for him to speak.

He stopped, turned, faced her, faltered in his courage, walked on a few paces further, stopped again, faced her once more, his heart beating, thumping through his brain, 'come on, come on, tell her you fool.' He placed both of his hands in hers, his gaze drew her to him, eyes met eyes, smile met smile, then, simply, he confessed.

"Sally, I love you."

The reply was also simple, as simple as ever it is, when a girl has heard such a long awaited, proclamation.

"I love you too Billy."

Two short sentences from two people who had uttered countless words to each other over the years, but with their speaking, it transformed a relationship. The long unspoken, little understood tension, which had always been present between them, dissolved. A blinding overpowering infinite range of delightful sensations surged through him. In Sally, it was a calm that swept her frame, an assurance that her long travelled quest was ended. She had gained the love of Billy Thomas, nothing else mattered in the world, nothing at all.

Now her love was gathering her in his arms, confident, certain of his actions. Placing his lips on hers, gently yet full of longing, he pressed her to him. Sally was aware of how her breasts gave way to the pressure of his chest. There was no embarrassment just knowledge. It was an awareness also gained inside Billy's consciousness. That first kiss, given as a mutual physical expression of their now confessed love, lasted an age. Neither wanted it to end. When, finally they separated, he could see her eyes were moist with the threat of tears. Looking at him, Sally repeated those wonderful words. She did not want him ever to forget the first time she made her feelings known to him.

"I love you too."

She remembered her conversation with her mother just a short time before when she was cleaning the dinner things.

"Sally, do not give your love away unless you are sure, but do not deny it either. Billy Thomas is a good man, he will be kind to you, I know so. Just be sensible, that is all, careful."

"I love you too Billy."

Again her affirmation, given to the speechless, wonder filled boy. All should have been perfect, but her mind was also enclouded with a dread of future days, it soured her bliss. Now she carefully prepared to voice her fears, before they were drowned in the flood of loving touches she knew were coming as surely as waves upon a shore.

"Oh Billy, at last, at long, long, last we have each other, found our life's love and it was we two all along, just as I knew it to be. Now at the very moment all my wishes, longings are fulfilled, you are to go away, perhaps forever. I could lose you without ever having time with you, without ever being your nuptial Eve."

The moment of her highest joy had swiftly become the time of her greatest fear, allowing despair to encroach upon this, her happiest day. Sensitively, awareness of Sally's paradox dawned. Billy gave thought to his reply, it would require to be composed of considered words.

"When I leave Sally, my dearest love, you will never be out of my thoughts. Your love, your most precious love, like nothing else on this Earth will sustain me. As long as you promise to wait, I shall come back. Sally will you wait, will you wait for me?"

"Yes Billy, of course I shall wait."

Billy sensed just how deeply, earnestly, his Sally had made her commitment. This was no noveletish scene he was a part of, it was life.

"And how long would you wait for me Sally?"

"Billy, I shall wait forever."

"If you wait for me Sally, I shall come back, I know that I shall come back."

"Billy, I shall wait for you forever."

Sally now began to comprehend the strength of the bond they had created, she was becoming totally immersed in her gallant lovers words. Billy tested her further.

"Wait for me all through the Autumn rains?"

All through the autumn, Billy I shall wait for you to come home to me."

And when the wind and snow of winter has come and gone, Sally my dearest love will you still be waiting for me?"

This time, no words came. Sally's response this time was to kiss his lips and looking deeply into his hazelled eyes, she nodded her assent. Still her enquiring lover pressed his plea.

"And when the spring is with you resplendent with bluebells, and primroses lace the woods. Then even when summer is upon us with the long days, will you walk here to this very place, remember me, read my letters and wait?"

"Yes Billy, yes, yes, yes, for you my dearest love, I shall wait."

Now came a darker question, one that Billy needed to know, yet realised would bring a shadow to this lovely girl. In softer tones, more slowly than before it came.

Sally, will you wait for me if my letters stop, if others stop waiting? Will you wait and hope and never give up?"

Soberly, sincerely, truthfully, simply the answer came.

"Yes Billy, yes I shall."

"If my mother and your parents say that I am not going to return, will you smile while they weep their tears of sorrow and still wait for me?"

"Yes Billy, my own dearest boy, my love, yes I shall surely wait for you."

Now came his final questing intercession. He summoned up all his moral strength to ask it.

"And if all your friends, and mine, say it is time to get on with your life and offer you sympathy whilst drinking to my memory, will you not listen, not join them, but wait for me?"

"Oh Billy, I shall wait for fifty years, more, forever."

"Sally, you and I must know, that whatever I face, and I shall surely face whatever comes, one day I will, of certainty, come home to you. I make this vow, my bones shall never dwell in foreign soil, however long it takes, by whatever means you shall ever know where I rest. What I am saying is that the only time you shall know that our love has ascended to a different plane, a metaphysical unity, is when my body is displayed before you."

"Whatever befalls me, whatever death spits at me, shells, flame, bullets or blade, whatever is used by the foe to deprive me of life, I shall defy all. I shall come home to England. I shall come home to you and you shall know, you shall see and you will be full of pride for me."

To Sally, listening to her beloved's words, it was as if a benevolent spiritual surety had encompassed them both. Somehow, she knew not by what means, Billy had uttered a profound truth. God was with them right here and now in the hills above Glossop. This undoubted truth brought her all the comfort she needed. It was Eden all over again, as long as they both walked in the way of the Creator, all would be well.

"Billy, it shall be as you say, I know, I really do know. I shall never stop waiting for you to come back to me, either in body or spirit, no force

118

or compulsion will ever separate us my dearest darling, never, never, never."

Having made her last outpouring, Sally collapsed against Billy's chest. She was sobbing gently, but her tears were a release made of hope, no longer an expression of fear. They clasped each the other for an age, feelings of eternal belonging flowing from one to the other. He was confused at the depth of it all, how profoundly ethereal it all was unspoiled by any lustful intent.

Before, he had wished to caress this mysterious being, to unfold his hands upon her breasts. Now all such desire was quenched, eclipsed by the unutterable unbreakable oneness that bound them as surely as they were clasped to each other.

Sally was looking to the hills, here, being held by her life's love it seemed as if they were by ancient Galeed, rather than above Glossop. Scanning the horizon, her eyes fell upon a distant cairn. Though far away, she felt the monument was a witness to their plighting of troth, to their promises they had made to each other. Pointing, Sally declared her sentiments.

"Billy, there lies our Galeed, that cairn. That heap of stones is a silent witness between you and I. Never shall I again walk here, pass this place and you not be with me, here by my side. Today we have made our promises to each other before God. Years from now, people shall come to this place and feel as we, for our love has made it holy. Whatever we do, whatever takes place between us, let the God of our fathers be our judge."

Truthfully, Billy was mystified with Sally's references but, for now, her sentiments were enough. No further explanation was needed, he just held her, by so doing he received all the assurance required. His thoughts were mellowed, complete of contentment. He knew that together, on this very spot the two of them had sealed a pact that transcended their love to the highest possible plain. He had been reading some lines of late by Herbert Trench, for him they summed up every aspect of what had happened that afternoon. He shared them with Sally.

Come let us make love deathless.

Sally understood completely and voiced not a single comment for none was needed. The silence said it all.

For the rest of that afternoon they ambled, mostly in silence, sometimes stopping to hold each other in loving embrace. At five thirty, as promised, they arrived back at Sally's home. Immediately Elizabeth realised that an understanding had come to them, a closeness she had once been aware of herself when first Nathaniel told her of his feelings. Something also told her that Billy had been the perfect gentleman.

119

Glancing towards her husband, she could see he was already in conversation with the young man whom, before long would become a part of her family. She would have long conversations with Nathaniel, in the coming night of that she was certain.

It was time for tea, who knows, even the medicinal sherry. Yes, a sherry would be good.

"Perhaps you and Billy would like a sherry Nathaniel. Sally, come and help me with the tea things."

Billy did have his sherry and his tea. Elizabeth and Sally fussed around him while he and Nathaniel discussed the war and football, with Billy attempting earnestly to steer all the conversation to their mutual interest in sport. War was for another day.

At seven Billy reluctantly said his goodnights Elizabeth scuttled her husband into the kitchen leaving the young couple to themselves. They expressed their farewell with another impassioned kiss and whispered devotions.

Walking home, Billy had never before felt such ecstasy, the war was a distant prospect but vaguely contemplated. For the moment Sally Hawkins commanded all his thoughts, his plans. In this manner he made his way home. It was not until he entered the door he realised, that he had yet to speak to his mother to tell her he had volunteered. Oh well.

CHAPTER 8

In the early days of the war, young men still played
their football matches while large crowds looked on and cheered.
Then they were called upon to come forward and play
the larger game. Thus they played a far nobler game
in defence of their Country, exchanging football fields
for the battle fields of France

Lieutenant-Colonel H.P. Treeby. 20th July 1916.

Glossop without its young men, was a town bereft of energy and life. Walking its streets, even on a busy weekend day all that could be observed were women silently shuffling, undertaking their chores, sometimes in the company of a daughter, an elderly parent or a child. Barely a family in the town still possessed a son of military age at home. Over two thousand 'would be warriors' had left during the month of September, in time more than half would either come home with terrible wounds of the body and mind, or, forever resting outside of England's shore, they would not return at all.

Silence descended, a gloom, enhanced by the onset of drizzled, cold, mistbound days. Culture was changing too. Women were being recruited for work previously the sole domain of men. The weaving mills were at full stretch, producing endless rolls of khaki cloth to be transformed into uniforms, pleasing the owners who saw their profits soar as production increased through the deft hands of lesser paid workers.

Some argued that the golden days of temperance had returned. With so few men as patrons, the inns, taverns and hotels were short of business and began to decrease the hours they were open. If that was not enough, the government shortened the opening hours anyway. Glossop was becoming a productive, quiet, sobrious settlement geared up to the war effort and supporting those who had gone off to the battlefield.

Those whose loved ones were already fighting, the regulars and their territorial comrades that made up the 'Old Contemptibles', a name they adopted after being so described by the Kaiser himself, before giving him a bloody nose on the Marne, now lived a life of trepidation. In addition to the brothers Peter and Paul Griffiths, two further war dead had now been announced in the Chronicle together with the names of numerous wounded.

By the second week in October, the first of these had returned, displaying an ugly disfigurement down one side of his face. Those who had spoken to him were assured that he considered himself to be 'one of the lucky ones.' All these early manifestations of war, were visited upon the innocent little town bringing a dark foreboding to a great part of its inhabitants. The comfort for such as Sally Hawkins and Gladys Thomas, was in the knowledge that Billy along with all those who had recently volunteered were safe for the moment in training camp, where, according to his regular communications, he was to stay for the foreseeable future. Their shared secret desire was that it would all be over before he was called abroad.

Pastor Livingstone could not help but philosophise upon the last two months and how it had so changed the life of his community. He recalled the day that all the young men boarded the train, completely crowding the little single platform station, at the end of the line, which was Glossop.

Here was such a contrast of mood. The volunteers, for the most part, were milling around, impatient to be off, eager for the adventure to start. Displaying embarrassment, they reluctantly accepted the kisses planted on them by distraught mothers and sisters. Some were sensitive to the mood of the moment, giving out an equal expression of affection.

He particularly noticed Billy Thomas. Not only was his mother there but all the Hawkins family also. Gladys gave her son a paper package, Gideon assumed it was his lunch. Nathaniel shook his hand, he was hugged vigorously by Elizabeth, before Sally gave him quite a display of unashamed farewell full on the lips, followed by a long period of resting her head on his chest whilst, seeking assurance, gently allowing tears to flood her face. A pitifully tragic scene, he thought, hopefully, please God, not to be followed by tragedy.

When, at last, the pair parted, he noticed that Sally complimented his mother in turn presenting her departing soldier with two packages. What they contained he could only conjecture upon, it looked as if one might conceal a small book. As Billy climbed into the carriage, Gideon noted how Sally still clung to him, how loathing of their parting was manifestly mutual. Not even the obstacle of Billy's newly acquired bundles, could prevent a last unashamedly interlocking embrace.

In truth, Sally was distraught, as the overburdened train began to draw away from the station, the possibility dawned, stark and vivid, 'I may never see him again'. The last carriage was barely free of the platform when, looking around she realised just how many women were as herself, utterly distressed. Dozens of her sisters were weeping for those who had left, full of fear and uncertainty, not knowing what lay ahead but dreading the worst. Sally was as one with them, sharing their sorrow, a part of this public display of communal sadness. Yet, as swiftly as despair had fallen upon her, it ceased. Billy's words of reassurance came back to her.

"I shall defy all. I shall come home to England. I shall come home to you and you shall know, you shall see and you shall be full of pride for me."

Billy's voice came to her, not as a memory, but through the ether, a sounding in her ears. It was as if he were still with her bringing the substance of a new certainty. If his voice could be within her, even though they were apart, then it would always be so. If distance could not separate them, then neither could anything else, no obstacle, not death itself. Sally, here on this railway platform that had witnessed so many partings over the past few weeks, had discovered a spiritual comfort born of faith. Faith in her love, a binding love, an inseparable, immortal high impassioned linking of two souls as well as hearts, fertile and God willing, in the coming years, fruitful.

Of this she was sure, Sally Hawkins and Billy Thomas had created something between them that transcended normal human bonding, giving her all the necessary strength and more to carry on patiently persevering until her love returned. She felt sublime, though sad for those surrounding her, who did not own the same assurance. but ironically, happy for herself. Her Billy was coming home to her and when he did so she would give him everything that a woman can gift a man. She blushed, realising what thoughts had entered her mind.

Elizabeth noted the smile that crossed her daughter's face, it puzzled her. Something was stirring within Sally's breast, keeping her from expressing sorrow. What could it be? She did not know, nor would she for many years to come. One day in the future the astonishing, profound, truth would be made known to her. Along with a privileged few, Elizabeth Hawkins would be a witness to the power contained of a love born between two mated souls, of which the spiritual dimension was every much an aspect as any physical manifestation.

For the moment, leaving the station, Nathaniel was largely unaware of what transpired in the minds of his wife and daughter. Practical as usual, his thoughts went to Gladys who was walking silently alongside.

"Elizabeth, Mrs. Thomas shall be coming home to tea with us?"

It was a question, allowing his wife to extend the invitation. Nathaniel could but conjecture the thoughts that were circulating in the mind of Billy's mother but he was certain that she was in need of companionship and comfort. Gladys Thomas was possibly going to be family in the not too distant future, now was the time to extend a welcome to her.

Elizabeth was pleased with Nathaniel's sensitivity. She had been so immersed in thoughts of Sally that it had not occurred to her just how distressed Gladys Thomas must be. The poor woman had already buried her husband and now her son was off to war. Tea was the least she could offer.

"Of course: Gladys, you will come back with us, will you not."

Before the dazed woman could answer, Sally took her arm exactly as she had held that of her son.

"Walk with me Mrs Thomas, let us chat about Billy on the way back."

Gladys felt cheered, the past few days had passed like a dream where she was a witness to events but unable to influence them or even contribute as they unfolded. When, at last, Billy had told her of his volunteering, she had known for more than a day. Nor was it merely that piece of news he conveyed. Sally Hawkins came with him, shyly unassuming, pretty, pleasant, undoubtedly good for her son. She saw in his eyes the same unmistakable illumination Joshua use to display at times when his thoughts turned towards intimacy. If Sally Hawkins was to be the chosen lifetime partner of her son, then God bless them both. No better girl could be devised in her mind for the best son a mother had ever born.

Gladys was indeed grateful for the invitation, all morning she had dreaded coping with Billy's departure. Now she could share her thoughts and feelings with others who were likewise affected.

"Thank you very much Mr and Mrs Hawkins, Sally, I would appreciate some fellowship at the moment."

Putting her other hand upon the arm that Sally had entwined in hers, she expressed, in a whisper, her wish to be addressed in more personal terms.

"Please call me Gladys, at least for now, you never know one day, not too far in the future we might be conversing even more informally."

"Just so Gladys, I hope so, I do hope so."

The two women walked together side by side. From that moment a bond joined them together, cemented by their mutual love for a young man, who even now was fast receding from them in distance but had never been closer in spirit.

The train had stopped at Dinting and Hadfield to take on more recruits. Now it was speeding non-stop towards Manchester. Billy was sat in a carriage full of recruits much the same as himself. They had all, for the most part, been sent on their way with the proud handshakes of their fathers and the tears of mothers, wives, sisters or Sweethearts. Jimmy Jones and Bill Carney were sitting next to him chatting furiously, full of excitement. Billy turned to gaze out of the window, he was in no mood for chatter, he needed to reflect, oh, and explore the packages given to him by Sally and his mother.

Gently stripping away the paper from the smaller package Sally had given him, he saw that the parcel was further wrapped in a chequered cloth bound by pink ribbon, neatly fastened in the most delicate of bows. Further investigation led firstly to the discovery of a book. Looking at the title, tears came to his eyes, it was a copy of Milton's poetical works, small enough to fit into a tunic pocket. He opened it to find an inscription, which contained a line from a contemporary poet whose work was loved by both of them.

To my beloved Billy, that you might remember other times
'Come let us make love deathless'

As he explored the volume, something small and white fell out. It was a linen handkerchief, neatly pressed and folded. In one corner Sally had stitched a heart motif together with an initial on either side, *B* and *S*.

His heart poured tears, though his eyes forbade any such thing, perhaps they would come later. Now for Sally's second parcel, which was soft and shapeless, wrapped in plain brown paper, tied with white raffia. Gradually his careful efforts revealed an item of clothing. It was a sage green woollen waistcoat with mother of pearl buttons and a single pocket, inside of which was a note, comprising the very first love letter he had ever received and that Sally had ever written.

> *My Dearest, Most Precious Billy,*
>
> *I earnestly hope you like your presents. There are three. One for faith, one for hope and one for love. Billy I shall always treasure our times together and now I have a confession to make. My love for you goes far back to those early days in the library when we were so young and the World a happier, more peaceful place. Yes, for all those years, I have loved you heart and soul, mind and body. Now you have me, there shall never be another, could be another, for our very souls are welded, forever entwined. This poor epistle expresses but a fraction of my love for you, the most meagre portion.*
>
> *Read 1. Corinthians chapter 13, it says all.*
>
> *'MIZPAH'*
> *Sally.*

Corinthians, yes, he new, vaguely at least, but of *'MIZPAH'* he had no idea. It had to be Biblical, he would find it, even if he had to read from Genesis to Revelations, he would discover from whence it came. He need not have worried, by that week's end, he was to find the reference within the first book of the Old Testament and in so doing discover such a wondrous declaration as would leave him brimmed with both hope, and love, attendant with an unendurable longing.

> *And Mizpah; for he said,*
> *The Lord watch between me and thee*
> *when we are absent one from another.*

The train sped through an increasingly urban landscape to arrive in Manchester in less than an hour. Here uniformed shepherds who ushered them onto a second train destined for Chester greeted them. The carriages this time were even more congested. Billy and his friends, being last to enter, had to stand all through the journey. In spite of the lateness of the year and the rain, which was now beginning to fall, the carriages were stiflingly hot, the air full of the smell of sweating bodies. As the journey progressed, tempers began to fray.

"Watch your feet you clumsy ox."

"Mind your elbows."

"Mind your own, or I'll mind them for you."

'So much for comradeship', thought Billy. He would be glad when the journey was over. Looking around him, he could see that his friends felt the same. Little did they know how fortunate they presently were.

At long last the train drew into Chester and the horde of men all attempted to pour out of the carriages at once, adding to the general frustration and anarchy. Opposite the doors, Half a dozen NCO's sporting red bands on their arms and caps struggled to gain control, their senior officer shouting out instructions above the buzzing swarm. It took almost fifteen minutes before he obtained some semblance of success, but not before a score or more of the most undisciplined among them were told how 'orrible' they were and how the guardhouse beckoned.

Chester railway station was some distance from the city itself. A long road, almost half a mile in length, ran in a straight line towards the distant Medieval walls of its inner boundary. All along this stretch of highway, men in various forms of dress and state of attentiveness were being collected in some sort of ranking. The first batches of Kitchener's finest had arrived to invest the city.

Chester had provided a base for marching armies over many centuries, but none so vast, amateur or undisciplined as these raw recruits now assembled awaiting their next instructions. Since before the birth of Christ, marauding tribes men came out of the hills of the Cymru to test the vigilance of the then small, ill prepared settlement. In those days the river was navigable far above the City allowing craft to harbour where the famous racecourse was now situated. This is what attracted the Romans to the City. They named it 'Deva', then 'Chester' giving the name 'Cestrian' to its citizens. It has ever since been thus.

For almost four hundred years Roman legions garrisoned the city, leaving much to posterity, including the remains of what was once a magnificent theatre. Chester was a strategic staging post to the Welsh coast, an essential outpost for replenishing supplies for the long march to the

Druid stronghold of Anglesey. When, at last Rome became overstretched and could no longer sustain far off military enterprises, the troops withdrew, soon to be replaced by new invaders who, in their flat-bottomed boats sailed up the Dee to invest the City.

The Saxons brought a certain splendour to Chester with probably the most magnificent array of diverse armed might that the English world, before the coming of the Tudors would ever witness. In the year 973 armies came, led by their Kings, Lords and Princes from all over England, Wales and Ireland. Thousands of troops speaking dozens of languages and dialects billeted in the City. Six Kings rowed the great Saxon monarch Edgar, up the Dee to Eccleston, displaying their homage. A field in the town where Edgar received them still retains his name.

Years pass, the Normans are masters now. That vacillating ruler, John comes to demand homage of Llewellyn Fawr, Prince of Gwynedd or of Wales dependant upon whose view is taken. They meet at the head of two armies, hundreds of mounted Normans, displaying their chain armour, opposing Welshmen armed with their feared longbows. King John desires more than mere fealty, he requires a trusted ally. At Saint Warburgs, Llewellyn takes Joanna, the fiery illegitimate daughter of the mighty Plantagenate as his wife. Their tempestuous marriage lasts forty years and more. Chester, once again, is a witness to history being made against the presence of a vast array of warriors.

Medieval England experiences its last upheaval, the War of the Roses as it is later named. Here comes Harry Hotspur, he of Shakespearean legend, Mortimer also, together with Owain Glyndwr, latterly Prince of Wales. They conspire to divide the realm of the Plantagenate Henry, fourth of that name since the Conqueror. It is in Chester, the miscreants supported by three armies, that the Bard records their grievous plot to partition the realm into three, and how before the day's march to Shrewsbury where Hotspur meets an inglorious end, he summarises the essence of battle.

> Sound all the lofty instruments of war,
> And by that music let us all embrace;
> For, Heaven and Earth, some of us never shall
> A second time do such a courtesy.

All are doomed, swept away and lie buried, unmarked in the Shropshire plain, undone by the future Henry the fifth,

The Medieval World passes, replaced by the Modern. Tudors then Stuarts reign and, with devious Charles are challenged by the rising force of democracy, Chester is once again invested by an army. Roundheads and Cavaliers fight throughout the County for supremacy. The contest lasts for over five long years before the victorious New Model Army again, like the

Romans of old, use Chester as a staging post, this time on passage to Ireland.

One final internal conflict between the Island Races sees the Jacobite uprising. Chester, loyal to the house of Hanover, supplies men to repel Charles Stuart. The nearest the conflict comes is to Preston and Crewe, but once again an armed camp depletes the City of its daily needs.

Now after more than one hundred and fifty years, ever patient, ever loyal Chester had opened her gates to another military throng. Thousands were gathering, more than could be reasonably accommodated. At the Headquarters of The Cheshire Regiment, the art of logistics was being strained to its limits. With each train came more men. Lord Kitchener's appeal had been an overwhelming success. From the Wirral, from North Wales, parts of Lancashire, Derbyshire, the volunteers were pouring in. How few, how pitifully few, would ever return, once they gave their leave of the friendly, hospitable, embracing walls of this ancient town. Almost two thousand years, so little changes, in the actions of men.

For, Heaven and Earth, some of us never shall
A second time do such a courtesy.

Lieutenant Thorpe arrived at the station completely unprepared for the challenge that confronted him. Having reported to Regimental Headquarters, he was given the simple instruction. It contained no advice, just the basic elements required to undertake his task.

"Take two senior NCO's, you will find them waiting outside. Proceed to the Railway Station, report to the senior officer commanding distribution of entrainment and count out eight hundred men. Organise them in columns, march them back past here and onto the racecourse. It has been duly sequestered as the base for the formation of the new 10th Battalion. A senior officer commanding, further officers as yourself and six RSMs. are to join you in a few days. Till then Thorpe, you are on your own, an opportunity to make a name for yourself. Step to it now."

Off he had gone, a single Lieutenant, two NCOs. and they were to form a battalion. He had been promised adequate tenting, boarding, cooking and washing facilities. Well he was determined to travel hopefully.

Crossing the Regimental square together with his two underlings he made for the City centre. Having discovered they were both regulars of long standing, veterans of Ladysmith and Spion Kop, he began to gain some confidence. They walked though the ancient streets of balconied, Elizabethan styled, shopping parades and onto the Cathedral square. The ancient Gothic monument brought him confidence, it appeared so secure, so reliant, in its age old red sandstone and granite, so English, pertinent of the realm he had so solemnly sworn to defend.

The Station was rapidly approaching, men were everywhere, some attentive others just milling around, becoming bored, complaining as they smoked endless Woodbines. He determined, he would get to the Station, obtain his eight hundred strong, good and true, then get back to the Racecourse as quickly as possible.

Reporting to the overwhelmed officer commanding disposal, he gave over his orders. The response was curt, no doubt born of pressure,

"Take one of my orderlies, count out eight hundred, sign for them and get them out of here as quickly as you can."

"Yes sir."

Thorpe could be brief as well if brevity was needed."

Now he was full of importance, he was here, in the city of Chester, forming the 10th Battalion of the Cheshire Regiment. It would be his name first placed in the Regimental annals when the records of the 10th were written. Turning to his NCOs., Thorpe instructed them to count out twenty blocks of forty. Farmers, pitmen, factory workers, shopkeepers, men from all professions, footballers also, for Billy Thomas and his friends were, alongside this diverse representation of humanity, here gathered to the bosom of Lieutenant Thorpe. Together they comprised the twenty Cohorts that now composed the New Army, 10th Battalion The Cheshire Regiment.

Thorpe was pleased, he and his two underlings, had, with great efficiency, undertaken phase one of their instructions in less than half an hour. Now to march them to the race course, a little matter of less than a mile distant. In truth the men were both pleased to be leaving and proud to be identified as part of a regiment, to be fully incorporated into His Majesty's forces.

Eight hundred raw recruits filled more with eager passion than expertise, tramped the thousand yards or so in best possible order. True, they were out of step, not yet instilled with the discipline that would only too soon be branded upon their every action. However, Thorpe knew such raw material, born of the free will that the volunteer brings with him, would soon be honed into shape.

Each man marched in his fashion for the first and last time. A single day spent being drilled would cure most of the idiosyncrasies of the individual and all of his indiscipline. This day they carried out the prime need of Lieutenant Thorpe, they all marched in the same direction towards his goal. Another half hour and eight hundred men, in all their various apparel were on parade at the race course in twenty blocks of forty, roughly facing towards the grandstand.

Fortunately the weather was now dry and reasonably mild. The men were called to stand easy, Which did not 'you 'orrible little man', mean you could put your hands in your pockets and light a fag. Patience was now needed, they would now learn another valuable lesson, waiting and life in the army were synonymous.

Another hour where little happened, then as the monotony was becoming quite unbearable to the keen would be warriors, three lorries drove onto the course. The tents, cooking and washing facilities, together with a number of uniforms, had arrived. A masterful Battalion Quarter Master came with them, a man of little humour, having a poor bedside manner and no ability to match the individual with the correct size of clothing.

Logistics: the army was at its best when having to distribute resources to enable its infrastructure to become operative. Eight hundred men, fifty-four tents, fifteen men per canvas. Split each block into two times fifteen, take five from the next and so on. One tent equals a section, a pair becomes a platoon, eight a company. From each tent Thorpe would select a temporary full corporal and a lance. Later, when the public school volunteers arrived, each platoon would be given a junior officer like he. In turn each Company, would be overseen by a Captain. All that then remained to be appointed was the Battalion commander accompanied by say six Drill Sergeants and the raw material for a battalion would be in place.

It was five of the afternoon, fifty four tents were erected in six rows of nine, all duck boarded, provisioned of bedding and Tilly lamps. Two further, larger tents were also in place acting as cook houses. Latrines had been dug and washing facilities provided in the grandstand which also acted as Battalion HQ. Thorpe had carried out his orders meticulously. He was pleased with his day's work as were the Brigadier and his staff, when they came to inspect affairs.

Billy and his fellow former team-mates found themselves pitching a tent near to the grandstand. Their companions were a mixture of Welshmen, mostly from the Wrexham area, three brothers from Chester itself, and some Mancunians who had travelled with them on the train. They all appeared enthusiastic, not given to complaining and mucked in together. They were not to know at the time, but this small group of hopefuls were to stay together as a unit, becoming a fighting brotherly band, coming to rely the one upon the other during several battles and skirmishes. They were starting out mainly as strangers yet time and war would see them end as comrades and friends smelted, as a single entity, from within the furnace of war.

When the 'Top Brass' Came to inspect them, they all lined up as best they could in two rows before the entrance of the tent. Lieutenant Thorpe came along with his two erstwhile juniors, while the 'Big-Wig' stopped periodically to chat randomly with a number of the raw recruits. He eventually stood before Billy.

"What's your name soldier?"

"Billy Thomas sir!"

"And what do you do Thomas?"

"A Private in His Majesty's Cheshire Regiment sir!"

The officer was taken aback, usually those questioned would answer describing their civilian occupation. Not so this one, was it cheek, subordination or initiative, no matter, this man was different, made of possibilities, possible Corporal surely.

"In civilian life Private Thomas, what were you in civilian life?"

"A footballer sir, professional footballer."

"Professional? Who did you play for, what position?"

"Glossop sir, centre forward. There are three of us here together in the same tent sir."

"All from the same team?"

"Yes sir, myself, Jimmy Jones and Bill Carney."

"Fancy playing for the Battalion or the Regiment Thomas?"

"Yes sir, of course sir, my colleagues also, no doubt of that sir."

"Good man, good man."

The officer moved off. Covertly he voiced his opinion to Lieutenant Thorpe that Thomas would make an excellent temporary NCO. Thus within a day of entering service Private Billy Thomas became a full corporal due to his prowess with a football. Nor was he alone, Jimmy gained a single stripe that day. Between them they became responsible for a Section of a Platoon of the Battalion. Thorpe was pleased his superiors were pleased, it had been a good day for the Regiment, a good day for him. All together he promoted fifty four full Corporals that day and the same number of men with a single stripe. Having no resource to any official army regalia he fashioned temporary stripes from strips of cloth, red for a full Corporal, green for a Lance.

The men of his Section soon accepted Billy as their leader. He became a good organiser and conduit for requests that went back and forth in both directions. Within two weeks his happy few were a welded unit, each looking out for the other. As the intake arrived from the Public Schools to become Captains in charge of a Company, Lieutenant Thorpe was glad to take a back seat merely being a junior officer commanding a Platoon. He requested of the new officer commanding the Battalion if he could take control of '3' Platoon, 'C' Company. His wish was granted, thus he became Billy's immediate superior, a relationship that survived and developed till death came to separate them.

At last the regular RSMs. arrived, late of His Majesty's Royal Marines, drill was initiated with all urgency. Square bashing, the endless marching to and fro, day in day out. Cross country running also. A morning run to Gresford and back, or even Northrop, was not unusual. 'just to separate the men from the boys.' Billy did his best to encourage the less able and fit in his section to keep up. Others in the Section assisted, providing a great team spirit or 'esprit de corps' as Lieutenant Thorpe termed it.

The Battalion commander indulged his love of football to organise a competition between all his Platoons. Led by Billy with Joe Gaffrey in goal, Jimmy Jones, Bill Carney and a huge Welshman, Harold 'Hacker' Evans, they beat all comers, by wide margins. Then the team progressed undefeated in inter Battalion matches, even defeating a team of City of Chester players. They became known as 'The Immortals' as October came to an end, no little fame came to '3' Platoon, 'C' Company.

All came to an end during the first week of November, the Battalion was to move to Church Stretton in Shropshire, a purpose training barracks. Fitness and discipline was now to be augmented with skill at rifle, bayonet and tactical teamwork. The entire Battalion was entrained to Shrewsbury, thence by means of a route march, the seventeen miles to Church Stretton, all in a single day. Those who witnessed their march, ancient warriors of The Sudan and Ladysmith, young girls who virtually swooned at the sight of so many brave uniformed young warriors, cheered and shouted their encouragement. Some of the more brazen country lasses would cry out their thoughts on a particular individual who took their fancy.

"Now there's a likely one, 'ow 'andsome 'e is, 'ow you be doing me lover?"

With one such acclamation, a young girl in a farm smock ran across the road grabbed hold of a startled Corporal Billy Thomas, to plant a kiss upon his unprepared lips. She was very full bodied but loosely clothed, her chested beauties all but released themselves from their inadequate entrapments before she retreated as quickly as she had come.

"Lucky devil you are Corp."

"Silence in the ranks."

A smiling yet disciplined Lieutenant Thorpe at the head of his platoon settled the incident with a mock admonishment. Truth was Corporal Thomas was a lucky blighter, wherever he went things happened and usually for the better.

Later that evening, Billy was to make one of the very few mistakes in his relationship with Sally. In his next letter to her, he mentioned the incident in all its detail. It had amused him, he saw no harm in it. Sally perceived it to be otherwise. In reply she questioned whether he had encouraged the worthless wretch, how often did such things happen?

Immediately Billy saw his error. His next communication which he sent that very day upon receiving Sally's reply saw him full of remorse and reassurance, he was distressed beyond endurance he told her, please, please, please, forgive him. Of course Sally did so. It was to be the first and last time she would ever feel jealous over her love. Every letter sent to her by the reprobate in future would contain enough protestation of his absolute and exclusive love for her, that never again would the green eye of the little yellow god rise within her.

While Billy and his comrades were developing their deadly skills as marksmen and military adversaries, November was entering Glossop, drearily and forbiddingly clothed in pessimism. At Chapel, not a single Sunday passed without the evidence being displayed before him of just how much Glossop, and his congregation in particular, had given to the war effort. So few young men now attended. Those who before mainly congregated by the entrance, standing together in order that they could be the first to leave had generally been the first to volunteer. Their absence was conspicuous. In the past he had admonished them separately or as a group, for lacking in concentration or even respect for the Lord in his very own house. O Lord that he could do so now. Without them the services were that more grey, colourless, as if an important element was missing, which indeed it was. A certain vibrancy had vanished, the unabashed, unashamed facet of life that heralds from young men, all too often deemed a distraction but quickly missed when absent, no longer displayed itself as a part of his flock. With their leaving anxiety reigned, his congregation, depleted of its undisciplined youth, bore an emptiness which it would possibly never regain.

Gideon mused, they had gone to war, mostly too young to even have gained the right to vote or influence the affairs that had led to the conflict, yet expected to give their all for its successful conclusion. He had seen so many leave, observing how young they were, some not yet of an age where a beard could form upon their innocent chins, despite their protestations to the contrary. Contradiction, opposing sentiments, loyalties, fought inside his mind for clarity and supremacy.

The tormented Pastor struggled with the certainty that this terrible conflict was a necessary undertaking where good men should support the side of right in order that evil would not prevail. Yet he was beginning to understand the extent of the price that may have to be paid. He saw the possibility of a whole generation of young innocents being sacrificed upon the altar in payment for national salvation.

His reasoning extended to the acceptance that other citizens of other Nations must be convinced as he was on their County's behalf. Britannia, would not be the sole Country at the end of this tragedy to mourn for a lost generation. France, the Balkan States, Austria-Hungary, Germany, Russia, now Turkey and others still to enter the fray, all would lose their dearest and best. The more the war became protracted, an ever greater number of States would be drawn into its web. Come its end, the whole continent, the World even, could be filled with the tears of mothers, wives, Sweethearts, sisters in lands bled white, their cities devastated.

All the young men, inadvertently both the engine and the fuel powering the dynamics of it all, yet, in paradox, innocent bright eyed zealots, having little concept of the true part they were playing, visioned their participation as a most noble and honourable test of their mettle.

Honour has come back, asking to Earth
And paid his subjects with a royal wage.

Words of a Cambridgeshire youth powered by profound poetic imagination, moulded with patriotic intensity issuing forth a recorded testimony, an insight into the mind of a generation. It was also, he was sure, a source of inspiration, which could send successive regiments of his peers to join the grand crusade. This army of latter-day knights considered themselves mightily privileged to be living in such times as these where they could lift themselves above the dross and tedium that was the monotonous lot of their forebears.

Now God be thanked
who has matched us with his hour.

Not 'this hour' but 'his hour.' Brooke conjectured that it was God himself that had brought about these times upon his people. How could that be so?

Question upon question, doubt upon doubt, all ran through his mind. Rather than praising their Maker for these events, the Nations of the World and their heralds should be heeding the warnings of past Prophets. Already, though the war was young, yet to fully flex its muscles, the mighty engines of war were levelling towns and cities. Liege, Mons, Ypres, all had been visited by the monster and left devastated, brining to mind the words scribed of ancient days by the Prophet Isaiah.

'Now I have brought it to pass
That thou hast laid waste the cities.
Bringing them to heaps of stone.'

Neither was Gideon convinced that this war would be confined to parts of Europe. His great fear was that the conflict would spread to many parts of the World, leading to a global conflagration as foretold by another seer of past times, Jeremiah.

'Look, disaster is spreading
from Nation to Nation.
A mighty storm is rising
from all the ends of the World.'

What hope then for the young men so determined to prove their manhood on the field of battle? What of little Johnny who goes off to fight the foe on the coat-tails of his older brethren, singing the torrid songs of his friends. He glories in being one of them, taking on any challenge that the rigours of training put upon him. Steadfast he stands in the face of all this, winning the praises of older, larger men who at first thought he would not survive the constant attentions of the merciless Sergeant Major.

Yes Johnny overcomes these challenges, he grows in stature and marches off to war an invincible warrior. Here he comes face to face with the reality of the great adventure. Dead men, mangled beyond all recognition, their gruesome remains rotting amidst vast destruction. At times, secretly, he pales when confronted by his potential fate, he becomes subdued, it was not meant to be like this.

Arrives the day when the Angels come to deliver him. Perhaps whilst returning from an excursion into no-man's-land, he is hit by a stray bullet. A good and brave colleague gathers him over his shoulders, carrying him to the safety of his friends. Back in the trench they examine his wound. Too late, his life's' blood is draining away. Now he is a child once more, calling for his mother but she does not come for she cannot hear him. Not once in his life did he call and she did not hurry to his side, but this time in his most urgent need she does not come.

As the blood pumps out from the gaping wound, his vision blurs, memory dims, his cries fade, then cease. Johnny, laughter filled Johnny, has gone from them. Because he was so young. even the most hardened of those who witness his passing are touched. It is as if they have each lost a young brother. In death, his face, no longer stressed or contorted he looks even younger. "Surely," they mutter among themselves. "It was a sin that he was ever here."

Now he lies before them dead, sleeping his eternal rest, a boy in a man's uniform with big clumsy hands out of proportion from the rest of his frame. Later, he is buried, his few belongings sent home to a grieving mother. These thoughts, and others, were ever invading Gideon's mind. What made matters worse was his certainty that such grief was reflected elsewhere.

It was also true, that at this very same time a wretched woman in Berlin or Hamburg is being informed how her beloved Hans has fallen, how bravely he sacrificed his life. She is told what pride she should feel having the knowledge that her son gave all in the service of his country.

Gideon concluded that war recognised no virtue in life, except as something to extinguish. German, French, Austrian, Russian or British, it was all the same to war with its monstrous insatiable appetite. For many hours did Gideon ponder such thoughts as these. As the war dragged on and Christmas rushed towards him, more deaths being recorded, more wounded coming home, dreadful in their state of distress, ever more countries clamoured to join the fray. It served to re-enforce his certainty that the titanic struggle unfolding upon the Earth would demand millions more in sacrifice before its dynamics were exhausted.

Such were the thoughts of Billy's Pastor. A man who though he considered himself to be both a Christian and a patriot found himself in constant paradox. Both loyalty to his religion and to his Country required faith. Faith required a belief, was possessed of truth. What to do when two basic concepts conflict? War was an evil, so was tyranny. Constantly the battle raged within him as surely as it ravaged in Northern France. It represented a paradox, which, for Gideon, was never fully resolved.

Meanwhile, those in Glossop close to Billy Thomas, prayed for his safety and sent him comforts. Truthfully, their fears for him were tempered with pride as his letters home, which came in reams equally divided between his mother and his Love, told of his progress and adventures. Whilst he was stationed in Chester and then Church Stretton, they felt no fear, just a sense of loss in not having him about them. Still Christmas was approaching, surely he would be allowed leave from his arduous training, surely Billy would come home to celebrate with them.

Sally and Gladys had become very close, exactly as the elder woman had predicted. Most evenings Sally would call after closing the store, either to read her latest communication or listen to Gladys reading hers. On occasion, Sally discretely missed a portion if it appeared to her more intimate than was proper to relate to another party, especially Billy's mother. When this occurred, Gladys always knew, and smiled inwardly. After all Billy was Joshua's son, manly passion was inherited was it not? Blessed Joshua never failed to tell her what physical pleasure he gained from their union, how during a particular absence he had so urgently desired her. Surely flesh of his flesh would possess the same longings and the need to profess them?

One evening, after the reading of a particularly long letter to Sally, Gladys sensed a certain turmoil in the young girl's breast.

"What is it Sally, what have you not read?"

Gladys was surprised at the outcome to her question. The young girl burst into tears. Through the sobs Gladys gained the substance of Sally's distress.

Billy doesn't love me, he kissed another girl. See here, what he has written."

Sally cast the offending pages towards Gladys who read them urgently. At the end she smiled, crossed over to the distraught child and placing her arms around her, gave comfort.

"Well, well, what a stupid son I have. There he is, marching along the King's highway, resplendent in his uniform and an ill bred country lass, no better than she ought to be, takes hold of him, offering herself. All this in the sight of a whole regiment of soldiers walking along 'quick march.' I hope nothing untoward occurred or he will have to pay the consequences."

"Surely not Gladys, surely nothing improper could have taken place? In front of all those men and they all marching so fast?"

136

"That's what I like about you Sally, able to answer your own questions. Billy is not guilty of any indiscretion with that young lady, or ever will be, not with her or any other. However, he is guilty of causing distress in his manner of reporting this inconsequential incident and, for that, he needs admonishment."

"Do you really think so Gladys; really think so."

"Certainly."

"Oh Gladys, it made me feel so jealous, I felt sure he was boasting of a conquest."

"What my Billy? Why he is so besotted with you he even forgot to kiss his poor mother goodbye at the train station, he was so enraptured of you."

Sally now became guilt-filled recalling her impassioned leaving of her love.

"Oh Gladys I never realised, I am so sorry."

"Sorry, dear child? No need for that. To see my beloved son leaving his home town, full of the grace of your love, brought me the deepest joy. It is what has kept me going these past months, knowing he has the undying love of a woman the likes of yourself my darling girl."

It was an age before Sally left that night. She did not wish to go but her parents would worry. In future, she decided, she would stay with Gladys every other night, her parents would understand, of that she was certain. As for that reprobate boy, he would get such a letter from her that never again would she be the respondent of the kind of information that had distressed her so. Smiling with the thought of Billy wrestling with his conscience, once he got her next piece of mail, led her to anticipation. Christmas was coming and her love would arrive with it. Thanks be to God. Little did she know of the next trick that fate was to play upon her.

Back in Church Stretton, Billy and his section, indeed the whole Platoon, were progressing apace with their training. Skill and fitness abounded among the men. Lieutenant Thorpe was especially pleased. His men were the best in the Company, the Battalion even. From the very first week in their new camp, the Platoon had been introduced to the possibilities that the Lee Enfield rifle presented. Most of them became proficient within a few weeks. Not only were many of them excellent marksmen but they came to know the weapon so well that they could dismantle it and re-assemble it in complete darkness. In their 'naming of parts' exercise the Platoon gained full marks, the only one in the Battalion to do so. Thorpe's pride in his men's abilities overflowed. Perversely, the very source of his satisfaction was to prove the cause of the loss of their Christmas leave.

Summoned to Battalion HQ., Thorpe stood to attention in front of his senior commanding officers and his Captain, together with the three other Lieutenants that made up the Company.

"Well gentlemen we have called you together to congratulate you all, especially Thorpe here, who has licked his men into great shape. Thorpe, your Platoon is officially the best performing one in the entire Battalion. Congratulations man."

Thorpe's cup overflowed, he had achieved his ambition. The Colonel continued, praise was to come attendant with the unexpected.

"Gentlemen, as you are no doubt aware, The Cheshires have been a part of the conflict since its inception. Recently there have been casualties that now need replacing. The 6th Battalion especially need re-enforcement's. I have decided to send 'C' Company overseas post-haste. As our best performing Company they will provide a welcome attachment to the 6th. You leave in three days time. Gentlemen, that is all."

Thorpe was overjoyed. Firstly his Platoon had been recorded as being the best in the Battalion, secondly the were now being given the opportunity to prove themselves on the field of battle much sooner than he had ever thought possible. Wait till the men heard, how proud and pleased they would all be.

What the single mindedness of the professional, full time Lieutenant would not allow him to realise, was the extent to which his men were looking forward to seeing their families. Most had worked and trained with all enthusiasm for almost three months; they wanted to see their loved ones. His news was greeted like a cold wet flannel in an open wash house in winter. He just could not understand it. It was as if he had brought news of a death of a loved one to them all. All his efforts to make them the best in the Battalion had brought forth fruit. Gratitude, or some expression of satisfaction was the least he expected. Instead his news was met with sullen silence, it was beyond comprehension.

After the Lieutenant had gone the section gathered around Billy for clarification. The dumbfounded Corporal was as speechless as they were. Looking forward to seeing Sally had kept him going these past weeks, now he had to write and say he was going overseas. 'Damn this war, damn this war, all he needed was a little time then it could have him body and soul, damn this war,'

Spiting all their wishes, three days hence saw the one hundred men of 'C' Company arrive at Victoria Station London in transit to Dover and the Continent. Fate was to decree that Billy would undertake a journey between these two stations on four occasions, two in either direction. For now the excitement of seeing London albeit briefly and mostly from a carriage window assuaged their disappointment at not gaining Christmas leave. The experience of pastures new, anticipation of foreign lands outgrew their disappointment at not seeing home.

Not so Billy Thomas, he felt a sense of loss at not seeing Sally, not being able to hold her, to be close, to hear her sweet voice consoling him. More than anything the war itself could provide, the thought of being away from her was almost beyond endurance. As he crossed the channel on a stormy night, the sensation of standing looking over the rail of the ship making him every bit as sick in his stomach, as he was of heart, he wondered if he would ever see the sweet girl again.

Then, in the gloom of an enclouded early dawn, he began to make out the skyline of Boulogne. It made him feel selfish. Not a pebble's dash from England was a country threatened with enslavement. Here was true pity, a task to be accomplished. Poor Belgium, France too, terrorised and threatened by a merciless enemy coming like a thief in the night. How many of their sons were as he, fighting far from their sweethearts. His sense of loss was replaced by shame. Coming to this foreign shore, he would do his duty and willingly. Under his breath he voiced an oath.

"Bring on the foe, Billy Thomas has arrived."

Back in Glossop two women had just finished reading his letter. Arms about each other, they grasped what consolation they could. son, lover, he would not be seeing home for Christmas, now but two weeks hence. Gladys woke them from their sorrow.

"Come on Sally, lots to do. Why if our man is to have a Christmas worthy of the name we have things to make, parcels to organise. Run and get your father, he will know all about sending things post haste to France. If Billy cannot come home to Glossop for his Christmas, then presents from Glossop can come to him. Trot off now, the quicker we start the sooner it will be accomplished."

Sally put on her coat and raced off into the night, only then did Gladys break into tears, fall to her knees to pray aloud.

"Lord Jesus, you know how much we need Billy Thomas, keep him safe and bring him home."

Contrary to her Protestant teaching, Gladys now got up, placed a candle in the window and lit it. When Sally came hurrying back with Nathaniel and Elizabeth they all noticed it and grasped its significance. From that day until Billy returned, either Sally or Gladys would light a candle in that window every night, until their man returned to them.

CHAPTER 9

No war, or battle's sound
Was heard the world around,
The idle spear and shield, were high up hung
The hooked chariot stood
Unstained by hostile blood.

On the Morning of Christ's Nativity
John Milton. 1645.

The stenching trench welcomed Corporal Billy Thomas and his fellow comrades. It comprised a part, a very small part, just fifty yards of a front, constructed of an unbroken line of conflict extending from the Flemish coast, past Ypres, to Armentieres, where the infamous Mademoiselle had residence. From thence it stretched onto Arras, Albert and the Somme where its guardianship came under French responsibility. Here it carved its arteries and all its lesser veins, without ceasing, until it reached the Swiss border.

This unique form of human torment had begun as a short term, temporary scar across the landscape. Initially it was designed to allow for a pause in the conflict bringing a halt to the exertions of the troops of the two vast opposing armies prior to a final last gigantic contest of strength, tenacity and courage which would resolve the war.

Ironically this maize of increasingly complex interconnecting ditches became the source, not of ending the maelstrom, but of extending it both in its timescale and in its devil born imagination to explore ever more ways of destroying human life and spirit. In truth the trench system became a vast pitiless complex trap for millions of men during almost four long horrific years, It rapidly evolved into an infernal device allowing perverted science to practice ever more sophisticated experiments upon the bodies and minds of men.

Here, in this, the most unfortunate place in Europe, was a witness to what utter horrors human beings can withstand. A test of how far and for how long patriotism, discipline and courage can be stretched. With each new fiendish weapon, barbed wire, the machine gun, gas, shells, bombs, mines, coupled with the worst that nature can conjure, incessant rain, mud, cold, rats, huge black despicable ever devouring rats, the answer to 'what is hell' was given, made manifest.

As the years passed and peace, once more, all be it a mere temporary respite, came to this corner of Northern France, the question was resolved. Young men, challenged to face all these trials, when given a purpose, can endure a virtually unlimited level of fear, pain, suffering, disease, asphyxiation, gashes, broken and dismembered limbs, anguish and heartache. Mankind discovered, virtually no threshold exists that could not be surpassed by such as occupied this place, save that of death, or the visitation of so great an injury as to leave the recipient incapable of further combat. Even then, an inexhaustible source of new sacrificial lambs were available to carry on the slaughter. This was the reality of trench warfare on the Western Front. Such was the prospect that first greeted Billy Thomas and his comrades on that early morning in December of 1914 nearby to the town of Loos as the first year of conflict drew to its close.

In the early days on that flat Reubenesque landscape, the trenches were dug from out of green fertile pasture. The two opposing front-line trenches ran almost parallel to each other, deviating in places because of the lie of the land. The most developed sections were fully provided with sandbags bringing relative security from natural collapse or penetration from bullets and other light projectiles. Communication trenches stretched away to the rear, perhaps a mile, or more, to a small town or village, providing access for troops being both relieved or arriving to take up their station.

It was now three months since the trench had first been created. In that time men had come and gone. Some simply served out a term of endless sentinel boredom, broken only by the regular outbreak of shellfire executed by both sides, which took an attritional toll of their comrades. Even if they were physically untouched at the end of their tour of duty, they left different men, having seen, heard and felt experiences that a whole natural lifetime should not be expected to endure. They left, full of the knowledge that they would have to return again, perhaps several times before either the madness ended or they were rendered incapable of any more tours of duty.

Others, perhaps the most fortunate, received a wound severe enough to return them to England, or Blighty as she was known. They came home to their native soil having 'done their bit for King and Country', never to return, yet, never to forget, feeling they were the fortunate ones. The next time that they were to visit this dreadful place would often be years after the armistice and when a second equally tragic conflict had been and gone.

There were others though, who had come and would never leave. Some would lose their lives by a sniper's bullet, usually through the head having forgotten how fatal it was to peer above the parapet. Such unfortunates were usually buried within the hour of their dying in the formal, civilised manner accorded by military protocol. Their death would be properly recorded and letters written home to loved ones. Death came for these in a relatively instant and painless fashion and their place of rest marked and recognised.

How different death could be for those taking part in an attack, either as a manoeuvre to gain and hold part of an enemy trench or a night patrol incursion which could leave you dead in no-man's-land, or worse, incapable of returning to your own trench, mortally wounded. For these unfortunates their only relief came with a protracted, welcome death, then, once the blood had ceased to course through the veins, their remains would rapidly begin to decompose, to be covered in flies, then their offspring. As more rain fell, the land becoming a mire, evidence of their existence would sink beneath the surface, leaving no evidence that they had ever been there, ever been part of that company, comprising two camps of humanity, each striving to gain superiority the one over the other.

In such an environment, upon which was once a most placid provident countryside, now subjected to mankind's most ingenious invention of despoliation, the unspeakable was created. Each yard possessed its own particular horror. Perhaps it was the realm of a corrupted cadaver, consumed by an alliance of birds, rats and flies then, finally, gratefully, by countless billions of bacteria, which, paradoxically, had produced so much fertility in times of peace. Thus the rotting flesh of the dead were returned to the dear rich earth wherein, in future years, it would become 'richer still.'

Before the end of the great conflict, such scenes as this, and worse, would be multiplied hundreds of thousands of times, each an individual variant, a piece of evidence portraying mankind's culpable inhumanity.

Neither would the decomposed incumbent corpse be allowed to rest in peace. Often his skeletal remains would be disturbed through the constant blanket shelling from both sides which rained endlessly from both sides until not a single field, copse, wood, ridge, valley or river bank was left untouched. For those wretched young men, whose mortal remains would never be found or identified by their kind, there was left a sole consolation. God, the ever loving forgiving God, he would know where they lay. He would find them on that final day of judgement when, once again, he would descend upon the World, gather up these innocent youths to their resurrection and eternal life in paradise.

This was the Western Front, thus was trench warfare, the ultimate test for a young man's courage, which, each in turn, came to confront, face to face, pitiless, graphic, unremitting. Here came Billy Thomas and his comrades, here came their time of trial.

The battalion had left Armentieres in the early morning, marching the two miles towards the front-line in a drizzled, grey, foreboding light. With over sixty pounds of kit upon their backs, feeling as if they were pack mules or 'scape goats' they mirrored the poor Biblical wretch. Cast out into the wasteland, this unforgiving wilderness, they carried their Nation's burden, resultant of her political failure, here to assuage her sins, with their sacrifice.

It was an analogy not lost on Billy or his friends that morning, though others saw their situation differently. For them the true state of their plight had not dawned, that would come later. On this day they saw themselves as latter-day Crusaders, defending civilisation against the descendants of Attila the Hun and his Gothic hordes. Not so for Billy's immediate friends observing how dismal, twice burdened, Jimmy Jones and Bill Carney appeared, he attempted to reassure them.

"The good Lord is going to see us through. we are off to do his work, he will look over us you know."

The pair looked at him in disbelief, nothing would console their miserable countenance this day. Truthfully, even Billy's heart began to sink as they approached the front and began to form up Section by Section, Platoon upon Platoon, Company by Company, taking over from the exhausted, filthy mud encrusted previous occupants.

An anonymous voice, coming from within the ranks of those who were passing in the opposite direction did little to instil confidence in their future.

"Welcome to Knightsbridge Corporal, the best of luck to you. God knows you will need it"

The ranks from which the voice had come looked to be at the end of human endurance, devoid of any further strength. Exhaustion, immense weakness, soothed by the relief to be leaving this place, was etched on every face. Their countenance could be seen in the wearisome way they moved, no light in their eyes, neither hope, in spite of the fact they were leaving this place for a while. If Billy had been given the time, he would also have observed the haunted, frightened expression, revealing men who had experienced horrors previously beyond their imaginings, beyond the endurance of normal men.

All this he saw, even before he gained the trench, it caused Billy to steel himself for that which was to come. It was the nineteenth of December, just six days before Christmas he realised. At home all those whom he loved would be getting ready to celebrate the Saviour's birth. Festivities would be muted he knew, but in truth, he would so love to be there with his mother, friends and Sally. Especially, he was thinking of Sally, his girl of all those years. For so long his feelings had failed to find expression, hers also, now that they had been pronounced, a war had come along to separate them for longer still.

Standing, here in Northern France, all seemed so distant, so unreal. He was waiting to take his place in the front-line that separated his loved ones from a terrible enemy, while Sally was at home in England fretting for his safety. Somehow he felt like so many past tragic players in literature, helpless against a gigantic uncontrollable backdrop of historic circumstance. He was moving on a vast stage where the enormity of events dwarfed him, mocked his sensitivities and desires.

Now was the time to perform his duty. Along the column he heard the Lieutenant call out his name and his section's identity. At the head of his men he took his place in the line. For the very first time they were now facing the foe. The words of the hymn came to mind, he softly sounded them.

I fear no foe, with thee at hand to bless.

One day, he knew, they would be ordered forward and within a few yards would come into contact with the enemy. Even now, he was possessed of naiveté seeing the conflict in terms of a clean brush with the opposing forces where right would overcome might in a fierce fought but straightforward clash of strength. The awakening was coming and coming soon.

Their particular length of trench had been vacated by a battalion of The Royal Welch Fusiliers, many of them territorials who in civilian life had been miners. They commanded a diligence and knowledge, which they utilised keeping their section in good order. It meant that all had been well maintained in the best possible condition, secure dry and safe as could be expected. The Platoon occupied their fifty yards or so, Billy taking the right wing, twenty-five yards of fire trench where they would propel any invader.

The nearest communication trench was fifty yards either side of them. It led back almost a quarter of a mile to the rear. All their supplies, the evacuation of their wounded, orders and any other materials came along these two lines. The Germans well knew this and consequently concentrated their barrages along the route. Subsequently both arteries were in poor condition in spite of being regularly repaired.

Intersected between their fire trench a second line ran in tandem. Here was the command post where the Company Captain issued his instructions and from where he ranged forth to inspect all the positions under his jurisdiction. A telephone landline ran to Battalion HQ. If it were not cut communications were reasonably effective, but if put out of commission, a runner, a particular kind of brave often foolhardy man would race the gauntlet to bring orders back and forth. Proportionally, this happy breed suffered more casualties than any other in the ranks. The only persons in a more deadly position were those of the rank of Lieutenant.

Billy had come to greatly respect his immediate officer Lieutenant Thorpe. Ever since meeting on that first day in Chester, Thorpe had taken a particular interest in Billy's training, with the result that the man from Glossop, whose marksmanship with a ball had become so legendary in so short a time, had emulated this with his prowess in firing a Lee Enfield. At fifteen rounds a minute Billy could hit centre target four times in five from one hundred and fifty yards.

Thorpe also taught Billy the finer points of leadership.

"Lead by example, from the front. The only soldier to see your back should be those of your own side as they follow you towards the enemy's position."

Thorpe's rule of command, like so many of his rank, was simple. Skill and intelligence, mixed with courage under fire. For the rest of his time on Earth, short though it was, he kept to that tenet, losing his life as he acted out that which he had preached to others. The Lieutenant was to prove a good servant of his Country, all his endeavours with training were not to go amiss. Soon it would all be put to practice, training, combined with courage, was to display its worth.

As sunset arrived the order 'stand to', was heard. This was a twice daily ritual, practised all along the Western Front, repeated at sunrise. The High Command rationalised that the most likely time of attack was towards dawn or dusk, thus the twice daily performance when every man, fully equipped, would look out over the landscape of no-man's-land seeking out any evidence of enemy activity, anticipating an attack.

The general depth of the fire trench was eight feet. It was planked with duckboarding which provided a sump of eighteen inches allowing water to accumulate without reaching the level of men's' boots. This worked well in the drier months but when the incessant rains came, and come they did, the system could not cope, the trench flooded far above the duckboards adding grievously to the misery of its occupants.

A step supported with panelling, boxes of all description or sand bags decreased the height facing the enemy to a little less than five feet six inches, allowing a man with his rifle to fire comfortably without unduly endangering himself, from slots within the parapet sandbagging. Sometimes an enemy head would appear in the sights of a sharpshooter who would immediately let off a round, often being rewarded by a scream and a barrage in reply from the enemy. Sniping was a one sided game though, paradoxically played by both sides. The victim stood little chance whilst the perpetrator suffered little risk. Long life and the Western Front had nothing in common.

Deep within the second trench, most times to be belatedly discovered not deep enough, were constructed the rest billets. They were often covered merely with bowed corrugated iron topped with earth. Inside they would be furnished with the most basic of bunks together with an improvised stove. It could accommodate upwards of eight men per Section at any one time allowing for sleep whilst off duty and a hot meal comprised of either dear old 'Bully Beef', or reconstituted Maconichi's Stew. Sleep never came easily, the cold and damp saw to that.

If poor food and general discomfort were not enough, then there was the constant shelling. Shelling never bought good news. If your own side was setting up a protracted barrage, then, usually it was the prelude to an attack. If it was the enemy disturbing the quiet, it was directed to

145

extinguish either you or your friends. The poor recipient of a sleepless night would be only too aware, that come morning, even if you were one of the lucky ones gossiping on the affairs of the night you would most certainly be notified of someone who had 'Copt it', or bought a 'Blighty.' Another dreary day had come to the Western Front and you were still alive to tell of your part in 'the casual comedy.'

Ritual, routine, shellfire, The Watch, Stand To, Stand Down, all part of the boredom soon to become the greatest of all enemies. The officers considered this and planned events to liven up proceedings. The night patrol consisting of a Platoon or Section would make forays into enemy positions hoping to induce casualties among the enemy, discover information or collect a prisoner or two thereby extracting some useful information.

Billy quickly came to know when a patrol was going out. The Captain would stay out after sunset armed, ironically, with a pair of German binoculars, one of thirty thousand purchased by the War Ministry through Switzerland. He would gaze in one direction, then another, staying at his post until it was almost dark. Soon shadows could be seen creeping and darting towards their objective. Later, the night sky would light up, gunfire rattling from every direction, flashes followed by deafening sound as mills bombs and their German equivalent were thrown in the skirmish being played out sometimes just yards away.

Later, if all had gone well, men would begin to return, crawling carefully towards their home trench, being challenged by the Sectional NCO or Platoon officer. Finally the enemy would retaliate with a bombardment or an incursion of their own. This could go on for hours. What was ever achieved, Billy never discovered. True, it kept men alert, he deduced, provided some intelligence, perhaps, none-the-less, it was a terrible nuisance.

Life, for some, death, so predictably fashioned, continued much the same for those first six days leading to Christmas. The night sky before the eve of that great Christian feast came clear and cold an enfrosted night producing icicles thinly formed from the misted air. Here Billy was to witness a phenomenon, one which, in later years, was to enter the realms of myth and legend. For the next two days and nights the ordinary men of both sides who composed these massive opposing armies, sought out peace one with the other.

During the daylight hours of December 24th. the front went strangely quiet. The shelling ceased, not a single missile flew over them from either direction. A single incident occurred bringing excitement to both sides when a large fleeting buck hare, flew out from his ground cover that he had been occupying to become the object of mutual attention.

Dashing and darting, zig zagging, both left and right, the doomed creature struggled to deny its inevitable fate. Eventually it ran in the

146

direction of the Germans where one of their snipers, to the great delight of his own lines, brought it down. A single shot and it lay there, still, exactly as so many of his human companions, dead, unheeded, unburied.

There it lay temptingly close, a good meal for some lucky German soldier and his friends. The British snipers waited. They had lost the competition to shoot the prey, but woe betide any German who had the courage to collect his prize. Anticipation heightened the silence, men all along the sector peered through their slits and waited.

Deathlessness was interjected by the sight of a tin raised upon a stick, above the enemy trench. It was vigorously shaken making a rattling noise, which reminded Billy of the game of 'Tin-pan-alley' that he used to play as a boy. Soon it was accompanied by a white flag that was waving urgently from left to right. Next, from over the parapet, to the astonishment of all the British came a wooden barrel, small it was, about half a firkin. Then, hands raised, a German stepped out from his position of safety, waving the white flag even more vigorously. He need not have worried, no shot would be fired. The Platoon commanders, mostly of Public School background, harnessed their sense of British fair play and instructed their troops to withhold their fire.

The young German began to roll his barrel towards the British positions. Passing the dead hare, he rolled his trophy until it reached mid-way between the lines. Standing up, he spoke to his enemies in halting English.

"For you Englanders, very good brandy, happy Christmas."

Waving to the lines of his silent startled foes, the German in matter of fact manner, saluted his enemies and simply turned his back, waved once more and walked back towards his friends in triumph, not forgetting to pick up the hare on the way. A unanimous roar of approval rang out along both trenches. One young man's gesture of friendship, an act of individual bravado, needing no little courage, had completely transformed the atmosphere.

Lieutenant Thorpe was standing next to Billy as the German disappeared back into his trench. He gave full voice to what he had just witnessed.

"Well Corporal, you do not see that every day. That one could almost have been an Englishman."

Billy replied in agreement.

"Certainly sir, but what do we do with the problem he has left to us?"

"What problem Corporal?"

"Why the brandy barrel Sir. It would be churlish not to retrieve it, would it not?"

Thorpe, considered for a moment, formulating a determined response.

147

"You are correct Corporal Thomas, we must go and retrieve it, after all the goods are designated contraband by the war office. We must get it now, in daylight. Whatever happens, we cannot be seen to be skulking now can we?, not when the enemy has acted in such a way in full view of everyone on both sides."

"No sir, not at all."

"Well Corporal Thomas, organise."

"Yes sir, certainly sir."

Billy knew just the man for the job. Wrexham George, Always boasting about his local beer he was, insisting upon its superiority over its English counterparts. He went over to the Welshman, fully knowing that the consistently inquisitive Celt had overheard every word of the conversation.

"Well Taffy, are you up for it? Don't want those Germans to have one over on us do we."

"No Corporal, certainly not, it shall be done straight away. Welshmen to the rescue, just as at Agincourt."

This latter reference was to the Welshman's persistent assertion, during conversation, that it was the Welsh longbow that won the famous Medieval battle.

"Just so George, be careful, it is only a barrel of brandy after all."

"Only Corporal?, no such thing when it comes to brandy."

A white flag was prepared and waved in accordance to unofficial protocol. Up the trench ladder went the buccaneering Welshman, ready to gain a legendary place in his Platoon's mythology. He was eager for his prize. He had never tasted German brandy before but at this moment anything had to be an improvement in the meagre ration of watered down rum that he was presently issued each day.

Again the cheers erupted from both sides. Like his German predecessor, Wrexham George strolled, seemingly unperturbed, towards the barrel. He arrived where it had been left, examined it in mock critique, stood up, faced the German ranks, bowed to them as a symbol of gratitude and began to roll his treasure back to his admiring, anticipatingly grateful comrades. The cheers rose to a crescendo especially from the trench he was encouraging the barrel towards.

Gaining his objective, the barrel was greeted by welcoming hands, which gently lowered it down, into its new home. With a final flourish, George turned towards the Germans, gave a final exaggerated bow and slipped back down the ladder. Hands were thrust in his direction, he was the hero of the hour, home again, or as near as he could be here in France.

A great sense of triumph swept through the sector following the successful mission. It was like an epidemic infecting all with a sense of victory, as if the war had been won and they were all going home for Christmas. The reality was that they had simply gained a few gallons of

German brandy, very good brandy, together with a stout barrel, beautifully coopered that would be adapted by the section as a food and card table, following them wherever fortune guided.

Later that day, the mood was even more uplifted with the arrival from HQ. of letters and special Christmas rations. Also came a host of individual parcels for several of the men in the section, including Billy. Never had bees more eagerly gathered around a pot of honey than this group of men impatient to see what they had been provisioned with from home.

Sorting out took an age. By the time it was completed only two hours remained before 'Stand to.' There was not a man who had not received something. The pioneers who had transported the Christmas fayre to the front had grumbled incessantly over all the chaos the additional post had created.

"Theybe jammed packed back there Corporal, just like Christmas back home."

This caused Billy to smile.

"Well it is going to be like Christmas here soldier, and a good thing I say."

He never received a formal reply, the soldier simply turned away mumbling something about it being all right for some.

"And a merry Christmas to you friend."

"Humbug."

"Well he was full of the spirit of Christmas."

The conclusion came from a festooned Jimmy Jones who was laden with colourful parcels of all shapes and sizes.

It was a festive Wrexham George, by now fortified by not a little brandy, who summed up the mood of the section.

"Those who don't like Christmas should keep their thoughts to themselves I say."

Billy's share of the booty came in the form of three letters and four parcels, blessings indeed. He decided not to open any until after 'Stand to.' Meanwhile he stashed them in his private area of the billet. This was a place and time when men shared things, where comradeship provided for complete trust, where personal valuables were perfectly safe no matter what they were or where they were left.

'Stand to' came, a clear sky containing a simple thin line of marbled cloud away to the western horizon allowed for a spectacular sunset, the last of this first year of the Great War prior to its first Christmas. About three miles away, an avenue of Poplars still, miraculously, standing, began to obscure the sun. As usual the men were all attentive, standing alert on their allotted portion of the fire step. The temperature was dropping quickly, it would be a hard frost this night. Cold, starlit, but thankfully, dry.

The setting sun brought out the stars on the eastern horizon. High in the heavens the brighter stars of the Great Bear or The Plough as others know it by, began to shine. The constellation, standing upright on its handles reaching out towards Polaris, dominated the sky. Soon the Moon would rise, silvering the air, foretelling of Angels, Shepherds, Kings and the King of Kings. Wrexham George approached Billy. The cold was bringing sobriety to him.

"Strange is it not Corporal? How quiet it all is. No sniping, no shells, it's like the clocks have stopped."

Billy stood still for a moment gazing heavenwards, his ears comprehending the accuracy of the Welshman's metaphor, its eloquence. It was as if the whole World was standing silent, contrasting previous evenings when it appeared as if whole regiments of Valkurie were screaming across the sky. Holding the small volume in his hand he spoke aloud whilst George listened.

'But peaceful was the night
Wherein the prince of light
His reign of peace on Earth began.'

Billy had taken to memorising passages from Milton's Christ's Nativity and in so doing visioning the face and form of his beloved Sally, realising, over and over again, what a precious gift the small volume was to him. George, quite a man of words, found listening to the verse, spoken in these surroundings, a most moving experience, yet he could hardly find words himself.

"Beautiful, Corporal, beautiful."

So still was the night and so heightened their senses that the pair began to catch fragments of sound from the German trenches. Alongside his Welsh comrade, Billy peered out towards the enemy. Now the last essential element for this night arrived, it began to snow. Gently, in huge flakes, magnified by their imagination, the snow wafting on the air, drifted groundwards to lie still, in perfect form upon the frosted ground. The English Corporal, mindful of all around him and all that was not, placed his gloved palm skywards, awaiting one for of the unique crystals to land upon it. Billy found it difficult to achieve his aim for a flattened palm creates an airflow, which inclines an object of low density to veer one way or the other.

At long last one of the almost weightless fragments found a resting-place where his determined patience had guided it. A perfectly formed flake settled shimmering with the reflection of the newly risen Moon. it appeared miraculous to him that such a fragile object could rest here in all perfection. Delicate it was, beautiful, bringing forth a delight within him, reminiscent of the sensation brought to him whenever Sally came into view. She filled his thoughts as he looked upon his glistered treasure. Bringing his palm towards his face, with the lightest of emissions he sent the encrystalled wonder on its way to settle anonymously among its billions of fellow entities.

The sound of men scuffling hurriedly towards him along the trench awoke him from his meditations.

"Hey Corporal, look what we have found. We saw them the other day when we were coming up. The apple orchard over the ways, or at least what's left of it is full of the stuff."

With the end of his excited newsgiving, Young Billy Carney, together with his other partner in crime, thrust up a large sprig of foliage almost into Billy's face. It was mistletoe, yes mistletoe, and it was covered in berries. The pair had bunches of the parasitic growth. In the moonlight it appeared they had hundreds of clusters of pearls upon them, fit for the most beautiful of women. Here they were on the Western Front, the most dastardly place on earth yet it was a world wherein a perfect, undamaged snowflake could be formed, where the humble mistletoe appeared as priceless pearls. Back in the billet were parcels and letters. If the enemy were to cease his aggression, for a while at least, if his side were to likewise desist, then all could experience Christmas, Hallelujah!

Wrexham George brought forth thoughts of a more worldly nature, but no less pertinent to his pondering.

"Well lads, all we need now is some ladies to kiss under that lot doesn't we?"

General assent to this remark echoed all around. Billy kept his thoughts to himself though they mirrored those around him, with respect to one very special girl.

Having been encouraged by the first reception to his comments, Wrexham George became more profound of thought.

"What we needs now is some time that is peaceable like so as we can have our Christmas proper. Not much to ask is it now?"

The Welshman had echoed all their thoughts and Billy agreed.

"Not much to ask at all George."

He did not want to mar the sentiment but he had to be practical, men's lives were in his hands.

"Now men, we must remain vigilant, I am afraid all has to be as usual with the watches, we must stay vigilant. Perhaps, indeed almost certainly, not all the enemy share our sentiments."

Having impressed upon his men the need to attend their duty, Billy turned towards the billet eager to read his letters and open at least one present. Not for the first time that day Wrexham George stopped his progress.

"Hey Corporal, look at this."

Together with all the rest of the section, indeed in unison with mile after mile of trench occupants, Billy stared over out into no-man's-land. He caught his breath, to both left and right, each side stretching out far as the eye could see, the enemy trenches were illuminated with multi-coloured lanterns and what appeared to be Christmas trees. The flakes of snow were still falling, weaving their way in the windless air, catching prisms of light in their falling, red, green, yellow, blue.

Lieutenant Thorpe came up to Billy's shoulder, his eyes reflecting the sparkled lights.

"Well there's a thing, there's a thing."

A voice broke the startled silence, one of them at least intended to take advantage of the enemy's festivities to create an advantage.

"We should get out our Lee Enfields, might get quite a few Huns tonight."

Thorpe spat out a reply, his honour, sense of fair play was outraged.

"Any man firing over there without permission, gets put on report, understood?"

A general approval echoed his instruction. The wretch who voiced the proposition slunk away into the darkness suitably admonished. Speaking quietly to Billy and the other section leader Joe Gaffrey, who had just joined them the officer advised diligence and caution.

"Gentlemen keep a good look-out, don't want the enemy taking us unawares now do we? Just make sure we do not fire first that's all.

He now again looked towards the enemy, dazzled as much in spirit as he was by the light.

"It is wonderful, is it not?"

Every man who saw these things, the lights of Christmas against the falling snow, felt full of childish wonder, indeed the child that is in all men rose to the surface, bringing them pleasured memories of past Christmas celebrations, private thoughts of home. These reflections were now intensified.

The frosted air, quietly at first, then more assuredly, became Carol filled. German voices sounded out to bring a familiar Christmas Hymn to the British lines, a song universally known in spite of them being sung in a foreign tongue.

'Stille natcht, Heilige nacht'

Thorpe was now of a mood to philosophise. Remembering the Latin and Classical Greek learnt at his public school. The Punic Wars, Homeric legend, Hector, Achilles, Ajax, poetic conflict all. Now here he was, opposite a mighty foe, capable of indescribable evil, yet celebrating the birth of the Savour of the World.

152

"Apt for the moment Corporal, yet a paradox. Silent Night, what chance in this place of all places. However, you never know, after all they profess to be Christians like us, and largely Protestants I believe."

A second verse began. Now in addition to German came the Carol voiced in another foreign medium. This time Saxon voices were accompanied by Welsh, for Wrexham George had fearlessly climbed the parapet to sing in unison with the men from the Baltic coast. His fine Tenor voice resounded over no-man's-land. Finally he concluded along with the enemy choir.

'Sleep in Heavenly peace.'

Spontaneous applause rippled all along both sides of the line. Wrexham George, silhouetted against the moonlit skyline, a fatal situation on any other night, took off his cap, gave another of his now famous bows, turned and in as dignified a manner as possible, lowered himself back into the trench.

Jimmy Jones, reflecting the mood of so many men of both sides, all to few of whom would not return to their native land to record the event, summed up his thoughts.

"Well that is something to write home about."

Write home he would, along with many others each having their own perception of the events of Christmas 1914 on the Western Front, each adding a new perspective to the legend.

Lieutenant Thorpe, still unaware where all this was leading, enunciated his sentiments in contradictory manner.

"Quite so Lance Corporal. What a bloody fool. What can he have been thinking of? Still, kept up our side well did he not? Welsh is he. Well that's the Welsh for you, exhibitionists all, they just cannot help themselves. Give them an opportunity to sing and they will never stop, never. Makes you proud they are on your side does it not. Still Corporal, have a quiet word wouldn't do to repeat the fashion of that now, would it?"

"No sir, as you say sir."

The Moon had climbed higher now, almost full, reflecting upon the frosted snow, casting shadows from a virtually cloudless night sky. Not a scenario on which to play the fool. On such a night a chap could, almost certainly would, get his head blown off. Billy was suddenly roused from his morbidity by an exclamation from Jimmy Jones.

"I say, look out there, we have got guests coming for supper."

Again Billy gazed out upon the wintry landscape. Sure enough lamps were moving towards them, held aloft by shadowy figures. From out of the darkened void, voices began to announce greetings as if they were passers by on any English street.

"Merry Christmas English. Peace, peace to all on Earth."

The Platoon stood to, shouldering arms. The leading light was now but a few yards distant. Time to issue instructions considered a confounded Lieutenant Thorpe.

"No shooting men, let us not be the first to undertake an uncivilised act."

How foolish were these ambassadors of the enemy. with one command, a single order these lamp bearers, bringers of light, could be swept from the planet. The spell gripped him also, brought a festive foolishness to him. All normal thought of caution, so grievously bred into him, fled from his mind. He was captivated by an unknown quantity far above his normal capacity of rational thinking.

Thorpe holstered his pistol, requested Billy to join him, climbed a trench ladder and began to walk towards the lights as a moth to a flame. Billy followed quickly behind him, beckoning Jimmy to follow him. The three men were now standing etched out on the skyline. At this moment a German sniper or machine-gunner could wipe them from the face of the Earth. The lamps were now in a line, shimmering flickering in a silvered ghostlike orange hallowed glow, which reflected the forms of the three English soldiers.

"Hold your palms outwards men and walk slowly towards the lights. Show them that we have no malevolent intentions."

In full view of the enemy, highlighted between the lamplight and the Moon these three wise men walked across the most dangerous landscape of all time armed only with a faith that their fellow Christian enemy would do them no harm this night. Normally they would not have remained alive for more than a few seconds. Today, thanks to the birth of a baby thousands of miles away, almost two thousand years before, their lives were as safe as if they were sat in a Cathedral pew, listening to the gloried praise ascending Heavenwards from the throats of choirboys.

Here they met their foe, the treacherous, barbaric Hun, halfway between the two trenches, previously the source of an unremitting, pitiless rain of death the one upon the other. The Germans held their lamps aloft, allowing the English to see their faces. They approached ever closer until they were but two yards apart. Here they stopped. The leading German saluted and made an announcement, a proclamation in perfect English.

"A merry Christmas gentlemen. I am Lieutenant Meinicke of the Third Westphalian Regiment, from which I send you all felicitations and the compliments of the season."

He spoke without any accent, almost as if he had attended an English Public School, which indeed he had. Lieutenant Thorpe replied in similar vein and introduced his two companions, after which he extended his hand, which was vigorously accepted. Immediately all became handshakes, handshakes of peace and goodwill. From behind the lanterns, dozens more Germans rushed to greet their English foe, to hug them in the customary Teuton manner. It was almost an embarrassment for the normally non demonstrative reserved English who, in addition, were kissed over and over on their reddened cheeks.

Jimmy was handed one of the decorated Christmas lanterns. So pleased he was at owning such a trophy to take back to his pals, he handed all his precious Woodbines over to the enemy, who flocked round him eager for an English cigarette. Eventually, having been carefully packaged, it would find its way back to Glossop where for many a Christmas it would proudly shine out from the front window of his home.

For now, in this darkened yet moonstruck landscape it cast warming, glowing colours that cherished and softened so many hearts that night. This moment would stay with Jimmy for the rest of his life, for years to come he would tell the tale, a story that would grow in its telling. His grandchildren would listen awe-struck, hanging on his every word. Long after the memory of these tragic, testing, yet august, times were past, faded in their intensity, passed into history and myth, they would be rekindled. Those who gathered round the ancient warrior, the sole survivor of this small party of celebrants, to listen to his tales of the great Christmas peace and his part in it, would relive, for a time that evening when peace came to the place of conflict.

The general fraternisation continued for fully ten minutes. The Germans had brought some chocolate with them and also cigars which Jimmy became ever more burdened with. In addition to Jimmy's Woodbines, Lieutenant Thorpe, had fully two packets of Players upon him. Both were quickly disposed of, the insignia of the sailor's smiling head peering through a lifebelt, and the outline of HMS Dreadnought on a distant skyline being of particular interest to the grateful recipients.

A bottle of what later Billy was to discover was 'Jager Meister' was passed round to each man, who in his turn, swigged a generous gulp of its warming contents. Eventually, the bottle, now less than half full, was given to the ever increasingly overburdened Jimmy Jones to take back with him.

All was celebration, some low singing and dancing began, three Germans linking arms and humming a folk tune on the Black Forest of ancient days. The German Lieutenant lifted his hand and all became silence. He was preparing to make a toast, together with a proposition. He did so in perfect English.

"As a fellow Saxon, as an officer and a gentleman, from now until sunset tomorrow, I give my word that we shall not fire or, in any way, carry out a belligerent act. All we ask is that you act likewise. In the name of Jesus Christ I offer you the handshake of peace."

The German's face was illuminated, not merely by the Moon heightened lamplight but through the expression of joy etched upon him. In the flecked beams, now seasoned by another gentle fall of snow, the

German officer appeared almost saintly. His greeting and bringing of peace was certainly one which tradition associated being delivered by such kindred.

Lieutenant Thorpe was deep in thought, then he smiled at his opposite number, extended his hand and shook that of his avowed enemy. With this gesture, he assented.

"Lieutenant Meinicke, I agree. If something to the contrary is about to occur, outside of my control, I shall have three green flares sent up as a warning to you. Happy Christmas, In the name of Jesus Christ may you all spend it in peace."

Now all was handshaking and hugging, laughter filled the air as if the entire Heavenly Host was about to descend upon these unfortunates. Truly Angels did not appear, but a tension was released, peace reigned in a small part of the battlefield for a short span of time. For a further half an hour they milled around, being joined by others from both sides. They exchanged gifts of regimental buttons, cap badges and the like. For Billy the scene reminded him of the title of a book he had recently read, for him it was 'a night to remember.'

Having returned to their respective trenches, even though the night was now well advanced, both armies continued to celebrate. The frosted air became carol-filled. English, German, Welsh, courtesy of Wrexham George. Nor were the musical renditions purely carols. A German baritone sang from Tanhauser. Against such a background it was as if the Gods themselves adorned the fleeting blackened clouds that scudded across low in the southern sky passing the Moon, as if harbingers of mystery appreciating the heralding of the Nordic myth of deeds above heroic.

The singer concluded, the vast train of Woden vanished away back into their misted past. Highlighted upon his parapet he appeared as if he were a God himself. Applause erupted all along the front from both sides of the line. Lieutenant Thorpe approached Wrexham George.

"Well Private Mancot, we cannot allow for such a performance as that to pass without a suitable reply now, Can we?"

In truth, the Welshman had already considered a repost. His father was at Rourke's Drift. Many was the occasion that he heard his father tell of the great Welsh response to the Zulu warriors constant chanting and how it had stopped the enemy in its tracks. Now a Welsh voice would be raised once more, upon another battlefield before an even more deadly foe.

"Certainly not sir!"

With just two or three bounds he was up the trench ladder and onto the parapet ready to exercise his lungs. If 'Men of Harlech was good enough for the mighty Zulu tribe, it would suffice for these Germans. Over Flanders Field drifted, in the most tuneful Welsh, the tale of Owain Glyndwr's beleaguered few, of how they faced an overwhelming host, of how they fell, how they became immortalised in legend.

As his impromptu performance continued, Billy sat down on a wooden biscuit box, his designated seat. Against the musical background he read from his Milton, turning to 'On the Morning of Christ's Nativity.' As the Welshmen's foes attacked time after time and the massive walls of Harlech Castle were being torn asunder, bringing its courageous defenders to the edge of their inevitable death, all in a language Billy did not understand he was immersed in the words of the blind poet of ancient days.

'When such music sweet,
Their hearts and ears did greet
As never was by mortal finger struck.
Divinely-warbled voice,
Answering the stringed noise
As all their souls in blissful rapture took.'

In the background, in his songfilled Welsh, Wrexham George concluded his epic song.

'As you fight with all your might
To faith and hope you're clinging;
With the foe towards you leaping,
You your valiant stance are keeping
All the Nation with you weeping,
Freedom will not die.'

Not one in a hundred who heard the words sung that night by Wrexham George could ever understand them, though many could conjecture on their gallant nature, their depiction of heroism, their patriotism. Christ in his Nativity, contrasted the image of Welsh soldiers battling against impossible odds, of Teutonic myth, where men fought monsters. Only he whose birth was the source of the peace that had come this night to these ragged, cold, unhappy souls, would have grasped the irony.

However, George Mancot was to redeem the situation. To conclude his recital he now sang the beautiful hymn 'Canol Lan', written by John Hughes the Welsh hymnist who had died just a few weeks previously.

'Canol onest, canol lan'
Honest heart, true heart.

His performance completed, George bowed to every point of the compass, whilst both sides of no-man's-land erupted in sustained applause, together with cries of 'hurrah, encore.'

So elapsed the night. Gradually, it became quiet as men tired or succumbed to alcohol. Soon both sides of the trenches slept, except for the sparcely placed solitary sentinel. All fell still, uneventful, save for the occasional shooting star falling to Earth, adding to the balls of lead and iron that were scattered in countless numbers throughout the landscape. Each and every one slept in a heavenly peace.

CHAPTER 10

Peace hath her victories
No less renowned than War.

To the Lord General Cromwell. John Milton.1652.

Dawn came crisp, cold, damp. A mist, heavily laden, skirted the landscape, collecting in shell-holes, even the trenches themselves. Providentially, it hid many of the stranded horrors, wilfully strewed out in the world of desolation, all too familiarly known by its now accustomed name, 'no-man's-land.' For mile upon mile this provided the barrier, the spectacle immodestly displayed between the two mighty armed camps. Once again dawn emerged, fitfully awaking Billy Thomas from his haunted sleep. He rose to greet the coming light that was now beginning to defeat the enshrouded sky. Automatically, he began his duties; those of ensuring all his section were awake and preparing to 'stand to.'

Within minutes the fire-trench was occupied by bleary-eyed, tired, shivering young men, gazing out towards the enemy with whatever diligence their state of wakefulness could muster.

"Can't wait for a cuppa."

The anonymous remark could not be traced, but all who heard were in total agreement.

"Fritzy won't be coming over today."

Another bodiless remark, from out of the firmament, that found no disagreement.

"If he does, he had better bring his own Christmas pud and cigars, or we'll send him back with a blinking flea in his ear."

Other likewise mutterings continued to come to Billy's ears.

"Did you hear them singing last night? Some of those Germans can voice a grand tune, eh?"

"Reckon theybe no match for our Welshman, not a patch."

"You're right there."

"Why don't they go off to their homes. It ain't right is it, them coming over here, trespassing, blowing folks to kingdom come, spoiling our bloody Christmas. It ain't right is it? Go home I say and let us go with them, surprise everyone at home. After all, that's what they told us, all over by Christmas. Truth is it hasn't bloody started yet."

"Language, language, it's Christmas day after all."

"Yeah, Happy Christmas everyone."

"Happy Christmas."

"Happy Christmas."

So the banter continued, uninterrupted, throughout the section. Then Billy spied the approach of Lieutenant Thorpe.

"Quiet men, officer on parade."

Thorpe and his section leader exchanged salutes.

"Good morning Corporal."

"Good morning sir, happy Christmas."

"And the compliments of the season to you Corporal Thomas. How are the men this morning? Ready for a good breakfast?"

"The moment stand-down is called. Today we have riches indeed. The men cannot wait sir."

Never the less Corporal, keep them on their toes. Would not do to be surprised by Jerry, this day of all days."

Billy left no evidence of slackness in his reply to the officer.

"Right you are sir, of course sir!"

"Well Corporal, carry on."

With that final terse reply, Thorpe was gone, checking on his other responsibilities and, if truth be known, hurrying back to his command post for a mug of hot coffee.

Stand-down was sounded. Leaving two unfortunates on sentry duty, the rest scuttled back to the relative comfort of the billet. Here the men became silent, engrossed in thoughts of home. Above, the cloudless sky was free from war's activities. No shells stormed overhead, or aircraft; no shots were being exchanged.

"There could be no war at all. Why can't every day be Christmas?"

"Why not indeed."

" 'Cos we would waste it, that's why, people always waste good things. Take them for granted they does."

"Happen you're right there, still happy Christmas all."

"Happy Christmas."

"Happy Christmas."

Once again all became silent. Men were thinking of past times, of children by open roaring fireplaces, taking sweets from stockings, awaiting such a dinner as they so seldom had. A time of games, visits to and from relations and long-time friends. Uncles, aunts bringing further gifts, cold meat in the afternoon with warm mince pies. It was not so long since, that they were children all anticipating such. Could it really have been be so short a while?

Leastways, today, food was not a problem. Not a single man of Billy's Section was to be disappointed with his share of the day's fayre. Billy had received from his mother, Sally and her parents two parcels from Fortnum and Mason, which he proceeded to open to the background of sizzling bacon, eggs and fried bread, mingled with the rich smell of proper steaming coffee.

He laid out his groceries. The centrepiece was comprised of a large tin of roast turkey. Soon it was surrounded with sausages, Christmas pudding, cream, biscuits, chocolate, and a handsome fruitcake, together with boiled sweets and other assorted confectionery. One other of the section had received a similar parcel. The two of them decided to share it out with all the rest, making them the heroes of the hour.

Additionally, each man had received a gift box from no less a personage than Princess Mary. It contained a pipe, packages of cigarettes, tobacco and, finally, a photograph of the Princess herself posing somewhat erotically, smiling wistfully, intimately, as if purposely, specifically, taken for the lucky individual recipient.

Further, extra rations had come up from the rear. They were awash with rum and plum puddings. Indigestion was going to be a greater foe for each and every one of the celebrants, dwelling in this hole in the ground, this day, than any malevolence that the Germans would rain upon them. The coffee was passed around, heavily laced with the prized German brandy. With this came Billy's Christmas toast.

"Merry Christmas men, may we, next year, be sitting in our own hearths of home, and all this around us just a bad memory."

"Hear, hear, good on you Corporal. That's one motion we all second."

Wrexham George agreed in his own poetical Welsh way.

"Heniarth bach."

"What's that George?"

"There's no English to explain really, it's just an aching of the heart that wishes for the sight of the lands of my fathers."

It was a deep sentiment and profound in its description, proper translation or no. There was not a man listening who did not know exactly what he meant. Jimmy Jones followed with a hopeful possibility.

"Well, if Jerry is full of spirit like what's in this here brandy, he is not going to trouble us much today, just as he said last night. Perhaps we are going to have a completely peaceful day."

The one responsible for cooking the bacon, around the makeshift cooker, none other than young Albert, reflected the thoughts of all that heard Jimmy's words.

"Wouldn't that be just something, just something?"

Billy agreed.

"Certainly would Albert, certainly would."

Hope, springing from the possibility of a restful, peaceful day, mingled with the ever-lingering sorrow that separation brought him, forced Billy back into a reflective, melancholic mood. He needed to re-read his letters; hopefully they would bring him some solace. The breakfast utensils were quickly washed in the icy water they traditionally used, a generous portion of brandy, 'God bless the Germans', was poured out for all and the men sat down to relax, each, once again, in his own world, deeply reflecting upon loved ones.

Likewise, Billy's thoughts were of home, of Sally, also his mother who had so recently written to warn him on the 'looseness' of foreign women and how he should steer absolutely clear of them. 'Would not do to have another confrontation as he had on his march to Church Stretton now would it.' 'Indeed not mother', he had thought, realising the extent of the female plot hatching against him at home. 'Rather face the wrath of the entire German horde, than an alliance of anger emanating from mother and Sally. His conduct would be, had to be, above any scrutiny that could lead to their admonishment. Drat that Shropshire Lass, no wonder all the men of that county spent their time at the plough, it kept them from troublesome females.'

He took up his Milton and was soon deep within its pages. He read purposefully, whilst holding Sally's embroidered handkerchief which bore both her initials and his. The day was advancing. A sadly limpid, sulphured, almost leather yellowed, milky sun struggled fruitlessly to gain height. It remained lingering barely above the horizon, having little of its warmth to grant to the poor unfortunates struggling for some of its usual comfort.

It was not even noticed by Billy Thomas, so engrossed had he become in his reading. It was Sally's face that swam before him rather than the thin reflection of Hellos. Christ's birth as interpreted by Milton soothed his soul, much as the Psalmist calmed the turbulence of his King, during that time when it was the Philistines who ravaged the world.

> *'For if such holy song*
> *Enwrap our fancy long,*
> *Time will run back, and fetch the age of gold,*
> *And speckled vanity and war*
> *Will sicken soon and die.'*

He considered the wisdom of England's greatest poet, moved to write such words, his inspiration drawn from the same event that had brought to him and friend and foe alike a fragile peace this day.

"If only it could all end now. End in friendship, clasping hands as last night. Shaking hands and both sides going home to unite with their families, bringing peace back to this forlorn land. If rather than a mere solitary day's respite, the message of Christmas could teach them all of the futility that was war. If only:

> *'And Hell itself will pass away*
> *And leave her dolorous mansions to the peering day.'*

It was another aspect of Christmas, which broke the key.
"Humbug Corp?"

The boyish frame of young Albert stood over him, hand outstretched, a tin containing black and white, striped, boiled sweets shining enticingly within its realms. Swept out of his thoughts, he reacted automatically.

"Why thank you Albert, Humbugs, just what I could do with right now."

Albert went on his way, delighted that he had been of service to his Corporal. Billy was always so kind to him, watching out for him in the early days, yet not so obvious that others noticed. He was glad Corp' liked Humbugs, in future he would always have one available to offer him, just in case.

Billy sucked on the sugary spiced sweet. It was truly pleasant, ironically bringing to mind the other occasion that humbug and Christmas are brought together. He recalled the first time that he and Sally read Christmas Carol together in the library, with Scrooge declaring, 'Christmas bah! Christmas, humbug.

'Humbug indeed, what a place to spend Christmas, here in this realm of desolation, covered in mud and slime trying your best to kill before you yourself are killed.'

He mused: whatever happened to 'Thou shalt not kill.' Watching the contented young retreating soldier who had offered him the confection, he wondered how small a time it must have been since he was wearing short trousers. The truth was that Albert was a toy soldier. His thoughts never strayed towards the delights to be found from women, or discussion of beer and other strong alcohol, his delight, his anticipation of enjoyment, came from exploring a paper bag full of black and white striped sweets. Here was the true reflection of affairs. Did this war really need the likes of young Albert to fuel its furnace? If it was so, then this conflict was a more sorry affair than he had ever suspected. It was indeed, to give it polite expression, Humbug.

His good friend Jimmy Jones, unwittingly became the catalyst who awoke him from this gloomy reflective surmising. He came, a messenger of startling news.

"Billy, come quickly, this you are not going to believe. In no-man's-land, you have just got to see this."

As if he was an automaton, Billy rose and followed Jimmy back to the fire-trench. The nearer he got, the more excited conversation became. Men were all heading to observe this as yet unexplained phenomenon. Suddenly, without any consideration for his safety, all precaution tossed aside, Jimmy scrambled up the ladder and onto the parapet. Billy tried to pull him down but his friend called back to him.

"Don't worry Billy there's no shooting today."

Then Billy remembered, they had agreed a peace. He followed up the ladder, taking Jimmy's extended hand, he, in turn was on the parapet and into the light. Here, he met the most unexpected scene. Staked high above the German trenches were three giant signs. He read from left to right. 'Happy Christmas Cheshires', 'Peace on Earth', 'Goodwill to all Men.'

German soldiers were lazily perambulating alongside their parapet. There were at least a hundred of them. 'In normal times', Billy thought, 'a sniper's dream.' He looked back. The same spectacle was evident on his side, men casually wandering around as if the place was a municipal park. The run of frosty nights had created a thin hard crust of the mud. Slight though the snow had been, it had settled, although the frost had made it too powdery to turn into snowballs. Just as well, he considered, yet God could be such a spoilsport. Better by far to throw snowballs at each other than to toss mills bombs. He chuckled at the thought of fighting with snowballs to decide the outcome of the war.

"Wagner's Gods are dismissed, our Christian God reigns today. Corporal!"

Lieutenant Thorpe had crept up on him accompanied by the Company Captain.

Billy saluted his seniors in the most correct manner.

"As you say sir, Thor, Odin and the entire Valkurie must be straining at the leash, their dogs of war tethered, struggling beyond belief.

The Captain observed this Corporal of Thorpe's, he had heard much of his prowess. No one had told him that he was also an educated man.

"How vivid Corporal, you know of the Gods of the Ring?"

"Indeed sir, I see them being entertained most days."

"Quite so Corporal, let us hope that the host of Valhalla remain restrained for a few hours yet, the men could do with a rest."

The Captain had been at war for almost sixteen months without ceasing. Firstly, he commanded regulars, comrades of long standing, now mostly dead, sleeping round Mons in the main. Then came the Territorials to replace them. They too were gone, on the banks of the Marne or buried in neat rows before Ypres.

When he was first told that fresh, green, barely trained troops of Kitchener's New Army were coming to replace this lost legion, his heart paled. If the Regulars, or the well-trained Territorials could not survive this new type of warfare, then what chance these lads who had never so much as seen a rifle but four weeks since. He was convinced that these, the first of the volunteers, would also soon join the others. 'God, surely sanity will soon return to the Earth.'

The Captain dearly wished, that for a while, at least, he could be back in England. It would have been so, but the powers that ruled upon such matters had decided that this poor unfortunate Company of innocent newcomers needed a commander with experience, so he had been asked to

164

stay. Without realising why, he agreed. He dearly missed his often-travelled Herefordshire hills, delighting the eye on their journey towards their larger brothers, the Black Mountains of Brecon. He wondered if he would ever see his daughter who had come into the world just two weeks after he had left for France He also deeply missed his dear friend Charlie Sorley. This surreal day, played out upon this Gothic stage by actors too soon to be ghosts, provided just the backdrop for the poem that dear Charles has written to him a few days previously.

> *'On marching men, on.*
> *To the gates of death with song.*

Try as he might he could not recall any other lines other than the last.

> *'So be merry, so be dead.'*

All about him, as he trod towards these friendly men who were his enemies, he was surrounded by merriment. Charles wrote of the 'merry dead', until now it was a concept that he could not understand. Perhaps here, in this place, against this bleak backdrop, this demonstration of fraternisation, he could grasp what his dear friend was trying to express.

Charles, like he, had come over with the first flowering from Albion. He had seen, experienced and given witness to much the same as himself. His words were much more profound than 'eat, drink and be merry, for tomorrow we die': of that he was sure. The contented dead, both glad and happy? How true in a place where death was your constant companion. How true also, it could seem, death coming as a visitor, bringing release from the eternal ceaseless torment that was the lot of those on the Western Front.

Boredom, discomfort, the ever present fear of the most horrendous death. Truly many seemed to welcome an instantaneous death, the like which came from a sniper's bullet. He had heard it so expressed himself, more than once. Yet to find words to convey this to others, to have contemplated it so deeply, that it becomes possible to give them expression on paper, that is surely another matter altogether. Poor Charles, to be so melancholy. He hoped, he prayed, that his friend would make it home.

His mind was drawn out of its meanderings; decisions had to be made. He was in the company of the good Lieutenant Thorpe, a man, he was sure, who would be careful of men's lives. Attendant with him was this extraordinary literary Corporal, even more so, for he was from the working classes. It was this man's illusory speech that had brought him to his own musings. Three men, of such difference of background and persuasion, each bringing an element of perspective to the day, a day that, in years to come, would seem fanciful, incredulously contrasting against the generally accepted pitiless conduct of affairs.

Nonchalantly they strolled towards the centre of no-man's-land, careful to avoid the wire, the remains of the unburied dead, to meet with these representatives of the enemy, hoping to formalise this one day's respite from conflict. Not one of them realised, or, if they did so, expressed the fact that they had no formal permission from above for this activity, it was an unspoken, mutually agreed task, they were set upon.

Rapidly approaching the three men were the same German officers Billy had met the previous evening. This time it was the Company Commander that was first addressed.

"Compliments of the season Captain, to your men also"

"Why, thank you sir. I trust both you and your men are well."

The irony of these opening exchanges was not lost on Billy. After all, for every moment of each day, since war had been declared between the Nations, these officers represented nothing but their leader's trading of insults and the desire to destroy one the other. In spite of all this precedence, contradicting the possibility of such civil exchanges and seasonal salutations, this extraordinary event was unravelling before Billy's eyes. Germans and British went back and forth vigorously shaking hands, whilst ever more soldiers came to join the throng.

The Company Captain and the senior German officer were fraternising wonderfully, the Englishman smoking a large potent cigar woven in Hamburg, his counterpart enjoying the first of a packet of Senior Service that was now creating a subtle bulge in his tunic pocket. Additionally, Lieutenant Thorpe had been divested of two further packets of Players and, in turn, was boasting the possession of ten rather handsome German cheroots. Flasks containing Schnapps and bottles of whisky were surreptitiously exchanged, mysteriously disappearing as quickly as they had emerged.

After ten minutes or so a regimental Padre came upon the scene. He also was not averse in greeting the Germans and after a short while whispered a suggestion in the Captain's ear.

"Would it not be a civilised and Christian act to bury our dead that have lain here so long in no-man's-land. Surely, while we are peacefully enjoying a respite from enemy action, we can find time to inter them, pay our respects and commend them to Almighty God?"

The Captain relayed these sentiments to his German counterpart, who softly consulted with his subordinates.

"Of course Captain, perhaps we could make up a joint burial party. We could inter our lost heroes in parallel lines at an agreed spot in the centre of no-mans-land as you call it. We could then both honourably agree to desist from shelling that particular spot, make it a mutually recognised sanctified patch of land unused by either side for any advantage."

Confirmation came from the Captain.

"I agree, an extremely civilised proposal. Padre, you could officiate for the burial of both sides could you not?"

"Of course Captain, God does not consider the nationality of the souls of men who have flown to him. I shall be honoured to give all the dead a Christian blessing, German and British alike. I shall go forthwith to prepare all that is required."

Having satisfactorily concluded his negotiations, the Regimental Padre, the Reverend David Railton, turned back towards the British lines to gather the necessary items for battlefield burial. Meanwhile the officers of both sides organised the collection and preparation of the pitiful remains of the 'happy dead', and where possible identify them, record and register their names for forwarding to Regimental HQ.

Men of both sides worked shoulder to shoulder using trenching tools to dig the graves. Others had the foul responsibility of collecting the corpses. Some bodies were relatively new and, in the cold weather, had not deteriorated unduly, still commanding the appearance of human beings. Others, being out in no-man's-land for several weeks, had decomposed to not much more than skeletons, grotesque in their contortions. Additionally there were the pieces and parts of bodies that had been denied life through shellfire or whose lifeless forms, had been shattered by later explosions.

In all over a hundred bodies, which could be identified, were gathered together, more than sixty of them British. Others, through their uniforms were at least recognisable in their nationality and regiment, if not in any personal fashion. There were others though, shards of men, limbs, torsos, which gave forth not a clue to personal recognition. These were gathered, as collections in sandbags, to be buried in a joint mass grave, at the end of both rows of identified dead. For them David Railton had prepared a cross upon which had been etched the saddest, yet paradoxically, most hopeful of inscriptions.

Here buried, lie the remains of soldiers of the Great War.
Known only to God. Surely, he shall find them.

Crafted for the remaining dead were crosses of varying quality, having been constructed by several different men from both sides. Some had a name carved upon them, others just their nationality perhaps with their regiment also identified. The day had become grey, the mist, in its dilution, rising to obscure the sun. The landscape grew colourless, cold, damp, in totality, reflective of sombre gravity, as if mother Earth Herself was about to join, clothed in mourning for all these lost young men.

As there were more British than German dead, some of the enemy made their way over to the side where Billy and his comrades were toiling to complete the required number of graves for the British fallen. A young

German Corporal found himself assisting Billy to excavate a grave. In halting English he articulated his thoughts.

"The dead are the enemy of no one. A dead soldier, no matter what his origin, is a lost comrade. Tomorrow, have no doubt, we shall be enemies once again, for no force can stop Germany striving towards her rightful place of greatness upon the world stage. But, here and now, the immortal dead offend none except in their unacknowledged state of exposure. They aid or attempt to obstruct none. Here they lie, frozen in the form where they met death. English and German, both are superior races, descendants of a joint ancestry. Far above the rest, both our races excel in courage, the craft of warfare and the science that drives our ambitions. For this reason we shall share the world, each possessing great empires. Our armies, our navies and now our airforces shall conquer the World, sharing the spoils of war, fairly, taking the lands of the inferior nations. That is our destiny."

Billy stopped digging, listening spellbound to the oratory of his German helper.

"You think this war a good thing?"

"Certainly, war purifies, allows the strong to eradicate or subdue the weak, to dominate those of inferior race. You British know this all too well, Africa, India, The Caribbean, wherever you stamp your mark."

Billy studied the soldier who voiced such a powerful, if frightening message. He was slight of build, less tall than himself, displaying a well-trimmed waxed moustache. Having finished his hypothesising, unbegrudgingly, without complaint he went back to the task of gravedigging with a methodical, almost mechanical, zeal, completing his task with a virtually religious attention to detail. He carved out the corners with architectural accuracy; his sides were fashioned perfectly perpendicular in manner, allowing the base to be of the same dimension as the surface. Billy had stood over the Corporal as he finished the task wondering how it could be that a man professing such views as he had heard, could take so much care in forming the last resting place of an avowed enemy. He concluded, the Corporal was sincere in his homage that the dead of war, no matter of what side, was a fallen comrade one to the other.

The task finished, Billy offered his hand to the German. It was accepted gladly. As the Corporal gained the same height as himself, their eyes met, less than a foot separating them. Billy's gaze became transfixed. It was as if the German could hypnotise him just by merely staring at him with his deep bottomless dark brown irises. Without further word, the Corporal offered a pristinely executed salute, did an about turn and returned to his comrades.

The excavations had continued for more than an hour, over one hundred and thirty graves had been dug, each in straight parallel lines.

168

Finally, men were placing individual corpses into their last resting place and the relevant cross was driven into the ground above them. The larger excavation had been filled with the unidentified body parts. All was ready for David Railton to conduct affairs.

The Reverend Padre had returned, having changed into his Anglican robes. A number of other Company Captains had accompanied him, together with the Brigade's Colonel. This eminent party came up to their German counterparts and all saluted in proper fashion, formally shaking hands with no small talk taking place. A brief, whispered conversation took place between the two most senior officers resulting in a formal line of men being made either side of the parallel graves. The atmosphere was now much more sombre, as if the arrival of the senior officers had changed matters. Looking across to the German lines, Billy could not help but notice that the German Corporal whom he had conversed with was now firmly stationed centre stage among the German hierarchy as if he were a natural member of their company. 'How strange', he thought, then he remembered those hypnotic eyes and a deep unfathomed sensation of disquiet fell upon him.

Lieutenant Thorpe interrupted his mental meandering.

"Corporal, could you please order up an honour guard along our side of the line. At the double, if you will, officer commanding wants to proceed forthwith. I want the men to act with all due solemnity, no undignified behaviour, understood?"

"Yes sir, of course sir!"

The funeral service was conducted with all correctness, full of sober emotion and dignity, complimenting the bleak landscape, and providing a certain reverence to the pathetic remains of what were once men in their appeal for Almighty God to take them to his bosom.

David Railton began the service, using the prayer book, which had already given so much service in a war yet young. The Germans had found a young Lutheran Pastor and had hurriedly brought him up from an earlier Christmas service behind the lines. He, like so many of the educated Germans, spoke good English and his prayer book mirrored much of the content of its Anglican counterpart. Both volumes contained all the Psalms, from which each read.

'Der Herr is mein Hirt; mir wird nichs mangeln.
Er weidet mich auf einer grunen Aue:
Er fuhnt mich zum frishen Wasser.'

As the two Padres had agreed the first three verses of the 23rd Psalm were read in German. David Railton took over at the beginning of the fourth. In this valley of cratered shadows, this vale of death, of evil, of apparent Godforsakenness, the Psalmists words echoed, in all its pathos, away from the huddled group way beyond no-man's-land, to the reaches of Heaven's gate. The surety of God's divine loving presence, his fathomless power of forgiveness, came returning to settle upon those who chose to believe. Finally the Psalm spoke of enemies sitting down to eat, one with the other, with God's blessing descending upon then with great promise.

> 'Surely goodness and mercy shall follow me
> All the days of my life: and I shall dwell
> In the house of the Lord forever.

Billy, brimmed full with the pity of the occasion; the Germans on one side of the lines of graves, the British on the other. He knew he was witnessing a unique event. He looked around him, noting how deep in thought each one of those gathered appeared. With helmets and caps hanging before them, heads bowed, friend and foe alike, it was as if brothers had come home for a family funeral. It was incomprehensible, a manifestation incompatible with this war. He knew, observing all about him, that he would not forget this day, more he would record its elements for posterity so that, one day, people could agree that this war possessed the occasional spark of God given grace which displayed itself in terms of humanity between sworn enemies.

Now came the committal, enunciated by The Reverend Railton and comprised of words all of them strove to believe in.

> "In sure and certain knowledge of the resurrection of the body
> and life everlasting: Amen.

A bugler sounded out 'The Last Post', German officers came forward to sprinkle earth upon the British dead as well as their own, which was likewise reciprocated by the British. Thus, the service came to an end, a joint plea from friend and foe alike, commending to God those who had perished, so wantonly laid waste. Many that day also fervently pleaded with their maker to forgive the heinous acts they had enacted upon their enemies.

As the men began to disperse, having been dismissed in a formal manner, one of the German officers stepped forward to present the senior British officer with a pennant from the sixteenth Bavarians. Embarrassed by this act of generosity, this symbol of friendship, the Colonel quickly folded a Union Flag, which had acted as an altar, and gave it to his counterpart. The German officer bowed, saluted and thanked him before turning to leave the scene.

The sun was now as high as it would climb that day, the time having just passed midday. Belatedly, it broke out through the mist, bringing a soft, welcome, though warmless glow upon the land. The men formed pale shadows as they speedily filled in the graves, British and German alike completing the task for a fallen warrior without any consideration of identity or nationality, the poor recipient being simply the object of belated charity.

Once again men milled round, mingling irrespective of which trench they had scrambled from. Conversation was wide-ranging extending to sport, motorcars and families at home, this last subject being attended by displays of photographs. A soldier would be asked his opinion upon the likeness of a wife or child, which would always find a positive response. The irony seemed to escape both parties, that soon the soldier being asked his opinion would be trying his utmost to turn their loved ones and offspring into widows and orphans. It seemed as if the men would find any excuse to extend this period of fraternisation. They spoke of football in the main, if conversation of family had dried up, anything but the war.

Billy spent his time observing the scene with mixed emotions. He knew that on the morrow he would be asked to go and kill as many Germans as he could and he would do so, it was his duty. Yet there was surely a higher allegiance. How could he keep to both loyalties? It was a dilemma that he would never fully come to terms with.

"Corporal Thomas."

Billy turned to see that once again he was staring into the abyss of those piercing eyes that were the commanding possession of the strange German Corporal.

"Wonderful was it not? The comradeship of the common soldier is a magnificent thing, prepared to toil and struggle together, each reliant on the other, even to the gates of death. It is mindful of Gotterdammerung."

"Gotterdammerung?"

"It translates into your English as 'Twilight of the Gods.' It is the title of a Wagnerian opera."

"Oh Wagner, 'The Flying Dutchman', 'Tristan', 'Valkurie'. Yes I agree, all around wherever you look, it is all very Wagnerian."

The Corporal's expression displayed great pleasure at Billy's knowledge, and not a little curiosity.

"And where are you from my English Corporal?"

Billy was not sure he should answer but then considered it to be of little importance.

"Glossop, a small town called Glossop."

"Ah the edges of Derbyshire, by the pass, well protected by the Pennines."

Billy was astonished and he could not help but make comment.

"You display a detailed knowledge of English geography Corporal. How come you know so much of my country?"

"I was there for about six months, two years ago, in Liverpool working in the docks. During this time I studied the important routes across the land, rivers, mountains, passes. They were all of great interest to me."

"And why such interest?"

A masked smile came across the Corporal's face, the only time his severe expression ever left him, whilst in Billy's presence.

"Well Corporal, you never know, I might need to get an army over there one day. I have a vast memory for maps, particularly routes that an army might use. I am full of intrigue for such matters."

"Fat chance of that ever happening Corporal, better get back to your dreams. German troops will never set foot on English soil, never."

The German considered, 'such defiance from an English volunteer infantryman. In future it would be better not to speak English or to even admit that he had visited the place. This Englishman was plainly full of courage and determination. It increased his admiration for the Island race of fellow Aryans. People, as he should be treated with much care. He now had no doubts left; Britain was a land of heroic men being led by midgets. How alike the two nations, Germany and England.' He felt the need to extend his philosophic concept of mutual racial superiority to this gallant Englishman.

"You are correct of course Corporal. There is no need at all for our two nations to be at war the one with the other. I feel our destiny is one of friendship and co-operation where together we have our rightful place as the rulers of the World. Germany and England, twin master races."

The more the German spoke, the more uncomfortable Billy felt. It was as if the man's plausible tongue was drawing him into a web as surely as the spider entices the fly. Implacable intent, coupled with persuasive oratory had confused him, he felt enticed towards the man's argument. In truth, although he was one of the first to feel so, within a generation millions would find themselves attached to this rhetoric, giving birth to far devastating effect than even this gigantic struggle was producing.

Thankfully, so many distractions were occurring that the short spell was broken. Billy almost fell back considering the extent to which the words of the Corporal had become impregnated in his mind 'twin master races,' how grand that sounded. Then he thought of little Belgium, the images he had of that poor country and the messianic words ceased to sear his brain. Of one thing he was now sure. If most of the Germans were like this one, then this war was going to be protracted. For now he felt he had to get away from this unholy individual, in him he sensed an evil more powerful than anything he had experienced before.

"Well Corporal, I had better be getting back to my men. For me this has been a most unusual conversation. It is my hope that all goes well with you."

The two men shook hands. Once again their eyes met, the German's stare almost paralysing the Englishman. They parted each to their separate ways. One was puzzled, discomforted; feeling profound unease, the other sensing triumph, yet concerned to get back to his regiment. After all he should not have been here. His 16th Bavarian Infantry Reserve Regiment was at this moment, belatedly, resting; he should have been with it.

He was satisfied however; his curiosity had been fulfilled. Here, on the Western Front, he had come face to face with a real warrior, one, whom in other circumstances, he would proudly have stood shoulder to shoulder with, in battle. A pity for the British, that such courageous men were so badly led. How fortunate for Germany that it was so, heroes in the trenches sacrificed by pathetic generalship. He often suspected that such was also the case in the German ranks, one day he would do something about that, then surely Germany would be the greatest force ever known to history.

War was a holy manifestation, to be fought one soldier flexing his courage and strength against the other. That is why he was so opposed to the use of undignified weapons such as gas. War was great and glorious, a trial of National, racial superiority. Gas killed everything; there was no dignity or glory in the use of gas. Should he ever be in command of Germany's forces he would never sanction its use except, perhaps, in the eradication of inferior races. For the first and last time he would warn a fellow Aryan of a coming new weapon, one of which he thoroughly disapproved of. Stroking his moustache, he entered the communication trench.

The Corporal would survive the war. He would be wounded and gassed but he would survive. A quarter of a century from now he would be gazing out towards Albion's shores at the head of an even mightier army than Germany possessed in 1914. His long urging to re-trample his feet upon her land would never find fruition, nor would any German warrior cross her ancient soil except as a prisoner. He would bring terrible fire and storm to her cities from out of the air but through all this Britain would remain firm and steadfast. Instead of surrendering to his hordes and becoming a vassal state, she would be transformed into a beacon of light, to become the platform from which his destruction would eventually come.

Likewise Billy walked towards his trench. Evidence of the continuing fraternisation was all around him. Jimmy had blown up his football, the very one which had been made from the pig, all those years ago. It was being kicked backwards and forwards from Englishman to German and back again. He joined in but his heart was not in it. The German Corporal had filled him with an unutterable, indescribable sense of foreboding, which could not be rationalised. More, he could not come to terms with the urging that had come to him whilst they were conversing, that of wanting to run the little fiend through with a bayonet, the one he had hidden upon him.

True, he felt ashamed with himself for almost betraying his word of peace, though, in paradox, he also felt that he had failed to undertake a service to his country. Those eyes, those evil, stern, illuminated, hypnotic eyes. Surely they would stay with him for a long, long time, no doubt of that. Somehow, reflected in that one man's philosophy, portrayed by his eyes, etched by his words, his very persona, came all the elements that brings war and gives it an insatiable dynamic. This was one man who could not get enough of conflict, death and what he would call glory.

One other thing about the man puzzled him. As they were walking apart the Corporal had shouted at him.'

"Corporal! If you ever see a sulphur coloured cloud coming towards you from our trenches, urinate in a cloth and quickly place it on your face. It could save your life."

Billy considered it to be the last outburst of a madman. In reality it was a legitimate warning from a future megalomaniac who saw war as an ancient chivalric pursuit where men of equal stature fought with god-like valour, not through the noxious use of chemicals. The Corporal was convinced that in such a test of stamina and courage the German races would always triumph. Such devious weaponry as some of the inferior races would stoop to held no place in the German armoury, he would never sanction their usage.

For now his warning fell upon deaf ears, yet, at the right time, they would be recalled and would save the life of Corporal Billy Thomas and many of his section. Other thoughts now entered the mind of the Englishman, brought to mind by his witness to the home made football now being used to entertain both sides of the great divide.

Billy recalled the day he became part of the death of the pig that was at this very moment supplying the sport for those who were kicking the ball. In truth, it had sickened him. He remembered how the blood overflowed the bowl designed to catch it, how it stained the trench, its entrails exposed for the world to see. Yet, its death was of use. It fed a number of families and gave so much pleasure to two young boys. Now it had found its way to a new place of slaughter, being kicked around by friend and foe alike. 'Poor pig,' he thought, 'poor pig. This coming night Billy was to write a sonnet to the unfortunate animal in an attempt to assuage his guilt, his discomforted conscience.

So passed Christmas day on the Western Front. It had been peaceful, almost enjoyable, in its expression of mutual friendship. Memories of those who survived the ending of the conflict would, later, be full of this one inexplicable day. The day peace came 'On the morning of Christ's Nativity.'

CHAPTER 11

Do but behold yond poor and starved band,
And your fair show shall suck away their souls,
Leaving them but the shales and husks of men.

William Shakespeare. Henry the Fifth

Billy Thomas came to write his eloquent, haunting, classically constructed poetry initially through his experience of Christmas 1914 on the Western Front. It can be noted that, uniquely among the war poets, the young man from the foothills of the Derbyshire Peak District never challenges the goodness of God. Rather the war seems to have enhanced his faith in his maker; it is man himself whose principles are brought into question.

His experiences of the unbearable conditions of trench life are stark. However, these stem from his recording of man's response to his fellow sufferer, rather than descriptive catalogues of rat infestation, corpses littering the landscape or the mud. The damp and cold he certainly experienced, along with all the rest of the tormented who graced the caverns between no-man's-land but it is the men themselves that he is concerned with, not the elements surrounding them.

Within his work can be found sensitivities and references that give credence to his wealth of reading and the undoubted knowledge that stemmed from it. Finally his words are forever fortified by his faith in God, it is unswerving, it never questions his earlier formed beliefs.

Like many of his contemporaries his work covers a very small span of time, just eighteen months or so. Sally, his beloved Sally, was the recipient of scores of letters and literary fragments; during the time he was training or stationed on the Western Front. Likewise, his mother received regular commentaries on his views from the trenches though it appears that he never sent any of his poetic works directly to her. This form of expression he kept exclusively for his Sally.

Except for a few works that Sally carefully selected and are published within this volume, they are not to be given into the public domain until a hundred years from 11th November 1920 when at 11.00am copies will be released on the steps of The Imperial War Museum, London. This may appear to be a dramatic gesture, but it is what Sally Thomas wished. Together with collaborative papers from Colonel Gell and Victor Grayson they will very possibly alter present historical perspectives, and understanding on the events which led to the outbreak of the great conflict, life in the trenches and matters surrounding the entombment of the Unknown Warrior.

Sally Thomas treasured her husband's letters and poetry, especially the poetry. In her later years she came to wish that a selection would be published and become popular. It led to this writer being given private access to all her papers, which she kept in twelve ancient Cadbury biscuit tins. She chose this writer, or so she said, because he was a descendant of Gideon Livingstone, who was a man she trusted above all others.

It was on January 8th 1915 that Sally received her first poetic verse from Billy Thomas. 'Poor Pig' brought tears to her eyes. She profoundly understood the analogy, the paradox between empathy, necessity and brutality, which is brought together in the work. After the war she showed it to Uncle Frank Potter who read it with deep understanding, having witnessed and participated in the event that it refers to, from a first hand viewpoint.

Having read them many times, the words became planted, so etched in his mind, that he referred to them years later. Towards the end of his own life he confessed how it so affected him that, 'from my first reading onwards, I never again ate pork.' Jimmy Jones and his father both gave witness to the impact 'Pig' brought to them. Jimmy saw the poem as a graphic attempt to relay the ghastliness of trench life to those who could never visualise modern warfare but could identify with the brutal death of a poor helpless pig.

Sally considered its contemporary publication but was dissuaded by the local editor of the Chronicle on the grounds that it could affect the sales of what was a completely home grown meat. The good woman accepted his argument, which is a shame for it affected her attitude towards later approaches on publication. A crass editor, afraid of offending his meat advertisers, lost to this country, for more than three generations, the poetic works of an expressive, philosophic, Great War Poet. Billy Thomas had important points to reveal and stern warnings to make that should have been offered for publication much earlier. One of his pieces in particular which, if it had come sooner to public attention, might, possibly have had a profound affect on subsequent world affairs.

'The Little Corporal', could have become a work of great historic importance. Alas it was not to be. The poetic work found its way back into one of the biscuit tins to accompany the rest of her catalogue of astounding documents. Imagine the possible impact if such a work could have been placed into the hands of Winston Churchill prior to the Munich crisis for example. A stark warning from a past hero being given new life from the lips of the great crusader against fascism, could have helped to open the closed eyes and ears of those who preached the then established British policy of appeasement.

A further poem, which is of undoubted historical importance, is his 'Two Thieves.' During the early days of the war a story came out of the trenches which quickly gained credence with the British public due to the hysterical manner in which it was portrayed by the National Press. It entailed the accusation that the Germans had taken a captured British soldier and crucified him to a barn door.

This writer does not know how true this was; it is a matter beyond the realms of this volume. It is however the point of some research being currently carried out by a colleague. What is not in debate is the fact that it created an outburst of mass indignation at the time. It was displayed by the media as another example of the depths of bestiality to which the Germans could stoop.

If the full truth of crucified soldiers were to have become known during the time of the conflict, there would have been a sustained outcry in Britain. There were over two hundred such cases but it was the British who perpetrated them. What is more astounding is the sad truth that the Army executed this act upon its own men as an example to others. The sin which was most commonly the catalyst for such punishment was one where the victim had been caught asleep on watch. Billy was a witness to one such act and its tragic outcome, hence the poem.

Unless the reader was to think that this assertion is an exaggerated one merely based upon one man's perception a copy of an illustration instructing exactly how the punishment was to be carried out appears at the end of this volume. It is fully authenticated, it emanates from secret War Office papers. Apparently, the High Command was concerned that the structure of this particular punishment had got out of hand on a number of occasions. The purpose of the illustrated Government manual was to regulate matters. If the poem is read, together with the letter from Billy Thomas that also appears within the body of this book and combined with an examination of the War Office instruction, then no conclusion can be formed other than such brutality as reported by an outraged press certainly was a feature of the war. Unfortunately it was their own side that was mostly responsible for such acts.

Billy's Easter poem, 'Emmaus Road' is in complete contrast to the above. He wrote it in the form of three sonnets carefully constructed in the manner of John Milton. It stems from his love of Henry Francis Lyte's ageless Hymn 'Abide With Me', which as stated elsewhere, obtains its inspiration from the Gospel of St. Luke. It is also from St Luke that I have taken part of a verse and chosen it as the title of the small selection of his poems, which appear at the end of this book.

Billy came to write the work one morning early in March 1915. A letter had come from Sally in which she described the singing of his favourite hymn in Chapel the previous Sunday. To Billy it was a wonderfully scripted letter. It contained not one word of pessimism or reference of the War. The letter simply spoke of her love for him and of memories and grateful reflections upon their times together. Sally had crafted it so well, she missed him, loved him and was waiting, living each moment upon his return. She blessed him, thanked him for her wonderful memories and said goodnight with an almost erotic tone.

What a contrast it was this lovely letter, here in his hand, to the recent events that had so recently unravelled on the Western Front. The day before the letter had arrived; little Tommy Smith was killed. He was the second youngest of his section, being just a couple of months older than was Albert. It was only a month since that he had obtained the legal age to be in the Army. The poor lad was so urgently in need of relieving himself that he forgot to take the usual basic precautions. A German sniper's 'dum dum' bullet almost ripped his head from off his shoulders.

No Padre being available, it fell to Billy to collect the pieces, put them together after a fashion and to bury the lad, with as Christian a service as could be mustered. Perhaps he had not officiated too badly for afterwards many of the men came up to him to tell him he had 'done a nice job' had 'done the lad proud, poor Blighter.'

Wrexham George summed up the thoughts of the section many of whom, though by now thoroughly battle hardened, shamelessly and openly wept for the poor mite.

"A shame that's what it is, should 'ave still been at school or at home with his Mam, why the little soul was no bigger than a tanner rabbit."

These words from the normally jovial Welshman haunted and tormented the NCO who attempted to find consolation from such painful duties and scenes by reading from the scriptures. Consequently it was no coincidence that he had been deeply exploring the New Testament when Sally's letter arrived. Later when seeking further solace from St. Luke, the idea came to him and the three sonnets were composed in an evening.

On Easter Sunday 1915, in the Independent Chapel in Fazackerley Street, Glossop, the Reverend Gideon Livingstone read the verses aloud from the pulpit to a packed congregation. Those who later recalled the event stated that there was not an eye devoid of tears. When the Pastor finished the recitation a spontaneous applause broke out. Later Sally took the pages back from her Pastor and, like the rest; they went back into a biscuit tin. They were not destined to be read by another Human Being for over seventy years.

It was now almost three months since the Christmas truce, through the most miserably damp ridden, cold shriven of winters, Billy and his section manned their trench, only occasionally obtaining relief. Many of the men had succumbed to bad chest complaints. Most had various debilitating levels of trench foot. Sometimes their condition became so bad that they had to be excused their watch, sometimes for days. This led to more pressure being placed upon the others who, though weary beyond belief, were deemed fit for duty.

Forays into no-man's-land, by both sides, reconnoitring each other's lines had led to new bodies being strewn over the disputed battlefield. The Christmas day's Christian spirit of brotherhood and friendship had long since vanished. Once again it had become a war being fought to the bitter end. It had, without doubt, developed into a fight of attrition, dog eat dog, not possessing a grain of mercy within its hellish bowels. In short, for all the participants, life was Hell, frozen over it was that cold, but here a participant had more than a glimpse of Hell, of that there was no doubt.

Morale amongst the men had become very low; gradually the desperate conditions had ground them down. Billy had never known them to be so sick at heart. The bleakest of winters, followed by unceasing rain had brought the condition of the trenches to such an inhospitable, pitiful state that it was dangerous to venture far. Water was now lapping more than a foot above the duckboards that in theory should have acted as a sump guarding against exactly what had now occurred.

Outside of the main walkways a man could slip and drown within seconds, disappearing without trace beneath the morass of mud. Perversely, it was also the mud, which made it impossible for either side to attempt any large-scale attack of any kind. The condition of no-man's-land forbade any manoeuvres that would have possibly broken the stalemate. Such was the state of the ground between the sides that it could have swallowed up a whole regiment of men without a trace. Life just dragged on and on with a seemingly endless monotony

Additionally, the incessant shelling, which was gaining momentum by the day added another dimension to the elements which strove to deprive men of life. Life, which for some, had indeed gone beyond endurance, became no longer to be borne. Two suicides had been rumoured to have happened. The circumstances were quickly hushed up but the gossip continued to proliferate none the less.

At long last, the entire Battalion was taken out of the line, initially just for a few days, but this became extended. The respite was welcome, for these were men who like so many of their fellow unfortunates were coming to the end of their endurance. Their state of bedragglement had become so stark that Billy could not but recall and compare the look of the men he had relieved those few short months ago, just before Christmas. He remembered how appalled he felt at the time when he, fresh faced, marched to the front. Now the rolls were reversed. His men were marching away. What must their relief be thinking?

They were given leave to Amiens where those who wished were given rubber 'Johnnies.' The medical orderly was most precise on the matter.

"If you go to a Brothel, don't go without one or it will seem later that you are peeing razor blades. If anyone comes back here with a dose of the Clap I shall personally place the offender on report. You have been warned."

Billy did not take him up on the offer, Jimmy Jones neither. They did not wish to have the company of such women. Billy had desire for only one girl and Jimmy said that he would wait for such things until the right one came along. This did not however, stop them conjecturing upon the function of a 'Johnny.' It proved to be a source of intense puzzlement to them for some considerable time to come.

At the end of March new orders came to the Battalion. As a result Billy and his companions in strife found themselves back in holes in the ground near a place called 'Loos'. The joke, said only half in jest, was that it got its name because of the stink. It soon obtained a nickname that was frowned upon by the officers. Wrexham George got away with it by calling the place 'Ty Bach.' In truth the weather was becoming drier and warmer, bringing inevitable consequences to the war torn landscape, which, in reality had become the largest and most unkempt cemetery in Europe.

What the occupants of this spread-eagled necropolis did not know was that their masters were preparing a number of new diversions for their entertainment. The first had already occurred a little way off from where they were placed, near to a village called 'Neuve Chapelle'. There, three days of fighting left over twenty-three thousand casualties on both sides and resulted in a British advance of six hundred yards over a two-mile front. A man's life destroyed for every ten square yards of territory restored to the French Republic. General Joffre was grateful, General Haigh was overwhelmed with pride in his achievement.

This great feat of arms was soon followed up with further likewise achievements, at Hill 60, Ypres, Aubers Ridge and Festubert. On each occasion the result was similar to Neuve Chapelle. A small amount of the sacred ground of France was recovered or successfully defended at a similar cost in ruined lives. One man for every ten square yards.

A letter had come from Sally telling Billy that his Uncle Frank and her father now jointly owned an allotment. It came to them following a government idea that families should have such plots of land to grow vegetables. Their plot was no less than a fifth of an acre, almost a thousand square yards! Billy felt like replying that the same piece of land before him contained a harvest of almost one hundred corpses. Of course he wrote no such thing, but he discussed his thoughts with Jimmy Jones who later recalled the conversation.

Against this background of intermittent yet spiteful engagements the year of 1915 slowly progressed. The nature of these localised but extremely costly Battles at last brought home to all the combatants, from Private to General, the indisputable evidence that this war, entered into with such high hopes, was going to be a protracted and bloody affair.

At Verdun the flower of French youth was being bled white from a conflict which appeared to find no resolution. Men were simply poured into the Battle as grains of sand through the slim neck of an hourglass and were never seen again. Likewise, on the German side, men flooded from the other side, again, simply to disappear. Gravity was being defied; the hourglass was being emptied both from above and below. All the grains, each representing the life of a young man, fell towards the centre and vanished. More than this, it was being constantly fed. Swarms of condemned souls, emanating as ants from the gigantic anthills that were France and Germany, unceasingly gravitated into the bottleneck to ensure the flow never ceased or lost momentum.

So 1915 progressed, by the beginning of September, the War on the Western Front was as far from being resolved as it had been in January. Both sides were now deeply dug in. The dry months of late spring and summer had allowed for massive improvements and greater complexity in the system of trenches. Men had now adapted to this existence of living as rodents deep underground in burrows. They were living more as moles than men, scampering from one 'Glory-Hole' to another.

It was to be at Loos that the British High Command decided, under great pressure from the French, to make its final effort of the year. General Haigh was already planning a massive attack for June 1916, one, which would ensure the final defeat of Germany. However he was also compelled to display British willingness to relieve the French at Verdun. Hence the Battle of Loos.

Corporal Billy Thomas and his section had just 'stood down.' Except for the usual two on watch, they were eating their breakfast. This day they were blessed with both bacon and eggs together with ample fried bread and tea. The experiences of the year had welded them into a close knit 'band of brothers' almost a 'happy breed of men.' Truthfully there was not one among them who did not hanker after home but it was never spoken of openly. They had come to possess a comradeship, seldom leaving each other to gain fellowship elsewhere. They knew that, one-day, it could be the man standing next to them who would possibly save their life. Therefore they reasoned, 'best to keep close by.'

The year, thus far, had been relatively kind to the men of the section. Except for poor young Tommy Smith, they had suffered no further casualties, not a single scratch. Life had been one of a few weeks living in the trenches interspersed by short periods of leave in Amiens. Despite the best endeavours of the medical orderly a couple of the men had caught 'a dose.' It made life difficult for them, constantly having to go for a very painful pee. The orderly had not exaggerated when he had described the action of relieving oneself as passing razorblades. The rest of the section saw their predicament as a source for levity, but each man privately resolved not to embark on the kind of pleasures that brought such consequences to the recipient.

It was September the Twentieth, a warm, quiet, late summer's day a runner came hurriedly into their canteen billet.

181

"Corporal Thomas, is there ha Corporal Thomas 'ere."

"I am he Private. What is so important that you hurry so?"

"Beggin' tha pardin' Corporal but you are a needed at Company 'eadquarters prompt like."

The runner who came from a small Surrey village was new to France, being a recent casualty replacement, the previous occupant having received a 'Blighty' just a few days ago. He was still more nervous of giving a message to the intended recipient than he was of making the actual run to deliver it. He would surely soon learn to reverse his priorities or else he would not last long in his chosen profession.

"I shall be along right away Private."

"Right o' Corporal."

The runner was off, he had to repeat this message many more times down the line.

"Sommat is most definitely hafoot."

Albert Hadfield was mimicking the poor unfortunate, who had so promptly left them without so much as a by your leave, causing his colleagues to erupt in laughter. The young lad could be such a scream when he wished.

Billy was away for almost an hour. When he came back he had a very grave expression on his face, not a good omen at all.

"What is the matter Corporal Thomas, not like you to look so stern looking is it?"

Wrexham George was speaking for them all; it was not like their Section leader to be so sombre.

"I shall tell you what I can lads. Some of you, four in fact have got to get training in the use of gas, immediately. Four of you need to volunteer right now. As for the rest of us we have got to learn how to use gas masks."

"Gas masks?"

"Yes, gas masks."

"Phew."

"Phew indeed."

Gas had become a dreaded word all along the Western Front that summer. Witnesses to the results of this new ghastly weapon had told the most terrible tales of its effects. The entire skin could be blistered off. You drowned in your own fluids. It took days of agony before some of the poor unfortunates perished. Bullets, bombs and shells were one thing, but gas? It did not bear thinking upon.

"Gas?"

"Gas."

"Phew."

"Phew indeed."

"So what does this gas training entail Corporal?"

"Forty or so cylinders have arrived at Company Headquarters, together with an assortment of valves and pipes. More than that I cannot say except that they are to be implemented in any possible attack, just like the Germans have been using the stuff."

"An attack?"

"Looks like it."

"Phew."

"Phew indeed."

"With gas?"

"Gas."

"This is dangerous stuff."

"We are all to be fully protected with smoke masks, those using the cylinders will get other special clothing as well."

"That's a relief."

"Gas?"

"Gas."

Billy's sombre mood, coupled with the news that he had brought back to the men, had infected the whole section. Gas was the greatest of all fears in this war of countless horrors, an aspect of perverse science, which normal courage could not deal with.

"No doubt we shall be protected, what with these gas masks and all"

"No doubt we shall. What think you Corporal Thomas?"

Billy thought for a moment, he was recalling the words of the strange German that he had met at Christmas.

"Urinate in a cloth and quickly place it over your face, It could save your life."

It was such a strange thing to say. He had referred to a sulphur cloud. No matter what he thought of the Corporal, if this warning was genuine, then it was his duty to tell his men. He would do so when the time came.

Over the next two days, Billy's section, like all the others in the Battalion, dug out a forward position out into No-man's-land. It was provided with a service trench so that easy access could be gained for those who were to man it. Four men had left the section to be trained in the use of gas. When they came back it was with a pair of cylinders equipped with valves and pipes. Thus was the sophistication of the new terror weapon displayed for all to see.

The plan was for the cylinders to be used by pairs of men. The first couple would open the valve of their cylinder once they had checked that the wind was blowing in the correct direction, away from their own trenches. The pipes would be extended ten yards or so further into No-Mans-land, in principle, allowing for the gas to flow over into the enemy trenches and completely incapacitate them. Following on, the British would simply cross over the divide and occupy the enemy trenches which would be full of coughing and spluttering troops, who would be unable to put up a fight.

Two of the three Keen brothers, Peter and James, would be responsible for the first attempt and, in recognition of their particular responsibility, they had been given a set of special protective suits. Billy considered the situation. In his view the strategy was full of anomalies relating to wind direction, dilution in the dispersal of the gas and, finally, reliance in the wind direction. He could recall helping his Uncle Frank start a bonfire on many an occasion. How often did the wind direction change? Sometimes it was as though the smoke followed them to whatever new position he went.

The night before the proposed attack, Billy got the section together. He had formulated his plan. Earlier the section's masks had arrived. Everyone could see how woefully inadequate they were, being merely wads of cotton pads soaked in bicarbonate of soda. When the men had seen them they realised immediately that they would afford little protection. Billy was determined to redress the balance.

"Men it looks to me as though come tomorrow we shall be involved in our first real battle. I know what you are all thinking upon, it is the gas."

The men were all nodding in agreement but they were listening, Corporal Thomas never spoke to them like this without good reason.

"This is going to seem daft to many of you but I for one think that it will work. Take a large piece of cloth, fashion it so that it can go right over your face and keep it by you prior to the battle. Just before you go over take a good pee all over the cloth and put it over you. I believe that the ammonia in your urine will alleviate the effect of any gas that you may inhale.

"Corporal you ain't serious."

"Deadly."

"What us go over the top dressed like I don't know what and breathing in the fumes of our own piss."

"Yes."

"Why?"

"It may save your life."

"Oh."

"Really Corp."

"Really."

"Piss?"

"Yes."

It was Wrexham George who broke the impasse.

"Corporal Thomas, I reckons you been right often as not. If you say piss in a cloth and put it over your head for it will save your life, the wearing a mask dripping with piss is what we does I reckon and lovely it is too."

Many of the troop nodded and to some degree they were reassured. They reasoned that they may be stinking by the end of the day, but at least they would probably live. That night the survival tactics adopted by Billy's section were sent by jungle telegraph up and down the line. Come morning, hundreds of men would be wearing an assortment of urine drenched masks over their faces.

Came the dawn and with it 'stand to.' At five twenty the pairs of cylinder operators were in position in their forward posts. The signal went out for them to release the gas. A further period of forty minutes would elapse before the signal to attack would be sounded. Everyone waited at his position on the fire trench for the order to be given.

Carefully looking over, Billy could see a yellow gas cloud forming. To his relief, it was going away towards the enemy, hopefully to serve two purposes, that of obscuring his vision and also to incapacitate him. Privately he felt an awful sorrow descend upon him, visioning what was going to happen in the German trenches in a few minutes time. 'Lord God be with them for no man deserves such a death as came from inhaling this fiendish substance.'

He was still gazing out into the misted man made cloud when an alarm was triggered in his mind. He could feel a breeze on his face; the gas was beginning to drift back in his direction. It was Uncle Frank's bonfire all over again.

"Gas, gas, gas. Quickly men, the wretched stuff, it's coming our way."

Panic came over the men, already a faint irritable smell was beginning to permeate the air. Yet Billy had trained them well, soon they all had their urine-drenched masks covering their faces.

"What a bloody War this is."

The remark, coming anonymously from behind an improvised lifesaver, summed up the feeling of every man present. Now to add to their woes the enemy artillery opened up. It was accurate to; one shell exploded just thirty yards in front of them. Immediately, Billy realised that the two men in front, letting out the gas, had suffered an almost direct hit. If they had been incapacitated then their gas in an almost pure form would soon be filling up the trench. If that were the case they would all be soon overcome. Even their improvised improvements would not protect them if that happened.

He made his decision; he needed to inspect the situation for himself. He began to go along the communications trench. Halfway along he could see that someone was with him. It was Jimmy Jones.

"No Jimmy go back, no point in two of us going, besides you need to stay with the men and keep their moral fibre intact."

He could see that his words had no effect whatsoever on his friend so he stopped and turned.

"Lance Corporal Jones, go back that is a direct order."

Jimmy was taken by surprise; Billy had never spoken to him in that way before. Startled, he did as he was told. Billy proceeded with caution. Now he began to see that something was very wrong. A yellow mist was all around him. Tightening his improvised life preserver he gained the small redoubt. Lying before him were the two Keen brothers. They were both lying on their backs dead, with the torn shreds of their protective clothing scattered around. Out of their noses, their ears and their mouths came streams of blood. They had both suffered massive concussions from the airblast of the shell and had died immediately.

Billy felt an extraordinary sense of sorrow dawn upon him, only for it to vanish in an instant, for there in front of him, teetering on the top of the crater that was once a strong point, was the gas cylinder emitting its fumes directly down the communication trench. The valve had to be turned off. As he reached the infamous object he could feel his lungs beginning to irritate him. The cylinder was just out of his reach in the most precarious of positions. As he touched it with the tips of his fingers the wretched thing fell on top of him, falling hard against his head and chest. He almost passed out but a certain stubbornness within him gave him the strength not to do so. Struggling with the valve, he managed to turn it off. Knowing that there was nothing that he could do for the Keen brothers he began to crawl back towards his men the pain of his head, chest and lungs growing with each step. Clutching the urine rag to his face he made it back. He was near to collapse, his vision blurred, then he found the darkness.

His section who were all to some degree incapacitated would play no part in the coming Battle of Loos. This was the case for almost three thousand of their colleagues; they had all been poisoned by the crass stupidity of their own commanders and a change in wind direction. Such was the fragility of life on the Western Front in 1915.

CHAPTER 12

Yea, though I walk though the shadow of death
I will fear no evil for thou art with me
Thy rod and thy staff they comfort me.

A Psalm of David No. 23

Spectres surrounded him tormenting, prodding, and spewing out a ghostly substance. Giant ogres possessing tongues, which produced red dribble, mingled with acrid sulphuric fumes, from their mouths. Some of the unspeakable monstrosities were shooting out sheets of searing flames that consumed all who came within their path. Slime was enveloping him dragging him ever further down into the endless pit. He was spinning, falling, leaving the light. Darkness was enveloping his world. It was as if his life's end was approaching.

Then, as the pit approached, suddenly an angel floated towards him, calling his name repeatedly,

"Billy, Billy, Billy."

"Is that you mother?"

The voice was similar, familiar somehow. Perhaps it was Sally. No it was not Sally; the sound of her voice was etched in his mind. Now he knew, it was an angel calling to him. The figure was coming more clearly into focus now. Yes, now he saw her, an angel, dressed in white, pure white. He had died and gone to heaven. The angel was welcoming him to the gates. Yes, he was sure now, this was the entrance to heaven. Having travelled through the land of desolation, this wonderful creature was guiding him through the last potential dangers and pitfalls of his final journey. A brilliant Red Cross streamed into view. She was shaking him, gently, but he was being shaken none the less. It was most uncomfortable.

"Billy, Private Thomas."

No, he did not want to respond. He was tired, his chest burned, his eyes were so sore. The darkness beckoned, comforting, restful, and everlasting. To the darkness he would return.

Yet, the angel insisted upon shaking him bring him from the darkness, awakening him to the light, the pain and the insufferable smell.

"Thomas!"

The voice was louder now, more insistent.

"Thomas! Can you hear me? Thomas!"

It was useless the voice had forced him to respond so he awoke, his senses returning to him. He had left the depths of hell, heaven was not yet ready for him thus the angel displaying her Christian emblem and covered in white had escorted him back to the living world.

"Thomas!"

There, his name again. He felt the need to respond but the attempt merely brought forth a whispering, inaudible in translation.

"Good Corporal Thomas, you are back with us, good. Take it easy you have not had the best of experiences, but you are back with us".

He struggled, surely he was drowning, and he had to reach the surface.

" Easy Corporal easy don't strain yourself everything is all right".

Billy's nose tweaked as it encountered a demonic stench.

"Don't worry about that Corporal Thomas, it is only the Carrel and Dakens solution. Smells terrible does it not? But it is the ointment treatment we have for gas gangrene, which, fortunately you do not have. It is being used on the patient next door".

'Carrel and Dakens, terrible,' thought Billy and then without thinking further he muttered his sentiments in a hoarse voice that he did not recognise.

"He's like a badly cleaned latrine on a hot summers day".

"That's the ammonia, ammonia and chlorine".

The angel was coming ever clearer into focus, a few more seconds, allowing Billy's mind to clear and the realisation dawned. The angel was a VAD, a nurse in an immaculate white uniform displaying the cross of her profession. He had awoken in a military hospital. The trenches had gone and with it hell, at least for the moment. He had been saved for another day. But the smell, god the smell it was simply awful. It reminded him of stale baby's nappies.

Nurse Grace Bufford, soon to be promoted to sister, quickly evaluated that this young soldier was possibly one of the few fortunate ones to come out of Loos, that terrible battle recently fought where the infernal Germans had used a terrible noxious gas. For some reason the gas had not penetrated this young soldier's lungs as intensely as some of the others, especially those poor Canadians that Dorothy Nicole had told her of. They had died from drowning as their own bodily fluids invaded their lungs. Dorothy had explained to her the dread and terror that those poor souls had suffered before they expired. Yes hopefully this young man would recover and be shipped to Blighty for a rest cure before being given a second chance to die for his country.

Even the few words that Billy had spoken produced a rawness in his throat that compelled him to seek relief from a drink. The nurse ever sensitive to her patients needs understood. She slowly administered warm milk to her charge and this seemed to relax him. Shortly afterwards he fell asleep once more only this time he was more relaxed, his sleeping hours now filled with dreams of a more placid kind. Visions came to him in which a young lady kept attempting to reach him, imploring him to come to her. Her face and eyes were smiling, her arms outstretched, welcoming him to her bosom. Then she receded back into the mist, calling his name ever more distinctly until he woke once more. This time, when he opened his eyes, at his bedside, along with his angel, a man in a white uniform came in attendance with a stethoscope around his neck.

"And how are you today Corporal Thomas".

The inquiry was matter of fact, monotone, reassuring. Billy felt as if he were in good hands. He still felt exhausted his chest seemed to be made of flames, his throat as if a rasp was being drawn along it with every breath he takes each word he spoke. He merely nodded acknowledgement of the question, which was all his doctor required of him.

"Just so young soldier, relax, no need to speak. We shall examine him now Nurse Bufford shall we not?"

"Indeed doctor."

The reply came simultaneously to the angel drawing herself over the patient where she began gently to unbutton his bed tunic. The Doctor viewed the general state of the chest. Severally the skin was yellowed suggesting a level of jaundice. Additionally, a large area of bruising was covering the lower ribs and upper abdomen region. Something had slammed into the patient but had not caused any puncturing or lacerations.

"Nurse we shall need to bind his midriff, this man possesses a cracked rib or two."

The yellowing of the skin was a cause for anxiety compounded as it was by the other symptoms and their potential complications. Softly he placed the stethoscope upon the patients' the patient's chest.

"Without causing you too much discomfort could you please take as deep a breath as possible, then gently let it out Corporal".

"Yes sir"

The strained reply and the energy that it took to make it, told the doctor much. In went the air and then the exhalation. As the doctor feared, the bubbling sound indicated a high level of fluid in the lungs. To provide some concern but not anywhere nearly the suspected level that some of his charges, his late charges, had displayed. There was hope for this lad. He would examine him again tomorrow and if no further complications had set in he would arrange for his transportation back to England for convalescence.

"Well Corporal, a trip to Blighty for you I think. We shall decide in a day or so, meantime keep still, do as nurse asks of you. See you in the morning"

"Thank you Doctor"

Again came the stressed reply, needlessly spoken for it was lost on the wind. In that instance the doctor was gone, so many changes, so many cases to get through. In the event Billy was to stay in the General Field

189

Hospital for a further week. By morning the next day, bronchitis had set in. Fortunately it was not to prove fatal as in the case of so many others that had faced this first experience of gas warfare. Ever-higher levels of fluid developed on his lungs exacerbating the bruising of his chest and the cracked ribs. He could no longer control the irritation

With his throat in such a state, fits of unabated coughing would take place, after which he would be sore, his throat feeling red raw and the pain around his chest not to be borne. That night was almost unbearable. The total dryness in his mouth made it so hot it was as if the sun itself was bearing down upon it, yet, perversely, he also shivered uncontrollably.

By the third night the crisis came. He felt as if he were drowning, as if water was filling his lungs. It gave him an extraordinary feeling of panic. He struggled for breath becoming blue in the face. For an entire night he tottered between the land of life and of death. Then at last, with the dawn, the effects of the irritants he had absorbed began to wane. By midday he was stable despite being weak beyond description. Numbness blessedly now invaded his throat, an intense pain still wracked his frame but he was on the mend. Nurse Bufford took his temperature, it was near normal. She observed how this young warding was now much more relaxed, how, as he rested, his breathing was becoming near normal. She gave thanks to God for she now believed that she was witnessing one of the hospitals' lamentably few successes with gas victims.

Next day the Doctor visited again. It was early yet, but the worst of the symptoms had appeared to have passed. In comparison to another charge, which had arrived at the same time as this young soldier, a miracle had occurred. The other, a Canadian, had been a case beyond anything he had ever encountered. The victim's terror had been so dreadful that it had left an imprint upon him that he knew would stay in his memory for the rest of his life. The poor man had driven so hard to defeat the effects of the gas, but in the end he had lost, defeated by the ever increasing level of fluid in the lungs, which, in the end, drowned him in a crescendo of screaming, gurgling helplessness.

By the week's end Billy was transported. The soreness of his throat had subsided to a level where his coughing was intermittent, still harsh, but infrequent. True the pain coming from his cracked ribs was, like the bruising, quite dreadful, but possible to be borne. The doctor gave permission for him to remove to England the next day. England, home and glory, the thought within the minds of so many soldiers in France these days and for endless days to come.

Two days later after a long bumpy painful tiring journey over the poorly maintained French roads, followed by a choppy channel crossing Billy arrived back on his native soil. Finally, after a rather more comfortable journey from Dover, he arrived at the convalescent home of Abbey Lodge in Bromley Kent. This quiet dormitory Kentish village, unmistakably English, with its rural public houses, its village hall, now boasted a hospital displaying its red cross flag. Next door stood the ancient Church and a little further on the mansion house, which too had been transformed into a hospital. This was the exact environment required for the recuperation of the Corporal Thomas.

This atmosphere of wellbeing was to be enhanced by the visit, just two days later, of Sally, her parents and his mother. It came as a complete surprise As one of the nurses, a certain Miss Hilda Pole, was completing the evening rounds of her ward, prior to settling the patients down for the night, she, in the most matter of fact manner, made the announcement to her jubilant charge.

"After dressing tomorrow morning Corporal Thomas at about 11.30 you will have some visitors to see you, a Mr and Mrs Hawkins, their daughter Sally and, oh yes, your mother also".

Billy was overjoyed, his various aches and discomforts forgotten, he began to consider how best to present himself. He was in a ward of eleven other casualties who possessed various fevers, skin diseases and types of injury. Each bed had a number placed above it together with the name, rank and regiment of its occupant. Mobile screens were available for dressing times and moments of intimate necessity. They were also used during visits.

Matron, a Mrs Trixie Button, had laid down an instruction that no more than two visitors were to be by the bedside at any time. But special cases were allowed, flaunting her commands and, in truth, she knew of them. Her orders had been formulated in September 1914 but as the war progressed, the casualties mounted above anything that was expected, she therefore relaxed things through custom and practise, and unspoken role changes. So many pathetic scenes had been witnessed by her and the staff, so many occurrences of great courage and fortitude, so many instances of bedside reunions concluding in the passing of the patient, that humanity demanded the rules should change.

Gas inhalation victims such as Corporal Thomas had the pitiful habit of taking a turn for the worse for no apparent reason. The patient would appear to be on the mend when a relapse would occur, bronchitis set in again, then phenomena, followed by a painful death. Matron felt however, that Billy Thomas was over the worst, physically at least. He would not be an addition to the growing list of fatal casualties that she had to painfully place in her records.

Death was the most arduous of visitors. It was the duty of Mrs Button to liase with the correct authorities, then arrange internment and finally, compose the necessary letters of condolence to relatives, which was coupled with the charge of forwarding on the often pitifully small and intimate personal remnants.

191

Good news can provide the catalyst for great improvement to a patient's general condition. With Billy Thomas there was a transformation. His thoughts turned solely to the coming host of visitors. They all had to see him at his best, especially Sally. Sheets, pillowcases, were all changed crisp, pressed and fragrant, he was fit to be visited by the King.

The volume of Milton, so treasured, was placed in a prominent position. A vase of fresh flowers had been picked by Hilda Pole and her four other sisters, who were also VADS and placed at the window above his bed. A jug of fresh water, glasses and some fruit cordial had found its way to the bedside cabinet. New pyjamas were provided for him. He and his surroundings were pristine; all was ready for his guests, come the morrow.

The night passed fitfully dragging by the hour. Visions of Sally when they were last together, her touch, her fragrance, the expectancy, the spoken and unspoken promises of love and its fulfilment possessed his thought, forbidding sleep, tranquilly of mind and restfulness. Eventually though, came dawn, the daylight and with it the first rustled expressions of the movement that warned of the coming preparation for the days tasks. 'Not long now' thought the young man.

He breakfasted, was assisted in his shave by the ever attentive Hilda Pole, who, in truth, had come to take a special pride in the recovery of this particular soldier in her charge. Almost it was as if he were a pet, a wonderful wild bird, like so many that she had tried to save before the war, which she had found in distress in the garden of her father's vicarage. She sensed how important this visit was for Corporal Thomas. She would ensure that all went smoothly.

Doctor made his rounds. One patient in the far bed was giving cause for concern. This morning he was displaying a high temperature, his major wound being a badly shattered leg, splintered in several places, was not progressing as hoped. Happily, in contrast, the other reprobates were 'coming along well'. He gave his instructions then departed in his rackety car for the other village hospital. As the vehicle sped away, they heard his parting cry.

"Keep up the good work sisters"

Hilda Pole made one last check of her charges and awaited the day's visits with almost as much anticipation as young Thomas was beginning to build within him. Then 11.30 came and no visitors 11.45, 12.00, 12.15. Billy began to think that something had gone wrong that they would not come this day. His morale, for the first time since he had gained his injuries, dropped.

Nurse Pole observed this, she was about to go over and begin to issue words of reassurance when the bell rang. Immediately she turned towards the exit. The ringing was, most certainly, the longed for signal that the guests of Corporal Thomas had arrived and she was wanted outside of the ward, to escort them through.

Hilda proceeded towards the lobby and came face to face with a party of strangers three women and a man. They looked flustered and agitated particularly the young woman. Hilda's sister Muriel was acting reception nurse that day and she introduced the visitors and guests of Corporal Thomas. Hilda shook the man's hands and he introduced himself as Mr Hawkins. She shook hands with the two older ladies and came to the youngest one a pretty, shapely, blonde headed girl of about her age.

"You must be Sally" she observed" Billy, I mean Corporal Thomas, has spoken so much about you, I see his glowing references were not exaggerated".

Sally blushed avoiding her parent's eyes.

"Why thank you nurse we should have been here earlier but there was a long delay due to a train taking precedence. It was loaded with big tractor things that had guns on them. Funny they were described as water carriers. Never seen the like before have we father?"

"Something for the war no doubt. Still nurse we are here now"

Hilda could see the party was exhausted, agitated even, eager to see the patient.

"Indeed you are and most welcome you are too. Corporal Thomas was becoming concerned that you might not have been coming at all today. Let us go through without further delay. This way if you please".

Sally brought up the rear of the party. Her heart began to beat rapidly. She felt as if she were blushing. A year and a half, two Christmases now they had been absent the one from the other. It had brought pain solitude and anxiety, more than enough for two lifetimes. From their separation had also come a longing, complete with urges and imagination that she was not too sure was right, certainly it was not lady-like. She knew now that a world without Billy was no world at all. He was her love, her life, her all. She was meant for him; to be his comfort, his sustenance, the one to spend his passion upon. She would go with him wherever he wished, be where ever he required, just let him say the words. 'Please God let him say the words.'

She went through the double doors that led onto the ward. There, half way along she could see her Billy, sat up waiting, eager and smiling. The urge to overtake the others and run to him proved irresistible. Sally overtook both her parents and Mrs Thomas, got to the bedside and enveloped herself gently in his arms sobbing uncontrollably. He responded without any restraint, embarrassment or awareness of the nurse, Sally's parents or his mother, all of whom had become astonished onlookers.

Elizabeth thought to herself, 'the sooner these two are married the better". She remembered how she had felt for Nathaniel all thoughts years ago, the urgency the need to be with him to be possessed by him. It had now happened to her own daughter. Nothing could control these two now and nothing should. She looked towards her beloved husband and he to her. His smile told her that his thoughts lay in the same direction as hers.

Gladys was just overwhelmingly glad to see Billy alive and on the mend. Sally could hold him for now. His life had moved on away from her towards the delightful young girl. She would make him happy, very happy. 'God bless them both' she concluded, in her mind.

At last the two young lovers entered, once more, back into the world of the ward, aware again of others amongst them. They broke off their embrace. Sally smoothed her white blouse, jacket and skirt, sat down by the side of her young soldier and held his hand. Gladys bent over her son and kissed his brow followed by Elizabeth. Nathaniel shook his offered hand. Nurse Pole fetched some further chairs, drew curtains round the party and begun to leave.

"Now be gentle with our young soldier here ladies, he is still on the mend you know".

Sally replied on behalf of them all.

"Like fine china, that is how we shall treat him."

"Good"

The nurses response, was emphatic, she did not want any complications to befall Corporal Thomas now that he was doing so well. She emphasised her point.

"That's what he is at the moment precious as fine china, and as fragile."

"I am well enough"

The soldier's retort came in the most defiant manner.

"Not yet young man, soon, but not yet. I shall bring tea in half of an hour."

With no further ceremony, or comment, the latter-day Florence Nightingale was gone about her other duties.

"Oh Billy, my poor boy, what have those nasty Germans done to you?"

Gladys was overcome now. The bandaging about his midriff was all too apparent, the jaundiced complexion of his face had paled but was still unmistakable and, as all mothers would notice, he had lost a lot of weight.

"They are feeding you in here Billy?"

"Well enough mother, very well indeed in fact."

He did not wish to tell her his appetite had vanished for days and was only now on the mend. "No need to fuss mother, they are doing a good job looking after the others and me".

So the chat settled down. Normal hospital bedside chat complied with talk of the war the dastardly use of horrific weapons by the infamous Germans and tales of life in Glossop. Billy was polite. He listened to all that was said, made remark's when it was his turn, smiled and tried to look as comfortable and healthy as possible. He spoke not one word of his brief battle experience of his fraternisation with the Germans. It seemed not appropriate for the moment. His wish was to be given some time with Sally. He had things to say only for her ears.

Tea came. Half an hour had gone by so quickly. Elizabeth took advantage of the break in conversation.

"A beautiful tea service Nurse Pole".

"Indeed so Mrs Hawkins, donated by the lady of the manor herself. Part of her contribution to the war effort."

"Very fine"

Gladys agreed, she had always admired fine china.

Nurse Pole pulled out cups for everyone including Billy.

"Would you be so kind enough to administer to the patient"

The enquiry was made of Sally. It was eagerly taken up.

"My honour"

The response came with a flourish, for indeed it seemed an honour to the young girl, as the Nurse well knew.

"I will leave you then".

Elizabeth interjected, stopping her departure.

"Just a moment Nurse Pole, tell me, what are the grounds like. It is a lovely day and I should so like to see them if I may".

"They are beautiful and you are most welcome to look around. Of course our hero here will have to stay in bed, but you are most welcome, to take a stroll.

"Well we shall do that after tea will we not?"

The stern request came together with a discrete nudge to Nathaniel's ribs.

"I should like to join you too if I may"

Gladys made a short but similar request, eager to join in the conspiracy.

"So would I."

"Sally looks more than capable of attending to Billy. "Would you mind so Sally?"

"Of course not Mrs Thomas, my pleasure".

The game was now played out, Billy; the victim was trapped without uttering a single word. He would be a willing victim, however.

Tea finished, and the parents departed. Their discretion was synthetic and woefully thin, obvious in its conspiratorial nature. The plotting had been too obvious and blatant to be portrayed as anything other than a manoeuvre to leave the two young people alone, in private, behind the hospital curtain. Gladys administered a kiss on her son's forehead and repeated the gesture with Sally. They left; Sally and Billy were alone.

Swiftly she fell into his arms, meeting her lips with his, their kiss urgent, impassioned, seemingly endless. His hand clasped the left mound of her blouse and he gently squeezed it. Her breast felt full. His large hand barely covering it. It surprised him how firm it felt. How pleasing it was to hold her so. Sally made no attempt to resist his touch indeed her mouth fell even harder against his lips.

Eventually they parted and a sense of mutual guilt swept over them. Billy remembered how, once before, above Glossop, on that glorious memorable day, he had wished to complete the undertaking he had just achieved. Never though, he thought, would he have the unaffordable pleasure of taking one of those objects of delight in his hand. Yet, if the truth were known, he had fanaticised as much in the trenches, on many an occasion of he holding Sally, just as now, and more, much, much, more.

Sally was feeling a wonderful tingling mystical urge, compounded with a sense of guilt yet wishing to explore her adventurous inclination, her overwhelming sensations of desire, further. She tutted inwardly. 'Of course it could not be, not here, not this way.'

Billy was whispering to her.

"Oh Sally I have wanted to kiss you to hold you like that for so long. I am so sorry it just overcame me, the need to hold you so."

The words took away his breath; his heart beat as never before sensations rose in him beyond his control.

Quietly, slowly, looking deeply into her smiling enticing eyes, he made the request that he had been practising for many months in France.

"Sally, my dearest Sally, I am here wounded, not fully able yet to give all I wish, all you deserve, Sally dearest Sally can I ask you if you will honour me by becoming my wife, my darling wife for ever and ever and then some more as well?"

It had at last been said, their unspoken understanding had been given form, he waited, he was sorely in need of a reply.

Sally looked again into those deep brown eyes. So full of love for him, she smiled with a glowing radiance as she answered.

"Billy Thomas, I have loved you since first we read books together all those years ago in the library. If I do not become your ever-loving wife loved by you, then my life is without meaning in this world. Billy Thomas I will marry you, of course I will. Do you really think that I would allow Glossop's finest budding poet to slip through my fingers"

This time Sally placed Billy's hand against her breast and kissed him once more. Again an age passed before their lips parted and she looked him straight in the eyes

"And it had better be soon young man, very soon"

His cup overflowed. God had provided him with his greatest wish, the greatest gift that the Almighty could ever have bestowed upon him. It was at this point that circumstances aborted their physical passion and not too soon either. With a purposeful clumsily constructed, noisily planned entrance their parents re-entered their curtained bower. Unfortunately it

196

disallowed him to pursue the subject of his poetry. Of this he would find out on another day.

"What a lovely garden it is out there."

Elizabeth volunteered the point factiously. Now observing her daughter she sensed something dramatic had happened between the two young people, as if the Rubicon had been crossed.

Billy grasped his courage two handed and with firm resolve.

"Mrs Hawkins, Mr Hawkins, I have asked Sally to marry me, she has affirmed her acceptance. Would you in turn be gracious to provide me with your permission".

Nathaniel was speechless. Elizabeth and he had spoken of this possibility but to be asked so soon after the pair had reunited, in a ward full of wounded soldiers, each having their ears pricked to attention. The words just escaped him, quite involuntarily.

"Well I ask you, here's a howdy do."

He was stammering, trying to find the words. Then Elizabeth caught his eye, frowned, nodded her head, and smiled. Her face instructed him on what to say she needed to utter no words.

"Billy, nothing would give me greater pleasure, nothing in the world."

The tension filled air evaporated, hugs and kisses swamped the room, a gentle but assured handshake had taken place between the two men. The contract was agreed. Tears flowed, Elizabeth first, quickly joined by Gladys, then Sally. The three women hugged each other in triumph. To win a woman so, takes daring, Billy Thomas had dared thus; he had won.

It was Nathaniel who's practical mind allowed him to descend from the height of celebration first.

"When and where?"

Sally looked at her mother, who noticed the slight dishevelment in her daughter's blouse and a button adrift halfway down. She smiled, nodded knowingly and was not in the least surprised when Sally said firmly.

"Glossop, as soon as possible by special licence if need be".

Again Elizabeth nodded in her husbands direction.

"Whatever you say Sally, you know I could never refuse you anything".

His wife, dear wife hugged him. He had executed every word just so. She would reward him in her own personal, most gratefully received, intimate way that she gifted her husband every once in a while when they were alone. Romance was not just for the young she reasoned with herself.

If anything is guaranteed to mend a broken bruised body, then it is the promise of love fulfilled entering into a young mans mind. So it was to prove the case with Billy Thomas. His parents to be, together with his beloved mother had once again, attendant with hugs and kisses, left their curtained paradise. One last long lingering kiss, intimate, full of promise, one final caress of Sally's breast, a pleasure he was all too speedily getting an appreciation of, and they had all gone. Now, he was sure, that as soon as he was well enough he would be coming home to Glossop to a wedding and a wife. Impatience now replaced infection as his greatest enemy.

Later that evening when Nurse Pole came to complete her final round for the day. He asked her, how long it would be before he was free to go and join his love, and how long a leave could he expect? Knowledge of his victory in love had spread throughout the ward with cries of, "You lucky beggar "and "If you need any advice about the wedding night just ask."

Billy took all this banter in good heart, assuring his tormentors there were no problems in any department, no problems at all.

Nurse Pole, virtuous maid that she was but tutted, admonished the more blatant remarks and assured their victim that all would be well. She informed Billy that matters could possibly be enacted even faster than presently hoped for.

"In the morning Doctor will be notified of the circumstances and, you never know, developments could happen sooner than you think".

Developments did occur but not exactly in the manner that Billy had anticipated. Two days later at about ten o'clock sudden panic broke out. Suddenly the ward was full of nurses and orderlies tidying, clearing, dusting, mopping and polishing. Clearly something was a foot. Billy managed to stop a hastily scampering Hilda Pole.

"What on earth is going on nurse?"

"Top brass that's what, due here shortly, spot check thirty minutes time. You would think they would warn us, give us more notice. Oh no not they and we are in such a muddle".

Billy could hardly grasp how an officer's inspection could cause such consternation. Then he recalled. It was not that much different at the front. In twenty minutes all was transformed, not a crease in the bed linen, not a pillow out of place. Everything in its ordered position, the floors made spotless. Not a moment too soon either for within less than five minutes of 'stand down' from action stations, through the double doors came the inspection party. Each of the patients was on parade, either or under bedcovers, or standing perfectly presented by their bed.

The leading officer, a general by all appearances, led the party. He began to stop at every bed asking the occupant the extent of his injuries, where he had fought and so on. Eventually he came to Billy's bed where he stopped.

"Ah Corporal Thomas I believe, the very man, recovering well I hope Thomas?"

"Yes Sir looked after right well we are sir".

"So it would seem, so it would seem." The general twizzled his waxed moustache winked and added a provocatively accentuated question.

"Nurses looking after you well Corporal?"

Missing the suggestiveness in the Generals comments and demeanour he confirmed his experience.

"We could not ask for better attention sir, they are most splendid".

"Magnificent Corporal, magnificent. Now I have a most pleasing duty to perform." Turning towards his adjutant he barked out an order in the most exact manner.

"Lieutenant if you will".

The subordinate stepped forward and offered his superior a small black box. Extracting its contents the General turned towards the newly recovered soldier staring out at him from the bed and extended his hand.

"Corporal Thomas, it is my great pleasure, that we today present to you for displaying great courage in the face of the enemy, above and beyond the call of duty, the Military Medal on behalf of a grateful nation".

With this he stepped forward and pinned the award to Billy's pyjamas. At once spontaneous applause broke out through the ward and the nurses, doctors, patients and the military party. A photographer from the local press took a picture he was most pleased with. Later it would blaze out from more than one National and even reached the Glossop Chronicle. When Billy reached home he would be an even more famous son.

A sense of great pride overcame the recipient who stammered out his acceptance. The general shook his hand, and made a farewell comment.

"Well done lad"

He went on to the next bed and within five minutes he was gone. General Douglas Haigh was a busy man and he had an offensive to plan. It would be one that would win the war; it was due to start at the end of June by the banks of a river called the Somme.

Within two days Billy had been given his discharge allowed twenty-one days leave and was being driven to the station to catch his train. He had left Nurse Pole, her sisters, their father the local vicar and all the other staff, on the steps of the improvised hospital, having not a few tears in his eyes and leaving a few behind him.

CHAPTER 13

'Think, this heart, all evil shed away.
A pulse in the eternal Mind, no less
Gives somewhere back the thoughts by England given;
Her sights and sounds; dreams happy as her day;
And laughter, learnt of friends; and gentleness,
In hearts at peace, under an English heaven'.

'The Soldier' Rupert Brooke 1914.

Hilda Pole knew she would miss the dashing, brave gallant young Corporal. For as long as the car was in view prior to turning the corner, which led, towards the station, the dedicated Nurse waved after it. Even when it disappeared from view she could hear the comforting, chugging, of its engine for a while longer. Then it too ceased to be, and she pivoted round to return to her present charges. She hoped that her letter to Mr. Nathaniel Hawkins would reach him in time for the young man's hometown to be aware of his award of a medal, prior to his arrival that day. The communication had been sent because she was so sure that he would not have said a word. On this point, Hilda need not have worried. The photographer, who had been present at the ceremony, had seized his opportunity that very day, sending copies of his work to the Editor of the Glossop Chronicle.

Such a dashing boy, modest as well, one of her ward's successes. Yes she would miss him as indeed she would miss so many before the war's end when her hospital would be dismantled and given back to be used once again for the original purpose to which it was designed. This conflict was to bring so many injured into her care. Some would survive others would not. Some she would remember with great joy, as this young soldier, others she would give witness to their passing.

One would steal her heart, making her his wife and a proud mother. Hilda would give birth to two sons, one of whom she would lose to another war upon a French shore as he bravely gained a liberating foothold with the allied forces struggling, once more, to free that unhappy land. Yet, content for now, she sped back to the duties for which she was so dedicated, blissfully unaware of what the future held. She was thinking that she had only played a small part in the life of Billy Thomas. Fate was to decree otherwise.

Nathaniel Hawkins, at that very moment, was in the process of opening his morning mail. It was a Wednesday not a busy time in the shop and it had become his practice to spend 'half day opening' at home catching up on stock levels, ordering accounts, seeing to the mail. He enjoyed these times, alone in the house, in the morning room with tea from

200

a white fine china cup. Hilda Pole's letter was before him, her words etching upon his mind.

"Well would you believe it, our Billy."

He had spoken softly to himself. 'Our Billy' had become 'our Billy' from the moment his future son-in-law had made the announcement of the coming marriage between him and Sally. He repeated the term.

"Our Billy. thought he could get away with a modest homecoming did he? Well we shall see about that."

Hat on his head, although the sun was dominating this spring day, a chilly wind was descending from the Pennines. He filed his papers together with his unfinished accounts, consumed his tea, and was off to the town hall. Billy would have a reception from the moment he stepped from the train, he would so, or Nathaniel would want to know why not.

In truth the startled mayor and the officers of the town were astounded by the illuminated Mr Hawkins armed with his baton. Just five minutes since, they had been examining the photographs that had arrived on the desk of the Editor of the Chronicle. None other than General Haigh had presented their very own Billy Thomas with the Military Medal. Time to mobilise forces. The town would be ready to welcome home one of it's bravest and best.

Photographers were summoned, newspaper reporters informed, flags bunting and school children rounded up. To their great pleasure the cadets were ordered from their school classes to the drill hall for practice as an honour guard. Mr and Mrs Hill Woods were located to head the delegation. All would be ready for the 5.15 p.m. from Manchester to arrive with their own local boy home from the war.

The newspapers were particularly interested, what with romance and marriage in the air as well. What more could an intrepid reporter require. The Chronicle would pull out all the stops. Nathaniel left the town hall only after repeated reassurances that all would be done as he wished all, and more. Eventually he left to break the glad news to his wife, daughter and Billy's mother who, now, also worked in the emporium.

Sally Hawkins could not concentrate on her work this day. Ever since that glorious episode in the hospital with Billy, that time alone together behind the curtain when he kissed her and she him, with his hand gently upon her breast, Sally had felt exquisite. Billy's kiss, his caress, produced the most wondrous sensation of desire, a desire which built up deep within her, creating an ache and a urge which was both profound and conscience driven, providing her with the knowledge that she could not refuse him anything he wanted. Whenever Billy wanted something of her, wherever he so desired it to be, she would give it to him. It was the blatant truth, if she was to go to her marriage bed a virgin, as she knew she should, as she felt she wished, then it was essential that they be wed forthwith.

Sally knew her mother was aware of how it was. The subtle hints the knowing eyes that both warned, yet bled for her daughter, were constantly being displayed. Her mother had become the engine that drove matters, persuading Nathaniel to drive through whatever bureaucracy stood in his way, to obtain a special, very special licence. "Bless father" she thought. How lucky she was. Still time was dragging, not yet midday more than five hours before her love was back in her arms.

Elizabeth Hawkins sensed her daughter's impatience and expectancy. She had watched her daughter over the last few days. No longer an entirely innocent girl, though still physically a virgin, of that Elizabeth was sure, she sensed that Sally's thoughts had explored the possibilities that all happily married women yearn for. Sally, she observed, was a woman whose desires had been ignited, just as Nathaniel had lit hers those days before their wedding, a wedding that was perfect in its bliss it's fulfilment. From the very first night of their marriage, Elizabeth had never ceased to look forward to Those blissful, intimate moments with her Nathaniel. Even to this day they were as intense together, than those early exploratory times, perhaps more so. Their throes of intimacy might be less frequent than before, but they were still intensely exciting and longed for.

Now Sally was ready to be a wife, a wife to a very good young man indeed, and the future was delightful. Elizabeth would love Billy as she did her own son, the one she never had time with, the one who for many years had been at rest in the small corner of the cemetery that she visited so often. Tears came at the thought, best put them away, think of the living. Hey-ho, Sally Thomas, a grand name for her daughter 'Mrs Sally Thomas.'

Gladys Thomas was working away measuring and weighing out various commodities into retail units. Wednesday was never busy these days, half day closing and all. She stared at the clock, just after midday, Billy would be home in less than five hours, God be praised. Glancing over towards Sally, Gladys saw that she was about to run on a few errands for her mother. What a beauty she was tall, slim waisted, a full figure, lush, long silky hair, intelligent, hard working. Yes she would make her son a wonderful wife. She would make a lovely daughter too.

In truth Gladys had come to love and admire the young lady who had stolen her son's heart. She had never seen him so illuminated, happy, so full of hope and confidence. Then there was Elizabeth. Gladys and she had become close friends, supportive, leaning upon each other, knowing that a tragedy for one would be tragic for the other. Their hopes and aspirations for the future, like those of their children, were entwined. Gladys went up to the window watching Sally go on her way.

Elizabeth put her hand upon her shoulder. In turn Gladys placed her hand upon that of her friend, remarking in a soft sighing tone."

"A grand lass, Elizabeth, a grand lass."

Elizabeth was overcome.

"Why thank you, what a pair we have, how fine they are together."

Gladys agreed.

"Indeed, a very fine pair indeed."

They each returned to their own thoughts, complete of contentment. Five minutes later Nathaniel burst through the shop door with such enthusiasm that it seemed as if the tortured bell would never stop. Elizabeth had seldom seen him so animated. Luckily the shop was all but empty now, just Mrs Rodgers, and she as deaf as a post.

"Gladys, Elizabeth, come and hear my news, great news, what a day we are going to have. Well come here we have little time to lose."

He was exasperated, looking towards the two women who had not moved, their mouths agape. Observing no visible response, his patience evaporated causing his voice to rise to an ever higher pitch in his excitement. Finally he pleaded for a reaction to his, as yet, unexplained outburst.

"Well ladies come, come,"

At last Elizabeth retaliated, full of admonishment.

"Nathaniel, what on earth are you doing here? And you so agitated".

"Great news great news come here, don't make me shout it out across the shop"

No longer able to restrain their curiosity they came dutifully as they were bid. Something in his voice demanded their obedience, a previously unknown occurrence. Nathaniel proceeded to explain the events of the morning. Nurse Pole's letter, the Medal, General Haigh, the Mayor and officials, Girl Guides, Scouts, Army Cadets, Flags, perhaps even the M. P.

"Well what do you think ladies? What do you think?"

Here Nathaniel enjoyed an even more rare experience. Total silence from the two women, it was long after he had addressed them before a reply was forthcoming, They were unable to speak, it was all taking time to absorb.

"Well?"

The constant need for repetition was tiresome, he was becoming frustrated now.

"Ladies please!"

At last Elizabeth found her voice, Nathaniel's tone had finally found its mark.

"Better close as soon as Sally arrives back. Gladys write a note for the door. 'Closed early, due to arrival from the front of the local hero'. Then it's home to get ready. Nathaniel, your Sunday best if you will. Gladys, anything you need?

"Just time Elizabeth, oh it's all a muddle, Billy, what ever next, I never cease to be amazed".

A few moments later and Sally arrived back. The startled girl had the story related to her and again panic set in.

"It's all got to be perfect, mothers"

Both women she now addressed as mother, considering them to be equal influences in her life, consequently, she appealed to both of them.

"I have to look my best, Billy has to be as proud of me as I am of him."

"And you shall my darling."

The assurance came from Gladys.

"We will do a proper job on you, won't we Elizabeth? A right proper job."

"Certainly"

Her friend took matters in hand.

"Nathaniel, lock up, pack the things away. We girls have a job of work to do. Quickly mind, be home as soon as you can".

"Certainly Elizabeth"

The bemused but obedient reply came from a man who knew not to argue in such a situation. Never contradict Elizabeth when she was like this. If the Kaiser had someone like her at home would have never been allowed out to play at war.

"Off you go ladies, all of you."

He virtually threw their coats at them and pushed them out of the door, to be followed by a startled Mrs. Rogers. She was never to understand the events that led to her being ejected from the shop, neither would she ever pay for the string of new clothes pegs that she later realised that she was holding onto. Some episodes in life are destined to remain, forever, a mystery.

As for Nathaniel, now alone in the shop, it was as if he were floating in perpetual animation. How proud he was going to be this day, proud of both his daughter and his new found son.

Not only the women and Nathaniel were in the state of hyperactivity, their condition was reflected by a great portion of the town. The legendary Billy Thomas, centre forward of North End, wounded hero, defender of the Belgians, holder of the Military Medal was coming home on leave. Not one dignitary, leader of a Baden-Powell pack, member of clergy, friend of family, old acquaintance, wanted to miss out. It was half day, time and opportunity to prepare properly. Glossop would do him justice.

All this time the unsuspecting object of all this preparation was innocently making his way home, enjoying the passing countryside from the windows of his carriage. Having changed trains at Euston he was even now speedily racing past the Potteries. Coming through Crewe he had also noticed the so-called 'water carriers' that had been described to him. As he observed these strange Gothic metal monstrosities, he was not to know that the euphemism used by the War Office would lead to these constructions and all their later generations being described as 'tanks'. At one siding there were ten of them being sheeted up with tarpaulin, on flat-bedded rolling stock. They looked to him like a terrible futuristic weapon of war, a moveable fortress. Six-pound guns, or so he thought, were positioned on each side, machine guns too. Thick armoured plating riveted in place. More like a ship upon the land, he concluded. He could only conjecture on their use and on what kind of mark they would make as they trundled across the landscape.

There! he considered, he had solved the puzzle. This war was the first truly mechanical one, perhaps these monsters were metal horses. Ironic, he thought, it has been four hundred years since armoured horses were used in battle. If this were so, what kind of tracks would they make? He pondered upon two lines from 'Henry the Fifth.'

Think, when we talk of horses, that you see them
Printing their proud hoofs in the receiving earth.

Now he was tiring, his eyes felt heavy, droopy; he was becoming drowsy. Eventually, he fell off into unconsciousness. Now his sleeping hours were full of delightful images, mystical sensations emanating from the darkness with a girl called Sally. Erotic visions focused his dormant mind; he drifted upon a nuptial sea. It was as if he were observing himself and Sally from behind a Muslin drape. Both were visible yet annoyingly blurred. His name was being called in a familiar voice urging him closer and closer. The two were entwined oblivious of the world around them. Then he awoke and behold it was a dream. Until now it had always been a dream hopefully it would soon become reality.

He sensed the train was slowing down, it was coming into Manchester. One last change, over to platform one and Glossop was less than an hour away. He felt as if tortured. What if everything did not unravel as he had so urgently wished, what if she had changed her mind or her father his. What if 'Shut up Thomas,' he told himself, 'you are approaching a state of paranoia.' Again his mind drifted back to the dream and he was re-assured. The prayer came.

"Thy will be done, oh Lord, Thy will be done, how shall I count the ways?"

Back in Glossop things had moved a pace. The Salvation Army had been recruited. Music too, would now meet the hero. Sally had been dressed in a mirage of pink with veiled hat to match, new shoes and a delicate cape. The skirt length was shorter than decorum had dictated before the war. Now only two inches separated her from exposing the knees. A vision of loveliness as a poet might say. The two older women were pristine in their dress, both still being very attractive though more modestly so of latter days. Nathaniel was also 'spick and span,' as Elizabeth would have commented so. He was wearing a black suit, a waistcoat with a silver pocket watch, and a dark blue tie. He resolved that he would present the watch to Billy on the evening before his wedding. A symbolic gesture he thought, passing such an object as his father's watch onto the next generation.

The local train seemed so slow to Billy, stopping as it did at every conceivable opportunity. Now, however almost in spite of itself it was slipping into Hadfield. One last stop and he would be home at last. It had all come so strenuously.

On to Dinting, now apprehension built up inside the warrior, he began to tap his fingers on the window. As the carriage came to a halt, Billy observed a worried looking party seeking someone from the train. Then he saw a young man, just as he, being helped onto the platform. He had lost an arm, he possessed a patch on one eye, and the hair on one side had vanished being replaced by a blotch of skin. Shame overwhelmed him. Whilst he had been sleeping in his carriage, not far away was a comrade, coming home like he, but to what? Aloud though only for his hearing, he made a plea.

"God forgive me, but that is a sight that is best forgot, for many people's minds no doubt. Then he remembered his Kipling, 'Lord God of hosts be with us yet, lest we forget, lest we forget."

It was not especially the soldier he was referring to. It was the sight of the young woman gasping in horror and the little girl running down the platform screaming that her daddy had come home a monster.

Thankfully, the train was off once more, departing to the spur that went towards just one destination, Glossop, Billy murmured a prayer for his tragically deformed comrade

"God help you son. You are going to need God's help right enough."

The sight of the wounded soldier greeted unrecognised, except by a few loved ones, would stay with him for a very long time.

Meanwhile, at Glossop the platform was full. So too the square outside. The band was playing 'I Vow to Thee my Country.' Sally, Gladys, Elizabeth and Nathan had been placed in a prominent position with room to approach the destined carriage once it had been ascertained which one held their precious boy. The dignitaries were prominent having agreed their pecking order. All was ready, the tension mounting by the minute. If the train were on time they would not now have long to wait.

Silence began to reign. The band stopped its medley. All listened out for the sound of the whistle as the train approached the viaduct at Dinting. It could always be heard from Glossop station if all was quiet. They waited and waited. Then, suddenly, it was heard. Funny how it only made a mollified sound, as it was going away, never when it was coming towards the town. Now it's sound was as if it were a prelude to a triumphant marching tune. Billy was almost home, safe and sound. God bless the engine driver, God indeed be thanked.

Steam and smoke was now visible. The engine's sound, the pistons fury audible but abating, pressure being released, slowing down, the wheels turn carefully coming to a gentle halt, for Glossop, literally, was the end of the line. To leave one had to reverse on the same rail as one had entered. The engine stopped, carriages clinked together, doors opened, Billy, Corporal Billy Thomas M.M. was home from the war.

The band struck up; 'See now the conquering hero comes' from Judas Maccabeus, flags waved, cheers echoed the stanchions, Glossop was greeting it's own. Billy could hear the noise above that of the engine whilst the train still had a hundred yards to travel. He suspected what was happening. What a contrast, he thought, to the welcome that the poor soldier had received at Hadfield.

He was leaning out of the open window now ready to exit as soon as the train stopped. Embarrassment began to rise within him. Then his heart leapt. Sally had come into sight, his mother also, together with Nathaniel and Elizabeth. Impatience now overcame embarrassment. The door opened and the second the train came to a halt he was in her arms kissing her full on the lips witnessed by all those surrounding him, waiting to shake his hand or pat his back. In turn he hugged his mother, Elizabeth and Nathaniel. Finally, he greeted all the assembly of dignitaries, in their order of ranking. Everywhere the young children enthused, played tag or stood to attention in their Baden Powell uniforms, trying to look as important as their elders.

Then came a Signal, the band struck up the Anthem and people lifted up then voices in salutation to their king. The crowd was so massed that it took a full thirty minutes for the party to clear the station and climb into a vehicle provided by Hill-Woods, which was to service the last few yards to Sally's house where they were now destined. Here the neighbours also had a welcome prepared displaying genuine hospitality with an assembly of banners, endless cheers, and impassioned repetitive cries.

"Welcome home Billy."

Eventually they gained the front door and it was closed behind them. Privacy at last, at least for the time being. Now Billy could relax. It had been an exhausting journey. In truth he should have waited a few days more before leaving his ward, so be it, for he was home, here with his family, his beloved Sally.

Discreetly the parents left them together on the pretence that it would take the three of them to prepare tea, a compassionate Elizabeth remarked wickedly as she closed the door.

"We shall leave you two young ones alone for a while to settle down."

At long last they were together, Billy and Sally in a private clasp, binding them in union, their warm moist lips caressing each other. She with tears in her eyes and untold love in her heart, he with anticipation, untenable desire. At last they parted, their lips bruised, their hearts, in unison, pumping away. For now he left her breasts untouched as if unspoken, their passion would not develop further until the day of their marriage, at least that was what they would strive to accomplish. Later passion just might have other ideas, at this very moment though, it was enough just to be together. Contented, released from the nervousness brought on by sexual tension, they both sat down upon the green two-seater sofa. It had been placed in front of the healthy warm coal fire, re-stoked by Nathaniel, blazing out its warmth.

Billy could now but gaze at her with love and admiration, disbelieving that he could be so fortunate in life. It seemed as if all that he had experienced in the trenches and would do so again was, here, given credence. If it was true that the Germans, with their barbaric hordes, were bent on devouring the whole of Europe, as that dastardly persuasive Corporal had suggested, then all that he loved required his protection. This was surely his duty; to defend his loved ones, his lovely one, Sally. Sally Hawkins, Sally of the library, his Sally that he had loved so long, who was to become his life's partner.

Here she was, impeccable in her beauty, smiling wistfully at him her blushing cheeks being reddened even more by the pulsing heart of the fire. A beautiful fire, he thought, blazing its coals, sending out its radiance to provide comfort throughout the room. He reminisced:

> *'What though the radiance*
> *Which was once so bright*
> *Be now forever taken from my sight...'*

Holding her ever more tightly, he vowed that no power, no foe, however mighty, however ambitious, would separate him from his love, not while he breathed God's good air, or stood on God's good earth. He again gazed at the source that gave heat to the room, and pondered. An awareness came over him that not all the heat that he was encompassed in was emanating from the ignited coals. Yes, even this wondrous display of blue, green, red and amber flame was dormant compared to the inferno that was rearing within his heart and his loins.

Sally smoothed down her skirt, adjusted her hair and held Billy's hand. She appeared the epitome of decorum, of respectability. How appearances could deceive. 'If mother could read my thoughts right now,' she considered, blushing even more at the images coursing through her mind.

Then, inevitably, the spell was broken; a knock announced the return of their parents. Tea, informally, in front of the fire was to be served. Nathaniel now sat upon the right of the pair pretending to give individual attention to the fire using the set of implements that, fortunately, hung nearby. He was pretending to be relaxed, allowing himself to be amused within the source of the flames. He was however, a man in flux, tormented by the paradox of Billy Thomas, the man who could bring such happiness to his beloved daughter yet also potential, indescribable sorrow when, as was certain, he returned to this war's battlefront that daily consumed ever more lives, ever more pointlessly.

He was heavy of heart, having to weigh the happiness of these two young loves with the devastation that widowhood could bring, almost certainly would bring, if this war continued much longer. This brave valiant youth, who had so captured his daughter's heart, seemed fearless of going back to Flanders to place himself once again in harms way, 'please God' he urged, 'let nothing injurious again befall him.'

How he wished that, at this moment he had a woman's perspective towards life and its various potentials. Women looked at the world as their imagination led them and not with the evidence that their eyes and their ears gave them at any specific moment, discerning not to vision the inevitability of life's vagaries. They were, in truth, accepting it's joys of the day and dismissing all thoughts of the sorrow that might also come to them from out of that very joy. The future, for them, was placed in trust with no consideration as to whether or not that trust was well founded. Still the decision had been made; there would be no black clouds created today, or tomorrow. Billy, like Sally, also had to give up his trust to God; surely, despite his fears his doubt's, the Almighty would ensure his blessed girl's happiness. Thus Nathaniel both pondered and prayed whilst giving the appearance that his sole concern was over the condition of the fire.

In truth, in quiet moments to come, the two mothers would also fall prey to periods of infortitude but, for now, both allowed the bustle of the moment to drive them on. Almost as sisters, which, in truth, they had virtually become, they visualised and planned together, driving each other on towards a single goal, the recognised, blessed, perfect union of their offspring. Tomorrow, they assented, rested with tomorrow. Today would be lived well. No tears, no fears, would be permitted to cloud the great joy brought through the love, enjoyed and displayed, by these their children. The other world, with its endless and growing capacity to destroy the lives and happiness of families, could wait. Gladys and Elizabeth would safely shut it away for a while. For now, death had been driven from their lives, love was to be permitted its triumph.

This day, the lives of those two women were dedicated towards love's victory, they would ensure it was triumphant. These two lovers, carrying both their hopes and desires, would have the most perfect of days, the most blissful of beginnings. Then and only then, would they be placed back into the world of uncertainty, cast of upon that sea of fate where all have to navigate in hope and faith.

Elizabeth, with the assistance of Gladys, had laid out upon the coffee table all the trappings of a fine tea. The cake stand was full of scones, fairy cakes and vainly presented, in all it's decorative pride, the most tempting Victoria sponge that surely could be wished for. 'A sumptuous tea then a conference' debated Elizabeth to herself. Tea was indeed a charming satisfying affair. Billy quickly forgot his trench manners, those of eating with a spoon out of a ration tin. There, it had to be consumed, with all haste, before it became cold or contaminated with flies. You had to eat against the background of unrepressed belching and wind breaking, eating with companions who between gulps emitted expletives or described what they would like to accomplish with the little VAD who distributed soup at that feeding station in the rear.

In stark contrast, Billy today portrayed the appearance of an accomplished practitioner of demure table manners, the result of his mother's constant entreatments when he was younger. Despite Gladys' fears, his conduct made her proud. 'Something not wasted in his up bringing,' she thought.

Talk was low key, a discussion of Bill's journey, what he thought of his reception, how did he find Glossop, the little, very little of what he had seen. "Wasn't it kind of Mr. Hill Woods to loan his car for the short journey home?"

To this Billy made no response, thinking of a soldier and his family, back there in Hadfield, not having his fortune or contacts to provide a lift home. Hadfield was also a part of Hill-Woods' constituency.

"Why were you not there sir?"

It troubled Billy; the war was going to create so many examples of such wounded men as he had seen on that railway platform. Still, such as Hill-woods would not be MP's much longer, not if he lived to have a say in the matter. For now he kept such thoughts to himself, it would not do to spoil so wonderful a tea.

Yes tea passed pleasantly enough, even if Sally, Gladys and Nathaniel all noticed Billy's thoughtfulness. Exceptions were to be made for an exhausted young man fresh home after such an enduring journey. In truth, Billy's contemplations were allied with his tiredness and he felt sleep drawing upon him. Sally leaned over and took his cup, Her love she observed was in the land of dreams. Talk could and would, wait till next day. Her young man was back safe and close to her. He was going to have as much rest as his tired frame required.

"Bless him" whispered Elizabeth. "Look, and we just gabbing on. What to do? We can't leave him there and he is too tired to walk home."

Nathaniel, not for the first time that day, became the decisive member of the group.

"Spare room, spare room. Come on ladies let us help him upstairs."

So it happened, gently Sally and Gladys took the exhausted soldier up the stairs, where Gladys dressed him in a pair of Nathaniel's pyjamas. He hardly knew himself, simply carrying out the instructions of his mother exactly as he had done so when he was a little boy. It was when Gladys took off his shirt that she began to realise the extent of his injuries. His torso was a mass of bruises, black, brown, red and yellow. Immediately she called out to Elizabeth who came running.

"Elizabeth, look at this."

Gladys pulled back the sheet to reveal Billy's upper half.

Elizabeth let out an involuntary gasp. She could not believe what her eyes were telling her. Her hand reached out to her friend.

"God bless us, what are they doing to our lads our there, Poor Billy, what have they done to you lad."

Billy heard not a single word, he was so deeply asleep. The ladies just covered the bedclothes around him, made him comfortable, hugged each other in their mutual distress and quietly left the room.

When they were once again on the ground floor Elizabeth declared her decision to the other three.

"Let him sleep till he is ready to awake. Gladys, Sally and I will see you home and tomorrow you and she shall stay here to administer to the lad. Nathaniel and I can manage the shop. Sally coats please."

There was no discussion, no further planning to be made. Elizabeth had announced her decree and that was the end of the matter. The rest of the quartet knew better than to argue the least point when Elizabeth's mind was so set.

The three ladies left the home, leaving Nathaniel alone to meditate upon matters. He knew that later when his wife and daughter arrived back they would let him know what decisions had been made. They would tell him what his duties were to be and who else was to be spoken to. 'Hey ho, such is life.' He went back to stirring the dying embers.

When Billy awoke the next day after almost fifteen-hours of sleep all was in place for him to accede to. The women had organised matters, he merely had to conform to their wishes, which was his pleasure. He was in ecstasy, so looking forward to the coming days. Once again during his sleep an angel had drifted in to his dreams, during the morning's small hours. She had stroked him and with her fallen gown displaying her upper beauty, she kissed him. In his trance like waking, he had responded to her invitation, his hand finding the gaps of her gown and placing itself upon one of those luxurious, warm, firm, responsive breasts. He had absently played with the long hard nipple that erupted from the crown. The angel gasped then whispered, pushed back his pyjama top and kissed his chest, then his neck. He pulled her shoulder straps to each side leaving both her breasts to please his eyes. Exited hands found both nipples, then, in turn, his lips discovered them. The angel whispered his name "Billy." Then the apparition withdrew with words full of the most exquisite promise.

"Soon my love, very soon."

Then she was gone. His excitement abated and in his exhaustive state he collapsed once more into a further long, deep, uninterrupted sleep.

Down the corridor Elizabeth was awake. Her husband's steady breathing let her know that he was beyond the noises that invaded her senses, be they ever so slight. She knew the young man had been granted a visit and a glimpse of passion, of promise.

"So be it Lord"

She whispered for her own ears. The interlude, played along the corridor, reminded her of that splendid time of delightful passion, spent high in the hills above Glossop, just a few days before she was to become the bride of the man now sleeping, so soundly, next to her. That was assuredly a God given day, blessed, pure, heavenly, being loved by the man that she was to give the rest of her life to. She turned towards him and clasped him, seeking reassurance. Sleepily, his arm went around her, drawing her ever closer. She nuzzled into his hair tufted chest and, within a few minutes, in company with rest of the house, sleep visited her till the sun rose.

On the morrow morn, around noon, the young soldier awoke. With his waking the realisation came to him. The future held no difficulties for him, He had merely to conform and all would be his. Truly no lamb ever went more willingly to its slaughter. Heaven upon earth was almost with him, he would undertake whatever was required to attain it.

Whilst Billy slept, the three women had worked upon the itinerary. Billy had but twenty days. It was Thursday, the license had been granted by the Registrar, having successfully been badgered and bullied by Nathaniel till he acquiesced. The date was fixed for a week Saturday, merely ten days hence, leaving the newly weds a further ten days honeymoon prior to the groom's departure back to his unit. Lots to do, things to do, to buy, not least both an engagement ring and a wedding ring.

"Samuel's in Manchester will do right fine."

Elizabeth was so excited, she was like a young child in a sweetie shop.

For once Gladys disagreed with her friend; she possessed a far better idea.

"For a wedding ring you may be right Elizabeth, but perhaps for an engagement ring we can do even better. Sally what colour eyes do you have?"

Gladys, of course, knew the answer. She just wanted her future daughter to confirm it.

"Why blue Gladys, but you know this".

"Quite so,"

A certain mischievousness of tone came with the affirmation.

"Just like mine. My late beloved husband bought me a ring he did, and such a ring it was. He brought it to my house, on the night he asked me to marry him. He had purchased it in Manchester the day before, said it matched my eyes perfectly. Pure Sapphire it is. My wedding ring, now on my right finger, goes with me to the grave. This, the very one he brought with him that night, my engagement ring, well, well"

The poor woman had stopped in mid sentence she needed to compose herself prior to continuing.

"This very same engagement ring, I want Billy to give it to you. It fully matches your eyes as well. I know how much it will please my Josh when I see him again. How, how, how, very, very, much."

Poor Gladys could no longer continue with her words, tears poured from her eyes. Elizabeth went to her side where they clasped hands.

"I am so sorry, silly me, dear, dear, dear, what must you both be thinking. I still love him so you see, my Josh, my poor, poor, Josh. Still what I do now will please him greatly."

With greater composure, summoned from out of her very depths, she took out a small black box from her apron pocket and handed it to Sally.

"There you are my darling girl. This is for you, a wedding present from Billy, from me, from my beloved Josh. I hope you like it "

Slowly Sally opened it, smiled, began to cry and handed it to her mother.

Elizabeth let out a squeal of pleasure.

"Why Gladys this is beautiful. What say you Sally."

"Lovely, It's absolutely lovely."

"Then it is yours."

Gladys was joyful again, her pleasure was complete. She had seen one of her most treasured possessions handed on and it was wonderful. Surely Sally Hawkins was the most worthy of inheritors.

"I shall give it to Billy this very day and he shall place it upon your finger himself.

"Oh Gladys."

Sally was overcome, her arms encompassed her future Mother-in-Law. All Three women cried uncontrollably so heightened was their happiness.

213

Billy, as he had previously rationalised, had merely to conform. Contentedly, conspiratorially, the two women witnessed the giving of the ring. In the back garden, surrounded by the flowers of spring, Billy Thomas knelt down on one knee and taking out the ring, lovingly worn for so long by his mother, he slipped it onto his girl's eagerly offered finger. Again, with his knee becoming more moist by the second, due to the heavy dew, he uttered the time honoured phrase that never changes, one which almost every woman wants to hear, at least once in her lifetime.

"Sally, my darling, darling, Sally, will you marry me?"

Came a moment of silence, lingering, oh so torturously, on the moistured air. Sally smiled at the man, who for an age had been the centre of all her aspirations. She gathered him up from off his knee and swept him into her arms. Then, placing him at arms length once more, a tear meandering down her cheek, her radiant sapphire eyes gazing deeply into his, she gave him the affirmation he so earnestly sought.

"Yes Billy, yes of course I will, did you ever doubt it my darling man.

The resulting embrace lasted a lifetime. At the window, both women turned away from the delightful tableaux that they had given witness to and looked at each other, knowing and letting each other know that they each knew just how close the pair had already become.

"Well that's, that then"

Gladys made her remark in a matter of fact manner.

It was with equal apparent nonchalance that Elizabeth agreed.

"That's that."

CHAPTER14

The world was all before them where to choose
Their place of rest, and providence their guide:
They hand in hand, with wandering steps and slow
Through Eden took their solitary way.

Paradise last BK xii

Above the meadows and stone walled hills of Glossop the pair meandered, holding hands and soaking up the ever-strengthening benevolent rays of a spring sun, unblemished by cloud or inhibited by wind. The season where nature re-arouses the dormant urges of her creatures was advancing apace. A certain fecundity was in the air. Swallows, Swifts and Martins were yet to arrive home from their winter quarters, but already the crows were gathering large twigs, relative in their size to pit props. Male Blue Tits clustered, chasing each other, impressing the females to come and nest with them. Larks had risen in their vertical flight, soaring to the heavens in delicate song. The Thrushes were occupying their mating quarters high in the topmost branches of the Rowan Ash. In the bushes and hedgerows, sparrows, wrens and finches were rediscovering the previous year's sparse lodgements.

Above all, just in case some were missing all these signs, hundreds of freshly born, ever bleating lambs were scampering; playfully unaware of how short life would be for them. The soldier, freshly returned from the fields of Flanders reflected on their coming fate. 'Lamb of God who takes away the sins of the world' came wistfully to the fore of Billy's mind.

They walked bonded, handfasted together for a lifetime. Billy considered: for age upon age to come, their love would cry out to a heartless World, to an infinite universe, glowing eternal, long after their bodies had turned to dust. In the darkest crevasses of the most forbidding place that creation possesses, love such as he was experiencing surely overcomes all, bringing peace and serenity, to even the darkest of all the recesses that occupy creation.

So, thought the young man. 'I can withstand all, endure all, and conquer all. With her love, I can suffer any trial, bear any toil, and never lose hope. This love my Sally gives to me, and I to her, forbids me ever to become enraged, jealous or envious. Surly this is humanity in its most high and blissful form of expression'.

Possessed with such thoughts, his abandoned conversation poured out upon his love. She listened, observing how diligently he chose every word, remembering the small boy who in spite of all, had absorbed such a wealth of knowledge, such mature understanding. This boy, handsome, opinionated, who had steadily won her heart, simply with a word and a glance. What wonderful days they were, the early ones in the library with Mrs. Lloyd steering them upon a collision.

She recalled those bleak terms at St Elphins where his image and words filled her every vacant, and sometimes, to the distraction of her tutors, her not so vacant moments. Memories came flooding upon her. Tearful nights spent wondering if ever they would meet again and if, in the event, he would be kind to her, to be as fond of her as she was of him. Sally also thought of those times as she grew into a young woman and here other fantasies of Billy would enter her dreams, with less than modest images.

Thus were her thoughts as they crossed fields full of dry, yet luscious grasses more than a foot high. They climbed over styles and walls needing, for a while to be as far away from the rest of the Human Race as possible. Eventually they came to a copse, with a dry bank tilting towards the sun, sheltered from the breeze and facing south.

The young man took off his jacket, laying it down for the girl. Shyly she accepted. Together they took in the sun, his arm about her waist, her head upon his shoulders. The wind, slight as it was, wafted Sally's spring skirt, taking it above the knee. 'What lovely legs she has, so he thought. Sally noticed his gaze and brushed the fabric down covering once again a part of her that he had never before seen.

"Enough of that young man"

Her voice was full of pretence, of mock severity, she reached out to playfully slap his hand.

"I never saw a thing, or at least nowhere as much as I think I saw, and touched last night".

"And what was that?"

The question came, erotic and enticing from the girl who had now fallen back upon the meadow grass with both hands behind her head.

"These"

The boy, without warning, placed both hands upon her breasts while he gazed into these deep eyes of blue. Sally smiled and gazed back at him, her gaze speaking more than ever could mere words.

"Well they do belong to you Billy, along with the rest of me. They always have and always will".

With that she brought up her hands and arms to place them behind his neck. She kissed him, open mouthed, encouraging their tongues to meet, which, of course, they did. For a full hour they lay there, kissing, stroking, caressing, fondling. Although tempted, and she would have allowed so, he did not place his hand beneath her skirt. Something within him forbade as much. Yet, she was so responsive, kissing his neck and his chest through the now open front of his shirt, whilst he nuzzled her wonderful adornments exposed for his pleasure.

His loins hardened, Sally could sense as much. She had never been fully enlightened upon the mechanics of love but she thought she knew what they entailed. The hardening that lay against her, she sensed, was part of it. Her hand drifted towards it, slowly, enticingly, she touched it through his trousers, enormous, warm, pulsing, moving with a life of it's own. She stroked it, which brought him great pleasure. She could see how delighted he was so she repeated the stroke over and over. He lay back; She drew over him, her naked breasts falling towards him. She stroked him again through his trousers. Suddenly Billy let out a great sigh repeating her name, "Oh Sally, Sally, Sally. Then he went limp, turning from her, breathing heavily.

"Have I hurt you love?"

He turned back. Not at all my darling, You are just the most wonderful thing in the whole of the universe".

In truth Billy did not know what to do. There was a dampness down there. He felt awkward. He lay his love back down onto his coat.

"What you did was this" and gradually his hand slipped down to her skirt and gently he even so slightly parted her legs. He then began to massage her and she, in turn, obtained a glimpse of how two people can please each other.

"Well?"

The boy was desperately curious.

"Well, well, well."

Billy waited impatiently for Sally to expand her reply, which, eventually, she did. "

Well I never, Billy Thomas."

Here her tone changed, becoming more formal, almost severe.

"We had better get going towards home before we do something we should not and us agreeing not to misbehave until our wedding night".

"Well we didn't. If you want to know what misbehaving is, wait until we are married and I will show you".

Now came another mock admonishment.

"You told me you were a respectable man".

"I am"

The reply, came full of assertion, but it did not forbid him one last kiss, or gathering her breasts once more in his hands before they were put respectfully back in place, ready to rejoin the world that they had left such a short time ago.

As they walked back down towards the town Billy stopped her whilst she was climbing halfway across a style. Holding her by the waist he swung her down, looked again into those eyes that made his heart beat so rapidly and promised.

"It will be wonderful you know".

"Indeed it will my lovely man, Indeed it will".

The journey to Manchester came and went. It was here that Billy was to learn true patience. The choosing of so simple an item took in over twelve shops in its accomplishment. A return to the seventh shop in their excursions confirmed which was the best, though in truth Billy could see little difference between any of them. Yet Sally was overjoyed in her final choice and that was sufficient for him.

"I have to wear it for the rest of my life Billy and then take it with me to my grave. It shall lie on my finger forever: One afternoon in its choosing is not much of an undertaking."

"Putting it that way Sally, you are right, what are three mere hours when compared to eternity."

On the train back, from Hadfield to Glossop they were the only occupants within the compartment, which gave them a little more time to explore each other. Billy discovered how Sally enjoyed her knees being gently squeezed and her inner thigh stroked.

'Marriage' he concluded yet again. 'Marriage to Sally was going to be so magically wonderful.'

On Saturday they spent the whole morning apart. Sally turned her attention to her dress, spending an age with Gladys and Elizabeth, Billy went to see his old friend and mentor Jack Lloyd together with his wife Ruth who now acted as the town's senior librarian.

Billy arrived at the managers' house at ten a.m. At once he was immersed in Ruth's ample frame, being hugged and congratulated. There was no match this Saturday for Glossop so Jack was idling away the hours in his garden. He had planned later to go up to his newly acquired allotment now proudly boasting the early shoots of onion sets, parsnips, peas as well as a wealth of giant winter cabbages.

The young man was shown into the front room sat down and asked to take tea, which he accepted. While Ruth was away making her preparations Jack asked the pertinent question.

"Well Billy what brings you here? You must be very busy with the wedding and such."

"Quite so Jack. It is upon this matter that I wish to speak. It just happens that you can render me a great service."

"What might that be then Billy?"

The question was full of a sense of intrigue as if he was being asked to accomplish a special mission.

"I need a best man Jack, a good wise, Christian friend who can help me through my wedding day. You've been like a father to me, much as Nathaniel, but he is Sally's father and I cannot ask him now can I?"

"Well not really I suppose."

So conjectured a pleased but surprised Jack Lloyd. He questioned the coming groom more closely.

"Are you sure its me you want Billy?"

"Certainly' none better Jack, will you do it for me?"

"Of course I shall, and be proud to, you lucky fellow."

He shouted through to his wife.

"Ruth come and hear the news."

The poor over burdened woman was struggling with a tray of sandwiches, biscuits and tea. Now she was hampered with her husband running towards the door captivated with excitement and asking her to come quickly, a task she was already in process of undertaking.

"Why sit down Jack Lloyd you are behaving like one of those young footballers of yours whose just scored a goal."

"That's it Ruth, that's just as it is. I feel I have just scored a winning goal. Billy here, he has asked me to be his best man, what about that then?"

Before she could answer Billy interjected.

"Mrs. Lloyd if it were not for you, Sally and I may never have gotten to know each other as we have. You brought us together as young children. Those Saturday mornings getting Sally to show me where the Waverleys were. Encouraging us both to read the rest of them. Also when Sally went away to boarding school you knew how much I missed her, You consoled me in my anguish whilst I waited for her return. You kept my hopes alive that one day we would share things together once more."

"Mrs. Lloyd do you know what Sally gave to me the day I left to go to war? It was this."

As he finished speaking he pulled out from his jacket pocket his small edition of Milton now a much-leafed, thoroughly read volume, courtesy of endless nights of reading.

"Without you Mrs. Lloyd I would never have gained Sally's love, or the love of such as this."

Billy leafed through the pages and gained the one he sought. He read:

*'With thy conversing, forget all time
All seasons, and their change, all please alike,'*

"The times that I have read these two lines, on trains, in billets, or when set upon by an enemy seeking my destruction and, all, Mrs. Lloyd, because of you."

His words had brought tears to Ruth's eyes. She sat down, Jack placing his arm around her shoulder.

"You are most welcome Billy. It will be my life's pleasure to see you united with young Sally Hawkins and Jack there by your side. My life's pleasure I say."

With this she burrowed her head into Jack's chest and began to sob.

Jack felt that he needed to explain this outburst of emotion to the embarrassed soldier standing before him.

"Never had our own you see. It was not meant to be. If you knew how often Ruth would speak of you both. It was like the episodes in one of those magazines; waiting to learn how things were going"

Ruth recovered her composure.

"Jack will make for you the best man anyone ever had, the best ever."

"I know Mrs. Lloyd. Just don't let him forget this on the day."

He hauled the newly purchased wedding ring from out of his inside jacket pocket and placed it into the hand of his friend and mentor. This was yet another signal for Ruth Lloyd, once again, to flood the room with tears. It took some time for her to gain her composure.

"As for the night before your wedding, you are to stay with us young fellow. We shall have you so polished up for the big day that people will think the Prince of Wales has come to town."

"Yes you shall indeed"

Her words, so emphatically endorsed by her husband, told Billy that it would be both fruitless and churlish for him to refuse.

"Thank you both very much indeed, I accept."

Ruth was deeply overjoyed; her previous tearfulness was overtaken by excited anticipation.

"What a day it's going to be. Jack, I shall need a new hat."

Jack looked towards Billy in mock admonishment.

"Now look at what you have done Billy Thomas, bringing all this additional expense upon this household."

Ruth looked shocked, but then she saw the mischievous grin that appeared on her husband's face. She poked him hard in the ribs with a finger. Jack instantaneously put matters right.

"And you shall have one my dear wife, what ever one you will."

Billy was so pleased with this resolution of affairs. Another mission accomplished, now it was time to meet up with Sally at the library, where else but there? After a brief wander through the rows of books, they would simply cross over the road to the Manse, in Fazackerley Street, to see Pastor Livingston. He spoke of the duties that Sally was undertaking that morning which brought another round of tears from the eyes of Mrs. Lloyd.

"I wonder how Sally is progressing, she has been trying on her wedding dress while I have been to see you."

Billy Thomas may have been the holder of the Military Medal and he may have assisted in holding back the might of the German army. His tactical foresight on the battlefield may have been quite extraordinary, but he possessed little knowledge upon the infinite differing catalysts that can bring tears to a woman's eyes. Again the overworked handkerchief came into use as Ruth's eyes filled with moisture once again.

Now he was impatient to see his girl once more. Making short work of the tea, he took his leave, bidding farewell to an emotionally overwhelmed household. Then he was off; enthusiastically waved away by the very happy couple, wrapped arm in arm on the step of their house, the delicate, sodden piece of white cotton being used as a pennant signalling his departure.

Billy need not have worried about events elsewhere. That morning from out of an aged dress box, tied with pink ribbon, had come Elizabeth's own wedding gown, together with its veil and accessories.

The two women fussed around their victim seemingly for hours, making adjustments, notations for alterations and exclaiming superlatives whilst Sally observed herself in front of a body length mirror. Elizabeth was to be the first to comment upon the final result of their efforts.

"You look a picture my girl, of course girls are a little more fuller in the bust these days, but we can let out the back a little."

"I don't suppose Billy minds about that."

Gladys winked most wickedly to her friend.

"I don't suppose he does"

Her partner in crime agreed, they were looking at each other, smiling and giggling mischievously like a pair of schoolgirls.

Sally just kept her thoughts within, not commenting upon the titillating conjecture of the two other women. She knew Billy did not mind, he did not mind at all.

Pins were put in place and the veil placed upon the bride's head. Once again the two women turned Sally to face the mirror. Both women made their closing remarks upon the image. Arms around each other they voiced, what had become for them, their traditional manner of expressing complete satisfaction.

Well, that's, that, then"

"That's that."

It was twelve thirty when the pair met on the steps of the library, The very steps that Billy had ascended so many times in the past, impatient to meet the girl he was now holding hands with.

"Well let's go and find some books"

"Like old times"

"No Billy, there is a profound difference between this moment and then. Now we know that we belong to each other, shall always belong to each other, completely belong one to the other."

Sally pondered. Memories of Billy's touch, his most intimate touch, still enthralled her. Who would have thought, those years ago that they should become so.

"A penny for your thoughts?"

"These thoughts, Billy Thomas, are worth a fortune."

"Are they now?"

"Yes they are."

"Well are you going to share them with me."

"Certainly not."

With this final authoritative refusal, Sally entered the building, stepping over the towns coat of arms, beautifully displayed in mosaic, 'Virtas, Veritas, Libertas.' The place was virtually as it was all those years ago. Volumes came to hand, placed exactly where they had always sat. For a while they were once again those two innocent children playfully each seeking out a work, one attempting to impress the other.

Suddenly, Billy took his love in both hands.

"See all these books in this vast library. Well I would not exchange all of them for this one volume."

With this he took out his Milton, kissed it, and then kissed her.

"Not for every book the place contains."

After half an hour or so, mostly spent in quiet reflection, they left. To the shocked sounds of tutting from an assistant who, obviously, knew not what historical events she was a witness to, the pair kissed each other shamelessly within the hallowed walls, and left. Going down the steps they kissed once more, smiled at the disapproving assistant and stepped towards the Manse, leaving their childhood behind.

Departing together, for the last time, somehow, above all Human knowledge and understanding, their spirits left something behind, translucent and benevolent, still abiding alongside those rows of books. These books, books that had provided them with so much pleasure and had inaugurated such love, were destined to reach a generation of other readers before, finally, falling apart, they inevitably became discarded and replaced. Yet each volume, at the time of its destruction, possessed a value above comprehension, for each had brought so much joy and consolation to this pair of star-crossed lovers and to so many others who were to follow in their wake. Rather than being a valueless article, of no further use or worth, every page within the tattered aged binding had become a treasure, a pearl of great price.

Now, the pair arm in arm, progressed on their journey. Endlessly, caps and hats were raised from passers by, as they proceeded to their destination. Strangers, never seemingly met before, stopped them. They experienced exchanges of shaken hands, smiles, endless smiles. All this and more graced their early afternoon stroll to the Manse, a distance of less than two hundred paces.

It was as if the entire town had taken these two young lovers into their hearts, adopting them, allowing themselves to reflect in the glow of their colourful, bountiful expression of hope and love in a world that ceasingly, day after day, grew ever more drear, grey, and mournful. It was as if these two young people had the answers to so many of the questions that the town was asking of itself.

222

"When would this war come to an end? Will my Johnny come home safe to us? Please say it is not as bad as it appears, surely if you two can be as this then, of certainty, our own will return and have the same."

All this expressed through this display of hope and love, in the actions, and open displays of affection by a young solider and his beautiful girl. Just through a smile, a smile at the end of a mile of smiles. Thus they arrived at the Manse.

Billy released the bell pull, bringing Mrs. Livingston to the door. Again the wide warm smile, the open door, the invitation to enter.

"Do come in the both of you"

The ample, motherly woman, pristine in her white blouse, blue skirt and apron, the kind Gladys always referred to as 'her pinny,' greeted them by kissing Sally on the cheek.

" Pastors waiting for you in the study, go through, I shall bring the tea."

'More tea,' thought Billy, 'thank goodness for the Suez Canal.'

The pair discovered Pastor Gideon at his desk finalising his sermon for tomorrow.

He looked up, an expression of great pleasure dawning upon his face.

"Sally, Billy, my, my is that the time already, one o'clock of the afternoon and me not ready, my how time goes. Well come on in, sit yourselves down and let us see what it is to be done."

Except for a glancing handshake on the station platform Gideon had not set eyes upon Billy for nigh on eighteen months. He had kept abreast of news of course through Gladys, Sally and her family. Nathaniel had called, of course, to tell of the wedding, to arrange the license and to fix the date and time. Now he had both his victims in front of him, nervous, eyes only for each other, shy.

"Come, come, tell the me all your news. It has been a long time Billy has it not."

"Indeed Pastor too long, in truth it feels an age."

"And is the war as bad as it appears Billy."

Gideon's own son was a doctor aboard a hospital ship in the Aegean. The letters he was receiving from him filled the Pastor with horror, anger and loathing that such things, as he had read, could be enacted, perpetrated, in a civilised world. Additionally, he had seen through his own eyes, so many wounded men coming home, crippled in mind and body. Yet, something told him that matters would get worse, much worse, before this conflict's conclusion came to pass.

Billy had waited a while before his reply, seeing that Pastor Livingston was in deep thought.

"Well it is bad out there, very bad, but we shall come through it Pastor, of that I have no doubt, no doubt at all. We are fighting a tenacious foe, intelligent, fit, well equipped, organised, and vicious, but we shall prevail never fear."

"And shall we prevail this year Billy, how long son, how long must it continue."

"I do not know Pastor. A great offensive is being planned on the Western Front, new weapons, more artillery, planes, and machine guns. I have great confidence in its outcome but I do not think it will bring a conclusion to affairs this year. I have seen the enemy; I have looked into his eyes. I have even sat down and eaten with him, spoken of his families and home, upon God also. At Christmas we even sang carols to each other."

"Many of the enemy, I know, would love to go back to normal times but this war has taken a great hold, gained a life of its own. No, nineteen-sixteen is not the year that will see the end, despite our greatest efforts. It is not going to be the year of our victory, but with the great offensive that is surely coming, the blockade, the attrition and our display of undoubted commitment, it is the year that we shall stop the Germans from winning."

"But we hear of great victories, thousands of Germans prisoners. Surely they cannot go on like that."

"They can, they do, and they will Pastor, countries have a huge capacity to absorb countless loss of life, of material. I am only saying this, and begging your pardon Sally. I shall say it. After the war, when we who survive return, it will be to a different kind of world. A world where many of the ancient monarchies will have disappeared, their systems and their values having collapsed with them."

"There shall be a new order. One where mankind looks after his neighbour, where greed and gain do not overwhelm men's motives, where Christianity, a true Christianity reigns, where men love their neighbours as themselves, where political philosophy and religious theology march together side by side towards the new Jerusalem."

Billy's oratory had both stunned and silenced his audience including Mrs. Livingston who, however, was the first to recover.

"Why Billy Thomas what words you possess. Gideon, he reminds me of someone I once met. A preacher without a church, a man with a mission, having nothing but his Bible and a dream to build a house of God where there was only a field. A man who addressed his congregation in all weathers, a congregation loyal, loving the lord, dreaming that same dream, one day to build a new Jerusalem. Where did that preacher go? What became of his congregation?"

" I see today, before us, the son of the man who capped our spire. His spirit is still with us. God bless you Billy and you too Sally, the next generation of our congregation shall be in good hands. God bless you both."

Gideon had listened silently to two orations. Now, before he could reply there came a third.

Sally leaned towards her beloved man and took his hands in hers. "Billy I have always loved you since that first time we met. You, scarcely in long trousers, me an undeveloped spotty wisp of a girl. Even then I thought of you as special, gifted, full of knowledge, full of dreams. Those dreams you speak of here with the Pastor and his wife, I accept them, and I will help you to develop them, be your strength and guide, always, ever by your side. I promise, I shall be a good wife to you, but I shall be more than that. I dedicate myself to being your life's partner in striving towards that goal of a New Jerusalem to banish the dark satanic mills."

Here Sally composed herself, her voice dropped and she continued.

"Billy this is my promise to you. I shall love you, cherish you, and keep you only unto me. Your battles will be my battles. We shall fight them together, each in unison one with the other, and if you are ever overcome, if God takes you from me, I shall continue in that struggle, knowing you are with me in spirit. I love you, I always have but, until this moment, I never knew how much."

"Pastor Gideon when you marry us you can do so with the knowledge that we are fully aware of the frailty of life, the uncertainty of longevity, particularly in such times as these. However long or short our time is proved to be, together on this Earth, you will have never, never, joined together two people more loving, more insistent in their wanting to be joined. Pastor please marry us, possessing joy for us in our life together in the certainty that if death parts our physical selves, it will never conquer our spiritual togetherness. That shall be eternal."

Mrs. Livingston could see that, for the moment, her husband was lost for words, she used the age old remedy that soothed minds at such times.

"Let us have tea shall we?"

Handing a cup to Gideon, once again it proved to provide the immortal English remedy to such situations. Never was tea more refreshing to Gideon than the cup he was handed. It truly was the cup that cheered, that and the delicious slice of home made cake he indulged in. Five minutes passed in reflective silence. Gideon composed himself and then responded.

"Well, usually it is I who gives the prospective Bride and Groom what advice I can. Having listened to the pair of you and to my good wife as well, what can I say? What can I add, to what has been said? I have known you both since birth. I baptised you both. I welcomed you both into the congregation when you confirmed your adult beliefs and commitments. I married both your parents and Billy, my wife and I had no little hand in bringing together your mother and father, God rest his soul,"

"It is with great pleasure that I shall minister and bless your union, the one with the other, My greatest pleasure. In doing so I shall feel deeply proud and privileged."

Here he concluded his philosophising and turned to more practical matters,

"Now we have some more formal things to discuss, hymns and things. Also tomorrow I shall bless you at communion and announce the date and time of your marriage. Now what hymns. What ones would you like?"

The good Pastor felt much better now that the conversation had turned towards utility. He awaited a reply.

It was Billy who spoke, looking towards Sally for agreement.

"Pastor I know that this is not a wedding hymn but it has become a great favourite at the front with all the men manning the trenches. I should like you to include 'Abide with me,' as much for the people who cannot attend, or who have gone before, as for as any other reason."

Sally agreed, squeezing Billy's hand as she did so.

"Well Billy, it is an unusual request for a wedding, but very apt under the circumstances, you shall have it. Did you know it was your father's favourite hymn also?

"Yes Pastor I do, one of its lines is engraved on his headstone."

Gideon tried to recall and then it came to him.

"Quite so, 'Point me to the skies,' if I remember correctly.

"That is perfectly correct Pastor"

"Abide with me', it is then. Sally, how about you? What would you like?"

"Love divine all love excelling', Pastor if you will."

"Marvellous, and the congregation at the end will all, 'be lost in wonder, love and praise'.

His wife agreed.

"Indeed they shall. What a day it will be, what a wonderful day."

Came Sunday morning and Billy, together with his mother, strolled together towards Sally's house, where they were met at the front gate. From here, Sally and her betrothed walked arm in arm before their parents.

Nathaniel looking proud and pristine, with a woman upon each arm, conducted them to their place of worship.

Upon the Chapel steps the now recognised routine of hand shaking, together with good will wishes and backslapping, took place. A beaming Mr. and Mrs. Lloyd were there, as was the Pastor waiting by the door welcoming the faithful to service and praise. He placed a piece of paper one into each of the couples' hands for safe keeping.

"You two shall read the passages today. Billy the first. Sally the second. They are notated on the papers."

226

They entered the place of worship. Billy looked around; he was seeking out a specific couple. He found them, excused himself from Sally for a moment and went to speak to them. Within a couple of minutes he was back, having made an appointment to meet with his friend Jimmy's parents on Tuesday evening.

The service was well underway. The time came for Billy's reading.

"The first reading is from psalm 121, a psalm of David."

"I will lift up mine eyes unto the hills
From whence shall come my help,
My help cometh from the lord,
Which made heaven and earth.

He will not suffer thy foot to be moved:
He that keepeth thee will not slumber.
Behold he that keepeth Israel
Shall neither slumber nor sleep.
The Lord is thy keeper:
The Lord is the shade upon thy right hand.

The sun shall not smite thee by day,
Nor the moon by night.
The Lord shall keep thee from evil;
He shall keep thy soul.
The Lord shall keep thy going out
And thy coming in
From this time forth and for evermore.'

The congregation was visibly moved. All those present knew of a young man's death at the front, or had loved ones, striving out there at this very moment, facing all manners of peril. To them, Billy's reading of this comforting work, dressed as his mother had insisted, in his full uniform, with his hat resting upon the lectern, poured forth a comfort to them all. The passage was tangible, yet also full of reverent mystery. When he finished he walked back to his place surrounded by absolute silence, a silence that was created by a sense of unexplained awe. It was as if the Holy Spirit himself had visited the congregation powering forth assurance and hope. Many felt for years afterwards than they had been witnesses to a remarkable occurrence.

Prayers were said, then a hymn. 'O God our help in ages past.'

Sally read from I: Corinthians chapter 13, finishing with the immortal lines.

227

"But now abideth faith, hope, and love, these three,
And the greatest of these is love."

Poignant and pertinent. Gideon had chosen well. He now had his congregation in the palm of his hand. Firstly, prior to his sermon he gave out the notices. The Spring fair, women's prayer groups, the knitting circle, the youth club. Then came the item that all ears were impatiently waiting for.

'On Saturday next the marriage shall take place of Miss Sally Hawkins, spinster of this town; and Mr. William Thomas bachelor. Let anyone who has any due cause as to why these two should not be joined in holy matrimony let them speak now. This is the first and last call under the emergency regulations now currently in force."

It was unheard of, unprecedented, but an immediate spontaneous applause broke out in congratulation, which led Gideon to remark with assumption.

"Well I gather that meets with the approval of all present."

It had indeed been so approved.

He now took up the text for his sermon. It came from the Psalm,

'My help cometh from the Lord.'

Later Ruth was to tell him that it was his best sermon in years, full of the passion and self-belief that had dominated his early outdoor orations. He was pleased, having torn up the sermon he had written prior to yesterday's meeting with the two beloved members of his flock. Late last night and into the early hours of the morning he had written words of inspiration, the like of which had not left his pen in years. After its end an exhausted Pastor announced the final hymn, John Bunyan's 'Who would true valour be'

The words, resoundingly sung, lifted the lofty rafters of the house of God, sending his congregation on their way with hope in their heart and with a new peace of mind.

On the steps looking out towards the library where it had all begun, Gladys turned back towards her sister in love, placed a hand upon her shoulder and said affirmatively,

"Well that's that then"

The usual affirmative reply came back with even more conviction.

"That's is most certainly that."

CHAPTER 15

Nor love thy life, nor hate,
But what thou liveliest, live well,
How long or short permit to heaven;
And now prepare thee for another sight

Paradise Lost Bk xi

During those last few days before their marriage Sally just would not be parted from Billy. She insisted that they went everywhere together. They were never separated during the daytime, and were often to be seen arm in arm, walking the winding lanes leading upwards to the hills, existing only for each other, dwelling in their own private world. Each of them sharing their dreams, the one with the other. Their mothers just sighed, knowing they had no control over the forces which drove the pair and with a shrug of the shoulders, simply let them go their way unhindered.

The protestations upon Sally's lack of attendance at the shop was met with a pair of huge blue appealing eyes, making the decision for them. Thus, until after Billy had left once more for the front, Sally was to have a total holiday from work. The Emporium would just have to manage without her.

So love was allowed a free reign and inevitably it look its course, opening avenues of awareness of each others needs and desires. Here among the hills and grassy meadows, sitting upon a blanket, smuggled out by the devious Corporal, they became engaged in intimate conversation. Their thoughts given voice, they probed the daring, explorative, erotic, and the suggestive, their language becoming ever more filled of promise upon promise.

They entered complete dialogues, leaving no doubt, each in the others mind, the realisation, that come their wedding night, the fulfilment of love's expression would be entire, and without condition. Sally would go to her marriage bed a virgin; pure in the eyes of God, yet their intimacy had become so graphically intense, that very little would be left on that night for them to guess upon.

On Monday evening they went to visit Jimmy Jones' parents, as Billy had arranged. Whilst they were there they also called upon Uncle Frank to inspect this years pig. Auntie Helen came to the door. Her face fairly beamed to see the couple.

"Uncle Frank is up the top feeding ' The Kaiser' but, be careful, he is a real grumps this one."

Sally looked puzzled and Billy explained that 'The Kaiser' must be the family name for this year's pig. He was very eager to see a sight, that was so much a part of his lost youth, that he immediately caught the startled girl's hand and rushed her up towards the pig-pen.

Uncle Frank was there as usual with both his neighbours. In fact they had two pigs penned up, both old spots as Billy informed his fiancé with a knowledgeable smile.

"Which one is The Kaiser?" he asked of his uncle.

"Why that one of course" he said pointing to a giant Porker with an oblong black patch beneath his nose. In truth he did look somewhat similar to England's greatest foe.

"And the other, whose he?"

"Why that's Hindenburg, who else".

"The Kaiser and Hindenburg, well at least this is one place where they will meet their deserved fate".

"Nothing less, Billy, nothing less".

They conversed for an age. Billy recalling and relating to Sally his first experience of the ceremony of the pig and how its skin and bladder had made a perfect football providing Jimmy and he with almost ten years of use.

"I often think of that first pig; how it brought Jimmy and I years of practice, honing our skills, increasing our stamina and strength. I doubt without such as he, that we would ever have become professionals".

Sally said not a word, she was thinking of Billy's poetry, a matter upon which, they had not, as yet, spoken upon. Now she remembered the very first poem that he had written to her and, had not yet shown to anyone because it disturbed her so.

"Poor pig", sighed Sally". "I often wonder upon how cruel we all are".

Billy made no reply. His eyes were full of images where men were being treated like stuck pigs, bayoneted in trenches or suspended by barbed wire. He would try to change the Subject.

"Mr Jones, is Mrs Jones at home? I promised I would call and see you both".

"She is my boy, expecting you this very moment. I suspect there is tea and perhaps a slice of cake awaiting for you".

"Thank you Mr Jones, we shall go right away. Uncle Frank see you on Saturday if not before. Oh, and nice pigs".

"See you Saturday Billy, meantime don't do anything I wouldn't do hear me now".

"As you are Uncle Frank."

Somewhat embarrassed, and avoiding Sally's frowning eyes he took her hand and headed towards Mr Jones' front door.

The blue door was opened awaiting their entry but Billy still felt it pertinent to knock whilst simultaneously calling out the name of the occupant.

"Mrs Jones".

There was a shuffling sound and a little rotund lady, wearing the obligatory pinny, came to the entrance. The, now familiar, burst of pleasant surprise came to her face. It fairly beamed.

"My, my, Billy Thomas, do come in, you too young Sally, we don't stand on ceremony here".

The little lady, was now somewhat more grey haired, and portly than Billy could remember from the last time he had last seen her. It had been at the Station, where she was bidding farewell to her son and all the other young men which comprised Glossop's portion of the emergent New Army. Along with what had seemed to be half the town, she had gathered there on that platform back in 1914, anxiously waiving goodbye to the cheerful, happy expectant young men who were so innocently unaware of what they were about to face.

"Happy days, happy days, off to France to get a medal back home by Christmas."

Now Billy was home to a great welcome because he was seen as a local hero whilst the rest were scattered all along the Western Front. Here they either anxiously awaited their time of trial, or already lay beneath their small corner of land that they had so dearly bought.

He had come to offer reassurance and consolation to his friend's mother. It would not be close to seeing her son here in the flesh, but before he went Billy would give Mrs Jones, a woman now fully aware of war's horrors, a personal message. It was all he could provide, except to add how fit and well young Jimmy was and how much he missed and loved her. The poor woman simply had to be content with this message from him as her consolation.

"Nice to see you Mrs Jones, lovely weather we've been having for the time of year".

"Almost like summer, tell me what is the weather like in France?"

Mrs Jones indicated for them both to sit down next to each other on the sofa.

"It can get much warmer than here Mrs Jones, but it can rain just as hard, you take your pick".

"And tell me of Jimmy, how was he last when you saw him".

"Very well indeed Mrs Jones. It was he that helped get me back to the casualty clearing station. Then he stayed with me until they placed me on a train, which was taking the wounded to a field hospital. That's when I last felt him. I cannot say that I saw him, for my eyes were completely bandaged. His last words were 'Lucky blighter, give my mum and dad my love when you get back to Glossop."

"He was fit and well and has now retired to Amiens for a long furlough. Hopefully I shall rejoin him there when I go back, so if you have anything for him I shall be glad to let him have it".

"You sure Billy that he has not been hurt at all?"

"Not at all Mrs Jones. I can assure you".

Mr Jones came in whilst the conversation was taking place.

"Thank you for that Billy, this is a great comfort to us both, isn't it missus".

"That is indeed a great comfort to us Billy."

Mrs Jones planted a huge kiss on Bill's cheek and exited to get the tea, wiping her eyes on her pinny.

"Thank you for that young Billy. The missus she's been right worried. Now perhaps she can calm down a while".

They had tea and cakes; everyone in Glossop was offering them cake wherever they went. Sally listened intently as they talked of the old days, the pigs, Chapel, Billy's father, and football. It was getting late. Darkness was falling about 8-00pm at the moment. They made their excuses, gave their hosts expressions of gratitude and made ready to leave.

Mr and Mrs Jones both came to the door to see them off, crying out to the pair as they began to descend to the town.

"See you on Saturday, God bless."

Back by the doorway the woman looked anxiously at the man and whispered what was almost a prayer.

Lets just hope she's long a wife and short a widow."

"Aye and let us hope that he and Jimmy look out for each other".

"Well" Jimmy could not ask for a better friend".

"That's very true my love."

Mr Jones gently ushered his wife indoors; there was a chill in the air.

In the gathering gloom Billy ushered his beloved on a circuitous route home. He needed a private moment with her. They went across the meadow that led to the small bridge by Partingtons mill. Here he kissed her, gently at first, then with fire, urgency, as if time was running out for days such as they were having. His love responded at first with giving such kisses herself and then, with words of love and assurance, she endorsed this moment of passion with promises of soon to be fulfilled desires.

"Not long now Billy, another day over. Saturday shall surely come, and come that evening you shall experience and know all of love's mysteries. Come on my love, it is getting cold, let us go now."

So, in the gloom, they left this little spot of England, so typical of the Country that the Man was fighting for. Walking alongside the stream, they passed the stark edifice of Partington's mill. Against the background of a skyline now almost devoid of daylight and filling with threatening cumulous it looked truly dark and Satanic. Billy thought of the contrast, the green and pleasant land above the town and the sight that greeted him now. Pondering, he put his arm more closely around his love and together they wound their way back towards her home, to her parent's house and an unexpected visitor.

Upon entering her front door Elizabeth announced that Mr Hill-Woods was here to see them both. Sure enough, when they went through, there he was, sitting in the room talking to Nathaniel.

"Well if it is not the happy couple, how are you both?"

Mr Hill-Woods or Colonel as his honorary title now proclaimed, stood up to shake Billy's hand. He was resplendent in his dress uniform with its white winged cotton shirt and regimental tie, Billy noted it carried the insignia of the Sherwood Foresters. Billy saw before him a man full of himself and his own importance. The type of leader that had led the world towards the mess it was in. He was the kind of man whose time was passing, whose day was surely coming to an end. A man who felt that he had the right to wear such a splendid uniform but did not feel the need to risk his life in perpetuating what it represented.

Yet, Billy determined, tonight he would be polite, distant, but polite. He was after all a guest in Nathaniel's house, he would not embarrass him by stating here, before this strutting peacock, the things he now believed in and how such a man as he, here offering his hand, had no place, no part to play in any future decent society. No Billy would not warn him tonight, of his sure and certain downfall, resulting from the implementation of the kind of new order, conceived by himself and so many of the others, who, one day, would return from this war, filled with resolve.

Sally could sense her partner's discomfort; diplomatically she offered an excuse for the inevitable disinterest that Billy might make to this man whom, she also, had grown to despise.

"I am afraid Mr Hill-Woods that Billy has gotten very tired. He is still not fully mended and I have insisted that he should retire very soon. I am sure you understand sir."

"Of course young lady. Billy I am very sorry I was hoping to have a word about an article for the local press but perhaps another time soon."

In truth, Sally was not far off the mark. Billy was going through one of his phases of unexplainable fatigue.

'Would you like lunch at the club sometime this week, perhaps with Nathaniel and I?"

"What of Sally, could she not come also?"

This perplexed the MP; he tried to explain the situation as tactfully as possible.

"But it is the Conservative Club. I am afraid they do not allow lady diners, except at certain times, when they can be escorted properly."

"Well I am going to respectively decline in that case sir. You see I am determined to spend every hour God grants me during my leave to be with my Sally and I have no intention of going to a place where she is not welcome."

Hill-Woods was quietly enraged, he had been placed on the spot and pushed into a corner. He knew he had to retreat gracefully. He was an experienced politician, he knew how to regroup.

"Quite so Billy. Then perhaps we can agree upon another venue. Nathaniel shall we discuss this further, tomorrow would be opportune. I will call upon you at the shop?"

The remark was a question the lifting voice indicated as such.

"As you will Mr Hill-Woods. Let us see what the two of them have to say in the morning."

"A Good idea Nathaniel."

The chastised politician had redeemed his dignity somewhat, but something told him that if he did not retreat immediately another assault upon it would quickly follow.

"Well must be going, not a spare moment these days. Goodnight Billy, Sally, Mrs Hawkins"

With this perfunctory farewell, he simply shook everyone's hands and headed towards the door followed by Nathaniel. The door was heard to shut and Nathaniel re-entered suppressing a grin.

"Well you two certainly put him in his place."

Billy felt the need to endorse the attitude that he and Sally had adopted towards the pompous, presumptive and manipulative M.P

"As will many others before much longer."

To his surprise Nathaniel agreed with him.

"Quite so, but you should have seen his face, it really was a picture. He is so used to people fawning over him."

"Well it is time that was put a stop to, times are heading for a change."

"I tend to agree Billy, but what do we put in his place."

"Socialism, Democratic, Parliamentary, Christian, Socialism."

Now Nathaniel, in his turn, felt relaxed.

"There's a thought Billy, one for us all to consider, men and women alike, but first the suffrage, universal suffrage. Women have waited too long. It's now theirs to have."

"Hear, hear," cried Elizabeth.

"Hear, hear," echoed Sally.

"Well that's two revolutions in one night. Too much for me, Elizabeth I'm off to bed. It's exhausted I am."

They all bade Nathaniel goodnight, listening to him ascend the stairs. It was Elizabeth's turn to say goodnight.

"Why you two, what a couple you are going to make. I will leave you now. Billy stay in the spare room, it is made up for you. You are both tired, don't be long now."

She in turn made her way up the stairs. 'Sensible children' she thought to herself, 'surely they will behave themselves these last few days and if not then, hey ho!'

The pair snuggled on the green sofa watching the dying embers of the flame. Eventually Sally reluctantly concluded that it was time for them also to go to their rest.

"Time for bed, its been a long day."

Up the stairs they went together then after one last lingering kiss they parted to their separate rooms. However a surprise greeted the boy as they disengaged at the top of the stairs, for Sally whispered a promise in his ear.

"I shall come along and tuck you in shortly."

This she did but when she entered his room it was to find him in a deep sleep. Sally lay beside the sleeping man, undid the top buttons of her night-dress and placed one of his listless hands upon her breast. Having it there, pressing upon her, had become one of her pleasures. Before daylight, long whiles before consciousness returned to the soldier, she had gone to her own room, one day less remaining, to becoming a wife.

'What a sensible girl' thought her sleepless mother, again sure that no ultimate union had taken place. The house rested, together with all the occupants, each having their own dreams, private, luxurious, wondrous, dreams.

Nathaniel was the first to awake, and then looking at the clock decided upon some minutes more. He turned towards his wife, who guided his hand, as had her daughter the hand of the soldier, love was not the sole possession of the young.

Tuesday merged into Wednesday when it rained all day.

In fact the heavens wept torrents, streams of her tears pouring water down into the town from the hills around ending in the high street by the square where the limited drains simply could not cope.

The roads became like the canal. No traffic could pass through. Billy thought of his friends in the trenches. Life on the Western Front was miserable at the best of times, but when it rained it elevated the misery to a level unbearable to even contemplate. He had experienced the almost soul destroying aspects of existence in the morass, and was so grateful to be out of it, even if it was to be for a short time.

Looking out from the rain streaked window, he remembered how, at such times, he had used sandbags to provide covering for his boots and further, up to his knees. Billy recalled that, in spite of this added improvised protection, he had still become enstenched in treacled mud. He could smell it now. He would always be able to smell it.

Still, in England, on half day closing, with your life's love having a complete holiday, and with the adults away to the shop, life was luxurious.

Tea and toast now greeted him, whilst still in a warm bed and the rain remained outside, merely splattering the ensashed pains of glass which rattled incessantly with the gale. Tea served by his lovely Sally, still in her loose dressing gown, well; a man could only think of heaven.

Sally noted the satisfied expression, the eyes that beheld her countenance with such appreciation.

"And what are you gazing at young man?"

"The tea and toast my love. Just what a man needs at this time of the day."

"Oh."

So came the disappointed and surprised response. Attendant with the singular expression came Sally's own retort.

"Well here you are then, and get up when you have had it. We have a lot to get through."

With this pronounced display of petulance, the tray was almost slammed against the bedside cabinet. Billy. highly amused, caught Sally's hand as she was turning to go. It was his time to pose a provocative question and to see where it led.

"And where are you going young woman?"

"To leave you in peace with your breakfast."

"Some chance."

He took hold of her hands and swung her down upon the bed clasping her waist and pressing his mouth upon hers. It was a small bed but he squeezed himself to one side leaving her room to lie beside him.

"Go on, get inside, It's a cold day, there's plenty of time."

"Why Billy Thomas,"

It was a refusal, an admonishment, mockingly so, but, none the less, she did as was bid.

They were lying under the covers on their sides, facing each other. Billy parted her gown, unbuttoned the fortuitively designed night-dress and with little difficulty withdrew both her beautifully displayed articles simultaneously from her person. She in turn without muttering a sound took off the top of his pyjamas, exposing his still battle bruised chest. 'If mother could see me now,' she thought guiltily.

Billy began to stroke the cleft between her breasts, then gradually, exquisitely, cupped her left breast in his hand. With his thumb he began to roll the nipple. It became erect, insistent upon further enticement, which he providently applied. Gently he turned her onto her back and rolled on top of her, supporting his weight. He spread his legs about hers, which remained, closed and slowly, rhythmically, moved his hips in a circular fashion around and upon her.

The sensation was exquisitely unbearable, enticing her to move with him, her breasts being flattened and massaged by his swaying chest. An urge almost beyond control rose within her She wanted to give him everything that she had to give right there, irrespective of their mutual promises. His lips were nuzzling into her lower neck, then her shoulders. He sucked at her skin as hard as he could; it filled her with an uncontrollable sensation an unutterable desire.

Sally raised his head, looked into those flaring, not to be refused eyes and offered it all to him.

"Billy if you want to; you can."

"Can what?"

The reply came erotically, asking her to be more precise in her language.

"You can do it to me if you want to."

There, it was out, scantily clothed, entangled in the most profound embrace; she had offered him the ultimate prize. It was at this precise moment, when all he had dreamed of night after night in the trenches was there for him to have, that Billy recoiled. He kissed his love with all the passion he possessed, brought his hand up to her flowing hair and made his decision.

"Sally nothing would please me more. I want you, desperately I want you and here and now just as we are. Everything I ever want or need is right here before me, fragrant, splendid, and irresistible. Even so I shall wait, nothing shall spoil the expectancy of our Marriage and the wonder of our wedding night."

Sally looked at Billy with complete surprise. Her mother had once told her that no man would never refuse to take 'advantage,' if offered the opportunity. Billy could see in her eyes that she was feeling some sort of rejection. He had to reassure her.

Sally, you are my ever eternal love. I want to remember the first time we become as one, each other unto the other, as so special, so very special. Three more days and I will show you what is possible from me as your husband. Let not my impatience, taking advantage of you like this, spoil it for us."

With that he slid to her side still holding her around him embracing her with his arms and legs.

Billy's words had succeeded. Once again Sally felt both secure and needed. Within herself, Sally felt what she perceived to be bitter disappointment, yet, in truth, her emotions were deceiving her. She was simply experiencing frustration, having become so deeply aroused by the sensations brought upon her through Billy's attentions. The intimacy, the thought of making her physical union to the man that she so loved, was wonderful.

Yet, paradoxically, in contrast, lying in the small bed cocooned in her lover's embrace, she also experienced a great emotive gratitude. This man, her Billy, felt so much for her that, even now, with her in his bed, he had held back, deciding rather to wait. Here she was ready to give him

237

everything, divested of almost all her modesty. She was a prize waiting to be taken and he had declined to take advantage of her, knowing what she really wanted.

Their marriage was truly to start on the evening of their wedding day and now the principle was set in stone. She kissed him gently, almost sisterly in her relief and gratitude. It was her Billy, her lovely Billy Thomas who, in spite of her enticements, remembered their mutual vow. When the final invitation was made, he had, with gentleness and consideration, displayed another aspect of his character, resolution. Now, for portraying such excellent conduct on the field of love, he was mentioned, in the most glowing of terms, in her despatches.

"Thank you Billy, you are the most wonderful, caring and considerate of men. Perhaps it is time to get up now?"

He agreed, reluctantly agreed. He got out of bed in nothing but his pants, the form of his manhood, still possessing an element of excitement, was there on display for Sally to muse upon. Its size gave her doubts upon the possibility of the final enactment of love, as she had perceived it to be. Seeing him so, the concept of lovemaking became just that little more intriguing.

He slipped on his shirt, trousers and socks. Sally thought men in socks were so funny. He went to the bathroom leaving her with the battlefield and her forces intact. However her outer defences had been breached beyond repair and, in the action of their demolition, had provided conjecture, and amazement about the strength of the enemy's artillery. She whispered to herself, smiling inwardly as she did so.

"What a resolution is coming, what a resolution."

Thus Saturday came so strenuously, time seemingly dragging on endlessly. Yet, in spite of the clock refusing to flow smoothly onwards, Friday afternoon eventually came.

Billy was packing his things in preparation to stay with Mr and Mrs Lloyd. Everything had been meticulously planned for, though Billy could be forgiven for thinking otherwise. Gladys was fretting around him like a mother hen, fussing, muttering to herself creating more problems than those she was managing to resolve. He had pressed and cleaned his uniform and borrowed a suit carrier from Nathaniel. Mother had polished his medal, cap and boots, despite his protests that he would clean them. Gladys thought him 'spic and span,' and ready to be paraded in front of the whole World. 'He is just like his father,' she recalled to herself.

When eventually he was ready to depart she asked him to sit down. Gladys could see that her son was eager to depart, but she protested at his impatience.

"Please sit down Billy, just for a moment."

Billy felt embarrassment beginning to descend upon him. 'mother, ' he thought, was going to tell him of his 'husbandly' duties, something that he did not need an explanation upon. He needn't have worried; it was not to be like that at all, From the way his mother began however, he could have been forgiven for thinking otherwise.

"son"

Billy braced himself. He was never called 'son' unless some serious talking was about to be undertaken.

"son, your father, God rest his soul. He has been gone these past fifteen years, taken from me whilst a young man, full of ability, hope, and goodness. He was a gentle man, kind, never venting his frustrations at home, hiding his fears and doubts from his loved ones. Yes, Joshua Thomas, my 'Josh' was a good man, a gentle man."

"People would ask me, when some time had elapsed, why I did not seek another marriage. Me a widow, and you a young urchin in short trousers playing football in the street, night upon night with that young Jimmy Jones. They would ask why it was that I did not find another man to help with things and give you a new father?"

"I would answer. When you have had the love of such a man as mine. When he has given you such a son as I now have. When a union like we were gifted with, had been created, perfect in every way, then nothing could, ever would, and never should replace it. I had one husband a beautiful and tender man, sped to heaven before his time. Yet there, I know he waits for me arm outstretched, reaching for me with his hand. He waits there for my time of coming. I was his, only his, I am still of him and will be, until the end of all ages."

"His flesh became united to mine and here you are stood before me, the indisputable evidence for what I am saying. But there was more to our union than a perfect physical union. We stretched out to span the bridge that links life with after life. Billy what I am telling you is that our love, the love that is Josh and I, still exists, it is greater than death. There was no man like he and even though, in this world, he is lost to me I am his forever, and he is mine for all of time."

Gladys had never spoken to her son like this before and she was speaking without interruption for Billy was spellbound with what she had to say.

"The good book teaches us to know that no trial is unbearable whilst we have our faith and hope. My faith is in the sure and certain knowledge of being reunited with my good man in a place where there are no tears, no sorrow, no pain and no fear. My hope of this world is placed entirely in you Billy, my beloved son, the living testimony of the love that my Josh and I had for each other. Tomorrow I give you to Sally Hawkins, to have and hold as I was once privileged to be possessed. She is a good girl, a wonderful daughter, proud of her I shall be, as I am proud of you, fruit of my union with that blessed man, who so surely waits for me."

"Love her Billy, be always kind, and never fear for the future. son, if in these sad and danger filled days the Lord sees fit to take you from us, there will be love and treasured memories for her to cherish, for all of us to cling to as now I cling to Josh. Whatever happens in the future we are secure in the knowledge, of the sure certainty, that we shall all meet again."

Gladys paused and indicated to her son to kneel down. Billy did so, he was profoundly moved, privileged, knowing that he had just been a witness to the most wonderful expression of faith. Gladys placed her hand upon the head of her son, whilst her tears fell upon his hair.

"son I give you my benediction, my blessing on both on you and your union. I know how long you have loved her, how painfully and patiently you awaited her, all those years you were apart. Now is your time. Take it, use it wisely, prodigiously, fruitfully and may your union be as blessed, as mine was with my Josh."

Here Gladys put both her hands upon her son's head and blessed him as only a mother can, with the holy tears of womanhood, pure as any water, freely given from deep within her soul, her heart.

"God bless you Billy, speed He you upon your way, in His way. May the great. powerful, all seeing God of the Christians guide you, guard you, and keep you until He wills you to his presence. Amen."

With his own tears streaming down his face to mingle with those of his beloved mother, Billy, moved beyond all understanding, acknowledged the gift that Gladys had bestowed upon him, in the most simple manner.

"Amen mother. Amen."

Billy felt humbled, yet full of grace and comfort. He kissed his sobbing mother with his own eyes full of tears. Now he made her a solemn promise.

"I shall make you proud. I shall be worthy of my father's memory. I shall do my duty as surely as my father executed his. Mother, never fear, I have three wonderful women in my life. From the very first there was you, sacrificing all for me, leading me unto and through the true path. Now I have my Sally who I shall love till my last breath. Finally I have Elizabeth, my beloved girl's mother, both kind and generous, trusting me with her only daughter."

"Three women, and the memory of a great, loving, kind and generous man; my father. There are countless others who have shown me kindness. Mrs Lloyd, Jack, her husband, Nathaniel. There are Uncle Frank and Auntie Helen, Jimmy whose friendship I so cherish and a host of others. Never was a man so truly blessed by such good fortune and worthy friends."

Emotionally drained by the experience they had created and the undoubted spiritual visitation that had come heavensent upon them, they both knew that it was time for Billy to depart. Thus, they parted, fully, mutually, hugged and kissed. As Billy left the house Sally was arriving with Elizabeth. He was allowed one short chaste kiss before he was instructed to be on his way. As he departed he looked back to see the three women who had been so provident in fulfilling his life waving him goodbye for the morrow morn.

He was now to visit Nathaniel before progressing towards Jack Lloyd and his last minute preparations. Five minutes later saw him knocking upon the now so familiar door.

Nathaniel opened wide the door and indicated for his future son-in Law to enter.

"Do come in Billy and what have we here all parcelled up?"

"My uniform and other essentials Dad"

Billy, for the first time, had addressed his host in the way that they had agreed.

"Well come on in son, hang up your things, sit thyself down. A small spot of the medicinal I think, Port?"

"Just a drop, thank you."

Never before had Nathaniel offered Billy such refreshment, in fact never before had the man offered the like to anyone other than Billy. He was entering a club with just two members. Nathaniel poured two crystal schooners, which he produced from out of his bureau, his own private domain.

"Well sit yourself down Billy. I have something to say."

For a second time that evening Billy felt he was about to be given one of 'those talks' that bride grooms were expected to receive. Again he need not have worried.

"The women are all together tonight Billy"

The man, who by the end of the morrow morn would be his Father in Law, was seeking for the right words and he had started off the conversation with a woefully obvious statement.

"I mean we have a while to ourselves before you proceed to Jack Lloyd's house. A good man Jack, none better to stand with you in Chapel. An Anglican of course, but none the worse for that."

The fact was that Nathaniel, along with everyone involved, was highly charged with emotion. He like so many was deeply proud of Billy Thomas. Now his fortune was to call him 'son.' It was time to show how much this meant to him.

"Billy my father was a wandering itinerant in the days when I was a young lad. A peddler I suppose. Horse and caravan filled with household goods, drapery and the like. He possessed a marvellous grinding stone, which I turned on many of occasion. Beautiful it was; in fact, it is still out in the back of the shop covered over. I shall have to show it to you one day."

"However, he was also the proud owner of a second valued item, one which he referred to many times a day. It was this."

From out of the drawer in the bureau he took a large silver pocket watch with gold edging. It was beautifully ornate. When he opened it the face was displayed, patterned with silver scroll work. The figures were in Roman numerals, the hands crafted in delicate fleur-de-lis. It was the most handsome watch that Billy had ever seen; he gazed upon it with awe.

"My father told me he obtained it from a French sea Captain. I never got to know how. He would always show me the movement from the rear case, see"

With this Nathaniel opened the backing and through a glass cover the movement of the timepiece with all its interlocking functions were visible.

"Look here,"

A gesture from Nathaniel invited Billy to examine it. He kept his thumb on the lower part of the inside case in order that Billy could read an inscription. It read, 'To my son Nathaniel on the occasion of his wedding T.S Hawkins.

"Well what say you, beautiful is it not"

"Wonderful? Why it is marvellous."

"There is something else to show you Billy" with this Nathaniel took his thumb away from the rest of the back casing. Now he could read what was a new inscription.

'To Billy Thomas on the occasion of his wedding to my daughter Sally, Nathaniel Hawkins.'

Billy was overcome; he sipped his port to fortify his rapidly filling emotions.

"Why I don't know what to say I'm sure"

"Thank you will do Billy, that and an assurance that you will always strive for Sally's happiness and safe keeping. She loves you so much you know. Has done for years."

"I know and I her, we are as one. Two fledglings in one nest looking out for each other, comforting each other."

"Quite so Billy. Well, you take her with my complete blessing. She could not have a better man. Now what about the watch?"

"I am overwhelmed. I really am, speechless, well almost. On behalf of Sally and myself I accept this wondrous gift. Thank you Nathaniel."

For the first and last time in his life Billy had addressed his future Father in Law by his Christian name. It was an intimate time for them both. They talked a while longer but the shadows were edging ever longer. It was time for the young soldier to depart.

Nathaniel took him to the door. They shook hands, clasped each other by the shoulder and Billy, with no little sense of awe, went on his way, the owner of a unique pocket watch. He would keep it and treasure it until, in turn, he would hand it on to the next generation. For now, in his safekeeping, were two of Nathaniel's most precious gifts. He would guard both of them well.

Jack Lloyd was on tenterhooks. It was as if tomorrow was bringing an important match, as indeed it was. It was his duty to manage and coach, to see that his team was best prepared. It should be fully aware of the talents of the opposition, have all its kit prepared and most of all it must be brimming with confidence. There was little real difference to sending a team into action or a bridegroom to his fate. Jack Lloyd had often proved his worth as skilled in the former. In the latter, his performance would be outstanding.

He was in his back garden checking his young pea shoots now protruding two or three inches above the ground underneath his glass cloches, which protected them from both harsh weather and greedy birds. Satisfied that all was well, Jack mused upon how much better these fragile shoots were given guardianship in comparison to all those poor souls over in France. When Billy, was ushered through the house by the exited and highly charged librarian, he was deep in contemplation.

"A visitor Jack, young Billy is here."

Jack, suddenly distracted from his intense concentration, closed the clip, which held the particular cloche together, and rose.

As he did so he felt the stiffness in his back. 'Not as young as you were Jack,' he summarised, stretching, weaving his waist from side to side, he turned to his guest.

"Ah, the victim has arrived and how are you young warrior?"

"Better condition than you appear Coach. I reckon it's the lack of exercise or the onset of age, fancy a three miler."

"Cheeky beggar,"

The retort came from a man who had put hundreds of young hopefuls through their paces; he was not going to let this young upstart get away with it. "Plenty left in the old fellow yet."

In truth, Jack Lloyd was a man no longer fully involved in his great love, the production of professional footballers and the exploration of every aspect of required skill. His past success had come from monitoring their practise onwards and upwards towards perfection, aiming to get each one to a point of peak fitness. Two years ago he possessed the embryo of a good solid second division team, capable of challenging for promotion. It contained individuals, who were being sought out by bigger clubs, top clubs, a time of potential greatness.

Then came the war. The season was but five or six games old when the majority of the squad had vanished, swallowed up by the New Army all destined for France, the trenches and God only knew where after that.

Now he coached a team, described by its benefactor, as a team of old veterans and aspiring lads too young for the front. They seldom played and, when they did, they hardly ever won. Now, stood here before him, full of youth, vigour and aspirations for the future was probably his greatest find. He still did not know exactly how the lad had got the ball to bend in flight. Now perhaps he never would.

To his knowledge it was a skill unique in football. Both left foot and right swerving in and out, A couple of seasons more and this lad would probably have become the most sought after player in the country. Undoubtedly, he would have gained an England cap and worn the famous white shirt. Now he would possibly never know how truly great this lad could become, never, never, know, unless this war concluded soon and Billy, along with all the rest came safely home to continue where they had left off. God hope it would be so. Meanwhile, it was true that, along with thousands of others, he wore his English shirt, only this one was khaki and the game much more deadly than mere football.

Billy sensed that his good friend and mentor was troubled in his mind and he guessed what it was. He would steer clear of the subject of football as best as he could.

"Troubled Jack, not lost the ring I hope."

"Fat chance. If I don't get you to the Chapel tomorrow on time, sober, properly spruced, together with that ring, I shall be a dead duck. The Missis, she said to me a while before you came, that she had not spent all those Saturday mornings nurturing you two, in getting you both together, for it to fall because of something I didn't do right."

"Quite so, good woman our Mrs Lloyd, we two owe her everything."

"Well so happen, right young fella lets get you inside and sorted."

Mrs Lloyd was a good cook, but she cooked nothing fancy this night. Nothing to upset a young bridegroom's stomach. Pie, mash and the last of the sprouts, then rhubarb tart and custard for a sweet.

"Now a drop please Jack."

"Quite so Missis."

From out of a cabinet came three sherry glasses and a bottle. The dark amber liquid was carefully poured out in three equal measures. He then set out a glass before each participant of the meal.

"Well Billy, a toast to you and your Sally. God bless you both in your life together may it be happy, prosperous and fruitful."

Their glasses clinked and a sip was partaken by each.

Mrs. Lloyd began the dinner table conversation.

"You see Billy, not having children of my own, Hubby and myself have so taken to you both, from very early on. It was, perhaps, due to the innocence of it all and the expressions of mutual shyness and your almost subconscious attempts to impress her sensitivity. Sally's undoubted growing feelings for you were so obvious to me but went so unnoticed by you.

244

Then came the day of your parting, her to finishing school and you back to your books. Bleak years they were. But I saw, you see, saw what you did not. Those tears of hers, dried by a small white handkerchief that day she departed away down those entrance steps. I remember it because Sally dropped it as she was passing by the counter and I recovered it from the floor. Embroidered upon it, in red, was a small heart and two sets of initials one either side S.H and B.T. I knew then she would be back for you whatever the span of time."

Billy was astounded by what he had heard from the grand lady.

"One minute if I may Mrs Lloyd,"

He went to open the small case he had brought with him and unfolded a waxed paper that was kept within. He took out the Milton and from inside this, he drew out the object being referred to by Mrs. Lloyd. Placing the piece of linen in Mrs Lloyd's hands he made an enquiry.

"Is this the one?"

Mrs Lloyd gasped gently in disbelief. In a disbelieving, haunting whisper that she announced her confirmation.

"The very one Billy, the very one."

"Sally gave me this and the Milton, on the platform of Glossop Station the day I left for training camp. It is so precious to me but I thought she had just embroidered it, she never told me, has never told me how long ago she made it."

"Why Billy that is so romantic."

"Indeed it is Mrs Lloyd, indeed it is."

Once again, on this, the happiest of days, tears flowed freely down his cheeks, dampening the white linen as before, many years before; it had absorbed his Sally's droplets.

Mrs Lloyd held her Jack's hand as she in turn was overcome. She felt, as indeed her husband sensed, they were in the presence of a profound revelation, a most intensely emotional, intimate, almost spiritual experience. Sally had loved her Billy from the beginning. The evidence had been unravelled, right here before them, for all to see that it was so. Mrs Lloyd had been privileged to be present at the birth of a romance that was proving more touching, vivid and intense than any novelist's work. It had proved so strong, bound by invisible ties that could not be readily explained away by the usual criteria. It humbled her to think she had been, in part, the catalyst for such a love.

Billy felt it also; his tears were those of humility. To think that his Sally had decided to love him all those years ago. He didn't deserve her, would never deserve her. Their love was one of grace, amazing grace. All he could do was to return that love, never wavering, or allowing it to diminish until the day he died.

The conversation after this revelation was inevitably filled with reminiscence. Over and over events were recalled. Tears, smiles and memories, the evening was filled with such. The sherry glasses were topped twice more and it was a happy, slightly tipsy young soldier who was shown to his bed by his friend.

A night of happy dreams followed, leading to a deep satisfying refreshing sleep. Mrs Lloyd, waking him with tea, to inform him that it was seven thirty, finally terminated his happy visions. His wedding day had, at last, arrived. What a journey he had travelled. What a day, he both hoped and prayed it would prove to be.

CHAPTER 16

Hail wedded love, mysterious law,
True source of human offspring.

Paradise lost BKIV

If ever a groom required friends to prepare him for his great day no pair could ever have been more helpful, encouraging and nerve settling than Jack Lloyd and his good wife.

Billy emerged down stairs washed, shaved and scented.

The upstairs bathroom, a luxurious rarity in Glossop, had been laid out with towels, soap, a specially purchased Eau de Cologne and other accessories, all designed to prepare the young man to a level of optimum appearance and fragrance. Dressed in Jack's borrowed dressing gown he came down stairs to greet his hosts.

The ironing board was in full use and for a second time in less then a day the soldier's uniform was being pressed. His boots were by the fireplace, once more polished to perfection. Bacon was being prepared on the range together with fried bread, black pudding and sausage. Two eggs were in the rack, ready to join their companions in the pan.

Jack offered a sentiment.

"A hearty breakfast for the condemned man. Its going to be a long time before you eat anything else young fella."

In truth Billy was extremely hungry, famished. He did not need any encouragement, what with that aroma wafting his way.

"Thanks Jack, how are we for time, mustn't be late today of all days."

"Indeed not"

So emphasised the woman looking up from her ironing.

"And neither shall you be."

It was Jack who made the confirmation, which was based upon his meticulous planning.

"We leave at 9.15 sharp. Arrive 9.30. Meet the minister in the Vestry, finalise the preliminaries, then wait and hope the young lady arrives. Eat your breakfast and don't worry about a cross or a dot. The General here will see that you go over the top on time."

"You've been reading too many dispatches from war correspondents Jack,"

Billy was joking, yet he could not help but compare how reminiscent, the feeling in his stomach was at this very moment, to the unsettled state it was in, prior to going into action against the Germans. 'Oh well, cometh the hour, cometh the man,'

Thus he steeled himself for the great endeavour that loomed before him.

Billy considered that it was a pity really that fate and circumstances had not bestowed upon Mrs Lloyd the title of Field Marshall and that General Haigh's responsibility never stretched further than getting a wedding off to a good start. 'If it had been thus,' thought Billy then the war could already have been won.

Exactly on time, 9.15, two resplendent, immaculately turned out men stepped out into the morning sunshine and with best foot forward began the walk to the Chapel.

Mrs Lloyd waved them off with a sigh.

"Thank goodness, now I can get ready; I ask you; men!"

Even though, in spite of her muttered protest, she felt a huge sense of pride looking after her two proteges disappearing over the brow into the town. Now it was her turn.

"Time to get yourself ready my girl."

It was as if the whole of Glossop was going to attend the officiations. Small groups of people were gathered on corners, or out upon their meticulously scrubbed house steps. The numbers began to grow as the two self-conscious men paced ever nearer towards the Chapel. Normally under such circumstances, Billy's natural desire to be inconspicuous and unnoticed in his personal life would have produced a self-conscious desire within him to be elsewhere, solitary, free from interference and notice. Yet today his thoughts were elevated to such a height that he was largely unaware of the interest his prescience, his walking of the streets of Glossop, on this morning of mornings, had produced.

Before his eyes was a vision of his beloved Sally as indeed it had appeared so many times during the last two years, longer, if truth were known. Today Sally and he would become one, one in aspiration, one in consolation, one in adoration, one in passion, one.

The war had fully tried his capacity for hope, for faith. Love of Sally, and her love expressed for him, had seen him through all the terrible times of trial, and despair. The power of love had vanquished these twin impostors in all their wiles. They had been magnificently defeated and repulsed. He had been through the tempter's wilderness. Now Eden awaited. Today would give witness to love's complete victory.

At last, the Chapel came into view. By now, Billy was in a condition of near ecstasy, a state, modified at times, by nervousness. It was a rapture of many facets; they would remain with him for the day's entirety.

Meanwhile, back in Charles Street, an area that Jack had ensured Nathaniel that Billy would not pass, his future father in Law had been prepared by his wife, duty inspected and told to sit down. He was instructed to do so without creasing or disturbing either himself or anything upon his person. Now he simply sat, looking from his chair to the window, where the beneficent sun filled the morning room with streaks of light. In spite of the day's benevolence a course of panic began to surge within him, leading him to disobey his dear wife's instructions and to threaten his clothes with the hint of a crease.

Upstairs, two women were quietly, efficiently and methodically transforming their bemused daughter into a vision of loveliness and grace. Alarms may be sounding down the stairs, controlled by the needs of promptness and planning, but they had no influence on the affairs above. In Elizabeth's bedroom all was calm. The women spoke in smooth, whispered, tranquil, comments. Requests for ribbon, needle and thread, all the fripperies of presentation were made with a precision that most men would have considered highly improbable of women in the circumstances.

Finally the two mothers stood back. To say that they were pleased with their endeavours, would fail to grasp their sense of achievement. Sally would be sent to the Altar perfect in every way. Both women kissed her and both gave her a blessing. Elizabeth tried to think of something that they may have missed but there was nothing. All was now ready for her daughter to descend the stairs. Earlier, the doorbell had rung and a beautiful poesy of white and red Carnations had been delivered interspersed with Lilly of the Valley, the scent of which, had filled the hallway.

Gladys considered that it was time for mother and daughter to be alone.

"Well, I will just go into the room and check on how presentable I am for the occasion. See you down stairs Sally."

She left the room, now the two other women could speak their final private thoughts.

Elizabeth enquired of her daughter as all mother's do so at such times.

"How do you feel Sally? Nervous no doubt about the ceremony and things."

Sally began to feel embarrassed.

"Nervous? Of what things mother?"

"You know, what I mean Sally, nervous about later."

It was Elizabeth's turn for embarrassment.

"Mother if you mean nervous about tonight when we are alone, not at all. It will be wonderful, and in case you are doubting, yes I am still a virgin, but I know how happy Billy and I will be together in the bedroom, or where ever else we find ourselves to be when we wish to express our love."

"Well, well, hey ho."

It was an instinctive reaction, Elizabeth considered for a moment and decided that she ought to add to the remark.

"All I hope is that you two will be as happy that way as I have been with your father. God bless you both, he is a good man your Billy, a very good man, hey ho, and away we go."

With that she picked up Sally's veil to place it delicately upon her head. Once again the loveliness of her daughter's innocent image peering at her through the veil took her breath away. At last, her mouth issuing forth the slightest of gasps, she gathered up the trail of the dress and guided the bride through the door, where both began to descend the stairs.

Nathaniel heard them coming down and made his way to the hallway. What greeted him took away all his worrying upon time and preparation. His daughter stood before him. His little angel. His little precious Sally who, as a child, went everywhere with him, sitting for hours upon his knee listening to stories, and being consoled over a bruised knee or a hateful boy who had pulled her hair. His little girl now a woman, a woman who today he would entrust to the love and duty of another man. His eyes misted with tears. Speech would just not come to him.

"Well Daddy?"

He simply stared at her, trying, without success, to withhold the tears.

"Well Daddy?"

Elizabeth endorsed the plea.

"Well Nathaniel?"

"Well, well, well, what a beautiful woman you are Sally."

"Today I am the most proud of fathers."

Sally came up to him to plant a kiss upon his cheek.

"And I father, the most fortunate of daughters. Thank you for all that you have done. All the effort you have undertaken in making this such a happy day for me and for all the things that you have done for me, all my life through."

Sally once more, delicately placed a kiss upon her father's cheek to acknowledge her gratitude.

Gladys had now joined them in the hallway and was adjusting her hat in the mirror. "Elizabeth, time to get to Chapel for us two."

"Indeed"

With the agreement came Elizabeth's awareness that she would never again see her daughter in this house except as a wife. As is the unexplainable tradition at such times, Elizabeth began to cry.

"Well we shall leave you both to await the carriage. All the very best of fortune for today Sally."

It had been arranged for the mothers to walk to the Chapel, whilst a carriage would arrive for Sally and her father at 9.55.

In turn both the women gently kissed the girl, whom they had so beautifully prepared, then; opening the door, they went out into the day. As they began to walk the short path to the pavement they became aware of the large crowd that had grown in front of the house, all eager to see the bride leave her house and proceed to her marriage.

Gladys and Elizabeth each noticed friends and acquaintances and waved to them in the crowd. On their journey they were accosted by many who shook their hands and providing expressions of good luck and wishes for a happy day. Thus, very slowly, the two women were allowed on their way. The short journey to the Chapel took about fifteen minutes. Finally as they approached the steps to the entrance, Elizabeth commented upon the other portion of their care.

"I wonder how Billy is coping?"

"How indeed"

It was a voice possessing no little trepidation that made the reply

In truth, Billy was coping well enough. He and Jack had met with, Pastor Livingston in the Vestry, where he too was the receptor of both advice and compliments.

"Why, don't you two look the bees knees and you Billy, you look resplendent."

"Thank you Pastor, you don't look so bad yourself"

Jack also returned the courtesy.

"Pastor, I do not believe, seeing us three standing here, that the Three Wise Men themselves could have looked any better."

"Right you are Jack, how very right. Well step through and let us make some final checks."

They followed him through into the little room. Gideon indicated to two chairs.

"Sit down gentlemen, if you will."

The licence was displayed before them on the small desk that had previously provided the sanctuary for those of both Billy's and Sally's parents. It already had their details reproduced in Gideon's registry, which had been kept in a locked drawer since the Chapel was consecrated. Billy was asked to check the details of his and Sally's matrimonial records. They seemed to be in order.

"I thought, as we have a little time, that you might like to see this."

Gideon opened an older looking registry to a section entitled Baptisms: registration of baptisms 1894 to 1906. There, within the covers, was Billy's entry and two pages further on Sally's baptism was placed on record.

Gideon looked at the two insertions and philosophised.

"Just goes to show you never know what the good Lord has in store. I baptise you both, confirm you both into the Chapel congregation. Billy, I bring your father into the congregation. He was an inspired youth whose mission in life was to create beautiful buildings, and never to cease in his efforts to assist the unfortunate. I marry him to your mother, and, yes, I give him a Christian burial him also. Sally's parents I blessed their marriage and what a happy day that was I can tell you.

Now you both are being solemnised with your marriage vows within these walls. So it continues: life progresses. How many more entries relating to you and your families shall I have to enter? Truly, I do not know. Then, after I have left this place, my successors will continue in their turn. Of course, I do not know what the future has in store for us all. I do know this however; whatever our calamities, or tragedies, misfortunes or achievements, life goes on. It always will, until the end of days and the coming of the Kingdom"

Billy felt humbled, Jack also. Billy realised that he was, of certainty, in a hollowed place where much of the destinies of himself and those whom he loved, was forged. He made a final observation of the little room within which were the sacred records of their past, their present, and where too their future and that of those around them would be placed. These records, magnified ten thousand times over, provided the bridge of continuity, of immortality, in a world full of danger and death. At that moment, Billy felt he would rather be in this room, in this building, than anywhere on Earth. His father had helped to construct it, had indeed been one of its inspirations. 'How many more of his future generations would enter these walls?'

Pastor Livingstone broke his musings with an appeal.

"Let us pray a moment gentlemen, let us pray in thanks for all that has been, for all that will be today and for our hope for the future."

In unison the three men knelt within the private confines of the vestry, each having his own thoughts, aware of his duties for the day and his tasks and pleasures for the morrow.

"Lord Jesus Christ, you who know of our every thought, our desires, our fears, our source of happiness, our hopes. Grant unto us all and those whom we love, the peace and happiness that surpasses all understanding. May all of us grow in your merciful countenance. May your blessing be upon Billy and Sally in their union. Help them keep their vows unto each other, supporting each the other during their life's journey, Amen."

"Amen."

"Well then Billy, Jack, it is time for you to take your places at the front right hand side. Oh by the way Billy, has Jack provided you with any practical guidance?"

"Yes indeed Pastor, all seen to."

Gideon mused for a moment, his right hand encompassing his chin.

"Good, good, see you outside them. Well, time to put my overalls on."

Gideon always referred to his vestments as his 'overalls.'

Billy and Jack took their places at the head of the congregation exchanging glances and smiles with several of the members who had begun to fill the Chapel. Glancing at his magnificent pocket watch, it displayed seven minutes before 10.00. At that moment Gladys and Elizabeth arrived walking down the aisle, being greeted at every row. Gladys took her place behind her son, Elizabeth in a pew opposite. Tension was beginning to build.

Outside the Chapel the bridesmaids had arrived, Uncle Frank's two daughters. Both in their mid teens, they waited, knowing their duties, prepared for the unexpected, if necessary. The carriage, to both cheers and applause from the gathered throng, arrived, drawn by two wondrously arrayed grey horses. It was immaculate, the driver wore a beribboned top hat, the reins decked in white satin and the carriage likewise.

In this warm Spring morning, the top was fully drawn back allowing the bride and her father to give full view to the crowd. More rapturous applause greeted the pair as they came to a stop.

The driver dismounted, opened the door of the carriage, to assist the occupants as they stepped down. The two bridesmaids drew up her train and with her arm resting on her father's, Sally began her walk up the steps of the Chapel. She had paced towards this entrance so many times in her life, yet she had never been happier than on this day and this was displayed in her radiance, for every single well-wisher to see. All the usual comments of such an attendance were uttered. Women smiled, some wistfully, others thinking back as they reminisced upon their day of happiness, when it was they who stole the show.

The young ones smiled with expectancy, anticipating that they too would, one day, walk up such steps as these, dressed like this young bride, on their way to solemnise their vows. For many girls of Sally's age, or younger, it represented the highest possible aspiration.

The shadow of the pair filled the open doorway, the organ struck up, and all heads turned, as slowly her father began to approach the altar steps. 'Cometh the hour, cometh the bride,' concluded Billy on time too." He looked towards the heavens to plead, 'Please God do not let me forget my lines.'

In truth the Chapel was packed, people were standing in the gallery. Almost a thousand had gathered to see the young lovers who had bought such hope and colour to the grey, stark existence of a small town living the second year of an endless, and by now for many, pointless conflict. Billy would enact his lines in front of the largest audience he had ever encountered, outside of a football match.

Now Sally was beside him. Her father stepped back to sit beside his wife. Sally's very presence brought Billy reassurance. 'When we emerge from out of this place she will be my wife,' he thought, with no slight sense of accomplishment.

253

Gideon approached the rail and stood facing the happy pair. He had absorbed the unique nature of the occasion. Never in all the history of this Chapel, had so many gathered for a service. It therefore required a special introduction.

"Dearly beloved, friends: I feel overwhelmed at the number of you who have come to witness the joining together in holy matrimony of these two young people. If I feel this, then we must consider how much more nervous Billy and Sally feel. Let us pray that they fulfil their avowed intent with joy and sincerity, possessing your good wishes and prayers for today, and for the future."

"We shall begin with the hymn 'Love Divine All Love Excelling."

The organist swelled the Chapel with the introductory notes and, perfectly on time, the congregation raised their voices in song. Words echoed the very air, profoundly affecting the pair upon whom all eyes and ears were centred. Notes rose and fell, the words filling Billy and Sally with assurance, with confidence. The final couplet arrived to find the two of them settled and prepared.

'Till we cast our crowns before him'
'Lost in wonder, love and praise.'

The small fatherless boy, who used to look forward so much on Saturday mornings to spending his time in the presence of the pretty young girl now stood beside her fully aware of the transformation that the years had brought upon her. The girl, who so loved to display her literary discoveries had returned to him, had returned to the confines of this Chapel to pledge herself to him. The aspirations that now enveloped the accomplished footballer and soldier were identical to those experienced by the immature, inexperienced, youth who, dotingly, used to wish for a single smile from the girl. Then he was casting off in his boat, upon the ocean of life, learning how to chart a course, to plot a destination. Now he was a man who stood triumphant before this gathered host with his prize beside him.

'To love one woman only
And to cleave to her, and worship her
With years of noble deeds
Until he won her.'

Sally also found her mind wandering back to the idolising underweight companion who often, on those wet Saturday mornings, would wait upon her every word

254

'Thank you Jesus for bringing him to me. Help me to be a good and loving wife.' Her contemplation and thoughts, suddenly, almost unwillingly, came back to the present, jolted by the words of Pastor Livingston.

Gideon, full of rapture, guided the two through their vows. Vows which generations of couples down through the ages, stretching back over 1,500 years of English history had enunciated in much the same form. At such a time as this, with so vast a congregation, he felt history's legacy descend upon the Chapel and all within.

The promises completed, he ascended his pulpit opened the Bible and read his text for the homily. It came from Psalm 45.

All-glorious is the bride within her chamber
Her gown is woven with gold
She is led towards her husband
Led with joy and gladness
She enters the room of her husband
Her son will take the place of his father
He will perpetuate his memory through all generations
The nations will praise him forever and ever.

His eyes lifted from the book. He surveyed his audience. Choosing his words with the greatest of care he began. Later in the week the Chronicle would print his oration together with a commentary. All those who listened to him that morning, felt privileged to have received his message for, although it was a blessing upon the newly married couple, additionally it acted as comfort to all who heard. Everyone who had loved ones away from home, facing danger in far off lands, were to leave the Chapel consoled.

It was as if the words spoken by Gideon had reached out in such a manner that many of the invited guests felt that they were uniquely theirs to posses and take away with them. The Pastor's words somehow kept in place a belief, an assurance, that the English way of life continued and would continue, steadfast and true. He spoke upon children, the continuity that they brought. How devastating it was to lose a child, even in the cause of the Nation. Words now flowed inspired by a congregation wrapped within his spell.

"Here displayed before us all, is living proof of this truth. Here we see evidence for faith, for hope, for love, especially as the Epistle maintains, for love. These two young people, now husband and wife one soon to return to war to face the battle's strife, the other reposed within her possession of faith, hope and love, These two, together with countless thousands of others like them, portray all our aspirations."

"We live in dark days but they will end. We live in a time of war, but it will cease. We also live however, in a time of great love, of sacrifice, of unity, of hope, that will never end."

"Sally and Billy take with them our hope, our faith, and our love. Bless them Lord Jesus. Guide them, guard them, and keep them. However long or short, fill their union with your love and they in turn will fulfil each the other, with all that marriage was destined to provide"

"We, the citizens of this town, this small town of Glossop, nestling in the solid strength of our Derbyshire hills, protected by our rocks of ages that keep us safe from infection and the envy of less happier lands; thank God he has brought these two together. We here today have been so privileged to see them joined in holy matrimony. Praise the Lord."

Gideon felt the words beginning to formulate for his conclusion. He needed to send Billy and Sally on their way out of this Chapel possessing total confidence in their future. He now also completely commanded his stage, his congregation; able to profess and enunciate a message to the entire gathered assembly.

"So as we leave this holy place, upon this holy day; we give them our best wishes for their future joy and happiness. Yet, we must also dedicate ourselves, rededicate ourselves, to the greater struggle, the struggle of which Billy and Sally are a part. We must, like them, commit ourselves, recommit ourselves, remembering our belief in God, and our duty towards our King and Country."

"We must also strive to ascend onward and upwards towards the greater peaks of honour that somehow have become forgotten against the landscape of this wretched conflict. We must, we shall, stand by our Country with duty and with patriotism as exemplified by these two young people here. But we must also strive to reach that greater pinnacle that is far above mere patriotism, never looking away, never conceding to fear. We must look up, scanning our eyes heavenwards and, with a straight and rugged finger, thus, pointing to the skies, the light of our souls, shall shine through the gloom."

His homily concluded; his outstretched arm and spired index finger fell limp. He now felt drained. He would announce the final hymn, give his blessing, upon the pair and the congregation then leave the rest to his God.

"Now we shall sing 'Abide with me' the wonderful hymn of consolation and reassurance that comes to us from the pen of Henry Francis Lyte."

The words and music seemed to fill the very souls and hearts of all within, not least Billy and Sally, husband and wife. They both sang, having eyes, solely for each other, yet even they were absorbed by the power of the hymn. It was a moment neither would ever forget.

Outside the Chapel the kindly sun once more greeted them, accompanied by a huge crowd of well wishes which had swollen in numbers since the service had begun. The photographer was diligent in his duties. Firstly taking small personal intimate plates, then expanding to take in the masses which had emptied from the Chapel. Later and in the years to come, Sally would look at them all, sometimes alone and other times with friends and family. One she would particularly treasure, that of Billy pictured on his own, sat in the vestry, portraying all his uniformed splendour, dignified, handsome, courageous, eternally hers.

Nathaniel had held nothing back in his generosity. Today was to be the most precious in his daughter's life and, hopefully, the most memorable. The carriage swept husband and wife towards the George Hotel where a scrumptious wedding breakfast awaited. As Jack had forecast, Billy had little appetite for anything except to gaze upon his beautiful wife. Later, that evening, he would be glad to have accepted his friend's advice when another hunger, deep within him, overtook the need for food.

The ceremonial was enacted to the full. The meal was followed by the grateful, appreciative, acceptance of the vast number of fine presents. Speeches and blessings came from Nathaniel, and Gideon. A fine oration was delivered by Jack Lloyd, who, in his capacity as Best Man, related the most unlikely stories. Mostly, they were based upon truth but, certainly, they were embellished with unashamed exaggeration.

He spoke of Billy's football career, his various school-boyish adventures and scrapes. He emphasised his knowledge of literature and his faith in, and love of God. He also, having being informed by his good wife, told of the long and obstacle filled romance of his protégé. How his young friend had been captivated at such early age by the loveliest of women.

Now he observed, how love had most assuredly triumphed in the wilderness that was life. Billy and Sally had brought colour to these long, grey, danger filled days, not only here in Glossop, but also wherever it had been spoken of. It had been displayed through the countenance of his friend as he read the letters from his beloved Sally, in France, in training camp or when being read to in hospital. Jack came to his conclusion.

"Their love shines through it all, as this telegram confirms. It is headed France 14th March 1916."

"To Billy Thomas, Corporal 9th Battalion Cheshire Regiment, and to Miss Sally Hawkins, on the occasion of their wedding. We send congratulations and are fully confident that a successful conclusion of all operations will be accomplished. From all at No3 Platoon 'C' Company, all success and happiness for the future."

This brought out a round of applause from the entire gathering.

Sally's eyes met those of her husband; she knew where his thoughts were at this moment, and they were not here in these lavish surroundings, that was certain.

It was early afternoon when the carriage left on the short journey back to Charles Street. Sally had by now changed into the most fetching of costumes, with a cream-matching hat, wide brimmed providing a hallowed outline to her form, encapsulating her smile, the light of her eyes and the trestles of her flowing, corn ripened, hair Once back at the house they kissed privately for the first time as a married couple. He discovered that he was suprisingly nervous. Sally sensed his shaking.

"Its alright Billy, I won't break you know, as later we shall see."

Suddenly, without warning, the parents arrived chattering excitedly all at once. Elizabeth however, practical to the last, decided upon organisation.

It was now 2.00pm; matters had still to be taken in hand if the day was to end as fulfilled and as happy as it had been thus far. She began to make decisions.

"Right tea I think."

Gladys earnestly agreed.

"Good idea Elizabeth, it has been a thirsty day."

Tea it was, the five of them seated round the small table in front of the fire.

Elizabeth made a last request of her daughter prior to her leaving her home for the last time as a maiden.

"Play something for us Sally my dear, perhaps the Chopin."

Sally had become an accomplished pianist over the years. A piano had been central to the furnishings of the morning room for as long as she could remember, yet for some reason she had never played in Billy's presence. She felt so nervous at the thought of carrying out her mother's request, but she prepared to do so. Sitting upon the stool, from which she had extracted the music, Sally prepared to play.

To Billy it was magical, with each note played, his love for her grew evermore. His heart now ached with such intensity that it was almost above endurance. His love for this perfect flower of womanhood found new heights of eloquence, new realms of urgency. Initially, the notes sounded out singularly, Sally's fingers tripping, gliding effortlessly from one key to the next.

Later the music changed, becoming evermore intense, even furious, or so it sounded to his ears. The intensity of the central notation now began to wane. Once more the keys were being manipulated gently and movingly. Chopin's Etude was coming to its fragile end containing within its promise, 'So deep the Night.'

The final note sounded, profound in its lilting, haunting compassion. Silence reigned, a sacred all embracing stillness, an immortal moment of quietude. From the recess of his memory, Billy envisioned a young girl departing from him, to go off to a place of learning, leaving him bereft and crestfallen. Unashamed, unnoticed even, his eyes filled with tears and he wept. Quietly, Sally, having noticed his distress and somehow knowing its source, came over to his side and held his hand. She whispered to him soothingly.

"Its alright Billy, We are forever one now."

All was still once more. At long last, Gladys broke the silence that had so overwhelmingly descended upon them.

"Well what an exhausting day it has been and what a beautiful conclusion you brought to it Sally. Now, after tea, we girls shall have to go and get things ready at the house."

"What things?"

Billy's question came of frustration. Just married for less than four hours and the two of them were taking Sally away from him.

His mother admonished him.

"Never you mind Billy, we will not be long. You two men can sit down and relax, have a chat, we shall see you soon."

With the objection dealt with, after the tea was savoured, the three women got up. Hats, coats, and scarves were wrapped around them and away they went. Billy was left alone with his father in Law. In truth there were matters he wanted to raise with Nathaniel. It would be opportune to deal with them now. He went to the door with his wife, kissed her farewell, watched the trio as they turned the corner, then returned back into the room where he found Nathaniel gazing out of the window as if into an abyss.

Standing alongside the man, who had been his sponsor, his mentor, his friend and now his father in Law, Billy also stood mute. The two men simply stared into the street which, having returned to normality, contained people going on their way upon such business as Saturday's tasks demanded of them.

Finally Nathaniel spoke.

"Thank you for that Billy, for being silent when silence was necessary. To look out there you would think all was normal and well. How far from the truth is that?"

"Just over the water and places elsewhere, a great carnage takes place, consuming men as never before in the whole of the history of humanity. We have been asked ever more, for further sacrifices to be sent to fuel an insatiable appetite. Attrition they call it. I have heard of it referred so. The war ends only when manpower, the resources, the equipment and the desire of one side is exhausted. Tell me Billy how near are we, our allies, or the enemy to that time. How long before one side's exhaustion forbids them to continue and peace is pleaded for?"

Another period of silence. Billy was contemplating. How to answer this man? Searching the window, for the answer to such an incomprehensible equation. How to reply? Emotively, patriotically, hopefully or truthfully? Billy decided upon the truth or as near as he could

259

bring it to his comprehension. His newly acquired father in Law would appreciate the sentiment of truth if not it's content.

"We know how great are the facilities that exist in the world to wage this war, the infrastructure, the willingness of our young, the determination of our government, the capacity of our industry, our ability to organise and distribute ordinance. Britain has a great resource of all these things. In addition we can add patriotism, we saw it displayed only today from the pulpit of a man who hates war, particularly this war. Reflected in the Pastor Livingston is the quintessence of our nation, of our allies also, in the main."

"Likewise Germany possesses much the same, more in certain aspects, if the truth be admitted. Austria, Hungry are also so proud owners of these attributes. Even Turkey, as the Gallipole campaign so painfully displayed, is garrisoned with the like. With all these resources, equally possessed by all the protagonists, each filled with desperation to avoid defeat, I make no mention of victory, a stubborn will dominates the affairs of Man. Here, and everywhere else. I see no end to the carnage, or at least no end in the near future."

"Before this war's end I believe it will encompass the World, both New and Old, East and West, North and South, land, sea and air. It will involve all the elements, new dastardly technology, fiendish, perverted inventions with, a never ending, greater capacity to destroy men's lives. Unless sanity is restored to the Nations of the World this war will last for years to come with neither gaining advantage. It will last until a Nation's economic capacity can no longer replace its losses, its people rebel, or an invention comes into the possession of one side so terrible that it sweeps its opponents away.

Till then, it's in the trenches of France that man's incapacity to settle his affairs peaceably will be experienced. Likewise the Balkans and the Alps, the endless wastes of the East, the depths of the ocean and the sands of the dessert, will give witness to his folly. It will be all thus and more. Mars has risen, he is not about to abdicate his throne."

This was a tour de force that Nathaniel had not reckoned on, coming from a man, who merely a few hours ago, was expressing his lifelong vows of love and fidelity.

"Eloquently voiced son. A most eloquent, if terrible, analysis Billy and one which I am compelled to concur with. Now what we have to address, is the question of how we face this future, You, I, Sally, Elizabeth, your mother, five souls, lives, all entwined, with you Billy, as its pivot. You and I have to explore what might come to pass and create resolutions for any conceivable situation."

Billy knew exactly what Nathaniel was alluding to. It was time to put the good man's concerns to rest.

"Nathaniel what you are referring to, is the matter of how will you all handle the event of my death, should events not go my way. That's practical and don't think that I have not given it much thought. Sally is far too much precious to me, for it not to have occupied my mind. It was for such a circumstance as you describe that I have written this."

From the inside pocket of his waistcoat he withdrew a letter, sealed in an envelope. It was addressed with a single word, 'Sally.'

"Father, should you obtain news of my sure and certain death at the hands of the enemy, sure and certain mind, then you must give this to Sally. It will be a comfort to her. We have both discussed such an event at length. The one matter we could not resolve was how it could be determined upon. My certain death, that is. How could Sally be sure beyond all doubt."

"Nathaniel it is the one task, the last task I hand to you. When to decide to give her this. When she reads it she will know what to do, how to act. This, and her faith, will keep her whole, and strong, strong for all of us, for herself."

Nathaniel uttered never a word. He took the letter from his son in Law went over to his bureau, took out a key from his waistcoat and secured the communication within. Only then did he speak.

"Billy it shall be as you have insisted, never fear, God help us that it may never be needed and that you come home safe and sound to Sally, to all of us."

He returned to the window and continued upon his observations. The afternoon was growing old, few people were now walking the pavements, he was hoping that the women would not be long now.

Billy, he thought, was taking everything in his stride. Without any bravado, or histrionics, his new son in Law had thought through the future, filled as it was with such uncertainty, and had planned accordingly. Sally was a fortunate girl to have the love of such a brave, loving, considerate man. Billy too what a woman he now possessed, beautiful, intelligent, determined just like her mother. Yes he knew how lucky, was Billy Thomas.

Time, he concluded, for a small drop of fortification.

He poured two schooners of port and handed one to his companion "Well good health, happiness and good luck Billy."

It was taken with gratitude. When thirty minutes later the ladies returned, the two men were completing their second glass, enjoying the warmth from the fire, and an inside warmth, provided by both the port and the warmth of easy gentle conversation.

Elizabeth's sensitive nose caught the fragrance from the glasses. She searched for signs indicating a lack of sobriety and found none. Even still, she gave her husband a knowing frown of disapproval.

Nathaniel decided to gain the high ground before critical words headed towards his direction.

261

"Ladies, back so soon, I trust all is in order."

His daughter decided to undertake her father's reprieve.

"Certainly is father, things could not be better."

Sally sensed her mother's agitation. She too had noticed the crystal glasses stained red and had decided to save her father from her mother's wrath. Her day had been perfect, due in the main to her father's generosity, her evening, her wedding night, she knew, would also be perfect. The three of them had transformed the house in Talbot Street into a delightful refuge for a married couple. Now all was ready for Billy and her to spend their first night together.

The newly weds sat together recalling the day with their parents. They were holding hands, feeling the need to be alone, but too polite to make a comment. Elizabeth, as so often had been the case of late, resolved the problem.

"Well you two, you had better be making tracks, or your dinner will spoil, last we saw, it was simmering gaily on the range. No doubt you can't wait to have a meal alone together."

She felt a rise coming, bringing a flush to her face.

"A gentle walk by the Chapel then round the library and past the Church would be nice. Supper should be ready by then."

It was Elizabeth's acknowledgement that now was the time, at long last, for the couple to go on their way.

So they left, two young lovers, arm in arm slowly stepping out into the sun's last rays, which now brought long shadows across the road. Clouds were ascending from the east, the freshly announced wind began to lift the newly sprouted birch leaves, which in turn wafted the thin lengthy branches high above the point where they joined the trunk. From the avenue the pair gazed on into the distance. Looking at each other their eyebrows raised in silent agreement that a storm was being brewed.

Kisses and hugs were exchanged and soon their silhouette began to disappear. The pair turned, waved to their parents and continued on their way. Nathaniel could feel the storm coming also.

"Let's get back into the house ladies, the winds getting up."

Elizabeth agreed.

"Yes lets."

Linking her arm with her friend the two women took one last look at their offspring.

"Well, that's, that then," stated Gladys, wistfully.

"That's, that,"

Her friend, confirmed the notion taking her handkerchief to her eyes.

Sally and Billy walked along Fazackerley Street. They stopped at the Chapel. Hand in hand they started towards the door where so recently they had stepped out to begin their married life. Without words, they crossed over the library steps where, again, they stopped. Here Billy took her in his arms and kissed her.

"I love you Sally Thomas"

"I love you too Billy Thomas."

"Time to get home my love, look at those clouds, they appear storm filled, it is going to tip it down."

They quickened their pace, the wind was gaining steadily in its force, becoming, along with advancing clouds, ever more menacing. Billy had seen this phenomena many a time, up in the hills above the town. Storms could fall upon the day, from out the Pennines, almost without notice. That was going to occur now. He needed to get his wife home without delay. As they passed the Church and entered Talbot Street the first streak of lightning darted down in the darkening distance followed immediately by a shattering outburst of thunder.

Who would win the race the, storm or they? The gathering clouds were now fast approaching, bringing with them a malevolent cloak, threatening to engulf them. Just twenty doors away from safety, ten, six, then two. Sally got out the key placed it in the lock, the door opened and in they went. Fifty yards away lightening struck the large elm at the corner of the road. It split asunder, its largest branch crashing down onto the railway line fully blocking it. The thunder crash that followed shook the very foundations, vibrating along the entire street. The air was charged with such a level of static that even, securely indoors, the hair on the heads of the embracing lovers crackled with sparks.

The storm had created a power cut. The newly installed electricity had failed. Sally gave Billy his first instruction as his wife.

"Stay there Billy, we have some candles."

Within moments two candles had been lit upon the front room table, followed by a further pair above the mantelpiece.

It was then that Billy noticed a 'contraption', as he was to come to call it, sat upon a cabinet in the corner of the room; boasting a large brass horn. He immediately recognised what it was.

"A gramophone?"

"A gramophone."

"With records?"

"With records."

"What records?"

"Look and see."

Billy examined the cabinet under the gramophone. Inside was a collection of about twenty records. He chose one; wound up the handle, placed the needle onto the edge of the spinning disc and sat down next to Sally. He held her hand and waited. From out of the horn emanated the most wondrous sound. Sat in the gloaming of candlelight, on this his wedding night, out poured music that filled them both with the highest, sensation of delight.

Later, when he examined the paper cover, he discovered that it was the Intermezzo from Cavalleria Rusticana composed, as the label signified by a gentleman called Mascagni. The pair instantly fell in love with the haunting melodic strains and for three minutes, whilst holding each other closely, intimately, they were held in a rapture composed from a delectable mixture of the music and their own expectant fecundity. By the time the increasingly emotive harmonics had reached their gentle impassioned conclusion, they had both become profoundly encompassed by, and ingrained with, the music's deep sentiment of transience. The silence that followed was unutterable, exquisite in its tension. It was gothic; it was also divine. Now they were ready to begin the great adventure that was their marriage. The great harvest of sap, rising, this spring, from the stem of the trunk of this sturdy, young English Oak, was to finally ensnare the nectar seeking bee, producing a golden honey, fragrant, glowing, and sweet.

The young soldier kissed his new bride; Mascagni had provided the last element, putting the final piece of the jigsaw puzzle into place. It had brought this perfect day to its conclusion, to its inevitable point of consummation; Flowing through the ether, it contrasted starkly to the elements that raged outside, placid, melodic, a bringer of peace, of reassurance. Billy went over to the gramophone and re-set the record to play this wonderful music, once more. Now was the time to claim his prize.

The aroma of a casserole wafted into the room but it failed to inspire the man. He was here with his wife, his long awaited wife, together, alone. The flickering candles, together with the repeated sound of the tonal poem, provided a heightened romantic aura around the lovers. Food was the last thing on Billy's mind.

As fortune would have it, eating had not entered Sally's thoughts either. Without further words they came together in an embrace. Here, as husband and wife, holding each the other, the reflection of the minute flames flecked their faces, creating reflections, ensparking their eyes. It also enflamed their passions, forcing their hearts to beat faster, their breathing deeper. Food could and would, wait.

"Hungry?"

The enquiring man looked into his Bride's eyes, hoping for a negative answer.

"Not at all Mr Thomas"

The mischievously enticing reply merely caused the man's passion to become more enflamed.

"Well then?"

"Well what, Mr Thomas?"

"Well why don't we go upstairs Mrs Thomas?"

"Why not"

"Why not indeed."

Swiftly Billy took their dinner from off the hotplate, swept up his young wife as if she were made of feathers and kissed her fully on the lips. Pacing himself, he carried her effortlessly, step by step, ever upwards towards his room.

He got to the landing and turned towards his destination. Sally interjected to change his direction.

"Wrong door husband, we women changed things around today, take me into the front room if you will."

Without a word, Billy did exactly as he was bid. Still effortlessly carrying his wife, he entered the large front bedroom that had been the private domain of his mother and father. It had been delightfully transformed. Standing in the doorway, his wife held aloft in his arms, he could, even in the twilight, make out the double bed, newly quilted, with the lace curtains wafting slightly in the draft that emanated from the partially opened windows.

"husband now you can love me, possess me fully, take all that I have, all that I am. Tonight I am yours. I belong to you, now and forever."

"Indeed you do my love as I am yours. Tonight and for as long as I live I shall love you as no man ever loved a woman."

He passed through into the room determined to place his lovely new bride gently upon the bed. As the strains of the Intermezzo began to fade once more, his nuptial torch now truly lit, with his foot he manoeuvred the door. It closed behind them.

> *'Thus these two*
> *Imparadised in one another's arms*
> *The happier Eden, shall enjoy their fill*
> *Of bliss on bliss.'*

CHAPTER 17

On she came
Guided by her heavenly maker
Sweetness of heart, nor uniformed
Of nuptial sanctity and marriage rites
Grace was in her step, heaven in her eye.
In every gesture dignity and love.

Paradise Lost Bk. viii.

Two souls, joined together within their matrimonial bed, slept. They had discovered that preparing to become a married couple is not something to be lightly entered into. Stress dominates the day, even in their joy, their rapture, duties, tradition, ceremony, acknowledgement comes to dominate the bridal couple's affairs. For Billy and Sally their tension was multiplied, so much was expected from their day of union, from family, friends, so it seemed, the whole town.

Then finally, after all the drama of their gallant dash to defy the storm, the storm that ravaged and pounded the valiant town they found themselves alone. Throughout that night the tempest raged, scattering anything that was not securely held down, levelling a dozen trees or more, disrupting those amenities which rely upon a benign aspect from nature. By the end of the day, with the sound and fury echoing above, the two newly wedded souls were entirely divested of their usual energy.

They should have simply collapsed, each in the others arms and swiftly flown to their rest.

Paradoxically, thus is the nature of human love, it is at such a time as this that a new force captivates the species. The cloak of exhaustion falls away, the sap begins to rise, the need to become of each other, each for the other, giving and receiving love's highest expression, overcomes listlessness within the mind, within the body. Billy and Sally found it to be so. The days leading towards their wedding had led them ever closer, ever more enticingly, temptingly towards love's final goal, yet in their desire to keep marriage, their marriage, a mystery they both came to their bed that night, innocent of experiencing the ultimate act.

Both had become aware of each other's needs, even of their capabilities, they had each witnessed the other's nakedness, or virtual nakedness, in the presence of the other. They knew the beauty of unclothed closeness, how the movement of skin upon skin provides such rapture. Yet still they had not explored that final mystery. Now, at the end of this, their wedding day's end, despite their tiredness, neither would disappoint the other.

Thus came the night, their nuptial night. The flow of love that, inevitably, had been so gaining upon them, breached the final barrier and poured through. Sally felt as if Billy had taken possession of her whole existence, her entire frame. Physically, emotionally, spiritually, his force consumed her. It became part of her, warm, pulsing, with a life of its own, an instrument which created the final link witnessing to their oneness that, for so long, had been her ultimate desire.

No pain emitted from such an invasion; the whole experience was wondrously gentle, without being passive or lacking passion. Billy displayed a delicate patience as he carefully explored his right of passage. He was so profoundly caring, that when, eventually, they became joined they were like two pieces of wax softly and slowly melting becoming forged and welded, each to the other, in their supreme fecundity.

They evolved their own unique fusion, which developed a perfect symmetry of grace filled union, formed into a single entity of joy filled humanity. Sally was enchanted, sensing their hearts beating in intense communion with the pulse of the Universe itself.

Sally's joy was of him and with him. His motion became hers, his words of love, his expressions of ecstasy, of calling her name.

"Sally, Sally, Sally."

His words echoed her calling out to him. She was as certain of the pleasure that he drew from within her being, as she knew he was aware of the profound fulfilment he had gifted to her. As they expressed their needs, they achieved their satisfied triumph time and again into the early hours of the morning. When at last sleep conquered them, they lay as Adam and Eve in the blessed garden conjoined, enwrapped dressed as on the day they were born.

Sleep brought dreams, dreams of loveliness, of each other, wandering naked under the warmth of the benevolent sun, hand in hand, enparadised, to the backdrop of the most wonderful music. So many times did the Mascagni come to be played over the next few days that it began to sound out imperfections, blemishes created by scratching or wear caused by the needle. The pair cared little. Mascagni's Intermezzo had become theirs; emblematic of the years they had spent together and the sole witness to the elevation of their love reaching its highest plain.

Now that very sun of their dreams, became reality. It burst its early rays through the curtainless window, bringing with it Nature's very own music that greets every such morning. Flashing, splashing sparkled, patterned, light, splayed across the room. The flickering rays began to disturb the man, his eyelids motioning, his body moving. First he stirred then stretched out his legs drawing down the sheets and blankets to expose his chest and his adored wife's back. Eventually his eyes opened and his mind drew back into consciousness. He awoke and behold that, which he thought was a dream, was real. Here she was his Sally, besides him in all her loveliness, warm, soft, gentle sighing in her sleep. His very own earthly angle. Thoughts drifted back to the evening before. He whispered softly, placing his lips upon her back, his nose accepting her exotic aroma, filling his loins with refreshed desire.

"What a wonderful woman you are Sally Thomas."

His kisses caused her to stir. Though still asleep she turned on her back an arm coming towards him, holding him. Her breasts came into his view delighting him with their curved fullness. Billy observed their darkened centres crowned with nipples that the slight breeze flowing through the open window caused to stiffen as a cairn upon a mountaintop. She was a delight was Sally Thomas and now she was his for all of time.

Billy knew that he could calmly enjoy this morning and whatever it brought, there was no need to rush, hurry or to panic over time. They had been excused from morning service. Instead, they would attend evensong to give thanks for the bounty that had befallen them. Thus, the day was theirs to use as they willed. Sitting up, he decided what he was going to do. Gently he placed Sally's arm back towards the centre of the bed and deftly got up. He drew on his new short under pants, 'what a good invention they are' his mind concluded, then placing on his housecoat he quietly went down stairs.

The warmth of the kitchen told him that the range was still alight. Within minutes he had riddled the grate, put on some new coals, opened up the grill and lifted the hot plate guards, ready to make tea and toast. Soon the kettle began to steam. The freshly cut bread exhibiting its toasting aroma. His head had gone under the tap, teeth brushed, the closet visited. He had a good wash with the remaining hot water. He then thoughtfully replenished the kettle for Sally's needs and prepared a tray set with plates, cups, butter and cosied pot. Triumphantly, he ascended the stairs with his morning offering to his bride.

Sally was coming into the world. Her arm had drifted to where her husband should have been and found nothing. In startled disappointment she had sat up to find the object of her search at the door of the bedroom tray in hand. Quickly she realised that her breasts were fully exposed to view and with a natural modest instinct she drew up the sheet.

"Shame to do that Mrs. Thomas, what with me being so recently acquainted with them."

Sally blushed at her husband's forwardness, yet she shamelessly relented and the sheets fell down, leaving her treasures for him to view to his delight. Billy sat down the tray on her side of the bed. Sitting down, he placed one of his wife's breasts in his hand and kissed her. 'Good morning Mrs. Thomas, and how are we today?"

"Why Mr. Thomas, and how do you think I should be?"

"Not ready to get out of bed yet I hope"

"And what on earth does that mean Mr. Thomas?"

"Wouldn't you just like to know Mrs. Thomas?"

Billy rose from the bed, poured out a cup of tea, which he offered to Sally, buttered some toast and handed that over also.

He then repeated the process, crossed over to the other side of the bed and placed his breakfast things on the bedside cabinet. Here he pulled away the quilt in order to get back under the blankets with his love. This movement exposed more of Sally than she would have wished. He caught sight of a blond tuft of hair, which intrigued him. There were things of womankind he had still to discover. It mattered not, Sally would lead him on in his pursuit of this new area of study, just as efficiently as she had on other aspects of life all those years ago in the library. By the time he left for the trenches he would be fully conversant with the form, manner and workings of womanhood or at least in all these matters, that had been deemed by the great creator to come within the realm of man's understanding.

Not until almost three in the afternoon did they emerge from that room except for further refreshment and the necessities of life. Eventually, it was Sally, with a practical need for Billy to go first, who gave her husband one last, long, lingering, kiss. She then, without warning, pulled back the quilt on his side, exposing his nakedness. She informed him that it was time for a wash and a shave, that mechanical function of men she had often observed her father undertaking, not with a little fascination. Self consciously, Billy got up, his manhood plain for her to see. This man amazed Sally, observing how he was built, or, more accurately, Billy in his nakedness, uniquely, enthralled her. It was like nothing that she had felt before. Billy observed his wife's self satisfied look. Her eyes appeared transfixed.

"Why it's a wanton I have for a wife"

He enunciated his words whilst quickly wrapping his dressing gown around him before Sally could espy the results that her curiosity was having upon him.

"I will bring up some hot water for you in the jug and basin."

"Thank you Billy"

Sally was grateful. Her husband's sensitivity was remarkable, as if he knew of the difficulties that she was experiencing.

Once he had departed Sally got up and placed her gown around her. Quickly she stripped the bed, grateful that it was no longer the tradition to exhibit the certain signs of her virginity for all to see. In this case they were so pronounced that none would have doubted her previous chastity. How could so much blood have flowed without any sense of pain at all? It was remarkable.

By the time Billy arrived with the hot water. The bed was remade with fresh clean sheets, the soiled ones had been placed in the laundry basket at the top of the stairs. Billy would never see the proof that he had deflowered his wife. Such evidence that virginal lovemaking provided, so stark an element of certainty would never come within his realm of awareness. In so many ways he would return to the trenches an innocent. In others, he would report back, a most accomplished husband.

Deftly he left his wife to finish her preparations. Downstairs on the range stood the long ignored, now simmering casserole. The aroma was exquisite, leading hunger of the stomach to take control over all his other forms of hunger and urges. The tempting dish, bubbling on the hot plate would soon meet its waterloo, then, and only then, could he truthfully say that every one of his requirements had been attained.

At last Sally joined him at the table. He served up a plateful for each of them, along with some cold cordial to accompany it. His wife was becoming ever more impressed with her new husband, with every deed he undertook on her behalf. Now in the calm of a Sunday afternoon, the food before them, they relaxed, contentment replacing passion and reflection for anticipation. It was now that the realisation came to him. For the first time in his life, he was eating a meal without his mother, here in this house.

This house, the home of his youth, of his earliest thoughts and aspirations, where for hours he had helped his mother card box upon box of hooks and eyes, had now provided for the enactment of his first lovemaking. This little home of his where he had read book after book by the fireside, upstairs, in his small back bedroom, had given witness to the fulfilment of his desires. Here he was, at last, alone with the girl whom he had dreamed of all through the long years when they were apart.

Like millions of families throughout the country he and his wife were having their Sunday meal in apparent normality, as if outside events were evolving in their usual manner. It was then, as he pondered upon the simple and uncomplicated mealtime, that the cloud of reality, once more, entered his mind returning him to the reality of life in the real world.

These were not usual times. At the very moment he had obtained his life's desires, events beyond his control, Could sweep it all away, forcing their parting. It was now, in the afterglow of his deep joy, that the thought, always in the recess of his mind, came to the fore.

Sally sensed that her husband's mind had drawn him into a mood of apprehension. She could see that he was deep in thought, distressing thought. Sally considered that she knew its source, it was time to give him comfort and assurance of another kind to that which she had ministered over the past hours.

She began her task, her voice, full of comfort, softly reaching out to him, as it had done so years before when, in the library, she informed him of her going away.

"I know Billy, I can see that you are troubled. You have made me so happy indeed, fulfilled my life's dream. Whatever occurs, from now on, nothing can now take you away from me."

"We can be parted. I can be left here to worry for you and, God forbid, grieve for you. Yet there is one thing that cannot be taken away from me, from you, from us, it is ourselves each with the other, for the other, a part of the other. That transcends above any separation, any parting. It is greater than death itself. Our love, our deep profound living love, can never be destroyed by mortal man or any of his infernal devices."

Her words produced the effect she had designed, calmness of mind came to him once again. He got out of his chair and, walking over to she sat, he knelt before her. Placing his head in her lap he quietly, openly, began to weep. Now she knew, it came upon her. This grown man, a soldier, holder of the Military Medal, he who had faced guns, bullets and all manner of danger, her Billy, was still, in many ways, the small fragile sensitive boy she had fallen in love with that first morning in the library.

Sally placed her hands upon his head, stroking his hair in the manner that womankind have been called upon to minister through countless generations. He was her man, strong, full of purpose, aspiration and courage. Yet, in paradox, he was also that small boy, she had first met all those years ago, crying out for the strength, sympathy, love and understanding which is only provided by her sex.

In such manner they acted out the pageant, he in her lap, she gently rocking him, sifting her hands through the strands of his hair. Their union was complete. Love finds expressions in more than the obvious manner. Now no barriers existed between them. They had exchanged their vows, vows they would keep forever. They had shared their joys, their coming together. They had become as one in a high, caring, sensual act, withholding nothing. Now they were sharing their fears, pouring out love and devotion as only humans can.

In this manner the couple communicated for an apparent age. Such expression possessed its catharsis. Gradually Billy began to emerge from her lap. He lifted his head towards her, meeting with those beautiful eyes, flecked, moist, sparkling, filled with empathy and endless love. Sally placed his head sideways, back upon her lap, so that his eyes could stare upon an endless horizon. All was quiet and still. Then, without warning, a question came from out of the firmament, seeming not to have any connection with what had gone before,

"Why Milton?"

It took a moment to absorb the words. Even so she still could not understand the question. There was nothing to relate to.

"Milton? My love, I don't understand?"

It was Billy's turn for a short silence, while he composed his answer.

"Why Milton? It is beautiful; I carry it everywhere with me. It is full of the most profound spiritual beauty, but why did you choose it? Why Milton?"

271

Now she understood. The small volume that she had purchased from Smiths to provide a comfort. Why did she choose that particular volume? Now, confronted with the question, she wasn't quite sure, or was she?

"Well it did fit into the pocket of the waistcoat I had knitted. Its dark green cover matched the wool."

Billy sensed her reticence. He would make another attempt at an answer; his instincts told him there was more of an explanation to come, much more. Also he wanted her to mention the white embroidered handkerchief without him having to prompt her. Gazing, once again, into his dear girls eyes he persued the point with a single word.

"And?"

Now she blushed, she was trapped. Not now being in command of the modesty of maidenhood, it might be possible to convey to her beloved man the truth, the whole truth. The words stammered from her, haltingly hesitant.

"Well if you must know."

She paused to look at her husband, who was nodding his head.

"If you must know, I discovered a copy in the Library at St Elphins. You understand we girls had a very restricted range of books in our small school library. Nothing of any nature which could compromise our innocence, or awake the curiosity, which most young maidens, seeking knowledge of the future contain within them, was allowed to exist within its walls"

"And what did you discover in your copy of Milton"

The question was not merely erotically mischievous; it contained a real sense of interested enquiry.

"Well."

Sally, knowing that she was trapped, decided to admit all.

"Where is your copy? I shall read to you."

Billy went over to his uniform jacket, which hung on a clothes conveyance that his father had made years ago. He took it from his hanger. Beneath was the knitted waistcoat, within it the volume, which he extracted.

"Here you are Sally."

He handed her the small book having kissed its cover.

Silence descended, only the turning of the finely made leaves could be heard, finally Sally let out a sigh, looked towards Billy with a sheepish smile

"Here it is, 'Book iv' from 'Paradise Lost.' I must have read it hundreds of times, those years we spent apart."

For half an hour she read. Billy in the warmth of the room, basking in the mellowness of lovemaking's expended passion, listened to every

272

word. Later, when, once more, he was far away from her, he would, again, recall to mind, extracts from her recitation.

> *'Thus talking, hand in hand alone they passed*
> *Onto their blissful bower. It was the place*
> *Chosen by the Sovereign planter when he framed*
> *All things to man's delightful use;......*
>
> *Espoused, Eve decked first her nuptial bed,*
> *And heavenly quoirs the hymenean sung,*
> *That day the genial angel to our sire*
> *Brought her in naked beauty......*
>
> *.....they went; and eased the putting off*
> *The troublesome disguises which we wear*
> *Strait side by side were laid nor turned*
> *Adam from his fair spouse, nor Eve the rites*
> *Mysterious of connubial love refused......*
>
> *Thus lulled by nightingales embracing slept,*
> *And on their naked limbs the flowery roof*
> *Showered roses, which the morn repaired. Sleep on*
> *Blest pair, and O'yet happiest if ye seek*
> *No happier state, and know to know once more.*

Sally's reading ended, she reflecting upon how exact Milton's description of the marriage bed was portrayed within the lines. Billy pondered astonished by his wife's uxorious, intimate reading of the thinly disguised revelation of the act of love.

"You see now Billy, just how much I was determined upon having you as my husband, even from the earliest of our meetings. In my school girlish manner you had been designated to me to become my love. I shall tell you something else. The embroidered handkerchief that I gave you within the volume. I had stitched it years earlier. On the day that I had to tell you that I was leaving for St Elphins, it was to be my momento to you. Unfortunately, the courage to present it vanished, in my anxiety that you would not wish to have it, or cherish it so, for within the stitching was my very heart. All the love I then owned, and since, have ever possessed, it was and is, yours."

Now the truth was out, Billy did not want to tell her that he already knew. Mrs. Lloyd words would go unsaid, here was his beautiful wife before him, undergoing a confession, opening her heart, her life, displaying a little of her mysteries, her ingenious manner. Yes beautiful she was, to be cared for, cherished, valued above everything, everyone. Sally was more precious to him than rubies, being her husband would mean that he would always be known at the gates, he would always praise her and bless the day he first met her.

How he loved her. How his heart would ache for her when, duty bound, he left Glossop once more. Before leaving he would have to commend to the written page the thoughts, images and emotions which so filled and overwhelmed him at this moment. Now all he wanted was to take his wife, dearest among women in his arms and wrap her in love, his love.

There she was fragile, fragrant, tears beginning to fill her. Sally had lived her dream, driven herself towards her destiny. Now here she was, everything fulfilled, all in place, love surrounding her, her Adam protecting her in this little Eden. Yet she knew, the Devil and his servants, were coming to attempt to take it all from her, to attempt destruction upon all she had built.

Billy could not sense or understand all that encompassed her mind that day, though he perceived, correctly, that she too was now being haunted by what the future held. Now his task was to be ever near, providing reassurance, to bring strength. It became his turn to hold Sally whilst her tears and sobs subsided. He hugged her tightly, his strength embracing her frame. Her head began to lift towards his, her neck stretched, lips seeking his. They met, warm, soft, smooth, caressing, then a compelling sensation rose within her. She could hear her heartbeat gaining momentum. The need for Billy to possess her once more was uncontrollable. Taking his hand, her eyes pleading for him, without a further word being uttered she led him up the stairs.

They were missed at Chapel that night. The general congregation did not realise the pair had promised to attend, but their friends and family were aware. Knowing smiles traversed the pews, even reaching the pulpit. The reading that night was from psalm 42, as the words echoed through the Chapel the two women glanced at each other smiling, wondering, wondrously.

'As the heart panteth after the water brooks,
So my soul panteth after thee.'

A few streets away, two souls were panting, having dashed like deer towards each other, quenching their desires in the waters of love. It would be Monday afternoon before both, looking sheepish, feeling guilty, emerged from their Eden in Talbot Street, to take the short walk into town and the shop where their parents worked, waiting excitedly, expectantly, to discover how married life was treating their offspring.

It was ten minutes after the shop was reopening from its customary lunch interval that the two young people walked through the door, their countenance vivid in its glowing intensity. Holding hands, their faces radiating an afterglow that both mothers recognised with warm fond remembrance. Neither had ever seen their offspring so illuminated with joy. Their eyes catching each other, they mutually concluded, without using words, that the two had found, within their union, all that they had dreamed upon, all they could ever, would ever, desire.

Nathaniel, looking over the counter, serving a startled customer, felt a great satisfaction as he observed the three women and his young protégé hugging, kissing, and squealing with joy, as they completed a reunion that marked a parting of the entire last two days. Once, after an extraordinary length of time, the excitement began to quell, Elizabeth took her daughter into the near stock room. Her head was full of questions, needing to know that matters were all agreeable. She quizzed her daughter on every conceivable matter, both those of a practical nature and other subjective aspects, which a young bride requires to meet her preconceived expectations.

"Mother he is wonderful, it is wonderful, everything is completely wonderful"

Sally enraptured her mother, as she fell into her arms, crying softly, gently.

"Then why the tears my darling?"

"Because mother, I have to let him go. In nine days time he leaves me and goes back to the war."

Her tears were more open now; Elizabeth sat her down upon one of the wooden crates that were stacked around the room. She could remember but one or two times previously in her daughter's life when she had acted as a counsellor, comforter, upon finding Sally distressed so. Consoling her daughter on this occasion was going to be very difficult indeed.

"Do you remember Sally the last time you parted from those that you loved made you so unhappy. The time when we had to pursuade you to finish your education at St Elphins? Well that time of parting of separation soon passed didn't it? This time will as well."

Her daughter's response was to surprise her.

"Mother even now you just do not understand. The reason that I did not want to go to boarding school was because of Billy. We used to meet every Saturday morning in the Library. We read books together, introduced each other to new writers, new poets. Saturday mornings became the highlight of my week, my life. I loved Billy even then, all those years ago. I wanted him, wanted him for myself. Now do you understand?"

Sally's words astounded her mother; she tried to put them into some perspective.

"Sally, tell me, just how long have you been attached to Billy? Are you really saying that this romance goes back to when you used to go every Saturday to the Library? Are you saying that this beautiful marriage you have just begun has its roots in a love that goes back to when you were so young?"

Elizabeth recollections were beginning to focus now. She had remembered how her daughter had always got up early on a Saturday and insisted on one of her best dresses being worn She recalled her daughter selecting a bangle or bow for her hair and scolding her if she did not prepare Sally's hair just so. Now Elizabeth knew and the realisation made her eyes well with tears. It was as if she had just completed reading a Bronte romance.

She had read Jane Eyre many times. Once, in their early-married life, Elizabeth had read it aloud to Nathaniel. For night after night, by lamplight, upstairs in their small bedroom, both of them had become engrossed with the novel's heightened romantic twists and turns. How finally, the brave yet reckless, dashing, Rochester, is brought down, disfigured and blinded, through the vengeful actions of his distraught, maddened wife.

'Reader I married him.' Elizabeth remembered the night she had begun that final chapter, in front of the fireplace, realising how little of the novel was left to be read and, how something would be lost to them upon its conclusion. How romantic it was, how loving Nathaniel had been that night, possessing her for an age, a beautiful wondrous age.

She had often thought that it was upon that evening when she became of child, when her daughter was conceived. 'If that was the case,' Elizabeth now considered, then her daughter, this most wonderful girl, sitting before her now, with her freshly gained womanhood, if that was indeed the case, then Sally was star-struck from the very beginning.

Her poor daughter. How many times must she have sat in her room plotting; planning ways of being near the young man who so filled her thoughts, her imaginations? She could only guess. Here she was now resting on her mother's breast having her hair stroked, caressed gently by the woman who had given her life from a union itself blessed by love, romance and gentleness. One thing only gave Elizabeth concern. The happy times, the fulfilled moments of Jane Eyre's story merely occupies but a handful of pages. The storm and stress of her life fills a whole book, her marriage but a few leaves.

"God please do not let that be my daughter's fate?"

The prayer was unwittingly whispered causing Sally to stir

"What mother? What did you say?"

"Nothing darling, nothing at all. Come on; time to rejoin our men I think. You will get to know more about them now you are a wife. They simply are not happy unless we are there fussing over them you know."

"Oh mother, if only I have the time and privilege to fuss over Billy, for him to show me how much he loves me, as you and father have had ,then I would greet the grave a happy and complete woman."

'How like Charlotte Bronte,' thought Elizabeth. It was as if she had entered the pages of a new book, written by her favourite writer, to witness the conflict, passion, triumph and tragedy.

"Come on now Sally, let us go back and find our men".

The truth of Elizabeth's insight on the ways of men was being made manifest out in the shop where Nathaniel was in conversation with his newly acquired son in Law. He had observed Billy pacing round the shop, tinkering with numerous objects, displaying impatience eager to have his wife back in his presence Eventually Nathaniel could not bear to observe the young man's self inflicted torture any longer. It was plainly time for him to provide some fatherly advice.

"It will ever be the case Billy. It's called women's talk. We just have to put up with it, could take an age you know."

"But what do they find to talk about for so long? What could take up so much time?"

"Why us of course. You and I. Sally will be telling her mother how happy she is. Elizabeth will be absorbing every word, asking her questions the like of which only one woman enquires of another. Billy they are conversing over you and your ways. Elizabeth will be recalling her early married life and they will be making comparisons. The longer they talk means the more we occupy their thoughts. Quite a compliment really."

Nathaniel was only being half-serious. If only he knew just how now near to the truth he was.

Gladys had overheard the conversation. She too had been watching her son. He so reminded her of her Joshua, impetuous, impatient for results, caring so overwhelmingly when he came home to her after an absence due to work. Yes her son was his father's boy. She felt happiness for him, so, alongside Nathaniel, she assured him that all had gone well and how happy Sally appeared. Having said that, it would not do to allow these two men to believe that the worlds revolved around them. That would not do at all.

Listening to the pair of them coming to conclusions that could only have been built upon vanity, Gladys interjected.

"That you two men should be so lucky. There is more to a woman's life than talking over their husband's I can tell you. Now Billy give me a hand here for the moment."

Occupy his thoughts with other matters was her answer to her son's impatience.

"Come on Billy. Idle hands lead to idle thoughts."

It was an almost sulky Billy that nonchalantly strolled over towards his mother, yet within a few moments, as had been his willing lot, his life, he was assisting his mother. Mindful once again of times past, he quickly fell into a rhythm with his mother, filling packages of seeds whilst she weighed them out.

At last his torment was over. A composed Sally came out of the stockroom full of smiles, pacing swiftly over to her husband and giving him a huge hug. Demonstrative behaviour like this had become more fashionable as the war progressed; bringing down the age-old Victorian convention that had so dominated public acts of affection between men and women. Once, not so long ago, even small intimacies as they now displayed, would have produced whispers of scandal mongering. Not so now, this day their hugs passed by without a second glance though, it must be said, both women reflected upon the closeness of their offspring with a great deal of satisfaction.

'Time to let them both go on their way' thought Elizabeth.

The day was developing into another promising, spring laden, experience.

"Why don't you two go for a long walk, its lovely outside. Spend the day together and come to dinner tonight?"

"Now is that not a good idea?"

Gladys affirmed her friend's suggestion.

"Off you go now."

She ushered them out of the shop as a sheep dog controls the movements of his charges, gently but firmly.

The grateful pair, wordless but knowing what the other wished, made their way out of town. They silently ambled their way up into the hillside over looking the town, those benevolent hills which had provided their privacy in the days leading to their marriage, the privacy which had allowed each other to discover the essences contained within human love.

After an hour's walking, a walk interspersed by intimate embraces and kisses, they arrived at the very spot where they had lain just a week before, where they had filled each other with so many exotic sensations. Once more Billy took off his jacket. Sally, invitingly, sat herself down upon the dry mossy grass beneath the beech trees whose roots and mantle sucked so much moisture from out of the earth leaving a firm yet comfortable nuptial bed. Here, they lay together under that English sky, so precious that regiments of young men willingly went off to defend its independence. All was still except for the song of birds mingling with the most intimate of whispers and sighs. It was here, in this blessed plot, that their daughter Daisy was conceived. Such love, such perfect love, expressed and fulfilled, completing the cycle of life.

High above the field, caught upon a swiftly rising thermal, two Hawks climbed towards the heavens. Their timid mewing came to Sally's ears. She opened her eyes. Her lover was upon her, her neck sensing his kisses, her breasts being gently caressed. He was, once more, of her, as she was of him, one flesh. She sensed his rising urgency. Locking herself, her legs pressing hard against him, surrounding him losing all awareness of

278

being, meeting her final joy with his. At last, at long last, they lay, expelling great breaths of air. Their joy was complete.

CHAPTER 18

'Till we have built Jerusalem
In England's green and pleasant land

William Blake.

Nine days can pass so swiftly. For the two newly weds it was especially true. Nine short days, but what days they were. Coming down from the hills, having gained the sanctuary of their home, they once again felt secure. They were giggling like children, feeling guilty about their unashamed lovemaking in the open, where, who knows who, could have seen them.

The shamefulness of unpassioned hindsight at what they had done produced a certain mutual guilt. Well, perhaps not guilt, but at least a certain self-consciousness. Both were sure that their parents knew they had spent the afternoon making love in their special place by the beech copse, isolated high above the town. This thought brought with it the idea that retribution, in the form of admonishment, would descend upon them.

In truth both women conjectured as much, but their thoughts went unspoken. As for Nathaniel nothing of that nature entered his mind and Elizabeth felt, as she had done so in the past, that what he did not know, would do him no harm.

As they lay together, their bodies each giving to the other warmth and comfort, a time of reflection came upon them. Sally told her beloved husband of her observations in the hills whilst he was spending his passion on her. How the Hawks had spiralled above them, how he and the Hawks had given her so much joy and pleasure. The Hawks invading the sky, thrusting the thermal, cleaving the air, seemed to her to be symbolic of their act of union. She spoke of all these elements, which had added to the delight that he had brought her, to produce the most captivating encounter with love that a woman could ever have.

Before he went back to France, Billy, having listened to her words, would compose a sonnet for her, of their time together in the hills. It would become a source of considerable comfort and fond reminiscence to Sally in the years to come. He titled it 'Above Glossop Moor.'

Sally was destined to read it countless numbers of times. It is now buried with her, clasped in her hand.

So Monday night passed in discovering many new enticements, born of their mutual explorations and discovery of novel sensual thrills, that a man and a woman can bring to each other. Truly they wandered in a Garden of Eden, complete with experiences and emotions reflective of their beloved Milton's pair of tragically dispossessed lovers. Sally adorned herself, for his delight, in a sensually thin translucent satin cream night-dress. It possessed a loosely tied ribbon which, allowing for one slight movement of hand, of which daily Billy was becoming more deft, parted the garment, in the most provocative manner. Enticingly suggestive, it promised further rewards, should the lucky recipient of the display have the courage to explore further.

'Made so adorned for the delight.
That, with honour, thou may love thy mate.

The words came to him from book eight, his favourite section of Milton's great work. 'How strange,' he thought, 'that it was Sally, so delicate, untouchably innocent and unapproachable who should have first discovered the wonderfully explicit, intimate nature of the great poem. He contrasted his own development in the understanding of the epic, with that of Sally's early comprehension. Whilst he, although memorising vast numbers of lines, was totally unaware of its truly personal, intimate expression hidden so resourcefully within its lines, Sally had discovered and developed an astounding interpretation, poetically revealing the original source of human needs and desires. Eve, commanded many a mystery, that most alluring of all womankind's attributes. These were destined never to fall within the realm of those matters that are understood by men. In turn, she had handed her secrets onto generations of her daughters until it had fallen to his Sally to embrace them.

Even after man had gained the most inner secrets of her charms, she would never be fully understood, or completely extracted of her every delight. Truly a man's wife, could provide him with all comfort, all reason of being. Adam, Milton, and now himself, had all approached Woman and been placed in awe of her. Adam's sons had loved her, placed her on the highest summit of grace and love but never had they come close to understanding her. Eve and her daughters remained a many facetted splendoured gift, God's most perfect gift. In gratitude, as with the other sons of Adam, Billy gratefully accepted her, treasured her, and would seek endlessly to please her. He would defend her, be ever faithful to her, ceaselessly strive to be of her and to be solely, exclusively, exquisitely, pleasured by her.

'The sense of touch, whereby mankind
Is propagated, seems such dear delight,
Beyond all other'

If only Sally could be with child before he left. How complete life would be. Filled with such silent musings, tiredness came upon him. Turning to his beloved, he discovered that she had already drifted away to the domain of dreams. Billy soon followed. Thus they slept, each entwined within the other, sleeping endlessly, complete of love, relaxed, spent. The sun would be well above the eastern horizon before either stirred having swam in seas of euphoria, in magic waters.

'Love leads up to heaven.'

Glossop's most favoured son, her hero, newly married to his beautiful, intelligent; charming wife, was not to be given a completely free reign with his time. In fact two opposing forces were plying for his attention and service before his time of leave was over. Firstly Hill-Woods and his Conservatives asked Billy to attend a patriotic rally, one thinly disguised to embarrass the Liberal government. They approached him in total assumption that he would give voice to their aim. The other invitation came through his Uncle Frank. The first he dismissed easily, if not without a measure of embarrassment, and the other, an offer to attend a Socialist patriotic meeting, grasped his imagination, which he readily accepted.

The meeting to be held on the Wednesday evening was expeditiously publicised. Two young Clarinettes cycled round the town with posters, paste, buckets and brush. Dozens of sheets were posted in prominent positions all around the town, having Billy's name centred on them in the largest possible print. Belle Maloney 'La Belle' of all those years ago, was to be the main speaker, once again extolling women's rights of equality.

Uncle Frank had now become chairman of the local Labour Party branch and a councillor, having dramatically won a by-election just four months before. He was to chair the meeting.

By prior arrangement they met in the 'Moon and Sixpence' half an hour before the rally. It was a Public House of course and Sally felt rather self-conscious as she stepped through its doors. Her parents had always told her that it was not 'ladylike' to be seen in such a place, but 'hey ho' Billy was her prime advisor now.

It was a rather small place, built just two years previously on the site of an older tavern that had burnt down. A Mr Somerset Maughan had come to town to direct a production at the nearby playhouse. The present owner met the promising playwright at the bar during the interval. Having told Mr Maughan that he was opening a new alehouse just up the way, he asked him if he could think of an appropriate name for the new establishment. The answer came back, 'The Moon and Sixpence.' It was the name of a play that he was working on. To the publican, it sounded exactly right for a playhouse tavern, so the name became adopted. It left the publican often wondering if his establishment would ever gain any fame through its name, he thought 'probably not.'

The rest of the speakers, orderlies, organisers for the rally were already gathered in one corner of the lounge. Each had a pint of plain or best, except for 'La Belle,' she drank tonic water.

"Would not do for the World to think that I climbed the platform intoxicated now would it? They regard me as a brazen hussy as it is."

"No Miss Malony, but no one could ever think of such a thing regarding your good self."

Billy's declaration took the woman by surprise as indeed it did for the rest of the group. One just did not make remarks so to an unknown female comrade without, at least, an introduction.

However, something tugged at the memory of 'La Belle' she turned towards the direction of the voice, a voice that created stirrings within her memory. She saw the handsome man, together with his lovely companion. Splendid he was, decked out in his uniform, with a medal on his chest. But, for all his added years of experience, love, war, maturity, nothing could disguise who he was. Her words formed a question, but it was merely rhetorical, she knew.

"Billy Thomas?"

She then repeated herself only much louder, much more enthused,

"Billy Thomas?"

'The very same ma'am."

Billy was so pleased she had recognised him.

"You two know each other?"

The query came from Uncle Frank; Belle Maloney obliged with an answer.

"Why yes, this young man once carried out a great service for the cause, he took care of Hercules."

"Hercules?"

Uncle Frank was becoming more puzzled by the moment.

"Our horse, our great, powerful, heroic Clarion horse. He is too old now Billy, for such duty. He has been gracefully retired, put out to grass. Where he can idle away the days. Besides, the caravans are not being used at the moment. These days we use the train."

Quickly she explained to Frank the story of her meeting with Billy

"It must be seven years ago at least."

"More"

Billy, interjected, he knew just how long it was. Then he remembered. How is Mr Robert Blatchford?"

"Not too well I'm afraid, but next time I see him I will tell him how his young sentinel matured. It will please him very much."

The conversation moved on, talk of the war, Billy's speech. It had been decided that he would sit on the stage alongside Sally and that at the end of his speech Belle would present both of them with their Labour Party membership cards. It would make such good press. Almost certainly, it would bring a large number of new members to the Party. Sally was nervous, she wished she was back home, but she was proud and pleased.

The group made their way from the Public House to the station, then down the cobbled square to the cross. Quite a crowd was entering Victoria Hall. Billy's name on the poster was proving to be a great crowd puller. Four men were on the door, each displaying a red band on their right sleeve. They were Miners, well built men, hard, able to handle unruly hecklers and meeting wreckers. Socialist meetings tended to have need of such men, in times like these.

The hall was full. It was not yet two years since that Billy, listening to Hill-Woods, felt drawn into the web of the devious man's spell of patriotism, and had enlisted. Now here he was, back from the front, married to his love, in his uniform, decorated for his bravery, and about to pour forth vitriol on all the very social evils that the local M.P stood for.

He took his place upon the platform, alongside Sally, Uncle Frank, 'La Belle' and a local trade unionist from the cotton mills. Billy looked around the hall. Scattered in amongst the crowd of men, their wives and some small businessmen, were men and women in uniform. These tended to huddle in groups, some on crutches, some with head bandages, and one in a wheel chair. There were a few in nursing uniforms, crisp, neat, proudly displaying their red crosses on their fronts, portraying a delicate beauty from under their white caps.

A sense of humility came over him. He was fortunate; God had given him talents, gifts of learning, skills in sports, in leadership. Now he would see how far these gifts served when it came to public speaking. Billy looked down at his notes. Sally, who had aided him in their production, smiled at him, giving him encouragement and support.

Frank rose, the humming in the hall ceased.

He began his address. His introductions. There was a polite applause for the trade unionist, followed by a more enthused reception for Belle Maloney, especially from a section of suffragettes. They had unravelled a banner to one side of the hall and propped it against a wall, adding to the red and gold Union and Socialist displays that were all around. The largest applause, however, almost rapturous, was reserved for Billy.

"Now it is my great privilege to introduce. Corporal Billy Thomas M.M here direct from the trenches, from Flanders field. He has seen this war at first hand, he has bravely faced the foe, and he has been wounded, and decorated for bravery. In short, he is a hero. Yet, for all this, he has come to see how patriotism and sacrifice should reap its reward and gain its recognition. Tonight, on behalf of all his colleagues in the trenches and all those who have already supremely sacrificed themselves for this land, he will insist upon their just rights. He will demand for them the dignity that good wages bring, that good job conditions ensure, safety regulations for the workers and decent housing for all."

"Ladies and gentlemen, Comrades, I have heard this man enthusing in private on how it ought to be, how he wants to see things improved after the war. Now I give you the opportunity to hear him in person. Comrades, I give you Corporal Billy Thomas."

What an introduction for the young soldier, the hall simply erupted. A voice from the back coming from a uniformed man possessing a single leg and supported by crutches shouted out at the top of his voice.

"Go on Billy tell 'em, tell 'em how it is out there, tell 'em the truth."

Billy rose, all nervousness gone, carried along by the enthused reception he was being given. Already the remarks of the wounded veteran had compelled him to drift from his prepared text.

"I am urged by my comrade here to tell you how it is out there. Well if you want to know, I shall tell you."

For ten minutes or so Billy described life at the front leaving nothing to the imagination. In his animated description, his audience was transported to Northern France, almost living the experiences of the soldiers, such was the graphic intensity of Billy's oratory, his detailed, graphically expressed memories. The trenches were full of British working class men, men who in civilian life worked on the railways, the mills, the mines, and the steel forges. They were clerks, postmen, farmers, some even ex prisoners or from the ranks of the unemployed.

All these men had been brought together, not by conscription but because, when their country needed them they had volunteered. They were the back bone of the New Army, they had courage, determination, they were God fearing in the main. They respected their King and loved their Country, and for all this they were prepared, if need be, to die, to sacrifice life, mind and limb on the battlefields of France.

Now Billy's knowledge of France, and his profound identity with past heroic deeds, enacted in that country by armies of the British, took hold of his oration. This was not the first generation to conduct its self thus, so selflessly, with patriotism, loyalty, with sacrifice, a thousand years of such example had carved this country of Britain, chiselled out its destiny, its desires, the aspirations of its people.

"We have ever been a nation of soldiers, brave men and women, yes women. See the example of Nurse Carvel."

This brought great applause. The execution by the Germans of this brave daughter of England had touched the hearts of every man and woman throughout the land. She was remembered now. Once the applause died down it was the turn of his endless hours spent in Glossop Library and the knowledge that it had brought him, to come into play.

"We are a nation of inventors and designers, of craftsmanship, explorers and researchers. We are a civilised Nation of free men and women, struggling to overcome dictatorship and oppression. We are a Nation fighting against all that is evil in the world. We are a Nation of epic heroes, men and women, known and unknown, recognised and unrecognised. Our efforts; efforts and examples of energy, time, strength, courage, sacrifice, all has been willingly offered and taken by a grateful Nation. We were asked, and we gave. We shall continue to give."

"We shall give freely for we are asked, not instructed. We shall fight, and many of us shall die, fallen in a foreign land. There are also those who shall work and fight the good fight at home to build the weapons that sustain the troops. We shall fight abroad, wherever we are needed, for as long as we are needed, until ours is the victory. Then, our task complete, we shall come to home to a land that is free, at peace with the world. It is then that we shall have to turn towards being at peace with ourselves. It is then that the hour will come when all this effort, all this sacrifice, will demand its recognition."

Now he lowered his voice, he was about to use, directly, a reference from his revered writer. I am reminded that there have been times when we so warred with ourselves that military conflict was the main expression of our society. In such a period voices were raised to attempt to restore sanity. Mighty Milton proclaimed as much on the occasion of Parliament's victory over the Monarchy. Like he, we must be prepared to construct the peace fairly and equitably, giving to friend and foe alike. Milton cried out to the Lord Fairfax."

'Yet a nobler task awaits your hand;
For what does war, but endless war still breed.
Till truth and right, from violence from, be freed.'

"Peace, truth, right. Is that too much to ask?! Is it too much to demand? For the honoured dead, for their widows and orphans, is it to much to ask that they be justly treated, justly provided for, given a voice, decent homes, education, jobs, and fair wages. Is that so much to ask?"

His question brought enraptured acclamation throughout the hall, particularly from the uniformed members. Cries came of "Tell 'em Billy, tell 'em 'ow it is."

"What is Victory? What is Victory to bring? Make no mistake comrades. Victory is our first aim. Nothing deters as from that task. But we must ask that one essential question. What is Victory? I say Victory is nothing, unless it is attendant of justice, freedom, peace, fairness between the nations, fairness between each and every individual in our society. Item one, the franchise must be extended to contain within it, all adults, men and women alike"

This brought the women to their feet. Led by Belle Malony who stood in uninterrupted applause. When, at last, it died down, Billy continued. He was existing now without notes, allowing the adrenaline and the atmosphere to draw him along.

"Have not women played their part in this war as much as the men? Have they not? The Voluntary Aid Detachment, nurses, the ones who brought me back to health so that I could go back to the trenches of France, have they not played their part? The fundraisers, those endlessly knitting articles, to provide the gloves that keep the fingers warm of the men whose rifles point, towards the foe. The women factory workers who replaced the men to provide the ordinance? Give them the vote, Let them sit in the debating chambers alongside the men. It is their right, their sacred right."

Again came the applause, together with stamping of feet and shouts of acclamation. Frank was thinking to himself. 'We have a new star born today for the cause'. Pride overwhelmed him.

Billy though was not quite finished with the issue of the franchise. Lowering his voice and slowing down his words, he made the most telling point.

"Tell me any of you, tell me Mr Asquith, tell me Mr Hill-Woods our esteemed MP, tell me any of you here tonight. Which of you, here or throughout the Country, would, if he came face to face with the dear brave, self-sacrificing Nurse Cavel, answer her no, if she, from her grave, asked for the vote? If she demanded that her voice be heard? Who among you, which one of you, would answer her no and deny her a voice in the Country that she so selflessly died for? Who? Who? who?"

The very building rocked with denials, Billy had won every person within those walls to the side of female suffrage. At last the noise died down and everyone, once more, took their seats. Billy continued to develop his theme."

"Yes all this and more. It is when the peace comes that the time for building comes. Hospitals, well equipped, enough for all. Homes, good homes, enough for all. Education for all, advanced technical, artistic education, for all those who so desire it. A good diet for our children. Let us make rickets a thing of the past."

Again came acclamation, combined with looks of astonished approval among those on the platform.

"As Milton addresses Cromwell. After the civil war had come to its end."

'Yet much remains.
To conquer still; peace hath her victories
No less renowned than war, new foes arise
Threatening to bind our souls.'

287

"New foes indeed, their names are legion. Poverty, hunger pestilence, ignorance, yes pitiful ignorance. We must carve out the peace magnanimously, giving all nations a dignity, a sense of worth. Furthermore, to all people, regardless of class, of origin, of ability, must come this dignity, this sense of worth."

Billy's speech was over running its allocated span but Frank, encouraged by nods from the rest of the platform, decided to give him his head. This young man, fresh from war had the meeting in his hand.

Billy's mind had now cast back to the time of the Christmas truce and the strange moustached men he had met there between the trenches on that one day of peace.

"You, all of you, have heard the tales of the Christmas truce. Some say it never happened. Well it did, I was there, a part of it. During that one day when the guns were silent, when enemies shook hands, I met this German soldier. Unlike many of the others, who if truth be known were as ourselves, possessing wives and families, hoping that soon the war would come to an end, this man had something evil about him, a determination, a pair of eyes that could transfix you.

He told me that the war would never end until we had bowed to Germany's will, that we would be totally destroyed if necessary. Amazingly, he knew of Glossop. He saw the town in terms of military strategy, guarding the pass over the Pennines. He was evil, evil but determined, having powers of persuasion. Ladies and Gentlemen when the time comes, as come it will. When the time of peace arrives, our leaders must ensure that the peace is honourable and equitable, that truly, this war, is the war to end all wars."

"We must construct an honourable European peace. For, if not, then people like that moustached Corporal that I met between the trenches, will come to power and champion his people. Then surely a new war, more devastating and terrible, than the first, will come to pass, a war that will bring a lasting ruin upon Europe, upon the entire World."

"So then let us strive, first for victory, secondly for a just peace, thirdly for a just society, a Democratic Socialist society. Let us reaffirm the words of William Blake."

'I shall not cease from mental fight
Nor shall my sword sleep in my hand
Till we have built Jerusalem
In England's green and pleasant land'.

Billy sat down, the audience rose. Some, it was true, were bemused by his interpretation of a just peace between the Nations but his vision of a just society after the war had inspired them.

When the applause finally died down. Frank stood, to introduce Belle Malony, she rose.

"Well ladies and Gentlemen, it is so reassuring that, despite war and injury, patience and daring are still greatly to be seen, displayed by our young men and women. To see just how much they are enduring yet keeping their vision, passion, determination and hope for the future brings, in its turn, to us here at home the same sentiments. Today we have heard a wonderful message, one that single mindedly urges us all not to forget that the first objective is to strive for victory, to bring an end to this terrible conflict, to win this war."

These words of hers, unusually measured and temperate, brought forth a recognition from her audience. She was following an inspired performance, and well she knew that, this night, it would not be surpassed. She felt her role was, on behalf of the platform, to enhance what the young solider exposed, to knit it together, to glue together, the loose ends.

"Billy Thomas has implored us not to cease in our struggle until all our young people return to us, enlarged with the recognition of their bravery, their victory. I second that. Especially I say to, our womenfolk, remember it is for your sons and daughters that you shine this day. Come the victory, come the homecoming, then it will be time to renew our struggle for equality for women, help for those mothers bereft of sons, of wives their husbands, aid for their orphaned children, for the wounded of mind and of body. Only when have obtained that just society, only then, and only then, can the epitaph of the fallen, be proudly written."

"So I implore you, join the fight for victory, but, also, join that greater fight for justice, join the emerging force in British politics, join the Labour Party, yes join with us. Help us to build that New Jerusalem."

Belle's speech was shorter than initially intended, but it served its purpose. Together, her message joined with Billy's 'tour de force,' their words had won over a host of new enthused recruits.

Not only did several score people join the cause that night, along with Billy and Sally but Nathaniel and Elizabeth joined the Labour Party also, turning their back on a life time of Liberal allegiance. Gladys joined the Party with pride, reflecting in her sons glorious speech, so too did Pastor Gideon Livingston, Jack Lloyd and his wife.

Ruth had observed the two young lovers; She had heard Billy's words. Her work in both encouraging his reading and in nurturing their love had been brought to fruition, both emotionally and intellectually. Ruth would go home that night a happy woman. Surely, this night, she had seen her acorn ripen into a strong, formidable, tree as sturdy as any in the forest.

Billy was sleeping soundly, deeply, full of contentment, having within him a deep sense of fulfilment, of achievement. The pair had arrived at their small house, having left their parents in Charles Street and walked intimately arm in arm to their home. Sensing his exhaustion, Sally offered that he go immediately to bed; telling him that she would bring him a hot milky drink.

Thus they sat up together in their treasured bed. Billy had brought up the gramophone and they listened once again to Mascagni's Intermezzo. The milk calming him, the music pacifying him, both came to dilute the adrenaline, that was still coursing through his veins. The cup becoming empty, Sally blew out the light. Her husband, once again, came to her, finding in her a most glorious comfort; the cup by the bedside may have been emptied but the one within him overflowed.

Now he slept, the moonlight casting a faint glow on his face. Sally watched him sleeping, her Soldier husband, her articulate crusader, her wonderful man; hers. She gazed at him, stroking his hair whilst he slept. For over an hour, Sally performed this ritual, then tiredness overtook her also. With her head upon his chest, she too slept; her breathing in unison with the man who lay beside her. The ambitions of her heart, the uttermost depths of her desires were fulfilled. Tomorrow, April's first day would arrive bringing nearer their separation; but that was tomorrow.

CHAPTER 19

Mizpah.

The Lord watches between thee, and me
When we are absent one from another.

Genesis Chapter 31 Verse 49.

The day of Billy's departure, of his leaving, back to the trenches of Northern France, crept ever nearer. In Sally's heart a sense of panic was beginning to rise. She was sometimes unwell when she awoke, lethargic and sickly, but she tried hard to disguise it and was largely successful. She did not know, of course, but nature was giving her early notice of her changing purpose, her introduction to the side effects of progressing future motherhood. It would be a few more weeks yet before the real evidence would manifest and a new source of joy would be added to her life.

For now she but pondered. The days approaching her marriage had brought her ever closer to Billy. The fantasising of how it would be, had been replaced by episodes of physical expression that had stripped away so much of her assumptions. Two weeks ago she was not even sure how men were made up, how exactly they differed. She had participated in conversations of conjecture at St Elphins but nothing that particularly prepared her for the unravelling of the great mystery.

Now she was a totally complete woman. She had been claimed by her life's love, as she had intended to be all those years ago. Being so possessed was wonderful, glorious. The sensations she experienced, when he took her, were beyond her powers of description. It was as if she had left her very body, as if her mind, in ecstasy, reached out to a higher plain. It left her exhausted, mellowed in contentment, in fulfilment, tingling in every part of her person. Now accomplished of love, he aroused her desires then satisfied them through his touch, his teasing and, finally, their fusion, euphoric in its luxuriance.

On Thursday night Pastor Livingston came by. He was sensitive to the nearness of Billy's departure. He also wanted to congratulate Billy on his performance on Wednesday night and to see if Sally would read one of the scriptures on Sunday morning. He came with a more important request of Billy, a further task for him to fulfil, before his taking leave of the Chapel, and those of the congregation who had so come to love and respect him.

Gideon discovered a home of highest contentment, a home full of love, complete of spiritual, emotional and physical happiness. He was made most welcome. Billy had answered the door and shown him into the parlour.

Sally was inside sewing buttons on some shirts. It was the man of the house who made the tea from the simmering kettle on the range and produced an immaculate tray containing all that was necessary to provide tea for three, including a variety of biscuits.

The Pastor made an observation.

"Well I have been here before in similar circumstances, I recall how I called upon your mother and father, what let me see now, over twenty three years ago. They were so happy those two. Both were very shy, my wife and I, almost corralled them together, but it was a very happy union, that of your parents, Billy."

"Your father was such a skilled craftsman, your mother is a delightful woman. I know how proud your mother is of you today. I can tell you Billy, with great certainty, your father too would be very proud of you today, very proud."

Sally responded for the pair of them.

"Why thank you Pastor, I am sure he would have been almost as proud as I am of my grand husband. Tell me Pastor Livingstone is he not just the most perfect of men?"

"Sure he is Sally, sure he is."

The Pastor confirmed her question, to do otherwise would have been churlish, the girl was obviously in raptures. This young man is so lucky, he thought, deservedly so. It was then that it occurred to Gideon just how alike father and son were, courageous, inspired, charitable, respectable and loving towards women in general and their own wives in particular. Yes surely, like father, like son. He decided upon making his suggestion to Billy, a suggestion that had gained birth of his experience of listening to Billy at the Socialist rally.

Gathering his thoughts together, he began to express them.

"Billy, I have an idea. I would appreciate if you and dear Sally would let me put it forward."

He took up his teacup, sipped the well-brewed refreshment and broke a biscuit and absentmindedly dipped it into the tea, a habit that his dear wife had often scolded him over. Gideon had gained the attention of both of them, he was ready to put forward his proposal. Sally had stopped her sewing. Billy came and sat next to her, taking her hand. The pair gave the Pastor their full attention.

"The rally on Wednesday. I have to say, Billy, you gave a polished, professional performance a credit to your undertaking. You held your audience in a spell. You spoke from your heart telling them what you thought they needed to know, not what was expedient to speak upon. They grasped your message, it gave them hope, satisfaction, that they had been spoken for. You identified with their plight, their sacrifices, all were fully explored and addressed. In short Billy, they were inspired, you performed a great service on their behalf"

"Well now you are soon to leave us, to travel back into the inferno. Having examined and formed expression of their good peoples earthly needs and desires, how about attempting to inspire their spiritual selves. Would that not be something? What I am proposing is that, on Sunday morning you provide the sermon for the congregation and you Sally; I would like you, once again, to provide a reading. I know how much has been asked of you both in the last few weeks. I know also how little time you have left, how little time you will have to prepare such an address. None the less I am still asking you to undertake this service for your fellow man, for the Chapel and for God."

Gideon completed his socialisation of the young man, took up his teacup and another biscuit remembering this time not to sink it into the tea. Munching crumbs and sipping tea, he awaited a response.

It came from Sally.

"Well Pastor Livingston, how could my dear husband refuse such a request. As for myself I shall be pleased to read for the Chapel congregation."

She looked into her dear husband's eyes, he reddened.

"Yes Pastor we shall both be pleased to do as you ask."

Billy agreed with a nod of assent in the Pastor's direction.

"Well that is agreed then, let us examine the message. I believe that what you extolled the other night has also a directly spiritual expression, perhaps we can emphasise that Billy?"

Billy now spoke for the first time since his visitor had arrived.

"Pastor, often in the trenches or back in billets, the men of my section, or some of them at least, would want to talk of spiritual matters, to have the Bible read and spoken upon. They needed to be reassured of their salvation, should they succumb to the war's desire to consume them. We would read from the Gospels, St Paul and the Psalms, especially the twenty third."

"Revelations we also explored, and studied upon in some depth. Yet, of all these times, I remember a discussion we had one night. I remember it especially because it gave great comfort to one of the youngest of the section. The day after, he was shot in the head by a sniper. The bullet almost took his head off. I buried him myself. Wrote to his mother on behalf of his comrades, shared out the pitiful few articles he had left behind."

"The scripture which gave him such comfort that night, before his death, was the first Peter, the second half of his first chapter. I would like to speak upon that if I may."

Pastor Livingston memorised.

"All flesh is grass.
And all the glory thereof as the flowers of the fields
The grass withers and the flowers fail:
But the word of the Lord abides forever."

"Precisely Pastor, perhaps we can speak around that?. Possibly my dear Sally can read that as her scripture."

"As you wish Billy, a most profound text. I shall look forward to your interpretation of it."

Gideon, having fully realised his task, wished now to withdraw and leave the two young people to their marriage. He was minded of his own early days of marriage, the need of two people to be alone with each other.

"Well thank you both, I must be getting on my way. So many people to see, in so little time."

He rose, shook Billy's hand, Sally's also, and was on his way. Sunday service would be grand. He would have Billy's name placed across the notices as the visiting speaker, attendance should be high.

As soon as he left, Sally swept into her husband's arms. She kissed him long, lingeringly, and passionately, displaying her need for his intimate possession of her again. No need of words, Billy brought down his arms, gathered her up and began to climb the stairs once more so effortlessly, as if she were made of nothing else but the most precious of silk and satin.

Sunday came, again the sun was kind, bestowing warmth and providing a golden glowing light upon all that had made the effort to come to the Chapel. In truth, as Gideon had suspected, there were many more in the congregation than usual. News that Billy was to preach this day had been spread far and wide. The news was bringing people to the Chapel whom normally never went to hear the word on the Sabbath, or went to other places of worship. Glossop was providing its own very special valediction to its favourite son.

'Oh God our help in ages past,
Our hope for years to come...

The strains of the hymn rang out around the Chapel walls. So vigorous were the vibrations coming from the combined throats of the worshipers that they resounded from out of the environs of the Chapel and far into Fazackerley Street. Later people were heard to say that it could be heard as far away as Norfolk Square. So great was the choired anthem, that angels residing in heaven itself could have heard the plea to God and, if their ears reacted to the song of praise, then the maker himself must have received it.

After prayers came Psalm 43:

'Vindicate me, O God,
And plead my cause against an
ungodly Nation.'

The question was asked why is the soul downcast when all you need is to put hope in God.

Now Sally read from the first Epistle of Peter.

Therefore, prepare your minds for action
... Love one another deeply, from the heart
For you have been born again you are imperishable...
...'All men are like grass....
But the word of the Lord endures forever."

The words expressed by Sally not only came out of the book, but from her heart also. The tremor in her voice was from emotion, not nerves. In this, the congregation enjoined and were carried up on each word, elevated to a height of meaning, and of understanding that later many could neither explain, comprehend, and certainly never forget. Her words floated like a personal plea they became, as its source intended, 'the living and enduring word of God'.

It was a stilled, reverent, congregation that faced Billy as he rose to address them. Having implored God to guide his words he began.

"Having a sincere love for your brothers
Love one another deeply, from the heart."

The congregation, listened silently, absorbing every word he uttered. He told of his childhood, of his love for his parents, his pride in his father, the stonemason who had capped the spire of the building in which they were sat. In a parable reflecting the words of Saint Peter he told them they were all living stones, warm, heart beating stones. Like the sturdy cold granite, in the right hands, they could all be shaped to serve the Lord. They could become precious corner stones, like those which held up their Chapel. They need not live in fear of rejection by fellow men for 'it was the stone that the builders rejected that became the capstone.'

Yes Jesus himself, rejected by humanity, was the keystone for their salvation. He continued with his theme

"The men at the front. Do they not stand sure and erect as stone in the face of the foe. Those who defend you armed with faith, truth and courage are as precious stones. One day all that will be of them, for future generations to remember will be their name carved on stones. In years to come, if the generations forget they will become meaningless names to most. Yet carved out in towns, villages, cities for all to see to look upon, to give thanks to, they shall live forevermore. For in dying, they looked heavenwards and they believed in the word of the Lord. In sacrifice they displayed the highest love, its most splendid expression. In dying for us, they die in the Lord Jesus Christ, they die in his word and 'the word of the Lord stands forever."

"So these souls are safe, those of my brothers who have died in the Lord. But what of those who remain who are the recipients of their love, their sacrifice, or being their Widows or grieving mothers are left behind? What of those whom they loved so much?"

"It is for us the living, on their behalf, to seek out a just society. Just in a godly sense. Just in a civil sense. I tell you all men are brothers. Yes all men. British, French, German, all are brothers. Only in brotherhood shall we find peace, only in peace shall we find justice, only in peace shall we be able to fully to serve the Lord, and in serving the Lord we bring peace, justice hope to all mankind."

"Forget your perishable riches, silver, gold and finery. Share in the world's bounty. Let no Widow starve, no Orphan go hungry or badly clothed, no wounded Veteran without the dignity of the necessities of life."

"I go back to the front in a few days time. Soon we shall be put to the strongest of tests. We shall be asked to give all we have, and we shall respond because we are asked, because we are all that is left to defend these shores."

"We shall respond because of our love for our families, our Country, our God. We shall respond, and in so doing many of us shall fall, never to see these green fields of England again. Do not, I implore you forget us. Pledge yourself to build in our memory, for a better world, a much better world than the one we have. Build in memory of us, we who gave everything. We who gave a physical, spiritual sacrifice acceptable to God because we do it in the name of his blessed son Jesus Christ."

'Greater love hath no men than this,
That he lay down his life for his friend.'

Billy concluded by blessing those who had heard him. He told them he would send back the love of them all, to his friends and comrades in the trenches. He told them not to worry. Even those who had fallen or those who were yet to fall would be safe.

'Do not let your hearts be troubled,
Trust in God and the Lord Jesus Christ'
Amen.

Gideon surveyed the congregation, Billy's words had sunk deeply into their minds. It had been a wonderful sermon. Over the years many within the congregation had given a sermon. The democratic manner of the Independents allowed so. He could not though remember such an occasion as this. All who had heard Billy's words were deeply touched, in a manner that would affect them for years to come.

Came the service to its end and Sally, Billy, their family and friends, together with dozens of well wishers, gathered on the steps of the Chapel. There were salutations, valedictions and congratulations completed with expressions for safe conduct, promises of prayers and thoughts. mothers, wives and sisters who had men at the front asked Billy to relay their prayers to them.

He did so knowing that he would never meet the overwhelming number of them. There were literally over a million men now crowded into that corner of France. Most of the soldiers mentioned were either in the Sherwood Foresters, Lancashire regiments or other battalions of the Cheshire's, but for the sake of the peace of mind of those whom he had been asked, he gave them assurances. They in turn for the most part, went on their way confident that a personal message to Billy for their loved one would be with him in a few days time. They believed and that belief gave them comfort.

Now it was home to dinner in Charles Street, a long farewell dinner with their parents, Pastor Livingston and his wife, Uncle Frank and Auntie Helen.

The meal was as sumptuous as it was traditional. The roast beef of old England, a marvellous array of vegetables and rhubarb crumble with the thickest custard Billy could ever remember, being served. Gideon offered up Grace, an impassioned affair, concentrating upon a plea heavenwards for Billy's safety and the safety of all the men at the front.

That afternoon, later to so occupy the memories of both Sally and Billy, was filled with fellowship, with sacred songs around the piano, so beautifully played by Elizabeth and her daughter. Simple songs of praise where all things were 'bright and beautiful' to urgent invocations to Jehovah, pleading for his guidance to be given to those pilgrims travelling through barren, foreign lands.

As the sun began to set and shadows lengthen, the pink glow ever shrinking, giving way to the grey of dusk, the singing continued. Jesus reigned wherever went the sun. David's twenty third in lilting Crimond flooded the room. In a solo, Sally sang of the light that kindly led and complimenting in his tenor voice, Billy reminded the reflective group that the Church had but one foundation.

The time had come for Gideon to part, his seven o'clock service was less than a half an hour away.

They sang finally, for the last time that fate would bring them all together, the parting hymn of Henry Francis Lyte, reaffirming the assurance that the Lord almighty God was with all of them, residing with them in both life and death.

Who like thyself my guide and stay can be?
Through cloud and sunshine, oh, abide with me.

The partings began, the tears started to flow, Uncle Frank and Auntie Helen escorted Gideon and his wife towards the Chapel. They all promised to be with Billy when the train left on Wednesday. Shaking hands, kissing, hugging profusely, they went on their way.

Leaving the house Frank and Gideon walked in front, their wives behind together, tearfully discussing the day's events. Frank had made a decision he spoke to Gideon of his determination.

"Pastor I have decided. I shall attend your Chapel each and every Sunday in future. I like the way you involve people, how you make them a part of the expression of worship. As a Socialist I feel more comfortable with you than with the Anglicans. Yes Pastor I am coming home to the Independents."

Gideon pondered, he was happy. He had always respected Frank and now, once again, he was going to be a part of his flock.

"And your good wife?"

From behind came a women's voice

"His good wife will be pleased to accompany him Pastor, very pleased indeed."

They walked the rest of the way in contented silence. It had been a most agreeable day.

Back home, in Charles Street, the depleted group was having one last cup of tea before the young pair left.

Nathaniel was concluding upon affairs with kind words of approval and praise. Gladys and Elizabeth, within their contentment listened like sisters each a mirror to the other. Billy and Sally, now always holding hands all coyness gone, totally evaporated, were attentive also. The shadow of his departure was being held successfully in abeyance for one last night.

"Well you two. You have brought some light into the lives of a great number of people, these last few days, though I must say it all pales when compared to the light that shines out from your eyes. Never have I seen two people more happy together, more suited and may I say it, more in love. Billy, I am so proud of you. Sally you also. All three of us here hold you so close, you are so very precious to us. You play out love's young dream so well. It is there for all to see."

He knew it was time to send them on their way, back to their nest in Talbot Street. Three days was all that remained for them, surely never enough.

"So, time for you two to go home, leaving me to be bullied on my own by these two, come on, hats and coats."

Off they went, arm in arm, back to their little paradise, waved off by their three parents. Three days, three nights to be in each other's embrace, but what days, what nights. Sally was to relive them over and over, again and again, for more than eighty years.

Wednesday morning came, inevitably, drizzled and mournful, cold as if winter had returned to mock them, completing Sally's depression. The previous evening had been one of calling on family and friends to bid them farewell. Even though so many would be at the station at twelve noon to wave goodbye, there were those who Billy had wished speak to personally.

For Mr and Mrs Jones, he was taking gifts back to Jimmy. Uncle Frank, who promised to keep an eye on things. Pastor Livingston and his wife, whose prayers were to sustain and comfort both of them. Gladys who hugged her son for so long, also had tears soaking her cheeks. Elizabeth too, she smiled at them both but tears were behind the surface cheerfulness. Nathaniel, shaking hands, being kissed by Sally on the cheek, emotion had welled in him. Breaking through, his tears flowed in their turn.

Now it was Wednesday morning. Billy and Sally had loved all through the night, never out of each others arms, wrapped together in their nakedness, no longer shy or nervous, displaying and giving all the love and passion imaginable. The suitcase was packed, the uniform immaculate. Sally was sending her man back to the front vested of perfect presentation, spent of all urgency and desire, fully comprehending how much he loved his wife, and was loved .

Her part in his homecoming was complete. She had given him everything that he had ever conceived of being blessed with, or granted, since that day when, covertly, she had kissed his wounded frame in that hospital ward, overseen by Hilda Pole, a nurse who well knew that men found their physical and mental restoration through more than mere medical procedures alone. In turn, these past twenty days had given witness to every anticipated fulfilment for his Sally. In all its entirety, the years of suppressed images of love that had been locked away deep within her, had found a permanent harbour.

The expression of every fanciful notion had been explored and confirmed. All she had gathered in her mind, from that day she first handed a book to her small friend, had come to pass. He who had been transformed into the heroic soldier who now stood before her impeccable, steadfast, courageous, so handsome in his uniform, had turned her into a complete woman. Today, despite his departure, it was a perfect world.

His photograph, which had been collected yesterday, was now framed. It displayed her man and immortalised him in a splendid, very English pose. His eyes so full of determination, softness too, but only Sally would know that; only she had seen him so, only she would ever see him so.

Now they stood, facing each other for the last time alone, soon their mothers and Nathaniel would come knocking to escort them to the Railway Station, but a five-minute walk away. The impending, inevitable reality of their separation now fully dawned upon them. Tears became compelling, no longer could they be held back. That day they were to flow alongside the gentle drizzle, mingling with the very tears of God himself becoming, between them, a holy sacrifice. They clasped tightly together, they kissed, he stroked her hair, and he spoke.

"My darling, darling Sally, my beloved wife. I leave you with so little, I take with me so much. My little girl who I have loved since that first day when, together, we explored those shelves of books. Those eyes, so beautiful, within your smile, yet even more so when glistened with these tears. My darling, darling Sally, I take with me so much."

"The memories of these past days with you, up in the hills, by our copse, here in our house, our bed. Nothing, no enemy gun, no soldiers bayonet, no violence of any kind that might be perpetrated upon this frame of mine, can take away one second, one sensation, one solitary deletion of that which you have given me. This is one soldier who leaves these shores complete of all he needs to fight for, to defend you my blessed girl. I have all of this, more than ever I envisioned, ever earned, ever deserved. Darling Sally, I take with me so much."

He had spoken, now she knew. It was of little comfort now, but in the days, the years to come, his words, here so wondrously expressed, would find written form in her notations and bring her repose and condolence, sustaining her grief, enriching her memories. Now she knew what she must do, become fearless, as fearless as he, her brave, brave man. She would put on her hat, her best smile, one of promise for the future. Then she would wave him goodbye, supported by her family, lest she appear weak in public.

Only later, privately, she told herself, would she weep again for her beloved man. If only she could tell him now what she suspected, that their love had further found expression in new birth but it was only a suspicion, she could not inform him till she was sure.

Now came the doleful, tolling knock upon the door, the moment had arrived, one last private kiss, one last clasp of his dear wife's breast and Billy went to open up the exit to that other world. A knowing smile of reassurance, mutually given, and Billy slid the lock, pressed the latch and opened the door. There the three expected visitors faced them with greeting smiles, thin lines barely perceptible, neither handling nor concealing their trepidation.

In they came to partake of tea, a muffled affair, of less than half an hour, then it was time to proceed. Billy opened the door for one last time and stepped out into the inhospitable drizzling rain. Hand in hand Billy and Sally led the small procession. Neighbours had come out onto their stone steps to bid him farewell, to shake his hand, to wish him luck, to urge him to 'give Jerry something he won't forget.'

The scene minded Gladys of another occasion more than sixteen years since when she escorted her beloved husband along the same street, she shuddered, the thought filled her with dark foreboding.

Gideon, awaiting at the station, was thinking back also. Looking along the platform he could see the black train approaching from out of the sorrowful mist. His thoughts were of that time when he stood in that very place awaiting the arrival of Joshua's coffin arriving home from Stoke. He too was full of sombre memories, trying so hard not to make comparisons.

Then, acknowledged by well-wishers, round the corner, came the young man, head erect, side by side with his wife both displaying a calm dignity. Applause broke out, hands seeking to shake his, to wish him well. It appeared as though the whole town was standing beside him. Gideon stretched out both his arms and placed a hand on each of their shoulders.

"May God himself go with you Billy Thomas, may he protect you in your duty, for it is his work you embark upon. May he bless you both, bring you calm of mind, may he grant you his eternal love. Amen"

He could not bring himself to mention the word 'peace'; it seemed not appropriate somehow.

He hugged them both, as did his wife. This young man who had filled him with so much empathy, as did his father before him, was once more entering the fiery furnace where only God could protect him. Sally too, so graceful, pretty, dignified, she was going to need as much help as he could muster in the days ahead.

The last hugs were put in place, then, by common consent, the public left them to their final farewells. Nathaniel, Elizabeth, Gladys also stepped back whilst, unashamedly, Billy gave his wife one last empassioned kiss and the words.

"Wherever I am Sally, wherever I go, there you go also. My mind is your mind, my eyes your eyes, my heart your heart, and ever it will be so. Each time you want me with you, just summon my name. I shall be there, we shall be together. Love, such love as we have, is indestructible, eternal. Love such as this, is greater than death, it will never let me go from you. God bless you my love until we meet again."

He then handed her a small box.

"Open it when first you are on your own. It is very special."

A last kiss and he was gone, to cheers and tears, one final paradox in a life of contradicting essences and emotions.

Later, when she opened the box, it held a small necklace containing a medallion. Upon opening the clasp, she discovered that it contained a miniature of both their likeness. It was engraved with the words 'Mizpah' and a note, which simply stated Genesis Chapter, 31 verse 49.

He boarded the train, holding his life's love's hand from the carriage door window. The whistle went, steam built up, the wheels turned and he was away. Sally ran alongside the train until the end of the platform, one hand holding on to him, the rain streaming down on her now hatless head, completely unnoticed. Finally, the speed of the train defeated her and she was left stranded, completely alone, waving frantically, shouting through the gloom, into the increasing distance.

"Billy, Billy, Billy."

The man waved until, turning the corner, the platform went out from his sight. He sat down, the tears flowed, no words escaped his lips, save one.

"Mizpah."

CHAPTER 20

'Does it matter? Losing your legs
For people will always be kind'

'Does it matter': Siegfried Sassoon
1916

Timothy Hyde was sixteen. He had been born on the first day of the new century. His parents ran the main post office in the High Street; a busy enterprise responsible for the mail, which daily, arrived at the Railway Station, and was then delivered throughout Glossop and the outlying villages. Ever since he could remember, Timmy, had assisted in the shop, cleaning or sweeping, running errands and sometimes helping at the sweet counter which had become the most popular part of the premises. He also delivered the telegrams.

People considered him to be a good lad, cheerful, polite, well spoken and enthusiastic. He must have been one of the most recognisable young boys in the town and would be greeted wherever he went. Timmy's life, like that of the post office, had become increasingly busy as the war went on. Charities had used the premises to organise the distribution of parcels to the troops. The art of letter writing had found a renascence as loved ones of those fighting overseas wrote daily. Local provision suppliers designed hampers and gifts to supplement the needs of the troops and families often clubbed together to send off these comforts in the hope that life would be more comfortable for poor Tommy Atkins.

In truth, Timmy saw the war as an adventure where battles were glorious, the soldiers brave, the enemy dastardly and victory inevitable. Countless opportunities for medals and fame were there to be had. All you were required to do was to volunteer, train, go to the front and perform deeds of daring do. Kipling, the press, the patriotic publications, although graphic, were full of heroism, victories and positive prophecy. One more push, one more great national effort and the enemy would run, back to Berlin, back to Vienna where they would beg for an armistice on any terms. Then the great British Empire, on which the sun never set, nor ever would, could once again become the saviour of civilisation, admired throughout the world.

Timmy, without even gaining a uniform, enlisting or travelling to the front was already a victim of the war. Kipling instructed him from the pages of his favourite illustrated Schoolboy publication.

'Play up, play up and play the game.'

303

The war hero poet Rupert Brooke had died fighting for the just cause, that all would return to how it once was.

'With hearts at peace, under an English heaven.'

Kitchener pointed, to such as he, to do his duty. For God, King and Country. Truth, at least to the ears of young lads such as Timmy, had indeed become the first and lasting casualty of this ever increasingly stubborn tragedy.

It was the war, as with so many of his age, that consumed Timmy's life, together with his work, and football. If anything could ever replace the war in his mind it was football. For as long as he could remember, Timmy had stood behind the East End goal watching his beloved team. He possessed programs going back over ten years. On the occasion of every home game he would walk to the ground with his father who, with his friend Nathaniel Hawkins, were avid supporters.

The Post Office and Mr Hawkin's store were near neighbours and so the two men would often find themselves accompanying each other to the ground. On many an occasion, Timmy would hear Mr Hawkins telling his father about a new player or giving his opinion on development in the club. The names of some of his heroes, Tommy Toward, Jimmy Jones and Billy Thomas often passed the lips of Mr Hawkins.

Yes, Saturday was eagerly looked forward to during the season. His father would guide him through the turn style insisting that his son was still of age when 'half price' was applicable. Timmy was now five feet ten inches high with a hint of fluff around the chin. Half price would not be possible much longer.

James Hyde was proud of his son. Timmy had been diligent at school having graduated from the technical college, which turned out high quality students ready for engineering or clerical apprenticeships. Timmy's final report had been excellent. He had excelled in literature, grammar and arithmetic, making him the perfect person to groom for the business.

However, like many parents with sons of Timmy's age, James Hyde feared for his son. He well knew how the war was going, miles of trenches, which never seemed to move, having casualties that seemed to mount in ever-increasing numbers. The wounded that had come home, photographs of the dead, which appeared weekly in the Chronicle, were a constant reminder that the conflict, seemingly far away, was also indeed being fought here in Glossop.

His wife, Jenny, came back home some evenings from one of her women's groups, with sad harrowing stories of evenings spent consoling mothers, sisters, and wives. He did not want Jenny to go through the grief that was a constant daily emotion for so many of the women of Glossop.

Therefore, he constantly prayed that the war would come to an end before Timmy was of an age when it would come to consume him also.

James had other plans for his son than that of being maimed or killed in the great conflict. He had come to hope that his son had a future on the football field. Timmy had played as a forward for his college and at that level had made a name for himself. Nathaniel had got his friend Jack Lloyd to watch him and he had been impressed to the extent that Timmy, having been given a trial, was now in line to play for Glossop's reserves next season.

Jack Lloyd had so few to choose from, having lost many of his best to the war effort, that he was prepared to give promising youngsters a go earlier than he would normally have done so. It would be two years before Timmy came of age for the army, so James prayed that the war would end before then.

In truth, although James considered himself to be a patriotic Englishman, he was gradually coming to see this war as a waste of young lives in pursuit of very little. Of course, he kept these thoughts to himself, not even divulging them to his wife. Little did he know that his wife held similar sympathies. As with so many couples, in these times, their fears for their loved ones was so intense that they kept them in silence, even from each other, lest expression brought reality ever closer.

Jenny Hyde had two daughters both younger than her Timothy. They were a great comfort to her, pretty, intelligent and helpful. Jenny was a suffragette, not a militant one but she was deeply committed to the pursuit of Universal Suffrage. Once she had travelled to Manchester, attending a great rally addressed by Emiline Pankhurst and other eminent leaders of the movement. Speakers argued that women would bring to politics a sense of understanding and empathy that the all-male leadership of the European Governments so sadly lacked. Her local branch consisted mainly of middle class, non-conformist, middle-aged women who for the moment argued that their protest must take second place to the need for victory over the enemy.

They theorised that once the nation realised the part that women were playing in the war effort, their case would be enhanced. It was true that the local membership had grown over the last two years, Jenny considered that this war was possibly going to be the final catalyst for the attainment of their aims. She saw great hope in the new tactics of the movement, with its new emphasis of organising groups that were designed to bring women together who had men overseas. The lack of suitable male candidates had also allowed women to have greater involvement in local government.

This had proved a great success. Glossop's Mayor for the past two years had been a woman. She worked tirelessly, organising those many varied female qualities, and abilities, all to long lain latent, as a part of the town's war effort. Now Jenny's good friend, Elizabeth Hawkins, had recently joined her Suffragette group, which pleased her very much. She and Elizabeth had been acquaintances for years, their husbands, having joint interests, encouraging their friendship.

Lately Jenny and Elizabeth had taken to having afternoon tea on Wednesdays, which was half day closing for them both. The privacy afforded by this 'get together' provided the opportunity for them to become close confidants discussing their fears and expectations. Elizabeth would talk of her daughter Sally and her son in Law Billy, sometimes for the entire afternoon. Conversely Jenny would let her guard down and tell of her fears for young Timmy.

These were times when their personal lives could be provided with an open perspective, without fear of criticism. Each of the two women had developed a confidence with each other that allowed their thoughts to be expressed, knowing that they would meet with a sympathy and support, not to be found elsewhere. In truth, before the two women had found this outlet for their private thoughts, they had felt within themselves an overwhelming guilt. Their feelings, their form of expression when discussing the war, their annunciation of their fears for their families, were idiomatically the opposite of all the propaganda that surrounded them. The messages displayed on the billboards, in the newspapers, the patriotic rallies and within general conversation, were generally alien to them.

If Wednesday afternoon did not exist, the intimidation of this war culture would have suppressed them into total submission and acceptance of their situation. Wednesday afternoon was an oasis of sanity, a sanctuary within the ever increasingly mad and insatiable desires and demands of the war and the society that it so utterly controlled. For Elizabeth and Jenny there was no avenue available outside of Wednesday afternoon that they could embrace, to bring forward their aspirations for political and social advancement, their desire for peace and the future of their young men that daily were being consumed by the war.

Wednesday the 18th of June 1916 saw Jenny leaving the post office at 2.30 p.m., and walk towards Norfolk Square. Reaching the cobbled incline, she began to pass the station from where she would start along Norfolk Street towards its intersection with Charles Street. She was musing upon her good fortune in obtaining two chocolate eclairs, which would provide a delicious addition to Elizabeth's sandwiches and confections.

As she passed the entrance of the station Jenny noticed a uniformed young man leaning against the wall, supported by crutches. He was missing part of his left leg. It was young Jimmy Jones.

"Hello Mrs Hyde"

The greeting cut through to Jenny's heart, she knew that Jimmy was one of Glossop's most promising players, having often listened to her husband's reports of matches on Saturday evenings. Now here he was back from the war minus an essential part of his person, a part that he needed to continue with his life. She could hardly believe who it was standing before her, struggling to maintain his balance on the cobbled stones. She replied to his greeting.

"Hello Jimmy, are you all right? Can you manage to get home? Would you like me to get you some help?"

She really did not know what else to say. She felt so inadequate standing by this young wounded soldier, sensing how near he was to tears, to collapsing. Others were passing by, ignoring him or just nodding in an embarrassed fashion, not wanting to be confronted by this side of the great conflict.

One of their own was home from the front, never to be the same, indeed bearing no resemblance to the enthusiastic cap waving youth that signed up, at their insistence, less than two years before. In truth, many of those passing by young Jimmy Jones, were guilt ridden at the spectacle he presented. If they did but know it, their guilt would soon become magnified as Jimmy Jones, multiplied hundreds of thousands of times, would face them on every street corner.

People were becoming weary. So many of them were wondering within themselves, 'when will it end.' Now they passed by, keeping such thoughts to themselves, silently afraid that the next casualty, that they were to meet, would be one of their own family. They passed on quietly, tormented, as much a casualty of the war as the one here before them.

Jenny just stood there watching, a sense of shame engulping her. She approached him intending to offer Jimmy her assistance, her recognition of the injury that he had gained, playing his part in defending his Country. Jimmy drew back almost clutching the wall. It was then that Jenny noticed how he was shaking and perspiring.

"I'm alright Mrs Hyde, one of the Porters has kindly gone to get my father from work. He will be here soon."

'Oh that is good Jimmy. But let me wait here with you. I am on my way to Mrs Hawkins, you know, Billy Thomas's mother in Law. You were serving together were you not?"

Jimmy was about to reply when Jenny stopped him.

"Tell you what, lets go and wait in the George. Have a glass with me. You can give me news of Billy in comfort."

She ignored his attempt to politely refuse. Informing the Station Master of her intent and having asked him to tell Jimmy's father where to find him, she assisted the young man across the road, opened the door for him and escorted him to the lounge. There she sat him down at the window table and went over to the bar to order drinks; something she had never done in her life before. Other patrons just stared at her whispering, their hands covering their mouths, embarrassed at the sight of this shaking, sweating, human being, who really should be in the Public Bar. She made her request to the barman, completely ignoring the scornful remarks all around her.

"A pint of ale and a glass of lemonade please."

As she asked the barman she felt she was shaking as much as Jimmy. She got a respectful and affirmative reply.

"Certainly Mrs Hyde, I shall bring them over to you."

The barman, John Hughes had two sons of his own, fighting with the Sherwood Foresters. They were both somewhere in France, good lads who wrote regularly to their mother, a woman who wept daily for their safety. He had watched the cameo from the window, an unsteady confused young man, in pain, momentarily friendless. Then this lady comes along and undertakes her duty, a duty that the town should have been responsible for.

Mr Hughes was determined to play, at least a small part, in the young lad's homecoming. He went to the back office, where the manager was going through his stock lists and received an affirmation to a certain request. Pouring out the drinks that Mrs Hyde had ordered, he placed them on to a tray and took them over to the window table.

"A pint of best for the young gentleman and lemonade for you Mrs Hyde. There is no charge, the George would not dream of asking for payment for the first drink of one of Glossop's returning heroes, neither for a Good Samaritan either."

Jenny was overcome. Poor Jimmy however, was almost at the end of his endurance; she would offer thanks on behalf of them both.

"Why thank you Mr Hughes. Most worthy of the George, thank you very much."

"A pleasure, a real pleasure I'm sure, nothing too good for this soldier, I'm sure, real sure ma'am."

Then he left, a lump in his throat, walking quickly in case anyone would notice the moisture forming in his eyes.

"Well that was a kindness Jimmy, nice to be appreciated isn't it?"

Jenny noticed how difficult it was for her young companion to grasp his glass. Her hair was feeling prickly she could sense the disapproval of the genteel class clients, who were all around them, taking their afternoon tea, having their sensitivities so crudely encroached upon. It appeared to her that they held not one hint of sadness or compassion. Jimmy was embarrassed she could see.

Jenny was passed embarrassment. She now possessed a certain anger that could, no longer, be contained. Speaking in a voice loud enough for all to hear she made here opinion of these latter-day Pharisees plain for all to hear.

"Now Jimmy what do you think of your welcome here on your first day back from the front. You must be impressed by the respect and gratitude that people have for you."

Jimmy did not know what to say. He was now both embarrassed and perplexed, completely self-conscious that he was the object of such disdain.

John Hughes could sense the embarrassment. In an action that he would later wonder at, being usually ingratiating towards his clients, he walked to the centre of the lounge to redress affairs. Employee or not, he would stand for this nonsense no longer

"Now here is Jimmy Jones back from war, wounded for his Country, his God and his King. I say that we stand and give him three cheers. Hip, hip"

Slowly at first, the occupants of the lounge rose. In the main, they were not demonstrative by nature, but by the end of the third cheer the entire company were all erect and applauding this latter-day Hector. With one simple, yet courageous act, John Hughes had completely changed the atmosphere. It was now relaxed, people nodding to each other in approval. Now all of the occupants of the lounge wanted to grasp the young man's hand and buy him a drink. This made Jimmy even more tired and self-conscious, but he disguised his feelings well. Truthfully, all he wanted was to see his father and to get home.

Such was the scene that greeted Jimmy's father, Michael. Walking through, the double doors, he gazed across the lounge and saw his son surrounded by well wishers. His was a mixture of pride, anguish and gratitude. He crossed over the room grasped his son and held him while applause, completely spontaneous this time, erupted once again. His Jimmy was home, wounded, but home. One of the clients shouted out "Another pint for the young man if you will Mr Hughes, and one for his father as well"

This allowed for another demonstration of approval and applause. John Hughes felt happy, he had done a good days work. Then a vision of the two faces of his sons came to him and his eyes misted again.

It was a tearful father also, that sat down with Jimmy and Jenny.

"Son, it's so good to have you home, Mum's waiting for you. I'm sorry that I was not there to meet you but you were on an earlier train."

"That's alright Pa"

Jimmy's reply was wearily conveyed. He was safe now, back at last, here with the familiar face of his father. All he wanted to do was to get home, yet he did not want the conversation to go any further without acknowledging the debt he owed to Mrs. Hyde.

"Mrs Hyde very kindly brought me here for a drink Dad, she has been very charitable towards me"

Mr Jones began to grasp that the good woman sat next to his son had indeed rendered him a service.

"Thank you Mrs Hyde, I am grateful to you"

They exchanged handshakes and warm smiles. Then turning to his son he repeated his greeting.

"Oh it's so good to have you back Jimmy."

Jenny now thought that now was an appropriate time to leave.

"Well Jimmy, I have to go. As I explained, I am on my way to Mrs Hawkins, you know, Billy Thomas's Mother in Law. You were serving together were you not?"

This time Jimmy was able to reply.

"You're right there Mrs Hyde, Billy and I were together the night that I got this"

Indicating to his empty trouser leg, he gave a brief synopsis of the events, which led to its severance.

"Seven of us went on a patrol six weeks ago. Billy is now an acting Sergeant and he was second in command of the operation. We've lost so many of the commissioned, that people like Billy, who shows ability and bravery, gets promoted in the field. Well we went over at night to try and discover how the enemy in front was organised and where their machine guns were placed. Then the night lit up. Billy gets us into a shell hole but the Germans must have seen us. Two of us get killed and I got one in the leg. Billy waits until the flares die down and tells the others to go on in front. Then he picks me up and carries me back. Must have shouldered me for over three hundred yards. I got safely back to the trench, losing blood all over."

"Billy is exhausted but makes sure that no dirt gets in my wound. He tears my trousers, puts on a tourniquet, washes the wound and fills it with brandy. The VAD's, told me that this saved my life, stopped any gangrene or poison, but the bone was so badly shattered that I lost my limb. Got my life though and all down to Billy, my mate Billy. I'm a testimony to his courage, a living testament. Seems a little unfair though. I get off to Blightly and Billy is still out there waiting for the next time."

Jimmy had finished his story and his second pint. He was shaking less now, more relaxed.

"Thank you so much for everything Mrs Hyde. Tell Mrs Hawkins that I will come up and see her, Sally and Billy's Mum as soon as I can. Billy spoke of Sally all the time. He's so happy, what with her being with child and all. He chattered everyday about the kindness that he was shown when he got married. Never seen a man so happy, tell them that."

"I shall Jimmy, look after yourself, have a good rest, you deserve it. You are a hero, as well you know. All of you are."

So she went, leaving the young man in the good hands of his father. As she left Mr Hughes nodded surreptitiously towards her in approval. Her heart was thumping, 'fancy Jenny Hyde going into the lounge of the George and ordering a pint of ale. Whatever next.'

Elizabeth had been looking out from behind her lace curtains. Jenny was late. She was never late. What had become of her?

At last she saw her friend climbing up on the left pavement, which was unusual. Perhaps she had been shopping. Still she was nearly here. Time to put on the kettle.

As Jenny had been climbing the hill, she felt a growing sense of sadness for the plight of all those young men guarding the trenches of France. Surely it must be over soon. Mankind could not much longer endure such tragedy, such horror. Today, listening to Jimmy Jones, the war had come home to her. His description was so graphic, she almost felt she was there with the shells, the flares, the machine guns, the mud, the blood and the pain. She had seen how deeply etched he was in the nightmare that he had lived through.

Jenny knew that the images of what he was forced to endure would never leave him, not for the rest of his days. Jimmy Jones would live a haunted life, experiencing a continual nightmare lived every day. Yet this Jenny surely knew, she had to be reassuring to her friend Elizabeth. Her son in law was over there in France, an exceptionally brave young man, facing all that the German's could hurl at him.

Jenny had to keep Elizabeth's hopes alive. She had to assist in furnishing that hope that Billy would return home safe and well. He would, she was sure, return in triumph to become a good family man, sober, kind and hard working, providing a happy life for Sally and their children, taking up, once more, his chosen profession.

It was a smiling Jenny that greeted Elizabeth as the front door of the house was opened.

"Hello Elizabeth, sorry I am late but I have just met a friend of Billy's back from the war."

Elizabeth's interest was immediately kindled.

"Oh do come in Jenny, the kettle will be boiling, sit down I shall bring in the tea."

Jenny offered her the eclairs, to add to the meal, and waited for Elizabeth to return. Soon they were both sat down comfortably, facing a delightfully presented afternoon tea with sandwiches, biscuits and cakes, peaceful and private, welcoming and sustaining. Jenny could not help but quietly consider the comfort of their existence here, with life in the trenches of France, where the young men of Glossop and all the other towns and villages alike, existed in daily danger of their lives.

Elizabeth had noticed how her guest appeared to be contemplating in a world of her own.

"Well, I will pay a penny for them"

Jenny was brought back out of her thoughts to realise she had been in her own world.

"I'm so sorry Elizabeth, but I have had such an eventful hour or so that I was carried away."

Elizabeth's curiosity was now kindled tinder dry.

"Never mind Jenny, but are you going to tell me of all that has happened. I would love to hear of Billy's friend and whether he had word of him at all."

"Indeed he did Elizabeth."

Jenny went on relate everything that had happened. When she had finished, Elizabeth was quiet for a while. Sally had received regular letters from Billy and had shown them all to her mother. Billy had mentioned the incident that Jimmy had revealed to Jenny, but he had desisted from writing of his part in the rescue, merely stating that young Jimmy had been wounded and would probably be home soon.

Having listened to every word that Jenny had spoken, Elizabeth was impressed beyond words.

"My, that's a wonderful story Jenny, to think that Billy, our Billy, has been a real hero all over again. It's the second time he has performed such a deed. What a wonderful boy he is."

"A wonderful man."

Jenny's echo of Elizabeth's sentiments was totally genuine. She had seen the look on Jimmy's face when he spoke of his friend.

"Billy Thomas is a real man, his friends and comrades must feel so secure around him.

Elizabeth replied to her friends eulogising observations, her voice full of pride.

"Yes, indeed they must."

Thus, afternoon tea passed, with both women expressing their thoughts on Jenny's experiences in the George with young Jimmy. They could not comprehend how embarrassed people could come to be when confronted with the actuality of conflict. How a wonderful soldier returning from the war that, outwardly, almost all supported unreservedly, could be ignored in his plight or even be made to feel unwelcome in their presence and deemed to be spoiling their afternoon refreshments.

They decided that Jenny's experience should be made more public and that an organisation should be formed to meet with the needs of such as Jimmy. All such young men, should be met upon their return and made to feel most welcome. The inhabitants of Glossop should ensure that the gratitude of the town was expressed to all. It would be a most worth while task for the people, who previously had seen their duty as merely supporting those at the front. Those who were coming home deserved the fruits of their efforts just as much as those abroad.

Thus, it was that Glossop came to provide an organised reception of the returning wounded, greeted by the illuminates of the town, supported in their needs, and that of their dependants.

The Council, the Churches and the Chapels, the political parties and the women's organisations were all mobilised to provide for those who had given so much. Later, once the war was over, out of that organisation came the committee that was responsible for the building of the memorial to those who never came home. Jenny and Jimmy, Elizabeth and John Hughes were the unspoken, unreported ones who brought this small example of humanity, to a town which was losing it's ability to cope.

Overwhelmingly controlled and organised by women, a powerful voice, an unremitting voice, an irresistible force emerged, which overwhelmed and defeated all those institutions that had denied the female suffrage, in the times before the great conflict had begun. It was perhaps, the only victory that emerged from the butchery, out living the age and becoming a permanent feature in society.

As far as Glossop was concerned, from out of that afternoon tea, a movement was born that was to so graphically endure that it finally defeated the bigotry expressed from, what was, a purely mechanical oligarchy. A wounded soldier, a sensitive woman, a barman with insight and afternoon tea. Such are the elements of history, of lasting change, far away from the battles, devoid of generals and politicians.

Elizabeth waved goodbye to Jenny at six o'clock, knowing that the events of the day had given birth to something profound. Her husband arrived home almost an hour later. He had been with Jack Lloyd all afternoon discussing their particular local crisis. Hill-Woods had announced that he would no longer be taking an interest in the Football Club, either administratively or financially. The MP observed, quite correctly, that the team had performed so badly in its regional matches this season and the attendance had been so derisory, most home matches being played before less than one thousand people, that it would never again play professionally.

So many of the promising team of 1914, both the first and reserve sides that had joined up , out of twenty five or so, only two remained and both of them were in their late thirty's. The rest of the playing staff was now made up of young promising locals and players previously retired. They were no match for their traditional rivals. Nathaniel now feared for the future of Glossop North End. As history would prove, his fears were not without foundation.

Then, as he and Jack left the Liberal Club where they had been meeting, they met with Pastor Livingston who told them that he had just been to see Jimmy Jones who had just come home. He told them of Jimmy's lost leg and also of how Mrs Hyde had assisted the young lad even buying him a pint in the George.

Nathaniel was taken aback. Both James Hyde and his wife were abstainers. He was sure they had never entered a pub in their lives.

"The George?" enquired Nathaniel

"The very same, but don't fret Nathaniel she provided the lad with refreshment for medicinal purposes. By all accounts the poor lad was on the verge of passing out. Your friends have made my sermon for me on Sunday, In these times examples of the Good Samaritan are few and far between. She played the part of a saint, what with Jimmy having lost his leg and shaking all over.

"Lost his leg?"

Jack gasped in disbelief.

"I'm afraid so."

The reply came full of understanding for Jimmy's special tragic experience. Jack, dumbfounded, repeated his first comment.

"Not lost his leg, football was his life. Such a talent such a waste. Nathaniel I will wish you good night and go to see him"

"Certainly"

Nathaniel could see how utterly distressed his friend had become. Best to leave him for now.

"I will come and see you tomorrow around six."

It was a thoroughly depressed Nathaniel Hawkins that walked alongside Gideon Livingston till they reached his home at the Manse.

"This world is falling apart Pastor. This war is going to consume us all."

Gideon could see how much his friend was troubled.

"Nothing will ever overcome the human spirit Nathaniel. It will be challenged yes, confronted by evil certainly, despair and tragedy also, but it will never be defeated. Trust me Nathaniel, when I say, trust in God, he will see us through."

That evening, Nathaniel, sat with Elizabeth, feeling chastened and full of foreboding. He was listening to her describing her afternoon with such an illuminated, highly expressive light in her eyes. So bright was she that her words insisted upon hope, her newly formed challenge demanded resolution.

They had both been confronted with almost identical bombardments to their empathetic and anger sourced emotions that day. Nathaniel could not fail to see just how differently they had dealt with them. His wife was forward looking, working out how to make life better for those around her. All Nathaniel could see was an ever-worsening world, dominated by ever darkening skies, laden with death. Nathaniel contrasted these, deciphering how men and women acted in a crisis. From that moment, he became a fully committed supporter of universal franchise. He did not know how life would be with women participating in the halls of power, but it had to be better than the world as it now was. It would be different, and difference with what the future currently held meant hope, and hope was what the World needed now.

314

Little did he know, but an event was about to take place, which would all too soon magnify the present horror. Death was about to visit more houses in Britain in one day than at anytime since the last great plague almost three hundred years before. Tomorrow was the first day of July 1916. The first day of the battle of the Somme. Soon young Timothy Hyde would be run off his feet delivering the black edged telegrams from the War Ministry. Like the Angel of Death, the presence of this well liked boy, riding on his bicycle would be announcing the end to the lives of so many of Glossop's sons.

CHAPTER 21

Then they that feared the Lord
Spake often one to another:
And the Lord harkened, and heard it,
And a book of remembrance was written.

Malachi: ch.3 v16.

"A home fit for heroes."

Jimmy Jones' Company Captain had used these words before. As he and his comrades marched to the front together that day in April 1916, the officer uttered the promise. He truly meant it, for him it was an honestly thought out concept, not a pipe dream or a thinly veiled suggestion of some ill conceived Eldorado.

"When you lads get back home, life is going to be different."

Jobs for everyone, better working conditions, better housing, land, health care, and pensions. Once we've defeated the Hun, once we have freed Europe from tyranny and our duty here is completed, we shall claim our rights. We shall go back home and build a better world for all of us. His speech was electrifying his men. He knew that they needed more than 'God and the King,' so he recalled a meeting that he had attended in Chester Town Hall back in 1915 before they had all sailed to France. Questions were asked for at the end of the rally.

Lloyd George had been the key speaker. He had eulogised for almost an hour, keeping the attention of everyone. After lambasting the enemy, extolling the virtues of democracy, he went on to talk of the future, a future after the war. The audience was spell bound. The little Welshman had brought raptures, lavish applause down upon himself.

The Captain had attended the meeting because, at this time, he was a staunch Liberal, and an admirer of Lloyd George, though recent events had filled him with disillusion. Consequently he was beginning to lean towards the cause of Socialism. He believed that, in the main, it was the common working men whose blood was feeding the war effort, consequently, it should be them and their families, to benefit from the day of Victory. So he raised his hand at question time. His uniform provided him with the opportunity. The chairman selected him.

"Yes"

The chairman pointed in his direction, and the inquisitorial Captain rose.

"Mr Lloyd George, I believe it is the common man who is providing the sacrifice out of which will come our triumph over the foe. Therefore I insist it is to him and his family that the rewards must be secured. When at the end of it all, when he comes back to his country covered in glory, when the hero returns, a new world must be built for him, a home fit for heroes."

The largely middleclass audience clapped him bounteously even if they were a little embarrassed, Mr Lloyd George rose to reply after making a notation on the sheet of paper before him.

"In that, you speak for us all, I assure you that is our aim. Tell it to your men before they go to face the foe. It is indeed our desire it shall be so."

More applause, more accolades for the little charismatic Welshman. It had been a good meeting. It would be well reported. Another fine piece of work, keeping the nation behind the war. As Mr Lloyd George left he folded up his piece of paper.

'A home fit for heroes.' He would use this little gem when the time came, a wonderful rallying call. He was like a spider was Lloyd George, spinning a web full of tasty sounding phrases, which, upon examination meant very little. The War had drained him of his idealism; he had become a quack political doctor giving out valueless prescriptions that cured virtually nothing. Plagiarism never once occurred to him, the Captain's phrase, came to be his words.

'A home fit for heroes' the words inspired Jimmy Jones. His Captain was a good man, in his mind, always having time for those under his command.

He was a strong disciplinarian, commanding a well-trained Company of troops. He took example from Wellington, consistently enquiring of his men, his ordinary, working class infantrymen about their families and homes. Yes, Jimmy would always remember him as a good man, a man with a conscience, having little control over events. Time would come to show whether the carnage and the sometimes senseless actions that he was forced to execute, would prove all too much for him.

What a contrast Jimmy had found, to that of his leaving, when he struggled from the train at Glossop Station. People stared at him, some nodded, but none offered to help except the Porter who had taken his case and asked the Stationmaster if he could run and get the young soldier's father. He stood outside the station wall for ten minutes balancing himself, shaking, unsteadily. If Mrs Hyde had not come along he might have fainted. Again he could sense the annoyance and embarrassment of the people in the lounge, not wanting to be in his presence. Mr Hughes had made him welcome, had changed the mood of those who sat there, enjoying their afternoon tea. Of all those he had seen in that space of twenty minutes or so, only two genuinely welcomed him home. The others just wanted to go on their way, simply wanting not to be confronted with such as he. Their sensitivities were attacked through having to face this personification of the war that they so passionately professed to support. 'A home fit for heroes,' indeed.

Jimmy had experienced a fitful night. His mother had helped him to bath, dress and get into bed. He was so exhausted by the time that he had arrived home he just wanted to rest. His wound although outwardly healed still pained him. He just wanted to be in bed, resting, reading, and thinking. Now it was morning, almost midday. His mother, Esther, had bought him eggs and bacon, complimented with tea, cup after cup of tea. He was feeling much better and, after an awkward struggle, he managed to climb down the stairs and into the sitting room.

Both his father and mother were there, his father reading the Chronicle, his mother sewing. Knowing how their son would refuse they never offered to help him. They just uttered a normal greeting.

"Good morning Jimmy"

In unison and waited for him to sit down in his usual chair. His father offered him the local epistle.

"Like to read the paper."

"Yes please, It's been three months or so since I saw a copy. Billy brought one back when he returned from leave."

"Another cup of tea?"

For Jimmy's mother, as with so many others, tea answered so many problems. It was calming and allowed for conversation. Calm conversation was what was needed now.

She went off to the kitchen not waiting for a reply. Michael filled his pipe, a ceremony in itself and Jimmy got out a woodbine and began to read. After a couple of minutes Michael decided to attempt a word.

"Glossop are not doing well at the moment, they've missed you and the other lads."

Jimmy's reply was to the point.

"Not surprised."

"It's a real shame, just as we had got together our best team ever"

Then quiet descended, Michael realised what Jimmy was thinking of his future, a future without playing football.

"Well son, after a few days we will have a chat about what's to be. Whatever comes about, me and your mother will always be here for you."

"Thank you Dad."

The reply came in a very matter of fact manner, and, as though not interested for now, Jimmy turned back to reading the paper.

The tea came in and was drunk mostly in silence although Esther noticed Jimmy had three digestives, he had not lost his appetite. Suddenly, Jimmy made an announcement.

"Mum, Dad, I want to visit Billy's wife and mother. He saved my life. I want to see them and tell them."

"Well Jimmy" said his mother "I will go and see Sally this afternoon and arrange something. In sure all Billy's family would be glad

318

to see you. I shall make some lunch, then go to the shops and go up to Talbot Street on my way back."

Jimmy agreed to her proposal.

"That would be a very good idea mother. See if it is convenient tomorrow, or as soon as possible"

"Yes"

And that is exactly what happened. She served lamb stew with potatoes for dinner. After cleaning away the dinner things, she left the two men sitting reading their papers and made ready to go on her errands.

Michael had been excused from work for the rest of the week. Gideon Livingston had put a support system into action as soon as he knew of Jimmy's return. He had seen Mr Partington, the mill owner where Michael worked and a message had come to the house to say that Mr Jones need not report to work before Monday. A letter accompanied the message explaining that Michael's wages would not be lost. Signed personally by Mr Partington. It also wished Jimmy, 'All the Best' and stated that, when he was recovered, he was to come to the factory office where a suitable position might be found for him.

Chapel, politics and a good nose for publicity were beginning to be mobilised for one of Glossop's war casualties. Men were in such short supply that a mill owner could afford to be generous to the likes of Jimmy Jones.

Partington had recently secured a new large order for Khaki fabric and needed his looms to work at their highest potential of speed and efficiency. Of course, what would happen after the war, when orders dropped off and the men returned, could not be foreseen, but for now a place could be found for a one-foot war hero.

Michael decided that it would be a good thing to show Jimmy the letter. Jimmy read it. Suppressing his thoughts, he offered a reply that sounded grateful.

"That's nice Dad, fancy Mr Partington offering such. Maybe in a week or so I will go up to the mill and see what's what."

"Good idea Jimmy, but only when you are ready"

'Perhaps' Michael thought, 'things would not turn out too badly for his poor lad.'

The afternoon passed in general conversation Michael not wanting to ask about life in the trenches and Jimmy, for now not wanting to speak of such scenes, that would come soon enough. It was a quiet, peaceful, warm, comfortable, afternoon, just what Jimmy needed. A stark contrast to the last few months, full of noise, cold damp and danger.

Esther returned at four thirty. She had seen both Sally and her mother in Law. They would both love to see him tomorrow afternoon together with herself and Michael. Jimmy thanked his mother. He was so pleased that he would be able to tell of Billy and take his love. Tomorrow could not come soon enough.

The walk up Talbot Street was achieved with some difficulty on Jimmy's part. Not only was confronting the cobbled hill a problem but today a number of people stopped to wish him well. He did not stand out so much when accompanied by his parents and people felt more at ease in addressing him. They usually did this via his parents with such phrases as "You must be very proud of him" and "It must be nice to have him safely home."

All Michael and Esther could say was "Yes" and "Of course."

In truth Michael felt patronised but he remained polite for the sake of his wife and son.

They eventually arrived at Talbot Street to find Sally waiting on the step. She ran towards Jimmy and swept her arms around his neck.

"Oh Jimmy it is so good to see you"

She was crying as if it was Billy himself who had come home. Taking his arm on his foot less side, she guided him over the step and into the front room. Billy's mother was sitting down and got up to greet the visitors. They sat Jimmy down in the best chair, making him the centre of a horseshoe, with two other chairs either side. A small table was placed in the middle with sandwiches and cakes covered by tea cloths. It was a most welcoming and informal presentation, designed to make Jimmy and his parents feel at ease. It succeeded.

Mother and Daughter in Law had become very close in the three months since Billy had left. Sally had made the decision to live in Talbot Street and prepare for the baby and for her husband's return. Gladys moved into the small new bedroom and the main bedroom had become Sally's room and a potential nursery. Elizabeth had suggested to Gladys that when Billy came home she should come and live with them. The house in Charles Street was a large one, far too big for a couple on their own. They would be glad to have her. It was a good plan, all they needed was the baby and the return of Billy.

All morning the women had prepared the tea. Gladys could see how excited Sally was becoming. It was, for both of them, as if a part of Billy had come home.

The five of them had settled down. While tea was being taken, the conversation consisted of small talk. Events in the town and general chat about Jimmy's return. They all agreed what a marvellous woman Mrs Hyde was. Gladys had to be convinced.

"Do you really mean Jimmy, That Mrs Hyde went over to the George with you, up to the bar and bought beer?"

"Yes Mrs Thomas."

The reply, still seemed to be greeted with disbelief, so Jimmy reiterated his assertion.

"Bold as brass she was."

"Well I never"

Thus uttered Gladys, so incredulously that she repeated her statement.

"Well I never."

Michael chuckled to himself. He remembered a political meeting that he had attended before the war, where speakers warned about allowing women the franchise.

"Beware the monstrous regiment of women"

The cry, fell upon a rapturous, baiting audience of men, who largely felt that women had their place. It was never far from home unless they were running errands. Now here he was, with his poor son, surrounded by a platoon of this regiment realising how different things could be, would be when the women took their place in the affairs of the world.

The table was cleared, the man allowed to smoke, and everyone sat down to listen to Jimmy's tale. He began by taking them back to the time when Billy first rejoined them.

"Our brigade had been pulled out of the line for relief, to a town called Amien's. A nice place, where we were welcomed. People called us the 'Valois' which means 'brave' or something like. It was there at the end of the March that Billy came back. He was full of it he was. 'Got married' he said to Sally Hawkins, the world's most beautiful girl. 'Clever and beautiful' he said."

When we were sat down together he told me how he had loved Sally ever since he first saw her and of his first time out with her, when he won her prizes at the fair. He said that with Sally he was a King, the happiest man in the world, married in such a short time, the best day a man could ever have. He was so full of joy, that the gloom of the war was gone when you heard him.

Glossop came flooding back in his eyes together with visions of all his loved ones. He was so grateful to Mrs Hawkins with all her kindness and the like. Reckon Billy could see anything through, now, I do. We stayed together a whole week in Amiens.

Some of the lads, beg your pardon ladies, wanted the comforts of the town if you know what I mean. Billy and I thought we would keep well away so we stuck together. We were billeted in guesthouses of sorts but the Patron was hospitable enough, plying us with good food and baths. I'm afraid we did have times with wine bottles, but nothing else. We just kept each other company with tales of our football and home.

Then one day the Captain got us all together and told us we were going back to the front. He said the big push was coming and we had to be prepared. Time to leave Amien's and swap it for a muddy trench.

321

Billy was now an acting Sergeant, on account of his action when he got gassed. It meant that he would be charge of a section of trench, setting an example to the rest. Three stripes on his arm. Like being a centre forward, only this time for real, no game."

Jimmy realised his audience getting impatient for him to progress but he felt he had to tell it all, tell it how it was.

"Sorry Ladies if I'm rambling on but I thought to tell you everything."

"That's all right Jimmy"

Sally wanted to hear everything. She did not want Jimmy to leave out a single word.

"That's perfectly alright. Take all the time you want. Theres no hurry at all."

Sally was happy to listen to every detail however graphic, however lengthy. While Jimmy was here, talking, Billy was here alive and real. Jimmy could take as long as he liked.

As for Jimmy, the longer he reminisced the more he embraced his experiences. It became graphic, he began to relive it all again. His mind drifted until he was back there on the open top deck of a London bus meandering back towards the front.

The soldiers never ceased to wonder at the efficiency of the army in the transporting its troops to the front. It was once they entered the trenches that the system broke down. Leaving Amiens, the troops mustered into columns, were issued with three days 'K' rations and then placed forty-six to a bus which drove in a convoy, single file, to their destination, the banks of a river called the Somme. Spirits were generally high. For these men, unlike so many of the others pouring in, this was their second year of campaigning, being veterans of Mons, Ypres, Loos and the Marne.

In relative terms, the past six months had been quiet. Poor Frenchie had been taking the brunt at Verdun the fortress town, which they had been defending with all they had.

To France the very name 'Verdun' installed national pride. By March 1916, it had consumed over four hundred thousand lives, half of them German. Now it was the turn of the British and Empire troops .The battlefield was to be the Somme. A mass attack would take place at the end of June, sucking the Germans into the gaps that would be created, relieving Verdun and giving the French Valois a breathing space.

Jimmy and Billy sat together on the top deck of their once red and cream bus, which was now covered in matt Army Khaki. They were told it was to be a short journey of about thirty miles, but the roads were so badly damaged in parts that progress was very slow. The signposts, which they came across at regular intervals, were pointing towards a place called Peronne. The landscape was flat, Billy considered it to be Reubenesque, which Jimmy did not quite get to grips with, but it sounded well.

Scattered around the skyline were rows of tall sentinel Poplars, in pairs, providing avenues. They were almost in full leaf, pale green, fresh. skylarks ascended flying into the sky. They could not hear them over the noise of the motor but they could imagine their delightful voicing, in praise of a new summer's day. Both of them had lazed in the spring meadows of Derbyshire and heard such song lifted in praise of the early morning from these most appreciative of birds.

Billy turned to Jimmy, after a period of deep contemplation. "Who would think that we are on our way back to war. It's so peaceful. One day we will bring our families over here for holidays. The land is so flat that we could ride on bicycles and travel for mile after mile everyday. This is a bad war but it has led us to places that we never thought of going to and would love to see once again, with our loved ones, when peace reigns once more."

"If only Sally could be here with me in a time of peace what days we would have, what days."

Jimmy brought a footballing perspective to Billy's vision.

"We ought to have matches with French teams every year. We could go on summer tours in all the French towns or even German ones. We could play all over Europe, have a cup competition like our own one at home."

Billy agreed most enthusiastically.

"Would that not be something?"

"Just grand."

Their bus travelled on rambling through placid rural pastures, as if the pair were on a day's excursion as in the days of yore.

Billy suddenly pricked up his ears.

"Can you hear that Jimmy?"

"What?"

"Guns, I can hear guns,"

Sure enough when you listened above the sound of the engine, you could hear spasmodic dull thumps of shells being expelled.

"That's our guns"

Billy was sure it was friendly fire that he could hear.

"The way they sound, the shells are going away from us. We're probably about ten miles from the front."

The reality of their returning to the war destroyed the little idyll that they had enjoyed. As the sound of the guns grew louder the sense of their own, flimsily protected mortality, came, once again, upon them. It was then that Billy voiced thoughts to Jimmy that were very close to him.

"The sadness of it all Jimmy, is that back home, I have everything a man could wish for. If this war were not in being, life would be perfect. I know that I joined up to help defeat evil, but what worries me now is my fear that the real evil is the war itself. As you know I met some Germans in the Christmas truce, just a few months ago. I looked into their eyes. I listened to their stories of their wives and mothers and then I came back to my trench trying to kill them. What does that make me?"

"But Billy, we carries out our orders, that's our duty. Our fight is for freedom we can only live proper lives if we are free."

Having listened to his friend, Billy felt that he should enlighten his best friend with the ideas that had so ravaged his mind since being hospitalised.

"And where does our freedom come from? You and I Jimmy, have a good life, what of all those around us in Glossop and all over our land. Those who live so badly that they know not of sanitation, education and sufficiency. What is this war really going to do for them?"

Jimmy countered with a cliché in reply.

"A home fit for heroes."

As an afterthought, he added the voice of authority to his assertion.

"You heard what the Captain said."

"Perhaps so."

Billy's reply came with a thoughtful air

"Let us hope so Jimmy."

The bus came over a small incline and suddenly, in the distance, the battery that was firing into the German lines, came into view. There were eight pieces, each expressing their ordinance in turn. Around them were heaps of exhausted cases being stacked onto wagons for their return to the rear and by each artillery piece a row of shells yet to be sent over. The column of busses stopped nearby and the leading car let out the brigade officer who joined his other officers for a conference.

Soon the lieutenants were issuing orders for the men to disembark. They would march from here to the lines. Their ride was over. Marshalled once more into companies and platoons the battalion was inspected by their immediate officers and, urged on by the senior NCOs, they began to troop.

It would be a distance of about four miles to the trenches and rain was now beginning, to fall, the spectres of past events and conditions began to haunt the men. Someone mumbled the thoughts of them all.

"Well it's going to be mud again, bloody mud."

"Quiet there in the ranks."

So roared a sergeant and quiet they were, once more each of the men deep in their own thoughts.

Now the landscape changed, craters began to appear, occasionally at first, then more and more until many of them overlapped. Then the mud got worse and they were jumping over large puddles and skirting lakes of oozing brown liquid. Then it was single file over planks. It didn't pay to look to closely at the ground either, occasionally a hand or foot was exposed where stretcher details had not yet been able to clear up. Every where was brown mud, occasionally relieved by a grey mass of chalk where a larger shell had pierced through the topsoil and exposed the chalk beneath. Overhead, the sky was overcast with a mixture of rain filled cloud and smoke. Here the trees were just stumps devoured of all apparent life, devoid of any leaf. It reminded Billy of Dante's inferno, which he had once read on a rainy afternoon in Glossop's library, where else? Amiens now seemed so far away to these squelching troopers. If it was Dante's inferno it was a cold, soggy one.

The Cheshire's were relieving, not for the first time, a battalion of the Royal Welsh Fusiliers over a stretch of front, which extended more than eight hundred yards. The twelve companies, which made up the Battalion, began to line up. To cover the area each Company split into four platoons containing approximately twenty-five men over whom there were two NCO's and a Lieutenant. As a platoon came up out of the trenches it was immediately occupied by its equivalent from the Cheshire's. At no time were more than a few yards left with no one to watch the enemy.

As Billy and Jimmy went down the access trench towards the main artery the Welsh were coming up and passing them with greetings "Best of luck lads, keep your heads down, watch out for those whiz- bangs, mind the bloody mud, glad it is I am that that's over"

The replies came back to the weary men from the Valleys and the Mines of North Wales.

"Thanks mates, hope you left it clean and tidy. See you in Piccadilly."

One platoon from each company went to the rear to act as relief, which meant that for one day in eight, soldiers were brought up out of the line for twenty-four hours rest. Just over half a mile behind their lines was a semi ruined building which had been commandeered as a special relief billet for A. and B. companies. How the men would look forward to their turn to occupy that farm. Why it would almost feel as if it were the Celestial City itself.

Billy's turn, for that day's relief, came after five days. Five days occupied with improving their environment draining the water and shoring up the sides. In truth with many of the Welsh being miners, the trench had been well maintained. Their predecessors had merely changed a covered trench, deep underground, for an exposed one. They had even considered it to be safer. At least here you could duck, weave and dive. If the coalmine got you that was it, usually there was no escape if you became trapped underground. No, there was little difference really, dying for King and Country or dying for the coal.

The real enemy for the trench soldier was the monotony of waiting. Endless days spent in the repair of trenches with a shovel in your hand, whilst ensuring that your head was never higher than the parapet. Shellfire would erupt consistently, often for hours, or, what was worse, seeming to die down, only to engage itself upon you, once again, without warning.

Sometimes a single stray shot would be forthcoming, to hit a sandbag nearby, reminding the poor unfortunate just how fragile life could be.

Snipers would let off a few rounds from time to time just for the hell of it. The new incumbents of the trench were warned to keep a constant lookout for raiding parties, but none had been spotted so far. Again, you could be wakened from the semi dream like state, that repetition would inevitably bring you, without warning. The chatter of machine gun fire or scattered explosions from nearby trench mortars, would often startle a shallow dream bestowed soldier from the little rest he was managing to gain. Finally, there was the rain, constant bloody rain, bearing down on you and everything around you, incessant bloody, bloody rain.

Each infantryman dealt with the monotony in his own way. If he could find shelter or if the rain actually stopped for a while he could read. That's what Billy did. He read, always his friends would see him with his small volume of Milton. He was engrossed. One day Trevor Roberts one of the Roberts brothers in the platoon asked Billy about the book

"What's that you're bloody reading then Billy?"

"It is the poet Milton."

"And what's Milton?"

David, the other Roberts brother, posed this question.

"Milton is a great poet, his work is full of images that can make you forget where you are. So I drift off from this place for a while and I read it over and over"

Trevor came to a conclusion. It was simplicity itself but profound none the less.

"Must be good then"

"Read some of it to us then Billy, doing so could just allow us to forget for a while as well. "

This remark came from another bored member of the Platoon, Harold Evans, lying on a settle bed.

Trevor also urged their NCO on, he was truly curious to discover what this Milton had to offer.

"Come on Billy read us some. I could do with forgetting this place for a time. I really could."

Billy hesitated. He was not about to be taken for a laugh

"I don't know lads, I've not read aloud since school."

"Go on Billy, read some of it to us."

Another urging, this time it came from Wrexham George, another unfortunate lodger of the shelter. It was followed by a much more immaturely voiced request.

"Come on Billy, help us to pass away some time."

This last plea from the youngest of the platoon, Albert Hadfield, someone who Billy looked out for, struck a chord and Billy agreed to read.

"I don't fully understand all that is in it myself but I will do my best. If it bores you then I shall stop. It's a very long poem in two parts called, Paradise Lost and Paradise Regained."

This led David Roberts to exclaim.

"Well we've lost Paradise right enough, lets see if we can find out how to regain it."

With that final sounding hope, Billy sat on one of the low wooden benches, opened his precious book and read. He read slowly and deliberately, letting his comrades absorb every word and absorb the words they did. They became spell bound.

> *'Of mans first disobedience, and the fruit*
> *Of the forbidden tree, whose mortal taste*
> *Brought death into this world, and all our woe*
> *With loss of Eden, till one greater Man*
> *Restore us, and regain the blissful seat.'*

Sally's precious present to Billy became a jewel, one possessed by all around him. It contained so many images faced by them every day. The comfort and resolution it brought knitted the group ever closer together. They would talk about what they had heard, sometimes for hours after Billy had finished a session. Particular passages would become grafted upon the listeners, who would learn them by heart.

> *'The dismal situation waste and wild*
> *A dungeon horrible, on all sides around*
> *As one great furnace flamed, yet from those flames*
> *No light, but rather darkness visible*
> *Served only to discover sights of love.'*

Common men from various walks of life, thrust together in this hell, began to understand hell, to withstand hell, to climb up above the stench and the mud, bringing freedom to their spirits. They became ever closer as a group, good sincere friends, looking out for each other. All this came to pass through the reading of a small book containing the words of a poet, dead for over two hundred and fifty years.

Day after day men the would wait for Billy to be free from duty, to be finished with his fatigues. They would often come up to him individually and ask him a question. He resolutely refused to become a teacher, to aspire to an authority, which he felt he did not possess. He would tell them that they were perfectly capable of reaching conclusions for themselves.

"Understanding is in the hearts and minds of all of us. We each see things differently. What gives us the spirit to acquire peace, to find acceptance of our time and for the future is ourselves. Talking together, listening to each viewpoint brings a richness, which improves us. We, each of us, have a gift that, when expressed as a whole, brings enlightenment, understanding, and fulfilment."

Jimmy was getting tired, he had talked for over two hours letting out all the emotions within him. His mind drifted back to his audience. Realising just how long he had spoken for and how little along the road of his story he had travelled, he paused, he was exhausted. The picture of him stood alongside Billy, on sentry duty philosophising on all they were experiencing, now commanded his memory. Recollections of talking in soft voices about Milton, whilst the clear star filled heavens glowed passively down on them and their sleeping comrades, flooded his vision. It was so intense, that it took a supreme effort from him to come back to this small room in Glossop, warm and comfortable, safe and secure.

"I'm sorry"

It was a genuine apology that he offered to his audience

"All this time and I've got nowhere, I'm sorry."

Sally reassured him.

"Well don't you be. Listening to you Jimmy has brought me such marvellous consolation."

Gladys agreed with her daughter in Law.

"Jimmy, if it's alright with you I am going to make a cup of tea for everyone and then maybe you could tell some more."

Esther agreed.

"Jimmy you brought it home to us. We were all there in France whilst you were speaking it was beautiful, terribly beautiful."

Michael had pondered upon all that was said. He was so proud of his son. Proud that he could live through such as he was describing. He had come back less a leg, it was true, but he was now safe, his mind whole.

CHAPTER 22

Eden raised in the waste wilderness.

Paradise Regained: Bk.1 l 7.

The tea refreshed the being of Jimmy Jones. Properly infused, an art perfectly performed by Sally, delicately presented and poured as indeed she did so, when sipped gently, it slowly refreshes the body. It can additionally replenish the spirit and that occurred also. That day the tea, passed to Jimmy by Sally, brought him round. He was exhausted, physically, mentally and spiritually. The tea dissolved his weariness and changed his empty frame, his tortured mind. It prepared him for the ardour's of his next set of recollections, recollections, which for many like this young man, would not normally be bearable.

Within Jimmy Jones, dwelling deep down in the darkest corners of his mind, were memories so terrible that normally they would never find expression. Yet here, with these three urgently encoring women and the strong protective form of his father, the tea gave him the courage to continue.

Sally was speaking of the Milton that she had presented to Billy on the day he first went off to war. The pleasure that Jimmy had given her when telling of its part played in the great tragedy, warmed her, allowing her breast to be calmed, her heart to beat more regularly.

"Esther was the first to speak of Jimmy's next task.

"Only continue Jimmy if you really want to, We shall understand, you know, if you do not wish to do so."

"Thank you mother, thank you, but there are things that need to be said and I feel that I must say them. At first I was merely going to speak of Billy. But we were all part of the story. All of us, all of the section, each and every man, should be spoken of. He sat back deeper into the upholstery of the chair and stared directly in front of him gradually drawing himself back to the trenches."

"Our turn came to be relieved of our watch and to fall back to the rear, to the deserted farmhouse. There were twenty-four of us, two Corporals, and twenty-two Privates. Our Platoon Commander went off to the officers quarters, well away from it all, but we were glad of that. NCO's were part of us, like us, not from the toffee nosed Public schools where the Lieutenants usually originated. We would all be able to relax more easily with just the Corporals overseeing matters."

Even in a small unit like ours the men split up into groups. There were those whose idle hours were filled playing cards. They called it a school. Never played anything but a game called 'three card brag' for hours they would deal, round after round, six of them. They seemed to be unaware of anything but the game.

"We had a couple of educated men, barrack room lawyers, politicians, constantly talking and arguing between themselves, a Liberal and a Labourite. They were the solitary ones. They never came together with anyone else. In their own world they were. Then there was us, poet's corner, the Milton men. We were mainly a group of five but from time to time others joined in. We had begun to talk of other things even sing a few hymns, and if truth were known many of us prayed, mostly in silence, but sometimes aloud."

"The farmhouse was a large building with outhouses some of which had become latrines. One small building had a boiler, which was kept continually lit. The people who had left their home had stocked it with huge quantities of wood and a couple of tons of coal, so keeping warm all day was not a problem. We could wash both our clothes and ourselves."

"Here was our sanctuary; here we could sleep soundly for one night having had good food. Mother, you would never guess the times I've spent in a trench thinking of us sitting down to Sunday dinner. There were times when I fed, just on the memory"

Jimmy and his mother exchanged glances. She smiled and something welled up deeply within her causing tears to drop from her cheek.

Jimmy continued with his story.

"Yes the farmhouse was like a palace to us. Built of stone, it was strong warm and dry, A real palace. Well one of us, that Trevor Roberts from Wrexham, I spoke of him before if you recall, he comes up with great idea. I tell you it was such an idea it ought to be invented over here. Every street should have one, maybe every house."

Jimmy was now deeply instilled into his recollections. Trevor's conversation returned to him and he could see him once again putting his idea to Billy.

"You see corp. I worked up at this place called Erddig. A great big house, with acres of land, filled with woods, cattle and sheep. This man, his name was Phillip Yorke. He was a man of ideas. He had contraptions for making bricks, cutting wood and all sorts. In fact, his place was filled with contraptions. He even had a car."

"Well, one day he says to me, 'Trevor can you build me a contraption for washing myself in hot water that just flows over men doing a proper job. Well Mr Yorke I says, reckon I can. Billy, I tell you, that night I sat down and drew this thing. I called it a shower 'cos it rains down on you gentle, like a shower, a hot shower'. Once I built it I tried it, just the once. It was great, I can tell you."

"Mr Yorke was made up with it. It only took an hour to make. He was like a little boy at the seaside, getting one of his servants to fill it up over and over. Well Corp reckons I can make one here. Looking around we got all the bits. What you reckon Corp?"

Billy considered for a moment, wondering whether to take this inventive Welshman seriously.

"Well."

Roberts was having none of this prevarication. He tried the Socialist approach.

"Ain't we good enough Corporal"

This did the trick; Billy was convinced.

"If it's good enough for Philip Yorke it's good enough for the likes of us. Take your brother and one other and build the thing. I'll get lots of hot water together."

It was with a great sense of pleasure that Jimmy recalled the building of the shower. He was sent by Billy to search for accessories and he smiled to himself as he recalled finding the cupboard in the large bedroom full of towels, soap, brushes and the like. He remembered rushing down the stairs, arms full with his trophies.

The shower was in an advanced stage of construction. It was about eight feet tall. It had a galvanised; two handled washing tub placed upon the top. Terry Gresford, one of the three manufacturing the object was a first class improviser. He was previously in the mines shoring up seams with timber supports. Men's lives had been placed in his hands, in his skill in shoring up the ever-extending tunnels of coal. He had made a great job of the platform. It consisted of four vertical posts with horizontal beams at its apex, which supported the now, perforated, galvanised tank. Into this the water would be poured raining down on the person stood beneath it, standing in a galvanised bath, wallowing in the luxuriance and the comfort of it all.

It had been built near to the large fireplace, which was now aflame with logs and coal. Not ever, even back in England, had the guests of this bleak farmhouse in France, experienced such an indulgence. Once it was finished Terry spoke up, an unusual occurrence; for he was one who usually kept himself to himself. He concluded his observation on a very positive note.

"That's going to work a treat, come on lads, let's get it started."

Young Albert was designated to be the first to test the 'washing machine' so baptised by Trevor. Under he went armed with a bar of carbolic, naked to the world, while hot water tempered with cold, to make it comfortable, was poured into the top tank. Sure enough water expressed itself through the holes and down upon the fortunate Albert spraying him with clean, hot, refreshing drops of water, which allowed him to soap himself and become clean, really clean for the first time in almost two weeks. He was like a schoolboy, which in reality, was what he really was.

Playfully splashing around the bath, whilst streams of hot water fell upon him, cleaning off the stench of the trench, he sang at the top of his voice.

It took ten minutes for the tank to empty. By this time young Albert was as clean as ever his mother would have seen him. Clean, warm and refreshed. What more could a trench incumbent, of this insane conflict ever to aspire to. Albert was as if he had passed through life and entered Paradise.

Nor was his experience unique. In turn the entire Platoon went through the process. Within four hours they must have become the cleanest, most fragrant Platoon on the Western Front. Oh happy band, it was an egalitarian experience. Each in turn having ten minutes of bliss upon bliss, exiting from above. Upon the completion of their turn, a reconstructed human being, a member of a civilised existence, emerged to partake in whatever else could be found to enrich this very special day.

"Well I reckons we all be going to heaven"

So announced Terry, as he completed his ten minutes worth.

"My mother always said it were next to Godliness, being clean and all that."

"As long as heaven doesn't call us too soon."

The ironic spoiler had inadvertently spoken to brushing off some of the acacia nectar, that all of them were swimming in.

"Got a lot of living to do yet, I hope."

The group of Kitchener's own were gathered around the fireplace, watching the flame lick around an old black cauldron, full of bubbling boiling soup. Leeks had been found in an outhouse, together with onions, carrots and potatoes too. Some bread brought with them that morning provided the rest of the meal aided by the joint surrendering of their stored victuals. Clean, warm and now soon to be fed. It could not get better. Well, in fact, it could.

By now it was four in the afternoon. Most of the men were sitting around the fire anticipating the sharing out of the broth. Suddenly a woman's voice cautiously cried out from the ether.

"Valois, Je Suis Madame Bertois; Valois."

The group of naked and semi naked men, veterans all, froze. Men who were constantly facing the worst that the Germans could throw at them, scattered in panic at the sound of a strange French woman calling out to them by the door of what was her home. She repeated her first statement with embellishment.

"Valois, il est Madame Bertois, il est moi mason, le Grande Flamengrie."

Billy, who unlike most was fully clothed, went over to the door where a stout, muscular woman of about sixty confronted him. She was armed with a two prolonged pitchfork and a wheelbarrow. "Englais?"

The good woman enquired of their Nationality, hoping that her answer was in the question.

Billy possessed library book French.

"Oui Madame, Oui nous avons Englais"

"Bon."

The lady replied looking both astounded and pleased both at the same time.

"Bon! Tu est Englais Chavaliers pour France."

Again came the reply.

"Oui Madam"

It was then that Madam Bertois decided to put the young man out of his discomfort.

"This is very good young man. Needlessly, I was worried about my house, but here I find it guarded by our brave English Soldiers."

Just at this moment, back in Talbot Street, there came a knock at the door. It broke Jimmy's concentration and the story ended abruptly. His listeners were so enwrapped with his tale that it took them a while to mentally come back into the room. Sally volunteered to go and see who it was. She opened the door and there before her was Pastor Livingston.

He stepped back from the house as if he could sense that somehow, he had broken a spell.

"I am so sorry Sally if I have interrupted something special, but I had heard that young Jimmy and his parents were making their way to your house and thought it might be opportune to call. Wish him well so to speak."

He was worrying needlessly; Sally was very pleased to see him.

"Oh Pastor, how wonderful of you to call. Yes they are all here and you are most welcome to join us."

She made way for him to enter and Gideon stepped inside.

"Jimmy has been telling us of happenings you would not believe. You really are most welcome to join us Pastor."

Gideon was ushered in to the front parlour to find the Jones family and Billy's mother waiting upon his entrance.

"Hello Pastor Livingston, welcome"

Gladys was the first to greet him.

"Do come in and join us you will be amazed at Jimmy's tale, real amazed."

"I don't know about that Pastor"

Up chirped up Jimmy, without any encouragement, he was already feeling much better. The telling of his tale was becoming a real catharsis for him.

"They all invited me up here to tell of Billy, and give them an entire history of trench life and all those I shared it with."

Gideon reassured the young man.

"Well Jimmy, that's how it should be. All our young men were urged to go to war. It is our duty to hear what they have undergone. If it is not intrusive I would like to join you and listen to what you have to relate. You never know it could help me with my address on Sunday which is on love and sacrifice."

Jimmy surmised for the Pastor's benefit.

"Well Pastor, I have seen a lot of sacrifice, and if it is right for men doing things for each other, looking out for each other, protecting each other, sharing things together, comforting each other and praying together to be called love. If it is right to call such as that love, then I have seen a wealth of love and I can give witness to it."

It was one of the occasions in his life when Gideon felt that God was humbling him. Here was young Jimmy Jones back from war, less a leg, but grown and profound beyond his years. He would listen more this day but even now he felt, if he could be persuaded, it should be Jimmy, Jimmy Jones who addressed the congregation this Sunday.

Who was more worthy, more accomplished, more justified in speaking on 'Love and Sacrifice' he or the young Jimmy Jones sitting here before him?' He would listen more. He would learn, But he was already aware that it would be this wounded scarred soldier, unpretentious and simple who, he would prefer his congregation to listen to this coming Sunday.

Sally had brought in a cup and saucer for her Pastor. Methodically she went through the ceremony of filling the cup, in his fashion, and presenting it to him.

"Jimmy has had so much to tell us Pastor, we've all listened. It's been like we were there, in France he's been…"

She hesitated, unable, immediately, to find the correct words.

"Jimmy has been so graphic in the telling of his story. It's not like we've been told at all. It's been as if we've lived every word of it."

This brought a minute of silence. Each of those in the room, who had listened to Jimmy, had experienced feelings and fears they could not entirely comprehend. Something had drawn them away from the comfort of this Glossop home, to take them far away to war, to a muddy hole in France. Soon they would return there, this time in the company of the Pastor Livingston.

It was in times like these that Gideon felt the presence of God very close to him, a real physical presence. During such experiences, it was as if holiness was descending around him, protecting him, consoling him or pushing him on. He and his God had built a Church from nothing. He had found for God the loaves and fishes. In return God had provided all his needs, that his aspirations and visions had required for fulfilment. Gideon had tried to walk with God and his God had surely walked with him, gifting both himself and his congregation.

Now was such a time. Gideon sensed Angels gathering all around, almost hearing the rustle of their wings embracing, guarding and protecting this small group. Each person within these walls was animated, and envisioned. Together with young Jimmy Jones, his tortured body and mind displayed for all of them to witness to, the Angels were blessing them as surely as the young man was being blessed through the sympathy and understanding of those listening. Now Gideon too felt blessed and privileged to be here, to play his part in experiencing the metaphysical awe, that encompassed the room.

Jimmy turned towards his Pastor.

"I am so glad that you have come Pastor, because you might best be placed to understand what I have to tell next about how twenty four men and an elderly lady spent an evening together in a ruined house in France. It was an evening that changed us all, probably for the rest of our lives, which will be short for some, but perhaps too long for others."

"This French lady was so kind and generous. We had invaded her home uninvited, built a great big shower there by her fireplace, helped ourselves to her potatoes, leaks, carrots and other more personal, things. Yet she was the kindest, most welcoming woman, a proper Lady, a French Good Samaritan. That was what she was. Straight out of the Bible she came did Madame Bertois, Straight out of the Bible."

CHAPTER 23

A virtuous woman, who can find?
For her price is far above rubies.

The Proverbs ch: 31 v.10.

For a short while only, it is time to leave the trenches of Northern France, and the small group of people listening to Jimmy Jones, in that little house in Glossop. The story of Madame Bertois, or Lucille Cressage, which was her maiden name, shall now unfold. From the time of her birth in 1856 she was beloved and worshiped by her parents who had no other children. Her father was almost fifty when Lucille first opened her eyes and her mother forty-two. A great surprise, a gift, a gift of God.

She grew into a pretty child, living a peaceful life in the luxuriant tranquil countryside west of Amiens, on the road towards Paix. When she was fourteen an event occurred that would change her life forever, the Prussians invaded France. Many of the population succumbed to panic. The last war to be fought on French soil was during the dying days of the regime of Napoleon, over fifty years previously. Then, Prussian cavalry, the infamous Brunswickers, dressed all in black, swept through Northern France to descend upon Paris, despoiling the countryside and its population. Tales of how they had ravaged the land and people, created an air of panic. They swept all over the land, bringing fear whenever they visited a community.

Now, once again the Hun was among them. The poor hid what they could and waited. The rich boarded up their homes and headed for Paris. Some of them even to London. Lucille's parents felt that they could not leave their large dairy farm and the tonnes of cheeses, which they had made and for which they were famed. Conversely, the Prussians had a reputation for taking all that they so desired. This included young French maidens, whose virtue held no barrier to their wanton desires.

Their concern, for their daughter, led them to the decision to send her abroad. They decided to dispatch her to a girl's school in England, one renowned for cultivating young ladies. It was Lucille's father who heard of the place when speaking to Henry La Fontelle the Mayor of Paris. Discovering that Monsieur Fontelle was sending his young daughter to England. He asked if he could arrange for Lucille to accompany her. Within a week all was organised and the two girls were boarding the ferry to Dover.

Lucille and her friend Marie attended Wycombe School for Girls for more than three years. Their grey and red uniform stood out whenever they were allowed to go on outings to town, or were in the congregation of the ancient

336

Parish Church, charming everyone whom they spoke to with their endearing accent that French school girls possess when speaking English.

The school often organised Charabanc tours to many of the beautiful villages that nestle among the beach woodlands of the Chiltern Hills. Burnham Beeches and Stoke Poges became two of Lucille's favourite places for an excursion. Walking through the endless acres of trees, firmly embedded in the chalk, spaced wide enough for grassy glades and mossy banks where, in late Spring, when all is lost in a sea of bluebells, gave her great pleasure. So ingrained were the pleasant memories of those verdant days that she fondly remembered them for the rest of her life.

The Churchyard, where England's greatest pastoral poet, rests was also a wonder for her. It was she who, on moving a stone made loose by years of weathering, found an original script, scribed from the very hand of Grey himself. It contained an unpublicised verse of his Elegy. Some Stanzas were crossed out and blotted by the scribed sooty ink and were never used in the final draft. One such discarded verse was still readable. Lucille was to come to the conclusion that, paradoxically; it was the Poets most beautiful set of lines.

> *'There scattered oft, the earliest of the year.*
> *By hand unseen are showers of violets found*
> *The red breast likes to sing and warble there*
> *And little footsteps, lightly print the ground.'*

The paper found its way into her pocket, to be discovered years later, after she had died, together with her own notation enclosed 'Found by Lucille Cressage Stoke Poges 1873 England.'

It was a small detail in the life of a young girl but it explains much of why she conducted her so affairs in her later years.

In the spring of 1874 Lucille returned home. She was shocked by how much her parents had aged and how their attitude towards her had changed. They now so controlled her conduct that she felt stifled. Lucille wanted to explore events as they occurred, and her emotions as they developed. Her parents declined her every request to expand her horizons, wanting to keep her closeby.

She was to be the inheritor of all they had ever earned, all the property that represented, the accumulation of generations of hard work and acquisition. They began to look around for a suitable match for their daughter, someone who would add to the farm's prosperity and bring them an additional worker. So they plotted and planned, but they reckoned without Pierre Bertois.

It was at the annual department's agricultural fair that fate decreed that the two should meet.

Pierre was a thirty-two year old dairy farmer who, famously, raised a prize herd west of Amiens. When they collided by the cheese exhibits in 1882, Lucille was piled high with ten rounds of her parent's famous Brie. Every year they sold over two hundred roundels at the fair. It was a major yearly event for them, one that acted as a pathfinder for the coming year. Lucille was walking blindly, the cheeses blocking her view; Pierre was leading his magnificent Friesian, which was stubbornly refusing to co-operate. The collision was dramatic. Cheeses went in all directions. Pierre came to rest sitting on one of the Brie with Lucille on his lap and the bull almost nuzzling them, attracted by the scattered cheese.

People stared, as they do when such a thing occurs. They stopped to gather round, gazing at the couple who were sitting on the ground surrounded by copious amounts of dilapidated Brie whilst being nudged by an enormous bovine.

Lucille stared into a pair of large brown eyes and a bristling moustache. Pierre looked back at a beautiful face full of innocence and mystique. Their eyes filled with laughter and spontaneously it came to the surface, Slowly at first, beginning, simply, with muted amusement, their mirth soon developed into giggles, then, uproariously, uncontrollably, came an eruption of full, totally uninhibited, laughter. They looked ridiculous, they knew it, and they cared not at all.

Pierre was the first to regain control and gather himself together. He offered his hand to Lucille, which was accepted and gently pulled her to her feet. La Belle de Amiens was enthusiastically licking one of the Brie, oblivious to the noisy interest of the crowd. A mixture of fear, embarrassment and an unfamiliar emotion began to descend upon Lucille. Fear of her parents and for the cheese, embarrassment at being the centre of a public farce and an emotional magnetic interest in the cause of her predicament.

It was a whirlwind, Despite the protest of her parents within four months Lucille married her Pierre and went to live with him at his large ancient farmhouse ten Kilometres east of Peronne.

Like many such relationships where love is so intense, it was a tempestuous marriage but their mutual physical attraction was such that any terse events were short lived, ending with expressions of deep, urgent and finally, spent desire.

They had five children, first a daughter, then three sons and lastly another girl who, sadly, died a few weeks after her birth. The family prospered. The early years of the new century were kind to them. Their meat and dairy products were sold effortlessly and the family lived contented, healthy, sturdy and strong.

Danielle, their oldest married in 1912 having found love in Paris with a rather eccentric artist. Life was good, the future full of promise. Then someone shot the Austrian Archduke and, once again, came war, threatening everything they had. As each new forbidding event unravelled, Pierre became quiet and thoughtful, and took to walking the bounds of his farm at eventide not coming in for his supper until it was way past dark. He would simply and silently eat his ham with potatoes or some cheese. His humour went from him, his laughter departed.

One evening in the third week of August he came in, took his wife's hand and walked out of the house with her. He said but one word.

"Listen."

Over the noise of the wind there came a gentle series of thuds.

That is the sound of German guns. I first heard them yesterday evening, which is when sound, travels more easily. Today they are louder. The Germans are coming.

I think our Valois will not stop them. Neither will our friends the British. The farm will be destroyed, together with the cattle. We cannot save the farm but the beasts can be driven to a safer place. Your parents farm.

Lucille's parents had died within three months of each other over fifteen years ago. Since that time the house and land had been rented in three lots, most of it becoming arable. Recently, one tenant, a single man, had finished a short-term lease and had not renewed it.

There is enough land on the Haux Poix, which we could use. If we take the cart, complete with the pails and the churns, we can milk the cows as usual, selling the produce as we go. The journey will take four, perhaps five, days. Lucille had her doubts; she did not want to go. This was her home, her place of happiness, of her husband and children. She did not want to go, would not go, and she told Pierre so.

"Perhaps the army will hold the Germans. Our British friends are coming over, more of them arrive each day."

Pierre brought her back to reality.

"My love, did you not hear the guns, daily they will get louder hundreds of them, then they will engulf us."

Lucille would not believe him but the next day the guns were louder and the day after that louder still. It was then she decided.

"Tomorrow we shall go Pierre, you are right, nothing will stop them."

She went to tell the boys Andre, Anton and young Louis. The response she got from them put her into a state of panic. Andre spoke up for himself and his brother.

"Mama, Anton and I are going to join the army we are going to the war. France needs us, She is bleeding we must go to the war."

Emotion burst forth from Lucille, now the coming Germans were not only threatening her livelihood but the lives of her children as well.

"No, my sons you must not go, you cannot go, I shall not let you go."

Calmly Andre put his strong arms around his mother's shoulder and gently spoke in the vain attempt to assure her.

"Mother we have to go. We are exempted from conscription for now, but our honour tells us we must go. We shall go with you and father to Poix then, we shall continue to Paris and join in comradeship with all the other Valois who are defending the precious soil of France."

Lucille was devastated; she knew how determined her boys could be once an idea had come to them. In truth she agreed with their sentiments but 'dear God' she thought to herself 'do not let my sons be killed.'

Early next morning, after milking, the procession left the farm. The cart was loaded with essentials and equipment, leaving one hundred and twenty cattle to be shepherded by the men. Once they had met with the main road they realised that their progress would be slower than they thought. It was full of people, using every conceivable kind of transportation and all walking or riding away from the sound of the guns.

The sense of panic that almost all the retreating mass felt was at first submerged, but as the day drew on and movement became ever slower it became audible. Pierre began to realise that the situation was hopeless. There was no way that they would ever reach their destination like this. He would have to take the cattle over the fields, cross-country and into the country lanes. There they would gradually progress towards the east. Pierre made his decision. Lucille would continue in the cart with Lois, while he and the other boys would drive the cattle.

Thus they parted. It took Lucille two more days to arrive at Haut Poix. Then she had to wait for her husband and the boys. Five days later they duly arrived, together with all the cows. They appeared like a trio of nonchalant cats, who having been fretted over by their owner because they have disappeared for days, just turn up by the back door and walk over to their feeding bowl as if they have never been away.

Pierre had brought good news with him.

"We met many soldiers on the way British and French. Yesterday I was speaking to a cavalry captain. He said that recent reconnaissance suggests that the Germans were turning back westerly along the Meuse. He was certain they would be stopped east of Amien but he thought Peronne would be taken within two days.

It took a number of days for the family to settle. There was a lot of work to do but within a week life had become fairly routine. At last came the moment Lucille had dreaded. It was at the dinner table ten days after they had arrived that the two boys announced they would be leaving in the morning. The parting was to overwhelm her. For the first time in her life Lucille had no control over family events. Death had taken her youngest, it was true, but it had been a natural death, paradoxically, part of life.

This was different. Her two sons were leaving, volunteering, to face uncertainty, danger and death. Once they had gone she could only wait for news. She was distraught. Their leaving took over an hour. Hugging and kissing her beloved sons, Lucille refused to let them depart. Eventually, Pierre had to gently but firmly separate her from her offspring and allow them to leave.

They had been well provided for with bread freshly baked, ham, cheese and pickles. Her last sight of them was when they turned waved and disappeared over the crest of the hill about one kilometre distant. It was the last she would ever see of them.

From that moment matters descended from sadness into tragedy. It was just two days later that Pierre had a heart attack. He was working in the milking parlour with young Louis when the pain came over his chest. Louis ran to get his mother. Between then they managed to get him inside the house and into a chair. He was semi conscious and not responding to their questions.

Lucille told Louis to take the cart and bring back the village doctor as fast as possible. Five minutes after he left; Pierre had a second and fatal attack and was gone. As his eyes misted over Lucille could feel him gently squeezing her hand acknowledging her presence. Then it relaxed; his spirit had left him.

Pierre was buried in a small cemetery overlooked by Haut Poix. As he was being lowered into a strange plot of ground, Lucille promised him that, once it was free, she would take him back home. That she would take him back, to his beloved farm, nearby to the fields he had so often roamed, where his spirit could hear the lowing of the Friesians that he was so proud of.

Louis played the part of head of the household. He had brought back Danielle and her husband from Paris. They had agreed to stay on and help with the farm. Lucille just entered into her own thoughts, unaware of events happening around her. All she would speak of were her sons and her husband.

Then in January 1916 came the next devastating blow. It came from the Ministry of War. The telegram simply stated that her two sons had fallen defending their country, side by side, on the same day at Verdun, repelling a vast German attack. In truth they had been part of a unit of one hundred and fifty men who had left their billets one morning to travel up the 'Vore Sacree'. They were not among the thirty who made it to the front. One of Krupp's infernal monsters destroyed them. Neither of them was to ever see a German or let off a bullet in anger. They were just consumed by the inferno that was Verdun.

The single two tonne shell, killed over thirty of France's sons, not one piece of flesh was ever buried not one man ever identified. The Captain simply checked the survivors, who had reached the trenches, noted the ones who had not made it and reported their deaths to divisional head quarters. The bureaucrats completed the exercise. Telegrams went out all over

France to wives and mothers. Then they were forgotten by the next day and replaced. By its end, Verdun would have created almost a quarter of a million telegrams, sent to families in France, in less than a year.

For Lucille, it was the end. She just lay in her bed grieving for her lost men. Her loving husband, her devoted sons gone. She sincerely wished to be with them, living no longer had any purpose. Danielle became very attentive. She never left her mother's side, soothing her constant sobs, her cries, her unheard plea's that her loved ones might return.

Then, one day in April, she suddenly changed. Lucille got up early, had a large breakfast, and then declared that she was going to visit her house by the Somme. She declared that there was much to do.

"The family safe must be retrieved, it contains thousands of Francs. The house must be checked to see all is well, it is what Pierre would want."

The horse had long been requisitioned, so Lucille decided to take the two-wheeled barrow and a pitchfork in case a Bosch should be stupid enough to confront her.

At once, the rest of the household tried to dissuade her, but her mind would not be altered. Danielle pleaded with her mother.

"At least take Louis with you."

At last she conceded this point.

"But only to Peronne."

Rising early next morning, the wheelbarrow was loaded with supplies and weatherproof sheeting. Mother and son were to take turns pushing the barrow the other would hold the pitchfork. The weather, unlike the past few weeks, was warm and dry. The spring solstice had long passed and the hours of daylight were greater than the times of darkness. Lucille hoped to cover twenty-five kilometres each day, making the trip a three-day affair.

Evening on the first day saw the pair having covered thirty kilometres, fifteen east of Amiens. Lucille knocked on the door of an ancient farmhouse. The clear sky meant that the temperature had become suddenly cold. A lady of about the same age as Lucille answered the knock. Once she had heard of Lucille's quest they were both welcomed enthusiastically.

Next morning they again set off early, having left a ham in payment. The woman who lived on her own, would take money under no circumstances, but she welcomed the ham. The wind had gained pace and clouds were rising from the west. Louis recognised them as cumulous nimbus; rain-bearing clouds. He told his mother as much. Sure enough by noon drizzle began to fall. They continued on but after two hours the rain was becoming torrential. Also lightning flashes were encroaching towards them. They managed to obtain shelter in a barn before the storm fully reached them.

Lucille had not witnessed such a tempest for years. The rain teemed down, sheeting almost horizontally. Louis lit a small fire in one corner. Keeping control of the flames they sat down by the flames, gaining a little warmth and began to dry out.

"Oh the poor Valois"

Lucille's whispered empathy was for her ears only. She was thinking on what it must be like to exist exposed in the trenches in such weather.

"Oh the poor Valois"

The storm ravaged the barn for the remainder of that day and through most of the night. Then just before dawn the wind dropped, the clouds climbed higher and, as the sun rose, the sky was more than half-blue.

"Thank you God"

Lucille extolled her gratitude heavenwards, it was 7.00am, and the sun was splaying its warmth upon the world. It picked up the spirit, previously depleted by her lack of appearance the day before. Consequently, it was two humans travelling hopefully that departed from their overnight shelter.

"If the weather remains like this, we shall arrive in Peronne by evening. Then tomorrow you will stay in the town Louis, while I go on alone."

Louis agreed by the nod of his head. By two in the afternoon Lucille began to hear distant gunfire.

She tried to remember how it compared to that other sound, last heard when she left the farm. It was sounding very distant certainly well past Peronne. Once she got to the town someone would know where the lines were.

Blisters were now forming on her hands from wheeling the barrow. Lucille examined Louis hands. His were also beginning to blister, probably his feet too. Well one more hour and they would be in Peronne she would find good lodgings for Louis and, if the weather held she would continue to the house, about another three hours walk further on.

They entered the small town at 3.00pm. Enemy artillery had produced some damage, but it was of small account. She left Louis in the care of a sympathetic landlady and continued on her pilgrimage.

The sound of the guns was very much louder now and the landscape was becoming cratered. On more than one occasion, she had to navigate round large water filled holes. In truth it was becoming more arduous by the minute but Lucille knew she was less than four kilometres away from completing her journey. She would not be defeated now.

The end of her task was upon her, fortifying her resolve for one last effort. Walking was now an automatic series of motions. Slowly Lucille felt she was losing all sense of pain and fatigue, indeed all sense of existence.

Sleep tempted her to stop, but she continued. Then, suddenly, surrounded by craters, deafened by shellfire, the farm was silhouetted before her. Oh so slowly, she began the walk up the drive.

As she got within a few metres of her front door, she felt she was hallucinating, Singing could be heard from within. Then realisation dawned upon her; it was occupied by soldiers. Furthermore, they were not French; the singing was in English. Tentatively she raised the knocker and struck the door. Immediately the singing stopped and after a short while, the door opened and a soldier, who was about the same age as her Anton, confronted her. The young man took on a startled expression and backed away into the room. Peeping round the opening in the door, she announced in French who she was, tentatively inquiring after whom they were.

CHAPTER 24

'The lord is my shepherd
I shall not want'

23rd Psalm

Jimmy had been speaking for some hours now; his chronicle of events was being related with intense detail. The reason for this was that whenever Jimmy began a new chapter of his story, he lost all control in its telling. The strength of the images that came before him drew him back to relive the events once again, as if he was no longer in the room.

So illuminated did he become, so distant did his voice drift away, that he took his listeners with him. Jimmy was elevated, transported, completely unaware of those around him listening eagerly to each word he uttered.

He fell into a metaphysical trance, born of self-hypnotic suggestion, which transported him back in time and back to France. Now, as the name of Madame Bertois came to his ears, expressed from his own lips, a vision of this most wonderful woman appeared before him. The face of this splendid, courageous woman who had trekked for miles in a pilgrimage to inspect her house and collect some of her valuables, once again, smiled at him.

It was as if he was back there and she before him, as if he was again standing, half naked, in that large room of the house east of Albert, witnessing how she brought with her assurance, comfort and love. Jimmy was once again reliving the day when this good woman became the mother of them all. Boys who, during recent times, had been half starved, often frightened, and fed up, were given a short time of normal human experience through the love of this good woman.

She added a new dimension to the bond that that had been forged between the youths that made up this platoon. These ragged urchins that England had sent to France to be the first line of defence against her enemies, for one night, found their very own Madonna. That night, Madame Bertois became the mother of them all.

It was not without considerable apprehension that Madam Bertios entered her home. She closed the door and with a slight smile, tentatively walked to the centre of the room. There was a miniature Eiffel Tower standing to one side of the fireplace. Her tin bath provided the base for poles which held her wash tub which now appeared to be full of holes. Slowly it came to her. It was an invention for washing bodies. The English soldiers had constructed a machine for cleaning themselves. She well knew what the weather had been like and how filthy the conditions in the trenches must be. The newspapers had been full of photographs showing how the Valois existed in this war, sometimes up to their waists in mud. This invention had solved the problem.

The young man who had opened the door had two stripes on his uniform and seemed to be in charge. In very proper fashion, he introduced himself.

"I am Corporal Billy Thomas, and who do I have the privilege of addressing Madam?"

"I am Lucille Bertois, this house belonged to my husband and I, our children were born here, our cattle milked in the parlour over the yard. Now, as you protect it from the Germans, you have a right to use it, to be its guests. You are most welcome."

Scuttling around, like so many bowls hit by a projectile, the men, who were in various stages of undress, tried as best they could to hide their nakedness as if they were the original inhabitants of Eden. Their visitor, a mother of three grown men was embarrassed not at all. In fact, she was amused to see the effect she had on soldiers who daily faced all manner of challenges and encounters. She had observed that these blushing heroes, assembled in her house, were little more than boys To see them reacting to her presence in such a manner, merely confirmed her observations

It was ten minutes later that some sort of order was established and Lucille was able to be introduced to all of the uninvited guests that had occupied her home. The afternoon was drawing on, the cauldron would pour forth its sustaining substance in about another hour. Clean and relaxed, the men began to break up into their usual groups.

Jimmy recalled.

"Six men had gathered with Billy to talk on Milton, Jimmy Jones, the Roberts brothers, young Albert Hadfield, Terry Gresford, our carpenter, and Vic. Vic who would always keep to himself. He would always help whenever he was asked and sometimes he would just assist voluntarily in a task that needed to be undertaken. Vic was no slacker, but he kept to himself. He never smoked or took the rum ration. All he did, or seemed to do when off duty, was to read from his book. A worn out book it was, dog eared, mucky, he was ever engrossed with this volume I tell you; engrossed. Someone once asked him what the book was, but he just said 'Politics' and glared back down the pages. So that was that and no one ever asked again, that was until Billy did so."

"He was a familiar figure to Jimmy; it was as if he had met him before. This indeed was the case. The last time Billy had seen him was in a semi-sober state as he helped him onto a train preparing to depart from Glossop Station. Victor Grayson had recognised Billy in return, but neither of them had referred to that evening in Glossop, where one of them had made a speech and the other had volunteered."

"A peculiar relationship had developed between the pair. Billy was deeply curious of the circumstances that had brought Vic to his section. He had arrived during the time that Billy was recovering and getting married in England. Vic was sincerely interested in Billy and how life had treated him since they last had met. Yet, without knowing quite why, neither had yet asked a question of the other. The time would come when each would reveal to the other all that had transpired, but the time was not yet right for such a conversation."

"This night though, Vic approached the group to listen to some of the Milton. For once he was in need of fellowship, and this group of men, gathering round together simply because they wished to explore the works of a metaphysical poet, intrigued him. The lads made the circle wider for him and also for Madame Bertois who came to join them. Billy started with a welcome."

Jimmy's eyes glazed over once more. He was again sat in this place of respite listening to his comrade.

"Well our group is bigger tonight, our new found friend, a lady of France and Vic, welcome Vic"

A nod of gratitude found its way to Billy and was accepted in the same manner.

"I thought tonight just to read a few lines then we can talk on it, explore it and see what we find. Everyone in agreement?"

There was expectant murmuring of acceptance and Billy opened the book.

'............... *The childhood shows the man,*
As morning shows the day. Be famous then
By wisdom; as thy empire must extend,
So extend thy mind o'er all the world.'

Jimmy, and the rest of the men, were spell bound. They had been listening for weeks now and Milton had got to them all. Now, whenever they heard the words they were mindful not only of their beauty, but also of their meaningful and deep essence, it was intense. The men, together with Madame Bertois, had listened to just four lines of verse and now their thoughts were busy, mindful of an inspired meaning, one to be unravelled. Terry Gresford asked Billy if he could repeat the verse, which Billy did. Terry began the discussion in a subdued voice.

"I suppose that what it means is that the way we are brought up, educated and all that, dictates the way we are when we become adults. The more we learn, the more we experience, and consequently the more we become enabled to play a useful role among our fellow men."

Billy sounded his approval.

"That's good Terry, you've understood that well, but it contains more than that. It goes on to state that what you have learned, all the good that you have accumulated, all the knowledge, emotions, triumphs and disasters, should go towards the application of its use for the benefit of people the world over."

The discussion went on for over half an hour with ideas being developed and expanded. It appeared that the group had gained that wonderful enlightened ability to master the art of dissecting literature thus exposing its full meaning, beauty and significance. To most of the mechanicals assembled there, in the most unlikely of circumstances, it provided for them, a personal perception of accomplishment. It brought forth a simple truth, which delivered a certain compensation from their time of trial.

Here they were, studying Milton, together, far from home, a time mostly spent being cold, wet and miserable, had come a short period of purpose. In their discussion they came face to face with what they were. It displayed a simple fact, that even in this hellhole, they could find a comfort in accomplishing a contribution to understanding it all. Now their pondering was about to be elevated to another, higher dimension, for up spoke Madame Bertois.

"If you would not mind, may I say something,"

"Of course Madame"

Billy's, confirmation brought universal agreement, So she began, using a new quotation drawn from out of the recesses of her mind.

> *Nor love thy life, nor hate; but what thou liv'st*
> *Live well, how long or short, permit to heaven.*

The group was dumbstruck. Here was their beloved Milton being quoted, from memory, by a strange French lady who had just happened on their seminar, as Billy called such a session.

Lucille continued, placing the quotation into context.

"It is from earlier lines in the Lost Paradise, but it better helps us to understand. Solomon was wise, but even with all his wisdom, his glories, and his wealth, he became as dust. It is good to grow wise, your wisdom aids the progress of man, but goodness, charity, love, these ascend above wisdom. They provide the purpose to wisdom. Love is the road to immortality, the gateway to heaven. It is towards love then, in all is aspects and manifestations, that we must all strive to become accomplished of. It is through love that we transcend above our decadence, our tortured existence, to discover rest and peace".

"Through love, all of us, all you young brave Valois, shall find your heaven, your paradise. Whatever your end my sons, however your end, your charity, your love, through faith, shall rise above the pain, above the mud, above the guns, above the fear, above death itself. In addition, reason, the reason for your being, your sacrifice, is made plain. You may have to forsake this 'Eden' such as it is but you will attain a far greater one a perpetual paradise through your charity, your love, your sacrifice".

She paused then concluded with a further quote.

> *..................'Will thou not be loath*
> *To leave this paradise, but shall possess*
> *A paradise within thee, happier far.'*

'A paradise within thee.' The group considered the words. They came warm and comforting. Finally it fell to Vic to speak up making a pronouncement, which, as befits a man of his profession, became an oration, a great oration.

"These words consume me, my brothers, my sister. I consider myself an agnostic. I do not know if there is a God or not, but I am convinced of our spiritual selves. It is surely that part of us which makes us selfish or kind, greedy or selfless, civilised or brutal. This place where we currently dwell, this place of mud and holes in the ground, this place, is as near to hell that I ever want to be."

"I also know those of our enemies, there on the other side, feel the same. We have left our earthy paradise, such as it is, with wives, mothers, families, friends and homes. Back there, back in England, or Wales, life can be hard and brutal, for some even like hell. But it is our home, it is familiar. You can go from one end of town to the other without being shelled or shot at, or covered in mud, though, it is true, some get daily covered in the black of the pit, the sludge of the quarry or breathe in cotton dust. Yet, in England, on the whole, I can stand up and speak my mind. If I have a wish, I can mount a Clarion caravan and shout out against injustices, with the hope that slowly we will improve things."

"Here, on the Western Front, if I so much as put my head above the trench, it gets blown off and no questions asked. Here they can make us food for the cannon, have us dwell deep in a ditch alongside the Somme, but, my brothers, my sister, what they cannot do, ever do, is take away our inner spirit the 'Paradise within us.' If we possess that, if we have that Paradise within us, cling onto it never to let it go, then we are 'happier far.' In truth, we become far happier than a man who lives on his knees, never discovering what he is, what he can become, his soul and body never known freedom of will, freedom of self, freedom of soul."

"Some of us are going to die here, maybe all of us. Our bodies could be blasted to a million pieces, left for the crows, if any of them are stupid enough to fly around, dodging the bullets, for scraps of our torn flesh."

"Our masters, German, British, French, consider us expendable, the price that has to be paid for their success. In short, we have served our purpose. We have fed the war. Yet in so doing we have become greater than they. Though our lives may be short, our deeds shall make us immortal."

"Whatever they say when they talk of us in pubs or on street corners, my brothers, my sister, they will say with pride and gratitude, 'this was a man.' Our remains, however small, known or unknown, will have had within them and still possess, even in the height of corruption, as we sleep, a Paradise within, happier far."

Vic had said his piece for the first time since he joined the section he uttered more than one sentence in open conversation, and what an utterance. His words had silenced the group. They had even brought over others from the troop, even the card school had ceased to deal. By the end of his oration twenty-four brutalised soldiers were listening to every word and now no one knew what to say for fear of seeming simple or crass.

It was to Lucille that the baton fell, to her the task of a response. Her words were not long in coming.

"Young man, I went to a school for young ladies in England over thirty years ago. We were taught Milton by rote, which is how I can bring forth quotations from my mind years later. Our literature tutor was devoted to Milton. Outside of class, we would sit on sunnier days, by the beech woodlands that made up part of the grounds and listen to him read lines from the great man. He would explain to us the meaning of the words, how precious they were, how valuable would be the sentiments they conjured later in our lives. With flowering description, he mused upon just how, with the passing of the years, we would be enriched by them".

"Yet, young, man I tell you. We never experienced such revelation and sentiments that you have gifted us with tonight. Truly you have a powerful spiritual being, agnostic or not. I only hope that my two dear sons lying asleep at Verdun grasped a similar sense of their spiritual selves before they fell. I thank you, most dearly, from the deepest recesses of my inner self, You have given me comfort today, resolved my despair, my grief. I can now accept that they are gone, that they went truly possessing 'a Paradise within them,' that they died, 'happier far.'"

Tears were flowing down the cheeks of Madame Bertois but they were tears of resolve. Peace had come to her distressed mind. Now she could remember her boys with fond memory and peace. No sacrifice, no death is pointless, even though a bereaved one, seeking reasons, may have to wait long and to search hard, there is a reason in every aspect of life simply waiting to be discovered. There is a purpose, however hidden, however disguised; it is love. Madame Bertios had come to the realisation that her boys still lived within her, possessed of her love that too is part of the 'Paradise within.'

The aged lady, widowed, deprived of her beloved sons, articulated all her sentiments to those who would hear. They flowed over the audience, ever increasing the tension of the moment, bringing an awesome atmosphere to the house. Conversation ceased, thought, deep profound inner thought prevailed.

It was the aroma, drifting into the room, from the large black cauldron of soup that broke the serenity of the moment. It led two of the audience to explore the status of preparation that it had achieved.

"Soup's ready"

-It was an excited, eager yell.

"Potatoes are soft, real cooked they are, come and get it."

Round the centre of the room was a table, large enough to sit most of the occupants of the house. Each man had washed his mess tin, and was in the process of collecting his portion when Madame Bertois stopped them all in their tracks, as if they were statues made of stone.

"What do you think you are doing? Guests in my house do not eat out of tins with old battered utensils. As you are my guests, we shall eat properly. Billy come with me, and bring another."

Taking out a ring of keys she crossed the room and went to the base of the stairs, which was enclosed with panelling. Upon opening the door she knelt down and pulled out a ring, which neatly fitted the space occupied by the enclosure. Using one of her keys, she placed it into a small hole in the flooring, turned her hand anticlockwise and 'Voila' the floorboards lifted to meet the angle of the stairs. Somehow she locked the trapdoor into place, stepped back and revealed a flight of stairs going down to a cellar.

"All my valuables are down here. My husband and I locked them away to keep them safe from the Bosch. Bring some candles Billy and let us go and see what we can find."

Taking a candle herself Madame Bertois began to descended the stairway, followed by Billy and young Albert. The rest of the men stayed above ground waiting expectantly, even more so, when as the minutes passed, they heard gasps of surprise and pleasure, coming from below.

The reasons for the sounds of delight were due to the sight that met the eyes of the two young soldiers. The cellar was large, almost the size of the room above. It was about seven feet high so they could stand comfortably. Wall to wall, reaching to the ceiling was full of bottles, row upon row. On examining the contents they discovered them to contain wine, both red and white you could take your pick.

"There is brandy too"

Madame Bertois was peering closely at some of the bottles.

"I never inspected them before, it was Pierre's domain. However, I knew of the cheeses."

Picking up a large heavy round object covered in muslin she handed it to Albert.

"Take that upstairs young man, and be careful."

"Certainly"

351

The reply came in an instant from the mouth of a boy who loved cheese. Albert proceeded towards the exit, full of excitement, for he could smell the strong scent escaping from around his arms.

As he ascended the stairs Madame Bertois gave instructions to Corporal Billy Thomas, who was staring around the Aladdin's Cave with his mouth wide open emitting expressions of disbelief and pleasure.

"Come here Billy, don't just stand there, take these upstairs with you."

Taking away a dust sheet, she exposed a huge quantity of porcelain and cutlery. Billy gathered in his arms all that she handed to him, and in his turn, he went up the stairs.

Twenty minutes later saw the entire troop all sitting around the large table, upon which had been placed a delicate lace cloth. Tablemats, a stand for the cauldron, finest chinaware plates and bowls, together with the huge cheese, and various bottles of pickles and silverware, were displayed before them for their delectation. They had also been served with cloth napkins, a first for most of them. Young Albert was the first to begin, but for the second time that evening Madame Bertois let out a cry of unbelievable astonishment

"Surely you shall say grace for such a feast as this. From all of you, believers and agnostic's alike, I have received your bounteous thanks"

This was entirely true, indeed she had been blessed by all the men time and again.

"Now it is time to thank he who he who brought me here in safety and will tomorrow safely return me to my youngest son in Albert. Who among you will say grace. Billy stood up followed by every one of his comrades, and with a sense of solemnity and serenity he blessed the food and those around him.

> *"Thou prepared a table for me in the presence of my enemies:*
> *Thou has anointed my head with oil.*
> *And my cup runneth over*
> *Surely goodness and mercy shall follow me*
> *All the days of my life*
> *And I shall dwell in the house of my God*
> *Forever.'*
> *Amen.*

All those present, card players, Milton men, loners, the declared agnostic prayed together, with their new friend and benefactor Madame Bertois. At the end of thanks they all diligently declared their Amens. Both the food and themselves were blessed.

That evening they were a happy band, once more 'a band of brothers,' full of fellowship. The wine, which it must be said Madame

Bertois rationed to two bottles a person, coupled with some brandy, made for a great party spirit such as they had never had, or ever expected. By ten in the evening, men were going away to their designated places of rest, fully fed, imbibed, at peace with themselves and each other.

Billy sat the entire evening talking with Lucille telling her of his Sally and of the small town of Glossop, at the foot of the Pennines. Together with Jimmy and Vic they conversed till eleven when Madame Bertois declared 'time for bed.'

By ten in the morning they would have to leave this place and go back to their trench, but this day, this one great, blessed day, would never be forgotten. Billy and Jimmy stood by the door and watched Lucille walk across the yard, candle in hand, and go into the barn. She had insisted it should be so, asking if they would meet the next morning at eight. Both of them assured her, promising they would be by the barn door at eight precisely. Together, they locked up the house and were asleep within five minutes.

CHAPTER 25

'I know a place where the wild thyme blows,
Where ox-lips and the nodding violet grows;
Quite over-canopied with luscious woodbine,
With sweet musk-roses and eglantine.'

Midsummer Night's Dream. William Shakespeare

Upon recalling how easily he had drifted towards sleep that night, Jimmy's mind came back into the room. He fell silent, along with all those around him.

Esther, who together with all the others in the group, with the sneaky exception of Michael, if truth be known, was aghast at the revelations made by her son.

"Jimmy do you mean to tell me that you and Billy, along with this lady and all of the other soldiers drank all that alcohol? Pastor I ask you" She turned towards Gideon to gain support for her sense of outrage.

"I ask you what do you think of our Jimmy telling such a tale and with you present as well?"

Her air of shock, of disbelief, sent the group into fits of laughter, which confused the poor women even more.

Gideon put her out of her misery.

"Esther, calm down, there's no harm done, indeed a great wealth of goodness has come from Jimmy today; spiritual goodness. I am overwhelmed, I am so privileged to have been here in this house, with all of you here, listening to your son."

"Jimmy your story has been a wonder to hear, and I know you have more to relate, much more. Let me tell you how I feel about what I have heard so far, how it has revitalised me. It is a profound experience for me to hear just how near to God you were. As for the drinking, well you know my thoughts on alcohol, I have preached on the matter many times.

Yet, I tell you, that that evening reminds me of another time when a group of men met to have a meal. On that occasion they were all invited to partake of wine and, no doubt, as that meal also proceeded a stressful occasion, some of those present may have consumed to much, who knows? On that occasion too the food and wine were blessed before being offered around. I tell you, I conceive of no sin at all in your tale. If Christ himself would offer wine at such a time, then this Madam Bertois can do likewise, without sin.

Yes Jimmy that's right I believe you were all near to God, very near. It must have been an inspired time and irrespective of how inebriated some of you must have gotten yourselves, not one of you must have left the house that next morning without feeling richer in spirit, greater in heart."

"That is probably true Pastor but it is not the end of the story concerning Madame Bertois and ourselves."

Jimmy remembered how he awoke that morning being shaken by Billy at half past seven.

"Water's hot if you want another of those showers."

Jimmy stretched, pulled away his blankets, and rose up from his ground sheet.

"See if you can stop me."

He ran, dressed like Adam before the fall, towards the now famous contraption, to indulge in his ten minutes of luxury. After he had dried himself and was dressed, he walked over to the empty doorway where Billy was standing, staring out at the landscape of France.

"It's a beautiful morning Jimmy."

Billy was feeling pleasured by the warming rays of the newly risen sun. It's only seven o'clock in Glossop. Sally will still be asleep dreaming of the baby. Jimmy, I am going to be a father. I should be there with her, looking after her."

"But you are looking after her."

His friend's reply was steadfast and assured. We are the ones who are stopping the Germans from getting to Glossop, from harming your Sally, our mothers, sisters and all of the others."

"You are becoming quite a philosopher Jimmy."

Billy was comforted by his comrade's philosophising, it had replenished his emotional well being as surely as the previous evening had restored his physical frame. For a moment they were allowed placid thoughts to invade them. Billy was about to break the mutually agreed silence when dear; precious Madam Bertois emerged from out of the barn.

"Good morning gentlemen" she cried out from across the yard. Billy observed that the pitchfork was back in her hand.

"Would you be good enough to accompany me please."

Picking up the wheelbarrow, she began to walk towards the rear of the cowshed, with the two soldiers falling in behind. The little procession continued until it came to a large heap of manure. Here Lucille stopped, picked up the pitchfork, and began to prod. After six or seven stabs the implement hit something metallic. A smile of extreme pleasure swept over her face. She began a little jig, grabbing hold of Jimmy's arm and swinging him round in joyful celebration, whilst crying out in simple triumphal exhortation but two words over and over again.

"My Franc's, my Francs, my precious Francs."

"Gentlemen perhaps you could help me please."

She began to clear around the object exposing it to the light. It was a safe, a small safe about twelve inches square. Jimmy and Billy grasped it together and placed it into the barrow.

Madame Bertois felt truly pleased, she had at last been reunited with her Francs, the Franc's that would pay for Louis's education after the war. Now she stood over the wheelbarrow with a young soldier either side of her. It brought back memories of her two soldier sons. She suddenly realised, never once, not even in a photograph, had she seen Andre or Anton in uniform. They had just gone off waving, full of hope, as they went over the hill, just that final backward glance, then 'darkness and silence.'

It happened exactly as the poet observes. This farm would never see them again. She would probably never find where they lay. If Verdun was like the front before Albert, then it would be an impossible task to find them. Perhaps, after the war, their country would erect a memorial to all those who had died at Verdun, and the names of her sons would appear on it. If that were so, then she would embark upon a further pilgrimage, just to touch the stone whereon their names were carved.

Billy and Jimmy watched their friend as she gazed into the distance. They could sense her grief. Billy guessed what her thoughts were.

"It is alright you know Madame, your sons are safely here, your husband also. They may even be watching over us now."

"This is true"

Yes it was so reflected Lucille. Men carve out the land, their daily toil enriches it, hallows it. Thus they become part of the soil, part of the land and, in return it captures a part of them. When, finally, they pass on the land retains a part of their spirit. What a comfort such a thought was how great a service this young English soldier had bestowed upon her.

"How wise you are for your years Billy"

"That is due to the war Madame, such things as we have seen, felt and undertaken, make you aware of the true value of our beliefs and principals."

"You are a good boy Billy" came the softly spoken reply.

"Your mother and Sally must be so proud of you, their brave son coming to France to face such danger."

"And you Jimmy, what of your family. Do you have a wife or sweetheart?"

In truth, until very recently Jimmy's life had consisted of football and football. Girls, so far, had played a small part in his thoughts, though he had noticed some pretty ones back in Amiens. He had considered that he would have liked to become better aquainted with them sometime in the future, under circumstances different to the ones he presently found surrounding him now.

Jimmy spoke of these musings and of his longing for home. During the space of several minutes this, the most compassionate of ladies.

Lucille Bertois listened with her usual deeply expressive sympathy and genuine interest. As their conversation progressed an idea came to mind.

"You two boys, come, follow me some more"

Her request was filled with an air of conspiracy.

"Let us see what we shall find."

Although numbers of shell craters were dotted around, providing evidence to the war all about the house, very little damage had been visited upon the buildings, save for one of the furthest outlying outhouses which had been transformed into matchwood. The three of them now walked to the rear of the house, passing into a small garden, hedged around with privet. Entering through a picket gate open by their host, the two men were struck dumb by the sight that greeted their war weary eyes. A scene met them so contrasting with the rest of the landscape, that surely it could not be a part of the same country. They had entered an area of about fifty yards square, untouched by a single encounter with a shell.

Spring was expressing herself in all the abundant glory of green, gold, orange and violet, that an English countryside provides in normal times. The ground rose towards them enabling the entire grounds and its gaily-dressed occupants to be viewed in its entirety from where they stood. Billy thought of Wordsworth and his daffodils, noting how exact the poet had been, in his classic description of the massed flowing yellow sentinels of Spring. Here before him came an experience to match that of the long dead Bard. His eyes beheld countless daffodils, as they 'danced' nodding gently, in the breeze that sprung out across from the West. Curling softly, towards the far side, and to the rear was a cobbled pathway leading to a rustic arch, under which an aged wooden bench rested.

Walking along the cobbles, Billy noted with inward silent joy, how the violets sneaked their small delicate heads from around the amber coloured stones scattered through parts of the garden, supported by the moss clinging to their solid hosts. He recalled Lucy Grey, and the pathos within the poet's imagery that had come to him when reading of her in Glossop library all those years ago. The Bluebells leaves were spiking out from their beds though, as yet, the flower heads had not blossomed. Clumps of delicate primrose accompanied the violets, minding him of Easter, his favourite part of the calendar supremely expressing, as it does death and sacrifice, hope and resurrection.

His thoughts were of Sally and her last letter, telling of how she was with child. Oh if only he could be with her now, holding her hand walking the lanes and meadows of Glossop. If only.

Jimmy's thoughts were of his mother. Remembering how delighted she would be, in times past, when, at this time of the year he would bring her home a small poesy of Violets and Primroses, and later a whole armful of Bluebells, how she would smile broadly, kiss him, and place them in vases throughout the house. It was his way of telling his mother how much he loved her without expressing the words. Now he wondered, casting his memory back to the enduring scene. Did she realise his motive in bringing home such masses of flowers? He hoped so, for somehow the words had never once left his lips, but he used to watch her staring at her son's gift, smiling as she did so. Here, in this small French garden, the words came to him at long last.

"I love you mother."

Now, ironically, Madame Bertois spoke, and the spell was broken. This fragile Eden, surrounded by all sides, by the pageant of war, had gifted both of them a moment of comforting reflection, but it was only a moment. They were back in the present knowing how little time they had left of their stay.

"My husband brought all of the Narcissus and Daffodils from Albert one autumn, about twenty years ago. He had gone off on his bicycle, laden with strings of our best onions hanging all around him. He could carry upwards of fifty kilos strung over his neck, on his back, by his waist and attached to the handlebars and pannier of his transportation."

"Once a week, during the middle of August and early September, off he would go for the day, visiting customers that he had got to know, people who admired his crop. He was renowned as one of the greatest onion growers this side of Amiens. It was the tonnes of cattle dung that he spread across the beds that produced such large pungent globes, or so he said."

"Well one day Pierre arrived back home towards dusk having, as usual sold every last one. However he came home with a sack full of bulbs of another kind on his back. He planted them singly all around the garden. What you see today is the ever-increasing mass of their offspring. They are beautiful are they not?"

Billy was minded of the famous biblical comparison.

"I tell you Solomon in all his glory was never arrayed as such as these."

Madame Bertois never replied, but she looked into his eyes and he knew she understood the reference. By now they had come to the area near to the garden seat and Lucille sat down, reliving the countless happy times spent here with her beloved husband, making love in the open air on summer evenings when the children were small. She recalled how Pierre was convinced, that young Louis had been conceived right here by this very seat. What days, what days. Here Pierre had taught Andre and Anton the art of playing Boule, using a makeshift sandpit on the path, Anton had become very adept, often coming home victorious after a day spent in Albert challenging the local rogues, who never seemed to be occupied with any other activity.

Such a lovely town was Albert, with its ancient church, where sat the famous Madonna atop the spire. Now a shell from the Bosch had almost toppled her and she lay sideways, teetering, threatening to come crashing down. Well, hopefully, the Germans would soon be driven back across the

Rhine; peace return to this garden of hers, and the Madonna made secure. Then she would come back to her home and restore the farm. Together, she with Louis, and, hopefully, the girl he chose to marry, would all live here, the farm would, once again, hear the voices of children and the world would go on.

The two soldiers could feel the mood of reflection that that this dear lady was experiencing, and wondered away also in different directions, each submerged in his own thoughts. Their musings were deep, distant, and full of the momentarily transitional nature of this solitary morning in paradise, one which they would all, so easily, each and everyone, to soon be forced to leave, returning to the inferno.

Then they were summoned. The strains of a softly spoken, enchanting voice calling them back to the seat, drew them both towards the lady once again, and this time they knew the spell was about to be dissolved, as if it had all been a dream. It was now about fifteen minutes before nine of the morning and Billy knew he had to return to his responsibilities. The time had come to regroup his section and ensure their appearance and correctness was compatible with the requirements of military regulations.

Madame Bertois was also aware of the situation.

"Now you two, we have to go our separate ways. I to Albert with my Francs back to Louis, you must return to where, once again, life will test your bravery. Tell me will you be able to visit my house at all in the future?"

"Hopefully"

Billy found himself having to explain that several other groups of men would enjoy here uninvited hospitality.

"We have been organised so that we have one days leave in eight."

"Well that being so, I shall bestow this upon you."

Her hand swept under her skirt and, after some investigation, she handed Billy the key to the cellar.

"Let us inform your comrades that this is the secret of all of you. You are all most welcome to any of the contents that this key provides passage to, so swear with all your friends to secrecy, and with God's help you will enjoy such a time again. There is one condition. Billy you will promise me, the table will be laid out correctly, none of those mess tins and you will conduct grace together with a prayer for my two lost boys."

"It will be done as you have decreed Madame Bertois, and I promise you will also be in our grateful prayers together with all your family."

"Then Billy, I leave in your debt. Life will now go on for me better and surer than if we had not met."

"That goes for all of us Madame, not because you simply refreshed our bodies but because you also enhanced our spirits."

"Thank you once again Billy"

Hesitatingly, the heavily laden emotional response brought up the good woman's arms, and she wrapped them round both the young soldiers' shoulders.

"It has been my privilege to know you two, Billy Thomas and Jimmy Jones."

Her tears became a flood, she knew that she was about to lose all composure.

"Now if you would perhaps be so kind, I could be left here for a little while as you return to the house. I shall not be too long my precious boys, I just need to bid my own farewell."

"Of course Madame"

Billy's throat was about to fill with emotion.

"Come on Jimmy, let us get back to the men."

They left together, saddened yet sustained and 'with wondering steps and slow, through Eden, took their solitary way.'

Back at the house, Corporal Joe Gaffney, in charge of the second section of Billy's platoon, was in a heightened state of panic. He rushed over to his fellow NCO and whispered urgently.

"Billy where the hell have you been, We leave in less than an hour."

Billy explained the events as they had occurred leaving, out the matter of the safe. He told his brother NCO what they had agreed and displayed the key. A smile came over Joe, he fairly beamed.

"Well that's alright them, In fact we have sealed it all up and replaced the carpet under the stairs. We've filled some water flasks with brandy but not too much. No one needs to know a thing. You see to your section and I will mine."

"Agreed"

Billy replied conspiratorially, Joe Gaffrey had been handed the carrot that would surely seal the secrets existing below the house for the duration of the war. .

"Just as you say Joe."

With that, short acknowledgement Billy went away with Jimmy, minding him not to mention the safe to anyone.

"Within half an hour all was completed. The house was put ship shape and Bristol fashion as Joe Gaffrey described it, the men sworn to secrecy, brandy filled in most of the flasks, everyone present and correct. At Billy's command they began, reluctantly, to file out of the house. There had been no shelling from the Germans for all the time they had occupied the house, and on the warm sunny day there was none now. God had been good, very good.

As they left they were confronted by Madame Bertois and her wheelbarrow. One by one they thanked her for all her kindness. She asked if they would be good enough to line up by the barrow. As they did so she spoke.

"It is perhaps that we shall never meet again my brave Valois. My dear boys are gone. I can no more bless them and wish them safe passage, but I can do so for you. As you go back to the front, I bless you all, for your mothers I bless you, for your sisters I bless you, for your wives and sweethearts I bless you, for France and for England also I bless you. Come to me one at a time please."

They did so, some sheepishly, some openly willing.

She kissed and hugged them all giving each one of them a Daffodil from her garden.

"Bless you my son, God be with you."

Repeating her phrase to every one of the twenty-four. When she had completed her task she said to them all,

"Go in peace my lovely boys"

Simultaneously with last this blessing, she went to take hold of the handles of the wheelbarrow, but she halted to add.

"Oh don't drink all the brandy in your flasks. Once my husband cut himself badly whilst ploughing the field, he immediately soaked the wound in his best Calvados. The same Calvados you have with you now. It hurt him so much as he poured the liqueur into the wound, that he fainted. But it never became infected. He told me the soil in this part of France is very fertile, full of bacteria. It will poison any wound with gangrene that it torches. The brandy cleans the wound and kills the bacteria. It will hurt but not fester. Mark my words, keep some of your precious liquor for this. One day, it could save your life."

With this she picked up her cargo and set off towards Albert. The last they saw of her was when she went over the top of a small rise, trekking as determined, dogged and straight as any man.

As her form disappeared the platoon turned and, with steadfast tread, marched back, in good order, towards the trenches.

CHAPTER 26

And you good yeomen
Whose limbs were made in England, show us here
The mettle of your pasture

Henry V act iii sc.1.

Jimmy fell into silence, pathos enveloping him. Tears began to fall for the memory of Madame Bertois, or his Joan of Arc as the men of the platoon had come to name her. It was just one day but what a day. Without that time his memories of France would have been totally filled with the horrors of war, with images of death and destruction. As it was, he knew that the horror would be perpetually with him but, because of the kindness of this grand old lady, they would be tempered by the vision of that solitary, beautiful day. God bless her and keep her he thought to himself.

"I have her address"

Jimmy informed his listeners, that he intended to keep in communication with Auntie Joan.

"Perhaps after the war, some of us can return to Madame Bertois home to thank her properly and to remember her kindness."

"Jimmy that is an excellent idea you have there."

Sally would go tomorrow if it were possible. This woman, Madame Bertois had provided for Billy, Jimmy and their friends when they had very little. Her generosity had been selfless. One day she would thank the good woman properly.

Gideon had become absorbed in Jimmy's story and, although his words had been so graphic that he would almost see the lady and her house, it would be marvellous to visit there himself. What he had heard in the last two hours or so was having a profound effect upon him.

Esther had also been completely compelled by her son's words.

She had formed a deep sense of gratitude for the lady, who had given so much to her son

"I would dearly love to meet this Madame Bertois myself" her words came so quickly almost a whisper.

"To have lost so much and to give so much, the woman must be a saint"

"Or an Angel"

The reply came from Sally. She knew of Angels who protected individuals and helped to bring their dreams to fruition.

"I think she must have been an Angel. I sometimes think she was a dream."

"Was her garden really as beautiful as you described Jimmy?"

For Sally the garden was most important she knew how much Billy would have loved being there among the flowers of Spring. It would have been precious to him. Just one thing puzzled her. She knew that Billy and Jimmy shared a mutual interest in birds, yet he had not once spoken of one.

"What of the birds Jimmy, you did not tell of seeing one."

Jimmy's face became very sad. He answered her slowly.

"There were none to tell of Sally. The birds have gone except for the occasional crow. Big black fat devils, eating unspeakable things."

"The birds of spring and summer, the swallow, swift, larks, tits and the finches. The birds that used to give Billy and I such pleasure, as we walked the hedgerows above Glossop when we were young, those birds have left. It might be due to the constant blast of gunfire or that the hedgerows have been devastated. The woodlands just sticks of matchwood in a sea of cratered mud. That the birds have gone is simply another confirmation that the trenches are a place of damnation, and those that dwell within are the damned."

Jimmy was beginning to realise that even now, after all they had heard, none of his audience were comprehending exactly what life was really like in Flanders and Picardy. He spoke to those around him with slow deliberation.

"I will tell you dear people of the trenches, how life is really like for its occupants."

Gideon felt he had to interject. Jimmy seemed far too distressed and exhausted to continue.

"Do not feel you have to proceed further with your revelations Jimmy, not for our account. The memories must be very painful to recall."

"They are Pastor very much, but if I cannot tell of the horror it will stay with me unassuaged forever. Speaking of those that I left behind, and of the conditions in which they live, is my Catharsis. Billy explained that to us in one of his 'Milton' talks. It is the means I use, my way of alleviating the pain, the terrible, emotive, soul destroying pain contained within me.

Yes, Billy told us of Catharsis. You find it in plays, and things of like nature, where great tragedy enacts a significant role. Well, first the tragedy is fully exposed, displayed before the audience or through the pages of a book. This is then explained through a combination of devises. The events and their links are further analysed and the total explanation brings comfort and acceptance to both the characters and the audience. That is what is happening here.

Sally recalled having a similar conversation with Billy years ago on a wet Saturday in the library. She knew what Jimmy was intent on doing.

"Tell us what you wish Jimmy, in the manner that you wish. But do it at your own pace, we have all the time in the world to listen."

"Thank you Sally. I want to tell it all. I really do but sometimes the memory strains my emotions, so bear with me. Dad you used to write to me about this big new garden that the council have given you."

"Yes son"

Michael affirmed his son's query, full of a mixture of pity and pride for the boy.

"They are called allotments. Up in new field there are about a hundred or so, forty yards by thirty."

"And when do you attend to them Dad?"

"Almost everyday, if the weathers right."

"So you won't go up there in the pouring rain then?"

Of course not, you would have to be mad to dig in the rain wouldn't you, getting soaked and full of mud. It would be a pointless task wouldn't it?"

"Just so Dad"

His son had led Michael exactly where he had wished him to go. Now he would paint a picture that they would all understand.

"Yet imagine those allotments with all the pathways clogged up. It has rained non-stop for a week and its raining still. You are ordered to go up there, and walk crossing over the mud yard upon yard of it. Then you are given a shovel together with some of your allotment mates. The rain is incessant, coming down in streaks from the Pennines. Well the order goes out to dig a hole, five maybe six feet deep. While you are digging the water begins to gather at the bottom. It gets everywhere does the water and the mud. Your socks are soaked, your feet wet, soft, and swollen. You get blisters that burst, bleed and fester. The rain never stops. Maybe you find some wood or corrugated sheet that keeps the rain from your head. Every hour you are ordered out of your shelter to keep sentry duty, because some maniac with a shot gun is taking pot-shots at you and perhaps he will sneak up and let loose with a blast, straight at you in the trench."

"Then the really bad news comes. The army has taken over the field for artillery practise and there's shells bursting in front of you, behind you and above you. Then this official maniac says you've to got run towards those guns over this muddy field that's full of holes, and dead bodies protruding from the ground. Oh and by the way there's barbed wire all over the place."

"You accept that you have got to do this and you get ready, but before you do the maniac comes along handing out rucksacks of potatoes, seventy pounds of them. He says you have to run with this lot on your back and by the way, just in case you are interested there are four nests machine guns that are going to rain thousands of bullets down upon you."

"If you can undertake such an experience, time and time again for weeks on end and come home with only a foot missing. If you could do all that and get home and cope with people ignoring you, the very people that you were undergoing this insanity for in the first place ignoring you, then you will know a little of how I feel."

Those gathered round Jimmy were speechless. not knowing what to say. His father never realised that even a fraction of what his son had spoken of, existed there in France. By re-situating the scene up there in his allotment field, it came to him graphic and cruel. How did they put up with it, these young men, most scarcely boys.

"So let me continue now."

So pleaded his son, he would get his wish.

"I need to tell you of how I lost my leg."

Here Jimmy relaxed, and in his dream like stance, went back to the trenches outside Albert, on yet another rain filled day. He recalled the Company Captain coming up the access trench to speak to the Platoon Lieutenant.

The platoon knew something was afoot for the two new officers went into the shelter to speak privately. It was thirty minutes before they reappeared the captain taking his leave with a sharp salute, retreating back to the company command post deep underground about two hundred yards to the rear.

Lieutenant Ted Marford had commanded this platoon, with few casualties, since it first came out over almost a year and a half ago. Now he had been given the order to take out one of his sections to deal with a bunch of German snipers that had been causing considerable casualties of late.

They were holed up, forward from the enemy trenches, in a group of ruined stone buildings. It was deemed that they were too close for artillery to deal with, so a patrol armed with mills bombs and gun cotton, were to eliminate them and demolish the remaining structures.

Ted Marford had decided to take out acting Sergeant Thomas' section.

Since their evening spent in relief at the farmhouse, four days ago, they had bonded into a closely-knit, mutually supportive group of men, with a much-lifted level of morale. He did not know how Thomas had achieved this but he respected his Sergeant's knowledge and bravery.

Once he had stood by the entrance of the section's shelter listening to Thomas discussing, of all things, the works of Milton. Yes, Thomas was an exceptional NCO leading a good section of men. He would take them. He called out for Thomas in order to brief him on the coming event's task. Billy came over and the two of them entered the sections shelter. It was a cramped but secure chamber well shored up and planked out. A number of chairs had been sequestrated somehow, and a small contrived stove had had been constructed in one corner, having a vent which extracted the fumes.

The two men sat down. Billy offered some tea from the stove, which was accepted. It was weak and sweet having no milk, but Marford found it sustaining and gratefully gulped it down.

"Sergeant, we have a job to do this evening. It's those wretched snipers who have been giving us so much trouble, shooting out of those ruined buildings their side of no man's land. H.Q. have given us the task of eliminating them tonight. Or I shall say in the early hours of tomorrow, 01.00 hours to be precise. We shall take out your complete section except for one to be left on sentry duty. The other section and adjacent Platoons, will all be on duty to assist with the return if needed. We shall have four of the troop armed with Mill's bombs and two others will carry gun cotton. The rest will be advancing, bayonets attached. The success of the mission will be judged by the elimination of snipers and the levelling of the ruins. Everything understood?"

"Yes Sir, perfectly, when shall I inform the men?"

"Get them together immediately and decide which of the section will have which task."

"Yes Sir."

Billy saluted and turned to go when the Lieutenant made a further remark.

"Thomas I know you and your section will put up a good show report to me here at 0030."

"Yes Sir"

Billy affirmed the compliment and strode off to address the men.

Vic Greyson was taking up some point with young Albert. The Roberts brothers, together with Terry Gresford and Jimmy, were brewing some tea to go with the bully. Three-card brag was commanding the attention of the rest of the section. Two of the lads were from Hadfield, who Billy had known vaguely in his football days. Joe Keen and Eddy Perkins. Joe was one of the three brothers who had joined the platoon that day in the Chester all those months ago. Now since he had lost both his two elder siblings at Loos he had become quiet, contemplating upon the frailty of life.

Gradually he had come back out of his shell. As the war progressed and almost daily, evidence of men's mortality visited them, he came back into this world of war, accepting the brotherhood of his comrades in the section. Now he looked to protect young Albert as best as he could continually explaining to him how he must be careful, lest his mother mourn a lost son.

His friendship with Eddy Perkins came from the familiarity of home, sharing copies of the Chronicle that had found their way to the front. Both were exactly aware how promising the football careers of Jimmy Jones and Billy Thomas were, having watched all the home matches played by Glossop in the 1913-1914 season. Now, in truth, all they wished for was the successful completion of the coming battle that would secure the victory, which would surely allow them to go home.

Both were fit, tall, strong and enthusiastic. Kings men the rest called them. They always toasted the King when first touching alcohol. The rest of the card school was made up of, Dickey Cross who was extremely prone to dysentery and expressed the most putrid air on a regular basis. It was said that if it was bottled it could be used to keep the Bunsen burner going.

The final pair sat around the table, were constant friends who looked after each other, always keeping sentry duty together. Fred Emsley was from Manchester, and Anthony Rawlings an apprentice Green Keeper for Lancashire Cricket Club. He had walked from Cheadle to Chester, in a single day, in order to join the regiment. His elder brother was a regular, who had left for France by the middle of August 1914, and had been severely wounded at the first battle of Ypres. He was back home now less an arm and with half a face. Anthony's mother wrote three times a week never ceasing to worry over her youngest son.

A section of thirteen men diverse by nature, by interest and by background, but securely welded together, each knowing that one day, he might need the courage and companionship of the men next to him. A sense of surety filled this section, breeding a mutual, respectful, sense of being, a team where each knew his place in the line, his part in the plan and his duty to the rest.

Billy decided that young Albert should remain behind on sentry duty, he explained to the young soldier that he would be as much a part of the foray as any of the others. Albert would have to ensure that hot tea was ready for their return, and he had to keep constant vigil whilst awaiting the completion of the mission.

The sense of importance and responsibility, that he had assured Albert, coming night's tasks comprised, assuaged the disappointment that the youth felt in not going over into no man's land.

Soon daylight left the trenches. That evening, darkness combined with a damp misty envelope of air that descended upon the unfortunate tenants of the trench. Billy was grateful for it. If the mist continued to keep its presence it would provide some cover for the section. Perhaps they would successfully surprise their target, deal with the enemy, and all safety return to their trench.

00:30 came and Lieutenant Marford with blackened face approached the take off point. The mist had not lifted which pleased everyone. Jimmy and Vic Grayson had responsibilities for the gun cotton and its charges. Perkins and Rawlings were armed with the mills bombs. All were ready for the off anticipating having a successful exploit.

"Give the Hun some of what we've been getting"

Ted Marford summed up the sentiments of many of the men.

"Right men. Follow me over, keep behind me. Whose got the cutters?"

The Roberts brothers came forward, they also possessed sets of mills bombs

"Right then you two, after me. Then the other mill's bombers followed by the rest. The gun cotton men were to the rear. Sergeant Thomas you are last. Keep the men up in close order."

"Yes Sir."

"Right men" he repeated again. "No more talking, no sounds communicate by signals."

The Lieutenant did not wait for a reply but went up the trench ladder, followed in pairs by the rest of the platoon.

Billy, like many of the others silently prayed to himself before he began his climb.

'In life, in death o Lord,
Abide with me.'

Then he was up and over the top of the trench. They had a distance of about three hundred yards to cover. The men snaked across the lunar landscape following on the footsteps of the Lieutenant. They had covered half the distance when the officer stopped. He was confronted by barbed wire. He beckoned to the Roberts brothers who began their work. Billy could clearly hear each snip of the cutters as, one by one, the strands were cut. He thought at any moment that the sound would alert the sniper nest, but no shots came and soon the path had been cleared and the column progressed.

They were now about fifty yards from the ruins, when the Lieutenant again came to a halt. He gestured for the column to come round in line abreast. The ground was moist but not sodden, having had little shelling and no armies going back and forth. In terms of the Western front, it was almost virgin territory. Billy estimated that if they ran, it would take them about six seconds to traverse the distance to the first building. Little enough time to catch the enemy by surprise.

Suddenly the Lieutenant let out a yell,

"Charge"

He was crying out at he top of his voice.

"Get at them men"

His urging worked, they were all running towards the ruins as fast as they could.

Surprise was almost total. Over went the mills bombs, and the Platoon fell flat. A couple of seconds later and a number of explosions blasted the other side of the walls. Then all was mayhem. The walls were reached without a shot being fired. Three Germans were waiting on the ground one was grasping a stump above the knee where a mills bomb had blown it off. The lieutenant fired his pistol, and he was dispatched, two bayonets finished the others.

Now all the anticipation and expectancy came to fruition. The defeated Germans were in full flight except for two who were holding their hands high crying 'Kamerad.'

Their rifles had been thrown infront of them. The Roberts brothers had flung themselves on the ground and displayed what good shots they were. One downed two retreating Germans, the other three. Very few got back to their own lines.

"Well that's that"

The lieutenant was very pleased.

"Eight enemy killed, two prisoners and no casualties on our side so far."

A shot rang out. One of the prisoners had picked up his weapon and fired. Immediately the Roberts brothers executed them both.

The Lieutenant turned towards Billy. A small round red hole had appeared in his forehead. The world was black; he never felt the impact of the ground as he came crushing down upon it. Life had left him instantaneously. Billy knew he was dead. It was now his responsibility to get his men back safely. He was determined to do so. He barked out his orders.

"Right men, get those charges laid as quick as you can. All hell is about to break out."

The men were disciplined. They knew their officer was dead, accepted it, and without question began to take orders from Billy.

A flare lit up the entire sky. Fortunately it could not penetrate the mist so they were still relatively safe for the moment, though it did not stop the enemy firing blind towards the ruins. Grayson shouted out the charges were set. It was time to leave. Billy asked Vic to lead the return. He needed no further encouragement and was off dashing into the mist. Quick as startled rabbits, over and away they went.

The unfortunate Rawlings was not to make it. A stray bullet hit him in the back of the head. It exploded showering Billy with brains. Again, Billy did not need to check closely. He could see Rawlings was dead. Very little was left above the neck and although the body was twitching he knew it was simply nerves.

Billy mounted the wall and was scampering, bent low, running carefully back towards the trench three hundred yards distant, possibly forty-five seconds from safety. He ran like the wind, like a winger with a ball ready to cross over to the enemies' goal. Then it happened. Shells began to burst around them. One came down infront of him. He saw one body lifted right into the air above twenty yards high. Then he heard the screams and ran into a newly created crater. He saw one of his men in his death throws holding his exposed blackened intestines before him. As he approached, the man's eyes glazed over, closing as he died. The other man was screaming holding a shattered foot. It was Jimmy.

Immediately he dropped his rifle, picked up his friend and slung him over his shoulder, then grabbing his gun again he was off once more. He was running with his friend who was crying out to the heavens. It seemed an age but it was less than a minute before he gained the refuge of the trench. As he did so the ruin behind him erupted. What he did not know was that the Germans had countered attack. Over one hundred died when the site went up. It was a good result for the British.

Billy however had no time to waste.

"Stretchers, quickly men, stretchers. Come on, hurry up."

Then he remembered the advice of Madame Bertois. He tied a tourniquet to Jimmy's leg, stopping the flow of blood. Opening his flask he flooded the massive wound, displaying its shattered bone, projecting through the shredded skin. He used the entire flask's contents of Calvados. As Madame Bertois had warned, Jimmy was, thankfully, unconscious. The bearers were now with him. They gave the new unconscious man a shot of morphine and left, hurrying their charge towards the nearest field hospital. Jimmy would be unconscious for two days before he would awake to a life with one-foot. However, no festering, no gangrene would take hold, the Calvados would see to that. The wound would heal quickly.

Meanwhile Billy took stock. He thought he had lost three men, plus his Lieutenant and one wounded, Jimmy. That was a correct summary. The Company Captain met him as he was seeing Jimmy being stretchered off. He saluted.

"Mission accomplished Sir, four dead and one wounded I believe Lieutenant Manford died from a single shot to the head. At least eight Germans were killed Sir, and the target was destroyed."

"Very good, sergeant"

The reply came from an extremely happy Company Commander.

"Get something to drink, Sergeant, rest and report to Company HQ at 0800. Well done Sergeant, very well done indeed."

With that Billy went for a drink of tea, laced with the life saving brandy. He had mixed emotions. His thoughts were with Jimmy and his dead colleagues. Even so he slept well that night.

Jimmy's thoughts came back into the room. His story was told.

"As you know I spent six weeks in the hospital. They were amazed how quickly I recovered. It was the Brandy of course. Whilst in hospital Billy and I wrote to each other. I have his letters here if you would like to read them Sally. I shall leave them with you."

"Thank you Jimmy I should like that."

Esther could see how tired her son was. It was getting late she should get him home.

"Well Jimmy time for home I think"

Jimmy agreed. He did feel tired. The telling of his story had taken a lot out of him.

"Perhaps you could come again soon"

Gladys was so pleased to have heard of her son. She was in Jimmy's debt.

"I shall see you Sunday no doubt Mrs. Thomas."

"Yes you shall Jimmy."

Gideon thought one thing further was required.

"Before you go, I think we should have a prayer for all those that were a part of Jimmy's story. I don't know how long this war is going to last, or how many more have got to die before the powers decide that enough is enough. It seems to me that Jimmy and all of his friends are powerless victims, facing the most inhumane conditions. The same could be said of other in the enemy ranks. They are victims also, carrying out the orders of their officers and generals. So let us pray for all of them, and their families and ourselves. Let us pray that this war ends soon."

And they prayed. For a time in silence each with their own thoughts. Jimmy grateful to be home, yet fearful for his friends back in the trenches of France. Esther and Michael prayed for their son, thankful that he was now safe, yet concerned for his future. Gladys could only think of her son, a brave leader of men. Yet he was vulnerable and defenceless against such terrible weapons, living in the most dreadful of circumstances.

Sally prayed that her baby inside her, would one day see its father in happier times. That Billy would come home safely to her and she would once again feel his warmth, give him her love, and together be a family. She prayed that God would protect him and all those who looked to him for courage and leadership.

Gideon felt the holiness of the moment. It was only after two minutes or so of silence that he interjected. He gathered all the diverse meditations and prayers of those around him in the room to a single expression. His words provided comfort and assurance. They brought peace upon the small house and the people within. He finally blessed them and commended them to God. As Billy would have said, the revelation that Jimmy had emitted through the telling of his story had brought a catharsis to all those who had heard them he, included.

As they were departing Jimmy warned Sally that Billy's letters were detailed and graphic. She should prepare herself before she read them. Thus all the visitors departed, each with their own thoughts. The war had come to Talbot Street that day, touching each and everyone of them. Their energies were drained. Departing into the glooming day they went to their beds that night, little realising what the next day, the first of July 1916, would bring.

CHAPTER 27

'A place called Golgotha.'

Matthew ch. 27 v 33

It was in the quiet of her bedroom, with the fruit of her Billy's seed thriving within her, that Sally took hold of the envelopes that Jimmy had left behind. She was filled with trepidation, knowing that she was about to witness an aspect of Billy's character that she had never seen before. How did men communicate with one another? How did men conduct their conversations when, day after day, they lived and breathed their lives so closely bound together?

She suspected that the comradeship of these two men had grown so close that every intonation of their desires and aspirations must, sooner or later, have been brought into their conversation. Taking up a single letter, she used it as a fan, trying to alleviate the uncomfortable warmth that had been brought on by the anticipation of what its contents may contain.

Sally remembered just how jealous she was when reading the letter from Billy about the wretch who had attempted to steal a kiss from lips that were not hers to touch. She recalled how, for an instant, the thought of pulling the 'no good's' stringy locks had been deeply appealing. Smiling, she knew that nothing of this kind was encased in any of these communications. Sometimes her total and absolute love for her blessed boy led her to think the silliest things.

Sliding out the pages from the first epistle that came to her, she little realised the shock that it would bring to her. However, the reading was to become a traumatic encounter for a completely different reason than any she had composed. Opening the folds of the leaves her eyes cast down upon the first sheet. Her heart was beating furiously as she began to read, its pace would increase rapidly as she progressed. For now the familiar hand welcomed her, a most blessed experience.

Somewhere in France. 10th June 1916.

Well Jimmy, I did not realise how much I had relied upon your comradeship. Without my fellow Glossopian to confide in, time passes so strenuously. I find myself in conversation with Vic Grayson quite a lot these days. He turns out to be a very interesting bloke, travelled far and wide he has.

We found ourselves on sentry duty together. You know two hours on, two off, so we got to talking. Once he found we had much in common Vic opened up. He remembered that we had a mutual acquaintance. Do you remember me telling of Robert Blatchford and the Clarion Van? I was eleven at the time or thereabouts. It was he who introduced me to reading so, indirectly, bringing me to Sally.

It had been almost two years since I had listened to Vic rallying so many of us to the colours. It intrigued me to discover what his past consisted of, and how he came to be come a replacement in our section. It turned out to be a most interesting tale.

Vic was born in Liverpool and got his education through the Unitarian Church. They soon recognised that he had a talent for public speaking so they asked if he would train for the Ministry. However, Vic had other ideas. He has seen so much poverty and has heard people speaking out against it, that he decides to become a Socialist preacher.

Soon he begins to get a name for himself, and is invited to stand as an Independent Labour Candidate in the Colne Valley. All the established Labourites wanted him to step down in favour of the Liberal but Vic, he refuses. Many independents came to rally for him, including Robert Blatchford and his Clarionettes. Do you know? against all the odds, he won.

Initially he is best pleased, he has defeated all opposition whilst campaigning as a true Socialist Candidate. Yet Parliament is a great disappointment to him. One night when we were on watch he told me how the system wore him down.

"When I got to Parliament the Labourites would not talk to me, some Liberals did, but no Labour people. It's a funny place is Parliament talk, talk, but no doing, not for the working classes anyhow. Parliament? Its all about keeping us under, under the thumb, I tell you, a hundred like me could have been there for fifty years and nothing would have been done, not for the likes of us."

"It's the likes of them whose factories churn out the guns, bombs, bullets and shells that have laws passed for their benefit. Laws that imprison strikers and those who champion workers rights."

I tell you Jimmy he spoke to me that night like a man possessed, possessed with a dream. If we both survive the war, then I would like to work with him and others of like minds. Together we can build this Jerusalem upon which so much is spoken.

Mind you I should like Vic to come back into the Party fold for it is through the bedrock of the movement that the battle shall be fought and won. Still, the Labour Party would be a poorer place without Victor Grayson in its ranks.

Vic's also got a marvellous sense of humour, working class humour he calls it. He knows so many songs. One went something like this.

'I am a man (a very fat man)
And I water the workers beer
What care I, If it makes' em cry

Or makes' em awfully queer
I am a man (a very fat man)
And I waters the workers beer.'

I tell you what, he had the whole section singing it, broke the tension, and something needed to. You see Jimmy, my good friend, you were not the only casualty that night of the raid. Besides losing Lieutenant Marford, we had three other dead. Dickey Cross was blown right up in the air by the same shell that got your foot. Anthony Rawlings copped it before we even started back, and Fred Emsley is missing. You know what that means.

Things have gotten very bad. Everyone is tired, endless shelling, repairing trenches, and expanding them. Something is afoot, being prepared for. Then came the most dreadful episode of this war that I have witnessed so far. We had a Court Marshall.

One morning there was an unannounced inspection by the Company Captain. He caught two young lads of 'B' section fast asleep. Just kids they were, I think they must have been younger than Albert. Well the Captain kicks up a great fuss, hauls them up before the Colonel. The up shot was No.1 field punishment for both, to be followed by the firing squad.

Jimmy you and I have seen a lot, been through a lot, but I tell you nothing prepared me for this. After the lads had been given their trial they were marched out about one hundred yards behind the front line. There they were crucified, I tell you they were crucified. Two sets of the stakes were driven into the ground to which each lad tied his arms outstretched. It was pitiful to see. They were crying asking for mercy, sobbing, their arms outstretched, they were I am telling you, pleading to be let go.

The Captain, with quivering voice, read out their sentence, to stay there tied with arms out stretched till seven hundred hours when they would be shot in front of the whole company. Two lads I tell you, not yet eighteen. The Captain addresses us all, saying that men who went to sleep on sentry duty put us all in danger from a surprise attack. We could all be killed in our trenches, he said, so an example had to be made. No one was to approach the pair under any circumstances no matter how much they pleaded. I think it was the cruellest thing I have ever witnessed.

That night hardly anyone slept. Gerry shells were coming over all the time but you could still hear the cries of those two lads. Then at about midnight, all the section not on watch came up to me, together with most of the others in the platoon. Terry Gresford spoke up for them.

"Sergeant, we've got to talking. It was wrong what those two lads did but, they don't deserve to have this do they? It ain't right, is it Sergeant, it ain't right?"

I had to think of my position what with discipline and that. But then I argued with myself there is something higher than discipline, it is conscience.

I replied to the questioning Welshman in the only way that I could. "No Gresford, I do not think it right but there is little we can do for them except pray that God will keep them"

Terry Gresford, understood. He accepted what I was saying, but he wished to pursue the matter further.

"Why, if we cannot tell them that we are praying for them Sergeant, cannot we show them?"

Wrexham George furthered the argument.

"It could be a comfort for them out there, crucified, with shells crashing all around then. Listen to them wailing, it's worse than the sound of the whiz–bangs."

I tied my hardest to explain.

"We can't tell them Gresford, It is against expressly issued orders. HQ would do the same to us"

The men looked down at the muddy ground, murmuring to themselves. I was worried that someone might do something silly. Then I had an idea.

"Men, we are going to concoct a service loud enough for the lads to hear, all in agreement?"

The men enthused at the idea, once again Gresford spoke up for them.

"You lead us Billy."

Victor calmly entered into the debate, with a few quietly spoken words that were to direct events.

"It has to be you Billy. You know what to do."

Well Jimmy, there we were twenty men or so. Hardened soldiers in the main, but more than one stream of tears fell that night. We sang at the top of our voices from the 23rd Psalm.

> *Yea thou I walk through the valley of the shadow*
> *Of death. I shall fear no evil*
> *Thy and staff they comfort me.*

Then I prayed aloud for all of us in the trench. At the end, I asked God to protect each man in turn, calling on those present to shout out their name. In an orderly and proud manner we all sounded out our names in full. No rank or military number just Christian and family names. Those on sentry duty also uttered for themselves. Then we turned away from the front and facing the two young sufferers Corporal Gaffrey shouted out the names of the two lads on their behalf. We felt both triumphant and deeply saddened at the same time.

The service ended with the Lords Prayer, which we recited loud and slowly. As it drew to an end, I turned around realising our Company Captain was with us, also speaking the words. It occurred to me he had been there all along. Our service came to a close with Wrexham George singing in his finest tenor tones from 'The Old Rugged Cross.'

'On a hill far away, stood an old rugged cross
The emblem of suffering and shame.'

It was most appropriate, but merely the annunciation of what was to follow, for then it happened.

Jimmy you have heard of the Angel of Mons, the mists of Gallipoli that took up the Sandringham troop to the realms of glory? Well none of them meet with what our eyes beheld. The 'Amen' was being said when a shell came over and lit the horizon behind those two lads. It may have been a trick of the light, with a column of earth being lifted skyward, but as we looked out at those pathetic pair of crosses, the image of a third appeared between then. Just for a second or two it was there, I swear so and shall do so till my dying day. Nor was it merely etched in my mind, though the vision had vanished as quickly as it came upon us.

The men just looked at each other full of amazement, wordless. We all saw it, this third cross. Later, some said they saw the image of a third man. Who knows? I don't think I did, but this I do know. That night I gained witness to something far above and beyond my understanding.

As the light from the shell faded I looked upon the face of our Captain, it was ashen grey with staring mouth and eyes agape. Upon noticing my gaze he came back into this world. Yet all who looked upon him knew that he was a lost man. He had played a large part in the torture of two innocent souls, and in so doing, he saw his own soul condemned. There was little time to rectify matters, for that he needed composure, which he readily obtained.

"As you were Sergeant, good service, a fine way to get round orders I must say. Look I'm going back to battalion HQ. See to things around here will you?"

Away he went, and here I was faced with a Platoon of men all of whom, like myself and the Captain, had been touched by something beyond their understanding.

Gresford came up to me, speaking in a voice full of trembling, stuttering out the words.

"Billy none of us can sleep right now, what with all that's happened. We want to keep a vigil for the two lads, to share the pain, so to speak. I agreed, sleep would not visit me that night either, I would keep a vigil also. That is how it was Jimmy, all through that night we kept awake, of our own volition. At 0430 dawn began to streak over the sky. As the first splashes of crimson and amber enticed the new day to arrive a voice began to sing from I know not where. Quickly we all enjoined.

'Swift to its close ebb out life's little day;
Earth's joys grow dim, its glories pass away;
Change and decay in all around I see:
Oh thou changest not, abide with me!'

Then it was that tiredness overtook us all. Sleep came if only for a hour. Suddenly at 06.00, just before 'stand to' our Captain awakened me.

"Thomas"

His voice full of electrified excitement.

"I've been to HQ and argued the case for the two lads. Its been agreed. Out there for one night is punishment enough. At 07.00 we can release them, they can return to their section admonished but intact. That suit you and the men?"

Well Jimmy I was much surprised I can tell you. I know just how set in their ways is HQ. The Captain must have done a good job. With a formal salute I thanked my superior, and told him he would have the everlasting respect and gratitude of both the men, and myself. I asked permission to be dismissed so that I could go and inform them. He readily agreed and off I went.

They were all together silent, each man deep in his own thoughts. I blurted out the news to them, in the hope of bringing some cheer to them. To my consternation it met with little reaction. I could not understand it. I turned to Gresford who was just staring blankly, his eyes fixed upon a spot in the trench.

"What's the matter now, Private"

"See for yourself Sergeant."

His reply came with a gesture, he was pointing towards the place where the two lads were staked out.

Peering over the reredos it struck me instantaneously. The crosses were gone, so were the lads.

"God preserve us"

The involuntary cry just came out. Taking a breath, the realisation dawned upon me. A shell had got them in the night, obliterating both the lads and their devises of torture. The belated reprieve had come to late, much to late.

Full of trepidation, myself and a couple of the lads went over to the sight. No risk now of breaking regulations, the two lads would not hear us now however much we shouted their names. They were numbered with the dead. The place where the stakes had been struck was now the sight of a crater. All that remained was match wood and small globules of human remains, together with shattered shards of bone.

As reverently as possible we gathered up what was left of these two poor boys. We could not identify what belonged to whom so we placed the decimated parts in a new, relatively clean, sandbag. It was not even half full when we closed it up.

I reported the affair to the Captain, he went from ash grey to ash white, all colour left his face.

"We should bury them sir."

I had stated the obvious, but it was to a man who could no longer hear. It took some time before he made reply.

"Thomas would you be so good? You see what becomes of such as this, This damned, damnable war, in which, as we become covered in its filth, in turn damns us. A home fit for heroes indeed, what must I have been thinking of. Thomas, I tell you we are damned, all of us, do you hear, damned. Yes please do, go and intern the fruits that have brought upon me, my eternal damnation."

The request came from a man no longer in control of himself, let alone a company.

I pitied him at that moment. He was a good man, I know, one that the war had turned into a monster, at least in his mind. None of us here in this hell were completely in control of ourselves, or others and certainly not events. I decided to do what was necessary.

"Sir, leave it to me. I know you have had no rest these last few days. I will ensure you that all that is required to be done, will be done."

"Thank you Thomas, I am deeply in your debt."

He paused, he was pitiful to behold. Something occurred to him. He opened the draw to the small secretaire that was in the shelter, and from it he took a small sheet of paper.

"Thomas, this instruction from the war office proves that what I did was in accordance with military regulations. You have it, should something happen to me, then I leave it to you to display as evidence to the depths of depravity that we have all sunk to. Those of us who have taken part in this disgusting conflict."

"Certainly sir"

I made that statement little knowing that the pair of us would never speak again. Not in this world at least. I felt as if I should have said more than two mere words of departure, but, in truth, nothing came to mind that would have been adequate.

The concentrated shelling of that night had produced casualties all along the line. The Padres were all overwhelmed. No one could be spared. To me, not for the first time, was given the task of providing those two lads their last words of commendation to God. I hope I did well in my task. I hope so.

Later the next night a single shot rang out near the trench, echoing through the gloom. Upon inspection we found our Captain. He had put a bullet through his brain.

It fell to me to report to HQ. The links in the chain of command had now been twice broken, and having no replacement yet for our lost Lieutenant, a subaltern from an adjacent Platoon ordered me to report the death, which I duly did. The lads and I had agreed not to mention the self-inflicted death. No good would come from that. So I reported that he was killed in the execution of his duty whilst inspecting the trenches at night. Near enough to the truth I suppose. Least ways I feel no guilt at having reported so.

We buried the Captain next to the two boys. A Padre conducting affairs this time. We explained that no one was available to bury the boys, save ourselves, so he blessed them and consecrated their earth, together with that which contained the remains of the Captain.

Well Jimmy, there they rest, the three of them together, and I'm not to make judgement. That will be executed by the highest of all commands. I am minded of Thomas Grey.

> *'There they alike, in dreadful hope repose.*
> *The bosom of their fathers and their God.'*

Will write again soon,
Billy.

P.S. I enclose the sheet of paper that the Captain gave me.

The last word read, Sally sat still her hand, instinctively, covering her unborn child. The War Ministry instruction was open in front of her. It displayed a young man upon a makeshift cross, exposed to the elements. It was later to prove a most important document.

She was never to read any of the other letters that her Billy had written to her friend. They came back into her possession later to be read by another. But that was a time far in the future.

For now Sally was tired. She heard the clock strike midnight so beginning the first day of July.

CHAPTER 28

Time is the strong destroyer
Of much that heaven sends,
And cherished treasures daily
Draw to their destined ends;
But youth shall live forever
In the trusty grip of friends.

William Noel Hodgson.
Died 1ˢᵗ July 1916. The Somme.

Preparations for the great Somme offensive were progressing with all expedition. It would come, in one way or another, to involve every member of the British armed forces massing in this small corner of Northern France that was the Somme and Picardy. In many places along the Western Front there was little more than thirty miles of open countryside to the Channel. This allowed for effective lines of communication and supply from England, but seen on a map such short distances displayed how vulnerable was the alliance to a German advance on the Channel ports themselves.

It was plainly evident, that a single determined effort by the Germans could split the Allies and dispatch the British back to their homeland. As Gallipoli had so starkly revealed, once expelled from the soil of France, there would be little hope of establishing a new seaborne front elsewhere. If the Germans could wheel the British round it would. In turn mean the defeat of the French.

At Verdun the French were being bled white as they had been for months. The cry fashioned by Marshall Petain 'On ne passé pas' was echoed by every French citizen in spite of the manner and number in which the dearest and best sons of France were being sacrificed. A British assault in great force upon the Somme would help to relieve the hard-pressed garrison at Verdun.

Success would also greatly extend the area occupied by the Allies, and exhaust the Germans to the point where they would first buckle then implode, finally retreating back beyond the Rhine. They would then sue for peace on terms favourable to the Allies, sign an armistice and lose the war.

Such was the vision that had occupied the Generals who gathered their maps together, drawing arrows displaying expected gains and objectives. Hundreds of thousands of British soldiers would leave their stinking muddied trenches and walk over to the occupy the German fortifications. The greatest artillery barrage in history would ensure that scarcely a single, German soldier would survive in their front line trenches.

A walk in the park, an orderly stroll over no-mans-land to take over the German positions. All in a day's work for the disciplined, well trained, British infantrymen, Kitcheners finest hand picked volunteers now possessing the benefit of eighteen months intensive training would become the pride of Britain and the glory of the World. They were fit, fashioned to absolute obedience, knowledgeable on tactics, on being conditioned to all the modern manifestations of battle.

Many of them had become fine shots, able to shoot accurately over two hundred yards at fifteen rounds per minute.

The Germans were going to get their shock of a lifetime. By autumn the Germans would be finished and back in their homeland, made barren by deprivation and the loss of a generation of its sons. So ran the plan.

There were those who secretly questioned both the tactics and the expected outcome. They were patriotic, full of desire to get to grips with the Germans though, for their part, they did not believe that the fight was going to be an easy one, as if it were a mere exercise upon Salisbury plain.

Captain William Neville of the 8th East Surreys was one such officer commanding a company of four platoons. He was coming back from leave returning to his lines opposite of Montauban in readiness for the attack. He had devised a novel idea to encourage his men who were virgins as far as battle experience was concerned.

Each of his four leading platoons was to be presented with a football and he would throw down a challenge. A prize would be offered to the first successful platoon to dribble their ball all the way over to the enemy trench. He knew how much his men loved the game. Almost all of them played, many being quite proficient, some even full time professionals. On more than one occasion he had witnessed heated arguments over the relative merits of two certain teams and the undoubted outcome of any future contest between them.

It was their enthusiasm for the game that impressed him so. Therefore, he had concluded, the way to inspire them in the forthcoming battle was to compare the contest between his troops and the enemy to a football match. A single problem remained; he had only managed to purchase three balls. Another had to be found somewhere.

It was June 20th, that morning he had left British Head Quarters at Montreuil and using a field ambulance, one of many moving towards the front, he had reached Albert, the town of the precariously balanced , falling Madonna, just two miles or so from the front. Tomorrow he would head south towards the village of Bray, then onto his company billeted west of Montauban.

He had found a room for the night to the west of the town, its furthest point from the front. The town was heavy with soldiers, Scots in their kilts, Irish flaunting their cockades, Welshmen marching by, singing

381

'Men of Harlech' as they did at Rourke's Drift. He came to hear accents from all over the British Isles, Cockney, Yorkshire, Lancashire, and Geordies all mingling together enjoying the calm before the storm.

Having found lodgings in this unfortunate place, Neville went strolling around the town. Soon the enthused sound coming from a large crowd attracted him. A well-organised game of football was in progress between a team in claret and white strip and one in red and green. It was even being refereed professionally by a uniformed official. He decided to enquire.

"What's the score?"

"Nil, nil."

"Who's playing?"

A man sporting the kilted uniform of a member of the immortal 51st replied.

"Canna ye no see? It's the great Hearts of Midlothian playing a Sassanach team."

He turned his attention back to the game.

"Go on there Jimmy Boyd, go on my son, now cross over to Ellis that's me boy. Now give it to Currie that's me lad shoot, go on shoot, go on, go on, that's it laddie shoot, goal! What a goal."

He turned to his no less animated friend to accept his analysis of both the player and the goal.

"Didna I tell ee didna I. What a canny wee player that Duncan Currie is. What a team. The best in all of Scotland, probably the World, Didna I tell ye. We never gets us beat. What a goal, what a goal."

Another man spoke up, this time speaking in a Northern accent. Although somewhat annoyed by the dismissive tone of the Scot, he never the less gave Captain Neville the rest of his required information.

"Watch what you're saying Jock that's the Cheshires that you are speaking of. Billy Thomas and his team. They will take some beating."

"And how long have they been playing?"

"Och, sure nay more than these past fifteen minutes."

"Thank you."

"Nay bother laddie."

Captain Neville, being late of a Public School, of course, played Rugby. In spite of this he watched enthralled for over an hour as the game progressed.

For the rest of the first half Hearts besieged the Cheshire's goalmouth. However the English defended as surely as their square did at Waterloo, with courage, dexterity and skill. Towards the end of the first period in one of their few breakouts, Billy Thomas deftly confused the right half , repeated the same confusion upon the centre, beat the famous Johnny Wilson, and slipped the ball to Bill Carney. Something inspired the lad that day, for he pivoted whilst still gaining complete control over the ball and, to the annoyance of every single Scot, Hearts supporter or not, simply lobbed the projectile over the head of the advancing keeper to place it perfectly between the posts. One apiece, just as the halftime whistle went.

The second half was even more intense than the first. Soon after the re-start Billy was given a long ball from Evans, which landed perfectly for him. He zigzagged round two defenders who were left bemused by his ball skills. As the unfortunate keeper advanced upon him, it was a matter of little difficulty to go round the stranded guardian and almost walk the ball into the goal.

Now it was the turn of the descendants of the vanquished of Bannock Burn to celebrate. Two one advantage to the English. The sons of Robert The Bruce would have to regroup. They duly did so. There emerged from out of their ranks two players who took their southern brothers to the sword over the next fifteen minutes. Norman Findlay and James Boyd, two terrifying charging Scots, passed back and forth to each other in rapid succession until they arrived at their opponent's penalty area. Boyd shot, the English keeper parried before the imaginative Findlay teased the keeper mercilessly back and forth until he simply placed the ball between his legs.

Neither was this the end of the unfortunate tormented Englishman. The feat was repeated just a few minutes later only this time the final humiliation was executed by Boyd. The Hearts players were ecstatic, enthusiastically shaking the hand of the victorious Scot who had so easily scored. The game was now theirs to be won.

Yet, as with most games of football, there was a further twist to be unveiled. It came once more in the guise of the Glossopian pair. It gave witness to the last time that a ball from the feet of Billy Thomas would rise in the air to bend away from the outstretched arm of a bemused goalkeeper, despairingly defeating the reach of his outstretched arm. Disbelievingly the victim turned as the ball sailed past to see it become the goal that equalled the scores. As the ball was picked up the final whistle went and the contest, so sportingly undertaken, came to its end.

The final score was three apiece which Neville, who had become ever more immersed in the game as it progressed, considered to be a fair result. Hearts were by far the best team, being a regular professional outfit that had been together for several seasons. The Cheshires on the other hand were mostly amateurs with a sprinkling of real stars. Billy Thomas, that young Bill Carney and the demon tackler Evans, put up quite a show.

The troops supporting both sides were generally satisfied.

"Ay a good match. That Thomas he's a real canny player."

"True enough Jock, another day and time he could have been playing for England. It was a good game, looks like the next one is going to be against Fritzy though, what do you reckon?"

"Weel English, no doot, and surely, we shall batter him between us."

"Reckon we shall at that Jock, reckon we shall."

With that the pair shook hands and went their separate ways. Yes, considered Neville, a good result, an even score and men brought together who would come to even up the score with the Germans. He wondered, 'what was the chance of getting his fourth ball from this lot?' He would go and ask.

As he walked away he noted a uniformed man with a large sketchpad in his hands. He walked over to the man to discover that he had drawn many of the individuals of the match in various attitudes of play. These drawings were really very good and he told the man so. Upon inquiring his name he was told that it was 'John Singer Sergeant'. Later these individual sketches would provide the background for one of his most important works 'Gassed'.

Billy was getting washed, together with the rest of the two teams, in a large improvised pool set up inside an Army mess tent erected by the Royal Engineers. Both teams were together, their rivalry having ended on the playing field. He and Duncan Currie were exchanging tales of past experiences, of their triumphs and defeats, their goals and near misses. For a while the war did not exist. Football is like that. Once a conversation gets started it tends to develop with such intensity that all other aspects of life are consumed by it.

Duncan was relating how the entire first team volunteered in 1914 just as Billy and many of his Glossopian team-mates had done. The war had already claimed the lives of two of his friends who played alongside him in their colours of deep burgundy and white. His great friend, Jimmy Speedie, a particularly promising player, had fallen at the battle of Loos, whilst poor Tom Gracie had succumbed to his wounds. At least poor Tom had made it back to Scotland before he died and was able to be buried by friends amongst familiar glens and mountains. Poor Jimmy, well he was never found. He was in an unmarked grave somewhere in Flanders.

Listening to the philosophical words of Duncan Currie led Billy to realise just how many footballers were here in France, defending her shores against the German Kaiser. He asked a question of his newly found Scottish friend.

"Tell me this Duncan, for how long do you think they will remember us all, those of us who gave up this beautiful game of football to come and die over here?"

Currie considered the question for a few moments, and then a profound thought came to him.

"Billy, I truly believe that those of us who perish here will become immortalised, our memories etched forever in the grateful minds of those who follow in our wake. It may well be that by the time that this conflict is over, very few of us will be left alive. But you see my dear friend those who restart the game will never forget that it was we who made it possible for them to continue the game in peace and freedom. Our life's blood will have made it possible. Every year will come an occasion whereby we shall be remembered, of that I am sure, every year."

Billy was deeply affected by what the brave Scot had said. The man appeared so passionate in his belief that, somehow, it was infectious.

"Duncan, I think that you are probably right. In a hundred years from now when such dreadfulness is past and Man no longer has the desire to blow his fellow Man's brains out, then the arguments and competitiveness between the Nations may well be settled on the football field, than in such a manner as this."

Currie too had become deeply affected by their philosophising, there was something compelling about this young Englishman.

"Billy, who knows. Perhaps, one day, football may come to be the most important thing in the world. Countries will compete to hold world-wide tournaments striving for National ascendancy through the means of scoring goals rather than shooting men."

A vision of such a world came before Billy's eyes. It was going to be too late for his generation but, God willing, the following one would live out their lives as this great Midlothian had foreseen. He had taken an instant liking to this philosophising gentleman of Scottish football who seemed so placid and assured in the righteousness of his cause, the purpose of his action and the truth of his vision. It was all truly infectious.

The pair shook hands vigorously, prior to their parting, both realising how short of time they were, how fragile their frames in the face of so great a storm of steel that was surely to befall them before the week was out. Billy's fellow adopted Cestrians were beginning to leave. He gathered up Jimmy's ancient football, which lay in a corner of the tent and ran to catch up with them. It was here that he was accosted by Captain Neville of the East Surrey Regiment.

The officer came out with his request without any preliminary courtesies.

"I say Sergeant, I don't suppose that you would do me a great favour would you?"

Billy was taken aback. What could this officer from a completely different regiment, a man that he had never before set eyes upon, possibly want from him?

"Sir what can I do for you?"

"Oh it's quite straight forward Sergeant, I would like to purchase your football."

Again Billy was puzzled, what could this officer want such an old ball for? He looked at it, really it was showing its age. However it was Jimmy's ball. The pair of them had played with it for almost ten years. To the world it was a scrap of a ball. To Jimmy and himself it brought back memories of a poor, bleeding, cut open pig and the image of a delighted face of a young lad as he was handed its bladder.

His reply was as instantaneous as it was emphatic.

"I am so sorry sir, but this ball is too precious to sell. You see it is almost as if it were a family heirloom."

Captain Neville was feeling quite frustrated; obtaining his last necessary football was proving to be the highest of challenges.

"How come Sergeant that so frail an object, that has obviously seen far better days, can be of such value to you?"

Billy duly related the story to him, which to be fair, the officer listened upon with great interest. At the end of its telling the Captain thought for a moment and remade his offer but this time in a manner, which Billy found hard to refuse.

"Sergeant you have convinced me of how much of our England is made up within this one solitary football. Not only was it gained through the efforts of a young English lad who was so determined to possess one, it was crafted through the effort and skill of one of those whom we are pledged to defend. It has given pleasure to two growing Derbyshire lads who through its application became extremely proficient at the game. It is now here on the banks of the Somme. It served as a catalyst for peace on the occasion of that famous Christmas truce. Now its owner has lost a leg and shall kick it no more."

"This ball is carved from out of History and the History of England too. I suggest to you Sergeant that it has one final role to play, that of being in the forefront of the attack that is to take place. Sergeant allow this scarred warrior of a ball to have its final hour of glory. Allow me to take it and with the others be kicked and passed across no-man's-land for the good of its country and the proud tradition of the great game that it represents. Sergeant give me your hand on it and let another chapter in our noble National game be proudly written."

Billy was lost. He recognised a man with the talent to mould words in Shakespearean fashion. Also he respected how he had so crafted his argument as to elevate the years worn object to a higher plane. He felt that the years had rolled back to the days of Agincourt and reminisced upon the reaction of great King Henry's final call to arms in the words of one of his noble Captains, Edward Duke of York.

My Lord, most humbly on my knee I beg
The leading of the vaward.

Billy knew what he had to do. Taking the ball, he placed it in the eager hands of the foolhardy Captain Neville. Using words, which were to continue to bemuse the fated officer for the rest of his short life, he handed the precious, coveted object to the grateful officer.

"Take it brave York."

Saluting, Billy turned and walked away, leaving Neville in possession of both the ball and the field. The Captain pondered. 'York,' what could the Sergeant be thinking of, there was no way that he could know that, although he wore the insignia of the East Surrey Regiment, he was only attached to them from the East Yorks. 'Remarkable,' he thought, as he carried away the all-important trophy, 'Quite remarkable.'

Not far away, having enjoyed the football match another of Britain's talented, but tragically doomed youth was sitting at his improvised writing desk composing his last letter home. He had espied the tableau of the exchange of ownership of the ball. Now words came to him once more, words that were to echo down the years. As William Noel Hodgson of the Devonshires was scribing out his final epistle he rewrote at its end a prophetic postscript.

Go, and may the God of battles
You in his good guidance keep:
And, if He in wisdom giveth
Unto his beloved, sleep.

CHAPTER 29

Boom, boom, boom, boom, boom,
Boom, boom, boom, boom, boom.
Boom, boom, boom, boom, boom,
Boom, boom, boom, boom, boom.

Private S. Baldrick. Royal Anglican Regiment. D. France 1917.

June 30th, ceaselessly, the shelling continued, as it had for seven days now, bombarding the German position with pitiless, endless ferocity. Chalk dust constantly drifted over the British positions, greyish white, as if it were composed of particles from a noxious gas. Dawn had come early about four thirty in the dewy hours.

The section 'stood to' a few minutes before six, gazing out with heavily laden, reddened eyes upon an erupting landscape where the yellow of wild rape, scarlet of poppy and the occasional green of tufted grass had all but disappeared. The shells had virtually destroyed them all, hardy a space existed between undisturbed ground out on the near horizon. All was now murkied grey.

Gaping holes in the ground, made the skyline appear as if giant teeth had been extracted by a butchering dentist, leaving cavities whose gums had become swollen, creating infected ridges, where once, the molars had been.

'Seven Days, more than enough,' thought Billy the entire German Army, or what was left of it, would now be vengefully waiting for them. This must have been the longest warning that unwelcome gatecrashers had ever given, to unwilling hosts, in all of history. If this was not enough, that Captain Neville, the one who had relieved Billy of Jimmy Jones's football, had been shouting insults at the Germans from his fire step for the last two days.

Now, under the shelter of the shelling he was displaying even more tactless bravado. He was standing outlined upon the parapet, his pistol in his hand, his arm in the air, crying out to the enemy. Continually, he composed insults upon their manhood and their parental integrity. He questioned their wives faithfulness, worrying them of the outcome when he came over together with his men, to present them with an eviction order. He appeared impervious to the enemy fire, as if nothing could touch him.

In truth, of course, the Germans, contrary to rumour, were neither stupid nor unprepared. They were, as Billy was sure, skulking deep in their dugouts, whilst the rain of death poured over them. How deeply they had dug down, Billy did not know, but even the largest shells could not penetrate that great a depth. Many of the Germans would survive uninjured, of that he was sure. How quickly, how many, how efficiently, and belligerently, would determine the outcome the battle.

Whether the British won or lost would be decided from the result of the first fifteen minutes action. How quickly and in what numbers the first wave of attacks could reach the enemies fire trench would be decisive. Surprise was essential and this brave, yet foolhardy Captain of the East Surreys, was warning the foe that he was about to invade them. He was constantly warning them that his foot would undertake encrusted mud aggravated injury upon their bottoms. So much for surprise.

The waiting was provisioning most of the stress that was beginning to manifest itself through the language and actions of the men. Originally they had been due to go over the top two days ago, but like Napoleon, a hundred years before at Waterloo, the weather had encouraged the Generals to postpone matters. Billy just prayed that the extra time was not being usefully employed by the enemy to prepare positions that would be engineered to repel the waves of British troops soon to be swarming towards them.

Considerable anxiety had occupied Billy's mind, contemplating upon how well his section would perform. They had become a well-knitted team ,each with their own skills, and him their leader. They were now down to eight from their original number of fifteen, although three new replacements from a battered section of B. Company had augmented their strength a few days ago. 'A football team,' he thought, 'and I their Captain.'

He remembered the men he had lost. The two Keen brothers those few months ago at Loos, Dickey Cross, Anthony Rawlings, Fred Emsley in the raid on the German stronghold jutting out in no mans land. Jimmy Jones of course, ever in his mind. His great friend, of all those years of childhood. His faithful lifetime's companion who so relentlessly practised with the home made football now in the lands of Captain Neville. His friend, who through persistence and practice had become a footballer of great promise. His friend, who was now less a foot, who would never play again. Jimmy Jones, poor Jimmy. His eyes misted and he wept for his gallant pal; Jimmy Jones, now less a foot.

Yet, it was true, Jimmy was out of the hell, which was so surely to come. Safe back in Glossop with friends and family, far away from this place of death. Who was the fortunate one? Jimmy or he? What price England, home and beauty? A foot? Tortured memories an uncertain future. Billy found himself praying for his friend, praying for all those back home, all those he loved.

Now his thoughts sped to Albert, young Albert Hadfield, so innocent and immature that he scarcely shaved. Poor Albert, how this war, seemingly with purpose, picked out the youngest, the innocent, destroying their lives in an instant, or worse, leaving them to suffer in an inaccessible place, crying pitifully for their mothers.

It had been so with Albert. Once they had been informed that a delay of forty-eight hours was to be made extending zero hour to 1st July, along with so many thousands of others, Billy had time on his hands, time to consider his fate, time to reminisce upon past events. Faces came to him of comrades gone, events, loved ones, and the loveliest one. He now often found himself reading his Bible quietly in a corner or whispering lines from Milton, whilst weeping into Sally's handkerchief.

Rain fell incessantly, reminding him of lines composed by Herbert Read, a brother soldier poet.

'All the world is wet with tears.'

Wet with tears, tears for a desperate world, for soldiers, their mothers, sisters, lovers, and wives. Tears for Albert, young Albert Hadfield. That night he wrote a sonnet to the boy's memory. What a lad, so proud, so fearful, must his mother have been. Now mournful on his loss, Distressed beyond description, dispossessed of his presence, his voice. In concert with countless other grieving ones, sisters, in tragedy, a 'world wet with tears'

So he had written his memorial sonnet to the young brave foothardy soldier, together with another that he had composed to the two young tired soldiers, whose bodies had been destroyed beyond recognition whilst being crucified as an example to others. But it was young Albert, whose face and the echoing memory of his pure soprano voice in full song, who haunted him. A particularly senseless death in an ever increasingly senseless war.

It was with the unthinking initiative of youth, that Albert had thrust himself over the parapet to aid the stretcher-bearers, who in bringing home a wounded comrade from a raid had themselves, fallen victim to a shell. Not for one moment did Billy believe that the German sniper, who began to take aim, knew that his latest victim was barely sixteen. It was all in a day's war, and after all the British were the present aggressors with their constant shelling and their nightly sorties.

So it was that, that the Saxon shot the young boy as he was making his way around the wire. The force of the bullet picked up his small frame from off the ground, forcing him to become suspended in the air then come crashing down upon the wire. There he lay, trapped in the barbs of this fiendish invention, with endless coils of wire wrapped around him. He was helplessly ensnared, for the evil strands were heartless, ruthless and totally efficient.

It was then, as his life's blood poured from him, that Albert's courage left him. He cried out for his mother, as he haplessly, frantically struggled to free himself, merely to encourage the wire to entwine itself even more intimately around him. The boys cries must have distressed, shamed even, the enemy who had fired the fatal shot, for indeed his pleas were the cries of a babe in any language. With the empathy that is shown to an animal in pain, a second merciful shot rang out silencing that pure soprano voice forever.

That night they recovered his poor broken body and buried him, not without tears, for he was the youngest of them. They blessed him, and commended him to his maker. Then they returned each one, to his allotted place to await, in turn, their fate. Sombre had been those last few days. The knowledge that each of the surviving members possessed upon their own mortality, their potential for confronting the kind of pain and suffering surrounding them invaded all their senses.

Yes the original survivors of the section now numbered eight. They had experienced more danger, displayed more courage, faced more trials, and lived in greater squalor than men of their young years should ever have experienced, manifested, or confronted. They came from many walks of life, religious persuasion and interests, yet now they knitted together as a unit, comrades united, ready to face the foe each dependant on the next in line, each prepared to cover for his friend. Truly they were 'a band of brothers' they had learned of laughter, gained courage, gentleness from one another. Now they too were ready, prepared to make richer still that land out there, that land belonging to no man, that foreign field ploughed by shell, furrowed by shovel, bonded by coiled wire.

Billy had put his house in order. Last letters he had written, to his mother, to Sally and one to his unborn child. He had collected all the communications from his section sending them to company H.Q for posting home in the event, …the event. Billy left the sentiment unexpressed, just as well.

They had stood down, darkness had descended, a warm dry night complete with stars. Stark, the outline of the horizon joined with gothic grey marbled cloud drifting across a warning moon, to create a portend for what that demented German Corporal would have described as Gotterdammerung, the twilight of the Gods.

Leaving the first two on watch, and increasingly becoming aware of the ever-increasing barrage of British shells, Billy told the men to stand down. The remainder of the troop went back to their dug out for hot tea and bully beef, perhaps also a drop of rum and a slice of cake from home, for now was the time to share out such good things, if even there was one of their number who would no longer pester them for goodies.

The cries of young Albert continued to haunt Billy. He could hear them still in his mind, even now, above the sound of shells. He recalled how the lad had first screamed out in panic, full of fright, formed of the knowledge that he was about to die. Then how his cries changed becoming quieter, more personal, dying slowly away until the sniper fired his second silencing round. mother! mother, Mum, Mummy....

As section leader, he had the duty to distribute Albert's belongings to his comrades, such was custom. What they found within his kit bag was so pitiful, that no one could touch a single item. Usually a dead man's bag contained cigarettes, some tins of spare food, even delicacies, a scarf, perhaps a diary, photographs of a loved one, useful items like soup or a razor.

Albert's Kit bag was sticky, full of boiled sweets, humbugs, hundreds of them, some wrapped others not, which had escaped into the recesses of the bag and contaminated it with stickiness and sugar. He had a Bible, inside its cover was inscribed the words 'To Albert from mother, ' dated 'Easter 1915.' Also inside the Bible was a letter, Albert's last correspondence to the woman whom he had called out for as his last breaths were expelled from his frame.

> *Dearest mother,*
> *I am in France thinking of you, what*
> *you are doing, sad because you are so far away.*
> *I'm thinking that even though the sea devides*
> *us keeping us apart the day will come, a good*
> *day when we will be together again never to*
> *separate.*
>
> *Mum it is here, without you, that home seems*
> *a dream as if it never was. Not having you has*
> *taught me about a mother's care loving, stroking*
> *my hair even when she knows nothing is really*
> *wrong with me.*
>
> *I will just say goodbye now, goodnight dear*
> *Mum. Pray that this war will soon end.*
> *Your loving son Albert loves you.*
>
> *Albert.*

Not one man's eye was dry as Billy read the letter, which had been the poor lad's attempt at poetry, aloud to his men. Some turned away spitting and cursing the Germans, the war. One was heard to swear, cursing God. They began to disperse having no further interest in Albert's belongings.

Billy stopped them.

"Wait men," he pleaded.

"As a token of memory and respect, I want each of you to take a sweet from Albert's bag. During his short life he had few pleasures. One was his sweets. He was always sucking them and giving them away. I remember when Dicky Cross tried to get him smoking, how it made him ill. He loved his sweets did Albert, and he loved us, his friends, companions, comrades. He treated each of us as his big brother. Nothing was too much for him. Always running errands he was.

So, I shall send home his Bible and his letter, to his mother.

I shall write from all of us telling her how proud she should feel. I shall tell her how we remembered him. How we each had a sweet of his and thought of him. How we shall all miss him. Now please, each of you, take a sweet."

The men turned round, in silence, each took a sweet from a grubby, crumpled, sorrowful looking, stained, paper bag and placed it in their mouths. It was almost like a communion service. In fact many of the men crossed themselves as they took from the offered bag, muttering a plea to God to bless their young departed friend, and to protect them from such a fate.

Billy's memories fled from this melancholic tableaux.
Now was not the time to spend ones thought on such examples of graceless waste of young life. He had to regain a sense of purpose, to do his best, his utmost for his men and their objectives. Far better to compose himself with thoughts of home.

Billy was not alone in his reminiscences. In the darkness of that last night, before the dawning of the mighty battle, each member of the section was contained within a shell of his own thought. Some mulled their considerations to themselves, others conversed in whispered snatches to their closest comrades. It was so with the Roberts's brothers, Trevor and David.

Trevor being the older of the two, had always felt so protective towards his younger sibling now, in the last few hours before the coming battle, he felt the need to reassure him, to comfort him. He began by recalling their life as boys together in the small hamlet of Trevalyn near to Wrexham.

Their father had worked in Gresford pit all his life, working for twelve hours at the coalface.

"Gresford pit is a dangerous place" he had told them one afternoon, whilst fishing with them by a small lake called the 'Flash'.

"One day there will be the most awful accident. I can see it coming. All those extensions, poor shoring, gas, water. I tell you lads' one day, not long from now there will be a great catastrophe. Gresfield will be full of weeping mothers, wives, children."

Old Emyr did not know it then, but he would live to see his prophecy fulfilled, not once, but twice. Tragedy would doubly come to visit that peaceful place north of Wrexham, famous for its bells. He would live to assist in the supervision of the attempt to save over two hundred trapped miners. He would also live to see his sons names carved upon a stone memorial, alongside others of the village who had fallen in their service.

All this lay in the future. For now, the two were recollecting that wonderful sunny afternoon in late spring, when they were ten and eleven. They had sat either side of the man who was their hero, whom they idolised. Each had caught a classic Roach, placing their catches in turn within the keep net, along with numerous small Dace, and a large Perch, which Emyr would persuade his wife to poach that night. For years afterwards the two boys would disagree upon who had caught the biggest Roach. Indeed, even now, here on the bank of the Somme, no agreement was reached; they hotly and keenly debated the matter, though it was in a manner of jest, of brotherly mocking.

Both knew, without need of the spoken word that, when the hour came, they would go over side by side, looking out each for the other, as they entered what they knew was to be their valley of death. They had jointly composed their last letter. It was a positive note, in spite of it being their final one. It was full of love for their parents, for Wales, for their duty as they saw it. They would not flinch from their duty, they assured their mother and father, they would do their duty and make both of them very proud.

Nor was their letter merely composed of formality of sombre thoughts. They reaffirmed their love for their parents, their gratitude to them, their love for the two sisters who, being older than either of them, were now both married to Gresford Miners both with children.

It was a long letter reminiscing upon their childhood.

Thoughts of home came onto the pages. Trevor and his work for Philip Yorke, he wondered how the estate was flourishing, David and Wrexham A F C. How was the team managing without his skills. Life at the Racecourse must be dull without his fluid runs down the wing. He spoke of his exploits against the Scottish football team whilst playing alongside his Chester and Glossop team-mates.

Now the letter was written and handed in to company H Q. Some rum had been consumed, and little more was left to say or do. They wondered if Billy was awake and willing to engage in some last conversation. Milton perhaps, followed by a hymn and a prayer.

On their way they met up with Terry Gresford. He had been writing home to his dear wife of three years, composing lines for her and their two children.

As his surname indicated his family had resided in that quiet fertile benign rural area of land that stretches from Wrexham to Chester. This pastoral countryside juxtaposed with silhouettes of coal faces, giving evidence to the rich black seams contained beneath the ground, contrasting with the delicate landscape that, from certain high spots, a courting couple could view Beeston Castle and the ridges at Frodsham and Helsby.

With considerable fondness he remembered how he and Jenny, his wife, first made love, impatiently, a week before their marriage one July afternoon. How beautiful she was, how innocent, how wonderful the act, how guiltily, yet sublimely, they had let their lovemaking last, how intriguingly erotic it was for them to recall the event when later they were coverletted together in their marital bed.

Terry loved his young wife, the mother of his children who, for his King and Country, he had left when he volunteered to fly to the colours. Now he was here ready, full of consternation, but never the less prepared to do his duty. Whether history would record his coming home to her welcoming loving arms, or would tell of her weeping upon his memory, he did not know. For this moment, he gave thanks to his God for the love of so beautiful a woman.

Now the three men conversed, two brothers and a man they called friend and comrade. All familiar with that part of their 'blessed plot' they had committed themselves to defend.

Joe Keen was keeping his thoughts to himself, remembering his two lost brothers, of his last sighting of the two as they had gone over the top at Loos. He recalled them having shaken his hand, never to return. Their bodies would never be knowingly found but left out there, in the land which no man held, to fall back into the dust from whence they had come.

There had been less than three years between the ages of the brothers. Joe being the youngest was always last in line, old shoes, patched trousers, darned socks, whenever he had any. There were disadvantages of course but plus points also. His big brothers had continuously protected him as a young boy. Joe was rather slightly built, but what he lacked in physical stature he gained in his ability for cheek, talking his way into and out of scrapes. He could scramble up trees, which was just as well at times, scrambling like a cat retreating from a pack of chasing dogs whose temper had been strained by the taunts of a lesser built, but more canny, tormentor. He had felt the need on many occasions to use the age-old threat of the defenceless

"I will get my big brothers onto you."

Luckily in Joe's case the threat was not an empty one which had led, on more than one occasion, to a larger enemy backing off.

The three had all joined Baden-Powell's Scouts, trekking over the Peak District, camping out in all weathers. Sitting in reflection, here on the Somme, his late brothers feeling very near, as if they were even now protecting him, Joe's memories travelled back to the time they were camping near to an ancient village.

They had spent almost a week walking over the peaks. They had climbed Mam Tor jutting defiantly, in its granite craggy form, firmly above all its surroundings. He became filled of nostalgia, reviving the sensation of being King of all he surveyed. That week it rained without ceasing, reminiscent of the climate here on the Somme. Now his eyes rained tears as his memory reformed the image of his dear brothers sharing much of his load on their backs that week.

Then his mind traversed another scene of that excursion. He, his brothers and the Scout troop had reached the legendary village of Eyam having come twenty miles or so south of Glossop. They were camped near to an ancient cemetery, one of several scattered around. Graves dotted all about the area, yet there were but few houses, merely a row of six cottages, aged, but beautiful in their historic simplicity.

That night, around their campfire, the troop leader recounted how, during the time of the last great plague, the very same that had ravaged London prior to the great fire, the village had become infected. The initial response of the villagers had been to flee the infection, till the vicar had called them together explaining that those of them who were susceptible to the plague were already infected. Nothing could be gained from fleeing the village. All that would happen, he said, would be that they would infect others. Better by far that they remain where they were, suffer what their destiny dictated, and face death together, proudly, defiantly, for the good of the rest of humanity.

They then decided that they would indeed share their fate together. Even now Joe could see the face of the storyteller, flecked by the flames, as he described how two hundred and sixty villagers, from a population of around three hundred and fifty, perished.

Next day, Joe remembered, they walked over to one of the grave sites and the three of them stood before one of the flat stones reading the commemoration, an inscription, part of which, became etched in his mind.

'Here lies a man
As love cost me
As you are now
Even so was I'

The three brothers had spoken of the brave villagers many times since that day. When they were together in the trenches they spoke of them and of how self-sacrifice was part of the heritage of the traditions of Britain. The Memorial to the plague victims was almost three hundred years old. It must have been read by thousands of people since the day it was first erected, coming to demonstrate how duty sacrifice and charity were natural aspects of Englishness.

Later they were to visit a nearby Celtic preaching cross, which had stood for over one thousand, five hundred years. They considered then, the countless Martyrs that the English Christian Church had been provided with. They were of England and now lay in English fields having defended her faith, through their ultimate sacrifice.

Now, having seen his brothers sacrificed for another English cause, Joe could not but contemplate upon his own mortality, exactly in the terms that the aged memorial had invited him so to do. A certain melancholia overcame him, a compelling sensation of utter loneliness. It was time to seek out the company of his fellow soldiers. Joe needed to hear the words, and contribute to the sentiments, that would undoubtedly be expressed that night.

Eddy Perkins had also, in his turn, been encompassed in thought. His last letter home had been written days ago. It was not his favourite occupation, or his greatest skill, but he was sure that he had covered his iterations as he had wished. His mind had been complete of regret. Regret that he had not lived his life as, he now felt, he should have done so. For too much of his life he had been a waster, always seeking out a chance. In addition, he loved his ale. Many was the night he had left the Norfolk Arms, being worse the wear for drink. Then there was the girl who had given him everything upon his word.

He had promised the world to Mary Green, a simple, plain, slight figured girl of his age, who lived just a few doors away in Colliery Row. His false plausible words had succeeded in his aim, that of seducing her in a field above Glossop. Subsequently, they had made love all through that summer before the war came. How she had not fallen for a baby, he did not know. Now Mary came to him in unspoken yearning. Full of remorse, he was now repenting of his actions; of his false promises to an innocent girl for whom he now felt a deep affection.

It was all too late. All he had now was a few short letters from Mary, dated before Christmas 1914, and a photograph of her smiling, her plainness somehow luring in its honesty. He had only once replied to her and that was a simple cursory note. After several attempts Mary had written a last letter explaining that she was no longer willing to continue in a one way communication, that she loved him, but was no longer going to waste her life on a man who thought so little of her.

At long last, eighteen months later, he had written back apologising for his behaviour and professing his love. He wrote to say that he was hoping that they would meet again after the war, should he survive. He was never to know, but he was to meet death before the epistle reached its designated destination. When Mary received his last words, she was to treasure them all her life. She remained faithful to this unworthy man, remembering days of love above Glossop, always leaving a solitary poppy beneath his name, etched upon the memorial in Norfolk square. She went to her grave over sixty years later, never having known another man.

For now, the repentant Eddy Perkins, observed the others of the section gathering together, and he turned to join them. He too had his part to play, he too would have his name carved in stone in Norfolk square, gazed upon, wept for, and remembered.

So they gathered together, one last time. Billy Thomas their leader, Trevor and David Roberts, Joe Keen, sensing he would soon join his brothers, Eddy Perkins heavy of heart, inwardly harking back to another place, another time, Terry Gresford home sick for his wife and children, nostalgic.

Now came three more, Wrexham George, Harold Evans and Victor Grayson, bringing up the rear.

George Mancot was famous in his hometown for his perfect tenor voice. This was the third section that he had been attached to since coming to France in August 1914, and it was the best yet, full of good lads and having a Competent NCO. Billy Thomas was sensible enough to ensure that his men were not meaninglessly led to slaughter, a highly important aspect of leadership in George's opinion.

He was the sole survivor of his first section having fought as a territorial at the Marne. He had them joined a new unit of the 6th Cheshire's but again he was the only member not killed when a shell burst into his trench. He had just turned a zigzag in the cutting when it fell concussing him and bursting his eardrums. Since then, from that first Christmas of the war, having fully recovered, he had been loyal member of this section of men, so welded together by their NCO.

In truth there was very little waiting at home except life as a collier and he had little love for the prospect of the pit. Lucky, as ever, he had survived a cave in at the pit face, where out of five others he had been the sole survivor. So often had George escaped with his life that he was seen as an emblem of fortune, defying death when all those around him had succumbed. Come the day, he was about to face his greatest test, playing his part in the greatest battle that men had ever devised.

George was not especially religious, although back home he regularly attended his local Welsh speaking Chapel singing in the choir and performing in concerts. His Cwm Rhonda, 'Guide Me O' Thou Great Jehovah,' and 'Canol Lan', were impressive. He had performed many a rendition, given at night time in the trenches, to the approval and applause of German and British troops alike.

He had no girl waiting at home. Once he had embarked upon an relationship with a young widow who had two children. She was six years older than himself. With her previous experience to enflame him, it had become an explosive affair. Finally, it had come to an end when he discovered that he was not the sole man who was privileged to have her delights unveiled for him.

In truth he was glad when the war had come. Glad for the opportunity to seek new adventures elsewhere. Yet, as he was about to face his sternest to date, he was not so sure. Northern France was a place where the Devil himself had unleashed madness upon earth, of that he was certain. It was a thoughtful man, full of melancholy, who now rose, spat profusely, lit the next in a long line of Woodbines, and went to join the others. He too was seeking comfort from familiar comrades of long standing, familiar in their predicament, their language, their fear and mutual never ending discomfort.

Harold Evans was deeply afraid, to the extent that his bowels were loose. Even the continual end to end smoking regime, that he had adopted for almost a week now, could not restrain his shaking. Further, he needed the comfort of alcohol. He had always required alcohol, even as a young man working in the textile mills of Glossop. Always one of the lads, ever a part of the crowd, drinking his wages, he lived with his poor widowed mother the only member of the human race who found no fault in him.

He was a man of few skills, little education or interest in matters that did not immediately effect his physical wellbeing. One month after he had left for training camp a telegram had come to tell him how his mother had passed away. Taking a three-day pass he travelled home for the funeral. Like himself his mother had found little time for Church yet the local vicar said good things over her coffin when officiating at the internment.

Few people were there, upon that lonely hillside, that cold rain filled day, where the wind, coming over the Pennines, riddled the body with spasms of frozen invisible darts. Now England, Glossop, held little for him. Considering himself to be worthless, yet not wanting the agony of a grievous wound or a bullet bringing death, tomorrow's events, the coming battle, now became an awesome prospect.

What little faith he had within him had been spawned of late by the readings and discussions that Billy Thomas had conducted over 'Paradise Lost'. The words had provided comfort, indeed more than that, the beginnings of a belief.

The decision came, formulated from necessity. He would speak to Billy Thomas. He was deeply afraid, even to the extent of being tempted to desert. Also, although he was unaware of the fact, he was a victim of the constant shelling, its appalling, concussing, aftershocks that made the very ground to tremble with malevolence.

Concluding that once killed he would never be missed, once obliterated, it would be as if he had never been, he needed assurance. It could only come from Billy Thomas. John Milton and the God who inspired and spurred both to pronounce confidence in their salvation, their inheritance of the next world. Hopefully, before this terrible night was through, he could find a little of the essence that flowed within his Sergeant and consume a little of it, then maybe, just maybe he would be provided enough courage to see through the coming day. The glow of the cigarette brightened as he got up. He drew upon it, filling his lungs with smoke and he too, in his turn, slowly walked towards the others.

Victor Grayson had been asked by Billy to check on the two men of the watch. They were both new to the section having been drafted from elsewhere in 'C' Company to replace the mills bombers that had been lost in the raid. The pair, Tommy Smith and Henry Stevens had been through much together, both being veterans of Neuve Chapelle and numerous raiding parties.

Talking knowingly of the build up they were witnessing, a massive shelling such as they had never before experienced, they knew that tomorrow represented a turning point in the war. They were both convinced that the Allies would have a great victory, get out of these abominable trenches and purposefully head towards Berlin and Victory. This time the Generals had got it right, more than enough shells, more than enough men to sweep the enemy away.

Victor approached them. There was a lull for the moment in the bombardment and it was easy enough to speak in quiet whispered voices.

"How goes it lads?"

"Well enough."

"Well the waiting will soon be over."

"Not too soon either."

"I shall bring a hot drink later lads."

"Cheers Vic."

"Keep your eyes peeled."

"Sure thing."

Victor left the expectant pair quietly, though confidently, discussing their coming fate, and went to join the others of the section that were gathering round Billy Thomas. So they came together, this diverse band of young men, fated as a single unit, to face the enemy, come the morrow morn. Each one was confronting the challenge in his own way, managing his fears, aspiring to his duty. They all had dwelt, in their own way upon their past and how the course of their lives had brought them here to the banks of the Somme. Now, in reality, all they had was each other, every man reliant upon the one next to him for success, survival and support.

They were surprised at just how hungry they were. Tin upon tin of Machonichis stew was opened, heated and consumed, enriched with bully beef. Strong rum was available to those who wished for its comforts. Hot tea, coffee even. They ate, they drank, for tomorrow..., tomorrow..., tomorrow..., no one wished to speak of tomorrow, least ways not yet.

So they gathered together, here in a dugout by a blazing fire which fed a steamy cauldron. Comrades in adversity. Billy Thomas, their leader, Trevor and David Roberts brothers from the womb, in arms also, Joe Keen full of the memory of his late siblings and soon, very soon, he was sure, to join them. Eddy Perkins full of regret, reconciled to an inevitable end. Terry Gresford determined to make his wife proud. His lovely wife, whom he so loved. Harold Evans, shaking, shell shocked, his mind so shattered he was no longer of this place, or capable of rationalising its consequences. Wrexham George observed them all as he had done so with others before. To him they looked lost men, merely awaiting their turn to become numbered among the dead, a part of the great slaughter.

Saddest, and most reflective of all, was Victor Grayson. He was a man whose life had shown so much promise, whose talent had flourished then dimmed, to evaporate as if it were an early morning Flanders mist dissipated by the sun. Out on the parapet, keeping watch, were the two newest additions to this tragic group Tommy and Harry staying alert, their minds filed with expectation, their bodies spurred by adrenaline.

It was fast approaching midnight. Least ways the weather was dry and warm. Together, the hot stew, tea and rum acted as a cocktail encouraging every man to begin seeking out some level of communication with the rest of his companions. It was Terry Gresford who first caught the mood of the moment.

"Billy, now would be a good time for a reading from the Bible or Milton, a hymn perhaps, a prayer also, before we all try and turn in."

Trevor Roberts joined in the request.

"What a good idea and a number from George as well. Come on Billy, lets show the enemy that we are ready for him, whatever he throws at us tomorrow."

Billy was easily persuaded that night.

"Good suggestion Terry. George, come on, give us your very best, give us Cwm Rhondda."

George was never shy in taking up a request. A few seconds later and the air was filled with his tenor voice. Each verse began with his solo rendition, taken up by the rest of the section when the repetitive lines came round.

'Guide me O' through great Jehovah.
Pilgrim through this barren land'

His voice ranged above the shelling, which, for now, had largely died down. It resonated out from the parapet over no mans land and entered the German trenches opposite. A Saxon warrior, determined that his race be not out sung, countered with the greater hymn of Martin Luther.

'A mighty fortress is our God'

Yet tonight, nothing, no one, was going to outshine the small khaki choir; led as it was by one of the finest tenors from North Wales. The great finale, repeated twice, resounded above all else in both decibel, pitch and content.

'When I tread the verge of Jordan,
Bid my anxious fears subside:
Death of Death, and hells destruction,
Lead me safe on Canaan's side:
Songs of praises, songs of Praises,
I will ever give to thee – give to thee!
I will ever give to thee.'

High above the battle's sound rose fine notes of purity, of the highest sentiment. How sad their maker must have been that night, the words uplifted to him in song from two sides both determined upon the destruction of the other. In German, not as accomplished, but every part as pertinent in its accolade, poured forth the retort.

' Though they take our life.
Goods, honour, children, wife,
Yet is their prophet small;
These things shall vanish all;
The city of God remaineth.'

The words of two great protestant Christians, Martin Luther and William Williams merged into a solitary anthem. Yet both were lost midst a landscape of destruction, spoiled for an age, a place called Armageddon where man tilled the soil with a trench shovel and planted it with lethal devises designed for a harvest of death.

'Win pfligon and win strewen'

'We plough the fields and scatter.'

On both sides of no-mans-land, countless men turned towards their God that night, that last night, before even this soul consuming war's ever insatiable desire for human flesh took a new grotesque path in its intensity, its desire to consume human flesh. For mile after mile men prepared for battle, thousands upon thousands of them reciting untold prayers pleading with their God to give them courage, to keep their loved ones safe.

In their small plot, Billy's section was gathered round, earnestly striving for a resolution to their nervousness, for their unresolved questions. Wrexham George in his display of tenor perfection had provided a sound beginning to their supplications. Now all turned to Billy to provide reassurance for tomorrow.

He had borrowed a Catholic Bible from Terry Gresford who had suggested a reading from the Book of Wisdom.

'But the souls of the upright are in the hands of God.
And no torment can touch them.
To the unenlightened, they appeared to die
Their departure was regarded as disaster,
Their leaving us like annihilation
But they are at peace...
God was putting them to the test.'

The passage completed, silence reigned, then up spoke Joe Keen.

"Corp, that was beautiful. If, as I reckons, I may join my brothers tomorrow, I shall be at peace, my family also knowing that we three are together, killed in this terrible conflict but at peace, having been put to the test."

"Well said."

The exclamation came from Trevor Roberts

His brother David shook Billy's hand.

"Thank you for that Billy. The worst that can happen after this day is that we shall all be together in the hands of God."

One by one, each in their turn agreed, each speaking up in unified agreement. All save one, Victor Grayson, who, for now, kept his council.

Trevor Roberts proposed a few lines from Milton to which Billy agreed, pulling out the now very battered volume. He read from the fourth book of Paradise Regained.

The men listened spellbound, absorbed by the tale of Christ's tormenting by Satan, who, using all his wiles, deceit, bribery, menace, thrusts Christ into the wilderness to face a barrage of devises from his allies, blasting the son of man from every vantage. Christ remains steadfast against the worst that evil can cast upon him and emerges triumphant.

'O' Patient son of God, yet only stood,
Unshaken, withstood the terror there,
Infernal ghosts and hellish furies,
Surrounded him, some howled, some yelled, some shrieked,
Some bent at him with fiery darts while he,
Sat unappalled in calm and sinless peace,
Thus passed the night so foul,
Till morning fair came forth.'

Not one men who heard the words failed to understand. Not a single word emitted into the ether in futility. Each digit was rich in meaning, association and consolation. Although manifest in diverse ways, every one who had given ear was now calmed, tranquil, infused with a certain faith, in the knowledge that, for them, one man had experienced this, and more, merely for the love he had for the sons of Adam.

They were speechless, all except Victor Greyson, the agnostic Socialist who professed his humanist beliefs whenever he was invited to explain the principals behind his political pronouncements. Now came the softly spoken voice of a changed man. He was still a man who believed in universal brotherhood and the concepts of equality and of Socialism, yet, also, it was the voice a of a man who had undergone a profound change in metaphysical belief.

"Billy I declare in front of all these present that I am an unbeliever no longer. I declare Jesus Christ to be my saviour, the saviour of all mankind. Of his charity I beg his forgiveness for all my past disbelief and beg him to allow me into the family of God."

With the end of his declaration he knelt down in the mud entirely unaware of being covered in the clinging filth. He wept, wept tears of joy. Others of his comrade's came over, placed their arms around him or shook his hand. Tomorrow Victor Grayson; rebel, Socialist, Parliamentarian, soldier, would go over the parapet into the face of hell, but it would be as a man saved, certain of the resurrection and his place within it.

All the section, nine soldiers, whom historians would later describe as doomed men, knelt, restored of faith prepared to accept their fate, their destiny. In extemporised fashion Billy intoned the blessing. Men wept openly, some crossed them selves, giving themselves up to God. Their bodies were undoubtedly doomed but equally, their souls were safe.

"Now we shall sing 'Abide with me' and turn in. It is going to be a long day tomorrow."

"Hopefully Corporal, hopefully tomorrow will be a long day for all of us a very long day."

Terry Gresford's remark was echoed and agreed upon by all those within earshot.

George Mancot began, leading the singing most worthily. Upon the air, each line, every last word, went out into the night with meaning, with purpose, providing consolation and assurance to those who could hear. When the last line of the final verse had been sung, Billy summed up the entire echoes of France Lyte's work.

"There is no death, no darkness, if you dwell with the Lord."

It was fast approaching one o'clock. Each man of the section shook the hands of his comrades in the universal, ageless sign of peace and the group dispersed to seek what rest they could. For a few short hours, a respite would come to them. Dawn would emerge at around 4am. They would meet again for breakfast.

CHAPTER 30

Even the youths shall faint and be weary,
And the young men shall utterly fall:
But they that wait upon the Lord
Shall renew their strength;
They shall mount up with wings as eagles;
They shall run and not be weary;
They shall walk, and not grow faint.

Isaiah ch.40 vs.30-31.

Sleep refused its nightly visitation upon Billy; he was so charged with the adrenaline that was flowing through his veins. It was fast approaching one o'clock. For now the guns were silent, the sentries on both sides, he was sure, were ever watchful. It was, for the moment, as peaceful as it could get, here on the Western Front. In less than an hour, he anticipated, the final great barrage would erupt, bringing fear to the enemy, raining death upon him. Who could tolerate such a long period of devastation? Unfortunately, he well knew the answer for he had seen his own 'happy breed of men' suffer so, far longer than an outside observer would ever have deemed possible.

Walking the trench this Saturday morn, a stark realisation dawned upon him. He was about to witness the making of history, more, to be a part of it. This day's battle, whether for good or ill, would, for all time, etch out its own niche in the edifice of British legend. The first of July1916, with its epic, breathtaking action would take its immortal place alongside Hastings, the Armada, Blenheim, Waterloo, Balaclava, Crecy, and Agincourt. Ah Agincourt, would that tomorrow would bring another such victory.

Here on the Somme, not far from the scene of that immemorial field of battle, like King Henry the Fifth before him, Billy strolled the lines, gazing towards the place of coming conflict, striving to gain resolve whilst reflecting upon his duty, his mortality.

'Stiffen the sinews, summon up the blood'

Words came to him. Deeply engrained they were. That England could not only breed so great a King, so mighty a warrior, but also, so immortal a Bard, to place into language words worthy of his, and his countrymen's deeds, was a marvel to him. He now envisioned that steadfast, ancient, dread, sovereign before Harfleur, re-arming his exhausted host with courage and purpose.

'Dishonour not your mothers, give attest that those
Whom you call fathers did beget you.'

No other language possessed by any portion of humanity, he was convinced, could convey so deep, profound expression, to so graphic a purpose.

'I see you stand like greyhounds in the slips
Straining upon the start. The game's afoot
Follow your spirit and upon this charge
Cry ' God for Harry, England, and St George.'

Indeed a majestic monarch, overwhelming in war, unparalleled in generalship. Yet, if Shakespeare was to be believed, gentle and kind, ever considering the welfare of his men whom he genuinely respected as fellow soldiers, all with their reasoned, motives and purpose. Billy recalled how the King displayed his humanity his insight into the troubled minds of his men.

'We must bear all, our lives, our souls, our children,
Our careful wives, our debts, our sins.'

Here, on the eve of another intrepid struggle, Billy was reminded how, in very similar vein to his own patrol of the watch this night, the King paced from group to group, crouching with them by their night fires seeking association, joining in the traditional conversations that men engage upon, prior to being put to the test.

'Bids them good – morrow with a modest smile
And calls them brothers, friends and countrymen.'

Here upon the Somme the young Section leader, honed from the weather smoothed granite and limestone hills of Derbyshire, was, in his turn, typographically reflecting the victor of Agincourt. Thus he went walking from Watch, to Watch, checking all was well attempting reassurance upon every wretch and pale faced youth who could not find rest, bringing with him comfort and comradeship.

He knew full well how great a force confronted them, the sense of hopelessness that some of his section must be experiencing. Approaching each one with words of reassurance, here in the stilly night, his calm, gentle manner restored many of them. Upon his face there appeared no sign of how dread an army was before them.

As he carried on towards the shelter, seeking out a cup of hot tea, King Henry's prayer came to him.

406

'O' God of Battles, steel my soldier hearts,
Posses them not with fear.'

Filled with these echoes from the past, he left the fire trench, determined upon getting, at least, an hours sleep. With him went 'a little touch of Harry in the night.'

That first July morning of the summer of 1916 gave witness to the Somme as, gracefully, she flowed interminably towards the sea. It had been so ever since the glaciers had retreated, forming the Pas de Calais, thousands of years before. The river was clear, as crystal, reflecting the young moon in countless fleeting sparkled facets. It continued flowing, over rocks, through weeds and drifting flotsam, conveying even the occasional corpse in its gentle current.

Billy did gain his hours sleep. However, it came fitfully disturbed. His dreams were elevated between nightmare and apocalyptic vision, where endless rows of corpses passed by, marching wearily into hell, their frames graphically displaying evidence of death's inevitable corruption.

Later, in contrast, came the angel's face of his beloved Sally, calling out his name, alas all too short-lived. Then crash, lightening, thunder striking, earth quaking devastation. He awoke with the realisation that the sounds surrounding him were not of the sleep filled world. Above him whirled projectiles of death.

Away to his left the sky was aflame. He staggered to his feet. All around him men were staring wide-eyed at the sight portrayed above them. They appeared as petrified trolls turned to stone, being centred amidst the tracered crescents of the awesome artillery ordinance, performing its last barrage upon the enemy. It was to continue so, well after dawn, not ceasing till a few moments prior to Zero hour. If any had doubted before, they fully comprehended now, Armageddon had arrived.

The young man, a veteran, in spite of his few years, was determined to enter battle looking his best. He would now shave, spruce himself up, consume strong hot tea, and then report to the Lieutenant for final instructions. Afterwards he would brace himself and prepare his men in readiness for the day, the day that had come so strenuously.

Half an hour later, together with Corporal Gaffrey, he presented himself to the officer who had replaced the departed Lieutenant Marford. Billy noticed his superior was shaking, he hoped that it was due to the cold early morning air. 'The man should have put on an extra shirt,' he thought, just as that unfortunate Stuart monarch had decided upon, before mounting the scaffold, on the day of his execution.

The sound and the fury was increasing by the minute. Salvoes of shells were coming over, ever more rapidly increasing in their ferocity. Now the trench mortars began their operations, adding to the mayhem.

Whump, whump, up and over, designed to drop down at a steep angle into the trenches of the despairing enemy. All these aspects of the overture simply added to the deterioration of the young officer's nerves. He was fresh from the Church Stretton parade ground and The King Edward the Seventh Public School in Lytham St Anne's, a pleasant academic institution on the Fylde coast. Now he flinched reactively with each shell's explosion. He had been uprooted from that placid place of learning, then henceforward to training camp and on to the tumultuous insanity that was the Somme. Graham Fawcett, now a leader of men had not been prepared, had not become near to being adequately acclimatised to the conditions of trench life or the realities of modern warfare.

On this day, he was expected to lead twenty-five or so men over the parapet into no–mans–land and on towards the enemy trenches. He was to calmly march through mud-filled, shell holes, and barbed wire, whilst encountering the mutilated corrupted bodies of others who had made vain attempts before him.

All this he must undertake with due expedition, while being rained upon by mortars, bombarded with shellfire, strafed with machineguns and the pristinely aimed bullets of snipers. He was barely twenty-one years old, never to see his next birthday, make love to a woman, vote in an election or again be with his mother. They would not even find his body, it would be parcelled up within the ground where he fell, alongside so many others of his doomed generation.

For the moment however, this bemused 2nd Lieutenant needed to issue coherent, meaningful instructions to his two NCO's. who presently stood eagerly and expectantly before him. Billy Thomas and Joe Gaffrey, they were men who were deemed inferior in rank in the eyes of the army, inferior in class according to society, indifferent in education designated by certificate, yet they were, in reality, so superior in their experience of warfare and the handling of men. Fatally, the knowledge and practical experience possessed by men such as these, so crucial to managing the events of the coming day, was being ignored by the High Command, adding to the legion of mistakes that were to compound the approaching tragedy

Fawcett had returned from his briefing at brigade HQ where he had been the most junior of all those in attendance. In sombre manner the Captains and Lieutenants were informed of what was expected. How they would organise their men in a straight line, each section having its leader at the far end of the platoon with their Lieutenant in the centre. In turn, each of the Captains, whistles in their mouths, pistols in hand, would lead their Company from the centre. At 7.20 the guns would fall silent, seven huge mines would then explode in specified strategic places along the battlefront, bringing a final devastation upon the enemy.

All the obstacles facing the attacking force, almost certainly, would have been destroyed. Very little opposition was expected, with the barbed wire being completely cut. Thus the Commanding Officer announced that the Companies would be formed upon the parapet in line, rifles to the front, bayonets attached. The army would then, with due order and discipline, simply walk over to the opposing trenches and occupy them, clearing out the dead Germans. Then, using the first trench as cover, they would fire upon what was left of the enemy in the succeeding defensive positions whilst following waves would pass over them and continue the advance. All would be ordered, they had a good plan. No battle had seen such preparation to ensure success in the entire history of warfare.

What Fawcett could not understand upon leaving the briefing and returning to his NCO's to relate instructions, was the absence of his own assurance. Moreover why were his bowels feeling so loose? He put it down to anticipation, a sensation he had often felt before in his life, prior to taking an examination at school or college.

Billy spoke up, sensing his immediate superior was overwhelmed by the situation that confronted him.

"Well Lieutenant, tell us the form"

Gaffrey and he looked at each other, their confidence in the officer draining by the second. It was not reinforced by the stuttering feeble reply that followed.

"Well, Sergeant, um well, well, its simple really, quite simple. The, the barrage stops at 7.20, we go over ten minutes later. Upon the sound of the Captain's whistle the whole company will join up in a line, walking over no-mans-land till we get to the opposite trench. Simple really, there are very few of the enemy left in their trenches, the barrage has seen to that."

The Lieutenant stuttered and hesitated all the way through his recitation of instructions, giving every indication that he believed not one word of that which he had said.

The two NCO's nodded knowingly to each other and prepared to leave, both of them wishing to be with friends and comrades with whom they were about to share so much. They saluted the young Lieutenant and turned to leave when the bemused man stopped them.

"I shall do my duty this day never fear"

He was looking towards them with tears welling in his eyes. It was the gaze of a small young schoolboy preparing to scrap with the playground bully so much bigger than he, yet although afraid, determined not to flinch in his task, especially as it was to be enacted before the whole of the class.

Joe Gaffrey and Billy looked at each other both fully realising the personal struggle proceeding within the tormented youth who had been given governance over them. It was Joe who gave voice to their thoughts.

"Of course you will sir and you shall have the full support of us both and all of the men of the Platoon. Have no doubt upon that."

At this they both stood to attention and saluted the doomed youth they called 'Sir' and from whom they took their orders.

Upon leaving, having travelled twenty yards or so, Joe Gaffrey took hold of Billy's sleeve and in a voice barely above a whisper he spoke of his doubts.

"Look Billy, if all is as they say then we shall walk over and be part of a cakewalk. If it is not, then we could all get killed or worse lie out there for days, our lives slowly ebbing away. If it does go wrong, lets adapt the tactics by creeping from shell hole to shell hole. Just one of those blighters firing a machine gun could wipe us out in five seconds if we just walk over there like a row of Aunt Sally's."

"Just so Joe. It is our duty to get to the enemy trench, but to get there alive. We won't be of any use to King or Country if we die without purpose."

"I'm with you there mate"

"Well best get back to the section, lots to do."

Then he added as an after thought

"Best of luck Joe."

"You too Billy."

They clasped hands together in the dark, brothers in arms, each mutually assuring the other, whilst the music of the shelling continued and overhead, projectiles were riding the air like so many Valkurie. It was the last time they would speak together, a poignant moment, as if they were enacting a final, tragic, Wagnerian operatic scene.

Billy arrived back at his section's dug out, discovering that many, like he, were having difficulty in sleeping. It was now fast approaching 3.00am. Before the next hour daylight would begin to emerge out of the eastern horizon highlighting their targets for the battle. He felt that the coming conflict should be forgotten for a while, approaching 6.00am would be soon enough. Hot beverages, should be served, laced with rum for those so inclined to partake. This needed to be dispensed now, together with anecdotes, remembrances of home, wives, family, sweethearts, anything other than talk of this cursed war.

So the time passed in idle conversation, sometimes comic and, at other times, not so. Some stories of love were related, of opportunities missed or, conversely, graphically described, probably fictitious, triumphs. Yet, irrespective of conjecture upon their provenance, they were all stories of home, each one bringing a wistful comfort to the listener. So passed the time until the first streak of light appeared in the eastern sky precursering the flight of the stars.

With all urgency, collective and individual preparations began to move apace. By now all the Section, excepting Joe Keen and Eddie Perkins whose watch it was, were gathered around the makeshift oven, drinking tea. A demonstrative attempt was made to fry bacon, bully beef fritters, or faggots as the men called them, fried bread, eggs and sausages, bringing a full breakfast to the wearisome, contemplative men. They might be going to their deaths, to their salvation, but they would not travel on empty stomachs, not these immortal men of the finest Section in all the Cheshire Regiment.

The book of military history reflects, in so many of its epic pages, upon deeds of great courage, from Leonadas to Horatio, Boudicca to General Gordon. Place names are also inscribed, that are possessed of immortal reference; Thermopylae, The Alamo, Agincourt and The Heights of Abraham. Now, the name of a new field of battle was to be added within its pages. With it came new names, countless names, each the name of a hero, each representing a young man who knew, that morning, that he was watching his last sunrise, and would never more see sunset. If these immortalised young men were ever to play football again, it would be upon a celestial playing field.

Alongside hundreds of thousands of their footballing comrades, from teams all over Britain, as part of the Edinburgh Citizens Battalions, the entire playing staff of Hearts of Midlothian had come to the colours. Football, as they knew it, was finally set aside. 'The Hearts' had performed in inter-regimental matches with great credit, undefeated in any game that they had played since volunteering their lives for God, King and Country. This day, the first of July 1916, they were to sacrifice themselves whilst displaying acts of supreme courage, discipline and determination, all aspects of character that their chosen profession had taught them.

Four were to fall this morning as, fearlessly, they crossed into no-man's-land. Torn asunder, their broken bodies were never more to rise. Fighting as part of the Royal Scots, their hearts steeped in courage, the team that had provided such an exhibition of grace and skill just a few days before, gave their all. With their last display on the football field, they had given so many others an essential diversion from the ardours of conflict, this morning they gave supreme example upon the field of battle.

Here on the Somme, no thought being given to their personal safety, they fully played their heroic part on much greater pasture than mere football turf. Their selfless undertaking ensured for all time, that their lives became elevated to a far higher estate than simply playing football could ever have achieved for them. Duncan Currie, who had so delighted all who saw him play, was the first to fall. Harry Wattie and Ernest Ellis soon followed him. James Boyd was so severely wounded that he was to succumb to death just two days later. Most of their remaining number came to have such injury of mind and body that, never again, would a football find their feet, to become as potter's clay whilst they moulded its action.

Hearts of the deepest red and purist white. Still in these colours, their worthy inheritors play to this day. Crimson in memory of their shed blood, white to typify their innocence. Should their colours ever change, let uproar be manifest all over Scotland, lest their sacrifice becomes forgotten.

Flanking the men of Edinburgh; the inhabitants of an even longer established town of footballing fame were falling side by side. The 'Accrington Pals' possessed many of 'Th' Owd Reds' of Accrington and the 'Reds' of Stanley in their ranks. They also, like their Scottish brethren, paid dearly this day. The little Lancastrian town, situated half way between the much larger inhabitations of Blackburn and Burnley, would pay an incredible price for their gallantry.

This day; almost six hundred souls from the small weaving town would become casualties. Two hundred and fifty of them would never again gaze upon the moors of their beloved Lancashire for they had flown to Heaven's gate, their crushed frames destined, forever, to lie beneath the soil of that countryside which is Picardy. Within a few short days, street after street of their mournful town would see the curtains being drawn in row after row of the small terraced houses, so allowing for the occupants inside to grieve privately for their lost loved ones. Though many of the town's football team had gone, never having wavered in their task, successors would come to take their place, joining the names of Accrington and Stanley to continue a proud tradition. Today, despite many past disappointments, a resurgence exists in that small town and Accrington Stanley are, once more, becoming a name worthy of footballing fame. In its new found success let not the names and deeds of their past heroic team be lost in this new found recognition.

These brave representatives were but a fragment of those of the dearest and the best of a generation from the Kingdom of the British, that fell by the Somme on that morning of the first day of July 1916. Thousand upon thousand advanced, their faces set firmly towards the foe, pitifully armed to withstand the modern instruments of death, which poured out their dreadful projectiles, against which there was no defence. Yet, in spite of all, still they were to go on, wave after wave, steadfast, fearless in spirit, overloaded with the burden of useless materials that were never to be used. Thus, against such abominable odds, these gallant youths may appear to have failed in their task, to have been fruitless in obtaining their objectives. When observed from the passing of so many years, it seems as if their lives were offered and given fruitlessly.

The truth could not be more different. The land, which gives witness to their sacrifice, has not seen war for almost three score years. Two episodes of mindless bloodletting, finally taught the Nations of this portion of the globe that there is another way to conduct the affairs of men. This is the great victory that emanates from the graves of these young men. Insults and challenges are now hurled from the terraces of stadia, rather

412

than from a battlefield. The scene, where so much national pride and expression is now displayed, can still be formidable, aggressive and challenging, giving rise to endless criticism. One ponders, then recalls the row upon row of crosses in Flanders and Picardy and the deliberation ends. 'What foolish men we mortals be.'

By the banks of The Somme, on the morning of this most fateful day, the time was fast approaching; it was 7.00am, thirty minutes to Zero hour. Billy gathered his group around them.

"Well men we have shared much in the past twenty months or so, and here we are ready to face our most challenging task to date. We have lost some good comrades, fine soldiers all. I for one was proud to have known them. Not one of them, even the youngest, failed in their task. Not a single one of them flinched when it was time for them to display courage and duty."

"Now those of us who are left gather here, ready and prepared for yet another test of our fibre. We have become a family, looking each one of us after the other. Let us not today forget that. Now I would like us all to join hands in a circle and, as we have done for so many times now, pray together."

Without any hesitation, having no feelings of embarrassment, the entire group formed a circle and recited the famous Psalm, which had become the section's prayer.

'The lord is my shepherd, I shall not want.'

At its end the Lord's Prayer was recited and they all exchanged handshakes, wishing each other good luck. As they began to drift away they were called back together for one final time as Wrexham George began to sing.

'Abide with me fast falls the eventide
The darkness deepens, Lord with me Abide'

The men had sung this hymn so many times that the words came flowing from their lips. Furthermore, all along their section of the front, men stopped to listen, taking comfort from the verses as they were sung, with those who knew the words joining in.

'I fear no foe with thee at hand to bless;
Ills have no weight, and tears no bitterness;
Where is death's sting? Where, grave, thy victory?
I triumph still if thou abide with me.'

Inspired by this small band of veterans, hundreds of men stood side by side, heads bowed, contemplating their, hoped for, immortality, many of them just a few minutes from earthly oblivion. The fine Welsh tenor finished the last line with a repetitive solo coda, his singing pure of tone and unquivering to the last. Then, as his voice fell silent so did the music of the guns. Ten more minutes, and they would all be climbing the parapets and crossing through the valley of death to meet with the foe.

Each man readied himself in his own way, some with a curse but most with a prayer. Names of loved ones came to their lips, Agnes, Mary, Blodwen, Hilda, Sally. Even though a varied count of names were given up to Heaven, the name 'Mother', easily outnumbered the rest put together, such was the age of these sacrificial lambs.

Whistles blew all along the eighteen mile front. Without hesitation and all fear now gone, the dearest and best of a generation of British youth climbed up the ladders to leap into the inferno. One after another they rose to face their Country's dreaded foe, braced themselves and began their advance.

Billy looked both to the left and the right of him. He saw, for as far as his eyes could scan, the young men of Britain calmly forming up, ready to advance. The sight of all these youths, their ranks steadfast and erect, now calmly walking towards the enemy, inspired in him a last prayer taken from the eighty fourth Psalm.

For the Lord God is a Sun and Shield
The Lord will give grace and glory
No good thing will He withhold
From them that walk uprightly.

It was at this point that the great spilling of blood began. The first to be killed from Billy's Platoon was his immediate superior. Forgetting all that he had been told, the 2nd Lieutenant ran heedlessly towards the enemy, waving his pistol in the air and screaming at the Germans to do their worse. They duly obliged. A particularly alert sniper had risen from his hiding place and, taking careful aim, dropped the poor unfortunate with a single shot to the head.

Now the real harvest of death began to be gathered. Machine guns opened up everywhere. They concentrated on those gaps in the wire which were drawing in bottlenecks of stranded soldiers. It was in such a place of obstruction as this that Corporal Joe Gaffrey met his end along with most of his section. Billy struggling to get through his own gap, saw Joe and his men fall in a heap.

"God speed you good friend."

The words came naturally as if he were by a grave in an English churchyard. Now it was the turn of his men to attract the machine-gunner's attention. He was through the wire along with four of his comrades when the bullets came. The rear members of the Section were caught out with nowhere to go. Some tried to take the direct route straight at the wire. Others kept to the small gap in the wire. It mattered not either way, the machine-gunner got them all; strafing their poor bodies long after they were dead.

Fell, Tommy Smith and Henry Stevens, the new arrivals. So too, in vain attempt to climb the wire, went Eddie Perkins and his good friend Joe Keen, joining his two brothers in the Regiment of the slaughtered. His poor mother would now receive a third tragic telegram and his father would go into the barn and hang himself. A further tragedy played itself out, for the Roberts brothers lay side by side, the younger David with his arm around the elder Trevor.

'Who like thyself my guide and stay can be?
Through cloud and sunshine, oh, abide with me.'

They were now but five, dashing headlong through this furrowed field of death. Above the battle's roar, Billy heard a new machine gun site open up, quite nearby. Before him a line of spitting earth was spitefully inviting, beckoning his troop to advance within its realm. As was its will, his remaining charges were speeding headlong into its arc. Before him emerged a small crater, he knew what to do.

"Dive, men, dive."

Flat on their faces his men did exactly as they were told.

For a short while their problem was resolved. Seeing them fall, the German gunner thought that he had added them to his gruesome harvest and turned his attention elsewhere. To his right a whole company of men, led by a swashbuckling officer were dribbling footballs towards him. Footballs indeed! He would soon put a stop to that.

It took the skilled gunner less than ten seconds to complete his devilish task. Captain Neville and his team had heard their last whistle. The cavalier officer hung lifeless on an outcrop of barbed wire with most of his gallant team around him. A football, pinioned by the heartless barbs lay adjacent to him, slowly deflating upon the wire. Later that day, two of the four balls that had kicked off their advance, would be retrieved and enter into legend. The one belonging to Jimmy Jones, made from a pig, itself slaughtered in a trench more than ten years before, was to become the centrepiece of the East Surrey Regimental Museum. 'Poor Pig.' Upon it had been written words that prefigured another battle that was to take place between these two warring Nations exactly fifty years hence in the summer of 1966.

'The great European Cup

In 1966 the English were to win four two. On this first day of the Battle of the Somme they were to lose by approximately 60,000 to 15,000. One could reflect upon which is the better way to solve the needs of National expression and ambition.

Meanwhile, Billy faced a grave dilemma. He and his depleted troop remained in grave peril. They were two thirds of the way across no-man's-land, still having over a hundred yards left to cross. He looked at his poor bedraggled band. There were but four of the section remaining with him. The crater they were in was shallow; providing some shelter against the incessant machine gun fire, but little enough from the trench mortars that were dropping all around them. In addition they still had their objective to reach. He realised that staying where they were was not something that he could countenance.

A hundred yards from the enemy lines, say twelve: fifteen seconds at the most. Billy turned to face his depleted force. One thing was certain; this day would not end in the great victory that had been promised. It was a disaster. To the left and right of him, he had witnessed hundreds of men being mown down, many, including some of his own, having travelled but a few short yards.

One hundred yards and he, together with his last few brother warriors, could get to grips with the foe. He looked at the remaining four. They stared back speechless, their eyes imploring him to decide what action to take. Wrexham George, Bill Carney, Terry Gresford and Victor Grayson, he felt as though their lives were in his hands.

"Right lads ten more seconds to catch our breath, then its back over the top and, fast as you can, on to the enemy trench, best of luck and may God be merciful to us all."

Whether by instinct or belief they all replied in response to his prayer.

"Amen."

"Amen."

Fittingly, it was the last word that Billy Thomas ever uttered.

They got up and began to race towards their goal, which was so tantalisingly close. The trench mortar exploded just five yards behind them. It instantly took the lives of Terry Gresford and the Welsh Tenor, whose voice had so graced these barren fields so many times, delighting friend and foe alike. A jagged piece of shell casing sliced through his neck to silence that fine voice forever, whilst his fellow countryman had his brain pierced by a similar projectile.

Tragically, Billy, in spite of all his training, stopped to see if he could help them. Victor and Bill Carney still raced on towards the enemy and were both to reach their destination unscathed, the young Glossopian putting a bullet in the head of the demon machine gunner who had reaped so great a toll for his masters.

The second shell landed so closely that it lifted Billy clean off the ground, bringing him back to earth flat on his back. His back was punctured with several pieces of shrapnel, including one which lodged in the base of his spine, paralysing all mobility yet, paradoxically, driving away all pain.

He lay there, in a small crater, his body covering a portion of Picardy, his arms and legs splayed to all four points of the compass. His eyes were fully open, he just lay there gazing at the kind old sun who would have given him warmth if he could but sense it. Sadly the mortal frame of Billy Thomas was well past receiving such a blessing. No matter, he felt neither warm nor cold. Peace began to come to him; the noise of battle faded, then disappeared altogether. His eyes were open, taking in a pure blue sky.

It was then the music came, followed by a succession of visions. Mascagni's Intermezzo flooded his ears, its strains as clear as the time he first heard them. There was comfort here, a surety that this was the prelude to heaven's gate. Words entered his mind.

Hold thou thy cross before my closing eyes,
Shine through the gloom and point me to the skies;

He was a young boy again, standing with his mother; beside his father's grave reading the text upon the headstone. Now he would join him, to await the others, left behind to mourn.

The music rose and fell. It was crystal clear, played by the violins and harps of the Heavenly Choir. He was in a place of books, sat next to a young girl who smiled and passed him a small white handkerchief upon which was a red heart and crimson lettering. It also contained her tears.

A lute now plucked some notes and he was passed a ball that fell to his feet. Swiftly it sped towards its preordained destination and a great roar of approval entered his hearing.

Again the violins gained their ascendancy whilst he stood in the Chapel that his father had helped to build, gazing upon this most beautiful girl as she turned to him, lifted her face, smiled and said, in a quivered voice, the two most precious words that he had ever heard.

"I do."

The music fades, and with it his final earthly vision. There before his face was his beloved Sally, holding in her arms her unborn little Daisy, their daughter. Mystically he felt complete of happiness. Their smiling countenance displaying such love, a love that would not let him go. A breeze brushed his face, it felt as if the lips of the as yet unborn child kissed his brow. Petals from a freshly blown poppy fell upon him, as if they were scattered by their own dear hands. He so earnestly strove to remain, but his spirit was telling him that it was the moment for him to go.

One final time the music came to him, sounding its last notes, it was his time. His lovely ones began to take their leave of him. As they drifted away, he raised one arm in a final gesture to continue to abide in the World but it was all too much. His devastated body could contain his life's force no longer. The eyes closed, the light went from him, the music ceased, the vision vanished and his soul departed his frame.

High overhead the Angels came. There was much to do this day. In less than an hour, Man's inhumanity towards his fellow had reaped a harvest of twenty thousand souls. It was not for the first time that he had conducted himself thus, neither would it be the last, Thus, as they gathered, looking down upon this ghastly place, Billy Thomas was but one lifeless speck among so many.

The Heart had been torn from Midlothian, The East Surrey footballers had fallen, along with their gallant foolhardy Captain. The Pals of Accrington were lain, huddled motionless, row upon row, leaving a town to mourn for them more grievously than most.

Coming from all over the Isles of Britain, fruit of her green and pleasant land, rose the souls of the confused dead, each seeking guidance on where next to go, each receiving a guide to speed them on their way. For mile after mile, in endless columns, a generation of doomed, innocent youth came to their glory in a way so little understood by those who had driven them there.

This was no place for the dead to remain; this morbid, desecrated landscape of the damned. Away from the monstrous anger, the indescribable carnage, they were gently flown, borne by their celestial rescuers, to sleep in peace until the trumpet sounds, announcing the great day of redemption. Thus, along with all those thousands of others, the soul of Sergeant Billy Thomas M.M., late of the Cheshires, son of the town of Glossop, born of the High Peaks, beloved by so many, took its flight. It rose, safely nestled in the all-embracing arms, of one, whose wings rustled softly as they sped him hence.

'Heaven's morning breaks, and Earth's vain shadows flee:
In life, in death, O Lord, abide with me.'

CHAPTER 31

It is the time of roses
And she goes by forlorn
Nor sees the summer splendour
Nor feels the breath of morn
The trees are fresh above her
But no more comes her lover
And hark! They mow the corn.

William Noel Hodgson. Died 1ˢᵗ July 1916 The Somme.

Sally let the paper slip from her hand and it fell onto the dressing table, pathetic in its isolation.

"Pastor Livingston there is no need, purely on my account, to worry over me today. I shall be strong, composed of dignity. My grief shall be an inward one, contemplating upon my great fortune, my fortune to have known such a man as Billy Thomas, to have belonged to him and he to me, on this Earth and in the next."

"I had his love, a pure blissful, perfect, wholesome love, I have it still and ever shall. What we had, what we have, is greater than death, greater by far. Yes, his physical presence is gone from me and nothing can bring it back. We shall never again be joined in that paradise which is physical human love, but you see Pastor we have transcended above that to a higher, more perfect existence."

Taking up the single sheet of paper, creased from endless use, she read.

'What though the radiance
Which was once so bright
Be now forever taken from my sight,
Though nothing can bring back the hour
Of splendour in the grass,
Of glory in the flower
We will grieve not, rather find
Strength in that which remains behind;
In the primal sympathy
Which having been must ever be;
In the soothing thoughts that spring
Out of human suffering;
In the faith that looks through death
In years that bring the philosophic mind.'

Gideon could see that her mind, for the moment, was not of this World, it troubled him.

"Pastor, you understand, Billy is still here with me and will ever be so. Moment by moment I hear his voice. Each evening, in the darkness, his visioned face glows before me, his whispered assurances, forever, lie within me. Yes Pastor I grieve, but not for his loss, for Billy is as much with me now as ever he was. I grieve because his physical death was so unnecessary, so cruel, pointless in itself. Yet even that may not be so, if in his dying and with the dying of so many like he, British, French, German, Austrian, all those pitiful innocent regiments of youth marching, marching, marching, we learn the lessons never to allow such again."

"As for Billy, my Billy, he leaves me in this world with his seed firmly planted within me. Also, the memories of a longed yearned for love that eventually found fulfilment are, forever, etched within me. Yet more than this, much more, his spiritual presence is here, residing. That will never leave me. No Pastor, we have witnessed a great tragedy, a continuing catastrophe unfurls daily before us. Yet I know that Billy is safe, safe where he will never again feel pain, nor sorrow, or loss. I know this, you see Pastor, because Billy abides with me, here in my heart. We are joined and ever shall be. Billy abides with me and I with him."

"See for yourself Pastor, I have his very own words to prove the truth of my assertion."

Sally now handed Gideon a letter placed inside a plain grey military envelope, the type of which the Pastor had opened so many times in recent years. He began to gaze upon the lines, written in that familiar hand, he knew so well.

"Turn to the end of the letter Pastor, what do you find?"

Gideon did as he was asked; there he found two stanzas from Tennyson's 'In Memoriam,' a work he had come to know almost by heart. He noted, in both cases, that Billy had altered the first word of the first line.

He glanced at the sentiments and realised how apt, how comforting those words must be to Sally at this very moment, he read aloud.

'For in my spirit I will dwell,
And dream my dreams, and hold it true:
For though my lips may breathe adieu,
I cannot think the thing farewell.'

" Together with the imitations of Wordsworth, 'In Memoriam' was a favourite work of ours, Pastor. We held its sentiments very dear. We still do so."

Sally took the letter from Gideon and read the final stanza, probably the very last words that Billy ever committed to paper.

420

'So hear at times a sentinel
Who moves from place to place,
And whispers to the worlds of space
In the deep night, that all is well.'

"You see Pastor Livingston, as I told you, Billy still abides with me and I with him."

A wistful smile came across Sally's face as she reiterated her previous conclusion. Standing alone with her, in this room of love, Gideon too was filled of an overwhelming assurance, of the certainty that Billy still resided here. He would always, in the future, whenever he spoke with Sally be convinced that, in her presence, there also dwelt her beloved Billy.

Their love having been blessed and sanctified by their Saviour, their God, had been stronger than death. Even though one of them was of this world and the other now dwelt in his grave, preparing for the next, they were not divided. He was reminded of the very last couplet written by Emily Bronte. Here, in this little room, he was lost for his own words, so he borrowed hers, they felt so apt. He uttered them.

'Then – thou art being and breath
And what thou art may never be destroyed'

Sally voiced but a single word in reply.
"Quite."
Pastor Livingston had come this morning personally, to escort Sally to attend her beloved's memorial service. Having no body to mourn over, no grave of his that was known, it had been decided that those who felt so moved should walk to the Chapel. The mourners would retrace the steps of the same route that Billy and his mother had taken, all those years before, on the occasion of his father's funeral. Gladys wished it so.

Gladys, along with Sally would lead the procession, proceeded by a single drummer marking their paces. Veterans and members of the armed forces, local dignitaries, old friends, would accompany them. It would be an occasion long held in the memory; that day when Glossop, of the High Peaks spake its farewell to a most famed and beloved son.

The day had dawned brightly, the wind still, a nip in the late summer air. Along with the saddened bereft little town, mother Nature was paying her respects.

Upon knocking at the door, Elizabeth had opened it for him. Silently he stopped through meeting Nathaniel, shaking his hand. Jimmy Jones was already present looking sombre, yet proud, in his uniform. He now had an artificial foot and would walk to the chapel alongside Sally with the aid of a stick.

Gladys was sitting down, staring into the fire. Ruth, who had accompanied Gideon, went and sat next to her, holding the hand of the gentle-weeping woman.

"And where is Sally?" enquired Gideon of Nathaniel.

"She is upstairs waiting for you Pastor. She asked that you go up she wishes to speak to you alone before we leave."

"Quite so."

The burdened Pastor passed by the group, clasping his hands. He ascended the stairs. As he did so, he recollected how poor Glossop had come to hear of so many deaths of her sons, in but a few short days. It had taken until the fourth of July for the news to begin to come in of the tragic events three days previously, but once it had done so it came in a flood.

As young Timothy Hyde began to cycle round with his telegrams, and the Church Ministers of the town were alerted, it became evident that a great catastrophe had occurred. In street after street, curtains began to be drawn, and the men of the cloth were called to administer consolation. Nor was the agony merely to be borne by the bereaved for many received word that their loved ones were missing. For some this was soon alleviated by good news, for others the agonising wait had to continue. Such was the case for Sally and Gladys Thomas. It was not until the end of July that Billy was pronounced 'missing believed killed.'

Even so, Sally firmly refused to accept the statement from the War Office, until one day she had arrived at the Manse and calmly announced that her husband, in the flesh, upon this world, was gone from her. Now, two further months hence, the memorial service for Billy Thomas was to take place.

Gaining the top of the stairs, Gideon saw that the door to Sally's bedroom was open. Upon quietly knocking, he passed through into the eerily still room. Sally was gazing out at the window, at the pollarded chestnut tree whose leaves were beginning to transform into colours of autumn.

She turned, sat upon the bed, her hands clasped together in the lap of her black dress. Not one word did Gideon utter. It was Sally who had spoken without interruption. She had related her thoughts in terms of such assured spiritual knowledge, that whilst he listened, he became absorbed of a supreme mystical experience. Later when he spoke of it to his wife, or reflected upon it in his study, Gideon could only explain it as being in the presence of the Holy Spirit.

All was calm, the early sun glinting in a beam through the lace curtains. It was as if a trance came upon him. As he listened to her words, it was as if young Billy Thomas was there present in the room with them. Sally was certain, of this he had no doubt. The young soldier whose body had been torn apart upon the battlefield, that was the Somme, now came to them in spirit, reaffirming their faith, their hope, the truth of the resurrection, to eternal life.

Gideon had never experienced the like before, and would do so never again. All through her oratory and the Lord's Prayer that they recited together, prior to escorting the young widow down the stairs, to face those gathered there, the sense that Billy was present with them was profound. It was so real that all through that day Gideon was convinced he was witnessing a miracle, the undoubted revelation that love, although it suffers long, bears all burdens, believes all things, hopes for all things, also endures all things. He knew, of certainty, by the end of that day that love conquers all, for the truth of the assumption appeared before him. It would never leave him, not for the rest of his life.

Now they were gathered together in the small room, the very same group which had met to speak of France and Billy the day before he died. The Pastor and his wife, Sally, now a widow, Gladys mourning for the loss of her son, inconsolable, not yet having the faith governing her daughter in law. Elizabeth and Nathaniel were calm, alert, each determined to be a rock of support to both Gladys and their daughter, whose pregnancy was now apparent for all to see. Jimmy Jones was there, prepared to escort Sally all the way to the Chapel. His two parents had accompanied him, each sombre, deep in thought, also ready to assist towards the smooth operation of the proceedings.

A further knock came from the door, it was, once again, opened by Elizabeth. In stepped Jack Lloyd with his wife, two other people who had played so crucial a role in the love story that was Billy and Sally Thomas. Catherine Lloyd had wept all night as indeed, she had for most of the evenings since the news of Billy's death had broken. In many ways she considered herself the catalyst of the love affair that had so gripped the little town. Now she was to be a participant in its final chapter. The grief she felt was unbearable. Only the strength gained from her husband helped her sustain the great void dwelling inside her frame.

Gideon now took out his pocket watch. Clicking open the case, he announced that it was time to depart. He led the small group to the door, followed by Sally, Jimmy and Gladys. As the door opened, the rays of the late summer sun poured through, bringing light and a little warmth. The sight, which greeted the mourners out on the street, amazed them. Opposite the house was an honour guard of local army cadets. Madame Mayor was there, together with Hill-Woods, and representatives of all the local political parties; Uncle Frank stood by the door just as promised. He had organised the procession.

It was to be proceeded by three veterans of Loos; Privates of the Sherwood Foresters, home on leave having recuperated from relatively minor wounds. One possessed a kettledrum muffled; the other two carried the Union Flag and the Cross-of St George.

Every door in the street was open, every pristinely scrubbed stone step occupied. A great crowd had gathered, all determined to follow the procession to the Chapel.

The group took their places behind the flag and became silent. Slowly, reverently, the entire street, the dignitaries, it seemed half of Glossop, fell into place. The drummer glanced towards Gideon who nodded. He sounded out a slow beat muffled on hide, dignified, static, dictating the pace.

Thus they left Talbot Street towards the railway line, turning left, so marching parallel with the tracks. The Station Master had decreed that a train, glistening in its black livery should be stationed on the platform, having delayed it in its preparation to leave for Manchester. Crowding its corridors were more young men about to depart, prepared to sustain the front. Silently, those who could do so, leant out of the window in acknowledgement of one who had gone before.

The engine driver had observed the approaching procession, full well, knew its purpose; there had been so many like displays in towns and villages throughout the land. Receiving a nod from his guard, he climbed back into his cab and when the leading party was abreast of his charge he gently let out three blasts on his whistle. It was his personal expression of respect, not lost on those passing by. Others on the platform turned towards the street. Those in uniform saluted, mothers, wives, wept, clasping closer those whom they had come to wish God speed.

Other than the sound of the drummer and the train easing its steam pressure; all was silent. Coming into the cobbled square, walking directly towards the George, a further host greeted all the mourners in silent tribute. The hotel staff, the stationmaster and his staff ceasing work, bareheaded, paying their respects.

The mourners began to step up the small incline leading towards Charles Street. For a moment they stopped at the home of Sally's childhood, its dark green railings reminding Sally of the time when she clung onto them while a small boy and his mother passed by on their way to burying his father. For the first time that day a tear slipped from her cheek to moisten the pavement. Leaving the junction, the procession progressed towards the Library and the Chapel. It was here, looking at those precious steps leading into the palace of books, that Sally staggered, swiftly to be steadied by Jimmy. For a moment she became full of the memories of happy days, of a besotted boy, loved by an innocent girl. Sweethearts in childhood, sweethearts in marriage, sweethearts in death, sweethearts for eternity.

Sally stopped, then stepped forward, taking the single red carnation she had been carrying, she delicately placed it upon the steps. Kneeling down she read, to herself, the motto, written in mosaic, upon which she must have walked so many times. She wondered why she had never noticed

424

the words before. Virtas, Veritas, Libertas, scrolled beneath the emblem that represented the arms of both the town and its football club. Upon the shield were what appeared to be three swords, embellished with crosslets and a stone crown. The shield was centred by a red rose, for Glossop, though firmly set in Derbyshire, was once part of the Duchy of Lancashire.

This icon, once the insignia of a faction during the time of a previous titanic struggle, was now enriched, embellished, proudly displaying Sally's symbolic, solitary red carnation upon its porcelain petals. Sally saw both as emblematic, representative of Billy's blood, and the life's essence of his comrades, spilt in defending both her and the citizens of Glossop. Virtas, Veritas, Libertas; virtue, truth and liberty; still to this day, proudly possessed of the town and its inhabitants forged from the sacrifice of her beloved and so many, many, others.

Having knelt a while in contemplation, Sally rose to continue on her way, her consolation now complete. The carnation would later be gathered up by Helen Potter, pressed and presented to Billy's daughter on the occasion of her wedding over twenty years from this day.

So came the mourners to the Chapel, filing in with graceful order, whispered queries as to their placing, taking up their orders of service. Gideon conducted Sally, Gladys, Jimmy and the others of the leading party to their pews in the front by the pulpit, which he then began to climb. Facing the congregation he sat down listening to the organist playing the last strains of 'Valiant Hearts,' which was to provide the service with its introductory hymn.

Voices rose solemnly, giving life to the haunting melody, and reflection upon those who sang.

> '*O valant hearts, who to your glory came*
> *Through dust of conflict and through battle flame;*
> *Tranquil you lie, your knightly virtue proved*
> *Your memory hallowed in the land you loved.*'

Elizabeth, her throat crumpled with emotion, could scarcely force out the words. The occasion was overwhelming her, so deep was her sense of loss, her sympathy for her daughter and the woman who was Billy's mother. Turning her head along the row of pews she was astonished at the sight that confronted her. Sally, with Jimmy next to her and Gladys on her other side, head held high, dignified, was giving full voice to the hymn. There was almost a smile on her face. Gladys too, although more subdued, frail even, was looking proud, providing a serenity that seemed to emit from her and encompass her daughter in law. It was at this moment that Elizabeth came to realise what later so many others would come to observe, that these two women joined together through the love of a man, would become inseparable. For the rest of her life Gladys would always have

Sally beside her, in support, at night by the fireside, in Chapel, wherever one went, the other would be there also.

Later, the scene would remind Elizabeth of how thousands of years previously two women came together, providing mutual assurance and solace. The Jewess and the Moabitess, giving example to another high human virtue, unselfish, unquestioning, unconditional love.

'Where you go, I shall go
Where you stay, I shall stay,'

The service progressed; Jimmy gave a reading from Psalm 15. His practised sentences voiced from his earthy North Derbyshire accent, long nurtured in the hills above the innocent little town in the days before war came to her, or on the football field shouting out requests for a pass or, as ever was his way, an admonishment to the referee. Now he was a experienced veteran of the Great War, a man who was listened to, despite being barely of an age to vote. No hesitation came, neither a halting in his voice. The words, very true and clean, rang throughout the Chapel.

'He who keeps his oath, even when it hurts.
He who does those things will never be shaken.'

Not one person in the congregation, who heard these words uttered, so steadily, by the young man, could fail but to admire him. He alone, of all in attendance that day, had placed himself in harms way, alongside the one they were remembering, sharing in the danger that was the Western Front, danger which had lost him a foot and a friend his life.

Gideon began to steel himself in preparation for his address. Sally had chosen Matherson's hymn of compassion and reassurance to proceed his homily. Its words of hope and restoration of the power light possesses over darkness, glided through the air filling the firmament with serene melody.

'O joy that seekest me through pain,
I cannot close my heart to thee:
And feel the promise is not vain
That morn shall tearless be.'

The essence had been provided for his address. He knelt for a few moments, urging God to aid him in finding the right words. Then he rose, as he did so his prepared text fell to his feet, not to be recovered. This day, he would speak from his heart, not from any page.

He summoned his strength and began.

426

"We hear the loss of Billy Thomas and feel empty, all of us who knew him. I knew him as a babe, a young boy, a promising lad. I also knew him as a man."

"Billy came to manhood most worthily. I have no doubt his part in that great battle, so recently fought, he played most bravely."

For an age Gideon spoke of Billy's attributes, of his special love for one who was amongst them. He also spoke of the promise that the young man was developing towards fighting injustice and iniquity. He recalled the night of his maiden public speech and how it was received. Then the Pastor returned to the subject of his standing with others.

" He was loved, is still loved, by so many and thus his loss is the greater. As we gather here today, within these walls he so loved, that his father helped to build, we know that never again, here in the place will his face be seen. Yet he is here, will always be here. At Communion, at our prayers, our voicing of hymns and psalms. He is here because we are here and he resides in the memory of us all."

"We have witnessed the departing of so many young men, lads as he. Unselfishly they have given up their lives, struggling upon the field of war, striving towards a more perfect world. Their deaths seem without purpose, or reason. Yet one day a reason may become clear. Meanwhile this I do know to be a most profound truth. Along with all these other lads, God will find work for Billy Thomas in another better World, a World far transcending above this place of sorrows"

"One day, surely, we shall meet again where the lion sleeps with the lamb and swords have been turned into plough shears. You all have loved him, for he lived amongst you. Now he is beloved of his God with whom he resides. This day, with certainty, he soars on wings of eagles, he runs and grows not weary, he walks never to faint. To this we cry heavenwards Amen and, again, Amen."

Gideon was exhausted. His eulogy had drained him of emotion. From below Ruth could sense it so. Through worried for her beloved husband, she kept her place, silent, prayerful. She was aware of the atmosphere surrounding her, of the presence of something more than the Chapel, or the congregation, of an essence ascending above human understanding.

The Anglican vicar of the adjacent Church led the prayers, for this was an ecumenical service. The whole town was bidding farewell to a lost son. He prefaced his words, using a verse from longfellow's 'Psalm of Life,' a work that two young people had once read together, listened to and enjoyed just a few yards away from this place, one wet Saturday morning so many years ago.

'Lives of great men all remind us.
We can make our lives sublime

And, departing, leave behind us
Footprints in the sands of time.

He prayed for the soul of Billy Thomas, for his family and all those who knew him. Appealing to God, he pleaded for the Christian community of all denominations within Glossop, the wider world. He spoke prayers for peace, for soldiers at the front, for understanding between nations.

The service was complete save the final hymn. There were no more apt words to lift in praise than those Billy Thomas would have chosen himself.

'Hold thou thy cross before my closing eyes
Shine through the night and point me to the sky's
Heaven morning breaks and earth's vain shadows flee
In life in death, O' lord, abide with me.'

Silence reigned, contemplation, now Gideon stepped forth offering a final sentiment, words gathered from a 'Shropshire lad,' words summarising the destiny of those lads like Billy Thomas who, in their prime of youth, with willing sacrifice, gave all.

'They carry back bright to the coiner,
The mintage of men
The lads who died in glory
And never grow old.'

Filing out into the midday autumn sun Sally and Gladys received the reiterated condolences from hundreds of people all wishing to provide a personal word of solace. It was a quiet dignified walk home. The two women, arm in arm, silent, each knowing that their future lay together. Each day the older woman was discovering new attributes within her daughter in law, that she so needed for her own consolation, the one whom her son had decided to love above all others.

. For many years to come, they would live their lives as Ruth and Naomi. With the exception of one occasion, over four years hence, the two women would never spend a night under a different roof until the day Gladys passed on to be with her Joshua.

The evening was spent with the two of them re-organising the bedroom. Soon it would need a cot. Sally decided that she was going to have her baby here where Billy spent his youth, his early manhood, his wedding night. This house, the room upstairs, their room, was where her baby would first see the world in which it was entering.

That night, after kissing Gladys goodnight, leaving her by the warm fire to weep over her memories, Sally climbed the stairway and entered the room. She felt Billy waiting for her and began to speak to him, telling of his memorial service, of the kind words that were spoken, the reverence that was displayed, and the spirituality it emanated.

Sally knew he was pleased, she felt so. Placing her hand upon her tummy, it was as if the baby moved, bringing to her the reassurance that Billy would never leave her, or ever could. His child's presence, its face, its familiar gestures, its voice and smile would ensure her that her beloved was always with her. His spirit would surround her, would stay with her until the day she came across to him in that world of spirits.

She spoke to her baby of its father, for an age she spoke, well into the early hours. Eventually, the tins were opened, the battered containers that kept her most precious possessions. The lids announced that they held Jacobs's biscuits, but they were Billy's tins containing his letters and other memorabilia.

His very last communication faced her on the very top of the pile. She took it, pulling the letter from out of the grey military envelope. That it had been scribbled hastily, she could tell by his ragged hand. That he had not found time to edit it, she knew from its form. That it had come straight from his heart she knew by its content.

You tell me, and it is a wonderful
Comforting sentiment you tell.
One that you think of me every day;
Yet I tell you, and it is no exaggeration,
I think of you for every moment of my life,
Of every minute of my existence.
Wherever I am, whatever I am doing,
Not a moment passes without your visioned face before me,
Your echoed voice sounding about me, your fragrance
Drifting around me your heartbeat within me.
Not for a moment does any of this cease,
Not for a single moment.
For:
Sally Thomas, my beloved wife
I love You
This leaves me and comes to you
With the sure and certain knowledge.
That should you discover
Death came to visit me
That at that very moment,
That precise moment,
My thoughts were of you.
Billy

CHAPTER 32

I have many times asked myself whether there can be
More potent advocates of peace upon the Earth
Through the years to come, than this massed multitude
Of silent witnesses to the desolation of war.

King George the Fifth 1865-1936.

The evening of October the 4th drew in, lashed by the driving rain, possessing winds that gusted, moaned and echoed round the now empty Abbey. It was an appalling night, having the appearance of coming straight out of Wagner's metaphysical imagination. Relentlessly, it came whipping round corners, and sweeping over rooftops like so many Valkurie riding out to avenge their Wotan.

Walking up the great Nave, Herbert Ryle, Dean of Westminster, could but lay conjecture upon how many such evenings this grand Gothic medieval structure had survived, embattled but unbowed, typifying how the Nation had come through the devastation of the Great War. He recalled another evening, such as this, almost four years ago when, alerted by a mighty roar of engines, he had gone out from his residence to see the giant monolith etched out against a full moon coming towards his beloved church full of menace, dreadful to behold.

The rejoicing and thanks, spontaneously given by him, that night, to God, came once again to his mind. He remembered observing, with the utmost horror, the small string of objects that spewed out from the mouth of the monster and the relief he felt when they merely landed harmlessly along the embankment or into the river. It was an example, the most wondrous example, of a miracle that had ever befallen his eyes.

On that night too, the wind had visited, pitching and tossing the mighty angel of death, as if she were but an inflated child's balloon. The enormous energy of the storm, took the controls of the mighty machine from out of the hands of its hapless navigator, to place them into the fickle and capricious domain of Nature, sealing its fate.

The storm, venting its anger above, reclaimed the image in his mind, drifting back to him vivid memories from those days of trial. The whole gargantuan spectacle was played out before him on that night. A bare ten minutes after seeing the bombs being dropped, his emotions had leapt from trepidation to pity. Without warning, the elongated globe spontaneously ignited into flame, slowly descending towards its last dreadful encounter with the earth. This it accomplished with an explosion which seemed to rock the entire city even though the machine must have been well over Hackney Marches at the time.

The horrific death of the aerial giant provided the first incident, that he could ever remember, which moved him to pray for a fallen enemy. He knew that along with the great ship, several souls had perished, enemy souls it was true, but souls belonging to God none the less. He had returned that night to the Abbey, to the very spot where he was now standing, kneeling, giving thanks to the Almighty that London and the Abbey had been spared. He also commended to their maker, the souls of those he was certain had perished within the bowels of the mighty bird of death. He prayed for them and their loved ones in Germany who would never see them again. That night he pleaded with God to alleviate mankind from the great slaughter, of which the episode that he had witnessed was but one small skirmish, as soon as it was possible, that it was right so to do in his eyes.

For the Dean it was only his only direct experience of the war's ferocity. True he had met the bereaved, the wounded, the returned, but this one incident had been his only face to face encounter with the possibility of death. Perversely, it had ended in prayers for the repose of a few of the enemy and their unknown German women grieving for their young Herman or Karl.

Now peace had come, almost two years of peace and tonight he had convened a meeting to decide upon the future form that his country's grief should take. Somewhere by the Hackney Marshes, shrivelled to nothingness, were the last resting-places of those unfortunate enemy aeronauts whom, even now, from time to time, he remembered in his prayers. In France, Gallipoli, The Holy Land, Russia, Italy and Salonica 'lay resting' countless thousands of his country's bravest. How best to commemorate them? Tonight's meeting would decide.

All was prepared for his illustrious guests. The private intimate Jericho room was waiting to receive the party. It would not be long now before they arrived. Secrecy had been all-important. His Majesty had insisted upon unanimity of decision. Thus, he required that the, meeting's existence be known only to those who absolutely needed to know. After it was concluded, he told the Dean, then, dependent upon its decision, would knowledge of the committee, convening here at the Abbey, ever be divulged.

The Dean went over to the door, which was used as the private entrance to his residence, to await the arrivals. As he went he prayed, in this most sacred of places, that God would give them wisdom that night. Turning along the short corridor leading to the entrance, he noticed that his secretary had already let in two visitors, both of whom he recognised. David Railton, and Sir Fabian Ware had arrived early.

Walking up to them he shook both their hands, bade them welcome and, after instructing his secretary to show his other guests into the Jericho room, he led these first two gentlemen to their destination.

The venue for that evening was small, warm and installed with books that went row upon row from the floor to the ceiling. The only furniture was an oval table, which had been set out with eight chairs, in front of which were eight note pads, glasses and pencils. Two decanters of water rested in the centre of the table. It was professional ordered and austere, reflecting the atmosphere he hoped would prevail throughout the meeting.

David Railton was invited to take a chair midway on the left of the oval and Sir Fabian one opposite. Soon the room began to fill. Sir Edwin Lutyens entered; followed by a man the Dean had never met before. This latest entrant was introduced to the gathering, by Sir Fabian Ware, as Colonel Henry Williams of his Majesty's War Graves Commission, a man who was destined to play a pivotal role in the night's events.

Prime Minister David Lloyd George became the sixth person to join the group, posturing and pontificating as ever, reflected the Dean, somewhat ungraciously perhaps. Problems were escalating for the diminutive Welshman, what with him being a prisoner of the dominant Conservatives and the ever-present Irish crisis demanding so great a level of vigilance on his part.

Finally the King arrived, escorted by his secretary Sir Alan Lascelles. Sir Alan had organised a secretive exit for the King from the Palace, utilising a non-descript conveyance to bring them both to the Abbey. He had succeeded in delivering his charge in total privacy, no mean feat on his part, for his charge was such a distinctively featured monarch.

As the King entered, the entire group stood, silent expectant and attentive. King George the Fifth was shown to his place at the table's head. As he did so more than one here, witnessing his presence, realised that an historic moment had arrived. He sat down and, with the one word "Gentlemen," he signalled for the rest of the gathering to do likewise. After a brief pause, the Dean rose and began with the opening pleasantries.

"If it pleases your Majesty, I shall be honoured to introduce all here present."

"As you wish Reverend Dean."

"Your Majesty, here assembled are respesentatives of all the pertinent groups and individuals relevant to the matters that we are about to discuss, Government, The Armed Forces, The War Graves Commission, The Church and Sir Edwin Lutyens, architect of the Cenotaph and Chairman of the National Armistice Day Committee."

He then proceeded to introduce each individual and welcomed Sir Alan Lascelles. The meeting was ready to progress.

"Firstly,"

With a single word the King, assumed the role of Chairman. In so doing he elevated the gathering's importance to a higher plain.

"This meeting, although one of great importance, will have no recorded minutes. Any decision that results in a positive acceptance of the proposal must be unanimous. We shall all leave here feeling that each and everyone and those they represent are part of this idea. If the outcome is one of acceptance, then the Church will announce the decision. That way Monarch, Government and the Armed forces will be seen to be supporting a concept that emanated from the established Church. No one individual group shall gain credence or advantage. Are we all agreed?"

All those present murmured in affirmation and the King continued.

"Well then let me see if I can lay out the argument as it stands for the moment."

He paused to reflect, gathering his ideas. The King did not want to be seen favouring one view over another, although he was, as yet, to be persuaded upon the idea of a common Unknown Soldier of, God knows what ancestry, lying in this place of national reverence. Of all the dead, lying in hundreds of far-flung battlefields, how did you decide upon selecting the one to be so privileged, above all others, and bring him to reside, in perpetuity, alongside the great, the powerful and the good?

"Gentlemen, Sir Edwin's committee has produced an excellent concept. Two years to the day, to the hour, to the minute, that the armistice came into being, the nation will cease in its motions and for two minutes every resident within our shores, and indeed across the empire shall stand silent. They shall do so to reflect upon our debt to the dead of the Great War, those that saved their Nation, fighting for their God and their King."

"After the awesome silence, buglers shall sound the last post at which time I shall step forward and unveil the Cenotaph. The central memorial to the honour dead. Gentlemen, within the Cenotaph, which in Greek means 'Empty Tomb,' shall lie no mortal remains of any kind. In so being it is symbolic of all those who died. It is a place where the individual can reflect upon the memory of their own personal lost one. Yet, Gentlemen, it too can be the focus for our entire national mourning. Here, annually, King, Government, Church, The Armed forces and all who play a part in working for those who have returned, can gather and remember together, in grand ceremony, those who were lost, those who made the great sacrifice."

"No doubt, throughout the land and across the Empire, local memorials shall be raised mourning the dead of a parish, village, town or city where loved ones can come and see displayed, carved out of stone, the names of the individuals who were taken from their homes, never to return. The landscape of our country will change forever, having thousands of such memorials erected, at the most prominent of places. That is good. Nowhere will a subject of this Country or a visitor to our shores be able to travel without coming upon such memorials. Thus the memory of the war to end

433

all wars, as Prime Minister Lloyd George has described it, will stay etched in the minds of people for generations to come."

"Not withstanding all these local monuments, it is to the Cenotaph that the Nation and all the representers of our Allies shall be drawn, each Commemorative Armistice Day, to pay homage and give our grateful thanks. Sir Edwin have I laid out the basic premise of the concept that you and your committee have so assiduously endeavoured to achieve?"

"Yes your Majesty, indeed you have, completely and perfectly."

Lutyens was pleased; the meeting was proceeding well, thus far. The King had given his monument great prominence in his opening remarks; his great Cenotaph would remain intact as the sole edifice for national remembrance. He felt sure his argument would win the day.

The King continued; now was the time to attempt resolution of the matter. He decided to achieve his aim and display his knowledge of scripture at the same time.

"There we have it gentlemen, the case for the Cenotaph, the empty tomb, as indeed became the cave owned by Joseph of Aramthea did it not Reverend Dean?"

"Quite so your Majesty, it is an image prevalent in Christianity bringing forth images of resurrection, immortality and ultimate sacrifice. Sir Edwin's monument is perfect in this respect."

Lutyens was becoming more and more confident by the moment, his argument was becoming prevalent he was sure.

The King had succeeded in his initial aim Crown and Church, thus far, were of one mind.

"Right then gentlemen, let us proceed. It is time, I think to hear from the Reverend Dean. Reverend, the floor is yours."

The King was signalling to the Dean that he would allow him to put his case without any preamble from himself that might colour later argument.

The Dean rose, surveying the assembly. Thus far the argument had gone well for the status quo, now a reasoned but passionate case must be provided for in defence of a tomb for the Unknown Warrior.

"Thank you your Majesty but if it pleases this committee I should first like to pass the baton onto the Reverend David Railton Vicar of Margate. He it was who first conceived this idea. Reverend Railton provided pastoral comfort for our troops throughout the entire war. He arrived in France during August 1914 ministering to the then small regular army. For the next four years, as the professionals were augmented by the territorials, the volunteers and finally the conscripts, David Railton was unceasing in his endeavours to sustain their courage to provide Holy Communion, send communications back home and commend the dead to their maker. Whatever was needed, spiritually or practically, he was there. Consequently, I believe no one is better placed to put forward the argument

434

for the entombing of a national Unknown Warrior than he. David the floor if yours."

A dignified silence greeted the slightly built, newly installed, Vicar of Margate. Without exception, the room was aware of the great contribution that the Service Chapliaincy had endowed upon the front line troops, at the first aid stations and in countless other rolls, so often unknown, unrecognised, yet absolutely essential. They would give this little known Cleric full respect and attention.

"Gentlemen, your Majesty."

David Railton began hesitatingly; he was a nervous speaker, addressing such an esteemed gathering in so covert a manner. Lloyd George inwardly frowned at the Cleric's incorrect opening address, placing commoners before Monarch, but looking at the King it did not seem to have upset him one jot, it was one of those nights, rare and ethereal. All those present had promised not to make any diary notes, however he would find a way around that.

"You must forgive me but I have never spoken in such illustrious company before and I wish to give my cause justice."

The King interjected in a deliberately informal manner, wishing to put the poor man at ease.

"David, I for one wish to hear what you have to say. Please take your time. From what I have heard of your exploits during the Great War you have earned, full well, the right to espouse your cause. As for this being an illustrious gathering here today, all I can remark upon is that we pale in comparison with the illustrious company on whose behalf you now wish to make an evocation. David, take your time, God knows the dead deserve that as least."

The King was warming to this sincere priest, 'maybe,' he thought, 'he will surprise us.'

"Thank you your Majesty, you are most kind and indeed you are correct. Today, in Britain we enjoy a reaffirmed freedom, endorsed by the blood of so many of our young men. It may not be perfect, this land of ours, but it is all we have. Today it remains free from any foreign force and the mistakes that we make are our own mistakes."

"That our women and children did not have to flee before the heel of the foe is due entirely to those young men who held the line. And what a line it was, this last line of defence between us at home and the enemy raging at the gates. It stretched for miles winding with the contours of the land. Thin and fragile in places, it undoubtedly was, but it held. Unlike poor Belgium and parts of France, the Hun was never visited upon this land, for the line was held by that precious band."

"It held this line, it held, but at what a cost. I do not refer simply to the dead themselves, but to the privations subsequently suffered by their families. I refer also to their grief, a grief which for so many is compounded by not knowing where and how their lived ones fell. It is for those, the doubly distressed that I appeal to you."

The room echoed to the voice of this gentle cleric, the tension was rising. David Railton could feel it. He decided to tell of the time when the idea first came to him.

"One day gentlemen, I was billeted in a small family hotel about ten kilometres west of Amiens. My hosts were very welcoming, continually expressing gratitude towards me and the number of other British soldiers who were also their guests. They did everything to make us comfortable and welcome. The rear of the hotel was comprised of a fine walled garden around which grew peaches, pears and apples all growing in the cordon manner. A stone pathway led round the garden the centre of which possessed a perfectly kept lawn."

"Realising that I was a Cleric, the family roped me into the saying of grace and into visiting my fellow guests. Initially the French must have thought I was a Catholic Priest for they addressed me as 'Father.' Upon informing them that I was a Protestant they came to address me as 'Father Huguenot.' Not wishing to complicate things I allowed this to stand."

A small chuckle from the Prime Minister, exposed to David Railton that this irony was not missed by at least one of the assembly.

"Following my first breakfast, I was invited into the garden. The Germans had, at this time, never got within twenty kilometres of the town, although, during their advance in the spring of 1914, I believe the place became the front line for about two weeks before we began to push them back. So here I was, enjoying the delights of an unspoilt, tranquil garden, encased by a wall, peaceful and secure."

"Then came the surprise. I followed the hotel owner to the far right hand corner of the garden."

"Father Huguenot," requested my host, "I would like to show you an English Valois. Our own dead hero."

"I did exactly as I was bidden and approached the shrine. Here I came across a meticulously kept grave being regularly tendered."

"This is our own brave English Valois, he died here, with us, from wounds which festered. It was during July 1916 when so many were dying upon the Somme and although we sent our son to the British Headquarters in Amiens they could spare no one."

"I was told that there had been no way of identification for the young man. A French priest, from the church that the family attended, had officiated at the internment and so here he was, their very own British Valois, a treasured family possession. Then, gentlemen, it dawned upon me, the irony of it all. Such was the strain of resources at the time, there had been no one who could tend to this poor soul except a French family and their local priest, who from their own generosity and gratitude took it upon themselves to sanctify his death and keep his memory."

"The grave was beautiful, headed by the cross of Lorraine and the words 'Un Englais Valois.' I complimented my host upon the sensitive way in which he had interred our soldier and how well he kept the grave. Apparently the particular serviceman interred below, had been found wondering the village, delirious from a shoulder wound contaminated with gangrene. Within two days he was dead and other than his uniform there was no identification upon him and in his delirium he had not given his name."

"His epaulettes were evidence that he was a soldier of the Sherwood Foresters, but that was all. These had been placed by his grave, together with other British regimental insignia and a mocked up Union Flag. I was minded of those lines composed by one of the Irish war poets."

'Greater than a poet's fame,
A little grave that has no name.'

"For all I know gentlemen, this man lies, to this day, where I left him. If so, I suspect that he is regularly attended to, thanks be to God. Yet, none of his family will ever know where he is. They grieve, having no knowledge of where he lies, how he fell, or indeed anything about his last moments. He will have simply been reported, 'missing, believed killed.' Gentlemen, I conjecture, what if Colonel Williams and his men exhumed him, discovered his identity, would not his family's grief be alleviated? If he were my son it would be so."

"Yet, with all of the titanic exertions of Colonel Williams, such a thing will not come to pass, for his task is too great, as he will, no doubt, explain."

David Railton had prepared his premise, now he would come to his proposition.

"Suppose gentlemen, that we endeavour to bring back home, to these shores, just one such warrior. We then inter him here, in this sacred place, could not all of those who grieve for their lost dead suppose, if only for the moment, that this one elevated warrior was their very own son, husband or brother?"

"Think on it gentlemen, how comforting the thought. No longer would those who mourn for their lost dead be doubly grief stricken. I suggest to you that with such a thought, within their breasts, their grief would be uplifted, metamorphosed, transcended towards pride and thankfulness that they once possessed within their midst, so great a man."

"The people will come to this place, old soldiers, families, the widowed, the orphaned. They will bow, in repose, by the spot where he lays and pray for he who dwells within as if he were their very own. Who here would deny them this? Who here? Who here?"

Silence met the completion of David Railton's appeal. It was as if the entire assembly had been stunned. The spell was broken by the King.

"Who indeed Reverend Railton, who indeed. Yet we must progress, anything to add Dean Ryle?"

In truth the King felt a certain persuasion, being drawn towards the argument that he had just heard. Yet it was his duty to uphold tradition, to tread conservatively in his ways. He would wait to see how the discussion developed.

Dean Ryle sensed that David Railton's argument had changed the very air within the Jericho room. He felt it was his duty to now drive the argument forward. He would do his best.

"Gentlemen, David Railton came to me with this proposal for a tomb encasing an Unknown Warrior some months ago. His eloquence, logic, and passion persuaded me to champion his cause, espousing, as he did, his concept in much the same manner as he had done today. However I have to say that his address to us this evening has for me, and I expect for many of you, left a deep, profound impression. There is comfort in death, but there is much more. The triumph of good over evil, over death itself."

"During the war, even in our darkest hours. I believed that we were fighting for a just cause. We were placing ourselves before the playground bully to defend the weak. We prevailed, but it cost the Nation dear. A generation of the best of our youth lie asleep in Flanders field and countless other places. Now, in victory, we need to make our triumph theirs. They are not merely 'The Glorious Dead,' as inscribed on so many memorials, they are the glorious victors, still a part of us, a part of the Nation. It is now eventide; I am minded of the verse from the hymn."

'I fear no foe, with thee at hand to bless;
Fears have no weight, and tears no bitterness;
Where is deaths sting? Where, grave, thy victory?
I triumph still if thou abide with me.'

"Gentlemen, the hymn's inspiration comes from the Gospel of Luke. It refers to a time immediately after the resurrection of our Lord. That war, the war over sin and death, was won, for indeed he did abide with us, as we most certainly witnessed during the great conflict. Now, I pray you, allow one of this fallen host, whose way of death was known only to God, whose resting place is known only to God, become a part of this great Abbey. Let one of them be elevated to take his rightful place amongst the greatest of our Nation in the holiest sanctuary our great country has to offer."

The case as perceived by the Church, had now been put to the assembly for its contemplation. Outside the great Abbey, the storm began to abate, the wind ebbing away. With the calming of the storm, the rain began to fall gently, no longer in rage but as if they were tears from the very eyes of God himself.

In the eyes of the King also, there was a certain moistening, and he was not alone. A presence had entered the Jericho room, beyond mortal understanding and with it, a sea change in the hearts and minds of those present.

One member of the room had been profoundly affected. He was Sir Alan Lascelles. Later in contravention of all convention, he would add his words to the debate.

Composing himself, the King still felt the need to appear objective. Who to call next? He decided upon the young army officer, that he was meeting here for the first time.

"Perhaps now that the Church has made out its case we should hear from you Colonel Williams. I know well the task that has been placed into your hands, and feel that now is the appropriate time for you to add to the debate."

Lieutenant Colonel Henry Williams had been called to this meeting to provide a briefing of the situation in France where nine out of every ten British casualties of the war had occurred. It was his gruesome task, utilising a force of five thousand men, mostly Colonials, to comb the battlefields, exhume identify and re-inter, in a British cemetery, as many of the fallen as was possible. In truth it was an impossible mission, as he would explain.

"Gentlemen the War Graves Commission now holds in perpetuity, on behalf of the crown, lands all along what was called the Western Front, for the purpose of interring our war dead in a consecrated field that is of Britain. They shall reside in a place where their remains will be cared for during the ages to come. Down the years, visitors shall come to lay flowers, to spend a while at a place where a loved one dwells. These fields of countless crosses shall become places of pilgrimage."

" For those who have no known grave, great memorials are being erected, upon which shall be carved the names of all those dead we do not find. For example, a great memorial is being erected at Mons. I have calculated that it will take over twenty years before the last name is engraved on that monument. The figures are astounding, the task Herculean."

"I have five thousand men under my command, five thousand men. We work in two ways. Firstly we actively seek out remains at places where we know they should lay, and we are finding them by the hundred. Secondly we react when a report comes in. Perhaps a farmer's plough has turned something up and we investigate. If fortune is with us then another name is taken from the list of those with no grave and a new headstone is created above where we have provided yet another last named resting-place."

"Eventually, gentlemen, there shall be hundreds of acres of graves, great corners of foreign fields that shall be forever England, or more exactly, of the Commonwealth. Yet I tell you. If we labour, as we are so doing, for the next sixty years, there could still be up to half of own dead lying in places unknown, unacknowledged. It is that great a task."

"In assisting you in coming to a decision today I recall a conversation that I had recently with Belgian farmer. He was distressed that he was to lose three or four acres of land from his farm because the War Graves Commission had been granted it. The day that we arrived to begin our construction he confronted me. In a mixture of angry Flemish, interspersed with expressions in English, he accused me and the Commission or robbing him of his inheritance. Land that had been tilled by his family for generations."

"Who was to compensate him, he asked, did we not wish to compensate him for his loss? It was his land, not ours, he and his ancestors had earned it, we should pay him for his loss. Gentlemen, part of my duties in the task that has been given to me is to liaise with local people in a diplomatic fashion. I assure you, in this object I have behaved as if my entire training had emanated from the foreign office."

"On all occasions except this one time, I have acted in the most diplomatic manner. Not this time, I was enraged. 'Pay for it,' I screamed at him, 'Pay for it! I tell you sir this land has been paid for a hundred fold, not in money, not in gold, but in blood. It is the blood of those who shall rest here that have paid for it, and paid for it for all time.' Gentlemen, if I may say so, never has an opposing force ever retreated so instantaneously from the presence of an English soldier. Of this I can assure you."

At this admission, murmuring whispered around the room, Colonel Williams too was making an impression. Lloyd George began to reflect upon the level of debate that he was witnessing this evening. The House of Commons itself would be proud to stage such a dialogue. How he wished for a hundred allies such as these in the House today. Colonel Williams was now ready to make his closing point.

"Gentlemen if you can condone such conduct from me as a representative of the Crown, then logic insists you accept this comparison. Our Glorious Dead are unconditionally deserving of such places from the French, from the Belgians without the need to negotiate, without further cost, except to our labour. Surely you accept this. How can you then refute the right of one who represents those unknown dead, to lie forever in this holy place alongside. His eminent predecessors whose lives are also an essential part of what we are now? The unknown dead have earned this right, they have paid for it with their blood."

"One of their number should now be brought home to lie here in perpetuity. Then and only then shall his brothers rest peacefully in those foreign fields."

440

Again, as at the end of the other contributions, the atmosphere was thoughtful. Each and everyone around the table was being drawn into a debate full of emotive sensation, National pride, and memories of dark days, recollections came to them, of newspapers filled with lists of endless names, of all ranks and levels of society. Pressure was building, it required a valve to alleviate it. Lloyd George obliged.

"Well I am told that patriotism is the last refuge of the scoundrel. It would appear tonight that patriotism, has been replaced by poetry anecdotes and its allusions."

The King countered the observations of Lloyd George.

"Quite so Prime Minister, but here poetry has its place. Without exception, as far as I can ascertain, all the words used have been those of fallen poets have they not?"

"Sir, indeed they have."

The King's assertion, so affirmed, an admonished somewhat embarrassed occupant of Downing Street, who in another place was capable of eating opponents alive with his rhetorical wit, withered and would have remained silent had his Monarch allowed so. The King had other ideas.

"Well then Mr. Prime Minister shall we now have your thoughts on the matter?"

Lloyd George had been quite unprepared to speak at this juncture. He had hoped to be called at the end of the debate, when he could add his weight to whom he supposed would be the victor. This meant that Edwin Lutyens would have the final word. It would not do, would not do at all! Yet he had become genuinely impressed by Railton and Williams. If he put the weight of Government behind them, they would probably win the day.

Before leaving Downing Street that evening, he had enjoyed a light supper with Frances. Having discussed the issue with her, asking for a woman's viewpoint, she had been drawn towards the idea of the Warrior's tomb thinking it romantic, gothic and like that delicate flower of spring 'heart easing'. The words stuck in the Prime Minister's mind. 'heart easing'. 'Let us see where that leads too,' he thought.

As he stood up to address the meeting, the contrast between the short stocky Welshman and the tall athletic Henry Williams could not be more stark. But Lloyd George did not rely upon physical parameters to create stature, his lilting Welsh oratory could command the attention of thousands. He was persuasive, reasoning, and steadfastly patriotic, words could flow in smooth unhesitating proslytisation, that brimmed with emotion drawing respect and admiration, even from those who were his most bitter and bitten foes.

"Gentlemen, I came here a sceptic. Honouring our nation's dead is the most serious of issues and needs to be undertaken with all the solemnity, pageant and precision that this Nation's capacity for ceremony can provide. Sir Edwin's committee has been more than a year in the planning. The Cenotaph standing strong, upright, subtly merging the Gothic with the Classic is majestic in its imperial splendour. It will come to dominate White Hall that great thoroughfare betwixt the squares that one Trafalgar and Parliament."

"No head of state leaving their embassy to visit the residence of the Prime Minister shall fail but to notice it and, in their observation, realise that this great country will never bow to the tyrant, or fail to step forward in championing the weak. It shall stand there for all time imposing and grand. It shall comprise so many facets. A monument of memory, a symbol of sacrifice, an edifice to our greatness as a nation, standing for all time"

"Now all is complete. The unveiling of the Cenotaph, as his Majesty has described, shall be the most famous of moments, etched upon the memories of millions for decades to come. Nothing can or shall be undertaken that would distract from such a moment."

Sir Edwin was now feeling very assured. This little Welshman, this village tyrant, this upstart from that most barbaric part of the Kingdom was going to endorse his project. Soon the nonsense iterated by the previous speakers would be forgotten and they could all go home.

Lloyd George continued.

"On the Eleventh of November, hundreds of thousands will flock to the capital to become part of the ceremonial. We must not let them down by complicating matters with an ill-formed, quickly prepared gimmick. The day must proceed perfectly."

Railton and Williams were now becoming very unsettled, it appeared as if the Prime Minister was about to shatter their aspirations. Yet the Welshman was made of sterner stuff, he knew when to grasp the imagination, when the opportunity for greatness was upon him. Now he felt was such a time, this, he sensed was the place. He would never have presented such an opportunity to provide the pivot in an immortal decision. A thousand years from now people would still flock to see the tomb of Britain's Unknown Warrior. It would have been him, David Lloyd George, of the land of the Cymru, who made it all possible.

Yes, this was his opportunity, he would take it. This was no 'Hall of Mirrors' he could, he would, win the day. Having made his decision he would now use all his powers of persuasion.

"And perfect it shall be gentlemen, in all respects. Conjecture if you will, the selection of such an Unknown Warrior, sped across France, brought across the Channel, taken from Dover to Victoria Station. A gun carriage progresses along Whitehall. It attends the unveiling. The ceremony is completed exactly as arranged, then the procession continues to the Abbey and the internment takes place."

"This enhances the significance of the Cenotaph. It remains empty but not before it is consecrated in the company of that one sole representative of all the unknown dead. It can be achieved. We as a Nation can galvanise ourselves to craft what ever is needed. I am going to endorse the vision of Reverend David Railton and Colonel Henry Williams. Gentlemen we should have a tomb dedicated to an Unknown Warrior within this great place. It should cover one of their number. It could and it should. Furthermore, it shall, if my Government has anything to do in the matter. I believe we must make it happen. Gentlemen, with your resolution, it is going to happen."

The King was astounded. His devious First Minister had just made possible putting into practice the aspirations of the proceeding advocates. Who would have thought it? If only the little Welshman had kept a faithful orderly family life, void of all innuendo and rumour, he could have been the greatest of his office since Pitt.

'Oh well such is life.'

The King mused; better to check that Lloyd George could handle the new development though. It would be a tragedy to agree on such a new direction, if all that was needed could not be made ready in time.

"Prime Minister, before I progress, could I ask you to reaffirm that you have no doubt at all that everything could be prepared in time? After all we have but five short weeks before the day is upon us."

Lloyd George swiftly realised what the King had done. By asking a question relating to logistics rather than principle, the King was intimating that he too had swung his opinion towards the Railton proposal. Now his mind was made up also, Railton was to win the day.

"Certainly your Majesty, upon that have no doubt."

King George was grateful, now he could allow the meeting to take its inevitable course, for Lloyd George would now deal with any objections based upon logistics whilst the rest of this gathering, with the possible objection of Sir Edwin, would organise the creation of something most remarkable.

Sir Edwin's mood was becoming blacker by the minute. The great edifice and its significance was in danger of having its central role diluted, he would fight to the end to avoid such a scenario.

At this precise moment, when history was about to be led towards a particular fork in its journey, a most remarkable incident occurred. Sir Alan Lascelles, who would never normally interject in discussing policy matters, decided to break convention and ask if he could add his opinion to the debate.

"If it would please your Majesty, I should wish for a word. It is unusual, if not unprecedented for me to speak upon such a matter, but a word if I may, for I too have my own son to mourn over, buried in an unknown, presumably unconsecrated place."

The King was taken completely by surprise by the interjection of his private secretary. It was known upon occasion for him to speak with

443

reference to dates and State protocol, but never had he heard the man intervene in a policy matter. He felt a little uncomfortable about provisioning a precedent, but he would allow Sir Alan to speak his mind on this occasion.

"Of course Sir Alan, please proceed."

The King was intrigued, perhaps he would learn something of the man who drove the machine that was his office. He hoped so.

"Thank you for your indulgence Your Majesty, I will not take more than a few moments. Gentlemen, my contribution is drawn from a very personal grief. It is a sense of loss profoundly typical to that, which has been described by the Reverend Railton. His words so touched me that I feel compelled to respond."

For a moment, the man who was the King's private secretary gathered his thoughts. Memories of the past flooded before him, Of the days of peace and how he so enjoyed the company of his beloved sons. Like so many of their generation, leaving full of passion and pride, his sons had marched away never to see the shores of home again.

Now he imagined them, together with legions of their comrades, marching towards the horizon's sky to fade into eternity. He knew that he must speak for them, or their admonishing vision would haunt him till the day of his own death.

"The Great War brought forth many graphic images, and symbols, never before visited upon the Nation. A new literary genre, born of a novel and supremely terrifying form of warfare, came into being. Poetry, scribed from the pen of the common man, carved from his tribulation, entered the language adding to the vast wealth that it already possessed."

"The Great War was also socially unique. For the first time in our history, the entire populous became involved in the Nation's struggle. It was truly the Nation's war, enjoined by civilians and military, men and women alike. Of this we British can be proud."

"We would not have been victorious if one arm of our Nation had not given of its best. Now we are left with the victory. We are also left with our memories also. The symbol of the Poppy, imaging those countless blooms erupting from out of the ravaged earth, the trenches, the mud and barbs of wire, the cratered landscape, all are still with us. It will ever be thus. The beaches of Gallipoli, the sight of great ships slipping beneath the waves, these will stay with us till we, in turn, pass on to become a part of the past."

"Yet, listening to this debate, here in this holy place, I have felt that a new and greater image is being born. Of all the great and noble artefacts and memorials that we are creating, the Unknown Warrior shall become the most symbolic. He shall be the most nameless and yet paradoxically of all the devices that we shall ever create, none shall ever give a greater, more clear cut image of reality."

"Everyone of us who have their own dead, sons, husbands, loved ones, who lie in unknown graves, shall not fail to see that they too will be able to escort one, who could indeed be their very own, to his last resting place. Gentlemen, after two years of waiting, each and every one of us, so bereaved, shall be able to place a wreath personally to the memory of their own loved one. Moreover it shall be one who lies beneath the Nave of this wondrous place. Within the great walls of our Nation's Abbey, destined to sleep among the good, the great and the powerful shall lie one of that Great Company."

Silence reigned, the King had never heard Sir Alan speak so, though they had conversed together many times, with the King often asking him for an opinion. After this, further eloquent example of deeply sustained oratory, only one decision could be made. It was to be hoped that Lutyens had seen the inevitable coming his way and would accept the situation. Now was the time to find out. Ignoring his Prime Minister for a moment, he turned towards the architect and uttered just two words.

"Sir Edwin?"

Indeed the architect realised that he could now in no way reason against such a collective of powerfully charged argument. How best to retrieve the situation? During Sir Alan's contribution an idea had come to him. He would try to articulate it.

"Your Majesty, I tend to concur with the general line of argument that the discussion has followed. Indeed properly instituted upon the lines sketched out by the Prime Minister it can do nothing but enhance the significance of the day's ceremonial. May I propose that the representatives of the War Graves Commission here today be co-opted onto the national committee ensuring that this new proposed addition to the day's events is faultlessly acted upon and executed. Meanwhile I shall contact those who need to know, in order that any alterations we may need to make are undertaken. Gentlemen, in short, I fully endorse the mood of this meeting."

The King was relieved, indeed he felt very pleased. It had all gone extremely smoothly. Now he would formally bring matters to a conclusion.

"Thank you Sir Edwin. Well, gentlemen it would appear we are agreed. Prime minister I shall leave the co-ordination of matters in your good hands. I am confident that all will proceed swiftly and smoothly. For my part I shall undertake two duties. The first is that once the Cenotaph in unveiled and the ceremony completed; I, my sons and all the male members of the blood royal shall walk behind the coffin for the rest of its journey. It shall proceed us into the Abbey. Thus shall the Country acknowledge the greatness of he who is placed within. Secondly I shall personally take responsibility for the construction of the coffin. It shall be produced from an oak that fell in the gardens of Hampton Court just a few days after the armistice had been declared. The bringing home of the Nation's Unknown Warrior shall be a great and solemn affair. Are we all agreed?"

His words were met with general affirmation, the business of the evening was concluded to the satisfaction of all. The Unknown Warrior was coming home, home to a faultless internment, perfect, except for one small flaw. It was an imperfection that would only become known to those who were to inherit the mantle of the few gathered here in the Abbey, on this stormy night that was now, symbolically, abating. It was a secret that would not be uncovered for almost eighty years.

CHAPTER 33

When faithless ones with all their vain delights
Are crying out under their hellish plights
Sing, faithful, sing, and let their name survive,
For though they killed thee, thou art yet alive.

John Bunyan: Pilgrim's Progress.

The decision having been made the engine of state burst into action. All the departments of government, the armed forces and the Church each took on their various responsibilities, interacting with each other through the chairmanship of the Prime Minister.

The King had, as promised, ordered that the fallen Oak be prepared for use as a coffin utilising the sawmill and workshops within the grounds of Hampton Court. He then personally searched for a master wood craftsman to oversee and carve the great coffin that would encase the returning hero. It would be required by the 4th of November, barely three weeks away. Consulting with his land manager, he decided to approach a man who had made a name for himself producing great works of carved furnishings and had also been responsible for the renovation of the ceiling in St George's Chapel, Windsor.

Having been despatched by His Majesty, Major Thornton Hemsley found himself walking up the driveway of a cottage called Hollyberry Grove, in the village of Holmer Green, deep in the heart of the Buckinghamshire Chilterns. He asked his driver, who had escorted him up the drive, to knock on the door and waited.

Master Colin Russell, as he was known by his apprentices, had just returned home from a long day's work at the small factory that he owned in the village. He was drinking his tea and eating blackcurrant jam sandwiches, which were a fetish of his, when he heard the knock.

Mumbling and grumbling to himself, which was another annoying trait that his apprentices detested, he got up from his chair and went, bad temperdly, to the door, which he opened. He found himself confronted by two uniformed gentlemen, one in an army officer's uniform, displaying a military moustache and carrying a case.

"And what can I do for you gentlemen"

His enquiry was abrupt, such was his manner.

"Are you Master Colin Russell?"

The reply came from the officer with the briefcase. Thornton Hemsley had been taken aback by the gruff, rustic speaking, working man.

"Happen I am"

The response of the disturbed occupant was no better mannered than his initial retort. In truth he was getting impatient, he did not like officers in uniform, speaking with a public schoolboy accent, at the best of times. This particular moment did not present itself as a 'best of times,' therefore he was not inclined to politeness.

"And who wants to know?"

"None other than his Majesty the King. I am Major Hemsley and I am here on the grave matter of state. May I come in?"

It was a gaping mouthed, speechless, admonished man who opened wide the door and indicated for his visitors to enter, which they duly did. Colin pointed towards a pair of resplendently carved Windsor chairs and his visitors made themselves comfortable within them. He then sat himself upon his favourite chair, again immaculately carved with gothic imagery, which rocked gently with the movement of his body.

At last he managed a sentence.

"His Majesty the King eh, what can I do for him?"

"Well may you ask Mr. Russell"

The Major replied in an almost schoolmaster's tone, as if he were addressing a badly behaved pupil.

"None other than create a wooden coffin, such as the nation has ever seen, from an Oak that has been harvested at Hampton Court."

"A coffin"

The unbelieving craftsman could but merely repeat the words that he had heard, it was all so confusing to him. Then it came to him, a coffin is always made with someone in mind.

"Who would that be for then?"

"I am afraid that is a national secret at the moment"

The statement was issued by the Major in a most authoritative manner, as if he was suggesting that the questioner should pursue his line of enquiry no further. However he decided to plant a sense of deep importance into the apparently over inquisitive mind of the mechanical whose services His Majesty was so keen to obtain.

"All I can say is that it will become the most famous coffin ever made. It must be superbly crafted. It must also be finished within three weeks."

"Three weeks!"

Colin was incredulous. One thing he was not used to was being hurried. In matters of time he was rather a Prima Donna.

"Three weeks"

The Major made the affirmation in such a manner as to leave no doubt in the mind of Master Russell of the importance of the proposed enterprise. He added another word to enhance the importance of the duty that the King had so decreed, was to descend upon this artisan villager, a man who had probably seldom travelled any further than Amersham or High Wycombe.

"If you achieve this task in the allotted time, the Nation will always be in your debt Mr Russell."

Colin Russell thought for a moment, fancy these men coming from out of the blue, bringing him orders from His Majesty to build a coffin. Well of course he could not disobey the wishes of the King for was not that treachery? Feeling rather pleased with himself now, he decided to affirm that he would undertake the task.

"My debt eh? Reckon I must do my best then. When do I get delivery of the wood?"

Now came the next surprise in a day of surprises. The Major's next statement was, once again, to knock him back into his chair.

"You don't, you will bring all the necessary tooling with you to the workshops in the grounds of Hampton Court. The necessary cutting machinery is available on the site. You will also have as many assistants as you need. There must be no delay, we would require you to pack your things and come with us tonight. Would you be prepared to do this? You will have most satisfactory living quarters at the palace."

Colin was now completely dumfounded. He had undergone many commissions before, but none such as this, with both its secrecy and urgency. Yet he was also a man who enjoyed a challenge and adventure. This military gentleman, sat before him, was offering both. He would agree to go with him if arrangements could be made for contacting those who would need to know. His wife Valerie was visiting her mother in High Wycombe. Hollyberry Grove would need to be made secure, and his workers at the factory given directives. His foreman would have to be given instructions relating to the work in hand.

The Major undertook to see to the solving of all these problems. People were told the next day that Colin was undertaking some urgent renovation work at Windsor Castle. His long-suffering wife, who for years, had put up with his strange idiosyncrasies, was also informed that he would be absent for a while. It came as no surprise to her. Who could be astonished by anything a man did, whose daily habit was to walk around with a lit pipe smouldering away, in his pocket?

So it happened, by next morning the woodcarver found himself being introduced to his assistants, and the machinery was at his disposal. As was his habit, Colin fell into a certain insularity whilst inspecting the workers, the machinery and the raw materials at his disposal. Suddenly, upon looking up from his allotted task, he realised all the other persons in the workshop were standing still and facing towards the door.

Colin looked around and six feet from him, looking towards him, was none other than the King himself. He was speechless, flabbergasted, a rustic mechanical, totally unprepared for such an experience.

King George immediately recognised the discomfort of his newly acquired master carver and instantly sought to put him at his ease. In fact his manner and suggestion had a completely opposite effect.

"No need to stand on any ceremony here Mr King indeed, as we both have to work together, may I suggest that I call you Colin and usually people I work with address me merely as Sir. Would that be alright with you Colin?"

"Yes indeed Sir"

A stuttered reply came from the still astonished craftsman, who none the less managed to partially recoup his ground.

"That would be perfect sir."

"Good"

With a smile the King affirmed that all was well.

"Then let us get to work, Follow me if you will Colin."

"Just as you say Sir."

It was a much more relaxed subject who followed his King into the office adjacent to the workshop. His Monarch offered him a seat and went round the large mahogany desk that almost filled the room, to sit down opposite him.

"Well Colin, I shall now tell you all about your commission and we shall discuss the base designs. As your work progresses I shall visit you whilst you are working, when the others have gone. This project will crafted solely by your efforts excepting the outer shell. It is in the after-hours possibly the early hours of the morning that we shall decide upon the subjects of your workmanship."

"As you say Sir"

The still largely disbelieving craftsman was putty in the hands of King George.

"I shall be at your disposal whenever it is convenient for you."

The King smiled at his enthusiasm.

"Well done Colin, let us get down to it then. But before we do so I should tell you exactly who the coffin is for."

It was at this moment that Colin became aware of the enormous importance of the task that he had accepted the commission to undertake. He felt humble and in awe that he should have been so chosen. From that moment he became the most dedicated worker that the King had ever possessed.

Colin worked every hour, that he had the strength for, over the next twenty days. The shell was completed by the fourth day, composed of solid oak, one and a half inches thick. The lid was like-wise manufactured having a slightly thicker depth of wood.

On the fifth evening the base was married to the lid. It was a perfect fit first time. At this point, the rest of the workers were dismissed and the workshop became off limits for everyone except Colin and the

King. Now he would transform this basic casket into a majestic refuge for the mortal remains of Britains finest.

For eighteen hours a day, Colin would work. He slept in the office and was fed from the King's kitchen. He lacked for nothing. Work would start at eight in the morning and continue into the early hours. His Majesty would visit the shop almost every evening, discussing progress and considering modifications to the designs.

The relationship between Monarch and subject became one of a similar nature to that of Pope Julius the second and Michaelangelo when he was given the remit of painting the ceiling of the Cisteen Chapel. Late at night King George would come to inspect the progress being made. He would even pass Colin the required chisel or perhaps a mallet. All protocol was swept aside, even to the extent that Colin came to call his patron, George. For the first time in his life King George found a friendship that was based purely upon mutual interest and requited respect.

Colin even taught the King to use some of the tools and, in all fairness, they were swiftly mastered. There was one essential difference however, between the work of Colin Russell and Michaelangelo. Millions have seen the work of the great Italian master, less than twenty have ever gazed upon the work of Colin Russell, for, with the exception of some work on the lid all the carvings were on the inside of the casket. The only witness, down the ages, of his masterly imaging would be the Unknown Warrior and he was to lie asleep until the day of resurrection.

One night the King brought an object that left Colin stunned in awe. Taking it out from its scabbard, the King displayed a mighty sword, fully six feet in length.

"This, Colin, is a Crusader's Sword, one of an identical pair from my own personal armoury. It is said that they were owned by two brothers who fought side by side to free the Holy Land from the Saracens. One was killed and buried in an unknown grave back in Palestine, the other came back to fight alongside Henry the Fifth at Agincourt."

"Ironically, it was a part of our victory in the Great War to, once again, take Jerusalem for Christendom I would like you to make a small bracket that shall allow it to be attached to the lid and allow for it to be interred along with the Unknown Warrior."

Colin took the sword in his hand. It was truly magnificent, long but so well balanced that he felt little of its weight.

"George, this is magnificent, a marvel. I have never held an object so beautiful; truly, it is a wonder."

The King observed how absolutely delighted Colin was with the object. Suddenly, he knew of one way of honouring him.

"Good; on the day of his last journey Colin, you shall have the honour of placing this sword onto the lid of the casket along with a standard army issue helmet."

At long last all was finished. By the fourth of November the coffin had been twice varnished and Colin had attached the iron furnishings. The King was most pleased. His own personal responsibility in the process of bringing home the Unknown Warrior was fulfilled. He could now pass it over into the care of the Prime Minister for embarkation to France.

Colin was employed in the final polishing of the great casket when the King came to visit for the last time. However, on this occasion he was not alone; another illuminary had come with him.

"Well Colin, still hard at it I see. You certainly are a perfectionist, but please stop for a moment. I wish to introduce you to another who is deeply involved in this solemn matter."

Colin put down his cloths and turned towards his new visitor. The King made his introductions.

"Colin may I introduce you to my Prime Minister. Mr. Lloyd George. Mr. Lloyd George this is Mr. Colin Russell a most remarkable wood craftsman. He has produced a wonderful piece of work, fully fit for the last sanctuary protecting our Unknown Warrior."

"Mr. Russell I am very pleased to meet you indeed. If his Majesty's description is any where near to the actual finished article, then you have produced a most worthy piece of work."

"Well perhaps you would like to inspect it sir" invited the creator of the casket, and he went to take off the dustsheet that covered most of his work.

"Just a minute, if you will"

The interjection came from the King.

"Prime Minister we stand on no ceremony here. Colin and I have spent hours in the evenings and mornings crafting this masterpiece together. He has even taught me how to use some of his tools."

"Well Colin,"

A wizened smile came across the face of the highest commoner in the land, and a glance fed its way to Colin. Bringing forth a look of one who was entering into a conspiracy. Once more he extended his hand to the craftsman.

"You should address me as David. In truth it will make a pleasant relief to be able to spend a short while in informal circumstances."

"Quite so"

The affirmation came from the King.

"Now let us all look upon and marvel at Colin's creation."

Colin took away the dustsheet and David Lloyd George let out a gasp. The oak had been splendidly finished in a varnish which emphasised the grain of the wood in golden, glowing, rich, almost bronze, highlighted lines. Four legs had been carved in the likeness of lions. They would not go to France but would be placed at the bottom of the excavation in the Abbey in preparation to take the weight of the casket.

Around the edge of the inside of the coffin lid were engraved the names of all the major battles which were fought during the war Arras, Cambrai, Somme, Ypres, The Marne, Mons, Gallipoli, Paschendale, Mesopotamia. On all four sides, internally, made only for the sightless eyes of the incumbent himself, were scenes of the war. They would be all too familiar to all those who had seen photographs of the conflict. Yet it was the internal face of the lid that left the Prime Minister speechless. The Royal Coat of Arms had been carved in all its resplendent glory, together with the motive 'Duet Mon Droit' In addition below was another Latin text that he was not familiar with.

"And what does this translate as Colin?"

The enquiry came from Lloyd George, still in the process of gaining his breath.

David, It translates thus: 'Though your name is unknown, your deeds are immortal.'

"Well, well, well"

So mused Lloyd George filled with humility in the presence of so great an artist displaying his greatest work.

"So apt, so apt, Colin you have the nation in your debt. It is a most wonderful creation. I am amazed. Your majesty, it is a masterpiece fit for a hero, fit for the first Abbey of the Nation, and within the time limit to."

Then he added, smiling with nonchalance.

"And I assume within cost?"

He made the remark whilst turning to the craftsman who was full of pleasure from the comments that had been offered on his work by both his King and Prime Minister.

"George and I have never discussed cost, David,"

Colin, very embarrassed at the mention of money, had instantaneously reacted and in so doing became the first and only commoner that Lloyd George ever heard call the King solely by his Christian name. However, he was not to be allowed a second to reflect upon the matter for Master Colin Russell was on, what those who knew him called, his high horse.

"I do not, I could not, take one penny for this labour. No I will not accept a single penny. It was a labour of love. During the war my factory, small as it is, produced thousands of rifle butts for the Lee Enfield works. How many of the young fallen placed one of my butts against his shoulder I do not know. All I do know is that I am not going to make a penny out of this coffin. It is my personal gift to the nations fallen. In fact I have already been paid in full. My freedom is my payment, my freedom and the freedom of my family."

The King was impressed, as indeed so was Lloyd George. It had been so refreshing for him to have been in the presence of such an unpretentious, undoubtedly skilled, yet modest man. Seeing this work come

453

to fruition, had provided for him one of his life's greatest pleasures. Now, in addition, his friend Colin asked for no reward.

"Well' he thought to himself, 'well, we shall see about that.' He took both of the craftsman's hands in both of his and looking straight into the eyes of his newly gained friend, made an emotional declaration.

"Colin, on behalf of the Nation I thank you. Your work is thus completed and you can go home to your family. Do not speak of this yet. You shall hear from me soon, and no doubt the Government also.'

This was confirmed by Lloyd George who, had been walking round Colin's creation time and time again.

He too came to shake Colin's hand.

"I am afraid I must get back to Downing Street, the Irish are being extremely troublesome at the moment, and the matter needs my constant attention. However I have been most privileged to meet you Colin and to have been in the presence of your work. I wish you well for the future. You will hear from me in due time."

The King then indicated that they should depart and, for the first time in days, Colin saw the sky. He also realised that the place had been under guard, for a pair of sentries stood to attention as they left the building.

The three shook hands and parted, the King crossing the grounds alone back to his palace, Lloyd George to his car, which took him back to his residence. Colin was placed in one of the King's personal vehicles and driven back to his cottage in Holmer Green. Within two minutes of leaving Hampton Court he was asleep.

Two days later, on the Sixth of November, the solid oak carved coffin weighing nearly three hundred pounds, left Hampton Court on its journey to France. It arrived that evening, at the small Chapel in the village of St. Pol Sur Ternoise, near to the offices of Brigadier General L.J Wyatt acting director of the Imperial War Graves Commission in France. The General conducted the coffin onto a catafalque placed in front of the altar. Then he left, locking the door behind him. He was in a hurry; Tomorrow would be a busy day, he would have to rise at 6.00am.

Once the meeting in the Abbey had dispersed, that night in October, it had been agreed that the army, represented by Lieutenant Colonel Henry Williams, would laiase with the Imperial War Graves Commission to select a totally anonymous corpse for entombment in the Abbey. Henry Williams had been responsible, since 1917, for the decent internment and identification of the fallen, sometimes as a planned mass operation, or as a result of the discovery of a single corpse.

As he had so eloquently expressed to the covert gathering, he had soon come to realise that his was an impossible, never ending task. He had over five thousand men at his command, many of them foreigners, whose sole duty was in enduring this unpleasant work. Yet even with these resources, Henry had soon come to realise that the work would not be completed in his lifetime.

He reasoned that, in a hundred years time, people would still be discovering bodies from the battlefields. He hoped that, even this far into the future, efforts would still be made to identify the corpses and give them a decent burial. A certain sense within him told him that it would be so. The sacrifice had been so long and enormous, the Nation would never forget its debt to those who lay in France and elsewhere. The cemeteries that he was helping to create would stand as emblems, being kept in perpetuity, as an everlasting memorial to those who gave everything for their Country.

Now he had been given the responsibility for providing the logistics, enabling General Wyatt to select an entirely anonymous representative for the fallen, The two of them had met on October the twenty-third and agreed upon the system they would use. Six parties of Henry's men would simultaneously arrive at the battlefields of the Aisne, Arras, Cambrai, The Marne, The Somme and Ypres on the morning of the Seventh of November. Once there, they would select, entirely at random, the corpse of an unidentifiable British combatant.

Then, at half-hour intervals, each party would arrive at the Chapel of St Pol, place their precious responsibilities as indicated and, instantaneously, leave without a word being exchanged. That way, once they had left, none of the staff at General Wyatt's Headquarters, would even know which battlefield the corpses represented. It would be the responsibility of General Wyatt to choose one of the six corpses for embarkation to London. It was a foolproof plan ensuring the complete anonymity that the Country demanded.

By the evening of the Sixth of November all was in place. Henry had dispatched his parties of six men each commanded by a commissioned officer to each of the battlefields. When they arrived at their destination they would find a row of twelve bodies. The commanding officer would select one at random, place it in a coffin and leave for St Pol. From twenty one hundred hours onwards, the parties would leave at half hourly intervals, having completed their task. They would then report to Henry at his command post twenty miles to the east. Additionally a further five detachments would be standing by to retrieve the unselected corpses and take them away for burial at a designated cemetery.

General Wyatt arose at his prescribed time, prepared himself immaculately in his dress uniform, took breakfast and walked over to the Chapel to meet with his second command for the day, Colonel Gell, who was to supervise the delivery of the bodies. A final conference would ensure everything ran accordingly to each letter of the plan.

Exactly on schedule Colonel Gell met the General on the steps of the Chapel. Saluting his superior, Gell gave a precise report on the present status of affairs.

"Sir we have taken delivery of six trestle tables and set them out in random fashion. Each is to be attended by a pair of NCOs and RSM Yorke will stay in attendance throughout the delivery. We have six Union Jacks prepared to lay out upon the coffins. The lids had been detached from the casket, which by the way Sir, is a magnificent affair. Also five vehicles each with two of Colonel Williams men are parked ready to receive the coffins which are not selected. Nothing has been left to chance Sir."

"Very well Colonel Gell, I shall be in my office in the Chapel Vestry if needed, carry on."

"Yes Sir"

Having affirmed his responsibilities, the Colonel saluted once more and left to continue his duties.

As the day progressed Wyatt became more and more tense. Word had come through from Colonel Williams, stating that everything was progressing normally. Nothing to do now but wait. The clock seemed to be moving so slowly, it was like awaiting zero hour prior to an advance.

He need not have worried, at 21.00 the first delivery was made. The party was greeted by a silent salute, both to the officer in charge and towards the coffin. It was placed on the furthest trestle and covered in a Union Jack flag. The escort party gave their charge a last salute, then left. Not a single word was exchanged. General Wyatt saw them off and watched them disappear into the distance. The entire process took less than ten minutes, enacted supremely, with the utmost military precision. If the other escorts displayed the same diligence, then the first part of the task would be completed perfectly.

That is how the process indeed progressed. Each party arrived exactly in accordance with the program. Each took less than ten minutes to complete their duty, and each retired without a word. By midnight General Wyatt had taken charge of six bodies, which were laid out in random fashion in the Chapel. Fifteen hours ago there were seventy-two bodies from six battlefields, now he had possession of six, not knowing which battlefield a specific corpse had come from. Thus far so good. Now for the second stage.

Wyatt went over to Colonel Gell, who was personally guarding the bodies. Entering the door the General issued his next command.

"Gell I want you to go outside, select six men as randomly as possible, and report back on the Chapel steps, together with your charges."

Gell disappeared and for the first time Wyatt was alone in the Chapel with the bodies. He felt the hand of history on his shoulder. Walking past each of the flag covered coffins, a sensation of humility overcame him. One of these corpses was destined to dwell for eternity in Westminster Abbey. In future years he would visit the Warrior's grave, knowing that he was one of the last persons to see the corpse before it was placed in his great oak coffin. He laid both his hands on each coffin in turn, saluted and whispered.

"Rest in peace gallant warrior."

Finally he turned, walked towards the entrance to make the next selection. This was to choose the person who would indicate which one from the six was destined forever to be paid homage as the Unknown Warrior. As ordered, six men were lined in single file below the steps with Colonel Gell at the end of the row.

As he walked out, Gell called the men to attention.

They stepped too. He addressed the men.

"One of you will now be blindfolded and guided into the Chapel. Within, there are six coffins. You are to walk around and select one. It does not have to be the first one you come across, that decision is entirely up to you. When you make your final decision stop, place both your hands upon the coffin and just utter one solitary word, 'this'. Then wait to be escorted from the Chapel. Your blindfold will not be taken from you until you are back at the bottom of these stairs."

"Is this understood?"

There was a unanimous affirmative reply from all six men.

"Right each of you will step forward one at a time and take one of six straws projecting from my hand. The one with the longest strand will stay. The rest will immediately dismiss yourselves back to your billets without a word."

"Is that understood?"

"Yes Sir."

Again came the unanimous reply. The men walked up one at a time as ordered and selected a straw from the General's hand. Once each had possession of a strand they compared lengths. A Corporal displayed the longest one and immediately the others left. Not a word was said. The Corporal came to the foot of the steps and, facing the door, stood to attention awaiting further instructions.

As previously planned, Colonel Gell stepped forward and blindfolded the young soldier. He then accompanied him up the stairs and assisted him through the door. The soldier advanced slowly, and encountered the first coffin. He passed it by and continued to progress, confronting two others but continued until he bumped into the fourth. Here he stopped, placed both his hands upon the coffin and uttered the single word.

"This."

At the sound of the agreed word, both Wyatt and Gell advanced to where the man was standing. Gell took hold of the soldier and began to escort him back from the Chapel; Wyatt placed a large Ivory Cross on the coffin and also left the place. It was one o'clock in the morning. The

457

adrenaline was now flowing through the General. His task was almost complete, he should keep going.

Gell returned to confirm that the Corporal had left for his billet without a word and Wyatt issued his next command.

"Right, Colonel bring in the men designated to take away the five coffins that do not have a Ivory Cross upon them.

"Yes Sir"

Solemnly came the reply, for the shadow of history had also fallen upon Colonel Gell. He left, soon returning with five pairs of men who, without a word, each taking hold of a coffin left in utter silence. Gell went with them to ensure that each coffin was safely secured, ready for its final destination.

For the first time, Wyatt was left alone in the presence of the Unknown Warrior. History overwhelmed him, it was as if a holy aura had come to settle upon the place. It was totally silent. He could almost hear the beat of his heart. He knew it was beating faster than he had ever experienced. This was a unique occasion, he knew that he would never have a more responsible duty than this.

It seemed an age before Gell returned, appearing sombre and grave. He too had become totally enraptured by the historical significance of the event. For a few minutes they remained silent, then the General gave his next command. In a quiet voice, almost a whisper he asked Gell to help him off with the lid of the coffin containing the corpse. Carefully the pair of them displaced the Union Flag and folded it up in the military fashion. Then taking a screwdriver Gell took out the fastenings one by one and placed them by the flag. Finally, the lid was ready for removal. With each of them taking an end it was removed without effort and placed upon one of the empty trestles.

General Wyatt peered inside. The four-year-old body was almost passed the state of putrefaction, but neither had all the flesh become dust. The outline of the man's face stared out at him. The empty eye sockets and the exposed teeth gave the impression of a hellish gaze accompanied by a sardonic smile. All the limbs seemed intact but the chest had been badly damaged. It had appeared that this man had died as a result of a large piece of shrapnel or a large calibre machinegun bullet having struck him. As he looked upon the corpse the General knew he could never grasp it. He turned away sensing the bile rising within him. With superhuman effort he recovered himself and began to attempt reason.

All the parameters had been carried out to the letter. This body was absolutely anonymous. His duty had been fulfilled thus far. For this moment, he could leave it for others to re-accommodate the soldier inside his great casket.

'Yes' he thought to himself I shall leave it to Gell and two others to oversee the transfer. He would inspect everything once the lid of the great casket had been sealed.

Gell had also been repulsed by the sight of the piteous remains but, unlike the General, he had first hand experience of such sights. His war had been fought leading men from out of the trenches towards the enemy. He had known what to expect, for he had seen what bullets, shells, gas and shrapnel could do to a man. This was nothing new to him but, none the less, a sense of utter pity rose within him for however many dead one witnessed, each time it was personal, as if it was indeed the first time such a sight had fallen upon your eyes. Each of the glorious dead had lived, hopefully loved and had been loved, had been as Rupert Brooke stated in those immortal words

'A body of England's breathing English air.'

Yes this was a desolate, decaying mass, but once it was a man. The General and Gell faced each other and Gell could see that the ghostly sight had placed his senior in a state of shock. He resolved to assuage the General's obvious inability to continue.

"Well general"

His voice came out in a matter of fact tone.

"Your duty is done Sir, at least for tonight. May I propose getting two orderlies to assist me in the transfer of the remains? I will report to you the second that the task has been completed."

"That is an excellent suggestion, Colonel, I shall be in my office waiting. I must now get on with preparations for greeting the French cavalry tomorrow."

This was true enough. It had been an offer put forward by, the French at the last moment when the designated ambulance had broken down and a replacement was unable to reach St. Pol in time. Immediately the French army agreed that they would, indeed must, hold the responsibility for escorting the Unknown Warrior to Boulogne. It was one of the many ironies that a photographer had already taken a picture of the vehicle.

Historians would record, erroneously, that this unreliable vehicle was privileged to be responsible for the task. The truth was that it did not leave St. Pol till a week later, once it had been repaired. Consequently, there were still final instructions to be given relating to the hand over and for refreshing the squadron before they took over their responsibilities.

"Well I shall wish you good luck and God speed Gell."

Thus the General, piously relinquished his final historical responsibilities and made a somewhat hasty exit from the Chapel.

Gell once again looked into the coffin and upon its dishevelled remains. He resolved to make the poor man more presentable before asking the orderlies to join him. The jacket, was in surprisingly good condition considering the time that this poor soldier had been in the ground, though there were no sign of epaulettes The boots could be made to face upright and the face could be covered. This man, these pitiful remains, were to represent all the dead of the last war. He spoke out from the grave demanding dignity. Gell would see that he got it, not only in public pageant but here privately in this Chapel.

Gell placed a mask upon himself and began his task. He straightened the legs, making them uniform. The arms he intended to lay across the chest covering most of the wound. It was as he was about to undertake this operation that he felt a lump by the right hand side near to the waist.

His curiosity overcame him and he decided to part the jacket. Upon doing so he discovered the remains of a woollen undergarment. He felt for the lump and extracted, to his utter amazement a grease proof wrapped package. His first instinct was to go and inform the General but then he considered the position. All the other bodies had been dispatched. He did not know what was inside the package. If he destroyed it, he never would find out. He would keep the package concealed it upon his person and examine it. Then, if the contents compromised the situation, he would destroy them later. Meanwhile he would continue with his task as if nothing had happened.

The package slipped easily into his tunic pocket and, without another thought, he went to get the orderlies. Between the three of them they managed to transfer the corpse in a dignified reverential manner. The lid of the great casket was placed above the shell and sealed. Everything, as far as the world at large knew, would ever know, had gone according to plan. Their duty complete the three men faced the casket, saluted and Gell dismissed his assistants. Then, before retiring for the night, Colonel Gell went to inform the General.

Wyatt was tired, it had been a long arduous day and there was more to do tomorrow. He dismissed the Colonel and ordered that they meet at the Chapel steps at 08.00 just six hours away. Gell began to feel exhaustion overcoming him. His had been a long day, full of both physical, organisational and emotional strain. It had all taken its toll. He collapsed on the small bed in the room, which comprised his billet. Laying down, he unbuttoned his tunic dragged off his boots, unbuttoned his trousers and by several near houdinic manoeuvres divested himself of his garments. He got up, splashed his face in the sink and sunk back into bed.

Later on, in the early hours, the memory of the package came back to haunt him. He recovered the item from his tunic and placed it

460

inside his kit bag. It would remain there untouched until, when sitting in St. James Park, in preparation for attending the service at the Abbey, Gell would be confronted with it once again. Soon he would be faced by a dilemma far greater than any man of his age had ever faced.

For now, however, the little package was safe and the arrangements for the entombment of the unknown warrior could continue, and progress without interruption.

CHAPTER 34

And some there be, which have no memorial
They are become as if they had never been born;
Yet shall their seed remain and their glory never fade.
Their bodies are buried in an unknown place
But their names liveth for evermore.

Adapted from Ecclesiasticus Ch.44 vs. 9-15

A drizzled rain befell the earth, barely perceptible in its falling. A heavy misted laden air that soaked a man almost unawares in its stilly penetration. Colonel Gell solemnly reflected upon how appropriate it was as an overture to the day's events. He recalled another day, seemingly long past, that last long summer before the world became insane when, deep in the throws of innocent love, he had escorted Miss Wendy Hamilton to an open-air performance of Romeo and Juliet in Regents Park.

What a summer that was. He fresh in the uniform of a 2nd Lieutenant, 1st Battalion the Royal Green Jackets, she wearing the prettiest of dresses. Intent upon the play none, that day, had noticed the storm clouds gathering over London. As the daylight waned against the background of the two star-crossed doomed lovers, the heavens opened uniting with Chorus and his summary.

'The sun for sorrow will not show her head.'

He recalled how, as the play came to an end, the heavens opened and he grasped the hand of his delightful companion, swiftly taking off his tunic, gallantly placing it round her shoulders. His memory sped back to the carefree dash that the pair had made in their pursuit for cover, how they found a small doorway, how he brushed the rain from her eyes and how, to his great delight, he had kissed her.

Truthfully, he had never kissed a girl before that day, nor since. The war came, they corresponded, but the letters from her became ever more scarce and less intense. Finally, the last one came, in which she told him of another who had taken her heart from him. How the wretched war had wrecked lives, his life. Just a small insignificant episode in the affairs of men, but Wendy Hamilton had once meant the whole world to him.

His personal melancholy mingled with his thoughts of the body that lay in the Chapel. Did that poor soul also have a love, a special, very special person? If so, had she been loyal and loving to the end. He hoped so. Did she still grieve for her lost one as if the light were gone, for all time, from her World? Would she be comforted to know that his mortal remains, together with his immortal soul were now safe? Gell recognised a truly remarkable scenario that was unfolding before him. The Warrior, here entombed in his magnificent casket, was both embraced by the compassionate arms of his Maker and accomplished of transcendence through the grateful acknowledgement of his Nation. How he wished it were so, just as he desired fervently to be kissing Miss Hamilton once more in a doorway while the elements rained upon them. Blessed the rain that brought him his life's sole enpassioned kiss, what a day that was, what a day.

Today was such a day; heaven's tears descending upon them all equally. Perhaps, even now, the sun would come to shine. The gallant one inside deserved that at least for his last journey. Against this grey backdrop he summoned the words of his dear late friend, Wilfred taking comfort and renewed assurance:

> *'Move him into the sun*
> *Gently, it awoke him once*
> *At home, whispering of fields unsown*
> *Always it woke him, even in France*
> *Until this morning and this snow*
> *If anything might rouse him now*
> *The kind old sun will know.'*

The ageless sun today was hidden, remaining so for a few hours yet. The unknown hero would begin his last journey in the countryside where he fell, with God's tears falling, falling on these fields of Flanders, of Picardy, this place of poppies, this scene of courage, and of death.

Though reflective, Gell was fully aware of the importance of the task that lay before him. He had awoke, prepared to enact his duty this day, his duty to his God, his King, his Country, but most of all to the elevated unknown soldier laying in that small Chapel across the way. The Unknown Warrior would be just as he had left him last night, guarded without by a team of sentries, totally dedicated to accomplishing their last solemn task for he who was to be elevated, to represent them, in perpetuity, among the greatest of the land.

The anonymous hero had not even begun his journey home, yet here in this small french town, a place virtually unknown in Britain, a mystical aura had already begun to surround him. His guards would remember, with pride, all the rest of their lives, their vigil, when, throughout the night, they spent their watch guarding their fallen comrade. Now Colonel Gell would take over their duty ensuring his charge left for Boulogne with all the reverence and honour his efforts could bestow.

He observed General Wyatt emerging from his billet just a few yards across the road from the Chapel. He had the appearance of a haunted wraith; haggard, red eyed, with a hint of an unsteady gait. In truth, the General had not slept well. Horrific images had flooded his dreams, spectres floated above him, clothed in rotten rags, faces displayed the same fixed sardonic smile that had stared out at him from the trestle. It was as if an evil had transferred itself from the corpse to himself and displayed its dread through him. Now his nightmare had become manifest in his appearance

It was all too apparent to Colonel Gell that his superior, for the moment, was in no condition to organise the preparations for the day's itinerary. He would have to bear the entire responsibility for everything, at least for the moment.

"Good morning Sir, just to report, everything is in hand. All will be in place for the handover. Perhaps you would like me to call in an hour for you to inspect the final preparations."

"Just so Gell"

General Wyatt was all too ready to agree upon anything at this particular moment.

"Keep me abreast of events if you will."

With this the General did an about turn and walked back in the direction of his accommodation. He reminded Gell of how Shakespeare describes Richard the Third emerging from his tent on the morning of Bosworth Field. Gell sympathised. This war still effected men, even in its aftermath, in ways yet to be fathomed by science and the medical profession. 'How long could such things last?' he thought.

But now duty called, time was moving on. Reaching the steps of the Chapel, he saluted the sentries and asked the Corporal in charge to summon the detail responsible for erecting the ceremonial Dais. All went splendidly, within the hour all was in place. The six pallbearers of the 51st had arrived resplendent in their tartan, headed by a lone piper who was, even now, creating some consternation by tuning his instrument. An honour guard was standing easy in full preparation for inspection by the foreign dignities and His Royal Highness the Prince of Wales, whose duty it was to hand over the coffin to a Squadron of French Cavalry. To them had fallen the honour of escorting the Unknown Warrior to Boulogne where it would be taken aboard a ship of the Royal Navy, which would transport it over the channel.

It was now 09.00 time to ready the General. The dignitaries were timed to arrive in thirty minutes. Gell prayed earnestly, that the General was now fully recovered. His worries were without foundation. Wyatt re-emerged from his quarters the complete commander. Resplendent in his dress uniform, extensively bemedalled, displaying his history on his chest, giving the appearance of commanding total control over events.

For two hundred yards either side of the road, men representing several British, French and Belgian regiments were keeping the ever-increasing crowd to the pavements. Children had been ordered from their schools all supplied with small Allied flags. Red, white and blue began to appear everywhere.

Still the mist would not lift, though the air had become drier, more comfortable. Gell estimated that vision was still less than two hundred yards at best. The wait continued. At last, the sound of a cavalcade of vehicles, those bringing the distinguished guests could be heard in the distance, long before it came into view. Colonel Gell ordered the men of the honour guard to be called to attention. All was ready for the ceremony of departure to begin.

The motorcade drove into view. Three vehicles, the second of which carried Edward Prince of Wales and his Excellency George Clemenceau, President of France. He had come to bid the cortege farewell at this point, because at precisely the same time that the British hero was to be interred his Country's 'Soldat Inconnu' was to be buried under the Arc De Triomphe. It was here that the Anglo french ceremony would take place, in the small village of St. Pol.

As the car drew to a halt General Wyatt stepped forward together with his adjutant, the honour guard clicked to attention and the greetings were made. After the formal inspection the illuminates climbed onto the Dias there to await the coming squadron of French Cavalry.

Colonel Louis St. German was fast approaching, together with his squadron. He, as with many of his men, had fought at several of the immortalised battle sites, Verdun, The Marne, the Ardonne, and The St. Quentin Canal.

Soon soldiers of his calibre, trained to the peak of excellence in horsemanship, would cease to exist, except for enacting ceremonial duties. One of the inventions that had sprung from out of the late conflict, the tank, was rapidly developing, coming to replace such as he. These iron monstrosities would, in future conflicts, completely come to dominate the role that previously mounted troops had performed. Be that as it may, no tank could ever replace the resplendent epic display of courage and daring of the cavalrymen dashing headlong across the field of battle. Neither could a squadron of tanks ever imitate the solemn resplendent dignity that, today, this group of men portrayed in their role as escort to their immortal British fallen comrade.

The Colonel dismounted from his pure black stallion and advanced towards the Dais at a gentle pace, holding the reigns of his mount. He headed a group of eight riding four abreast. Immediately, to his rear, came six splendid black horses, harnessed in pairs to an artillery ammunition carriage. Upon each right-sided mount sat a cavalryman controlling his pair. Behind them came another eight horses again four abreast. Bringing up the vanguard, was a Lieutenant, sabre drawn, his arm extended.

The sight of this troop was simply magnificent. France had fully exercised all her skills of pageantry, displaying, splendidly, her duty this day. Each of the horses, were perfectly groomed, jet-black, possessing white nose flashes, the exception being the team of six pulling the carriage. These appeared to be entirely black without blemish of another colour, magnificent Arab stallions, strong, intelligent, highly disciplined. They provided a grand sight, vibrant, courageous, complete of solemnity, of dignity, such as St Pol had never before witnessed, or would do so again. France, undeniably, was giving of her best in bidding farewell to the one who represented the bravest of the brave.

Clemenceau rose to the occasion, his black suit and waistcoat allowing his flourishing ermine moustache and bushing eyebrows to stand out. He was rather short in height, and stocky, the exact opposite of the young, dashing, tall, slim Prince of Wales, perfectly presented, resplendent, displaying the uniform of the Colonel in Chief of his Regiment. Both men stood to acknowledge the salute of the young Colonel, as he came to a halt in front of the Dais.

The Prince was first to speak.

"Colonel, on behalf of his Britannic Majesty King George the Fifth we hand into your care, one of our dear lost warriors of the Great War. Our two nations fought side by side during four years of mighty struggle. Many men fell, from both of our countries, who have known grave within the realm of the knowledge of man. Such was the fate of the one we hand into your safekeeping. We ask that you guard him well during his last journey through this France, this Country where he fell, and for whom he gave everything. Vive La France. God save the King."

Applause spontaneously greeted his twin acclamation. Having, at last died down, Clemenceau rose to reply.

"Your Royal Highness, on behalf of the people of France I accept this most precious charge."

He turned to face his Colonel of cavalry.

"Soldiers of France, to you now falls the task of guarding this brave soldier. You shall defend him with your lives you will not cease in your vigilance until he is safely restored into the care of the forces of his Country. Your duty is clear. Shall you accept this task soldiers of France?"

Colonel Louis St Germain stepped away from his horse, the bridle being caught by his adjutant. He came crisply to attention, took off his helmet, brought his staff to the horizontal and in a clean voice, speaking in perfect English, with scarcely an accent, acclaimed his proud and solemn undertaking.

"Monsoir Le President, your Royal Highness, on behalf of France and her citizens I take upon this great duty. Our fallen brother is accepted

466

into our safekeeping. We shall guard him diligently with our lives as, surely, he gave his for us. His holy remains shall be handed into the care of his Britannic Majesty's Navy in Boulogne. Until that time he becomes one of us, one of our squadron, a brother soldier, a citizen of France."

Colonel St Germain repeated his last two sentences in French saluted the Dais and turned to face the Chapel. Once again, spontaneous applause broke out among the civilian onlookers. Hats went into the air, and flags were waved uncontrollably by the enthusiastic young. They were then to be as suddenly stilled, as the tones of the bagpipes of a lone piper began to play. The tune was familiar to all of those in uniform; indeed many of them had heard it on too often an occasion.

'The flowers of the forest.'

Slowly, proudly wearing his VC., the 51st Regimental Piper marched towards the Chapel steps, whereon he turned, facing towards the Dais. With meticulous symmetry, the two sentries opened the doors and shouldered their arms. Proceeded by a Lieutenant, sword drawn, the coffin was brought out, draped in the union flag carried by the kilted Highlanders.

The near side of the carriage was lowered and carefully, reverently, the body, encased in the mighty Oak casket, was secured in readiness for its departure. The very air was stilled, not a sound or flutter from any flag, nor movement from any child, a woman wept but it was as if a reincarnated Mary herself was crying at the foot of the cross.

This dead solider, dead yet immortal, famous for all time, was in their presence, mute, without movement, yet dominating all he surveyed, filling minds with memory, gratitude, providing catharsis. A solitary, pathetic corpse whose life had been blasted away in a moment, unseen, forever unknown, yet loved by all who would come into his company, for generations to come. An unspoken awareness, paradoxically both awesome and benign, touched each participant witnessing the occasion. A profound, unexplainable, metaphysical occurrence was unfolding before their eyes; an event forever to brand its impression, to become indelibly imprinted upon their minds for the rest of their lives, young and old alike.

Yet this ceremonial was not merely a spectacle provided of human expression. As the side of the carriage was raised, the mist lifted, taking with it the gloom of the day, allowing the 'kind old sun' to burst through. It brought a beaming glow onto the flag covering the coffin, drawing the eyes of the people upwards towards the heavens then onto the horizon and beyond where lay Arras, the Somme, Paschendale, and Ypres.

The countless white crosses that now dominated these fields of battle, row upon endless row, flooded the mind. The imagination filled. It was as if those endless regiments of dead, sleeping in the soil of France, were bidding farewell to their comrade, wishing him Godspeed determined, in the knowledge that such as he forbade the fading of their sacrifice, forbade the generations to come, ever to forget.

Louis Saint Germain grasped the moment. With one sharp word his men remounted their chargers. One last salute to the Dias and the troop turned about bringing their procession to face west towards Hesdin and on to Boulogne. With complete precision and the ever strengthening sun, gleaming reflectively upon their helmets, the squadron began to leave at a slow trot. The splendour, that was France, went with them leaving the crowd stunned into silence.

Suddenly an elderly lady ran out from the mass, a single red rose flew through the air to land upon the flag draping the coffin. The cry was heard.

"Bon voyage Mon brave Valois, Soldier Inconnu, bon voyage."

Instantly the spell of solemnity was broken. The silence was ended by the spontaneous applause that followed this unrehearsed salutation. Tragedy became transformed into triumph, accolades, cheering echoing the woman's words. Thus, to great acclamation, the cortege left St Pol Sur Ternoise. It was to be more than two kilometres distant before the sounds of farewell faded from the earshot of the escort.

Madame Lucille Bertois was pleased with her action. The red rose plucked from her garden the night before, her personal tribute to the fallen, remained with the cortege. It had now become an emblem of France. It would still be alongside the coffin when, eventually, it filed past the Cenotaph in Whitehall, London.

The horses now broke into a crisp trot towards Hesdin. A small town, one which had acted as host to thousands of British soldiers during the Great War, witnessing thousands of freshly embarked, marching young men as they strode, courageously towards the front. Bright eyed and expectant, these youths headed, seemingly heedless, into battle, many never to return.

Hesdin had also provided sympathetic shelter to endless streams of wounded, on their way back home. It was a town that had never been ravaged by war but had been, all too graphically, an observer to its consequences.

As the troop entered the town its entire inhabitants came out to pay their homage. The streets were lined three or four deep with its citizens, all eager to display their respects, their gratitude. Hesdin was an ancient town with a huge cobbled market square, Church bells began to toll and seeing before him a reception of dignitaries, gendermerie militia and other uniformed services, Colonel Saint Germain knew his column would have to receive the welcome of the town.

Motioning his men to come across four abreast, his splendid force came to a halt in the centre of the square. Louis St. Germaine was beginning to realise that the journey to Boulogne would be full of incidents springing of spontaneity. He concluded he would have to extemporise his itinerary at each and every town as circumstances unravelled.

They were delayed in Hesdin for thirty minutes being showered with speeches, flowers and applause. Eventually, the squadron successfully proceeded through to Hesdin's outskirts speeding away towards Campagne-Les-Hesdin where they swung north, riding parallel to the coast. The ancient town of Montreuil proved to be especially enthusiastic in its welcoming of the squadron. Here they were presented with a huge wreath almost two metres in circumference which was attached to the rear of the carriage.

Whilst they were stationary, receiving the plaudits of the town, a distraught young woman, clothed completely in black, forced her way through the cordon and, with superhuman endeavour, gained the side of the carriage. Immediately a pair of gendermerie grabbed her and began to force her back towards the crowd. Colonel St. Germaine, observing the event, dismounted and went over to her, asking her stewards to release her.

He put his arm around her waist and conducted her back towards the carriage. Here he allowed her to bury her face in the flag of Britain whilst she sobbed uncontrollably. For fully two minutes the pageant was played out. Finally, slowly, the sobs ebbed away. Gently, calmly, empathetically Louis, still closely holding the woman to him, escorted her back to the awaiting crowd. Here he placed the grieving widow into the comforting arms of a pair of Sisters of Mercy. The crowd erupted, mobbing him, shaking his hands, kissing him, and embracing him. Louis was overcome.

It was through a supreme effort that he gained the stirrups of his horse and remounted. Gradually the troop managed to progress to the far end of the square and proceeded along the narrow streets. Again, they were mobbed. It appeared as if every vantagepoint was being taken by an observer, keen to be a part of the event. Eventually they arrived at the outskirts of the town and bade it farewell. Upon leaving, Louis knew he would never forget Montreiul, its people and the woman whose tears of France now stained the flag that covered the Unknown Warrior.

So sped the squadron, on towards Samer where fresh greetings and homage were lavished. Finally they gained a clear road for Boulogne and their task's end. At the outskirts of this harbour city, they were to rendezvous with six British infantrymen, each a holder of the Victoria Cross. These gallant warriors were to accompany the carriage, three to each side, on its last few miles to where the cortege would hand over its charge to the Royal Navy.

But, Boulogne was not to be outdone by its smaller sisters through which the convoy had passed. Boulogne would excel herself. The spires of the ancient city were coming into view almost three miles distant. Yet, even now, small groups of people had gathered to watch as the procession passed, their numbers increasing the nearer they got to the city's environs. The city crest, perched upon a high post, designating its bounds, now came into sight. Here Louis could see that a multitude had gathered, civilians and military alike.

It was evident Boulogne had a great parade in mind. 'So be it,' concluded Louis, as long as his task was not jeopardised in any way.

"Let Boulogne have its day of fame."

A day of fame indeed, to rival the past armistice celebrations and that day almost twenty five years in the future when, once again, this time after four years of occupation, British troops would stream through the city streets as an army of liberation.

The City Mayor, continuing the tradition established by others of his eminence along the way, greeted the convoy. Positioned upon a hastily constructed plinth he prepared to read a citation. The leading horse came upon the civic leader and stopped, behind, the rest of the party settled to a halt. Louis hoped this would not take long.

At least this request, silent as it was, was granted. The Mayor spoke for less than ten minutes speaking of the city's gratitude to the Unknown Warrior and all the countless dead he represented. It was only when the civic dignitary finished that the Colonel realised just how great and memorable these last few kilometres would be. A possession almost half a mile long began to congregate behind the carriage. This multitude would slow down the pace but, considered the Colonel, the rendezvous with the British Navy should not, hopefully, be unduly delayed.

A large brass military band of the Coldstream Guards, led by a Regimental Sergeant Major in full regalia proceeded the parade, followed by the mounted column with its charge. Six British soldiers, all holders of the VC., flanked the carriage. They would act as pallbearers, taking the coffin on board ship. The huge white wreath given by the people of Montreuil would now be carried by residents of that town, followed by an even greater wreath, donated by citizens of Boulogne lifted aloft by uniformed Valois, veterans of the Somme and Verdun.

Following this impressive display came the Band of the Royal Marines, together with an escort from the French Foreign Legion. The vanguard comprised of another French Cavalry squadron, ensuring that the host of the marching civil dignitaries kept apace with the remainder of the procession. Thus the Unknown Warrior entered the last city of France that he would ever travel through. After Boulogne lay the Pas-de-Calais and the white cliffs of Dover.

The procession began, slowly winding through the streets of Boulogne; shops and tramways were closed. No traffic was seen upon the streets. Pavements were lined up to ten deep with, sometimes silent, sometimes cheering, applauding crowds. Children, parents, civilians, veterans, all had arrived, wishing to pay their final respects and to assuage their grief in yet another display of emotion. The entire city had come to a halt, providing the British hero his last farewell from French soil.

The parade entered the final street leading to the docks. Here, guarding the way, were scores of holders of the Croix de Guerre, silent, uniformed, standing to attention. As the coffin passed, each in turn, saluted in final recognition to a fallen comrade. At long last, the procession came to a halt, alongside the immaculately presented destroyer, which was to take the coffin home. Colonel Saint Germain's squadron lined up alongside the ship, reversed away from the coffin and dismounted. Walking across to the gangway where the coffin was to be piped aboard the Colonel met the British Commodore. They exchanged salutes, then shook hands. The final ceremony on French soil was about to take place.

A line of soldiers of the French Foreign Legion from English speaking countries, all wearing the Croix-de-Guerre, made up an honour guard, stretching from the carriageway to the gangway.

Their officer commanding stepped forward and, facing the carriage, gave a poignant recitation.

'I have a rendezvous with death,
On some seared slope of battered hill,
When spring comes round again this year
And the first meadow flowers appear,
And I to my pledged word am true,
I shall not fail that rendezvous.'

The words composed by Alan Seegan an American comrade fighting with the Legion, falling early in 1917, some months before his own country became involved, completed the ceremony of words for the Unknown Warrior excepting the officers final retort.

"To you brave warrior, whose name shall never be known, who did not fail that rendezvous, we give our final salute."

With this last accolade, all came to attention. The two National Anthems were played, followed by the last post. The escort then gathered the coffin and it was carried aboard the ship to the traditional piping that traditionally, for centuries, welcomed senior officers aboard. Whilst this last act on French soil was played out, all the regimental and civic banners were brought to earth. The coffin was now safely aboard. It was secured and a guard was placed at each corner, each an able seaman, veterans of the battle of Jutland and the Falklands. Raising the Ensign by half, the destroyed weighed anchor and began to leave the harbour.

It was at that moment Colonel Louis Saint Germain observed the name upon the ship; 'Verdun.' This gleaming new destroyer had been launched bearing the title of the greatest single conflict fought by France in the Great War.

Defending that vast complex of forts had cost France more dead than any other battle in her entire history. More men had been lost defending this corner of France than had Napoleon's retreat from Moscow a hundred years previously. The name 'Verdun' was, forever, seared to the hearts of both her soldiers and citizens alike. This ship and her place in the ceremony, displayed Britain's respect for the part played by her ally. A fitting token, a final, most precious display of the friendship and respect that was felt between the two nations.

Colonel Louis St. Germaine bade farewell, watching 'Verdun' pass out of the harbour walls giving one last blast of her horn. Finally, she was free and out into the open channel, steaming towards those cliffs of home. Little did the gallant Colonel realise that in less than twenty years hence, off the shores of Dunkirk, he would meet up with this destroyer once again as she assisted in the evacuation of British and French soldiers in the face of yet another invasion from that deadly enemy.

He could not know as it disappeared over the horizon, how, in turn, that very destroyer would carry him to safety away from the German guns bringing him towards the very same shore, that she was, at this moment, carrying the Unknown Warrior. He could not foresee how a few weeks later, whilst German and British planes were screaming overhead, fighting to secure the skies, he would find himself standing in Westminster Abbey beside the very tomb of his charge. Neither did he know that he would take off his epaulette, an insignia of the Free French, the Cross of Lorraine, and place it upon the grave.

Neither, could he foretell how his life would conclude, having later returned to France at the head of a victorious force of Free Frenchmen where, side by side with General De Gaulle, he would enter a liberated Paris. He could not now crystallise upon his final life's action. How on espying a sniper aiming at his chief, he would throw himself upon the General and, taking a bullet in the heart, receive his death wound. All that was in the future in a new war whose seeds, even now, were being sown.

Meanwhile, out in the Channel, the brave destroyer was rapidly gaining the horizon and disappearing from view. Taking one last glance, Louis St. Germain turned round to face the dear land that so many had fought to keep free and, with an air of complete satisfaction, walked back towards his awaiting men.

A good day's work completed, he would now return to his barracks, content in having done his duty for that land a mere few kilometres across the sea. A loyal ally, this steadfast, beloved Albion, now at peace, complete and free.

It was enough, more than enough, to be accomplished of the assurance that these two great countries England and France would remain firm allies, friends, after so many centuries of belligerence towards each other. He knew this because still sounding in his ears was the acclamation voiced from the loud hailer of Verdum as she set sail. The final words of her Captain Commander Thompson echoing the order of the day spoken by a Marshal of France

'On ne passé pas.'

'They shall not pass.'

CHAPTER 35

With proud thanksgiving, a mother for her children,
England mourns for her dead across the sea.
Flesh of her flesh they were, spirit of her spirit.
Fallen in the cause of the free.

Lawrence Binyon: For the fallen 1914.

For centuries, sailors from the Isles of Britain have compared the complex and varied disposition of the English Channel to that of a woman. She displays many moods, several modes of appearance; differing facets of temper. Her humour is capricious, continually altering from the pacific to the tumultuous, from the benign to the tempestuous. Before more than one wretched mariner, the Channel has been as a mirrored glass one moment, only to change, without warning, into a mountainous ravine, complete of treachery, containing within her depths the potential for death and destruction with every powered towering surging wave.

The Channel, England's champion, her greatest defender for a thousand years, guarding against numberless enemies each, in turn, striving to reach her shores. Ever since the days of the Conqueror, this short stretch of water had forbidden so much as a foothold to those alien hordes that would have enslaved her. A moat carved out of ice, acting as a mother, she has maternally, ceaselessly, protected her sons and her daughters 'against infection, the hand of war and the envy possessed of enemies, from less happier lands.'

Now in the stilly morning of a misted autumnal November day, another mood overcame these precious waters, that of the coyly veiled bride. The chalky cliffs chiselled from out of the channelled sea remained shyly enshrouded, concealed from view. Even though her waters were tranquil, danger still emerged. On such days the air is frantically broken with the demented sounds of warning horns pleading anxiously for others to steer clear.

Verdun, becalmed mid Channel, was waiting for the mist to lift. She had plenty of time, almost two hours to idle away before she was due to dock in the ancient encastellated harbour that, even now, was filling with souls, impatient in their waiting for the return of their dead hero, their son, brother, husband, sweetheart, comrade.

Gradually, with affection for the occasion, but less eminent than in former months, the kind old sun began to penetrate to the surface. Gently but purposefully, the dampened fogginess was retreating, the rays of the sun pushing visibility further and further until land could be observed almost five miles off.

The destroyer raised her engines revolutions, and began to gain the English shore. Now the harbour boom, protected by its block ships, came, invitingly, into view. Here six of Verdun's sister ships gathered in line astern to escort her home.

At first all appeared grey, doleful, provisioned of mourning, but the nearer the custodian of England's chosen nameless warrior approached the harbour entrance, the more the sun triumphed in her battle with the mist laden air. Streaks of glowing beams finally reached the ground, warming, bringing a less dismal light to the occasion. A yellowed hue came to be granted the scene and in so doing, light emerged as an important element to the event.

So came he home, the Unknown Warrior, in sober yet triumphal acclamation. The tears and gentle sobbing of Widows, mothers, Comrades, enriched the moistured atmosphere, and the echoing cries of the Gulls. Moving alongside her berth, Verdun appeared to simply drift in tranquillity towards her designated spot. At her bridge Commander Thompson viewed the scene in company with a tired but accomplished General Mac Donogh. Commander Thompson felt history upon his shoulders. Today he truly was the most privileged of men. He was indeed exceedingly lucky to still be on this Earth at all. Back in 1916, whilst commanding HMS Surprise, he had been blown overboard by the force of a mine which hit his unfortunate ship whilst it was rescuing survivors from the 'Torrent.' He was one of a very few survivors, fortunate enough, to be picked up out of the water by the crew of HMS Radiant.

Now was to be the day, which would witness the enactment of the greatest honour ever to be bestowed upon him during his long and eventful life. He was to inform his Country that the great task was complete. From ship to shore went the signal to those waiting on land. 'Verdun to Harbourmaster, we bring home our Unknown Warrior; permission to come alongside with our charge.'

Soon Commander Thompson's responsibilities in this matter would be complete having been faultless in their execution. The Navy, through centuries of diligence, had provided its motherland with countless deeds of heroism and service. This one act, small in itself, in the hearts and minds of millions, would rank alongside any of its previous distinctions.

The docking was smoothly accomplished, photographers representing all the newspapers of the day recorded how serenely, solemnly, yet passionately the Unknown Warrior came home. Led by General George MacDonogh, sword drawn; The Royal Marines brought him ashore and bore him down the tramway to the sombre tones of 'The Death March of Saul.'

A small white wreath, enlaurelled with clustered bay leaves rested upon the Union Flag draping over the coffin. The parade abruptly halted. With the greatest of care, the Unknown Warrior was placed upon a catafalque and the wreath and flag were taken off in preparation for entrainment. This left the coffin in full display, its strapped oaken wood, dark, solid, and weighty. Once more the band struck up, introducing Pomp and Circumstance. To the strains of Sir Edgar Elgar, with one voice, the words that so sum up all that is of the spirit of Britain rang out.

'Land of hope and glory, mother of the free.'
How shall we extol you, those who are born of thee?'

Full of voice, albeit quivering voice, the words were given song. Tears streamed down the unashamed cheeks of civilians, veterans and serving officers alike. Here was dignity, but also unrepressed emotion, expressions of kinship and comradeship displayed by every man woman and child, representing a mournful yet mighty Nation welcoming home its lost hero.

'God who made thee mighty
Make thee mightier yet.'

From Dover the coffin was entrained to Victoria Station London, to be guarded throughout the night in preparation for the young man's last journey. As the steam pressure rose, with turning wheels, steel upon steel, accompanied by a mournful whistle, the precious cargo left Dover pulled by the magnificent jet-black, meticulous, gleaming engine, Raven.

That day as it sped across the Garden of England, the Downs, past Box Hill and on towards the capital, thousands lined the route respecting, each in their own way, he who passed by. A young anonymous dead soldier, was grieved for with pride and passion. Unknown, yes; yet, in some metaphysical way, known to all who looked on, as he sped past them towards his eternal resting-place.

November the 11th 1920 dawned still and bright. The clear skies of night had brought a frost; yet by 8.00 the sun, although low, was beginning to allow the temperature to rise. Along the embankment the pollared chestnuts would lose their leaves as the day wore on, the melting ice severing them from their parent. Each leaf, in its turn, would float lifelessly to the ground, in a slow melancholic spiral, coming to rest in a forlorn heap by the base of the trunk, there to await the road sweeper's inevitable attentions. Gathered together in their mass grave, they left behind their, as yet, undeveloped buds precariously encasing the embryo of future generations. Thus life's cycle continues.

Sally and her father were walking alongside the river near to the American embassy. They heard the chimes of Big Ben. A skein of pigeons swept over the water coming to rest on Westminster Bridge. It was cold but not unbearably so. Linking arms with Nathaniel the young mother and

476

widow felt no pangs of sorrow here, on such a day, but rather a gentle pride, a gratitude that she had been so loved, so desired, so needed by one of her Nation's heroes.

Now she had given birth to his daughter, blessed little Daisy, today looked after by two doting Grandmothers. Daisy had been born on the day before Christmas 1916 and immediately became the centre of attention for all those of her family who had so admired and loved the child's father. She came into the world in the very same room that her parents had shared during those ten short days of idyll.

That same evening Sally had taken her daughter to the window and, as she fed her with her own milk, snow gently fell against the glass. It was here that Sally introduced their daughter to her husband, where she felt his presence beside her. Now they were a family once more, mother, father, daughter, together delighting in each other's company. Memories of loveliness, of love enacted, merged with the evidence of its fruitfulness. Greater than death was their love, undivided by death were their souls. So it undoubtedly was as she prayed to her God that night, 'how great Thou art.'

Almost four years were passed upon since the day of Billy's great sacrifice. Though the invitation had come for her to represent the bereaved of Glossop and its district without any forewarning, she had readily accepted. Having left little Daisy to willingly be cared for by her doting Grandmothers, she had come to London full of expectancy. Sally would not be missed by her daughter today, neither should she be. This day was hers, for her and Billy.

father and daughter had come down to London yesterday. The longest train journey Sally had ever undertaken, for it appeared to stop at every station on its route. As she gazed out onto the countryside, she wondered how Billy had felt as he journeyed down all those years ago. Had he marvelled at new sights, at the hills, valleys, rivers and woods of his England, the England he was to give his life for? She did not know, but she hoped so.

It was the second time that she had made the journey, the first being on the occasion that she had visited Billy as he recovered from his wounds in that lovely hospital in Kent. She blushed many times to herself as she recalled with erotic fondness, the daring intimacy with which Billy had held her as they kissed. What days, what glorious days, memorable days, they were.

Last night they had stayed in a small comfortable guesthouse in Albany Street. When the landlady discovered their purpose she could not have been kinder.

"Lost two dear sons of my own, you see me dear. My husband, poor thing, could not face it, passed away himself last year."

She explained she had two daughters, both married both having presented her with grandchildren.

"But it's not the same me dear, not without my two lads God bless em, wherever they be."

Sally explained that they were to stay one more evening, then travel back to Glossop on the twelfth.

"You are most welcome, stay as long as you wish me dear. Company like yourselves stays so seldom."

The empathetic response from the poor woman, was so sincere, so full of the understanding that can only come from a fellow human being who has also experienced their own unutterable loss.

"People, as yourselves, proper ladies and gentlemen, are always welcome here."

Nathaniel and his daughter were not to know so, but when it was to come to the time for the bill to be settled, the good woman would refuse to take a penny

"My own memorial to my dear sons, you would not take that away from me would you, me dears? No, of course you won't. Now have a good journey home and God bless you both"

They could not deprive their host in expressing her gratitude in such a manner; so they abided by her wishes. Nathaniel used the money later when donating to Glossop's own memorial to the fallen. The result of their landlady's generosity was the beginning of twenty years of regular correspondence and meetings. Sally sent a card every Christmas and one would come back till they suddenly stopped in 1940. Upon investigation, Sally discovered that Mrs. Peel of the Regis guesthouse had been killed in the blitz. War was not to be a stranger to London for long, the demented Corporal would see to that.

For now however, the hospitality that they had received was a comfort, here beside the flowing artery of the Nation's Capital, sustained, as they both were, by a full traditional London breakfast. Sally was contemplating the coming day, when the accident happened, an occurrence that was seen as emblematic of the day's events.

Across the river from where they were walking, without any warning, came a great resounding crash. On the sight where the new hall for the London County Council was being built, one of the mighty cranes, inexplicitely crashed to the ground. Looking over towards the far embankment, Sally and her father saw a great dust cloud beginning to rise. Men had been working on the project in spite of the fact that others had decided not to so in respect for the sacred occasion. Now the crane had fallen, just like Babel's tower. It was seen as a rebuke from God himself, no one would work further at the site this day.

Sally and her father had decided to walk around the city for a couple of hours, before arriving at the Abbey by 10.00. This would give them plenty of time to find their seats and acclimatise themselves to their surroundings. From here they would leave the river and would walk up to

Westminster, past Parliament Square, then along Whitehall where the enshrouded Cenotaph was situated. They would then go on to Trafalgar Square and St Martin's in the Field. Finally, by walking down The Mall, coming by Buckingham Palace they could turn back to Westminster by means of St. James' Gardens.

Sally had read about all these places and seen pictures of the now to be visited sites. All in a single day she would see them, all because her beloved Billy had died for his Country and now lay in an unknown grave in Flanders field. Sally realised, all this, it was pre-ordained. Today she would see many of the places that they had so often spoken upon or read of in the Library. Yes, she would see these sights for both of them and later she would speak to him of the wonder of it all. Even now, among the bustle, which a gathering throng inevitably brings with it, Nathaniel and Sally had thought, but of one, conjuring up his face, recalling events that he had been central to, had dominated with his personality.

Nor were they alone, hundreds of thousands of others were beginning to gather for the occasion, each having a personal memory, a grief to be assuaged. They would line the route from Victoria to the Cenotaph from Whitehall to Westminster Abbey. The coming home of the Unknown Warrior had captivated the hearts and minds of the entire Country. Mere pictures, or descriptions in the newspapers, would be insufficient for later recollection; people just had to be here to witness the historical occasion for themselves.

The pair were walking aside the Palace of Westminster. Nathaniel was dressed in his black trilby, dark grey overcoat, his best dark suit and wearing a black tie. Sally complimented him clothed in black from head to foot save for a small piece of white lace decking her collar. They were as sombre in appearance as the Nation, moving slowly, thoughtfully, pondering upon the past few years of upheaval and the death that had so changed their lives.

As they entered Whitehall, two men were looking down upon them. Sir Alan Lascelles was speaking to his guest and friend, Philip Gibbs chief political correspondent to the Daily Chronicle.

"Just two of the day's mourners Phillip, came well prepared I dare say. So many women will today be convinced that it is their very own son, brother or husband who soon shall dwell in the Abbey."

"Quite so, Sir Alan, quite so."

Below, Sally and Nathaniel passed by the flag decked Cenotaph now protected by a squad of Scots guards, aided by quietly spoken policemen ushering people past in order that no congestion accumulated. By the time the two of them reached Trafalgar Square, Big Ben struck 8.45, within fifteen minutes, the Unknown Warrior would begin his last journey.

At Victoria Station preparations were underway. The cortege was to arrive at the Cenotaph for precisely 1030am, when the service would begin.

As Sally and her father turned towards the Mall, a man and a woman coming from the opposite direction made way for them. Nathaniel would never know so, but the man who raised his hat was none other than Siegfried Sassoon, the war poet, escorting his fellow writer towards the Cenotaph, she was Vera Britain.

"Quintessential Siegfried"

So observed Vera as father and daughter passed by them.

"The quintessential mourners, proud, full of memories. This day is for them, for all those, who like them, contain such compounded grief, not to be assuaged by common means."

"Vera as usual, you have struck the chord for today; your insight never fails to move me."

The two writers moved off in silence, listening to the hour being sounded from the Nation's timepiece.

As they approached The Palace, Sally became immersed in its unposing grandeur.

"The King is still in residence Sally, he has not yet left for the Cenotaph."

"How do you know father?"

"The Standard still flies, and at full mast too. It signifies the Monarch is still in residence."

Nathaniel's statement was quite correct, at this very moment His Majesty, King George the Fifth, was completing his dress, resplendently attired in the uniform of a Field Marshal, just the two of them in the realm. He and Haigh 'Let us hope Haigh remembers his place,' he thought with a wistful smile.

Turning left, Nathaniel and Sally began to progress towards the Serpentine. As they did so they passed a soldier dressed immaculately in the uniform of a Colonel, he was sitting on a bench gazing at a number of objects wrapped in a grease proof package. Contained within, were a small volume of Milton's poems, an embroidered lace handkerchief, and a hand written poem, together with a letter.

The book contained the name of a woman and an address in Glossop, Derbyshire. Colonel Gell was contemplating the significance of the items he was holding and what he should do with them. He knew he could not destroy them. Once they had been the most precious possessions of a brave man facing certain death in his country's cause. No he could not destroy them, but if he returned them to the person who had given them to this dead fellow soldier and to whom the letter was addressed he would be running the risk of destroying the anonymity of the Unknown Warrior.

To intensify the war being waged in his mind Gell recalled the words of the Reverent David Railton when he came to visit him in France just two weeks prior to undertaking of the process of selection. Railton had impressed him; he was a man born of a mission. Sat here before going towards the Abbey the cleric's words flooded his mind.

"Colonel Gell, It is a great and noble venture that we embark upon. No one shall ever know the rank of the Unknown Warrior, not his wealth, neither his class. There shall be no knowledge of his history or academic achievement. Such things will not have any place upon the spot wherein he shall lie."

If, in handing over the precious bundle to the proper owner, he told the poor unfortunate woman how he came by them, he would be endangering the whole concept of this day's undertaking. Colonel Gell was a man perplexed by a tortuous dilemma. Many more days would pass before he made his final decision. However there was mention of a certain Pastor Livingstone in the communication. Perhaps contacting him would help to provide the solution.

Unbeknown to him, the very person he was considering making contact with was, at that very moment, passing by. Together with her father, she was on her way to the Abbey, one of one thousand such honoured guests. The pair strolled by the Serpentine where mallards, geese, even swans, came towards them hoping to be fed. London and its inhabitants might be sombre of mind and apparel today, but the natural world continued on its way resplendent of colour, seeking out its daily needs. Once more, life continues, again, the cycle is maintained.

They approached the Abbey; its doors were open awaiting the guests. Both passed through the entrance, giving their credentials to the usher who serenely showed them to their seats. As they did so, they walked beside the open place of internment, where he, who was the essence of the day's events, was to find his last resting-place. As she did so, Sally paused to gaze around her. What a splendid place this was, strong yet peaceful, grand yet solemn. A mighty hall for so worthy a warrior.

At Victoria Station all was activity. When it comes to such ceremony few, if any, can excel Britannia. Today she would surpass anything ever before achieved. Today the entire Nation would, in unison, both grieve and express pride as it acknowledged its debts to those countless young men who had paid, so highly, the price for her liberty.

The previous afternoon Siegfried Sassoon had been at the station to see the coffin arrive along with a host of others. He was to write of the scene in typified terms.

'The great train arrived in silence,
A silence that deepened.
No one seemed to move.

481

A smothered sound of weeping covered
By the swirling smoke and steam
As the funeral train came to a halt.
The air itself was so stifled, all was so silent.
Silence can be seen as more than a physical state,
It can be transferred to the metaphysical. Silence is
The appropriate state of mind for honouring the dead.
It is a state where differences are superseded,
All is concentrated on death's transcendence.'

The Unknown Warrior had been left overnight within the confines of his railway carriage, guarded unceasingly till 9.00am when, before the gathered throng, the doors were opened and, carried by eight of his former comrades, he was taken out and placed upon the gun carriage.

Colin Russell, creator of the magnificent, outwardly plain casket, had been given the responsibility of ensuring that the brackets he had crafted were secured correctly. Now in addition, once the Union Flag had been draped, he had the honour, given to him personally by the King, of placing the ordinary tin hat atop the coffin, to unsheathe the magnificent sword and to place it on the bracket that he had provided.

Now all was ready for the fallen one to embark upon his final journey. The capital's great bell sounded out once more. It was 9.30. The hero, for now, known only to God, began his last journey. Again, as in France, six black horses led by muffled drums drew the gun carriage, whilst the band of the Royal Marines, playing Chopin's funeral march, followed in its wake. The entire capital, the work both of state and commerce closed, transport, communications, all came to a deadened halt.

'A great calm fell.'

Thus reported the 'Manchester Evening News' the following day. Slowly, each step a measured pace, the stately cortege progressed towards the great square, itself a memorial to the nation's greatest naval victory. Atop of his column, the great Admiral himself appeared to look down upon on of his Nation's sons, as if he was personally acknowledging his homage.

At the Cenotaph, now gathered together the great and the good, resplendent in their uniforms, pristine in their suits, yet, for a time, limited in their usual sense of importance. He, who approached where they stood, encased in oak, outweighed them all in importance and his presence upon his arrival, reaffirmed their humility. Today was the day when he would be immortalised to a plateau vastly higher than any that history would ever set for them.

As the coffin turned into Whitehall, Vera Britain stood at the junction; her gaze reaching out to Nelson, she was later to write.

'The dead seemed very near.
Were not the fallen gathered here?
To take to their shore.
The Victory they had died to win'

The poignant creator of penned remembrance contemplated upon the words she had composed on the day that the armistice was declared. They seemed more powerful to her now, than at any time in the past.

'Shall I listen to the merriment that victory brings?
Or with a heart that breaks and ears, that strain
To keep out the mirthful sound?'

She wept uncontrollably, nor was she alone. Slowly the procession approached the Cenotaph. As it did so, above the silence pierced only by the drum and hooves of horses, came a sound of rustled wings. It sounded the passage of the entire flock of pigeons that, well known to all, reside in Trafalgar Square. Soaring the heights in their transcendent thousands, they flew down Whitehall is if in homage. Below, countless eyes lifted heavenwards.

Along they came in winged salutation, passing high above the mourners towards Westminster. Here they peeled away, to depart back hence, to their regular haunts. More than one grieving widow, gathered here in Whitehall, envisioned that, soaring above them, the souls of the lost were winging by, in graceful acknowledgement of their part in the day's ceremonial. Angels disguised as pigeons, bearing their loved ones on high, an easy concept to grasp.

The carriage now came to a halt. Again the great bell sounded 10.30. Precise to the second, the honoured guest had arrived to take his Nation's homage.

The massed band struck up, the theme echoed, announcing the great anthem to be sung. It was to provide the Nations plea to her Almighty Sovereign for future sustenance, based upon the certain knowledge of past mercies issued unto her.

"O' God help in ages past
Our hope for years to come."

The King was standing adjacent to Lloyd George and Asquith. One the current holder of the supreme common office, the other a past recipient, they stood as if frozen solid. He knew they loathed each other, that, given a chance, they would not flinch to destroy their opponent's career. Although he had many reservations on the Welshman, he was glad

483

he had taken over the reins of office in 1916. From that time the war had been prosecuted in a much more professional and determined manner. After the end of hostilities, he had proficiently held his own in the world's councils. Sooner or later, he knew the Tories would plunge in the dagger, but for now, what with Ireland and the need to placate the resurgent aspirations of the labouring classes, he would do nicely.

The hymn ended, it was time to lay the Nation's wreath. His own hand was upon the inscription, reverently surrounded by red roses and bay leaves scented with Rosemary, he had given much thought to the words portrayed.

> *'In proud memory of those warriors who died*
> *Unknown in the Great War. Unknown and yet*
> *Well known, as in their dying, behold they lived*
> *George R .1.'*

As he laid the wreath, pipers played 'The flowers of the forest.' It was only later that a particularly observant civil servant noticed that the wrong wreath had been laid. Very secretly, it was later switched with the one that had been laid in Westminster Abbey and no harm was done.

The Crown having placed its tribute, those of Government, the Armed Forces and the Public Services followed. Now the hour approached eleven, Big Ben rang out and silence fell over Whitehall and London. Simultaneously, the stillness was mirrored all over the Isles of Britain. Big Ben struck out the hour sonorously and slowly, the fret and roar of city life ceased, men bared their heads and all remembered. Humanity stopped in its stride, minds filled with tender and elusive memories of dear ones who had made the ultimate sacrifice. The sun shone hazily, all was still, not even a flutter from a single flag interrupted the silence.

From the most humble commoner, to the highest in the land, came thoughts, memories that flooded the mind, both sweet and sharp, they broke the heart, almost unbearable in their poignancy. From countless lips came a name, from some emerged more than one. Lloyd George reflected upon his armistice speech.

> *At eleven O'clock this morning came to an end*
> *The most cruellest and most terrible war*
> *That has ever scourged Mankind.*
> *I hope that we may say thus, this fateful morning,*
> *Came an end to all wars.*

Poor David Lloyd George, even as he recalled his words he knew just how idealistic, how illusory, they were. Already a new-world order was coming into being creating new tensions, fresh rivalries. Peace would not last long, of this he was certain. Perhaps, through the will of good men, peace could be preserved for a generation, but not more.

A writer of epics, based upon innocent rural settings, now gone forever, was also contemplating in the silence. Later he would recall his musings through the written word.

> *'A great calm came from Heaven, distilling clemency*
> *Here was peace and silence rising to the skies.*
> *People held their breath, lest it be heard in the stillness.'*

Emiline Pankhurst, her fight for the suffrage won, stood next to Thomas Hardy as he crafted the scene in his mind. The service at the Cenotaph, in the presence of the Unknown Warrior, bore heavily upon her. She saw the coming burial of such a one as a memorial for her bereaved sisters. Later that day she was to turn to the man who wrote of the unfortunate 'Tess,' to voice her sentiments upon the service that they had witnessed.

> *Thomas, this was not so much a memorial*
> *For Unknown Soldiers, but to Unknown mothers.*

The silence continued, the spirit of memory brooding over all. Philip Gibbs continued to observe the ceremony above Whitehall in the offices of Sir Alan Lascelles. His words, later penned in the Daily Chronicle provide a lasting image of the events that were enacted below him.

> *'It did not seem an Unknown Warrior whose body*
> *came on a gun carriage down Whitehall. He was*
> *known to us all. It was one of our boys, not warriors,*
> *but boys, as we called them in those days of darkness*
> *that was lit only by faith. To some of the women weeping*
> *a little in the crowd after an all night vigil, he was their*
> *own boy who went missing one day and was never found*
> *till now. To many men wearing ribbons and badges in*
> *civilian clothes he was a familiar figure, one of their own*
> *comrades.'*

His lifelong friend, secretary to the King, watching beside him was to pen his thoughts more privately in his diary. As the two minutes silence came to an end, signalled by a bugler playing 'The Last Post,' the procession moved off towards the great Abbey. The King fell in behind walking at the head of a host that represented the entire Nation. Sir Alan Lascelles composed a notation of the scene.

*'Pipers marched before him, Admirals and Field Marshals
on his right hand and on his left all of London stood
bareheaded as he went, while on the coffin lay the steel
helmet which all of us wore and the long Crusaders sword
selected for him alone from the King's armoury. Of all the
symbols, he is the most nameless, the most symbolic; yet
few that Man has ever devised can have given such a clear
cut image of reality. For every one of us who has his own
dear dead, we could not fail to see that they too went with
him; that, after two years of waiting, we could at last lay
a wreath to the memory of that great company.*

So left this unknown man on the last stage of his journey. He who but a few days ago was nothing, yet now was everything, filled the hearts and minds of all those seeing him pass by. Through Parliament square he went where that great King of Warriors, Richard the Lionheart, stood astride his horse, his sword held high in salutation for one of his own. Finally the shadow of the ancient Abbey, wherein kings and poets slept, fell over the coffin. The Unknown Warrior was home.

Sat pensively in her designated place, holding the hand of her father, Sally's intimate thoughts were disturbed by the sound of the grand organ raising the introduction to Judas Maccabees 'See now the conquering hero comes.'

Standing with the rest of the congregation Sally saw the outline of the cortege highlighted at the entrance. Along with one thousand other bereaved Widows, her heart stepped up its beat pattern as the great coffin came down the Aisle to be placed before the Altar. One hundred holders of the Victoria Cross lined either side of the last path granted to the Unknown Warrior as he was carried down borne by eight serving soldiers of the Coldstream Guards

The coffin, having been safely brought to rest, the first hymn was sung

*'Abide with me fast falls the eventide;
The darkness deepens, Lord with me abide;
When other helpers fail and comforts flee,
Help of the helpless, oh, abide with me.'*

The words of Henry Francis Lyte rose, mellow of tone, from the voices of the congregation, upward the music drifted into the rafters of the mighty Abbey. From there it filtered skywards, Heavenward, to be heard by He for whom it was sung. Of all the occasions that it had been sung in the past and was to be so sung in the years to come, never would 'Abide With Me' sound so poignant, so eloquent, so earnestly pleading in tone, so majestic, complete in its certainty. That day, Lyte's portrayal of the constant struggle between death and life, darkness and light and the certain victory that is to be won over the grave, was given its supreme rendition.

For Sally, who had sung Billy's most favoured hymn so many times whilst in his presence, or away from him, it brought a special comfort. As the words were sung, she knew that somewhere, so very closeby, he could hear them. Yes, Billy was here, in this very place, of this she was sure; so she gave voice to the music and sung for both of them.

Nor was this to be her only comfort gained this day for a reading was given from the book of Revelation concerning the innocent dead. Coming from out of the great tribulation, they rise once more, clothed in robes of purest white, to stand before the throne of God. The reading ended with the immortal assurance.

'They shall hunger no more, neither thirst any more.
Neither shall the sun strike upon them, nor any heat.
For the Lamb shall be their Shepherd.
He shall guide them unto fountains of living waters
And God shall wipe away every tear from their eyes.'

During the momentary silence that followed the reading, there were many in the vast throng who could no longer restrain their emotions and, before the address was given, many a handkerchief was brought out to wipe away a tear. Sally saw the irony in this. If the scriptures were to be believed, and she thought that they were, then Heaven was full of tearless warriors, it was thus left for the living to have teardrops falling from their cheeks.

Her mind, her gaze, wandered from the service to explore the wonderful Abbey. The ceiling was remarkable, the columns huge, strong, reassuring, towering high in their ancient Gothic grandeur. She recalled how, one day, long ago, when Billy came out onto the Library steps with her, looking sheepish, too shy to hold her hand, how he looked up at the Chapel steeple and pointed to its pinnacle.

"My father put the final stone on up there, he was a very brave man don't you think?"

Sally remembered how she had agreed with him. How long ago that was, all those years, where did they go? The World was innocent then, having no idea what was in store, what tragedy would soon befall it. How long ago it all was, when the World was young.

Nor was Sally alone in allowing her thoughts to wander back to an age that would never return. Back in Glossop, Gladys, Elizabeth and little Daisy had gone down to Norfolk Square to pay their eleventh hour respects.

A service was taking place at the site where, soon, the town's own memorial was to be erected. During the service, Gladys had gone into a trancelike state and had wandered to the front. Pastor Livingstone was there and heard her as she spoke to the Lady Mayor, during the silence, to the background of a host of whispered shushes.

"All this silence for my poor boy. My Sally is not with me today, you know, she has gone down to London you see, for they are burying him in an Abbey today. Lots of people are going to be there, including the King you know. I would have gone up to witness it, but I am far too old"

It was here that the poor woman finally broke down. She began to weep uncontrollably.

"Why doesn't someone take her away."

Gideon quickly stilled the anonymous voice.

"Do you not know of whom you speak, that poor woman is the mother of Billy Thomas."

"Oh."

"Oh indeed."

The Mayor acted for the whole town by placing her arm around the distraught woman. The two minutes silence came to an end and she turned to Gladys Thomas, mother of, potentially, the greatest son of Glossop to wear a pair of football boots, making an invitation to her sobbing sister.

"Come on now Mrs. Thomas, let us go and lay this wreath to the memory of your dear son and all his friends."

That is exactly what happened. The two women, walking side by side, each holding on to a side of the wreath, duly paid their homage. As they did so, something happened in Glossop that day which has never occurred since, the crowd spontaneously erupted in applause. Many in the crowd at that moment had a vision of a young man being passed a ball that immediately sped goalwards with a certain wizardry, which deceived the wretched keeper to fall into the net. A reporter, who remains forever nameless, reported the scene.

'Both Mayor and mother laid the wreath.
Sisters under the skin; acclaimed by all those present .'

Simply another day in the history of a small town, now long forgotten, repeated in similar fashion through all the land.

Back at the Abbey, the service was coming to its conclusion. The coffin had now come to its designated final resting-place. It was lowered down to the words of Dean Ryle reciting the eternal reassurance that is the property of all Christians.

"I am the resurrection and the life saith the Lord, whosoever believeth in me shall not perish but gain everlasting life."

A final hymn was sung.

'Lead kindly light amidst the encircling gloom
lead thou me on.'

Whilst the final verse was being sung the King stepped forward. Taking off his glove, he ignored an offered sanitised, token, sample of earth. Without ceremony, he plunged his hand deep into one of six barrels, which contained soil from the battlefields of France. Stretching out his arm, he allowed the soil to gently flow from his parted fingers where it delicately fell upon the oaken lid.

His hand now soiled, he saluted the Unknown Warrior who now lay below, his coffin sprinkled with the first gesture of the earth that was to cover him. For possibly the first time in all the history of Britain, the King came to represent a complete unity between the classes, a unity built from sorrow, certainly, but a solidarity formed also from pride.

A bugler played Reveille and Kipling's recessional was sung. The Archbishop of Canterbury proclaimed the blessing and all came to an end. The great ones departed, leaving behind a throng, all wishing to imitate their Monarch and reverently toss a little of the sacred earth upon the coffin. In her turn Sally did so, Nathaniel also, it was a precious moment for both of them. For a seeming age, with the organ playing without ceasing, thousands walked past the open grave all repeating the symbolic act of the King. It was several hours before the great doors were finally shut and silence descended upon the Abbey.

All was completely still save for a ghostly echo of the words of Kipling. Kings, Queens, Poets and Artists slept alongside the soul of the Unknown Warrior.

'The tumult and the shouting dies;
The captains and the Kings depart:
Still stands thine ancient sacrifice,
An humble and a contrite heart.
Lord God of Hosts, be with us yet,
Lest we forget-lest we forget.

EPILOGUE

Thither shall all the valiant youth resort;
And from his memory inflame their breasts,
To matchless valour and adventures high;
.........Visit his tomb with flowers.

Samson Agonistes. John Milton.

A week before Christmas, Daisy would soon be four years old. Sally saw so much of Billy in their daughter.

"She's as bright as a button, that one."

Sally could not recall how many times that Gladys had said as much whilst perching her beloved Granddaughter on her lap. Poor Gladys, over the past few weeks she had changed so dramatically. Sally would find her talking to herself by the window of the morning room.

"Mother, what's to do?"

"Waiting for Billy to come home, war's over now."

Then she would take the poor woman in her arms and hold her while she wept unremittingly. Elizabeth once found her up at the cemetery, lain across Josh's grave, while the rain sheeted down and her without a coat, talking to her two lost men. This had made her physically unwell and now she was confined to bed. Not all the casualties of the Great War were either immediate or obvious.

It was late afternoon. Daisy was fast asleep, safe in her bed, a warm fire was glowing in the hearth. Sally was stitching a small sampler, crimson on white lace, when the door was rapped. Getting up, she crossed the room to open the door. Here she found both her mother and Ruth, Pastor Livingstone's wife.

"Good evening Sally, can we come in?"

"Of course."

Sally was somewhat taken aback, it had been Ruth who had made the request.

The two women entered, but did not move to sit down. Again Ruth spoke.

"Sally, I have come to take you to the Manse. The Pastor has a visitor and he instructed me to come and fetch you, apparently it is most important that you meet this gentleman right away. I stopped off to collect Elizabeth so that she could sit for you whilst you are gone."

"But I do not understand."

Elizabeth interjected.

"Just do as Ruth asks of you Sally, I shall look after everything till you return."

490

Still in a somewhat bemused state, Sally went to get her coat. Soon she was walking towards the Manse, full of questions for which Ruth could not find a reply. It was a woman full of inquisitiveness and having almost run out of patience, that was shown into Gideon's Study. Immediately she entered, a tall slim handsome man in army uniform gallantly rose from his seat. The Pastor got up out of his chair and came round to make the introductions.

Ruth closed the door, this was not a matter for her ears, or ever would be.

"Sally, this is Colonel Gell of His Majesty's War Graves Commission: Colonel Gell, may I present Mrs Sally Thomas."

The man, smiled and extended his hand, which she took. As she did so, Sally noticed that he held a small volume in his other hand. It was, somehow, familiar.

The End of Book One.

THE DAY
IS FAR SPENT

***

BILLY THOMAS MM. DSM.

1895 - 1916
***

HIS POEMS.

TWO THIEVES

Two thieves they were, nor yet gained twenty years
Who stole the watch, they fell asleep, none to greet
The enemy, to meet the Hun patrol.
If Gerry called their comrades shot. Their lot
Courts Marshall, the firing squad. "Line them up.
Send them to God". But first the night, in fright.
"Pin them against a cross". Field punishment.
Nor to relent, displaying, discipline,
Revenge to vent. Two lads who fell asleep,
Who stole the watch. Now crucified. All night
They cried, with shell and whizzbang lighting sky.
Just at the dawn they died, the sky went black
To take us back. Golgotha's Sacrificed
Came, taking them, enparadised, to live.

LOOS 1915

Upon an English field a football game
Progressed. Those dressed in red, determined,
Played to cross the line, advancing upon
The foe, and hence to go towards their goal.
Mission fulfilled to score once more, to breach,
That each in triumph be, their head high held.

Now stand within a foreign land hurled forth
Another foe more dangerous to meet
To tackle with nimble feet, gun held fast
And bayonet, to greet, to thrust his heart
With lead or steel to fleet his soul to meet
Our maker his and mine. What goal to score
And more, for now he is divine, Heaven sent
Whilst I by that great referee dismissed.

———————————

THE EMMAUS ROAD

Two towards Emmaus trod, a troubled
Walk, Jerusalem seven miles and more.
Conversing, great events commanded them,
When He of whom they spoke drew near to hand
You understand, this not they knew, that such
Was in their company when thus he spake
In curiosity "Jerusalem?
You speak, what news today? Illuminate."

Still, they stood, sad-eyed, confounded. "Know not
The news?" Cleopas did astounded cry,
"He Jesus the Nazarene, crucified,
Our hope, redeemer of Israel our land.
Betrayed most wickedly by those our priests
Now, not the least, three days are passed upon."

II

"And what became this Jesus, friend of yours?"
"Amazed we are" Cleopas replied, "Gone the
Crucified, vacant his tomb, hence no more
His body to be seen, our gloom, so sore.
Our women searched, though none his form could find
Spake they of one who cried, He is alive".

He mused "O foolish men remember this,
Suffering to come again in glory,
Bliss, refrain from disbelief. It has come
Of that, which Moses and the Prophets spake
Awake, composes all the scriptures told."
Now set the day, the stranger turned away.
They cried, "Abide with us the evening star
Shines over," Urgently, they cried, "Abide."

Harking their plead, the stranger came unto,
Sat at the head, their bread to break, so broke,
He spoke and sharing it they saw, once more,
The crucified amongst them standing there.
Yet but a glance, then disappeared from sight.

Faith enhanced, nor were their words spurned, untrue.
For the eleven also knew, Simon
Had related his Lord's appearance too.
Cleopas, his companion both, witnessed there
Of how they knew. It was the breaking of the bread
His manner, they said. Then he came again.
"Trouble not, doubt not, touch me and see
Together we shall dwell, Abide with me."

POOR PIG

Poor pig, so innocent you were when led
Unto your slaughter. We had fed you scraps
You had gobbled, apparently with great content.
Then you were sent, grunting, by those you knew,
Yet knew you not, save that as bacon cured.
We lured you on till came a muddied trench.
Still not you knew your fate. Scenting nose
Fell and rose seeking out some last delight
That might assuage your torment, when, fast
Held without relent, the hammer swiftly
Swinging down upon your head bursting blood
And you were dead, warning none. No more
For you were gone, your blood staining foreign soil
And now we toil to cut you up, poor pig.

ALBERT

Taffy, the fusilier, sang baritone.
Wrexham George, Welsh too, with tenor voice sang.
Albert, soprano he, you see, because
He was barely sixteen years, a choirboy,
Should be lifting song to God, Cathedralled.
It was his joy to pale the lark with his voice
And truthfully we did rejoice, our hearts
Uplifting hearing his voice, clear, crisp, sharp.
But now accompanied by harp, faultless
Only his God with Angels hears his tune
Gathered making Heavenly choir. Shot was he
Upon the wire, for his mother cried and then
He died, lifted high on Angel's wings, flown
To his eternal home. Left us in Hell.

———————————

THE LITTLE CORPORAL

His image haunts, strange man of stranger land.
Meeting between the lines, this corporal
And I. His eyes seared mine compassionless.
Now attempt description, to understand
How voluntarily came he that Christmas day.
Sighting his English foe, he came to call.

So small a man, waxing his black moustache,
His mouth spat venom. Hatred ruled him then,
Loving war, for sake of war, victory
The accepted, only aim, the very best
For Europe, the World. He would come again
He said, with war once more, armed with dread
And fearfully the World would shudder at
His conquesting Kreig, Europe, England too,
For those who would withstand him, far too few.

———————————————

ACKNOWLEDGEMENTS.

So many people and organisations have made this work possible and references have also been drawn from a great number of literary works, if anyone has been overlooked I apologise.

The individuals.

Firstly to Frances, who was an inspiration, a refuge and a comforter during a time of great trial. 'The half was never told.'

To my brother Colin, without whom, this work would not have begun.

To the staff and archivists of Glossop Library. A special mention must be made to Mrs Sue Essex whose courtesy; local knowledge and enthusiasm were invaluable to me:

To Mrs. Ruth Gordon of Derbyshire Library Services, for her work relating to the Glossop coat of arms.

To Michael Margerison of Lancashire County Library Services. A credit to his profession.

To Hugh Hornby and the staff of The National Football Museum, Preston:

To Chris Robinson, Chief Executive Hearts FC, and his archivist. A man to whom the game is more important than a mere business.

A special thank you must go to my friend Kalvinder Singh Uppal, who kept every promise:

To Julie Perez who so diligently worked on the script.

To Norma who proof read the final draft so thoroughly.

To my brothers, sisters and Pastor of the Seventh Day Adventist Church Preston, for their many manifestations of kindness and unconditional friendship.

To Linda Johnson, whose never-ending objective comments have come to be deeply appreciated.

To Maria Tambe, who re-typed the final draft.

To Rob Macauley who illustrated the cover and to Colin Davies who prepared the book for publication.

To Geoff Quansoon and all the staff at Concept and Design Solutions, Blackpool, for their attention to detail in every aspect of printing this volume.

Finally, to a little frail old lady and her biscuit tins: also to a portrait of a young man, so full of life and hope, now sadly lost.

Bibliography.

John Milton: The Complete English Poems; Everyman's Library.

The Holy Bible: (Authorised King James Version.) Cambridge University Press.

The Holy Bible: (New Jerusalem Version.) Darton, Longman and Todd..

Martin Middlebrook: 'The First Day On The Somme.' The Penguin Press. If you read only one book on the battle of the Somme, make sure it is this one.

Michael Gavaghan: ' The Story of The Unknown Warrior.' Alder Press, Oxford.

Malcolm Brown, Shirley Seaton: 'Christmas Truce.' Leo Cooper, Secker and Warberg.

Edmund Blunden: 'The Undertones of War.' Penguin Modern Classics.

Malcolm Brown: 'The Imperial War Museum Book of The Somme.' Sidgwick and Jackson.

Christopher Martin: 'The Battle of the Somme.' Wayland Publishers.

Lyn Macdonald: 'The Roses of No Man's Land.' Michael Joseph, London. This book brings out the pity of it all.

Martin Gilbert: 'First World War.' Harper Collins London 1995. By far the best general work of the conflict, even though he mistakenly identifies HMS Verdun as a French warship.

The Glossop Chronicle: All the pre war football match scenes, together with many of the featured speeches, owe much to reports extracted from this exemplary contemporary example of local reporting.

Dave Twydell: 'Rejected F.C.' Vol. (1) Juma, 1988. This volume contains the best account of the history of Glossop North End that I could find. It lies in the reference section at Glossop Library No. 796. 334.

Lindsey Porter: 'The Peak District.' David and Charles, London. 1989.

P. Anderson and D. Shimwell. Wild Flowers and Other Plants of the Peak District. Moorland, 1981.

John Singer Sergeant: Gassed. A truly remarkable painting which displays the tortured effects of gas warfare upon the human frame. If one looks carefully at this work, far away in the distance men are playing a game of football as if the war was not happening.

Brian Gardner: 'Up the Line to Death, The War Poets 1914-1918' Methuen, London 1964.

BBC Publications: 'Blackadder Goes Forth.' Video 1995

Immanuel Geiss: July 1914 The Outbreak of The First World War, Selected Documents. B. T. Batsford, London 1967

Robert Graves: 'Goodbye To All That' Cassell, London, 1929

Tony Jasper: Editor. 'The Illustrated Family Hymn Book. Macdonald and James, London. 1980.

Finally, to all those who gave me advice from time to time and to the countless articles, web sites and magazines that have provisioned my understanding and extended my knowledge of the First World War.